W9-AWI-012

IN MY MOTHER'S HOUSE
by Elizabeth Winthrop

Winner of the prestigious PEN Award for short fiction

"WRITTEN WITH SENSITIVITY AND INSIGHT!"
—*Washington Post*

"A lovely book—rich, subtle, funny, and moving—a very convincing picture of a world now largely, if not entirely, gone."
—Larry McMurtry, author of *Lonesome Dove*

"Explores the fearful legacy of child abuse in the lives of three women ... the author ... writes with the ease and narrative punch of a practiced storyteller."
—*Kirkus Reviews*

"WONDERFUL ... this is a real novel ... her living, breathing characters are strong, interesting women."
—Frances Fitzgerald, author of *Fire in the Lake*

"A WONDERFUL, RICH NOVEL, old-fashioned in its breadth and sense of history—contemporary in its understanding of the truth, which binds and separates family."
—Susan Shreve, author of *Queen of Hearts*

⊘ SIGNET   (0451)

THE BEST IN MODERN FICTION

☐ **LULLABYE AND GOODNIGHT by Vincent T. Bugliosi.** Sex, murder—and New York in the Roaring Twenties ... Emily Stanton came to this city of bright lights with a dream of Broadway stardom but instead found fame in the dazzling but dangerous underworld of speakeasies and mobsters. Inspired by a true sex scandal that rocked New York, this is the sizzling novel of crime and passion by the best-selling author of *Helter Skelter*.
(157087—$4.95)

☐ **IN COLD BLOOD by Truman Capote.** A riveting re-creation of the brutal slaying of the Clutter family of Holcomb, Kansas, the police investigation that followed, and the capture, trial and execution of the two young murderers. "A masterpiece ... a spellbinding work."—*Life*
(154460—$4.95)

☐ **MUSIC FOR CHAMELEONS by Truman Capote.** This bestselling collection of writing includes thirteen short stories and a nonfiction novel. "A knockout ... the most enjoyable book I've read this year!"—*Newsweek*
(161807—$4.95)

☐ **FEAR OF FLYING by Erica Jong.** A dazzling uninhibited novel that exposes a woman's most intimate sexual feelings. "A sexual frankness that belongs to, and hilariously extends the tradition of *The Catcher in the Rye* and *Portnoy's Complaint* ... it has class and sass, brightness and bite."—John Updike, *The New Yorker*   (158512—$4.95)

☐ **SONG OF SOLOMON by Toni Morrison.** A novel of beauty and power, creating a magical world out of four generations of black life in America. "*Song of Solomon* belongs in the small company of special books that are a privilege to review. Wonderful ... a triumph."—*The New York Times*
(158288—$4.95)

Prices slightly higher in Canada

Buy them at your local bookstore or use this convenient coupon for ordering.

NEW AMERICAN LIBRARY
P.O. Box 999, Bergenfield, New Jersey 07621

Please send me the books I have checked above. I am enclosing $_____
(please add $1.00 to this order to cover postage and handling). Send check or money order—no cash or C.O.D.'s. Prices and numbers are subject to change without notice.

Name_____

Address_____

City _____ State _____ Zip Code _____

Allow 4-6 weeks for delivery.
This offer is subject to withdrawal without notice.

In My Mother's House

ELIZABETH WINTHROP

A SIGNET BOOK

NEW AMERICAN LIBRARY

A DIVISION OF PENGUIN BOOKS USA INC.

PUBLISHER'S NOTE

This book is a work of fiction. Names, characters, places, and incidents either are the product of the author's imagination or are used fictitiously, and any resemblance to actual persons, living or dead, events, or locales is entirely coincidental.

Copyright © 1988 by Elizabeth Winthrop Mahony

All rights reserved. For information address Doubleday, a division of Bantam Doubleday Dell Publishing Group, Inc., 666 Fifth Avenue, New York, New York 10103.

Excerpt from "Always on My Mind" by W. Thompson, M. James, and J. Christopher, © 1971, 1979 by Screen Gems-EMI Music Inc. and Rosebridge Music Inc. All administrative rights controlled by Screen Gems-EMI Music Inc.

This is an authorized reprint of a hardcover edition published by Doubleday, a division of Bantam Doubleday Dell Publishing Group, Inc.

SIGNET TRADEMARK REG. U.S. PAT. OFF. AND FOREIGN COUNTRIES
REGISTERED TRADEMARK—MARCA REGISTRADA
HECHO EN DRESDEN, TN, USA

SIGNET, SIGNET CLASSIC, MENTOR, ONYX, PLUME, MERIDIAN and NAL BOOKS are published by New American Library, a division of Penguin Books USA Inc., 1633 Broadway, New York, New York 10019

First Signet Printing, July, 1989

5 6 7 8 9

PRINTED IN THE UNITED STATES OF AMERICA

To Alison Cragin Herzig,
that rare combination,
a great editor and a true friend

ACKNOWLEDGMENTS

A book of this size and scope requires the assistance, input and support of many people. I would like to thank them here.

For sharing their stories and knowledge with me, thanks to Mrs. Orme Wilson, Mrs. Paul Hammond, Julia Freeman Fairchild, Aldo and Dora Morelli, Willie Gold, Oliver Thompson, Augusta Alsop, Anne Anderson, Carole Nichols, Judith Brown, Frances Deane Alexander, E.C. Deane, Susan Crile, Judith Goldman, Susan Alain, Chuck Malliband, Charlotte Craig, Sheffield and Bobby Cowles, Frank Mellana, and Doris Betts.

I am also grateful to the Virginia Center for the Creative Arts for giving me a peaceful haven in which to work; to John Alsop, Josephine Coy, Russell D'Oench, Dr. Peggy McGuirk, Patricia Alsop, Anne Milliken, Jane Lawrence Mali and Darlene Phillips for their careful reading of the manuscript-in-progress: to Margaret Robinson and Elizabeth Ann Sachs for their constant support and invaluable editorial advice through many revisions; to Wendy Weil, my agent, and to Carolyn Blakemore, my editor, for their unshakeable patience and faith when I had lost both.

And above all, I want to thank my husband and children, who have seen me through more than one novel but never before with such fortitude and understanding.

When Lydia Franklin married George Webster in 1909, she took her journals with her from the dark brownstone on East Thirty-eighth Street to the plain white farmhouse in Northington, Connecticut. Besides Lydia, the only two people who ever knew the journals existed were Dr. Stevenson, who told her to write it all down in the first place, and Agnes Becker, the housekeeper, who found them under Lydia's bed after she died.

Agnes knew as well as anyone in the Webster family how to keep a secret. She arranged the four leather volumes in a cardboard box that had once held mason jars and hid them in her own closet behind the shoes. At night, in the weeks that followed Lydia's death, Agnes sat in the straight-backed desk chair by her window and puzzled her way through the loops that could be an *l* or a *t*, because Lydia often forgot to cross them, or even an *s* gone haywire. Surrounded by the familiar voice floating up to her from the books and the familiar noises of the house she had shared with her employer for forty-seven years, Agnes went on talking to her in that half-teasing, half-angry tone she had always used with Mrs. W.

"These books are just as bad as those scribbles of grocery lists you leave for me in the morning. How's a body expected to make anything out of this heads-and-tails handwriting? For a lady brought up as fancy as you were, you could have used a few more penmanship lessons.

And that sharp tongue of Mrs. W.'s would flash right back at her from the dark corners of the room, as if she were sitting next to Agnes just waiting to get in her two bits.

"So I suppose your handwriting is a model of legibility, Mrs. Becker?" Lydia only called her Mrs. Becker when she meant to tease, sometimes even to hurt, because they both knew that Harry Becker had run off and left Agnes when she was barely married and only two months pregnant. Most of the time, Agnes was just Agnes to everybody in the house.

It took Agnes three nights to read through all of the books, and when she was done, she put them back in the box and sealed it off with strapping tape.

"I'm going to leave them for Molly," she said out loud as she wrote the name of Mrs. Webster's granddaughter in black Magic Marker on both sides of the box. "If you had any sense, you would have done it yourself a long time ago. It might have saved all of us a lot of aggravation."

"I meant to." For once, the voice sounded apologetic. "But I didn't plan on dying so soon."

"So you thought you could plan your dying, the way you planned a committee meeting?"

The voice said nothing.

The next day Agnes asked Frank Delbianco to stop off at Mrs. Webster's lawyer's office on the way home from their weekly trip to the grocery store. She had been to see him once before when Mrs. W. had insisted that Agnes make a will.

"You going to be long?" Frank asked. He lived with his wife, Angelina, in the caretaker's house down by the calf barn. He had been hired after the war to look after the Webster place, and he and Agnes were always sparring. "Want me to go and come back?" he asked now. "I've got other work to do."

"So do I, Frank. I won't be long."

That's how it came about that Agnes Becker's will included a letter dated August 5, 1970, that read:

"I also leave the cardboard box in the back of my closet to Molly Webster Taylor, who can be found through her mother, Mrs. Charlotte Taylor of 17 Mill Pond Road, Riversville, Connecticut."

"What if Miss Taylor is deceased?" the lawyer had asked.

"That's hardly likely, Mr. Belmont, since she is thirty years old and I am sixty-nine."

He had shrugged. "Stranger things have happened in

10

my business, Mrs. Becker. It's my job to think of all contingencies."

"Then put down that the box is to be burned without being opened."

"Are you sure?"

"Absolutely. But knowing Charlotte, she won't pay any attention to what I say, not even if I'm talking to her from the grave. She never has."

PART I

1888–1906
LYDIA

1

If Lydia Franklin had any memory of her mother at all, it would have been that there was no room in her lap for a two-year-old. Pregnant with her third child, Elizabeth Franklin's belly swelled early to a rounded point that was noticeable even under the three layers of underclothing topped off with a loose taffeta gown. Her husband, Charles, tried not to let his eyes drift below her waist in those last months. One evening when they were dressing for dinner, he caught sight of her as she turned sideways to study her naked body in the mirror and he wondered how her skin had another three months of stretch left in it. He took responsibility for her discomfort the way he did for everything else that happened to her, and the more cheerful she grew at the thought of another baby in the house, the more he seemed to blame himself for inflicting it on her.

"It's a boy," she told him one night. "I remember feeling this way with John."

"I hope he gives you less trouble," Charles said from behind his newspaper.

"I don't mind the labor pains so much. Dr. Maxwell says if they come into the world screaming, they are ridding themselves of the devil. That's certainly true of John. And the reverse is true of little Lydia. She was an easy birth and she's been a terror ever since. Nurse told me she said her first word today. You will not be surprised to learn that it was 'no.' "

"She comes from a long line of women who get their way by one method or another," Charles said, putting down the paper at last.

"Charles," she said. "What could you possibly be talking about?"

15

Elizabeth Winthrop

Elizabeth, for all her coy smiles and decorative ways, was no fool. She knew, first of all, that her sister Katherine was madly in love with Charles Franklin, which made the winning of him all the more pleasant. She also knew exactly why Charles had been attracted to her in the first place. He would get the entrée into society that he wanted, but then it was an even exchange. She would get his money. Despite their important connections, the Livingston inheritance had been drained away by the large crumbling house on the Hudson River and her father's unwise investments.

In a way, it had been a surprise to everyone that Charles Franklin married at all. When he landed in New York in 1877, his only objective had been to triple the income from his father's copper holdings and it was not long before he made himself a name down on Wall Street. But the money and the respect from his daytime companions could not break down the barriers of New York society and the smart young man from Chicago learned quickly enough that the big deals were made at night around the dining-room table after the ladies had gone upstairs. Elizabeth Livingston was a daughter of one of the oldest families in the Hudson River valley, and Charles was attracted to her at first because she would smooth his way into the drawing rooms. He had never intended to fall in love with her.

When he finally admitted to himself that he had gotten in too deep and that he no longer even wanted to get out, he asked her to marry him.

"You'd do best to turn me down," he had said bluntly. "I was brought up by a common-sense, practical, down-to-earth woman. I don't understand the softer ways," he added, his eyes following the curl of her satin hat ribbons.

"Well, then, I shall have to teach you," Elizabeth had said as she laced one of the ribbons back and forth through her thin, pale fingers.

When the labor started early one morning in March, Lydia was taken out for a long walk by Nurse so she would not hear the screams from her mother's bedroom. The weather was unexpectedly warm and Lydia squirmed so under the extra blankets in her carriage that Nurse

16

lifted her out and let her toddle up the sidewalk beside her, clinging to one black gloved finger. They ate lunch down in the kitchen with Mrs. Sanders, the cook, and Lydia burnt the roof of her mouth on the pudding that the two women had forgotten to cool before they set it in front of her. Their eyes and their attention were all upstairs, where the cries had weakened to a faint whimpering. Dr. Maxwell and the midwife agreed privately that things were not going well, but they said nothing to Charles, who sat outside in the hallway.

In the late afternoon, at Dr. Maxwell's urging, he went for a long walk up Fifth Avenue. When Nellie O'Shea, the parlormaid, let him back in the front door, she had to brush the snowflakes off the shoulders of his dark coat.

"Most incredible thing," he said to her. "Spring in the morning and winter at night. It looks as if we're in for quite a blizzard."

"Yes, sir," she said, keeping her head down. She didn't want to be the one to say that there had been no sound at all from the room upstairs for the last hour.

Charles was too late. Both his wife and the baby, who had been caught in transverse position for too long, had been dead for fifteen minutes. When her waters broke, the blood poisoning which had been growing undetected in Elizabeth's system for the last month spread quickly to the baby boy, who died first. In desperation, Dr. Maxwell had attempted an emergency cesarean but Elizabeth, weakened by the agonizing labor and the tremendous loss of blood, died under the ether cone.

Dr. Maxwell administered a sedative to Charles and after a brief consultation with Harrison, who served as both butler and groom, he sent for Nellie.

"The undertaker is on his way," the doctor said. "I understand that you were Mrs. Franklin's maid."

"Yes, sir."

"The midwife was concerned about traveling in this storm, so she left early. I have tidied the room as best I could." They looked at one another for a moment without saying anything. "My coat and hat, please."

Nellie shut the door on the doctor's black back and stood without moving in the cold front vestibule. Harrison came up behind her.

Elizabeth Winthrop

"Mr. Franklin is resting in the guest room. Did Dr. Maxwell speak to you?"

Nellie nodded. Harrison let his hand rest for a moment on her shoulder. "Are you going to be all right?"

"Yes. I'll go up now."

The dark room stank of ether, and despite the snow and the cold wind, Nellie opened the curtains and cracked one window to give herself some air. She straightened the room first, avoiding the bed, where the bodies lay under a white sheet. Then, as she had done so many other nights in the last year, she went to the drawers and selected her ladyship's nightclothes, the silk knickers, the pink camisole, the dressing gown. On the bedside table, she laid out a basin of warm water, a sponge, the two jars of cream, and the ivory-handled hairbrush.

Before she lifted the sheet, she sank to her knees by the bed.

Then, trembling, she set about her work. Stripping away the sheets, she washed the baby first and dressed him in the white flannel nightgown Mrs. Franklin had chosen from the layette two nights ago. She laid him in the cradle that Harrison had carried down from the attic just last week. Then, slowly and lovingly, she sponged her mistress's body, patted it dry, and rubbed the crème rivière into the skin which in the last months had been stretched thin by the growing baby.

When her grandmother was paralyzed with a stroke three years ago, Nellie had been the one who bathed her once a week, so now she knew how to lift each section of Mrs. Franklin's body to pull the dressing gown over her head and down across the recently closed wound in her belly to her feet. Sitting on the edge of the bed, she raised the upper section of the body so that she could part the lady's hair and pull it to the front. Mrs. Franklin's head fell forward onto Nellie's shoulder, and for a long moment, Nellie did not move but cradled the heavy weight in the crook of her own neck as if to comfort her.

"There, there," Nellie whispered. The sound of her strained voice in the darkening room reminded her of how silently she had conducted this nighttime ritual even when Mrs. Franklin was alive.

The lady would sit at the dressing table like a porcelain statue while Nellie brushed her hair, massaged her neck, attended to her. Once Nellie understood exactly what was expected of her, they no longer needed to speak or even look one another in the eye.

Now she laid the body carefully back against the linen pillowcase and turned the thick hanks of hair into two neat braids that rested against the shoulders of the satin gown.

She gathered up the dirty sheets which the doctor had piled in one corner, stuffed them into a pillowcase, and set it down by the door of the room. Downstairs, she heard the front bell ringing. The undertaker was here. She had finished the laying out just in time.

She stood looking around the room.

"Will there be anything else, Mrs. Franklin?" she asked. "No? I'll just take these to be washed, then," she said, lifting the silk knickers and the camisole and adding them to the pillowcase. After a moment's hesitation, she put in the porcelain jar of crème rivière, the bottle of perfume, and the hairbrush. Nobody would miss those little things in the confusion.

"Good night, then," she whispered as she always had. For the first time, she leaned over the bed and kissed Mrs. Franklin's smooth forehead before pulling the sheet up across her face.

The snowfall that started in the late afternoon continued into the night and for much of the next day. Within hours, the city was paralyzed. The undertaker worked as quickly as possible in the upstairs bedroom with one eye on the swirling snow collecting on the windowsills. After her ordeal upstairs, Nellie had been allowed to retire early to bed, so it was the nurse who let the undertaker out into the storm. He hesitated for a moment on the stoop.

"I expect the Madison Avenue car will have a hard time of it in this," he said. "I'd better walk."

"Do you have far to go?" she called against the noise of the wind.

"Sixty-third Street hard by the river," he said, wondering if she might suggest he spend the night.

19

But "Good luck to you, then," was all she said before she shut the door firmly behind him.

In the kitchen the next morning, the women of the house (now there were only three of them, four if you counted the little girl) gathered to discuss the whole question of the two bodies upstairs. Mrs. Sanders and Nurse treated Nellie with more deference than usual, and she took advantage of this unusual situation by sitting slightly apart. She knew they were longing to hear something of what had gone on in the room upstairs the evening before, but she gave them no satisfaction. Let them ask, she said, knowing they would never dare.

"Harrison says that the streets are impassable. Nothing can make it through now, certainly not the hearse," said Mrs. Sanders. "That means those two boxes are going to stay upstairs for the whole day without even a decent prayer said over them. It's indecent."

Nurse liked the congenial chatter in the kitchen. She had never held herself apart from the rest of the staff like some of those high-handed English women she met in the park. "Where is Mr. Franklin?" she asked now as she tucked the child's bib up under her chin.

"Upstairs in the room with them. Just sitting in the chair. Harrison says he's been there since he woke up this morning," Mrs. Sanders said. She glanced at Nellie, who said nothing. "Thank the Lord Master John is staying with his grandmother Livingston. A thing like this an eight-year-old child would never forget. We are fortunate this one is too young."

But Lydia knew something was wrong. She had been making circles in her porridge with her spoon all through breakfast, but nobody had said a thing about it. And why hadn't Nurse taken her to that cozy room on the way down to breakfast so that she could be lifted into her mother's arms for a kiss. She liked the smell of her mother's skin, the tiny white bumps in the linen sheets that she tried to capture between her index finger and her thumb, the smooth blue bows on the frilly pillows. She liked her mother's voice, higher than Nurse's and always teasing. "Mama," she cried out one morning when

20

Nurse lifted her away and her mother laughed and clapped her hands.

"You finally learned my name, you little minx," she said. "Give her back to me for one more kiss, Nurse."

"Mama," Lydia said now. Conversation around the wooden table stopped and three pairs of eyes turned at once on her.

"Oh, you poor child," said Nellie, and suddenly Lydia was lifted out of her high chair and crushed against the stiff pleats of the chambermaid's chest.

"Mama," she said again, this time louder, and when everybody began to wail and dab their eyes, she cried along with them although she didn't really know why.

The funeral was delayed almost a week because of the blizzard. Without newspapers or telephones, the normal methods of communication had been wiped out, but also with the snow knee high in the streets, the chain of neighborhood gossip broke down. Since Nellie did not sweep the front steps for days, she did not see Missy, the chambermaid from next door, to tell her what had happened. Nothing at all was delivered, so that Mrs. Sanders's usual spot of chatter with the milkman or the butcher boy was eliminated and another strand in the web of local gossip was broken. Harrison ventured out a little farther each day and returned with grisly stories of the stiff bodies they were digging out of the snowbanks.

So we're not the only ones with stiff bodies, Mrs. Sanders thought, but it was too awful a thing to say out loud.

At last, the city began to untangle itself and Harrison managed to get out to bring back the hearse.

Charles stood in the room and watched them carry the two coffins away. The smaller box was light enough for one man to handle. Although the assistant lifted it with all due reverence, Charles imagined that the white bundle inside, no bigger than one of his wife's fussy pillows, must be shifting back and forth as the men took the stairs. She had been right about the boy.

"That was the reason that her belly looked so, well, pointed," Charles finally brought himself to say to the doctor weeks later. "The baby was lying across her from side to side."

"We'll never know for sure, Charles. I'm sorry. Some day soon, you will be able to put this all behind you and pick up the threads of your life again. There is nothing that any of us could have done."

"Nothing you could have done," Charles muttered as he left the office.

The day of the funeral Lydia was kept upstairs in the nursery. The house was crowded with people dressed in black who sat with Charles in the front parlor and spoke in quiet voices to one another. Along with neighbors and good friends, the family had gathered. Cousins from Boston, two maiden aunts of Elizabeth's who lived in a large house on Washington Square, her old nurse who had only left their employment a year before. Charles's parents did not attempt the long train journey from Chicago, but James, his younger brother, had sat up in the coach car on the night train from Richmond, where he had been staying with friends. Elizabeth's sister Katherine and her husband, Arthur Jay, brought young John down with them from his grandmother's house on the Hudson. Most of the afternoon he stood like a sentry at his father's elbow until Aunt Katherine sent him upstairs to the nursery. Elizabeth's mother, Sarah Livingston, had taken to her bed when she finally heard the news, and the family doctor refused to allow her to attend the funeral because of her weak heart.

From his chair by the fire, Charles stared out at the faces around the room. Every thought that occurred to him took a very long time to be translated into action, so that, for what seemed like hours, he considered raising his finger to scratch his ear before he could manage the movement and relieve the itch. He studied the people in the room, the crackling of the logs in the fire, the spreading puddle of a spilled drink the way an infant helplessly watches his own hands rise slowly up to punch his own nose.

Once in a while, he would open his mouth to say something, and all around him, the conversations would stop instantaneously, but then he would change his mind and say nothing and the mourners would lean back toward one another and begin murmuring again.

They were talking about the snow, about the children,

about Elizabeth. Sometimes his own name surfaced like a piece of wreckage washed ashore by the storm.

"What a terrible time for this to happen. I understand the bodies have been in the house for days because the hearse could not get through."

"—the most awful time further uptown with all the telegraph lines down."

"The Irvings' maid never managed to get home from her day off. They still have not found her. And Mr. Williams the undertaker. He was on his way home from here, I understand."

"Charles worries me."

"It was such a shock for him, poor dear. Now he's left with those two children to cope with."

"The boy will be fine, I'm sure. But the girl is quite strong-minded. Elizabeth spoiled her dreadfully."

"Well, I expect Katherine will step in there and arrange things. She's always been far more practical than dear sweet Elizabeth."

Upstairs, Nurse had reached the end of a very long day. Normally her charge would have been out for at least two long walks, but Mrs. Jay had given her strict instructions to keep the little girl out of sight in the nursery. "Very well for her to say," Nurse muttered as she worked the wool tweed leggings over Lydia's black shoes. "But she hasn't been stuck away up here without a breath of fresh air or a body to talk to for the whole day the way I have. We are going out."

"Out," Lydia crowed, and for once, stood still as her wool hat was adjusted and tied in place.

Down the stairs they marched, past Nellie, who was headed up to turn down the bed in the guestroom for Mr. James, past the big dark clock just ringing four, past the carved banister rails which Lydia had often clung to in order to protest something as unpleasant as a bath or cod-liver oil on cold nights. They had almost escaped into the front vestibule when the parlor door opened, releasing a cloud of stale air and weary voices.

"Look who's here," said a deep voice, and Lydia was swept up into someone's arms.

"We were just going out, Mr. James," Nurse said

nervously, wondering what Mrs. Jay would say. "She's been cooped up all day and she's quite testy."

"Testy?" said the voice, now so close to Lydia's mouth that she breathed in the smell of his Altoid peppermints mixed with cigar smoke. "Not my little Lydia. I won't keep her long, Nurse. I'm sure she'll be a welcome sight for everyone in here." With deft fingers, he undid her hat, slipped it off her head, and handed it to Nurse. "There are the pretty curls I remember," he whispered, smoothing them with a gentle hand. "Now a big smile, little one. For the crowds."

They went around the room together, the tall thin man with blond hair and the dark mustache, his head close to her brown curls, his lips whispering encouragement in her ear. "And this is your dear Aunt Katherine and Uncle Arthur. Put out your hand, that's my girl, and give your aunt a kiss on the cheek."

Lydia was mesmerized by his thick voice tickling her ear, his firm hand on her thigh. Nurse did not hold her so tightly, never held her at all except to lift her in and out of the high chair or the crib. She would do anything as long as she could stay up high and safe in his arms.

"I told the nurse that the child should not be brought down at all today," Katherine whispered to her husband.

"Isn't James divine?" said one of the ladies to another. "He could charm the birds out of the trees if he took it into his mind. I've never seen that little girl acting so docile and sweet."

Charles had remained silent through the whole performance, watching them draw closer. His younger brother had always been blessed with a flair for the dramatic, a sense of timing as sharp as an actor's.

"Now, little one, here is your father," James said, leaning over and beginning to undo the little girl's hand from his neck. "Sit with him for a while."

James could not know that his brother had never held this child, almost never even touched her except for the obligatory pat on her head when she was brought to him at Elizabeth's insistence for a good-night kiss. But Lydia saw the look of alarm that crossed her father's face when he realized what James expected him to do, the way he shook his head as they approached. She wound her other

24

arm around her uncle's neck and held on as firmly as if the blond man were about to drop her off the side of a tall building. For a few agonizing moments, while everybody watched, James continued to try to unclasp her tightly laced fingers, to talk her down into her father's lap the way an experienced groom talks his horse backward into the shafts. But she would have none of it, and Charles, at last, put a stop to the ridiculous charade by ordering James to take the rigid child back out to her nurse. His silent retreat signaled to the frozen audience around the room that a decent amount of time had passed and they could now leave Charles to his household. The men pulled watches out of their pockets and snapped their shirt cuffs, the women hunted by their feet for dropped gloves and prayer books, and Charles was so swept up in the general tumult of leave-taking that he did not see the look of fear and dislike that settled on his tiny daughter's face as the gap between them widened.

"So, I hope you behaved yourself, young lady," Nurse said as James set her back down on the floor in the front hall. He hunkered down next to her, took the hat from Nurse, and slid the long velvet ribbons into the fold of soft flesh under her chin.

"Absolutely, Nurse. She was just what the doctor ordered, weren't you, little one?"

Lydia nodded solemnly.

"Now," he whispered, ignoring Nurse, who was shifting impatiently just inches from his arm. "Can you say my name? Uncle James."

She shook her head.

"Try it," he urged.

"I really must insist, Mr. James," Nurse said, taking the little girl's hand in her own. "It's almost time for her supper and I want her to have some fresh air today."

James stood up, hands thrust deep in his pockets, and watched them maneuver their way through the first glass door. At the last moment, before it closed behind her, Lydia turned around and said, "Shames," in a small clear voice. The pleasing sound of her uncle's laughter followed her out into the evening street.

2

Charles Franklin had never been able to tolerate messes of any kind, particularly emotional ones, and although Elizabeth's sudden violent death left him feeling oddly unfinished, as if he had lost half of himself, he went back to the world of men with a certain sense of relief. Downtown, in his office, he was surrounded by men, by concrete problems with concrete solutions. He went shooting with men in Georgia in the fall and the spring and fishing with them in the summer. He took many of his meals at the Metropolitan Club and afterward he would slide gratefully into the red leather armchairs in the reading room, surrounded by the rustle of newspapers, the smell of pipe smoke, the occasional click of a pocket watch. His sister-in-law, Katherine, invited him for dinner constantly, but he turned her down as often as he dared. Charles did not plan ever to marry again. He decided soon after Elizabeth died that he would limit his intimate entanglements with members of the opposite sex to regular but discreet visits to a high-class brothel on Twenty-third Street.

Once Katherine had cleared out all of her sister's clothes, Charles moved a single bed into his dressing room and shut the door to Elizabeth's bedroom for good. He was shutting away the only time in his life when he had allowed his feelings to govern his actions. Throughout the nine years of his marriage, Charles had found himself continually unsettled by the breadth of his wife's emotions. She cried often and for no apparent reason, and some casual remark he might make one evening over dinner could send her into an inexplicable and childish rage. She sulked for days and he would come upstairs to find her sitting on the floor playing with her doll. She did it to torment him. She would not get up or look at him, but would tell the doll secrets in a stage whisper. "Here comes that mean, awful man, Clarissa. We won't speak to him, will we? We'll just turn our backs on him."

He could not bear it when she acted this way. The pouting and crying twisted inside him, and despising himself all the while, he would plead with her to tell him what he could do, how he could make it up to her. She played him like a fish, and once she had decided that whatever offense he had committed had been atoned for, she would smile, reel in the line, and land him on the shore, gasping and exhausted.

After she died, he found the presence of his children just as unsettling. Children couldn't be counted on to bottle up their emotions. They fell, they cried, they interrupted and disrupted. Or they acted like his son, John, who stood on the other side of the newspaper and waited with a solemn expression until it was impossible to ignore his patient shallow breathing. But children could be controlled. They could be kept at bay.

Nobody ever talked to Lydia about her mother and she remembered very little of the years that followed her death except the darkness. Dark hallways, black clothes, an airless, musty smell that seemed to seep out of the very walls of the house. The closed door to her mother's bedroom trapped all the morning sun which normally would have flooded the upstairs hallway, so that the servants had to turn up the gas jets in order to clean properly the crevices of the carved banister rails. Lydia always thought of the second floor when she recited the psalm in church about the valley of the shadow of death.

When she was old enough to know that she was breaking some unspoken rule of her father's, she would steal into her mother's room in the mornings after he had gone downtown to work. She played with the glass boxes on the dressing table, she read the titles of the books in the bookcase, she spilled the shiny black-and-white dominoes from their box and stacked them in different piles. Sometimes she even lay down on the bed, on top of the delicate dancing patterns that the morning sun projected across the room through the lace curtains, buried her nose in the linen pillowcase, and tried to smell her mother.

All that came to her was the clean and slightly scorched odor of the laundress's heavy black iron and a faint smell of gardenia.

The servants let her play there. "I don't see the harm in it," Nurse said to Nellie. "It's unnatural to shut the room up that way."

Nellie said nothing. After all, she made her own pilgrimages to that room for her own reasons.

One morning, when she had tired of her usual games, Lydia tiptoed around the corner to the dressing area. After a moment's hesitation, she reached up and pulled open the wardrobe doors. The dresses had all been removed, so that she could step inside the large space, empty except for a row of padded hangers, and pull the doors to until they almost closed behind her. In the dim light, she explored the back wall with her outstretched fingers, until they closed around the knob of another little hidden door and, trembling, she pulled it open. Still on her knees, she backed her way out into the light of the room, dragging along the wooden trunk she had found.

The top tray of the trunk held a pile of small, carefully folded clothes, and in the bottom she found the doll, a beautiful porcelain girl with long brown ringlets and jointed limbs that bent and turned. With a little cry of pleasure, she picked up the perfect creature and held it close, letting her hand slide down across the soft hair that felt real. She had seen dolls like this in her cousin Emily's room, but she had never had one of her own. She had never even held one before. She turned the porcelain body over on its stomach and began to unbutton its pinafore.

Usually, by this time Nurse would have come looking for Lydia, as it was past the time for their morning trip to the park. But on Tuesday mornings, the staff gravitated to the kitchen, where Mrs. Dickson, the laundress, always set up her ironing board, so that they could hear the latest tales of her other family's troubles. This particular day, she was deep into a juicy description of a wedding and everybody was so engrossed that they did not hear Mr. Franklin let himself in the front door.

The sleeves of the blue satin dress had been gathered too tightly at the cuffs, so Lydia had to concentrate very hard on working the doll's fingers through them and she didn't notice the footsteps in the room behind her.

"What are you doing in here?" His voice was very quiet. Lydia flinched and started to turn, but before she could look up or speak, she was swept up from behind, still clutching the doll with one hand. Holding her away from his body, her father carried her out of the room, shouting for Nurse. At the top of the stairs, Lydia was set down and smacked sharply on her bottom. The spanking did not hurt at all because of the layers of her petticoats. It was the fear on Nurse's face as she rushed up the stairs toward them that brought home to Lydia just how badly she had misbehaved. She began to wail.

"Nurse, I have told you that nobody is to go into Mrs. Franklin's room. I found the child in there with this . . ." The doll was snatched from her right hand and handed over.

"I'm so sorry, sir. I was busy downstairs and did not know. I never . . ."

"You know what I expect, Nurse. If I cannot trust you to keep this child in line, then I shall have to find someone else. Do you understand me?"

"Yes, sir."

Mr. Franklin had never raised his voice like this before. Downstairs in the kitchen everybody had frozen from the moment they first heard his voice in the house. Even the voluble Mrs. Dickson had been silenced in the middle of her story, her black iron suspended above one of Mr. Franklin's new Oxford weave shirts.

Still crying, Lydia was bustled past her angry father and up the stairs to the third floor, where the nurse took the time to pull down her petticoats to be sure the spanking would not be cushioned by her clothing. Nurse poured all of her own fears for her position into that spanking, so that the red marks on the little girl's bottom did not fade away for two days. When at last she was allowed to crawl into her bed and sob alone into her pillow, Lydia sorted through the experience in her mind trying to untangle her different feelings. It wasn't the humiliation of her first real punishment or even the loss of the beautiful doll that pained her as much as the memory of the way her father had held her out in front of his body like a dog that has made a mess on the rug. She never wanted him to touch her again. "I hate him," she whispered fiercely into the thick pillow. "I hate him for ever and ever."

As for Charles, he went back to the office furious with himself. The sight of the child on the floor playing with her mother's doll, the same one Elizabeth had dragged from her childhood bedroom into her marriage, had made him lose control of himself for the first time since his wife had died. And now he had taken out his frustration on the little girl and the nurse, who was sure to tell the rest of the household, if they hadn't already heard his outburst. It was intolerable behavior for a grown man and he was determined not to let it happen again. Soon the boy would go off to boarding school. He needed some backbone. And Lydia. Well, she had probably learned a good lesson today.

The routine of Lydia's days did not vary much. She had breakfast with her brother, John, in the kitchen on a small table separate from the staff's. In the morning, she did lessons with Nurse until she reached the age of nine, when she joined six other girls of her age at the Gridley classes. Mr. Gridley taught his students in his dark front parlor room on East Twentieth Street.

Years later when her granddaughter, Molly, taped her reminiscences for an oral history report in the ninth grade, Lydia remembered her early childhood this way:

"With Mr. Gridley, we learned Latin and read poetry. Science consisted of turning an empty glass over a candle, which taught us that fire could not exist without oxygen. Geography meant filling in a map of the country with all the names of the states. There were long passages of recitation from Tennyson and Shakespeare. A very eccentric and spotty kind of education.

"My nurse picked me up at eleven-thirty and we walked home from Washington Square up Fifth Avenue on the nice days. If the weather were bad, Harrison would call for me when Father did not need the carriage or we took the horsecar home. After lunch, I lay down to rest. In the late afternoons, I took piano lessons from a stern German lady who rapped my knuckles with a stick when I hit the wrong note. My favorite moment in the whole week was my art lesson with sweet Miss Sterling. She always whispered at me as if we were sharing some wonderful secret while we sketched the still life she had arranged."

"Did you miss your mother terribly?" Molly asked.

"I don't think so," Lydia answered quickly. "She died when I was two, so I expect I didn't know her enough to miss her. And I had my Aunt Katherine. She always included me in any plans she made for her daughter. Emily and I were not really close friends. In fact, I always suspected that Aunt Katherine rather liked me better and Emily knew it and was jealous. I stayed most of the summer with my grandmother Livingston up in her Hudson River house near Garrison. I loved the times there. The groom hitched Flower, my favorite pony, up to a wooden cart and I drove him along the forest trails and we swam every day in a deep quarry pool. Father came up only on the weekends, but Aunt Katherine was there all summer as well as Emily and her brother, Henry, who was just my age and an annoyance most of the time. He was killed in the First World War. And my brother, John, of course."

When Molly listened to the tape again after her grandmother had died, she could hear even then the slightly sarcastic note about brother, John.

He was six years older than Lydia and they never had much to do with each other, partially because of the age gap but mostly because they were so different. John craved his father's approval, and even when she was very small, Lydia remembered the way he stood at silent attention in the library, waiting for his father to put down the newspaper so that he could show him some paper he had done at school. Charles would give it a cursory glance, pat the boy on the shoulder, and send him away. Lydia was always waiting in the hallway to taunt him.

"He didn't even look at it."

"He did too. He said it was very good."

"He doesn't give a hoot," Lydia would say, determined to wipe that self-satisfied smile off her brother's face. Then he would punch her in the arm and she would punch back. They fought fiercely but silently until Nurse found them. Because she was just as mindful as the

Elizabeth Winthrop

children of Mr. Franklin's insistence on peace in the house, she always pulled them apart without a word and marched them upstairs, where she could give them a proper scolding in the sanctuary of the third floor.

"You must learn to act like a lady," she would tell Lydia. "You must walk away from him."

"She's the one who starts it," John said. "It's just because Father pays more attention to me. She's jealous."

When he said that, Lydia would go after him again until Nurse gave up and sent her to bed early without her supper. Nobody was more delighted than Nurse when John was packed off to boarding school at the age of fourteen.

"Dealing with one of them is enough," she told Mrs. Sanders. "But the two of them at each other's throat all the time. I can't abide it."

"Seems to me you've been left with the tougher one," the cook said. "That girl has a mind of her own. She's a mischievous little thing."

The business of the spring rabbit all started one warm day in April when Nurse had taken the child down to Stern Brothers in Madison Square to buy her Easter dress and bonnet. Lydia had chosen a daring dress of green-and-white-striped plissé and a large silk hat to match and Nurse had given in against her better judgment.

"I'm sure Mrs. Jay will never approve," Nurse said as Lydia led her gaily back onto the street. "It's too sophisticated a style for a nine-year-old. I should never have let you convince me."

"Don't go on so about it, Nurse. Doesn't it look pretty on me?" Lydia refused to let the older woman ruin the excitement of her day. For once, they had escaped the dark house and now had the whole morning to savor before the normal dull routine reclaimed them. Madison Square was filled with Easter shoppers, with children rolling their hoops along the diagonal paths, with the sound of the organ grinder on the corner of Twenty-second Street, the perpetual squeak of the carriage wheels against the cobblestones.

Nurse steered her through the crowds of shoppers, past the loud red-faced man who waved a bottle at them from his high perch on the back of the park bench, past the flower carts parked by the curb, the chestnut man calling out his prices. Lydia hung back, wanting to stare at everything, to touch, buy, reply, to get swept away in the dizzying colors and activities of the city stretching in the spring sunlight. When they stopped at the corner of Twenty-third to wait for a coach-and-four to trot past, hoofs ringing against stone, she managed to slip out of Nurse's grasp and twist away to the rabbit lady.

Every spring the rabbit lady set up shop on the Square. She sat on a tall wooden crate, her feet dangling, a dwarf woman with large childish eyes and a high laugh. In her lap and in the cages all around her, the white baby rabbits sat, sniffing, their pink unblinking eyes turned up to the commotion high above them on the street. Lydia knelt beside the crate to look.

"Pat one," said the rabbit lady, and Lydia obeyed, smoothing down the ears, letting her finger slip into the dip behind its head and then rise slowly out again on the bumpy road of its backbone. Without seeming to move, the gnome lady leaned over and dropped a small white bundle into Lydia's lap.

"Miss Lydia." Nurse's voice above her was annoyed but not half as angry as Lydia had thought it would be. She didn't answer. The silk fur lifted a little with the electricity of her hand.

"Only twenty-five cents, miss," said the rabbit lady. "If something unfortunate should happen to the little one, you bring it back and I refund your money on the spot."

Lydia rose to her feet holding the soft trembling against her chest.

"Whatever do you do with the dead rabbits?" Nurse asked.

The lady leaned over behind her wooden crate and brought up a basket piled with what looked like unspun cotton. "Doll muffs," she said, plunging her hand in and lifting out a small circle not much larger than a spool of thread. "And boas." This time a long thin snake of rabbit fur dangled from her fingertips.

Nurse said nothing for a moment, a frown starting between her eyebrows. The image of a small, sharp knife

33

sliding between the fur and the pink wrinkled body formed in her mind.

"You skin them yourself, then?" she asked, fascinated.

The small woman raised a finger of warning and glanced at Lydia, who had lifted the rabbit up so it could nuzzle in the dark space under her chin. "Yes," her lips said silently.

"Please, Nurse, I want to take him home."

If the sun had not been so warm between her shoulders, if she hadn't been caught up in the gay mood of the Square, if the child in her charge and the quivering rabbit hadn't gotten somehow muddled in her imagination, Nurse would certainly have said no and stuck to it. But she hesitated. And Lydia pounced.

"I could keep him in the garden the way the Wilson girls do down the street. The wall is high enough so he'll never get away. And I know he won't be any trouble at all. We don't have to tell Father. It will be our secret."

The older woman smiled, and the rabbit lady, smelling a sale, hopped down from her crate with a surprising agility. As she showed Lydia how to lift the rabbit properly and explained to her about water and feeding habits, the nurse watched without a word. She was remembering a conversation the day before with her employer.

"Mrs. Jay has spoken to me about the need for a proper governess for my daughter, Nurse. I frankly think our current arrangement has worked fine up to now. Do you agree?"

"Yes, sir," the nurse said quickly. "I hope Mrs. Jay is not dissatisfied with my performance."

"No, I don't think so. She merely feels that a governess would be able to continue the child's education at home, but I have decided to enroll Lydia in the Brearley next year. From what I hear about the course of study there, that should be enough education for any girl. Do you think she's clever, Nurse?"

"Oh yes, sir."

He went on almost as if he were talking to himself. "She'll never look like very much, I don't supppose. Such long legs and arms and that determined chin. But Mrs. Jay says the girl has a different kind of intelligence. Not like most women."

"I do think it would be hard on Lydia if we were to change people on her right now. We've gotten very close, you know, since the death of her mother."

He nodded and dismissed her. That last wasn't true at all, but sometimes, on a day like this, Nurse did feel a bit sorry for her.

"Thank you, Nurse," Lydia said as they made their way up Madison. "I've never ever had a pet before. Only Flower the pony up at Grandmother's and he's not really mine, you know."

"That rabbit is not to come in the house, Miss Lydia. I'm sure your father wouldn't approve. We are going to march straight home now before you convince me to do some other impossible thing."

By this time, Charles was well pleased with his life. His loyal staff, his well-run household, and his friends all contributed to a sense of being settled that he had not felt since before his marriage.

Then, one day, a letter came in the post from Dwight Franklin, Charles's sturdy, demanding father, who lived with his wife in a thick-walled dark house on the outskirts of Chicago. "James is back in trouble again and I'm afraid I have to ask you to step in this time. As his older brother, I feel you would exert more influence over him than either your mother or I. Take him into your home. Set him up with some work in the firm."

Dear Father [Charles wrote in reply to the letter of March 18, 1895],

I do understand your continuing concern about James, and of course I will take him in here if it seems the only possible solution, but I wonder what a widower with two children and a very sedate life will do for him. Surely, he will chafe under the constraints of this limited and rather lifeless household.

Despite the continuing unrest over the gold reserve, I suppose with my connections on the Street I could get him some useful employment, but James must understand from the beginning that my reputation is at stake also. Unless he is willing to change his ways completely (I am referring to the excessive drink as well as the gambling and the women), then I will not be able to put him up for anything at all.

I leave this decision up to you, Father.

With affection,

Charles

It did no good, as Charles was sure it wouldn't. James arrived on a sunny afternoon early in April, a day ahead of time. There was nothing his younger brother liked more than keeping people off balance.

3

When he discovered that the front door wasn't locked, James let himself in without ringing and left his bag and the gift box on the carpeted stairs. He pushed open the parlor door. Nothing had changed since his last visit. Dear brother Charles didn't seem to notice that the peacock feathers in the brass stand had begun to look bedraggled and dusty or that ruffled lampshades had gone out of fashion since Elizabeth died. James had a visual sense, an eye for color and design, and normally his fingers would have been itching to shift the furniture about, to throw open the heavy curtains and let some light into the room, but in his present penitent mood, James welcomed the familiar, slightly shabby feel of the place. It confirmed his sense of safety, of homecoming.

This is where I shall sit in the evenings, James thought as he passed into the dark red study. A fire in the fireplace on the cooler nights, my newspaper, my glass of port, my brother and I in congenial silence, interrupted only by the occasional pop from a pocket of air in a green log or the sound of carriage wheels on the street outside.

James had run through the last of his money betting on a friend's horse down in Virginia and then there had been that uncomfortable business about the little Blanchard girl. God knows, he was only trying to give her a good time and she was so cuddly and lovable, but the mother had accused him of the most terrible things and threatened to have him arrested. When his father's telegram arrived saying he could move in for a while with Charles, the plan seemed very appealing to him. He knew he had made a mess of things so far, but this time he was going to change. He was absolutely sure of it. He had spent all of the long train trip from Virginia arranging in his head

37

how things would be now that he had been taken in to this dark, serious house with its overtones of regular hours, church on Sunday, and wholesome family ideals.

And the little girl would help. She had liked him from that moment on her mother's funeral day when he had carried her around the room like a princess. Since then, he had come back every six months or so, always with a present that made her eyes shine. One time he had produced a wooden marionette princess from Paris with flat black eyes and legs jointed at the knees and ankles. Another time it had been a fur-trimmed velvet hat and cloak that Nurse clearly disapproved of. That time, Lydia had thrown herself on her uncle with such a mixture of alarm and delight in her face that he had almost cried. This morning with the extra spot of money he had borrowed from his friend in Raleigh, he had ordered the horse cab to stop at Turlow's on Sixth Avenue, where he found an exquisite porcelain doll dressed in layers of white lace. He smiled now, thinking of the look of eager anticipation on her face as she dug down through the tissue paper to the hidden treasure beneath.

Charles had no idea how to make a child happy. James saw himself stepping in as the loving uncle. He would read her stories by the fire and play endless games with her ever so patiently and buy her candy on his way home. "Which pocket?" he would say, and she would point shyly to the wrong one and he would shake his head and pretend to be angry and she would turn away and then he would snatch her back and give her the licorice with a kiss.

All of these scenarios he had gone over in his mind a hundred times during the long sleepless night, creating and re-creating and polishing the images so that the picture of his reformed self was detailed and complete. In fact, he was sure that by thinking so much about it, he had actually already finished the job. He was a changed man.

The rabbit was hiding. Lydia poked a stick under the bushes, whistling for him. He didn't show himself right away, but she was content to play hide-and-seek for a

38

while. Nurse was off. Mrs. Sanders and Nellie were gossiping in the kitchen over a tableful of silver to polish. They had forgotten about her.

The afternoon sun in the garden was warm on the girl's face, and as she made her way along the flagstone path, she stopped now and then to look at the flowers. The orange tulips that her mother had planted years ago had opened the day before. A thin layer of pollen dust covered the inner bowl of the flower. Lydia looked closer. A black center ringed by a thin yellow lining and then the shock of the orange curving upward like six fat pleading fingers. How amazing. She had never looked inside a flower before.

The rabbit hopped out onto a flagstone just one away from hers. With a swift, silent pounce, she scooped him up, lifting him under the forelegs with her outstretched palm. The rest of his body hung limply against her side until she knelt down on the path and gathered all of him into her lap.

When James pushed open the garden door, he took in her curved back, the way her ruffled skirts were tucked in between her high-buttoned black shoes and her bottom. He said nothing to her for a while, savoring the tiny sense of power that a person gets when he is the undetected witness to a private moment.

She was curled over, talking to something. He stepped forward to listen, but her voice was pitched too low.

"Hello, little one," he said.

She turned her head and he saw a look of fear cross her face in that instant before she recognized him.

"Did I scare you? It's only your Uncle James."

She struggled to her feet, lifting the rabbit with her.

"It's the rabbit, Uncle James. Father doesn't know about him. When I heard your voice, I thought—"

He kissed her on the forehead and leaned down to admire the rabbit.

"Do you want to hold it?" Lydia asked eagerly.

Without a moment's hesitation, he slipped his hands under the rabbit's forelegs and lifted the animal like a baby up to his face. Nose to nose, they eyed one another.

Lydia was enchanted. Nurse had refused to touch the rabbit, saying it was dirty.

"She's beautiful," James said.

"Do you think it's a girl?"

"Of course," James said. "No boy rabbit would have such soft clean fur."

She looked up at him quizzically.

"What's her name?" he asked.

"Rabbit," Lydia said sheepishly. "I couldn't think of anything else."

"Oh, that won't do at all. She must have a proper name." He handed the rabbit back into Lydia's receiving arms. "How about something romantic like Cassandra? Or Felicity?"

"You decide," she said.

He stroked the furry back, once and then again, as he thought. "Natasha," he said after a while. "A Russian rabbit."

"Natasha," Lydia repeated softly. "That's good."

"Now, put her down," he said. "I've brought you something."

"You always remember."

She sounds like a little old lady, he thought. So solemn.

She let the rabbit down softly with a final loving stroke and took the box that he held out. "But Father said you weren't coming until tomorrow."

"You know me, I like to surprise people. Particularly your father," he said with a smile. His left eye closed involuntarily, a twitch that had developed when he was eight years old and afraid of horses, something his father did not condone. She watched, fascinated, as the eyelid slowly opened again and his pupil readjusted itself after a momentary wandering.

"Aren't you going to open the box?" he asked, and she realized she'd been staring.

The doll was pretty, but she did not lift it out of the box. After the soft fur of the rabbit, she was reluctant to feel the smooth unyielding surfaces of this pretend human being. Her memory of dolls was not a happy one, but of course Uncle James could not have known that.

"You don't like it?" he asked.

"Oh, I do, Uncle James. She's beautiful," Lydia said,

touching the doll's cold perfect forehead so that she
wouldn't appear ungrateful. "Thank you." She had let
herself dream for days about what he would bring and
had settled on a stereopticon with a whole box of cards of
distant places like Arabia and Finland, places she never
expected to visit any other way.

"Miss Lydia, come in now." Nellie's voice preceded
her into the darkening garden. "You'll get a chill and I'll
hear no end of grumbling from Nurse." She stopped
abruptly and dropped into a quick curtsy at the sight of
James Franklin. "Mr. James, sir, you gave me a fright.
Mr. Franklin told me you were expected tomorrow."

"Hello, Nellie."

There was the tiniest pause before anybody spoke again.
Lydia looked around for her rabbit, but she had found
shelter for the night under the corner boxbush.

"Where is your luggage, sir? I'll have Harrison take it
up to your room."

"It's being sent on from the station."

"Then I'll just go up now and make sure the room's
tidy," Nellie said.

What was Nellie so flustered about? Lydia wondered.
She took her uncle's hand. "Come on, Uncle James. The
rabbit's gone to bed. She likes to hide under that bush in
the corner."

The feel of the girl's small firm hand in his brought him
back from a momentary daydream.

"Will you be staying long, sir?" Nellie asked.

"I expect so," he answered brusquely.

At the doorway, Lydia pulled him back to let Nellie go
on ahead. "Please, Uncle James, don't ever tell Father
about the rabbit. He would be very angry with me."

James hunkered down so that his face was close to
hers. "You mustn't ever worry about me, little one," he
whispered. "Now that I'm here to stay, you and I are
going to be such good friends. And we are going to share
lots and lots of secrets."

Lydia shivered. There was something both appealing
and terrifying about the way he said it. When he did not
move or speak again but kept his eyes on her, she kissed
him quickly on the cheek to break the spell.

*   *   *

Nellie O'Shea was getting restless. She had worked for the Franklins for eight years, and although the job was pleasant enough considering the horror stories she heard from her friends, she was ready for a change. She had never wanted to go into domestic service in the first place, but at seventeen when she had to get out of the house to make room for yet another baby, she didn't have much choice.

"Nice girls don't take work in factories," her father had said. John O'Shea was a janitor for the local church, a steady job, which meant he came home on Friday nights with a regular paycheck, but spending so much time with the priest made him irritatingly preachy and religious. Sometimes Nellie even wished he would loosen up with the other men down at Neal's Bar on Friday nights, but her father had sworn off liquor.

Nellie's friend Julia was working in the shoe factory on Allen Street. "The work is hard and the hours are terrible, but your life is your own when you leave there," she warned Nellie. "You take work in one of those fancy houses uptown and you're their prisoner. Look at Rosie. She says that Mrs. Jay is much better than most of them, but Rosie only gets one afternoon a week and part of Sunday for church. You're never going to meet anyone that way. Besides, I don't think you could get a job at the factory," Julia added with a little frown. "Because of your hand."

Nellie had already thought of that. Three fingers on her left hand had never separated. She had grown quite clever at hiding her deformity, so that most people never even noticed, and there were very few things she couldn't do as well as anyone else, but in the shoe factory she'd be working with machines. She'd have to keep up with the rest of the line and she didn't have the dexterity.

In the end, Rosie got Nellie her first job with a family on Washington Square. She started out at the bottom as a scullery maid, washing out the big iron pots and chopping the vegetables for the cook, but when she was fired after a year for talking back to the butler, Rosie came to her rescue again.

"Mrs. Franklin seems nice enough," Rosie said. "She's

Mrs. Jay's sister. She says she needs a parlormaid and I told her you were just the girl. But no nonsense, Nellie. I'm not going to put myself out for you again."

"You'd better teach me a few things," Nellie said. "I never got out of the kitchen at the Frenches' except to go upstairs to that measly bedroom that I had to share with the parlormaid. Two of us on the one skinny mattress. I might as well have been back at home again, except it was worse, because she was fatter and smellier than my little brothers. But I need a new place soon, Rosie. The babies are always yowling and my father reads the Bible to us every night. And looking at Mother gives me the creeps. She's so dragged down with the four children already, and little Pat has the whooping cough. I'm never going to end up like her, I swear to you."

After two lessons from Rosie on serving and deportment ("Yes, ma'am. No, sir. Can I take your coat, sir? Mrs. Franklin is out, sir. Would you like to leave your card?") Nellie presented herself at 19 East Thirty-eighth Street. She was hired after a brief interview with Harrison and Mrs. Franklin and moved in the next day. She had been there ever since.

Nellie had an eye for beautiful things and she thrived in this new position where she could spend hours turning the chamois cloth around the gold globe of the brass andirons or in and out of the filigreed rivulets on the silver fork handles. In the late afternoons when she was sent up to draw the curtains in the front rooms, she stood for a moment alone and buried her face in the smooth blue velvet, inhaling their musty richness, turning the extra folds of the material around her waist to simulate a gown. Sometimes, she stole little things just to keep in her room for a week or so and pretend they belonged to her. A silver picture frame. The carved onyx elephant from the back of the curio cabinet. Nobody noticed. In this house, she had her own small room on the top floor and she was always careful to keep her door closed and to put things back before they were missed.

Mrs. Franklin's old nurse had been pensioned off just two months before Nellie's arrival.

"That woman treated Mrs. Franklin just like a baby," the cook told Nellie. "The way she coddled her was ridiculous. Now that we've got a proper nurse for the children, I expect Mrs. Franklin will hire a proper lady's maid too."

But, to everybody's surprise, Elizabeth decided to train Nellie for the job. Every night after the Franklins came in from dinner, Nellie was called down to help her mistress undress and to brush out her long thick hair. At first, she felt uncomfortable and awkward performing this kind of intimate task for another woman, aware of the husband's footsteps on the other side of the door, the knock of his silver brush against the top of his bureau. Nellie knew he was waiting for her to be gone so that he could enter the bedroom, and she would try to do her work quickly. But Mrs. Franklin seemed to be in no hurry.

"Don't jerk the brush, Nellie. You must give each section of the hair the same number of strokes right from my scalp down to the ends. Like this, my dear. One long easy movement." Her head rocked back slightly with each journey of the brush and Nellie could see down the white skin of her neck to where her breasts rose and fell under the dressing gown. "That's good," she whispered. "Now the next part."

One night, Mrs. Franklin caught sight of Nellie's disfigured hand in the mirror and without any warning she reached back and pulled it toward her across her own bare shoulder.

"What happened to you?"

Their eyes met in the mirror. "It's always been that way, ma'am. They grew together like that."

"How terrible for you," she said, running her own smooth fingers across Nellie's rough ones. Nellie trembled.

"It's not so bad. This hand is not as strong as the other one, but I can do my work. Most times, people don't notice."

"I'm sure an operation could be performed. It would be very simple really." She turned it over and examined the palm quickly before letting it go.

Nellie picked up the next section of hair and went on with her work. "I'll speak to Mr. Franklin about it," the other woman said.

But as far as Nellie knew, she never did, because no

more was said about her hand, although sometimes, during their evening ritual, Mrs. Franklin would reach up and pat it unexpectedly.

In the warm nighttime room, Nellie would remove her lady's clothing carefully, taking the time to put each layer in its proper place in the room; the blue damask ball gown on the padded velvet hanger, the rose-colored silk petticoat trimmed with chiffon ruching folded in thirds lengthwise and draped over another hanger, then the two extra lace-trimmed petticoats pinned at the waist to a third hanger. In the beginning, Mrs. Franklin would undo the ribbons of her camisole and slip out of it herself, but as time went on, she let Nellie do more and more, while she stood immobile in the center of the room. Their work was done in almost total silence. The only sound was the gentle release of breath when Nellie unhitched the corset, which Mrs. Franklin insisted on wearing one hook too tight so that it forced up her small breasts. Then she would lift her arms and allow the silk chemise to be pulled up over her head, and the knickers and the embroidered silk stockings to be rolled down her smooth legs.

At first Nellie had been embarrassed by the sight of the other woman's naked body and had tried to hurry through that gap between the stockings and the dressing gown, but in time she learned to follow Mrs. Franklin's lead. Sometimes the lady would sit naked in her chair and unpin her hair so that Nellie could brush it out. She taught Nellie how to massage her neck and shoulders, and in the months before she was pregnant, she showed the girl how to apply the Princess cream, which claimed on its label to be unrivaled for the "enlargement of the bust." Later on, when her belly began to swell, she would lie on her back on the bed while Nellie rubbed in the crème rivière across the spreading, pale brown stretch marks.

As the baby grew, their nightly rituals became more drawn out and elaborate. Nellie knew Mr. Franklin no longer troubled his wife with his nighttime attentions and the girl was able to concentrate completely on her lady's comfort without worrying about the husband's impatient pacing on the other side of the door.

Elizabeth Winthrop

When Mrs. Franklin dismissed her at last, Nellie would creep upstairs to her small room, where she relived the sensual rituals of the last hours. She undressed slowly, lay down on the bed, and treated her own body to the same erotic massage until she finally fell into a deep, drugged sleep.

Nellie never spoke to anyone about these evenings. She pushed away the uncomfortable thought that perhaps she was committing some kind of sin. She had certainly heard what happened to girls who touched themselves in those places, but she convinced herself that Mrs. Franklin, who was a well-brought-up society lady, must know the proper thing to do and Nellie was only following her lead. Although she often wondered whether, for example, Rosie did this kind of thing for Mrs. Jay, she certainly never dared ask her. In front of the rest of the household, she and Mrs. Franklin behaved toward one another exactly as a lady and her maid should, and when they were alone together, they barely spoke at all. But their rituals awakened in the young girl a drive which the clumsy kisses of her boyfriend, Patrick, did nothing to satisfy.

But Nellie did not mourn for Elizabeth Franklin the way Mrs. Sanders did.

"She was a good lady, better than most," Mrs. Sanders would say months later. "She gave us those nice handkerchiefs at Christmastime and she always remembered to ask about my family."

Nurse and Nellie exchanged glances behind the older woman's back. "You've got a short memory, it seems to me," Nurse said. "How many times did we have to sit down here and listen to your complaining about the impossible menus and the plans changed at the last minute and the three extra people for dinner?"

"I'm not saying she was perfect, mind you."

"Well, I'm just as happy with the way things are now," Nurse said. "Mr. Franklin doesn't interfere. He lets us do our jobs. Don't you agree, Nellie?"

Nellie nodded without speaking. Her mind had drifted up to that closed bedroom. The gas had been turned down. That silent perfect body lay stretched on the bed. I miss that, she said to herself.

46

One night, with her candle in hand, she tiptoed down the stairs to the bedroom. Mr. Franklin had gone out right after dinner and she knew he would not be coming back for hours. Upstairs, Mrs. Sanders had fallen into her usual noisy sleep and the crack under the nurse's door on the third floor was dark. Nellie took great care on the two flights of stairs, testing for each creak with her outstretched toe.

The room still smelled of Elizabeth Franklin's favorite perfume, a sweet gardenia scent that clung to the bedclothes and the curtains months after she was gone. Nellie set her candle down on the dressing table and slipped off her heavy muslin nightgown. Dressed in just the camisole and the silk knickers that she had stolen the night Mrs. Franklin died, Nellie lay down on the bed and, with her eyes closed, undressed her mistress once again and massaged her cool white skin.

From then on, the bedroom became Nellie's secret stage where she relived the dim dreams of her nights with Mrs. Franklin, a place she visited as often as she dared. But she longed for something more, and finally, out of desperation, she gave in to her boyfriend, Patrick. He had learned his lovemaking techniques from dirty pictures and barroom boasting. When he was all finished and lay panting beside her, she cried silently, wiping the tears away with fierce swipes of her palm. He would never guess that, lying there on his thin dirty mattress, she was not weeping for her lost virginity but for the way the sensual connection with another woman's body had ruined her for anything else.

When James Franklin came to live in the house permanently, Nellie began to get ideas. In the years since Mrs. Franklin's death, he had stopped every six months or so when he was passing through New York on his way to Europe. Nellie could tell from the beginning that this man was very different from his older brother. He had a dandified air about him, and the way he teased her when she took his coat in the hallway made her wonder.

"Still here, then, Miss Nellie? I thought you had grander ideas than parlormaid to an old widower," he said on one of his more recent visits.

"What do you mean, sir?" she replied, not daring to look him in the eye.

"A face like yours," he said, lifting her chin with one outstretched finger. "It shouldn't be wasting away over a bucket of soapy wash water."

She didn't know how to answer but didn't dare pull away. They stood frozen for a moment and she smelled the liquor on his breath. Upstairs a door slammed and she very gently took his hand from her face and went to hang up his coat.

But nothing else ever happened between them. In those days, he seemed to be using the house just as a way station and kept his visits brief.

One afternoon, soon after James Franklin had moved in permanently, Nellie went down to see her friend Rosie on her afternoon off. Rosie had left the Jays two years before when a gentleman named Mr. Russell, a young friend of Arthur Jay's, had set her up in her own place on West Fifteenth Street. She had real velvet curtains and the nicest kind of furniture that you ordered from McCreerys on Sixth Avenue. Even a piano in the corner of the living room with one of those fringed shawls draped over it. Nellie loved going to see her there because it fueled her dreams that one day the same thing might happen to her. Why couldn't James Franklin be her Mr. Russell?

"Sometimes, I look up and he's just standing there watching me," she told Rosie. "Gives me the shivers. He comes on me like a ghost. But it's not the same as before. He doesn't flirt with me the way he used to."

"Maybe he's seeing if you're available," Rosie said. She leaned across the tea table to hand Nellie a flowered china teacup. "Help yourself to cream," she said, nodding at the matching pitcher. Nellie knew her friend loved being able to show off her latest acquisitions. Mr. Russell was very generous.

"Give him some time," Rosie advised. "These gentlemen are always worrying about their reputations. Remember how long it took Mr. Russell to come around to me."

"Patrick's started to talk about marrying me," Nellie said. "But I don't want to be stuck in Brooklyn with a lot

of squawling brats during the day and rich ladies' embroidery at night. I've seen what's happened to my mother.
That's no life compared to what you've got."

Rosie smiled, enjoying her friend's obvious envy. "So
set your trap for Mr. James Franklin. He'll fall in sooner
or later."

4

When he first arrived in New York, James amused himself at theater parties and opera benefit balls, but it did not take him long to tire of the same old conversations every night. With men, one discussed the Street, the gold reserve, the latest horse race in Jerome Park, the upcoming show at Madison Square Garden, where Fletcher was sure to win the tandem rig race with his matched geldings. With the women, one discussed the play, the next trip to Europe, or who had been seen leaving the Windsor Hotel last Sunday afternoon with Mr. Taplin, that tall man visiting from Pittsburgh. At the end of a season of this, James began to look elsewhere for his entertainment.

Despite the genteel movements of its privileged Four Hundred, New York in the late 1890s had long since lost its small-town feeling. The population was registered at one and a half million people and it was now a city of tremendous contrasts where anything could be had for a price. James developed an insatiable appetite for all of it. Still, the brownstone at 19 East Thirty-eighth Street remained his "safe" house, the place where he kept himself in check, and for some time his little niece continued to symbolize for him all his potential goodness.

He lived a divided life. During the day, he went dutifully downtown, where he sat at the large oak desk in a sunny corner of the building at 17 Park Row and signed papers about the size and destination of copper shipments. Charles seemed preoccupied with his end of the business and the continuing unrest on Wall Street, and once he saw that James was behaving himself, he let him come and go as he pleased. They both knew that James's position had been created for him, and if he chose to leave the office at three, Charles did not object, especially since his younger brother seemed to be spending most of his time with Lydia.

"I hope you're not spoiling her, James. She can be very stubborn."

"I'm just giving her a little company. It's lonely for her in that big house."

Charles shrugged. "I never knew you had such an interest in children."

"Perhaps I am getting sentimental in my old age," James replied with a laugh.

In the afternoons when he got home from work, he usually joined Lydia down in the garden, where they played with the rabbit. It was clear that the nurse disapproved in some way of their relationship and yet she did not dare say it outright.

"Nurse makes me come in so early for my supper," Lydia complained.

"She's jealous because you and I have such a good time together," James said. "But you must do as she says for now. We don't want her reporting us to your father, little one."

Lydia frowned. "Father doesn't want you to play with me?" she asked.

"I mean about the rabbit," he said, touching the small wrinkles in her forehead.

The child's eyes grew wide with dismay. "Oh yes."

One afternoon, they couldn't find the rabbit although they called and whistled and poked about for almost an hour.

"Maybe Natasha's run away," Lydia said sadly.

"She'll be back tomorrow. There's no way she can get out of the garden," James reassured.

The next afternoon, he came home to the sound of screams from the garden. He found the nurse shaking the girl by the forearms. "For God's sake, Miss Lydia, hush up." James stepped in and picked up the sobbing child. Holding her close against him, he walked her back and forth along the garden path until the fearful screams slowed to a rhythmic bubbly sobbing.

"Can you talk now?" he whispered, brought close to tears himself by the weight of her limp, sorrowful head on his shoulder.

The tip of her nose brushed his smoothly shaven cheek and she breathed in a pleasant odor, a mixture of imported shaving soap and his new brand of cigar, the dainty Rosa Bouquet. "Natasha's dead," she said.

"How do you know?"

"I found the body." She pointed behind her without turning her head. "Under her favorite bush."

"I'm going to put you down now, little one. Can you stand?"

She nodded, and once he was certain that she wouldn't fall, he went over to the corner to investigate. The nurse watched all this from a safe distance. The whole matter of Mr. Franklin's inclusion in the rabbit secret had made her very nervous from the beginning and she was frankly relieved that the miserable little animal had had the good sense to die.

"Go upstairs and find me a box, Lydia," he said. "The very least we can do is give Natasha a decent burial."

When Lydia had left, Nurse stepped forward.

"Can you see any marks on it, sir?"

"Nothing at all," he said as he turned the limp body over with a stick. "Heart failure probably. Where did it come from?"

"A lady down on Twenty-third Street. Funny thing is, she said if it died, we could bring it back and she would replace it. Makes me wonder whether she knew it would. She skins the little bodies and makes doll muffs and boas with the fur. The whole thing made me feel quite sick. Luckily, I don't think Miss Lydia heard her going on about it." Nurse was trying hard to be conversational. She did not like this man with his dandified airs, the way he took over with the little girl whenever he felt like it, but she also did not want him for an enemy.

"How interesting," he said. "Do you think I should get her another one?"

"Oh no, sir," Nurse said quickly. "I don't think it was a wise idea on my part. I never thought she would become so attached to it, don't you know? It's the first time I've ever done something behind Mr. Franklin's back, and to be honest with you, I'm just as glad the poor little thing has died. I do hope you won't mention—"

"Do be quiet, Nurse. I'm not going to say a word to

my brother." Not unless I find your very small transgression useful to me in the future.

They placed the rabbit carefully in the purple hatbox which Lydia had found in the top of the hall closet and covered her over with tissue paper.

"I shall bury her later," James said to Lydia. "I don't want you to think about it anymore."

"Don't put a cross on top of her," Lydia said solemnly. The brown stone cross on her mother's grave always worried her when she went with her father for their increasingly sporadic visits to the cemetery. She had once asked Nurse if it hurt her mother to have all that stone pressing down on her, but the woman had only reprimanded her for asking ridiculous questions.

"You can leave us alone now, Nurse," James said.

"It's almost time for Miss Lydia's supper, sir," she said.

"I will bring her up in a minute."

The woman hesitated as if she were considering pressing her point but seemed to decide against it. Once the French doors had closed behind her, James sat down on the stone bench and held out his arms. Lydia crawled into his lap.

"Feeling better, little one?"

She sniffed. "I guess so."

"I'll go down and get you another rabbit tomorrow."

Lydia straightened up. "I don't want another one, Uncle James."

"Why not?"

"Because I just don't."

"Why, this time, I shall pick out a very healthy rabbit. Poor Natasha must have been born with a weak heart."

"I think it was my fault. I don't want another rabbit," she said in a shaky voice.

"Whatever you say, little one. Not another rabbit shall darken the doorway of this garden." He pulled her close and rocked her back and forth.

"Sometimes, I think it was my fault that Mother died," she whispered into his shirt.

"And why is that?" he asked gently, knowing she was letting him in on still another secret.

"Because Father seemed so angry with me afterward."

Elizabeth Winthrop

James said nothing for a long time. He was thinking about all the times in their childhood that Charles had triumphed over him. Charles was his father's favorite son. He was stronger and smarter, and in any contest between the brothers, Charles always won. James knew from an early age that his was a lost cause. Even though, as time went on, he not only accepted but embraced the role of the family scapegoat, he was continually rankled by his brother's achievements and his prizes, the biggest one of all being the family business. At last, James had found his revenge. The child curled up against his chest would belong to him, not to his brother.

"Don't worry about your father, little one. You've got me now," he said. "No matter what."

The next day, he took the purple hatbox down to the rabbit lady in Madison Square. It wasn't until the following Christmas that he gave Lydia the white fur boa and the tiny cozy muff for her doll.

"Thank you, Uncle James," she said sweetly from her corner next to the Christmas tree. Later that afternoon, to please him, she dressed the doll in her new winter finery and brought her downstairs to show him.

"They fit her perfectly," he said, running his finger down the thin track of white fur that hung from the doll's neck. "Do you like your present, little one?"

"Oh yes," she lied. "The fur is so soft."

Nurse was the only one who guessed where the doll clothes really came from.

"You're making the whole thing up," Nellie said when she heard Nurse's suspicions.

"I can't prove it, of course. But I wouldn't put it past him. He's a disgusting, morbid man," Nurse said.

"For God's sake, stop complaining," Nellie said. "He spends every afternoon with the child. It certainly makes your job a lot easier, doesn't it?"

What Nellie said was true, of course. Once Mr. James got home in the afternoons, she didn't have to worry about the little girl until dinnertime. It was none of her business if the child's uncle had a twisted mind. No use going out of your way to borrow trouble, was there?

She never mentioned the incident to anybody else. The child didn't care much for the doll anyway, so a few days after Christmas, Nurse moved the offensive thing up to one of the top shelves in the bookcase where it could be admired from a distance. Lydia never once asked for it to be brought down.

Together Lydia and James explored the myriad, wholesome entertainments that the city had to offer to children with dutiful uncles. In the wintertime on the days that the park-bound horsecars posted their colorful skating flags, they took to the ice on the Central Park lake. Sometimes Uncle James pushed her about in a rented ice chair like an elegant baby, but most of the time they held hands and turned wide exhilarated circles around the more timid skaters. During her spring holidays, they rode bicycles up Riverside Drive to the Claremont Inn, where they ate a sumptuous lunch on the terrace overlooking the Hudson and James made up ridiculous stories to tease their waiter. "I'm so sorry, my niece is quite deaf. An unfortunate accident at birth. You'll have to shout quite loud if you wish her to hear you," or "Could you please bring us an extra chair? My niece wishes her pet cricket to have a seat at the table." Lydia always played along, her lips pressed together to hold back the giggles. In the early summer, before Lydia was sent off to live with her grandmother, they made a ritual visit to the Central Park Zoo to welcome the hippos back from their winter home in Florida. Many of these adventures included a stop at Huylers for a chocolate soda or a discreet visit to Maillard's Confectionery under the Fifth Avenue Hotel, where once a week Lydia filled her pockets with toffee drops that had to be smuggled past Nurse into their customary hiding place in the back of the bookshelf.

Because James's own childhood had been as joyless and rule-bound as Lydia's, he threw himself into these excursions with genuine enthusiasm. Before one was finished, he was planning the next, enchanting Lydia as much with the description of their next outing as the trip did itself. She returned home from these afternoons with flashing eyes and color in her cheeks, so that even Nurse could only mutter halfheartedly about "overtaxing" the girl. Charles did not condone or condemn the trips. In fact, he rarely mentioned them except to warn James again to watch that he didn't spoil the child.

Once he felt that Charles had been lulled into complacency by his proper behavior, James began to explore the evening entertainments that the city had to offer. After a glass or two of brandy in the study and some desultory conversation about the office, James would excuse himself and leave the house again, pretending an engagement at the theater or an after-dinner cigar at the club. Even though Charles suspected that his brother was lying about his evening's destinations, he did not object, as he often had plans of his own. On many occasions, James was just flagging down a hansom on the corner of Fifth when Charles shut the front door behind him and turned toward Madison.

During those rides down the quiet avenue, James would flip through his options for the evening in his mind the way a child examines the entire contents of the confectionery counter before he makes his final selection. Except for Chicago, which he left when he was barely eighteen, he had never lived in such a great big candy store of a city with such a variety of entertainments. In the beginning his forays into New York's nightlife were quite tame: a stop at the tawdry brothel on the south side of Union Square where the girls came from the Midwest and the madam forbade any "games." Her rules were "do your business, pay your girl and go," and if you doubted them, you only needed one meeting with her square-jawed face and her swollen red knuckles to set you straight. From there, he often took a turn at the faro tables in one of the downtown Broadway establishments or stopped for a show at the Bowery "museum," where for a few cents you could watch a lady cross her ankles behind her neck.

He avoided the higher-class establishments such as Canfield's, where the millionaires gambled in private upstairs rooms, partly because he didn't want tales of his wanderings to find their way back to his brother but mostly because James had a penchant for the seamier underside of life. He preferred dark ale and garlic to wine and perfume, and by the time he had finished a day in which his every gesture and inflection seemed limited by one unspoken rule or another, his body longed to be in places where nobody knew him, where no matter what he did or said, the people he rubbed shoulders with had seen or heard worse.

Gradually, he developed a whole new group of "downtown" friends who took him to places he never could have conjured up, not even in his wildest dreams. Places where naked women danced for him, massaged his body with oils, entwined as lovers while he watched, then beckoned for him to join them. He sampled the Chinese opium dens down on Mott Street, where sailors gambled on simple domino games and Orientals lay on the mattresses for hours in stupefied bliss with the wooden pipe at their lips. Twice he visited a tattoo lady on Crosby Street who traced the lines of an extravagant silver fish on each of his hipbones. His evening ladies giggled in delight when he manipulated the creatures so that they rode the waves of his skin.

He discovered a whole network of pleasure palaces, where he could gamble for high stakes in one room, take steaming baths scented with heliotrope in the next, and in the third join a group of ladies who were equipped with a battery of pleasurable instruments that ranged from a bouquet of soft feathers to tickle his body to a wooden pin that they rolled ever so slowly down his backbone.

Many nights he stumbled home and fell into his bed fully dressed, but he was always careful to appear at breakfast, properly shaved and cologned for the trip downtown. He believed that as long as he kept his life separated into these neat compartments, he could maintain his status in the house as the cozy uncle, the dutiful younger brother. And as the months went by and the city sank its pleasure talons deeper and deeper into James, he grew terrified that Charles would find some false reason to throw him out. Like the addict who robs or murders to get his next fix, James played the good boy for his.

He never knew that Nellie O'Shea was watching him.

"Sometimes he comes in at three or four in the morning. I hear his foot on the stair and it seems that just minutes later I hear the milkman rattling his bottles under the stoop," Nellie reported to Rosie.

"Where is he going?"

Nellie shrugged. "He's up to no good, I'm sure of it. For a while, he and Mr. Franklin used to go out to dinner parties together, but they've given that up. Mr. Charles never did much of it after Mrs. Franklin died anyway. I expect he just started when Mr. James came so that he could be properly introduced to society. Now they go their separate ways after dinner."

"Is he paying any attention to you?" Rosie asked.

"Hardly at all. He spends every afternoon with the little girl. I tell you, he's giving that lazy nurse an easy time of it. It makes my blood boil when I see her lying around watching the rest of us do our work." Nellie shrugged. "Of course, now the child's up visiting her grandmother for the summer."

"Well, you can't just wait for him to come to you, Nellie. You've got to let him know you're available." Rosie smiled. "You know what I'm talking about."

The next afternoon when he rang for the tea tray, Nellie offered to take it up.

"All right, then," Harrison said. "I've got to go around to the stables and check on the victoria. It slipped a bolt when Mr. Charles was out riding yesterday."

James had settled himself in the study. He glanced up when she came in. "Oh, it's you, Nellie. Will you open the windows, please? It's damned hot in this room."

"Yes, sir," she said, brushing close to him as she lowered the tray ever so carefully, her deformed hand cleverly turned under so that it was hidden from him. She was sure that he had never noticed it. "They say the heat is supposed to keep up like this all week."

"It's unbearable," he muttered as she crossed the room behind him.

"I'm sorry, sir, could you help me here? The window seems to have swollen."

They stood next to one another, their arms lifted, and he couldn't help noticing the way she leaned against him just the slightest bit when the window gave. She was a pretty girl, he thought as they worked on the next window. Two curls of her dark hair were pressed damply against her neck.

"I expect you must feel the heat in all those clothes," he said quietly.

Her hands trembled slightly. "Yes, sir. My room in the attic is very close on days like this."

He slipped his finger under the curls and lifted them from her damp skin. She did not move or look at him when he pulled out his handkerchief and patted the beads of sweat from her neck.

"It's a shame," he said, mostly to himself, and she wondered what he meant. He turned abruptly to the next window. "I'll take care of this one," he said.

"Yes, sir." She busied herself straightening the tea tray, and when it looked as if he weren't going to speak to her again, she started for the door.

"Nellie," he called sharply to her.

She turned, her heart pounding. "Yes, sir."

"I suggest you behave yourself in this house. I wouldn't want to have to speak to my brother about you."

"No, sir. I meant no harm," she said quickly, and fled from the room.

Too bad I can't take the chance, James thought as he flung himself back into the chair. It's not often such a pretty one makes herself so available to me.

On Lydia's tenth birthday, a bright day early in February, Uncle James came home earlier than usual from work. He found her upstairs doing her lessons.

"Come along, little one. Nobody should be studying on their birthday. I have a special trip planned for you," he said. "To see an old friend of mine."

He had hired a hansom cab, and they sat together in the musty interior without speaking. Whenever she tried to ask him their destination, he just put his finger to his lips and smiled. She gave up after a while and stared out the window at the passing scene. He loved his secrets, and if he had decided to surprise her, there was nothing she could do to worm it out of him.

The hansom took to the narrow streets of the Village south of Washington Square and then turned down into a section of the city that Lydia had never seen before. Even though it was winter, the streets were crowded with children and peddlers pushing their carts. The women were wrapped in dark shawls and they hurried from one cart to another, shoving their way up to the front and shouting at one another in a foreign language.

"Who are those people?" Lydia asked, pointing to a group of men with beards and flat round caps.

"Jews," Uncle James said. "We're in the Lower East Side. Mostly Jews and Italians and some Hungarians live here."

The cab slowed to a crawl and then finally stopped outside a white clapboard building with an awning that said "Sister Maria." Still mystified, Lydia got down beside her uncle while he told the driver to wait. Then he walked in a side door of the building and led her up a steep set of stairs past two children squabbling over a piece of wood in some foreign language.

They stepped into a dark, candlelit room which was hung with fringed shawls of various colors. In one corner, a lady sat behind a table which was also covered with two or three layers of dark material. She was smoking a thin black cigar. Lydia wrinkled her nose at the sharp smell.

"I've brought you my niece," Uncle James said, stepping toward her. Lydia pulled her hand away and hung back.

"This is my friend, Sister Maria," James whispered, urging her forward. "She's not going to hurt you, little one. She's going to tell your fortune. Come on."

"Is this the surprise, Uncle James?"

"Yes, this is my birthday present to you."

She didn't want to hurt his feelings although she was disappointed and scared. She didn't want to be in this dirty, funny-smelling place on her birthday, but she allowed him to settle her in one of the chairs across from the strange lady, who paid no attention to her at first. Before he sat down in the third chair, Uncle James slipped a bill into Sister Maria's outstretched hand and she tucked it into some secret place under her skirts.

There were two candles on the table between them. One was lit, and Sister Maria indicated that Lydia was to pick up the lighted candle and touch the flame to the other wick. The woman nodded as the flame flared up for a moment and settled down to a wavery glow. Then she pushed a deck of very old worn cards over to Lydia.

"Divide them. Two piles," she said. Lydia glanced up at the sound of her thick accent, but the woman still did not meet her gaze. Even to Lydia, Sister Maria looked surprisingly young. The fortune-tellers she had read about in books had crooked yellow teeth and nasty hairs sticking out of their chins. Sister Maria's skin was clear and unmarked except for a small tan circle in the very center of her forehead.

"That's the mark the spirits left when they gave me the sight," Maria whispered, touching her birthmark. Lydia looked away. Hadn't Nurse told her it was not polite to stare?

She allowed her hands to be placed palms down, one on each pile. They waited in silence for a long time. Lydia wondered what she was supposed to do now, but she did not dare ask. Suddenly, the woman grasped her forearms. "Concentrate, child," she whispered. "Let the cards reveal themselves to you. Tell me. Which pile feels warm?"

Lydia closed her eyes. Her head was pounding and she felt faint in the close room. She wanted to yank her hands away and run from the room, but she knew how angry and disappointed Uncle James would be with her. She must play this game for his sake.

"This pile," she said at last, moving her left hand.

Sister Maria put aside the other pile of cards and slowly laid out the smaller pile. Lydia counted ten large cards. Strange symbols had been cut out and pasted on top of one another. Uncle James leaned forward, and again in deep silence, the three of them stared at the cards.

"There is no mother," Sister Maria said.

Lydia shivered.

"This is a happy day for you, child."

"My birthday," Lydia whispered. "I am ten years old today."

Uncle James laid a hand on her arm and she knew she was meant to be quiet.

"There are happy days ahead for some years." She picked the cards up one by one, and Lydia was directed to cut them into two more piles.

"You have someone who is very good to you, very close."

Lydia glanced up at Uncle James and he winked at her.

"But you must be careful. I see danger ahead with this person."

Suddenly, Sister Maria swept all the cards into a pile and put them on top of the others. "That is all."

Uncle James stood up quickly. "There was something more. You saw more."

The woman shook her head, but Uncle James reached across the table and grabbed her wrist. "I have paid for the fortune, Sister. You must tell it. All of it."

"The child is too young," the woman hissed. "I told you it was not good with one so young."

Lydia was frightened. "Let's go home, Uncle James," she said, pulling on his coat. "I want to go home now."

"Quiet, Lydia," he said sharply. "If I know what it is," he said to the woman, "then I can protect her."

"Nothing changes the cards."

He tightened his hold on her wrist.

"Very well, then. I see fire. And death. Not hers. But someone else's." At last, Uncle James released the woman's hand, and in one silent motion, she rose and slipped away through the curtain that hung behind her chair.

On the way home, they stopped at Huylers, where Uncle James ordered a chocolate soda and a big piece of cake for each of them. Lydia played with the cake, dividing it into smaller and smaller sections with her fork while Uncle James tried to amuse her with a long story about a monkey, but his gaiety was forced.

When they got back into the cab, he put his arm around her shoulders and pulled her close for a quick hug. "I'm sorry, little one. I meant it to be fun. It was a silly thing to do on such a pretty day."

"What did it mean?" Lydia asked, close to tears. "The fire and—"

"Nothing at all," he said abruptly. "She's a silly young woman who doesn't know what she's talking about. We won't tell anyone where we went today. We'll put it out of our minds."

Lydia nodded, but for once she was grateful when she got home to the warm noisy kitchen and Nurse's grumblings.

"Your father has asked to see you in the study after your supper. He was not pleased that you were still out when he got home."

"What does he want, Nurse?" Lydia asked.

"He didn't tell me, Miss Lydia." Nurse reached across the table and lined her knife and fork up side by side on the plate. "Where did your uncle take you this time?"

"On a ride downtown," Lydia said. "May I be excused?"

"Yes. Go and brush your hair first."

Her father was standing by the fireplace, one elbow on the mantel.

"Hello, Father," she said from the doorway of the room. "Nurse said—"

He whirled around. "Yes, I was looking for you earlier. You went out with Uncle James?"

She nodded. "Thank you for the hat," she said, hoping to deflect him from questions about her afternoon. This morning she had found the box tied with bright ribbon by her place at the breakfast table. He never watched her open her presents but left them somewhere for her. Maybe he didn't want to see the expression on her face. "It's very pretty," she added.

"I hope you like it. Your Aunt Katherine picked it out."

They had run out of things to say. A log popped in the fireplace and they both looked down at it.

"I called you up here because I wanted to tell you that I've entered you in the Brearley next year." He sat down in his favorite chair, the one she often found Uncle James in when her father was out. "You look pleased," he said. "Have you heard of it?"

"Yes, Father," she said. "Two girls from the Gridley classes are going. And Emily." She did not say how she had listened to them all talk about it, how she had longed for just this one thing but did not dare ask for it. He had never shown the least interest in her clothes, in her plans for the day, in her illnesses, or in what she was or was not learning. She had thought that he would leave her with Mr. Gridley the way a person left an umbrella at a friend's house by mistake, until she was obviously too old for it anymore, and that would have been the end of her education.

"Of course. I had forgotten that your cousin is there."

She did not move, waiting to be dismissed. For once, he was not engrossed in one of his newspaper articles or on the way out the front door with his coat half on.

"I expect that the work will be more rigorous than with Gridley. There are many people who do not hold with Mr. Croswell's thinking. Apparently he feels that you should have the same kind of education as a boy."

"Yes, Father."

"Do you agree with him?"

Lydia hesitated. Her father had never asked her opinion about anything before. Was there a perfect answer to this question, some way to make him see that she was a good girl after all, a person he could take out riding on Sunday afternoons the way Uncle Arthur did with Emily, a daughter who could accompany him to Madison Square Garden when the circus was in town?

She clasped her hands behind her back and spoke with distinctly clipped syllables the way Mr. Gridley had taught them to do recitations. "I think I'm just as clever as John. So why shouldn't I be taught the same things?"

"That's a good answer," he said, turning his hand over to study his fingernails. "Work hard, then. Off you go."

The answer must not have been good enough, though, because after their talk, the fragile soap bubbles of their separate worlds floated apart again and she watched from her third-story bedroom window when he climbed into the green victoria for his Sunday turn around the park. One day she would sit beside him on the smooth leather seats. She would pull her driving veil down over her chin the way the ladies did and sit up very tall and nod to this passing carriage and then to that one. And he would be proud of her.

But until that day came she had Uncle James.

"So what was the Brearley like, Grandmother?" Molly asked, pronouncing each word very carefully before she handed the tape recorder back to her grandmother.

Lydia's laugh was clearly audible on the tape. "I was happier in those early years at the Brearley than any other time in my childhood. I think it must have had something to do with the quantities of female companionship. Girls my own age, the endless buzz of chatter in the hallways, the confidences whispered in the library alcoves, the rumors about who was to be invited for tea at Miss Ann Dunn's this week. Miss Dunn was the English teacher and we all had a crush on her from the beginning. She was not beautiful by any means, but the faraway cast in her eye when she read to us from Tennyson or the evil curl her eyebrows took when 'the highwayman came riding up to the old inn door' could make us fall far more deeply in love with her than anything as superficial as looks."

"What about the art?" Molly asked. "Could you take art there?"

"You would ask that, wouldn't you?" Lydia said with affection. "Yes. We drew from models."

"Naked ones?" Molly's voice sounded appalled.

"No. Of course not. Girls from other classes would come and sit for us. I can't remember the teacher's name, but I do remember she loved charcoal. 'Let your hands flow with the line, girls,' she would cry. And our hands all dipped and soared in unison."

"How did you get to school?"

"Nurse walked with me up Fifth Avenue to the corner of Forty-fourth Street, where I fell in with a group of other girls for the last half block, and from the moment I saw their faces and felt the warmth of their bodies crowding next to me, I knew I was . . . How can I put this? I was safe, included, part of something else. It must sound silly to you, Molly."

Molly didn't speak.

"In any case," Lydia went on, "it was the first time I had ever felt that way.

"Our mornings were occupied with English, history, music, and art. Then lunch and a short rest when we lay on pallets on the gymnasium floor down in the basement while Miss Bender read to us, usually from one of Dickens's novels. In the afternoon, there were calisthenics and Latin, and one day a week Mr. Croswell addressed the entire school on some question of ethics.

"I do remember I was sent down to his office one day

65

because I could not remember the dates of some obscure Persian war. He looked at me sternly over his spectacles and said, 'Well, Miss Franklin, since you do not know this fact, do you at least know how to find it out?' I nodded numbly. 'Very well, then. Nothing matters, you don't need to know anything in life as long as you know how to find it out.' It seemed a funny thing for the headmaster to say to me, but I was so relieved not to be sent home early in disgrace that I fled from his office without another word. Now I think back on it, I realize he was absolutely right.

"Girls from the Brearley were considered ahead of their time. We were encouraged to question our teachers and they were equally encouraged to give us a great deal of work. Delicate girls chose instead to go to Miss Spence's, where, it was said, they were taught how to serve tea properly and how to instruct the servants in the correct setting of a dinner table. They probably still are, say I maliciously. I couldn't care less about how to set a table, but I am glad to tell you I still know Lady Macbeth's famous speech entirely by heart. Shall I recite it for you now?"

"No, Grandmother," Molly said in a stern voice. "I don't think that will be necessary."

" 'Out, damned spot! out, I say! One: two: why, then 'tis time to do't. Hell is murky. Fie, my lord, fie!' "

"GRANDMOTHER!"

" 'All the perfumes of Arabia will not sweeten this little hand.' "

"I give up," Molly said with a giggle just before she turned off the tape.

5

In the spring of 1898, Americans waited eagerly for the Court of Inquiry's report on the blowing up of the *Maine*. Theodore Roosevelt, the Assistant Secretary of the Navy, was convinced from the beginning that the explosion had been an act of Spanish treachery, but popular opinion in the country adopted a "wait and see" attitude and down on Wall Street there was solid resistance against any intervention in Cuba. On March 17, Senator Proctor, a conservative from Vermont who had recently returned from Cuba, rose in the Senate and delivered an unemotional but disturbing speech about the horrors he had witnessed in that small country. What he had seen, he admitted, had totally reversed his original isolationist viewpoint. This quiet description did more to convince conservative senators and businessmen that America had to intervene in Cuba to force the Spanish Government to accede to the demands of the revolutionists than all the fiery speeches of the preceding months. When the Court of Inquiry finally concluded three days later that the *Maine* had indeed been blown up by a submarine mine, the cry of "Cuba Libre" was already on the lips of the country.

From the beginning, Charles Franklin had been one of the few men on the Street in support of the war. He had met Theodore Roosevelt on many occasions and had been fascinated by his definitive book, *The Naval War of 1812,* so that when Roosevelt and Colonel Leonard Wood began to muster troops for their volunteer regiment of horsemen, Charles was one of the first to volunteer.

At first, James looked on it as a "delicious lark," which enraged Charles.

"Somebody's got to show these blasted Spaniards that they can't just trample on human beings as if they were pebbles in the road. Roosevelt wants good horsemen and I can certainly satisfy that requirement."

"Absolutely," James said briskly. Who was he to make fun of Charles's little war? After all, it would get his watchful brother out of the house and there would be nobody to limit James's nighttime activities. His head began to reel with possibilities and he had to force himself back to the conversation. Charles was going over arrangements, and if there was anything James needed to do right now, it was to prove to his older brother that he would be a responsible person to leave in charge of the household.

"I will be taking Harrison with me and have asked him to start looking for a temporary replacement. Someone to come in by the day."

"Fine," James said.

"The childen will stay the summer with Mrs. Livingston as usual. She will let you know when they are to be driven up. Nurse, of course, will go with them, but Nellie and Mrs. Sanders will stay here to see to your needs." Charles pushed his chair back from the table. "I admit I am ready for a small adventure," he said. "The business is going along well enough and this war is sure to wear itself out in a matter of months. Why the hell not?"

"Exactly," James said, a bit too heartily.

In the midst of various preparations, which included a uniform fitting at Brooks Brothers, Charles informed his two assistant partners that James's duties in the company were to remain exactly the same during his own absence.

"In other words, keep him busy," said one.

"Precisely. I shall leave him in charge of the household," Charles said with a cynical laugh. "Surely he can't muddle that up."

The morning he and Harrison were due to leave for the muster camp in Texas, Charles came down the stairs to find the staff assembled in the front hallway.

"Why are you all standing about?" he demanded.

"Mr. James suggested we wish you goodbye, sir," Mrs. Sanders said.

Sentimental theatrics, Charles thought. And of course he's still up in bed. His first instinct was to dismiss them all and give his brother hell, but he held back. After all, if James were to be left in charge of the lot of them, it would be better to treat him like a competent manager instead of the child he knew him to be.

"The uniform suits you, sir," said Harrison, who was standing in the back.

"Why, thank you, Harrison. I hope I don't disgrace myself in it."

There was an embarrassed moment as they stood there, blocking his way to the door, shifting uneasily in the silence. Suddenly they heard Lydia starting down the stairs from her room on the third floor. She was reciting a speech from *Macbeth*, the morning's assignment for English class. Miss Dunn, the teacher, was the young girl's latest crush and she must have emphasized the need for enunciation and projection, because each of Lydia's clipped consonants was clearly audible to the small audience hidden below.

"To the last syllable of recorded time," she intoned as she banged on Uncle James's door. This made up part of their morning ritual. She woke him as she went down so that he could join her at breakfast. Timing was important because the conversation was always more jovial if her father had already finished his meal and gone back upstairs. "And all our yesterdays have lighted fools the way to dusty death," she shouted through the keyhole. "Up, up, brief uncle! Life's but a walking shadow, a poor player that struts and frets his hour upon the stage, and then is heard no more."

"Out, out, desperate niece," they heard James call back to her. "You are a tale told by an idiot full of sound and fury, signifying nothing. Do not stand upon the order of your going but go at once. Get thee to a nunnery."

"Stop it," Lydia called back. "You've mixed them all up. Hamlet says that to Ophelia."

The contrast of that spontaneous offstage scene with the frozen farewell tableau James had engineered filled Charles with sadness and rage. In the two years that had passed since James came to live with them, Charles had watched his daughter open up to her uncle like a flower turned toward the sun. Sometimes she was coy and flirtatious; at other times the sharp-tongued tease, criticizing his taste in cologne or the color of his new ascot. But around her own father, the girl remained silent and proper.

At first, Charles had been tolerant of James's attentions to the little girl. After all, Lydia should have some fun in life and he was just as glad to have James do the job. He certainly had no patience for childish expeditions to the zoo. But lately he had to admit he had grown irritated by the sound of their combined laughter in the hallways, the beguiling voice she saved for James.

Last night he had come upon the two of them in the study. She was reciting the *Rubáiyát of Omar Khayyám* and James was sitting cross-legged on the sofa, entranced by her performance. Charles stood in the doorway behind her and listened. Her hands flew about, her voice alternately roared and whispered, and she seemed to be so caught up in the poem that he thought, for once, she would not notice him. He slipped so quietly into the corner armchair that she wouldn't have stopped if James had not deliberately let his eyes wander away from her face with that little warning shake of his head. As if to say, Charles thought later: Careful, we are no longer alone.

She turned around. "I didn't hear you come in, Father," she said as she retreated behind the dutiful-daughter façade he had begun to dread.

"Go on," he said. "I want to hear it too."

"I was really done," she murmured, backing toward the door.

"Well, then, start again," he said, slipping into just the role he no longer wanted to play. Obediently, she plunged in again from the beginning, but the life had gone out of her voice and they were all forced to sit through what sounded like the stiff recitation of an unimaginative schoolgirl.

If Lydia were to turn the corner at the top of the stair now to find this little crowd of people looking up at her, Charles knew that the veil would drop over her face again. Damn James. Damn them both. He began to say a hurried goodbye, determined to be gone before they came down, arm in arm, giggling at some private joke like newlyweds.

By the time Lydia got downstairs, Nurse was the only

one left in the front hall. "Your father looked awfully smart in his uniform," she said.

"Has he gone already?" Lydia asked. "He never said goodbye to me."

"Go look. They may not have started yet."

The carriage was just pulling away from the curb when she got out to the front stoop, but Lydia did not run after it. If he couldn't wait to kiss her goodbye then she wasn't going to chase after him like an eager puppy.

If Uncle James had been in that carriage, she would have hallooed and jumped up and down and made such a spectacle of herself in the middle of the sidewalk that Mrs. Wilson next door would really have had something to gossip about in the parlors up and down the block. But then Uncle James would never have left without saying goodbye to her.

Harrison glanced back toward the house as the carriage took the corner, and when he saw her, he touched the horsewhip to the brim of his black hat.

The household machinery cranked along just as smoothly without Charles as it had with him. Unlike his wife, who had approached the maintenance of the house in an inconsistent and whimsical way, Charles ran his home the way he did his business. He assumed that Mrs. Sanders knew more about cooking than he did and Nellie was much the best person to determine the most effective polishing method for the woodwork and so on and therefore he delegated tasks and trusted the staff to carry them out. For their part, the staff responded to that trust, particularly the women, who remembered well Mrs. Franklin's disparaging comments about some minuscule spot on their uniform or the times she had canceled their day off at the last minute.

Collins, the daytime valet and groom, stepped easily into Harrison's shoes. A perceptive man with a good deal of experience in this kind of temporary position, he knew that a successful transition depended entirely on how smoothly he was able to assimilate himself into the established hierarchy of the household. It did not take him long to figure out that Mrs. Sanders wanted to give the orders and he was delighted not only to let her do it but also to compliment her on her efficiency. Unlike Harrison, he did not hold himself apart from the others. He liked to settle down with the ladies for a cup of afternoon tea at the kitchen table instead of requiring that Nellie bring it to him in Harrison's small front room.

In the weeks immediately following Charles's departure, James amused himself playing at lord of the manor. He walked around the house with Collins, inspecting the polishing job on the fire screens and rearranging the furniture in the front parlor room.

"Are you absolutely sure about this, sir?" Collins asked. "Mr. Franklin gave me no instructions about redecorating."

"He left me in charge, Collins, if you recall. Here, Lydia, take these faded old things and throw them in the dustbin," James said, snapping the stems of the peacock feathers in two and then again.

"Uncle James, we've had these forever," Lydia said, tickling her palm with the dusty feathers.

"Exactly my point, little one. Not only are they out of style, they are filthy. Now, where do you think this table should go? We can't put it between those two chairs because it would block the study door and I can't stand the thought of it smashed up next to that heavy armoire." He looked around the cluttered room with an expression of despair on his face. "If only I had a little extra money, I could work wonders in here. I'd order some of that marvelous pale French silk to cover the chairs and get rid of that ridiculous old sofa and those heavy blue curtains. Open the place up. Let some air in."

With Charles Franklin gone, the atmosphere in the house did loosen up considerably. James gave several dinner parties, which put Mrs. Sanders into a frenzy, as Mr. Charles never did any entertaining at all. For the first one, a small affair for twelve, Collins brought in two girls to assist Nellie and even Nurse was pressed into service to help with the silver polishing and the laying out of the dishes for each course. Lydia managed to sneak down and find a quiet place in the corner of the kitchen where she could watch everybody rushing about and bumping into one another.

"The soup was cold," Nellie called softly down the

dumbwaiter shaft from the butler's pantry. "I heard one lady telling the gentleman next to her."

"Not my fault," Mrs. Sanders grumbled. "Mr. James insisted on all these courses. Use the warming oven," she shouted back up in such a loud voice that the hollow echo of her words startled the people in the dining room.

Lydia watched it all from her corner, hugging herself and giggling. No matter what, Uncle James always made life interesting.

But James was not having as much fun as his niece. The excitement of the parties lay in the planning, when he picked out the flowers and fussed over the menu and the seating. But there was nothing he could do to move the conversation into more interesting areas and he was sick to death of news of the war. His first party coincided with the headlines about Admiral Dewey's defeat of the Spanish squadron in Manila Bay, and the gentlemen at dinner could talk of nothing but cruisers and gunboats until, to everybody's shock, James rose and led the ladies into the parlor, leaving the men to shift for themselves with a brandy decanter and the humidor.

Soon after John returned home from boarding school in early June, Mrs. Livingston sent for the children. James and Lydia shared a mournful goodbye breakfast, conscious of John's silent disapproving presence at the other end of the table.

"Uncle James puts on too much cologne," he said to Lydia on their way back up the stairs.

"You're just jealous," she said, an echo of their old arguments.

"Don't be absurd." John was going to Harvard in the fall and had adopted what Lydia called his "above it all" attitude.

James stood on the stoop to call out his goodbyes. Lydia hung out the window of the hansom cab, waving wildly all the way to the corner, when Nurse's arm reached out and pulled her back inside.

"Poor little chicken," he said to himself. "Stuck with that insufferable brother and Nurse all summer. I shall have to organize some fabulous expedition for the two of us in the fall. But for now, I intend to concentrate on Uncle James."

Nellie settled into a congenial way of life with Mrs. Sanders and Collins. For a while, she had cozied up to him, thinking that a butler was a better catch than a Brooklyn policeman, but he let her know very gently and firmly that he was not interested.

"I think Collins prefers men to women," Nellie confided to Mrs. Sanders one morning when they were lingering over their coffee.

"Well now, my pretty, what makes you say that?" the old cook could be coy herself.

Nellie shrugged.

"I saw you snuggling up to him when he first arrived. It was all Mr. Collins this and Mr. Collins that. What happened?"

"I only wanted him to feel welcome," Nellie replied with a smirk.

"If you ask me, you'd better marry that policeman of yours," Mrs. Sanders said. "You're not getting any younger, Miss O'Shea."

"Oh hush," she said halfheartedly. Maybe the old woman was right. If somebody else didn't come along soon, she'd be sitting in this kitchen in twenty years, going deaf and complaining about her joints just the way Mrs. Sanders did. Ever since her encounter with Mr. James, she had gone out of her way to avoid him. He could get her fired, she was sure of that. She had even cut down on her visits to Rosie, whose easy life had made her stout and even more patronizing toward her less fortunate friend.

But the oppressive heat in her attic room and the reduced population of the household stirred Nellie up again and she went back to her nocturnal wanderings. Mr. James came in from the office to change his clothes and went out again almost immediately. She knew he often did not return until three or four in the morning. Mrs. Sanders always retired early with a cold compress on her forehead. Usually, when Nellie tiptoed by, the light from her candle showed the old woman's mouth hanging open with her chin tipped toward the ceiling as if she were waiting for someone to drop her a grape. The lower floors were cooler. Nellie wandered freely from one room to the next with the light held high, pretending that the house were hers, the rooms available for her detailed inspection, the furniture hers to push about in different positions. Because she did not have to creep down the hallways, avoiding loose floorboards or sleeping children, she walked with purpose, always saving Mrs. Franklin's room for the last.

One night she went all the way downstairs, set the candle on the side table in the front parlor, and in her dressing gown played the lady. "Oh yes, Bridget, put the tea tray down there, please. Mrs. Clavell will take some more buttered toast, won't you, Rosie dear? So nice of you to drop by. You haven't come to see me in months. Did you get to the theater last week? Oh no? Well, you missed the best show that's been here all season." When she tired of this game, she led her guest into the dining room and over to the sideboard. "A little nip of wine will cool us down, won't it, Rosie?" she said as she lifted the heavy crystal stoppers from each of the three decanters. "Which shall it be? The port is awfully heavy this time of year. Just a little red would be nice, don't you think?"

Nellie had rarely drunk spirits. Once or twice, Rosie had given her a glass of sweet sherry in the afternoon, which had sent her back to work with a tingly feeling in her legs and, later, a headache in her left temple. Her father never drank, so except for the fights that broke out in the street and the bums she swept past on her monthly visit home, she had no experience with liquor. She picked up one of the decanters, propped the cut-crystal glass upside down on top, and retreated upstairs to her ladyship's bedroom to play her favorite game of all.

James broke away earlier than usual. In the suffocating heat, the two ladies he had been assigned did not please him. Despite the cologne he sprinkled on them, he could smell their skin and for once he longed for his own bath and the cool dark recesses of his brother's house.

"The heat's gonna keep up all this week," the cab-driver said when James reached up to the box to pay him. "All over the city, I've seen the people sleeping out on the roofs."

James nodded without answering. From below, he had noticed a light in the front bedroom and he was eager to investigate. Nobody ever went into his sister-in-law's room. Dammit. Could Charles have come home unexpectedly? They had heard nothing from him for a month, not since the June letter from Miami saying the cavalry was leaving the next day for Cuba.

He let himself in and walked quietly up the stairs.

Nellie had fallen asleep across the bed, still dressed in Elizabeth Franklin's camisole and silk knickers, now yellowed by repeated secret washings. Her dark hair was spread out on the pillow like an opened fan. The empty decanter stood forgotten on the bedside table next to the candle, which had burned out in a pool of white wax.

James stood in the doorway without moving. For the briefest moment, he thought this was the ghost of his sister-in-law, spread in sleep across the bed. When he stepped closer, his eyes finally adjusted to the gaslight from the wall sconces, and saw who it actually was, he smiled.

"Well, well," he said in a quiet voice. "What do we have here? Somebody playing games at night when nobody's watching."

When she woke there would be all sorts of confusion and talk between them, decisions to be made, so he did not move or speak again. It was too much fun to just stand here and look. How old was she? he wondered. Twenty-five maybe. Her skin was clear, a pale rosy pink, flushed as she was with the heat and the wine and whatever else she had been doing. Along the edges of her scalp, the thin wisps of dark hair curled easily against her damp forehead. And where had she found such fine underclothes? Stolen them probably. He felt a tug in his groin. Where his evening ladies had failed, this girl, abandoned in sleep, was succeeding. He leaned over, ever so carefully, and smelled her skin, which was perfumed with an oddly familiar scent. He could not place it, but he knew he had smelled the sweet gardenia on someone else.

Nellie was still drunk when she woke to somebody stroking her bare legs. She kept her eyes closed, unwilling to break up this dream although part of her was struggling up from the drugged sleep, reminding her it was time to drag her heavy self back up the stairs. When she lifted her head at last to see James leaning over her, the years of training about peace in the house kept the scream locked inside her.

"Nellie," he said. It was a statement. "Lie down."

"Mr. James, please. Please let me go. I promise I won't ever—it was so hot in my room."

"And you must have been awfully thirsty," he said, nodding at the decanter.

"Mother of God."

"Seems to me you're beyond prayer, my girl." His hand continued to move up and down her leg. "Now, since there's nothing else you can do, why don't you lie back down and let me take care of you."

Gradually, the tracks of his four fingers dragged her mind away from Mrs. Sanders asleep upstairs, from how this night would change tomorrow and all the days after. Wasn't this just the thing she had longed for? She knew already that James Franklin was no Patrick with his clumsy fumblings. His hands were teasing her, inching their way further up the road of her thigh with every pass. By the time his fingers finally slipped under the silk band of her knickers, she had given herself over to this one moment in time, and if in a sudden attack of conscience, Mr. James had pulled away, she would have not allowed him to stop.

He unlaced her camisole, and taking a dark nipple into his mouth, he tugged on it with his lips while he flicked the tip back and forth with his tongue until she moaned and swore at him. When at last he entered her, she reached around, and pressing her outspread hands into the tight flesh of his buttocks, she pushed him deeper and deeper into her. Their bodies rose and fell together with such exquisite timing that his long final release exactly matched hers and at the same moment their bodies grew still and he slept.

Nellie was left alone with her thoughts. She knew that the man who lay beside her now controlled her life.

Elizabeth Winthrop

Tomorrow, she could be packing up and taking herself back down to that crowded tenement on Norfolk Street. If she had struggled or fought him, he would have raped her and it wouldn't have made any difference at all, because who would believe the word of a parlormaid against a gentleman? Even if she had been forced to pretend that she enjoyed his lovemaking, she knew she had made the right decision. It was all too obvious that Mr. James was experienced with women, but she knew just as well that she had given him pleasure. Her body was the only weapon she could use against him. After all, hadn't Rosie done the same and look where she ended up.

The summer stretched ahead of them. Mrs. Sanders would be no real threat. She always slept heavily but even more so in hot weather. Twice this week, Nellie had gone back upstairs to wake her so that she would be downstairs before Collins arrived. Nellie smiled to herself. If Mr. James should ever tire of her, thanks to Mrs. Franklin she had a few tricks up her sleeve, certain enticements that were sure to bring him back.

He stirred beside her and she pulled her damp arm out from under him and rolled off the bed. He woke while she was dressing, and propped up on both elbows, he watched her struggle into her muslin gown.

"Miss O'Shea is not as innocent as I had thought," he said with a smile.

She didn't answer.

"So, you won't tell me where you learned your tricks. Never mind."

"It's late, Mr. James. I'd better go upstairs."

"I suppose you had. Too bad."

"What are you going to do?" she asked, trying to keep her voice steady. "I mean about me."

Pushing the covers off, he sat cross-legged in the bed. She forced herself to keep her eyes on his face. "Now, I could dismiss you immediately, of course," he said. "It would be my word against yours, and Collins is hardly going to put up a fuss about the loss of one easily replaceable parlormaid. Is he?"

"No, sir," she said, hating the way he made her agree with him.

"But why should I do that? I never imagined that exactly the thing I was looking for downtown was sleeping two floors above me."

"I gave you a chance before," she reminded him, even though she knew it was unwise. "When you first arrived."

He grinned. "So you did. But we were more restricted then, weren't we? Imagine that, Miss Nellie O'Shea. Nobody but Mrs. Sanders to worry about all summer."

She didn't tell him that she had already figured that out. Her body was beginning to tremble again and she knew if she didn't leave now, she might not get herself upstairs until the morning. It was foolish to take a chance like that so early on.

"Good night, then, sir."

He watched her go without answering.

In the beginning, James told himself that he would only let this go on for the summer. When Charles came back, he would say a word to him about Miss O'Shea's advances, and then he could return to his safe divided way of life. Always before, he had tired of a girl after a month or two anyway. Why should it be any different with Nellie?

She waited for him every night in the front bedroom. At first, he continued his forays downtown, moving from one place to the next in a leisurely way, amused by his power to keep her there until he arrived. But gradually, that part of the game paled for him and he came back to Thirty-eighth Street earlier and earlier in the evening. He had to admit that he found her far more enticing than any of the ladies downtown who seemed to tire in the long heat of the summer. And unlike the other inappropriate women he had attached himself to in the past, this one never mentioned the word "love." She seemed to harbor no romantic fantasies about what they meant to one another. Theirs was a relationship designed purely for pleasure, and in that, they were perfectly suited. He could not know that Nellie's sexual energy had been fueled by years of frustration and that she was actually forcing herself to move slowly, to hold out some of her more exotic tricks until he grew bored with the conventional ones. Once she had given in to him, Nellie did not look back but set about making up for the years of loneliness.

"Why do you always use your right hand to touch me?" he asked her one night.

"The other one is ugly," she said. "It makes me think of a duck's foot."

He took the hand and spread the last three fingers gently apart as far as they would go. Then he kissed the rough web of skin between them. "I like it," he said, placing it on his thigh. "Rub me with it."

She shrugged and did as he asked.

"You're looking tired, girl," Mrs. Sanders said to Nellie one morning.

Nellie blushed. "It's the heat," she said. "I'm not sleeping well at night."

"Oh, is that it? I thought maybe you might be sneaking off somewhere once I'm asleep."

"Where would I go?" Nellie asked, keeping her voice low.

Mrs. Sanders shrugged. "Off to see that fellow in Brooklyn. Lord knows, I don't care what you do, but I don't want you getting into trouble while I'm in charge."

Nellie stood up quickly and cleared the table of their breakfast dishes. "I broke off with Patrick. He's never going to amount to anything. I don't want to waste my time with him anymore."

"Is there somebody else, then? Usually, a girl doesn't throw one fish off the hook before she's landed another one."

"Not this girl," Nellie said. She pushed the wet rag around her plate, searching for a way to change the subject. "Would it be all right with you if I took the afternoon off, Mrs. Sanders? I want to go see my friend Rosie. I haven't been down to her place for a while and Mr. James won't be in until after dinner."

Mrs. Sanders frowned. "When did he say that? He never mentioned it to me."

Nellie froze. She had to be more careful. "Yesterday afternoon when he came in," she said quickly.

"That's the first time he's ever given us any notice. Aren't you the lucky one to be honored with such privileged information," she grumbled. "All right, then, you might as well go off once you've finished the downstairs. I'll tell Collins."

Rosie was glad to see her. "I wondered if you had given up on me entirely, Miss Nellie. Too busy to find time for your old friend?"

They settled themselves in the dim front room, where Rosie kept the curtains drawn against the heat. She served up lemon squash and watched while Nellie gulped it down.

"You can't believe how hot it is out on the streets. A woman fainted on the horsecar when I was coming down."

"It's no wonder with all the clothes we've got to wear. I've got nothing on under this dress. Oh, don't look so shocked. Who's to know except the people who should? Besides, it's much cooler that way."

Nellie giggled. It felt good to be back with her old friend, especially since she had such a lot to tell her.

"I told you he'd come around," Rosie said when she heard about Mr. James. She beamed at Nellie.

"Don't look so pleased with yourself," Nellie said, touching her friend on the knee. "It wasn't all your doing, you know."

"But I was the one who told you to keep working on him, don't forget. Now remember what I said. Don't give him everything he wants all at once. If you do as I say, I'll be coming by to see you for tea in your own little place one of these days."

Nellie smiled but said nothing. She did not tell Rosie that Mr. James was not a romantic like her Mr. Russell. Far from it. If he ever did fix her up in a place of her own, it would be because her body was as indispensable to him as his other addictions. That was one of the reasons she had come down to see Rosie. She knew what happened to girls like herself if they didn't take precautions.

"Rosie, I wanted to ask you something."

Rosie leaned forward with a smile. There was nothing she liked better than dispensing advice.

"You told me once that there was something we could do about—" Nellie hesitated. "You know what I mean. About babies."

"Is that what's happened to you?"

"No," Nellie said. "But I want to be sure it doesn't."

"I've never found a way to stop a baby before it starts. Only before it's born."

"What do you mean?" Nellie asked.

"There's a lady on Fifth Avenue who will get rid of it. It hurts, I'll tell you that. I've had to go twice. Mr. Russell told me if he ever heard about any children, I'd never see him again." Rosie patted her ample stomach. "I think she fixed me for good the last time, because it was almost two years ago and there's been no problem since."

Nellie stared at her. "What does she do?"

"Listen, why do you want to think about that now? If you ever get into that way, just come and see me and I'll arrange it for you. She's expensive but your Mr. James will pay."

"Julia told me once that the rich ladies all know a way to stop the baby before it starts growing," Nellie said slowly.

"Well, dearie, if you ever find out what it is, you be sure to tell me about it. Now come on, have some more lemon squash and tell me all the gossip. That's the only thing I miss about being down here by myself."

On the way home that afternoon, Nellie thought over what her friend had said. Rosie had a much higher opinion of Mr. James Franklin than Nellie herself, but then Nellie had made him out to sound as fine as Mr. Russell. She couldn't let herself think about babies. Maybe what they said about doing those things to yourself was true and she wouldn't be able to have them. Anyway, she couldn't stop now. She didn't even want to.

6

On August 15, a letter arrived from Charles.

> Base Camp
> West of El Caney
> August 1, 1898

Dear James,
   Colonel Roosevelt is agitating with the government in Washington to have us shipped home quickly,
as so many of us have come down with the malarial
fever. I have been taken sick with it twice myself but
am sufficiently recovered now. Far too many of our
troops have died of the fever, rather than from any
Spaniard's bullet. It has been a miserable, nasty
business.
   By now you must have heard news of our assault
of San Juan Hill. It was done with great bravery and
I managed to escape injury despite the fact that
many soldiers were felled all around me and Colonel
Mills lost his eye while turning to give me an order.
Harrison has suffered a shrapnel wound in his left
arm but he seems to be recovering quickly, considering the conditions here.
   If all goes as planned, we expect to reach Montauk
later in the month and Harrison and I shall be home
sometime after that, although I cannot give you an
exact date.

> Yours,
>
> Charles

James asked the three members of the staff up to the dining room at dinner and read the letter aloud to them.

"So we should be prepared at any moment to welcome home our heroes," he said.

"They have done awfully well, sir," Collins said. He was shocked by Mr. James's cavalier attitude about the war.

"Absolutely, Collins. Most commendable."

Mrs. Sanders stayed behind when the other two returned to their duties. "I was meaning to ask you, sir, if I might have some days off before Mr. Charles returns. My sister has been taken ill in Connecticut and I would like to go and see her. Nellie could do the cooking while I'm gone."

"That won't be necessary, Mrs. Sanders. I shall take my dinners at the club." He glanced at her. "In fact, it would be more appropriate if I spent the nights there also."

"Well, sir, I hate to put you out, but I expect it's what Mr. Charles would say." She looked down at her feet. "It being just the two of you in the house and all."

"Precisely. When would you like to go?"

"Next week, sir. I will come back as soon as I can."

"Don't worry yourself. We'll somehow manage to muddle along without you. Better you should go now and take care of your business before the household fills up again. The children will be returning early in September, as John must get up to Harvard by the eighth." James smiled at her and she went away thinking better of him. The poor man had always been under his brother's thumb and here he was, managing things very well really.

"It shall be a lovely honeymoon, Miss O'Shea," he told Nellie when they met a few minutes later in the upstairs hallway. "The whole place to ourselves, don't you know," he added in imitation of Mrs. Sanders.

Perfect, she thought to herself. She would get the extra time she needed. He meant to have her dismissed once Mr. Charles came back, she was sure of that. Before he was driven back to his downtown pleasures by his brother's reappearance, she had to inject herself as insidiously into his bloodstream as a drug. She knew this even more surely than before, because if she left here, she no longer had any place else to go.

On the last visit to her family two weeks ago, she had met a strange-looking child on the front stoop.

"Are you new here?" she asked the little boy. His long dark hair was plastered down on his forehead in separate sweaty strips, and when he looked up at her, she could see the pox signs on his cheeks. "Do you live here?" she asked again.

He shrugged. *"Non capisco."*

She stared at him in amazement. The Irish had managed to keep the Italians out of this neighborhood. Her father was always talking about people keeping to their own kind as if the city of New York should set up boundaries between different kinds of immigrants. She hurried up the stairs past two more dark-haired children, who drew back from her in fear.

The door opened slowly to her pounding. A strange woman peered out through the crack.

"Who are you?" Nellie cried. "Where is my family?"

The woman shook her head, but when she tried to slam the door, Nellie slipped her shoe in the opening. "Do you speak English?"

"Italiano. Immigration?" she asked, her eyes wide.

"No. My family used to live here," Nellie said, trying to speak slowly. *"Madre* and *padre*. Here. Where did they go?"

"Sorry." Nellie pulled her foot away and the door closed.

At last, she found an old woman on the floor above who knew something. "You're the daughter. I remember you now," she said, peering at Nellie more closely. "They moved last week. The landlord kicked a lot of the people out and moved in them Italians. Terrible people. They scream at each other at night, and the police had to come last night and take two of the men away. They had a fight over something. I don't know what it was. I stay behind this door at night. I have to push my chair against it because the lock won't work no more."

"Where did my family go?" Nellie was shaking with frustration. She knew that people could get lost in this city, tumbled from one squalid place to another like the dust balls she swept down the stairs from the top floor.

The old woman frowned. "They didn't say anything to me. One of the babies was sick again. Kept up the crying all night before they left. Your father was here all the time. Maybe he lost his job."

Nellie spent the rest of the hot afternoon waiting outside the back door of the shoe factory where Julia worked. Their families were friends. Maybe she would know something.

When the bell inside rang, Nellie positioned herself next to the door, which swung suddenly open and disgorged a tightly packed crowd of tired women. Searching their dazed blank faces for her friend, Nellie felt grateful once more for the ease of her life uptown. She would rather be a prisoner in an uptown house than finish the day like these women who looked beaten down and destroyed by whatever those machines made them do inside.

She reached into the crowd and pulled Julia toward her.

The girl's face brightened at the sight of her. "Nellie, what are you doing here? Don't tell me you've been fired too?"

"What do you mean?"

"Your father was put out of work last week. When he couldn't pay the rent, the landlord threw them all out. With just one day's notice. He moved in a lot of Italians—"

"I know, I was just there," Nellie interrupted. "Where did they go?"

Julia sank down on the bench by the factory wall. "The heat in there is something terrible," she said, as she reached back and untwisted the two top buttons of her shirtwaist collar. Nellie gave her a handkerchief which had been dipped in the gardenia perfume.

"This smells wonderful," Julia said.

"I put it up to my face sometimes on the horsecar when I get that faint feeling."

"Gotten used to your high living uptown, I suppose?"

"Don't start that," Nellie warned her. "Where did my family go, Julia?"

"The little one had to be taken into the hospital. He

had some terrible cough. To listen to him, you thought his whole stomach was going to come up. The three older boys were moved in with some cousins of yours on Morton Street." Nellie nodded. "I expect your mother and father will have to stay there too until he finds work."

"Keep the handkerchief," Nellie said. "I've got to hurry. I'm supposed to be back at work in time to help with dinner. Thanks, Julia," she called as she hurried up the street. Her friend waved the white cloth with a listless lift of her hand. She looked like a weary soldier calling for a truce.

By the time she got to Morton Street, Nellie could only stay a little while. The baby had died and her mother seemed half crazy with grief. The whole family was staying in one small room in the back of the apartment.

"Your father's out looking for a job, but there's no work around here. I told him to try down at the docks. I can't keep them here forever, Nellie." Ann, her mother's cousin, was a kindly woman, but she had her own troubles. A husband who drank and was always drifting from one job to another. Her ten-year-old boy was already working in a factory and the youngest shined shoes on the street.

Nellie gave her all the money in her purse except for the nickel she needed for carfare home and went into the back room again to say goodbye to her mother. She knelt beside the chair where the tired woman was huddled.

"Mother, I'll try to come back soon. You be sure to tell Ann where you go so I can find you. Do you understand me?"

The woman's eyes swept around and stared blankly at her daughter.

"Thank God, you can't have any more babies. Another one would kill you."

No answer. How old was her mother by now? She must be close to fifty. The little one had just turned four. It was sickening.

"I've given Ann some money to help with your food. You try and get some rest."

Her mother leaned close to Nellie. Her skin smelled dank, dead, like an animal's breath, and Nellie turned her face aside. "They took him away from me," her mother whispered.

"Who did, Mother?"

"The angels took my baby away from me."

Nellie struggled to her feet. "Try to sleep now. I'll be back."

But she hadn't gone back, even though she knew Mrs. Sanders would give her the time off. She had no more money to give them and it made her guilty to think of the way they had to live while she ate three meals every day and slept in a bedroom all to herself. There was nothing she could do about it, she knew that, and yet she couldn't bear to go see them. She had her own business to attend to if she wasn't going to end up on the streets herself.

Collins hired Mrs. Dickson's sister to come in and help Nellie with the housework during the day while Mrs. Sanders was away.

"Not that the old woman does much anyway except the kitchen," Nellie said to James.

"Never mind. I want you to be taken care of," he said with a thin smile, often followed as it was now by the slowly closing left eye that made her shiver. In fact, the more appealing she found this man's body, the more she feared him, although she was careful not to show it. He seemed to grow more attentive and loving, particularly when Mrs. Sanders had gone. It was as if he were playing at a real honeymoon. Several times he brought her flowers when he came in from his club after dinner, and once he arrived with an entire set of new underwear.

He held the box behind his back, enjoying her impatience to get at it.

"You have to promise me something before you open this."

She drew her hand back quickly as if it had been burned. "What kind of promise?"

"Nothing so bad. When you open this, you must promise to tell me where you got the others. The things this will replace."

She knew then what it must be and she hesitated for a moment. Well, why not? She didn't think he would use stealing against her. After all, she had committed much greater offenses with him than a little petty thievery. She went out of the room with the box and came back dressed in her new finery, a pale beige camisole that dipped into a deep lace-edged valley between her breasts and a pair of short knickers to match. In the bottom of the box, she had found three decorated handkerchiefs and two pairs of colored silk stockings with stripes of appliquéd flowers.

"Thank you, sir," she said with a pretty smile. "I like them very much."

"They suit you," he replied, his eyes roving across her body. "I chose well. Now, keep your promise."

"I took a few things from Mrs. Franklin's bureau after she died. The doctor sent me up to wash her body."

He seemed shocked. "Why you?" he asked.

"I was her lady's maid. The midwife had to go home early because of the weather. Remember, she died in the middle of that blizzard."

"Just the underclothes?" he asked with a sly smile. "What else?"

"Some perfume. Her hairbrush. Only a few other things. Sometime I will show you."

He led her to the bed, and after they made love, he whispered a question into her ear. "What does a lady's maid do for her lady?"

"Many things," she replied coyly. "I had to wait up for her when she went out to dinner. Take care of her clothes. Undress her. Brush out her hair. Mrs. Franklin was very particular about what she wanted me to do."

"She was a child, really," James said, rolling over and clasping his hands behind his head. "I never understood why my brother married her. It was so unlike him."

"She was very spoiled. Before I came, her nurse, Hattie, used to pay as much attention to her as she did to the children. I heard that Hattie still gave her a bath in the evening."

"Did you ever have to do that?" James asked, the breath of his question passing over her hot forehead.

"Yes. Sometimes. Plus other things."

"Show me," he said.

"Not now," she said. "I'd have to go upstairs."

"Go on." His voice had slipped from an interested

request to a command. Bring me more tea, Nellie. Open the window, Nellie. Go upstairs, Nellie.

She rolled out of the bed and pulled the top cover around her body. When she lifted the candle to light her way, he called after her. "You look like a goddess dressed that way," he said. She didn't answer.

She knew he would love the creams. He had the same sensuality about hands and skin that Mrs. Franklin had taught her. "My sister-in-law made you do this to her?" he groaned as her fingers moved across his belly, down along the fish tattoo, and back up over the hipbone.

"For her stretch marks. And the bust cream for the breasts."

"I'll do that for you," he said, lifting his body over hers. "Although these globes are big enough for me," he muttered as he kissed first one and then the other.

So at last, she received the same caresses that she had been commanded to give all those years ago. That night, she let go, screaming with pleasure before he even entered her.

During the time Mrs. Sanders was away, they took possession of the house. As soon as Collins left, James appeared.

"You must be waiting around the corner," she teased him.

"Thank God, Collins is a punctual man," he replied, taking her into his arms. "Which bed shall it be tonight?"

She gave him dinner. Sometimes they ate down in the kitchen because it amused him. Once, she served him in the dining room. He lounged at the head of the table in his dressing gown while she moved about, dressed only in an apron. When she leaned over to offer him the meat platter, he gave her a sip of wine out of his glass while he slipped his hand under the apron.

"You're making it difficult for me to concentrate, Mr. Franklin," she said with a giggle.

"Precisely my plan."

They acted like newlyweds, roaming through the house as if they owned it. During the day, when he went out and she slipped back into her role as parlormaid, she straightened the beds they had slept in, dusted the tables where they had set down the decanter, scraped off the candle wax that had dripped down the side of the holder. She left Maggie, Mrs. Dickson's sister, to concentrate on the lower floors, fearful that she would find something suspicious upstairs.

The last night before Mrs. Sanders was due to return, he took her up on the roof. Most of the brownstones in the city were connected by a common roof line, and on the hottest evenings of the summer, people moved up into the open air, looking for some relief from the closed-in rooms below.

"Somebody will see us," she said, hanging back.

"It's too dark." He unlatched the tiny metal door and helped her crawl through. "Wait here and I will make sure."

When he came back, she was still huddled in the corner of the back dormer window. "Nobody out tonight."

"I can hear voices," she whispered.

"Three roofs down. I can't see them, so they won't be able to see us. Don't be frightened," he said, and for once, his voice was almost gentle.

She had always been afraid of heights. Many nights in previous summers, Mrs. Sanders had suggested they go out onto the roof, but she had refused. Now, in the darkness, she clung tightly to his hand with her own good one.

"Let's not go too near the edge," she said.

"But that's the whole idea," he replied with a laugh. "To look down onto the street. I used to play this game all the time in Chicago. It was the one thing I could always do better than Charles. We had an air shaft between our house and the next and he was too frightened to jump it."

He pulled her hand through his crooked arm and led her like a bride down the aisle to the cornice. "Stop trembling. I won't let you go."

She couldn't turn and run. She knew this man well enough. He was the kind of person who was stimulated by someone else's fear.

"Now lean over and look down. Come on, this wall comes almost up to your waist."

Down below, the streetlamps gave off an eerie glow in

the steamy night. A carriage turned onto the street from
the corner and made its slow, noisy way down the block
toward Fifth. He slipped his arm around her waist and
moved it slowly up to her breast.

"Let's go in again," she whispered, trembling.

"Not yet. It's so cool up here."

"Please, Mr. James. Don't let's do it here."

But he was already aroused and turned her body
toward his. "Where's my wild Nellie gone?" he whispered
in her ear. "There's nothing like a little lovemaking in
the open air. It's the only place in the house we haven't
claimed yet."

She pretended to let go with him, and when his body
pressed hers harder and harder against the rough stones
of the roof surface, she had to bite her bottom lip to keep
from crying out in pain. He would have his way with her
when and where he wanted. For the first time since their
false honeymoon had begun, he left her afterward and
went back downtown, and she lay awake in her own bed,
trembling with fear. She should pack her things now and
run away. But where could she go? Not down to lie on
the dirty floor of her cousin's back room with brothers on
either side of her.

Later she woke to the faint smell of liquor.

"Who's there?" she called.

"Don't be scared," he said. "It's only me. I was watching you sleep." What did he want from her now? she
wondered as she fumbled for her candle. When the wick
caught fire and brightened, she saw him crouched in the
corner of her room.

"I thought you had gone."

"I came back," he said with a shrug. "Can I sleep in
the bed with you?"

He had never asked her permission before. She threw
back the sheets and he curled against her like a child.
They did not make love again, and as she lay awake, his
head pressed in heavy sleep against her shoulder, she
realized it was his way of apologizing. See, Nellie, you
have no reason to run anymore. The trap is sprung and
the animal is caught.

7

In the carriage next to the window, Lydia sat knee to knee with Nurse, who was fussing with her hair. Pieces of it kept slipping out from under the straw boater which was anchored with only one hatpin.

"I, for one, shall be glad to get back home. Three months in the country is entirely too long for me. All those bugs and the heat."

"The heat is worse in the city, Nurse."

"Perhaps. But it's what I'm used to."

"You say that every year," Lydia reminded her.

"Don't be fresh, child."

Lydia turned her face back to the window. She longed to pull down the glass partition and hang out, but Nurse had told her twice already to put it up. Besides, she knew that was childish and she was no longer a child.

Word had come last week that her father would be arriving home just a few days before she did. John had already gone up to Harvard, but she had stayed with her grandmother longer than usual this year because of an epidemic in the city.

"Little one," her Uncle James had written in answer to her last letter, "I'm longing to see you too, but it would be wiser for you to stay in the country a few more weeks. The heat this summer has been simply awful and typhoid has broken out in a few of the immigrant districts downtown. Of course, there's no real danger in our neighborhood but I know your father would agree that it would be safer to stay where you are. Don't worry. As soon as you come back, we shall have all our good old times together again."

Uncle James did not know it yet, but things were going

to be different between them now. She was growing up. One night this summer before she changed into her nightgown she had seen the two small bumps of breasts beginning to show themselves on her chest.

Her cousin Emily had come into the room to find her studying her body in the mirror.

"What are you doing?"

Lydia struggled quickly into the nightgown she had dropped on the floor. "Nothing," she muttered from under the safe folds of cloth. Emily was two years older, and this summer she already wore a corset with shoulder braces instead of the loose girlish chemise. She put up her hair now and Lydia watched when Nurse helped her secure it with the pins.

"Can I wear my hair up too, Nurse?" Lydia asked one night when the woman was braiding it.

"Of course not, child. Your cousin is two years older. Besides, your Aunt Katherine is very free with her. Some girls are not allowed to put their hair up until the year they come out."

"Well, I'm not going to wait that long," Lydia said.

"We shall see. It depends on how you behave. You can't expect anyone to treat you as a grown girl when you still run outside in bare feet and wrestle with your cousin Henry and ride that pony across the fields whooping and screaming all the while."

"I don't see what that has to do with it," Lydia said as she flounced out of the room. But from then on, she worked very hard at curbing her high spirits, at least in front of the nurse and her grandmother. She stayed away from John, who had the power to tease her into a rage, and when Henry complained that she was no fun anymore, she just smiled at him with as patronizing an expression as she could summon. But still, when nobody was watching, she rode Flower bareback down to the quarry and jumped off the highest ledge into the water.

And now when the carriage at last turned onto Thirty-eighth Street, she restrained herself from pushing down the window and leaning out to see if anybody was waiting for them on the stoop. She would have been disappointed. With the arrival of Charles, James had gone back to applying himself at work. It was only three o'clock in the afternoon, and these days he did not come home until after five. When his carriage finally pulled up to the door, she had been waiting for what seemed like hours from behind the parlor curtain.

"Good afternoon, Nellie," she heard him say. Then there was a long pause when she wondered what they could be doing. After all, in this warm weather, he had no coat. "Have they come yet?" he asked at last, his voice low and breathless.

"Yes, sir. They arrived at about three."

"Where is Miss Lydia?"

"I don't know. I expect she's upstairs in her room."

Lydia couldn't bear it any longer. "I'm here," she called gaily, and when he popped his head around the corner and put out his arms, she did not see the look of fear on Nellie's face as she crossed the hall to put Mr. James's hat and cane in the front closet. Lydia didn't throw herself at her uncle as she would have in the old days. She forced herself to walk slowly toward him and take both of his hands in hers. Then she very solemnly kissed him, first on one cheek and then on the other.

"My, my, who could this possibly be? I was looking for my favorite little girl. Do you know where she's gone?"

"Now, stop teasing, Uncle James. It's me."

"Well, then, if you are truly my Lydia, you won't mind a good hug from your old uncle." And despite her protests, he crushed her against him for a long suffocating moment.

She wriggled out of his arms. "Uncle James, let me go. You're wrinkling my dress." Of course, it wasn't really the dress. She wanted him to know that things had to be different between them. He had to treat her like the young lady she had worked so hard to create over the summer. Besides, he smelled too sweet, as if he were wearing perfume.

He stepped back and looked at her again. "It's a pretty dress."

"Aunt Katherine brought it up to me last week for Grandmother's summer party." She held it out with both hands and turned all the way around so that he could admire the graceful way the folds fell from her waist. "Did Father come home with you?"

"No, I expect he'll be along shortly. He told me he wants you to eat dinner upstairs with us tonight. So I guess he realizes how much you've grown over the summer."

She beamed. There was good old Uncle James. It never took him long to understand her. "Have you been behaving yourself?" she asked with a stern frown.

"Yes, Nurse. I've been awfully good. But I'm glad you're back. I haven't been to the zoo or the circus or anywhere exciting all summer. It's been very dull in town without you."

"Oh, I'm much too old for the zoo, Uncle James."

He feigned surprise. "What shall we do, then?"

"Why, the theater, of course. And the opera. And lectures about literature."

"Sounds too dull for words," he groaned.

"And you must take me riding in Central Park."

"If you insist, Miss Lydia. But I swear to you, we won't have half as much fun as we used to."

"Don't look so sad," she said, touching his shoulder as she went out the door. "I must go up now and dress for dinner."

James stood a moment longer in the front parlor, remembering his arrival here now more than two years before. He had never stayed anyplace this long, not since he was a child. Should he pick himself up again and move on? He hadn't been to Paris in years and he knew there were old friends he could dig up there. But that would mean untangling his connections here. Although Lydia's childish affection for him had always given him great pleasure, he found her appealing now in a different way. Her body had lengthened out over the summer and he was sure that under the shirtwaist and the chemise, her breasts had begun to grow. His little Lydia, the one who shared all her secrets with him. He could not just pick up and leave her.

And there was Nellie. That woman had twisted herself around him like a snake. He was still in control, of course. It would take just one word from him to have her fired, and yet, he was not quite done with her. Just the idle thought of her during the day could send that familiar ripple of desire through his gut, and even though he made occasional trips to the downtown brothels, mostly to make her jealous, her night tricks had totally spoiled him for the tamer women there. If she were jealous, she did not show it but opened her sheets to him with that calm knowing smile on her face as if to say, I knew you'd be back. With Charles and Harrison back in the house, their meetings had grown increasingly dangerous, but James was reluctant to make any move that would further entangle himself. For the moment, he went to her when he could, and when she had an afternoon off, he borrowed a friend's house downtown. Even the danger of it seemed to excite him.

Now, of course, it would be even more difficult with that ill-tempered nurse back in the house. Well, he would see to that. It was ridiculous for a twelve-year-old girl to still have a nurse.

Charles also noticed the physical changes in his daughter. At dinner, she sat between him and James, and when she tilted her face to speak to him, he saw the two spots of pink in her cheeks where the sun must have slipped under the wide-brimmed hat that girls wore to protect their delicate skin. Unless he was deceiving himself, she seemed less scared of him, and when he commented on her dress, she looked him directly in the eye to acknowledge the compliment. Always before, she had answered him while staring down at her feet. She was also the only one who seemed the slightest bit interested in tales of the war.

"What was Colonel Roosevelt like, Father?"

"A good leader. Lots of bluster, but when the Spanish bullets began to find their targets, he was right out there in front with the rest of us."

James stirred noisily in his chair but Charles ignored him. "If you get me some paper, I shall draw you a map of our assault on San Juan Hill."

Actually she found his description quite boring, but she sat absolutely still with an attentive expression on her face, her mind racing to form one question just as he was answering her last. James left them at the table and settled himself in the study with a great rattling of the newspaper and impatient murmurings about war stories.

"Miss Lydia, you must come upstairs now," Nurse said timidly from the dining-room door. She had waited an extra fifteen minutes past the girl's normal bedtime for fear Mr. Franklin would be displeased with the interruption.

"We lost track of the time, Nurse. Off you go, then, Lydia."

"Yes, Father. Thank you for the explanation. It was awfully interesting."

"Good night," he said, keeping his head down. The enthusiasm he heard in her voice might lead her to kiss him in front of the nurse and James, who was still making a pretense of reading the paper.

"That girl is too old for a nurse," James said when Charles joined him.

"I expect she is, but what does it matter?"

"I'd be careful, Charles. Lydia has reached that romantic stage when she can get awfully attached to someone. After all, didn't Elizabeth bring her nurse with her when she married?"

Charles did not move from his position at the window. "Yes. The old woman was harmless, really."

"Oh, I'm sure she was." James had the sense not to press his point. He had planted the idea in his brother's head. That was enough for the moment.

The next day Harrison reported to Charles that the nurse had requested some time off. "She has been with the children all summer, sir. I suppose if you feel we could spare her, she does deserve a short break."

"Certainly, Harrison. Miss Lydia will be back in school and we can arrange to have Miss Jay's maid bring her home. You can take her in the morning in the carriage."

"Yes, sir."

The timing is perfect, Charles thought. We'll see if James is right. Perhaps it was time to do some rearranging in the household.

"Harrison, keep an eye out for another parlormaid, will you?"

"Are you displeased with Nellie, sir?"

"Oh no, on the contrary. I am considering making her Miss Lydia's maid. She knows what to do, of course, since Mrs. Franklin trained her, and I will expect her to oversee the cleaning, but she will need some help."

Their eyes met. "Don't say anything about it downstairs, you understand. Just make some discreet inquiries. I have not made up my mind definitely yet."

"Certainly, sir."

"How's the arm?" Charles asked genially.

"Better sir. It aches now and then but nothing to worry about."

"Good. The jungles seem very far away from here, don't they? Three months ago we were discussing troop movements instead of household problems." Harrison, always discreet, allowed himself a small smile. They had grown comfortable together in a different way, sharing tents and water as they had, and yet Harrison had slipped easily into his old position once they returned.

"It's good to be back, sir. I didn't mind the fighting as much as the heat."

"I couldn't agree more," Charles said. "Bring the carriage around, will you? Mr. James will be coming with us this morning."

"Very well, sir."

Lydia was delighted to be rid of Nurse for a while. Nellie did not fuss at her if she played in the garden until dark or came in late for supper because Uncle James had kept her too long riding in the park. And dear sweet Uncle James had already taken her to see *Cyrano de Bergerac,* which had just opened at the Garden Theater.

"The girls at school are going to be jealous," she said riding home in the carriage. "Wasn't Richard Mansfield wonderful?"

"You'll have to find someone else to do the opera with you," he warned her. "I cannot abide all those people caterwauling at one another. I have no ear for it. You see, there are limits to your beloved uncle's endurance."

She reached up and kissed him on the cheek. "You've been awfully good about it, really, Uncle James. Maybe we should have one little jaunt to the zoo. Or a bicycle ride to the Claremont, just like the old days."

He held himself very still, pleased by the feel of her

thin body leaning comfortably against his. "My Lydia," he said quietly as she prattled on about the play.

After her summer in the country, Lydia felt constricted by the dark walls of the house, by the boundaries set on her by the city streets and the restrictions of her own new ladylike self. To Miss Freundlich's delight, she spent hours at the piano, allowing her body to float away on the waves of music. Propped up on the window seat in her room, she sat late into the night, sketching the street scene below. With Nurse gone, she was allowed to roam freely through the house and one afternoon she discovered the roof.

Indian summer lingered in the city that fall, and when Lydia stepped through the small door, the afternoon sun struck her full in the face. She smiled at the sight of the brownstone roofs stretching west all the way to Fifth Avenue and the city beyond, its skyline interrupted occasionally by a church spire jutting up here, a water tower there. At last she had found her city fields, a playground where she could hitch up her skirts and stride along the edge of the sky. There were nooks and crannies to explore, parapet walls to crawl over, dormer roofs to slide down.

She kept her roof excursions a secret for as long as possible.

"What have you been doing in this skirt, Miss Lydia?" Nellie complained. "I'll never get the dirt out."

After that, Lydia hid one of her old short skirts in the top of her closet and changed into it every afternoon on her way upstairs.

One night after her supper, Uncle James stopped her in the hallway.

"Where are you when I come home in the afternoons?" he said. "I never see you anymore. You promised me a trip to the zoo."

She put a finger to her lips. "Meet me tomorrow in my room at four," she whispered. "I have a secret to show you."

When she started up the attic steps the next afternoon, James hung back for a moment. Had she been poking about in Nellie's room? "Where are we going?" he asked.

"I'm not telling," she said. "It's my turn to show you something."

When she walked right past Nellie's bedroom, unlatched the metal door, and presented him with the roof, his laugh was one of relief, although Lydia took it as pleasure at her discovery.

"Isn't it wonderful?" she said. "You can walk all the way to Fifth Avenue from here. Come on, I'll show you."

They made a funny sight, the young girl leading her well-dressed uncle by the hand on an obstacle course across the rooftops. "I come here every day. It's my secret place."

She had turned into a little girl again, scrambling over the parapet walls, playing hide-and-seek behind the brick chimneys, and he joined her games, oblivious to the dirt that rubbed off on his trousers, his soiled cuffs. She showed him how to maneuver his way up the back side of the slanted dormer roof.

"If you lie on your stomach up here, you can look down on the street and see everything going on."

"You can also see everything by leaning over the parapet wall," he muttered as he struggled into position beside her. "It's a little easier."

"But this is more fun," she said. Across the way on the north side of Thirty-ninth Street, a maid was hanging her laundry on a rope strung between an iron pole and a chimney top.

"Name that building," Uncle James said, pointing north up Madison Avenue to a church roof, dotted with towers.

"That's easy," Lydia said. "It's on the block one up from the Brearley. The Church of the Disciples. How about that one?" she said, pointing further north up Fifth.

"I have no idea," he said. "Churches are not my strong point."

"Collegiate," she replied with a grin. "There's the Windsor Hotel. You can even see the reservoir from here. You can't beat me at this game," she said, their faces close together. "I've been at it for ten days."

"So this is where you've been hiding out. Lucky that

sour nurse is off visiting her relatives. She'd never let you soil your clothes this way."

"That's why I wear this old skirt. Nellie already complained about the dirt on my school pinafore."

"Maybe the nurse won't come back," he said thoughtfully.

"Why? Did Father fire her?"

"I don't think so. But you are getting a bit old for a nurse, don't you think, Lydia?"

"Oh no, there's Miss Freundlich coming up the street. I've got to go downstairs for my music lesson. Watch this." She turned around and slid down the roof on her bottom. Uncle James chose to inch slowly backward still on his stomach.

"You'd better wash before dinner," Lydia said, dusting off his shirtfront.

"How do I look in the back?" he asked.

"Dirty," she said, slapping ineffectually at the black soot on his jacket. She gave him a playful spank. "And your bottom, Mr. James. What have you been doing?"

"You're no better, miss," he said, turning her around and spanking her three times. "Naughty girl," he muttered.

"Stop, Uncle James. That hurts."

"One more for good measure. My old nurse used to spank me just in case I had done anything wrong."

"Uncle James, let me go," she said, frightened for a moment. "I don't want Nellie to find me up here." She wrenched away from his hand, too tight on her forearm, and headed for the door.

"Does Nellie know about your visits to the roof?" he asked on the way downstairs.

"No. You won't tell, will you?"

"Of course not, Lydia. We'll just add it to our list of secrets."

Later that night, lying in bed, Lydia thought about Nurse leaving. She was an old sourpuss and Lydia loved to complain to Uncle James about her, but she was the closest thing to a mother that Lydia knew.

"Father, please let Nurse stay a little longer," she blurted out when she met him in the hall after breakfast the next morning.

"Who said she was leaving?" her father demanded angrily.

"Nobody," Lydia lied. "I just—"

"Don't you think you're getting a little old for a nurse?" he asked, more gently.

"Well, yes, of course, I am quite grown up now," Lydia said, caught between the child and the newly created young lady.

"Never mind," he said, patting her clumsily on the shoulder. "Don't worry yourself about it." She was left not knowing what would happen.

The fall was unusually warm. Every day, after school, Lydia crept upstairs with her books and curled herself up on the old blanket she had stolen from the top of the hall closet. This year Miss Dunn was teaching them poetry.

"I do not feel you can possibly understand poetry unless you learn to struggle with it yourself," she had announced the first morning the class met. "Therefore, I want you to write a poem every week and turn it in to me on Monday mornings."

Lydia wrote more than one, scribbling them into the black leather notebook and decorating the margins with illustrations. She loved her moments alone on the roof and came to dread the sound of Uncle James's voice calling softly to her from the attic steps.

"I can't play today, Uncle James," she would say. "I have to study."

"Nonsense. Why do you want your head stuffed with all those words and numbers," he would reply, and taking the books right out of her hand, he would urge her to her feet.

How could she refuse? This was her beloved Uncle James, her garden companion, her best friend.

One day, when he came up, his face was pinched into an angry expression.

"What's wrong?" she asked, closing the book without an argument.

"That Nellie is getting above herself," he muttered, taking her two hands in his and pulling her more roughly than usual to her feet. They headed west for their stroll to the Fifth Avenue corner. He held tightly to her hand, and when she tried to pull it away to climb over the parapet wall, he lifted it up as if assisting her into a carriage. "You must learn to let a gentleman help you, Miss Lydia. I expect those maiden ladies at the Brearley teach you nothing about the ways of the world." His face brightened with a new idea. "We shall have a class in deportment. Right now."

"On the roof?" she asked.

"Why not?"

Another of Uncle James's games, she thought.

"You are at a dance and a gentleman requests the pleasure of a turn about the floor. Now you stand there, looking pretty." He backed up and then advanced on her again, humming a waltz tune. "Miss Franklin, may I have this dance?" His hand slipped around her. "Very good. Now you must always let the gentleman take the lead. Even if he does not dance well, float along with him. Relax. Feel the music." She tried, but she was aware of his outspread hand on her back, how his body moved and rubbed against hers. Her foot caught in the edge of her skirt and she stumbled.

"Hitch up those skirts," he said.

"I can't, Uncle James. Not up here."

"Nonsense, nobody can see us on the roof." He reached down, swept up the front edge of her skirt, and tucked it into the waistband, exposing her petticoat.

"Uncle James," she cried, but when she tried to snatch it out, he had moved both hands around her waist. He was no longer pretending to dance, but with his feet planted, he swayed with her from side to side.

"Please stop, Uncle James," she whispered. "Let me go."

But her old Uncle James had gone somewhere and this stranger half danced, half dragged her to the side of the roof, where he pressed his body along the length of hers.

His breath was hot in her ear. "Uncle James is going to play a new game with you, little one. He's going to make you feel all nice inside." His hand slipped inside her waistband and she felt it moving, digging, exploring like a small animal burrowing through the layers of her underclothes. When one finger found the middle button of her combinations, she screamed, "No!" and in that instant of his hesitation, she twisted out of his arms and ran

104

for safety, for the roof door. She vaulted one parapet wall and scrambled over the next, like a horse taking the jumps, cantering for the gate. At the door she looked back, but he was not following her. With his eyes closed, he still leaned against the chimney wall, one hand cradling that place between his legs.

Once downstairs, she closed her bedroom door very quietly and then pushed the bureau in front of it. She stood there shaking, waiting.

Then it came. His footsteps on the stairs, his voice soft outside the door.

"Lydia."

"Go away," she said, trying to keep the tears that were running down her cheeks out of her voice.

"Open the door. I brought your books down."

"Do you promise not to come in?"

"I promise." After a long moment, she pulled the bureau back just enough so that the door swung open to expose his face. He smiled and the left eye closed. Her good old Uncle James.

"I didn't mean to scare you, little one. I was just playing a game. You won't tell anyone, will you?"

Tell anyone? What had happened up there had no words attached to it.

She shook her head.

"That's my girl," he whispered, reaching his hand in across the bureau top to put down the books. She jerked back.

"You're not scared of me, little one?"

She shook her head again and the hand withdrew slowly. Watching it, Lydia was reminded of the snake she had surprised sunning itself on her grandmother's terrace this summer.

"I have to get ready for supper," she said miserably.

"I kept my promise, didn't I? I didn't come in the room. So you must keep yours, little one. You don't tell anyone about our little game, you understand." His voice was gentle, but she heard the warning edge in it. "Another of our secrets."

She nodded numbly. Then he was gone and she stood rigid, the wooden bureau knobs pressed against her ribs, until his footsteps had receded down the stairs.

When Nellie came looking for Lydia, she found the girl curled into the corner of her bed, close in against the wall.

"I've been calling you for supper, Miss Lydia. What are you doing up here? Don't tell me you're sick. I'm dead on my feet already and you lying up here."

"I don't feel well."

Nellie lifted the sheets. "Why are you dressed in these old clothes? I declare, if that lazy nurse of yours doesn't come back soon, I'm going to have to speak to Harrison. What with the downstairs to clean and running after you . . ."

The maid's grumbling voice soothed Lydia and she allowed Nellie to pull her clothes off as if she were a baby again. Her body felt limp from the crying, and when she put up her arms for the nightgown sleeves, it was all she could do to hold her arms rigid against the material, which caught on her outstretched fingers. Nellie gave her a sponge bath, but when she lifted the nightgown to wipe off her legs, Lydia jerked away.

"Don't, Nellie," she whispered, the tears starting into her eyes. "I'm so tired. Just let me go to sleep."

"All right, Miss Lydia. Mrs. Sanders will be angry about the wasted supper, but I'll fix it with her."

"Thank you, Nellie," she said as she rolled over toward the wall.

Later that night, up in the attic, James pulled back in the middle of a kiss.

"What's that?" he whispered in Nellie's ear. She held still and listened.

"Miss Lydia crying out in her sleep. It's all right. She didn't feel well tonight. I put her to bed early."

They waited a little longer, but when there was no sound, he laid Nellie back down against the bed and ran his fingers across her bare belly. "Nothing is going to stop me tonight," he muttered. "I have been wanting you all day."

She smiled to herself. "You have to be careful, Mr. James. Harrison was in the butler's pantry when I let you in the front door. He might have heard us."

"Dammit, I wanted to lift your skirts and have you right there against the wall of the front hall."

She pulled off her nightgown, smiling all the while, and pressed his head against her warm breast.

For the next few days, Lydia avoided Uncle James. She did not go back to the roof but set her books up on the side table in the kitchen.

"Now what are you doing down here, Miss Lydia?" Mrs. Sanders said. "With all the work I've got to do, I can't be tripping over you every minute."

"Could I please stay?" Lydia begged. "I promise I won't get in your way."

The poor child. Mrs. Sanders let her be, and when Harrison wasn't looking, she set the mixing bowl down so that Lydia could lick off the last of the cookie batter.

At night, when Lydia went to bed, all alone on the third floor, she very quietly pushed the bureau back in front of the door, but sometimes even that extra protection did not help her sleep. It was all her fault, of course. She should never have gone up to the roof. She had done something very wrong to make her Uncle James turn into that other person. Now, when they met in the hallways, he winked at her and smiled just the way he used to. After a while, she began to miss his company and the other thing that had happened between them floated a little farther away like a dead leaf carried by the wind.

They went to the zoo together just as he had promised. They laughed at the fat hippo blowing and snorting in his muddy water. They drank sodas at Huylers and walked home up Fifth Avenue.

"Winter's coming," he said, pulling her cloak around her shoulders. For a tiny instant, she froze at his touch through the thick cloth, and when he took his hands away, his face looked sad.

She slipped her small hand into his big one and squeezed it. "The zoo was fun today, wasn't it?"

"Yes, little one. Anything with you is fun."

And that was all he said.

So she would be his little girl, she told herself. It was trying to be that grownup person that had made things go funny between them. Next week the poem she handed to Miss Dunn was called "The Zoo with Uncle James."

When she gave him his own copy, he pushed the edges of the lined paper into the corner of his mirror so that the little picture she had drawn to illustrate the poem showed them dancing together along the wooden frame.

"That way I can read it every morning," he said.

8

When the nurse came back, she was in a terrible mood. Everybody in the house noticed it, but Lydia suffered the worst.

"I don't know what Nellie was thinking about, letting you do your work in the kitchen that way. How many times do I have to tell you, Miss Lydia, that you are a young lady now? You must learn the ways of a lady."

Lydia did not tell her that she had given up that project. She took refuge in a sullen silence that seemed to drive Nurse into a further rage.

"Look me in the eye. Stand up straight. See how you slouch over. You must show yourself off to best advantage."

"You make me sound like a racehorse," Lydia said.

The woman threw up her arms in a dramatic gesture. "I do not know why I came back here. My sister is doing so well with that little store in Pennsylvania. I have half a mind to walk out on this job and go live with her."

One day, Lydia came into her room to find the nurse leafing through her poetry book. Without thinking, she snatched it away.

"That is my private book," she said vehemently. "You are not allowed to read it, ever."

Nurse smacked the child across the face and instantly regretted it, but she was too far into it to pull back now.

"Don't you ever talk to me that way, you nasty insolent girl. I have been instructed by your father to oversee your studies and that is exactly what I will do. Now give me that book."

"No," Lydia said, backing away. "I won't."

The woman advanced, and before Lydia could stop

her, she reached around behind her back and yanked the book down and out of her hands.

"I hate you," Lydia screamed. She slammed the door behind her and hurtled down the stairs smack into Uncle James, who had just reached the second-floor landing. He swayed a little at the force of the impact.

"What is it, Lydia?"

Lydia was so angry that she stood without speaking, her fists balled in fury. "Come in here and tell me all about it," he said, leading her quietly into his room and closing the door behind them.

"It's Nurse, I hate her. You must tell Father to get rid of her. I want her fired."

James smiled, and settling himself in his armchair, he put out his arms. "Come sit."

With his comforting arms wrapped around her and her aching head settled against his shoulder, she poured out the story. Uncle James rocked her gently, and when she began to cry, exhausted by her fury, he reached up and stroked her hair.

"There, there," he said, his voice husky. "Uncle James will take care of everything."

Slowly she became aware that his body was moving under hers, that his hand had slipped down onto her thigh, and she stiffened. There was that smell on his breath that she used to tease him about.

"There now," he whispered. "Close your eyes and go to sleep. I'm going to make you feel better." His hand reached down and slipped up her leg, up under the petticoats to that place he had been searching for before. She squirmed, but this time he was holding her very tight.

"Please, Uncle James. Please let me go now."

"Hush, little one. Hush." His voice was so gentle, even his fingers were gentle as they twisted the button open and slipped into her crack, but she wanted so much to get away. "When you sit still like this, you're a very good girl. My little Lydia."

Underneath she could feel that lump rising between his legs. She began to cry again, very quietly this time. He pressed her head back down against the bones of his shoulder, and with her nose pressed into his neck, into the cloying sweet smell of his cologne, she shut her eyes and prayed. Please God, make him stop. Make him leave me alone. Take his hands away. Now the exploring hand down there cupped her and pressed her back against the lump that dug at her through the layers of petticoats, pushed and pushed at her up and down. His breathing was coming quicker, and with one last arch of his back, he moaned and sunk with her, deeper into the chair. She felt the hand inside her pants go limp and she pulled his arm out through the twisting tunnels of her underclothes. His eyes were closed now. Shaking, she slid down out of his lap and crawled to the door, terrified that he would reach out and drag her back, his hand landing on her ankle like an animal jumping for a branch.

"Lydia," he said, his voice drowsy.

"Yes," she whispered.

"You're my good little girl now. Remember what I said before. No telling."

Anything, she would promise anything, if she could just get out of this room.

"Yes," she said.

Upstairs, Nurse was waiting for her.

"I suppose you went crying to your Uncle James about me?"

Lydia stood and looked at the floor. "I'm sorry, Nurse," she said, her voice shaking. "I won't ever do it again."

"I should hope not," Nurse said, softening at the sight of the sorrowful child. Something had drummed the defiance out of the girl for the moment. "Here is your book," she said, handing it back. "Now go and take your bath before supper."

Lydia lay in the warm water for a long time. With the rough washcloth, she had scrubbed the place his fingers had touched until it felt raw and burned. She wanted to stay in this safe locked room forever. But she couldn't. Already Nurse was banging on the door. She thought of praying, but she wasn't sure she believed in God anymore. After all, how could he let Uncle James do that to her? Nurse always prayed to God's mother. When she was younger, Nurse had taught her that prayer about the Mother of God. "Don't ever tell your Aunt Katherine, mind you," Nurse had said. "Why?" Lydia had asked.

"Doesn't God have a mother?" Nurse looked confused by the question. "Just do as I say, Miss Lydia."

"Dear Mother of God," Lydia whispered. "Please help me. Please don't let—" But there she stopped because she didn't want to put those probing fingers into words. "Please keep me safe," she ended.

Just as before, Uncle James acted as if nothing had happened between them, but from the moment Lydia got home in the afternoons, she stuck close by Nurse.

"Where are you going?"

"Down to the kitchen for a cup of tea."

"May I come with you?"

"I've told you you must do your studying up here at your desk, Lydia. Why do you look so scared, child? You're acting like a frightened little rabbit these days."

While she was gone, Lydia would sit rigidly at her desk, listening for the slam of the front door, the sound of Uncle James's footsteps on the stairs. If she heard anything at all, she darted into the bathroom and locked herself in until Nurse banged on the door.

"What are you doing in there?"

"I'm coming out, Nurse."

She tried very hard to be good, to please Nurse. The woman did seem to soften toward her.

"I think I've finally gotten through to you, Miss Lydia. Your manners have improved lately."

"Thank you, Nurse."

Sometimes in the middle of the night, some noise in the house, the creak of the attic stairs might penetrate her dreams and she would start up from her sleep and call out.

"Can I sleep in your room, Nurse?" she would ask when the woman came to settle her down again.

"It was just a dream, Miss Lydia. Lie down now. It won't come back."

But the nightmares did come back.

Would Uncle James have the nurse fired? After all, Lydia had told him to do it, had screamed that she hated the nurse. One afternoon, she wrote a formal little note to her father.

Dear Father,

I am sorry to trouble you but I have a favor to ask you. I love Nurse very much and I want her to stay with me for as long as possible.

Your loving daughter,

Lydia

Charles was puzzled by the note. That night after dinner, he showed it to his brother.

"What do you think it's all about?"

James shrugged and threw it on the fire. "Remember I spoke to you about the romantic attachments girls seem to get at this age? This is what I meant. I haven't bothered to tell you before, but the nurse has not always shown good judgment with Lydia."

"Whatever do you mean, James?"

"Very small things, really. They weren't worth bothering you about."

"For God's sake, stop beating about the bush."

"For a while, she allowed the child to keep a rabbit in the garden. Lydia knew you would disapprove and the two of them kept it secret. Nasty dirty animal. I made the nurse get rid of it when I found out, of course."

"Not a great transgression," Charles said thoughtfully. "But I don't like servants disobeying my orders, going behind my back."

"Precisely."

But Charles put the decision off once again. At this point, he was too busy to be bothered with household details. In the last month, he had worked hard for Roosevelt's campaign, and now that his old colonel had been elected to the governorship, it was time to turn his attention back to his own business. The United Mine Workers strike in Illinois had made Wall Street edgy about investments in copper, and for the first time Charles was spending a good deal of time restoring investors' faith in his company.

The reports from Mr. Croswell about Lydia were very

positive. Miss Dunn, her English teacher, was particularly pleased with the girl's work. Very well. If she wanted the nurse to stay, why shouldn't she?

Nellie was beginning to worry about Mr. James, who seemed to grow more reckless every day. He was drinking a great deal, and one night, just a few minutes after he slipped into her room, Mrs. Sanders had pounded on her door, calling that she heard somebody on the stairs. With Mr. James hidden under the bed, Nellie had gotten the old woman back to her own room.

In the beginning when she'd brought up the idea of her own place, he had gone into a terrible rage.

"Trying to blackmail me, Miss High-handed O'Shea?" he snarled. "I can put you out on the streets like that," he said, clapping his hands together two inches from her face. "Don't you dare try anything like that with me."

It had taken her the rest of her afternoon off to calm him down and now she did not dare suggest it again. But he lay in wait for her in the house, taking every chance he could to slip his arms around her, rub himself up against her. She began to wish he would go back to his downtown ladies, if only to release some of his pent-up energy, but he told her over and over again that nobody else took care of him the way she did.

One night, Nurse stopped her on her way upstairs. "Come into my room for a moment, Nellie. There's something I wish to speak with you about."

"Is it important?" Nellie asked wearily. "I've had a bad day with all those curtains to rehang."

"I won't take too much of your time."

The nurse did not ask her to sit down, so Nellie leaned up against the closed door.

"I know what you and Mr. James are up to," Nurse said. "I've been watching you. I intend to speak to Mr. Charles about it unless you give me a reason not to."

Nellie's face had frozen the moment she heard his name. "I don't know what you are talking about," she said very slowly, wondering whether she should protest more loudly.

"I saw you this afternoon in the downstairs hallway." Nurse looked away. "Disgusting."

"Why, you little spy, sneaking around the house—"

"I was hardly sneaking, Miss O'Shea. I was coming downstairs for my afternoon tea. Thank God Miss Lydia was not with me. I don't know how I would have explained that behavior to her."

What a prig, Nellie thought. You could bet she'd never had any fun in her life. "So what do you intend to say, Nurse?" she asked recklessly. "Do you think Mr. Charles will take your word against his own brother's?"

"Of course he will," she said firmly, but Nellie could see a shadow of hesitation on the other woman's face.

"I'd be careful if I were you. Harrison told me and Mrs. Sanders that Mr. Charles is considering some changes in the household. Everybody knows Miss Lydia is much too old to have a nurse anymore. A lady's maid would be more appropriate at her age, don't you think? And guess who that might be?"

The nurse was beaten and she knew it, but she drew herself up anyway. "You had better watch yourself from now on, Nellie O'Shea. The next person who sees you carrying on like that might not be so understanding."

On her way upstairs, Nellie laughed out loud at the old maid's ridiculous posturing, but sitting up in bed that night, she had second thoughts. The next day after breakfast, she followed James upstairs and pulled him into Mrs. Franklin's room to tell him what had happened.

"That old cow," he muttered. "Never mind. I'll take care of her."

The plan he devised went off almost too smoothly. The nurse, of course, swore that she had never taken the silver spoons, that someone who wanted her out of the house had put them in her room. "Let me talk to Mr. Franklin," she demanded of Harrison. "I will tell him the real truth about what's going in this house."

"Mr. Franklin left me in charge. He has gone on a business trip. I frankly am surprised, but when Nellie discovered the spoons were missing, she came straight to me."

"Why didn't you just ask me?" Nurse demanded. "I have done nothing wrong. Have I ever given you any dissatisfaction, Mr. Harrison?"

He turned away without answering. Scenes like this

115

made him uncomfortable. Soon the woman would burst into tears and start in about her sick aunt. But this was a clear case of theft. Harrison himself had found the spoons hidden in the woman's top drawer. Besides, he knew that Mr. Franklin had been considering a change in the household and he had left Harrison in complete charge. The most upsetting thing turned out to be the little girl's reaction.

She clung to the nurse, screaming and babbling incoherently. Luckily, Mr. James walked in in the middle of the scene. Harrison took him aside to explain the situation.

"You've done absolutely the right thing, Harrison. I'll take over from here." Stepping in from behind, he undid Lydia's grasp on the woman's skirt. "Come on, little one," he said gently. "Let Nurse go quietly. Don't make it harder on all of us."

Nurse was the only one who saw the terror on the girl's face as she felt her uncle's hands on her, and even in the midst of her own fury and confusion, she wondered what had changed between the two of them.

"I am shocked by your behavior, Nurse," he said over Miss Lydia's head.

"You are a disgusting, loathsome human being," she spat back at him. "Ask him about Nellie, Mr. Harrison. Ask this man what games he is playing with the parlormaid." Her voice rose to a hysterical pitch, and Harrison stepped back into the middle. Mr. James clearly had his hands full with Miss Lydia, who was trying to run back to the nurse. Harrison picked up the woman's traveling bag, and with a firm hand on her elbow, he guided her out the front door, kicking it closed behind him with his foot.

"Let me go," Lydia screamed, and the moment she felt his fingers loosen, she tore for the stairs, tripping and stumbling up them without daring to look back. From her window on the top floor, she could just see Nurse stepping into a horse cab at the corner of Madison.

What would happen to her now that her last protection was gone? She huddled in the corner of the window seat, the last sobs heaving their way up her throat. When the door swung slowly open, she screamed.

"Miss Lydia, it's me, Nellie," the woman said softly. She crossed the room and gathered the hysterical girl into

116

her arms. "There, there, that's better," she murmured, rocking the long body back and forth until the sobbing had died down to an occasional involuntary hiccup.

Once again, she undressed the girl, sponged her forehead, and put her to bed. "Now, I'm not promising to do this every night, mind you, but I'll get Mrs. Sanders to heat you a little broth and I'll bring it up to you."

Until she came back, Lydia sat rigidly in the bed, staring at the open door, listening for footsteps. Downstairs, somewhere, she heard Uncle James's voice and then Harrison's. The front door closed again. She scrambled out of bed to the window just in time to see her uncle walking up the block in the fading light.

After Nellie had taken away the tray and turned down the gas, Lydia crept to the door and very quietly pushed her bureau in front of it. With the last shove, her mother's picture frame tumbled off the bureau onto the floor. She picked it up and put it away in the top drawer. After all, she would be moving the bureau back and forth every day from now on.

Later that night, Harrison and Mrs. Sanders drank a last cup of tea together. "To calm my nerves," the old woman said. "What a day. I would never have guessed it of that woman. I didn't like her much, mind you. After all, who ever heard of an Irish girl as a nurse?"

"It was Mrs. Franklin who took a fancy to her from the beginning. Remember, old Hattie had left just a little while before." He stretched in the chair. "Long time ago now. She didn't seem like a thief, though."

"Maybe she was stealing little things all along, Mr. Harrison. You never know about people."

He shrugged. "What did she mean about Nellie and Mr. James? Did you hear that?"

"Clear down here," Mrs. Sanders said. She certainly wasn't going to admit that she had been standing at the top of the kitchen stairs during the whole scene in the front hall. "Probably just jealous. Nellie's still a pretty girl. She may catch a husband one of these days but not that Bridget," she said contemptuously. She had never used the nurse's real name before. "There was no hope for her. Something happens to a woman who knows she's going to end her life an old maid," she added with a self-satisfied smile.

"I suppose so," Harrison said, struggling to his feet. He had been married himself once, but the girl died of pneumonia six months after the wedding. "Good night, then, Mrs. Sanders."

"Good night to you, Mr. Harrison."

In the years that followed, Lydia became the good girl, all that Nurse had ever wanted her to be.

On her thirteenth birthday, Uncle James took her to a photographer's studio. Before he ducked beneath his black shroud, the man posed her against the false Corinthian column, a rose hanging down from her fingers, her head tilted at a romantic angle that showed off the satin bow in her hair.

"For God's sake, Lydia, try to smile a little," Uncle James teased from his position in the corner.

"Yes, Uncle James," she said, and obeyed. Years later, when her granddaughter Molly would study that photograph, she would see how false Lydia's smile seemed to be, how brave the front she put up.

She stood up straight. She did her work at school. She curtsied. She never spoke too loudly. When her brother came home from school, she didn't even bother to tease him anymore. Some people noticed the change.

"Lydia seems so quiet these days," Katherine said to Charles. "Up in the country, she never even wants to play outside anymore. It's as if she's scared of something."

"She's growing into a young lady," Charles said, pleased with his serious, proper daughter. Without any help at all, he had managed to raise the kind of woman his wife had never been. "Isn't that what she's supposed to be?"

"Even young ladies laugh occasionally," Katherine replied caustically. But she had her own family to worry about and Lydia was so good that it seemed ridiculous to even bring it up.

She did not eat well and grew thin. Some days, she stayed in bed with some unfocused complaint. She was tired. She felt dizzy. Her stomach hurt. The doctor would come and examine her and prescribe rest, and Maggie, the new chambermaid, would grumble her way upstairs with meals on a tray, muttering about malingerers.

Lying in the bed, Lydia wondered whether she might just disappear. On the days that he found her, that he played with her, she closed her eyes and wished that it could happen. His hands would be groping, tickling, pulling at her clothes, and she would suddenly be gone and he would be touching nothing but air.

She knew it was her fault. She tried so hard to be good, but something she was doing was very, very wrong, something that was so bad and ugly it made Uncle James sick too. She hid her growing breasts from Nellie as long as she could because she knew it meant the corset cover, the webbed cage that pushed her up and out, just the thing she had longed for two years ago when Emily first wore it. Now she wanted to stay little forever, to hide the lumps of flesh under the loose baby chemise. But Nellie wasn't fooled for long.

"Your mother had beautiful breasts, Miss Lydia," she said softly as she adjusted the side laces of the corset cover for the first time. "She wore her corset too tight in order to show them off better." Lydia nodded numbly, the silent tears tickling their way down her cheeks. She did not stand up as straight anymore but curled her shoulders around to hide her front.

She still wrote poems, even though her new teacher did not require it. She scribbled them into her black notebook, which she hid in the back of her bookshelf, the place where nobody would think to look. On the bad days when Uncle James had come looking for her, she would make a mark in this book on the bottom of the page, a round black circle like the spot of the sin she knew must be growing on her soul, that invisible place where God kept his records.

Sometimes, for just a moment, down below the layers of fear and guilt, she would reach the anger, a round hot ball that burned day and night like the molten core at the center of the earth. But alone in the sickbed, the anger terrified her more than anything else. It swept across her, it made her body shake, it made pictures of mutilation come into her head, it took control of her as firmly as Uncle James's hands did. Once, in the grip of it, she stole

Elizabeth Winthrop

a carving knife from the sideboard in the dining room and hid it under her pillow. But the very next morning, trembling with remorse at the things she had dreamed of, she tiptoed into the cool empty room and put it back again. When the rage swept over her like that, she knew she could not be trusted.

She developed a twitch, an unconscious habit of rubbing both her thumbs across the other fingers, back and forth, back and forth until the skin made a squeaky noise.

"Lydia, keep your hands still," her father would say at the dinner table, and she would clasp them in her lap in shame because she had not even known she was doing it. Perhaps people saw other things about her in her face or in the way she walked, secrets that she was sure were deeply hidden but were actually just as exposed as her flying fingers. Uncle James saw things. She knew that, because in front of the others he always stared at her with a thin smile and the slowly closing eye she had come to dread because it seemed to her now to be a conspiratorial wink. He never looked at anybody else in the same way. She kept her chin turned away, her voice low, when he asked her a question at dinner.

As for James, he had taken down the wall so carefully erected in his early years in the house. He convinced himself that, as long as he adhered to certain rules of propriety, he no longer needed to keep one side of his life divided from the other.

"I think we've had quite an effect on you, James," Charles said one morning on their way downtown. "Off you go to work every day, home for dinner, even an occasional church service on Easter morning. Positively dull," he added with a chuckle. "How do you bear it after all those years of high living?"

James grinned. "I've turned aside from a life of sin. Saved by my respectable older brother."

"That's not entirely true, old boy. God knows where you go or what you do at night. I hear you dragging yourself up the stairs occasionally. But as long as you don't make any kind of scene, go right ahead and have yourself a good time."

"I intend to," James replied, irritated by the permis-

120

sion his brother thought he had the right to give. Right under your sanctimonious nose. In fact, right above your sanctimonious head on occasion.

Nellie continued to amuse him. She had been moved downstairs into the nurse's old room, which made it much easier for him to visit her at night, as Lydia was the only other person who slept on that floor.

"For God's sake, keep your voice down," she cautioned him. "What if the girl wakes up?"

"We don't need to worry about Miss Lydia. She's a great keeper of secrets. She would hide a murderer in the closet if I told her to. Besides, she's such a scared little thing these days, she would never poke her terrified nose outside that door. No fun at all anymore."

As for Lydia, he had convinced himself that he was doing her a favor. By the time she found a husband, she would be ready for him, thanks to her good old Uncle James. And if she never did, which wouldn't be a surprise since she never smiled anymore, then he would give her the only fun she'd ever get in her life. Just as he always had. Her crying and pleading infuriated him, which she must have figured out, because now her body was as rigid and silent as a board when he touched it.

"You should soften up, little one," he whispered to her one day when he had her alone again. "Like this," he said, taking the old doll down from her dusty perch on the shelf. "Remember this present?" he asked, stroking the little fur muff that hid the porcelain hands.

She nodded numbly.

"Feel it," he said.

She obeyed.

"It's soft, isn't it?" he murmured, moving his hand over to her arm. A whimper escaped from her lips and that familiar look of fear and then resignation crossed her face. It gave him a little thrill of power. She was still his Lydia, which made up for the times Nellie refused him.

Although he told himself he could get rid of Nellie whenever he chose to do so, deep down he had begun to recognize that he was addicted to her. Often when he had stayed away from her just to show her he could live without her, he would come crawling back up the stirs after a week or so. She would get out the jars of cream, pull off his clothes, and give him what he had been missing without her. Lately, he had even talked about getting her a place.

"You could have me all the time then," she whispered. "Anytime you wanted. Just like the old days. When we had this house to ourselves."

He had smiled at the memory.

9

Lydia lived the life of any upper-class girl in New York. Two days a week, after school, she was taught Italian by Signora Francese and this lesson was followed by piano, still with Miss Freundlich. On her fifteenth birthday, she was told by her father that on certain nights of the week she would eat dinner upstairs. She began to attend tea dances at the age of sixteen, where the young gentlemen filled out her dance card and she turned solemnly about the room with them, discussing the latest play.

Nellie taught her how to put up her hair, how to attach her stockings, and when the time came, how to arrange the thick cotton pads in her underclothes.

That morning Lydia refused to get out of bed.

"What is it this time, miss?" Nellie asked impatiently. The girl was always sick. "Another headache?"

Lydia shook her head. As soon as she had seen the blood on her nightgown, she had pulled the bedclothes back over her body.

"Well, come on, then, up you get." Nellie was in a bad mood. She had been up most of the night with Mr. James, who had stumbled into her room drunk and didn't want to leave.

Before Lydia could stop her, she yanked the bedsheets off and pulled her roughly to her feet. The maid followed the girl's eyes down to the brownish-red spot where the blood had dried.

"Something inside me is bleeding," Lydia whispered. "Will I die?"

"No, silly girl, you won't die. This is just the beginning. It means you're a woman now."

So along with the horrid corset and the stockings that caught in her fingernails and the pins that poked into her scalp, Lydia had to learn how to count the days between one bleeding and the next so she wasn't caught in the streets without protection.

During that winter when she turned sixteen, Uncle James left her alone, and a little tiny hope had begun to grow in her that those times were finally over for good, a little hope like the last wisp of smoke from a dead fire. She still pushed the bureau in front of the door on the worst nights, but under the heavy layers of blankets, she felt safe and warm.

Then one night she came up slowly from her sleep like a swimmer pulling toward the surface. She stirred and a hand came down over her mouth. Instantly awake, she gagged at the familiar smell of his skin. Even on his palm the liquor seemed to seep out of his pores. His other hand turned slowly under the covers, moving something wet and warm in larger and larger circles around her belly. He had never come in her room at night before. She had not even heard the bureau being pushed aside. Now she would never look at this bed, at her safe haven again, without thinking of him.

"It's better when you're asleep, little one." That awful name. Would he never stop calling her that? "Your skin is so soft." As his hand moved up toward her breast, she tried to twist away.

"Oh no, you don't," he said, digging his fingers into her ribs to pull her back.

"Somebody is coming," she lied. "I heard someone on the stairs. Maybe it's Nellie."

He swore, and sliding his hand away, he went to the door. Quickly she got out of the bed and tiptoed around behind him. There was a voice.

"Mr. James?" It was Nellie. "What are you doing in there?"

That was all Lydia heard, because he went out of the room, pulling the door shut behind him.

She spent that night in the bathroom, the only place in the house with a lock on the door. Terrified that the running water would wake someone, she sponged the white cream off her body and from between her legs with a dry washcloth, crying quietly to herself. How she had grown to hate this body with its lumpish breasts, its dark protruding nipples, the stiff hair below.

The next morning when Nellie came in to help her dress, their eyes did not meet. She sat in front of the mirror, looking down at her hands while Nellie undid the dark braid and began to brush her hair out with long smooth strokes. Normally, the ritual soothed her, but this morning, she could not keep still. What was Nellie thinking?

"I'm scared of Uncle James," she said finally, staring past Nellie's alarmed eyes in the mirror.

"I'm sure he means no harm, miss," Nellie said carefully, and Lydia knew then that the maid had guessed something.

"Please don't tell him I said anything," Lydia whispered, the tears prickling at her eyelids. "He makes me keep secrets. He would be very angry if he thought I told anything."

The woman put down the brush and rested both hands on the girl's shoulders. "Poor child," she whispered.

Lydia caught sight of the maid's bad hand and closed her eyes. Those extra webs of skin disgusted her, but she tried not to let Nellie know. After all, she couldn't help it, could she?

Later on, when Nellie was making the bed, she found the jar of cream which he had stolen from her room and her stomach twisted with sickness. It made sense all of a sudden. The girl's hysteria when the nurse left, her solemn, terrified face, the way she avoided her uncle.

Nellie said nothing to him at first. She had to pick her time carefully. The next week on her afternoon off, a bright early spring day, he met her down at his friend's house on Bleecker Street. They ate lunch together at a little café around the corner. Usually these were her favorite moments with him. She was sure that the people going by would look at them laughing together over a glass of sherry and think: What a handsome young couple. She took care to dress well so that nobody would ever guess it was just a maid the gentleman was entertaining. Later, when they were lying in the bed together, and he had just told her once again how good she was, she asked him about the cream.

"I found the jar under Miss Lydia's bed," she said carefully.

"I don't know how the hell it got there. Are you accusing me of something?"

"No," she said, cautious already. She knew about his temper. "Do you think she could be stealing things from my room? The girl seems to be acting awfully queer lately."

He burst out laughing. "That would be a new twist, wouldn't it? The high-class girl who steals from her maid. What a perfect circle of thefts. You steal from her mother and she steals back from you."

Nellie stared at the ceiling. That look of fear on Miss Lydia's face haunted her. Nellie knew what it was like. There had been that time all those years ago when her father, her high-and-mighty God-fearing father, had made her lift her chemise and show him her breasts. She shivered now to think of his hand squeezing the one, pinching the nipple until it hurt.

"Cold?" he asked, pulling her close.

"Leave Miss Lydia alone, Mr. James."

"Now the maid is telling the master what to do, is she?"

"Please. She didn't say anything to me, but I see that look in her face. She's just a girl. Leave her alone."

The first slap landed on the hinge of her jaw, making her ears ring. Then, looming over her, he turned her face and hit her again on the other side. "Don't you ever tell me how to behave, you little whore." She pulled away from him, catching up the bedclothes because her naked body suddenly seemed an obscenity in the close room. "Come back here," he roared.

She had never seen him so angry before. Why had she said anything? The girl was nothing to her. "Mr. James, it's getting late. I've got to get back."

"Not until I tell you. Do you understand, Nellie? You're mine. I can tell you what to do and what not to do."

"Yes, sir," she said, trying to humor him.

"Now lie down here and spread your legs for me the way you usually do." He reached out and ripped the covers away from her. "In fact, I think I'll give you a spanking for good measure. Lie on your stomach."

*   *   *

He finally let her go two hours later. When she crept in the kitchen door, Mrs. Sanders's expression told her how bad the welts on her face must look.

"What happened to you?" she cried, putting out a hand to touch her cheek and then pulling back.

"A man beat me," she whispered. "He took my purse." She had tucked it under her coat just outside the kitchen door as soon as she realized she had to make up some kind of story.

"My God, child, you look awful. Go up to your room and wash. I'll tell Mr. Harrison what happened. He can get Maggie to serve the dinner."

In the small rectangular mirror above the sink in her room, she stared at her face. Her eyes were swollen from crying and the welt at the corner of her jaw had already begun to turn blue. He had beat her across her bare bottom with the belt and then raped her, driving himself into her dry insides until she thought she would faint with the pain. Not caring about the house rules anymore, she locked herself in Lydia's bathroom and ran a bath. The warm soapy water soothed the bruises on her body, but she could not make the sick feeling inside her go away.

Men owned a woman's body. It had been foolish of her to think she could do anything to keep him away from the girl. She could not even protect herself and now she had ruined her chances with him. That night she propped the chair up under her doorknob and sat up with the gas lit. She fell asleep finally, slumped against the wall.

Mrs. Sanders woke her the next morning.

"You overslept, dearie. It's past nine. But don't worry, I spoke to Harrison and he said for you to stay upstairs and rest today. Mr. James has gone away on some kind of trip and Mr. Charles will be out for dinner."

"How long will he be gone?" Nellie asked wearily.

"Mr. James?" Mrs. Sanders shrugged. "Nobody told me."

He did not come back for two weeks, and by that time, Nellie slept with a knife under her pillow. One afternoon, she had taken the horsecar down to see Rosie, who had listened sympathetically to her story but had no advice to give.

"He sounds like a bad one, Nellie. What about your family? Could you move back in with them?"

Nellie shook her head. "My mother's gone crazy. The boys are all out on the streets and she sits in the same chair all day long, picking threads off her dress." She shivered. "It's pathetic, Rosie. My father finally got a job in a factory. They live in one room on the Bowery. There's no place for me there." She looked around Rosie's comfortable room once more. "I guess I'll start looking for a new job. But if I quit, Mr. Harrison won't give me a good letter, I'm sure of it."

"You could tell him about Mr. James, couldn't you? Say he was forcing his attentions on you?"

Nellie threw back her head and a harsh grating laugh came out of her open mouth. "A gentleman's word against a maid? You've been away from the real world too long, Rosie. I suppose I couldn't move in here with you for a while, could I? Just a little time to tide me over?"

"I couldn't do that, Nellie. There's no place for you to go when Mr. Russell is here. He wouldn't like that at all."

"I guess not," she said, standing up carefully. The bruises on her back had still not healed. "I guess I should have married Patrick when he asked me. But it's too late now, isn't it? Goodbye, then, Rosie."

She began to read the newspaper advertisements surreptitiously, but every one of them said "References required." Well, she would wait a little while. Maybe Mr. James was done with her. Suddenly her life in this house seemed luxurious compared to any other option. If only he would leave her be, she would do her work and be happy with it. But no matter what happened, she would never let him do that to her again. She would kill him first.

He came back unexpectedly one afternoon. Lydia was practicing the piano in the study, lost in the music, in the temporary safety of the house. In the middle of a measure, she heard his voice in the front hallway and she snatched her fingers from the keys. If he hadn't heard the music yet, she had time to get away.

"Good afternoon, Harrison. Spring has finally arrived, I see."

"Yes, sir. Did you have a good trip?"

"Very good. I needed the rest and Richmond is beautiful this time of year. In fact, I managed to make a little money on a very special horse. You're partial to horses yourself, aren't you, Harrison?"

"Now and then, I've been known to put a little money down, sir. Will you be having dinner here, then?"

"Absolutely. Back in the bosom of the family." As their voices drew closer, Lydia slipped off the piano bench and out the side door.

From then on, without ever speaking about it, Nellie kept an eye out for the girl, so that when Mr. James came back in the afternoons, Lydia was down in the kitchen helping Nellie polish the candlesticks or practicing her music while Nellie dusted the furniture in the study. They both knew that their sense of safety was a false one, that if he chose to, he could order Nellie out of the room, but Lydia took comfort in the other woman's presence. For a while, he left them both alone.

Summer came early that year. The heat began to build in May and it never broke. Nellie did not feel well. Underneath her uniform she wore only a loose pair of knickers and she dragged herself through the days with the smelling salts in her skirt pocket. The heat was trapped in the house by the heavy curtains and the thick rugs, and every night she peeled off her uniform and went down to sit in the tin maid's tub in the backyard shelter until Maggie banged on the door, calling out that it was her turn. The roof door was left open to catch the breezes, but down on the third floor Nellie and Lydia still slept, their doors closed and barred with pieces of furniture.

One night, Nellie heard the door move slowly toward her and catch on the chair back. She slipped her hand under her pillow and felt for the knife.

"Nellie." He was back. "Let me in, Nellie."

She got out of bed and crept to the door. "I'm going to scream, Mr. James. If you do anything, I'm going to scream. I don't care what happens anymore."

"Nellie, I'm not going to hurt you. I just came to say I'm sorry. I promise I won't hurt you."

"I don't want it to start again, do you hear? It's all over now between us."

He said nothing for a moment. "I've been missing you, Nellie. Nothing is as good without you. Please let me in. I promise I'll be good."

Something stirred in her and she trembled, betrayed by her body. How could she want him again after that last time?

"Remember all the good times," he said softly, his face against the keyhole. "We could have them again."

She put the knife back under the pillow and let him in.

He was gentle that night, almost humble. He touched and caressed and waited until she was aching with the need for him inside her and then he entered her, and every crevice of her body was full of him. It wasn't until later, after he had left, that the fear came back. And the regrets.

Mrs. Sanders succumbed to the heat early in June. Nellie found her with her head on the kitchen table. "I can't get up," she said. "The pain in my chest. Don't let them take me to the hospital, Nellie. If I get in there, I'll never get out." But when the doctor came, he ordered the ambulance and she was carried out of the house, crying like a baby.

That night, Charles and Lydia ate dinner alone together, as James was out.

"I'm going to send you up to your grandmother's next week, Lydia. I know it's early but this heat is unbearable."

"Yes, Father." One more week, she thought to herself. One more week of sleepless nights, of the nightly ritual with the bureau. "Will Nellie be coming with me?" she asked.

"I think she will travel with you this year. We don't need her here, as she has trained Maggie well. But she won't come up until the end of June. She'll have to do the cooking until I see what's to be done about replacing Mrs. Sanders. It's too bad. The doctor told me she really can't work anymore, so as soon as she gets well enough, I shall be sending her down to live with her sister." He lined his knife and fork up on the plate and sat back in his chair. "So, just one more year of school for you. Your reports have been good, Lydia."

"Thank you, Father." She liked sitting here alone with him. Uncle James almost completely ignored her these days, but when the three of them ate dinner, the brothers often got into a fight. James liked to make fun of his older brother's political pronouncements. "Father, do you think Uncle James will always live with us?" The question amazed her. She had not known it was coming.

"Would you rather he didn't?"

This was the time to say something. Down in her lap, her fingers were working again and she laced them together to keep them still. "I just wondered," she whispered.

"I expect he'll move out sometime, although he has shown no inclination to. I like to tell him that we're a good influence on him. Your uncle has not always been so well behaved."

She longed to be able to tell him everything, but the words would have been as disgusting as if she had vomited on the table and she dreaded the look of horror and disbelief on his face. He would hate her because he would see as clearly as she did that the things that happened must be her fault.

He pushed his chair back and folded his napkin. "Harrison and I will be away at the end of the week for a couple of days. He's driving me up to Rhinebeck to look at some land," he said.

"Yes, Father."

As he passed behind her chair, he patted her on the shoulder. "You're a good girl, Lydia," he murmured, and she trembled.

On Friday, Nellie fainted while leaning over the sink. She came to, her cheek pressed against the cool tile of the kitchen floor. Her left thigh ached and by the afternoon a long blue bruise appeared there. She must have hit the edge of the tub when she went down. But she knew it wasn't the heat anymore. Her monthly bleeding was over a week late.

That night, she lay in bed counting the days backwards and in her hysteria she laughed out loud at the irony of it. All the times she and Mr. James had lain lovingly

131

together and he got her pregnant the day he raped her. She knew he would visit her tonight. With Mr. Harrison off for two days with Mr. Franklin, there was only Maggie on the top floor. She had gone off this afternoon and she wouldn't be back until much later. Maggie had one of those "sick mothers" in Brooklyn that occupied a great deal of her time. Nellie had her work cut out for her tonight. First to please him and then to get some money from him.

Across the hall, Lydia lay in her bed with the windows and the door open. She knew Uncle James was out, and until she heard his movements in the house, she would take advantage of the light breeze that blew through her room into the hall. He had not come near her since his trip away. She had only three more days to go.

The weather broke that night. The breeze swung around and came down out of the north around nine. James felt it when he stood in the street after paying off the hansom. A lady's hat cartwheeled toward him. He put out a foot and caught it on the wide brim with one toe. Picking it up, he waited there until its owner, a stout lady puffing from her exertions, arrived to claim her property.

"Madam," he said with mock politeness. "I believe this belongs to you."

"Yes, thank you. Such a wind all of a sudden. It caught me by surprise."

"A welcome change from the heat, though."

"Oh yes, sir."

On Madison, the store awnings snapped like flags in the wind. The cabdrivers, high on their boxes, shifted their reins to one hand and held on to their hats with the other. On the rooftops, the white lines of laundry danced up and down like ghostly kite tails.

At the top of the stairs, James hesitated. Lydia had fallen asleep with her door open for the first time, her skin cooled by the breeze. In the gaslight, he could see one side of her face circled by the dark crown of hair. The skin on her cheeks was soft. Nellie must have taught her about the moisturizers a lady uses to preserve her face. He took a step into the room.

"Mr. James."

He turned around. Nellie was standing in her doorway, dressed only in her knickers. Their eyes met.

"I was waiting for you," she said. "Close her door."

And he obeyed.

Before Lydia opened her eyes, she felt the heat, and stirring, she pushed with her bare feet at the linen sheet, which was already bunched at the bottom of the bed. She dragged her eyes open and saw that the door to the room was closed, but she had forgotten to push the bureau in front of it. Halfway out of bed, she turned back to see the flames crawling up her curtain and she screamed.

Across the hall, Nellie heard the scream and froze. But James forced himself deeper into her. "Don't stop now, for Christ's sweet sake."

The wind picked up the burning curtain and it billowed out into the room. While Lydia watched, the flame crept sideways and then, fanned by the breeze, it jumped the airspace and began to crawl up the other side on the back of the second curtain.

The old fear still held her. She must have fallen asleep with the gas jet on and now, because of her carelessness, the curtains were on fire. She had to do something before anybody found out. In the bathroom, she found Nellie's bucket under the sink and she filled it, cursing the slow trickle of water. By the time she got back to the room, the door she left open had sucked at the fire. A burning twist of dotted swiss had ignited the rug and her bedspread was already burning. When she threw the bucket of water, half of it fell uselessly onto her bed. A corner of the bedspread sizzled into a black puddle but the wind continued to drive the flames along ahead of it. She backed out the door, slamming it shut behind her.

Halfway down the stairs, she remembered Nellie and started back up. She did not scream again. Uncle James would wake, and even in her fear of the fire, she could not risk that. Much later and only in the journals, she admitted to herself that she wanted him to die. Much later in the safety of Dr. Stevenson's sanitarium she dreamed that he was trapped in the fire, the hot fingers snatching at his body as he backed away into the corner.

As she groped her way along the dark hallway toward

Nellie's door, she could feel the heat like a force straining to explode through the wood of her own door. There was only a muffled answer to her banging, and in her frustration and fear, she broke all the rules and threw the door open.

The sight of Uncle James's bare skin, his legs scrabbling to find the floor, the curve of his bare bottom as he lifted himself up and away from Nellie, Nellie's large breasts flattened by the heat and his weight on her—all these things Lydia saw and then locked away into some compartment in her mind.

Nellie's voice was surprisingly calm. "What is it?" Across the confusion, their eyes met and Lydia did not look at anything else.

"My room is on fire," she said. "The curtains blew across the gas jet."

Uncle James spoke first, but whatever he said was lost in the explosion behind them as Lydia's door finally gave way to the heat.

"Oh, my God," he said.

"Run, Miss Lydia," Nellie screamed. "Go down the front stairs. Hurry."

"If Nellie had been there alone," she wrote in the journal, "I never, never would have left her. But he was with her and I could not look at him. So I ran and ran, stumbling down the stairs, tripping over the hem of my nightgown."

By the time Nellie and James were dressed, the hall carpet was already on fire. He gave her a blanket to press against her face. "We'll have to go up," he said, his voice close to her ear. "Keep your head low. The air is clearer down by the floor." In the confusion, Nellie remembered something. "Maggie should be up there," she called back to him, but if he heard her, he didn't say anything. "For God's sake, move," he yelled, pushing her with his hand from behind so that she tripped and fell against the edge of the attic steps. When she picked herself up again, she felt a cutting pain deep inside her as if something too tightly held together had snapped.

There was a splintering crash. "Your bedroom door," he muttered. "We'll go out the front balcony. I can already hear the fire engines in the front."

"Maggie," she screamed, throwing open the door. The room was empty, which even in the confusion made Nellie smile. Some sick mother.

They stood looking down from the small stone balcony that the architect of the house had added at the last moment because the symmetry of it pleased him. Down below, as a crowd gathered, the confusion mounted, and it seemed that hours passed before the small figures found a ladder and maneuvered it into the right position. It was not long enough.

"I'll have to let you down on to it," he muttered. A fireman was starting up the ladder to help them.

"I think I'm going to faint," Nellie said, her body swaying against his.

"Don't look down. Just turn around and go over the wall backwards. Keep looking at me," he shouted over the noise. From the house, the constant crackle of burning wood was punctuated by the occasional explosion of breaking glass.

She did as he said. He took her by both forearms and carefully lowered her. "Hold on tighter," he yelled. "Your left hand is slipping."

"I can't," she screamed back. "My hand." But by that time, one foot had found the top rung of the ladder.

"Keep coming down, miss," the fireman said. "I'm right behind you." He put his hands on the very top of the ladder, so that in the short distance between when Mr. James released her hands and they found the first wooden rung, her body slipped down under his like a letter into an envelope. "There now," he whispered. "Are you secure?"

She nodded, still staring upward toward James, who was already sitting on the stone railing of the balcony. "Wait as long as you can, sir," the fireman called back up to him. "The ladder won't hold the three of us."

"Right you are, Captain," he called gaily, his eyes on Nellie. With a wave of his hand, he blew her a kiss.

In that moment, Nellie's heel caught in the hem of her dress. Reaching down with her good hand to release it, she slipped and fell. With one long wailing scream that sent a shiver of horror through the crowd below, her body hurtled down, knocking the fireman off with her.

They hit the sidewalk separately and the crowd rushed forward. In the confusion, the men below released the ladder, which slipped away and caught on the second-floor balcony of the adjoining brownstone. Behind him, James could feel the heat pressing at the window. It was only a matter of time before the glass went.

"Get the ladder, damn you," he yelled, but nobody looked up.

The roof. Why hadn't they gone out on the back roof? He picked up Nellie's blanket, and wrapping it around his face, he dove through the window shoulder first. On his belly, he scrabbled along the smoke-filled valley between the front window and the metal door, searching for that inch of clear air near the floor. With one blanket-wrapped hand, he shoved the bolt on the door and pulled it in. He stumbled out onto the roof, but the open door lured the fire out too and he was almost knocked down again by the wave of heat and smoke exploding in the air behind him.

The fireman broke both his legs and a couple of ribs, but Nellie died in the fall. Her skull was crushed by the weight of her body, which turned upside down during its long descent and drove her head first into the pavement.

Once the roof door sucked the fire upward, the men working below were able to contain the damage on the top two floors. By the time somebody remembered the man on the balcony, he was shouting at them from the front of the house on the corner of Fifth Avenue. The maid from that house, who had come running out when she heard the bells, went back in and unbolted the roof door for him.

10

When Lydia looked back on those years between the fire and Dr. Stevenson, she remembered the silences most of all. Big empty rooms in her head where she had locked the bad doors and pushed the furniture in front of them.

She had spent that first night with Mrs. Wilson, the next-door neighbor. The doctor came and gave her a sedative and she slept, once the drug had melted away the noise of the bells and the screaming and the crackling. The next day, they moved her up to the country and she lay in the upstairs bedroom, where the green dots of the wallpaper soothed her. She followed the dots for hours, jumping from one to another with her eyes like a frog on his lilypad path. Emily sat next to her bed in the afternoon and read aloud, and her voice wound its way in and out of Lydia's head as she followed the dots, but she paid no attention to the story.

Her father came and sat by the bed. "The damage wasn't as bad as it could have been. Only the top two floors actually burned and there was some smoke and water damage down below. You know, I should have had the house electrified years ago. I just kept putting it off. This will give me a chance. You won't recognize the place when you come back in the fall."

He was trying to say that the fire wasn't her fault, and she watched him struggling with it as if he were calling to her across a great distance.

"Nellie?" she whispered.

He looked down into his lap. "Don't think about anything else now, Lydia. Just stay up here and get your strength. Uncle James said he wants to come up and see you soon."

She had built little rooms in her mind now. Uncle

James was trapped behind one of those doors and this time it had a lock on it. He stayed in there. But Nellie stood in the middle of the empty space calling to her. She didn't want to lock Nellie away.

"Did Nellie get hurt, Father?" she asked again.

"A little," he said, but his voice was shaking. "She'll get better again soon. But she won't be coming back to us."

"Father," she said. "Please tell me the truth."

He stood up and she shrank back from the sudden motion. Up above her, he seemed so tall, but she could see the glisten of the tears standing in his eyes. Nothing she had ever done before had made him cry. She rolled away and curled herself into a ball with her knees pulled up tight against her chest. She did not see the way he reached his hand out to touch her, how it hovered there for a moment above her shoulder, how finally it bunched itself into a tight fist that returned to the pocket of his trousers.

Later when Aunt Katherine came up with her dinner tray, Lydia was sitting up in bed. "Did Nellie burn up?" she asked.

"What did your father say to you?"

"He said she was fine, but you'll tell me the truth, won't you?"

Aunt Katherine set the tray down on the bedside table and caught the lamp before it tipped over. They had put her in the wing of the house that was electrified because she could not fall asleep in the dark. "The doctor said not to upset you, Lydia."

"I dream about her, Aunt Katherine. She's screaming at me to come get her."

"She fell off the ladder." Aunt Katherine sat on the edge of the bed and took one of Lydia's limp hands into her own. She stroked the back of it, over and over again, and the only sound in the room was the sliding sweep of their skin against each other as constant and rhythmic as a broom on a wooden floor. "She died in the fall."

What did it matter how someone died? But Lydia had dreamt of her still trapped in the room, of the bedsheets burning, of her screaming and batting uselessly at the little flame monkeys that jumped from one fold of her

138

skirt to another. "It must have been because of her hand," Lydia said. "It was always weaker than the other one. Poor Nellie," she said again, and for the first time, began to cry.

Aunt Katherine did not try to make Lydia stop. She got into the bed beside her and held her, and when the door opened, she shook her head at the maid, who had come to collect the tray.

By the time Uncle James came, Lydia had gotten out of bed. For most of the day, she sat on the terrace with her grandmother, who was senile and almost completely deaf and shouted orders at her granddaughter through her ear trumpet as if whatever trauma she had suffered had made her deaf also. They made a funny pair, the thin pale girl always with a book in her lap but never reading it and the round wrinkled woman wrapped in blankets even on the warmest days. From time to time, like a scientist examining a specimen, the old lady peered at Lydia through a gold lorgnette that she wore around her neck on a black ribbon. Grandmother Livingston soothed Lydia. Nobody had told her about the fire for fear the shock of the story would further damage her weakened heart. In any case, she wouldn't have understood, and Lydia found it comforting to sit with somebody who didn't know what had happened to her and who didn't care. All she worried about was whether her lunch toast had been sufficiently buttered.

"How do you stand it?" Emily had asked. "She screams at you all day."

"Does she?" Lydia shrugged. "I guess I don't notice."

So when Uncle James came for a visit, he sat on the terrace too, the large woman planted next to him like an enormous angry toad.

"Let's go for a walk," he said to Lydia the first afternoon.

"I can't leave Grandmother," she explained. "I'm in charge of her."

"She can't hear us, can she?" he asked.

"No," Lydia said.

"Who are you?" Mrs. Livingston bellowed, and James explained again.

Then she settled back into her wheelchair with a rumbling noise and dozed off in the sun.

"I'm going away, Lydia," Uncle James said. "To Paris. I'm tired of New York."

She nodded, unsure of the answer he was looking for. To still her fingers, she traced the letters of the book title in her lap.

"What happened that night?" he started.

"What night?" she asked sharply. Which night, which secret are we going to talk about, Uncle James? There are so many of them stretching like a necklace all the way back to the little white rabbit in the garden.

"The night of the fire," he said patiently as if she were a child again and he needed to go over something very carefully with her. "You haven't said anything about Nellie?"

"She's dead," Lydia informed him.

Uncle James frowned. "I know that. I mean about Nellie and me. Before the fire."

She didn't answer. That closed door opened for a moment and she caught a flash of white, something backing toward her before she slammed it again. "I don't know what you mean," she said with a little smile that he took as a sign of their old agreements instead of what it really was, a smile of triumph that she was so strong, so good at keeping the right doors closed.

"That's my good girl, Lydia. You always did keep a secret when Uncle James asked for it."

Lydia stood up suddenly and went to the wheelchair. "It's time for Grandmother's nap." She pushed the chair toward him and seemed for a moment to lose control of it, so that he jumped up and out of the way just as she made the circle and turned it toward the house.

Funny, he thought as he watched her maneuver the old woman through the narrow French doors. I think she's gone a little mad. Poor girl. She has been through a lot.

He sat back in his chair. That's settled. She'll never say anything. And Nellie can't. He had come out of the fire a hero. The crowd on the street had all told the story of how he sacrificed himself for the maid, of how he had waited to be sure she was safe before he tried to save himself.

But he couldn't stand the house anymore. He believed in ghosts and Nellie's had moved in already. He was sure of it. Just two nights ago, he had heard her laughing at him from the top of the stairs.

It wasn't until years later when he was dying in a cheap Paris hotel and his nightmares could no longer be tricked away with drink that he remembered Sister Maria and the cards.

In the fall, Lydia went back to the Brearley. Her father had not wanted it. In fact, he had already withdrawn her from the school when he mentioned his decision in passing to his sister-in-law.

"You must not do this, Charles," Katherine said sternly. "I have been with Lydia all summer. You should have consulted me before you made such a decision."

"Dr. Maxwell believes that too much education is not good for a girl. It stimulates her already active mind. With all she's been through, I thought it better for her to stay at home more and be tutored."

"Stay at home?" she asked with a harsh laugh. "Don't you think that might stimulate her active mind, as you put it. After all, she lived through a fire in that house."

Charles frowned. He wasn't used to his decisions being questioned by a woman.

"She has talked all summer about going back to the Brearley." Katherine heard her own raised voice and wondered why she was fighting for this with so much vehemence. Perhaps it was because she had only recently sprung herself from a prison of enforced lassitude. A woman could go mad lying about the house waiting for her next social engagement. Katherine nearly had, and even though she knew her contemporaries laughed at her work in the tenements, she felt completely alive and satisfied. "The only time I have seen a light in her eye all summer is when she reads poetry to me on our afternoon rides."

"The house looks quite different now. I have redecorated it and I have moved her into Nellie's old room, which faces out over the garden. I thought that since the

141

fire started in her room it would be wise to get her out of there."

Katherine softened a bit. "I am sure you've done a wonderful job, Charles. And she is getting better every day. But please don't go through with this. She must be allowed to return to the Brearley."

He shrugged, mollified by her praise. "If you think so, then perhaps I shall reconsider. Mr. Croswell did seem disappointed. She is one of his best students." His obvious pride touched Katherine.

"I'm sure of it," she said.

At the Brearley, Lydia felt safe again, surrounded by the familiar rooms, the smell of books, the innocent affection of the other girls. The senior class was small. To Mr. Croswell's fury, many of the parents withdrew their daughters in the last year so that they could prepare for their debut into New York society and, beyond that, their real role in life, which was marriage.

While at school, she did not have to work so hard to keep the bad doors closed. The empty space in the middle room of her mind was taken up with poetry and oil painting and the consideration of the causes of the French Revolution. Every afternoon, she dreaded the return home.

Her father had led the way upstairs that first afternoon. "I've made some changes, Lydia. You will be in here from now on," and she had to stifle the scream that rose to her lips when he pushed open Nellie's old door. When she did not move from the doorway, he took her gently by the elbow and led her into the center of the room. "It's pretty, isn't it?" he asked.

And he had tried. She could see that. The room had been repainted in a pale peach color that matched the new flowered curtains. In one corner he had installed John's old school desk.

"You once said that if you were as smart as John you ought to be able to study the same things. Do you remember that?" he asked.

She nodded, staring up at him with wide frightened eyes.

"I gave you John's desk so you would have a place to do your work in the afternoons. Here's a new book for your poetry. Your Aunt Katherine told me that your other one was destroyed." He moved bravely to the end of that sentence. After all, they couldn't go on never mentioning the fire. She still did not move but continued to stare fixedly at him as if too terrified to shift her eyes from his face.

"Go on, Lydia." A note of irritation had crept into his voice. "Look around you."

"Yes, Father." And she did. She put one foot in front of the other, she touched the linen scarf on the bureau, she opened the closet door and looked in, then closed it again.

"I rearranged things a bit. The bed seemed better next to the window. That way you can look right down into the garden."

When she didn't answer, he backed out of the room. "Janet is the name of the new maid. She will be up very soon to help you unpack."

The bureau had been placed on the opposite side of the room from the door, and when the maid came up, she found her new charge, still dressed in her traveling clothes, struggling with it.

"What is it, miss?"

"The bureau. I want it over there, next to the door."

"But there's no room there, miss. You'll knock into it going in and out."

"Still, I want it there."

Mr. Harrison had told her of the girl's sickness. Very well, they would move the bureau if that's what she wanted. Janet knew better than to argue with her new mistress the very first time she laid eyes on her.

At night with the bureau shoved securely against the paneled door and the new electric light filling the room, she could sleep well enough. But although she had always wanted a desk of her own, she could not make herself work in that corner with her back to the door. She kept turning around, sure that someone was creeping up on her from the hallway. She knew she was too old to take her books back down to the kitchen, and with Mrs. Sanders gone, she felt unwelcome there. The new cook, Mrs. Dayton, was friendly enough, but she clearly expected Miss Lydia to stay out of her territory. Each room of the house seemed to hold its own ghostly nightmare, and Lydia wandered distractedly from one to another, settling down for a little while and then getting up again until she was called for dinner.

In June they began making plans for her debut, which was to be held in September up the Hudson in the big house. That's where Emily had come out, after all. Lydia listened to the talk of her dress, the wrangling over the list of people, the discussions about whether they should hang ivy baskets or ropes of smilax down the front-hall banister.

"What do you think, Lydia?" Emily asked. "After all, it is your party."

"I don't mind," Lydia would murmur. "Whatever you think." She was so terribly tired from controlling those doors all the time. Now that she had graduated from the Brearley, it was difficult to know how to fill all the hours of the day.

"What do you do all day?" she asked Emily, and knew from her cousin's quizzical look that it was one of those wrong questions that she was always asking.

"You are so peculiar sometimes, Lydia. I don't know what to say to you."

"I know," she replied with a sigh. "I don't know what to say to myself." And there's so much empty space to fill.

As it turned out, the party had to be canceled that year. By the end of the summer, Lydia was no longer up to it.

"I can't understand it," Charles fumed. "She just lies in that bed all day, staring up at the ceiling. She won't even talk to me sometimes."

"She told me yesterday that everything feels too heavy," Katherine said quietly. "Her arms, her legs."

"It's what I told you would happen, Katherine. I should have listened to Dr. Maxwell when he warned me about her last summer."

"Charles, this didn't happen while she was at school. Only when she stopped." She didn't say how panicked she felt when she looked at her niece lying in the bed. It was as if Lydia were slipping away from them all, falling backward off a cliff, and she looked out of eyes that saw less and less of the real world and more and more of the world inside her head.

Katherine knew too many neurasthenic women, the ladies who took to their beds complaining of mysterious pains in their legs, attacks of dizziness, terrible headaches. The doctors descended soon afterward and the women were lost forever. They would recover for a little while, but it was only a matter of time until they succumbed once more as a result of a long heat spell or too much excitement.

The course of the disease, which is what they called Lydia's condition for want of a better word, was erratic. Every day that Lydia took a meal downstairs or went for a short walk to the barn and back was matched by a dark day in her bed when she was unable to lift her head or answer the simplest question. She never complained, although Katherine did not admit to Charles that the last time she had read out loud to Lydia, the girl had begun to cry silently, the tears slipping out of the corners of her eyes as she stared at the ceiling.

"What is it, Lydia?"

"The doors. It's so hard to keep them all closed."

"Then let them open up. What's behind the doors?"

Lydia shook her head and did not answer.

With Charles's permission, after they moved her back to the city Katherine began to call in specialists. They poked and probed at her, asked questions, and each of them gave a different name to the disease, calling it "neurasthenia," "neuralgia," "nervous collapse," "hysteria." Katherine did not trust any of them. They all seemed to agree that the cause was excessive emotional stimulation. "Of course," they said when they heard the story of the fire. But they disagreed on the cure. One recommended his massage treatment, another a strict diet of vegetables and mineral water combined with electrotherapy, a third a regimen of cool baths and abstinence from all animal foods. Lydia endured their examinations silently, although she clung to her aunt's hand throughout these ordeals. Katherine thanked them for their opinions and dismissed them all.

The winter dragged on. The light in Lydia's room was kept on day and night because she could not bear the darkness. She grew thinner. The constant feeling of nausea combined with a sharp jab of fear whenever she relaxed for too long. Her body was not hers anymore. No matter how hard she tried, she no longer had the strength to push the bureau in front of the door. Twice, Janet had found her collapsed on the floor, beating her forehead against the dark wooden side of it.

Her legs jerked in spasms and sometimes she leaned over without any warning and vomited into the pail that Janet kept next to her bed. In the evenings, after work, her father came and looked at her, asking Janet warily from the doorway how she was today. There were other visitors, Emily sometimes or friends from school. They never came alone and they always talked to each other over her head, which gave her the feeling that her old wish had come true and she had in fact, at last, disappeared. Aunt Katherine was the only one who spoke directly to her no matter whether she was able to answer or not.

One day, in the early spring, Aunt Katherine brought a man with her, another doctor.

"Lydia, this is Dr. Stevenson. He wants to talk to you."

He seemed to be very tall, standing next to her bed. He pulled up a chair, gave her a cursory examination, and then spoke to her.

"Why don't you try to tell me what's wrong, Miss Franklin."

She stared at him without answering. I don't mean to be rude, Doctor, but you see, I have so many things to watch out for. I can't get distracted by talking. Please don't keep staring at me like that. She turned her head away.

He came again once or twice. He did not talk to Aunt Katherine over her head the way the other people did. Even when she could not answer him, he asked her how she was feeling and whether she had eaten anything that day.

After the third visit, he met with Katherine and Charles

downstairs. "Although it is impossible to pinpoint them directly, her physical symptoms are a constant nausea, frequent headaches, and exhaustion brought on by malnutrition. Add to that a very deep melancholy."

"What is your prescribed course of treatment, Doctor?" Charles asked from his position by the mantelpiece.

"I operate a private sanitarium on Broadway near Thirty-fifth Street which is attached to the New York Orthopedic Dispensary. I recommend that you allow her to come to me for a rest cure. She will be there for at least a month and can receive no outside visitors or mail during that time. As I mentioned to you in our earlier conversation, Mrs. Jay, I believe Miss Franklin is afflicted in both body and mind and both must be treated. She needs regular daily exercise and massage to tone her atrophied muscles. She must begin to eat as soon as possible. The more she is able to consume, the sooner the nausea will go away. Right now, her stomach is literally eating itself. I will also prescribe large doses of malt and iron to improve her physical stamina. It is hoped that with the physical improvement, she will be able to face whatever emotional crisis she is avoiding by the sickness."

"Sounds like a lot of nonsense to me," Charles said.

Stevenson smiled. "That's just the beginning, Mr. Franklin. I have not told you about my experiments in the treatment of the mind."

Katherine didn't say anything for the moment. She liked the way this doctor talked. He was honest. He did not seem to care one way or another whether they chose him to treat Lydia. So many of the neurasthenic doctors she had heard of wormed their way into the patient's life and never left. Of course, it was to their advantage to keep the lady sick.

"You'd better tell us everything at once, then," Charles said. He still did not look directly at the man. Lydia's malaise was an embarrassment to him. It brought back uncomfortable memories of her mother's manipulations.

"Well, to describe my theories in detail would take far too long, so I will be as brief as possible. I am a follower of Sigmund Freud, a young Viennese doctor who has made some startling discoveries about the power of the mind over the body. He believes, as do I, that the effort required to avoid and contain the fears connected with a traumatic event can literally drive a person mad. I would try to lead her back through hypnosis to relive the event."

"But we've done everything we can to avoid that," Charles said.

"Naturally. You would be taking a risk if you let her come to me," he said simply. "The study of neurasthenia is a very new science."

"We have consulted many other doctors in the field," Katherine said. "They all seemed to prescribe a different treatment, but the one point they all agreed on is that she should not be allowed to think of anything unpleasant."

"I am sure they also told you to put all her books away," he replied with a harsh laugh. "My colleagues have some surprising ideas when it comes to the capacity of the female to withstand emotional excitation, which, of course, includes any kind of intellectual stimulation. Let me assure you both from the beginning that I do not agree with them."

Charles stepped forward, indicating the interview was over. "Thank you, Doctor. We will let you know our decision once we have had a chance to discuss it." When they shook hands, Charles still did not look him in the eye.

"What a lot of nonsense he talks," Charles said when the doctor had been shown to the door.

"He is young," Katherine said. "But some of what he said makes sense to me. Particularly the part about intellectual stimulation. Why don't we ask him to treat Lydia here, concentrating on her physical symptoms for the time being. Then, once her body seems stronger, we can decide about the other part."

Charles said nothing. He was deeply frustrated by the failure his sickly daughter represented. She had seemed to him to be just the opposite, a strong, intelligent girl. In the last years as James's hold over her seemed to loosen, she had turned ever so carefully back to her father. He remembered drawing her the battle map at the dinner table. Although he would never admit it, not even to himself, he missed her.

Katherine was waiting for an answer.

"All right, but you handle it, will you, Katherine? You

and Dr. Stevenson seem to understand one another. Just get her better, for God's sake."

"Charles, she's not a business problem," Katherine said.

Thank God sister Elizabeth won you away from me, Katherine thought idly as Charles helped her into her cloak. My quiet college professor and I are far better suited to each other than you and I would ever have been.

Dr. Stevenson was disappointed when he learned of Mrs. Jay's decision to keep Lydia at home.

"Considering the circumstances, I will do my best," he said. "But to be perfectly frank, I hold out no real hope for her cure unless you allow me to treat both the mind and the body."

"We feel this would be the best," she said hesitantly. "Mr. Franklin finds the entire situation very difficult."

"I gathered," he said wryly.

Stevenson knew that the girl's father was condoning his increased presence in his house and his unorthodox treatment in a moment of desperation. He suspected that Charles had a horror of any behavior that deviated from the acceptable social norm. As long as Lydia remained quietly sick, another delicate member of the weaker sex, he would not resort to any drastic measures. Mrs. Jay, on the other hand, seemed genuinely concerned about Lydia's mental and physical health. She had told him of her work with the visiting nurses down in the Italian tenements and he was pleasantly surprised by her rudimentary knowledge of medicine. This was not a woman who would allow herself or her niece to be chained to the sickbed.

In March, just a month after Lydia's eighteenth birthday, Stevenson's physical regimen was instituted, and although there were still days in the weeks that followed when the trays were returned untouched to the kitchen and the prescribed daily walk around the block ended at the first corner, Lydia did seem to improve for a while. A massage therapist came every day to tone her muscles. When the woman first laid her large calm hands on her back, Lydia began to tremble violently.

"I can't help it. I can't control it," she whispered. Dr. Stevenson had said this would help and she wanted so much to get better, but just as she was able to will one limb into stillness, another one would start. To her amazement, the woman paid no attention and gradually, under the pressure of her steady hands, Lydia relaxed.

In June the nightmares began. Charles was woken in the middle of the night by someone pounding on his door.

"What is it?" he called, pulling on his dressing gown.

"It's Miss Lydia, sir," Janet called. "I cannot calm her down."

When he got upstairs, he found Lydia tangled in her bedclothes, pulled back into the corner next to the wall. She screamed when she saw him coming toward her.

He reached over and shook her roughly by the shoulders.

"Lydia, stop it. It's me."

"Don't touch me," she screamed. "Don't," and in her fear, she twisted so violently that he let her go.

"Good God," he muttered to himself. "How long has she been like this?"

"A good hour or so, sir. I was sleeping across the hall because sometimes, when she's scared, she asks me to do that. I woke up when she first started to scream."

"Send Harrison for Mrs. Jay."

"Now, sir? In the middle of the night."

"Right now," he shouted. "For God's sake, hurry up."

"Yes, sir."

Charles sat in the chair next to her bed, trying to talk to her, trying not to let the fear show on his face. She looked like a small trapped animal. Her fingers picked incessantly at the bedclothes and she stared at the door of the room. Whenever he reached his hand out to calm her, she shrank back from him and screamed again. By the time Katherine arrived, he had moved his chair even farther from her bed because the greater the distance between them, the quieter she became.

"What is it?" Katherine asked Lydia in a low voice.

The girl mumbled something they could not hear.

"She won't let me touch her," Charles said, and his voice sounded so sad that Katherine put a hand on his shoulder for a minute. "I'm sorry I had to call you."

150

"Nonsense. Leave her alone with me."

Once the door had closed behind him, Katherine slipped into the bed beside Lydia and held her. It must have been an hour later when she felt the girl's body finally go limp with sleep.

The next morning, they called in Dr. Stevenson, who recommended an immediate move to the sanitarium. This time Charles did not object.

Lydia was under Dr. Stevenson's care for the next two years. She stayed in the sanitarium on four separate occasions, for anywhere from two weeks to two months, and during those times, he conducted daily hypnosis sessions with her. He never discussed with her what she said while under hypnosis and at first he was inclined to dismiss the stories about her Uncle James as the workings of an intelligent but overactive mind. But the descriptions did not change, and as he worked with her over a number of years, he began to believe that she was telling the truth about something that had actually happened to her.

Although Lydia's mental and physical health continued to improve slowly, the hypnosis did not seem to give her complete relief from the nightmarish memories of those years. The last time she took refuge in the sanitarium, they talked about this. By that time, Stevenson was coming under increasing criticism, not only for his unproven theories about the human mind but also for his espousal of a woman's right to birth control information. Although he did not tell her, he knew that if he continued on his present course, his sanitarium would soon be closed for good.

"Tell me how you are doing, Lydia?" he asked one afternoon soon after she arrived.

"Better. Ever since I started the work down in the tenements with Aunt Katherine and Dr. Baker, I feel calmer, more purposeful. Father is quite upset about it, as he feels I should be concentrating on finding a suitable husband." She managed a small smile. "I don't think I ever want to find a husband."

He smiled back.

"I feel I have no real right to be sick," she said quietly, "when I see what other people have to endure. The other day, we found a woman whose husband had thrown a pot of scalding water at her back." Lydia shuddered. "She didn't want to show us the sores on her back. Dr. Baker did what she could, but she thinks the poor woman will die of the infection."

"Perhaps it's too much for you."

"I expect that kind of answer from Father, not from you."

He shrugged. "We still have not found a permanent cure for you," he said. "I am beginning to lose faith in the powers of hypnosis because you are not consciously aware of what you are saying to me. Do you understand what I mean?"

She nodded. After her last visit, he had sent her away with two of Freud's pamphlets on the causes and cures of hysteria, and once she read them, she began to really understand the role hypnosis had taken in her recovery.

"I remember you telling me once that you used to write poetry."

"Yes, I was very proud of it. But when my poetry book was burned up in the fire, I never started it again. Now I prefer to stick to my painting."

"What if you were to spend this time writing a journal? Put down in words everything that happened to you. From the beginning. Wherever you want to start. I do not intend to read it unless you wish me to. It will merely serve as a method of exorcism for you."

She smiled. "A place to put all the ugly baggage," she said.

"Precisely."

During that final visit, which lasted close to two months, Lydia spent every afternoon in her room writing in a black leather book very much like the one that had burned in the fire five years before. As soon as she finished one book, she started another. When she left Dr. Stevenson's sanitarium on West Thirty-fifth Street for the last time, the bottom of her valise was lined with four identical books. Every page was filled from top to bottom with the loopy schoolgirl handwriting that had never been up to the Brearley's standards, those "heads and tails" that Agnes would complain about years later. Although Lydia never wrote in the books again, she carried them with her everywhere the way an old soldier carries the twisted piece of metal he happened to have in his pocket the day of the big battle. The one that stopped the bullet.

PART II

1906–1929
CHARLOTTE

11

"How many years did you work down on the Lower East side?" Molly asked during one of their taping sessions.

"Three. Four. I can't quite remember. By that time I was living with my Aunt Katherine and Uncle Arthur."

"Why?"

There was a pause and then Lydia drew breath close to the microphone. "I suppose because it was easier. My father was traveling a great deal then and I didn't like being in the house alone." Another pause. "Besides that, Aunt Katherine and I worked together every day. She was the mother I never had."

Molly cleared her throat. "So tell me what the work was like."

"Very scary at first," Lydia replied in her usual brisk voice. Anyone listening could tell that she felt she was back on safe territory. "You must remember that I was a girl who had been sheltered from any obvious unpleasantness. Sheltered the way girls of that time were. No television, no movies, no radio. We traveled everywhere with chaperones, we wore hats with veils, were taught to lower our eyes, avert our gaze. The worst thing I had probably ever seen was a drunkard in the park or a driver beating his weak horse. The smells and sights of those tenement rooms were almost indescribable. Too many sick children, not enough ventilation, no place to clean yourself or just be alone."

"But you kept at it."

"Yes. If Aunt Katherine hadn't been with me, I might not have. Frankly, the only other option seemed to be lying about at home waiting for gentlemen callers, and I had no interest in that way of life, I can assure you. We worked with a remarkable woman named Sara Jo Baker, who was one of the first female doctors. In fact, she became director of the Department of Child Hygiene for the city of New York just before I left to marry your grandfather. I was taken on because I spoke Italian, so I could communicate with the Italian women, our reasons for being there. They were all terrified of the immigration officers, so Dr. Baker and Aunt Katherine were having a hard time just getting into the apartments."

"What exactly were you doing?"

"Well, in those days, there was an incredibly high infant mortality rate. Dr. Baker had worked out a system with the Registrar of Records so that each morning she received a list of the names and addresses on the birth certificates issued in the district the day before. Even though most of the women gave birth at home, they were eager to register their babies as having been born in this country because it granted them instant American citizenship. We went around to check the babies for health problems and to alert the mothers to the dangers of unventilated rooms, contaminated milk, unsafe drinking water. The kinds of things people take for granted nowadays."

"Lunch," said Agnes's voice in the background.

"We'll be there in a minute," Molly said.

"Don't be long or it will just get cold."

"What kinds of things did you see?" Molly asked.

"A woman with a badly scalded back. Her husband, in a fit of rage, had thrown a pot of boiling water at her. Babies with dysentery dying of dehydration. Garbage on the staircases. Rats and cockroaches everywhere. And lice. Twice my head had to be doused in kerosene and then shaved for lice."

"I never imagined you as a nurse," Molly said.

A short laugh. "No, I'm really not the type. I was the interpreter and the one who distracted the children. I always took suckers along in my pockets. More often than not, it was the candy, not my Italian, that convinced the children to open the door."

"I guess we'd better stop," said Molly. "That's the second time Agnes has called."

"I know. I can feel her fuming all the way from the kitchen."

*   *   *

In the evenings, Lydia sat with Aunt Katherine in the comfortable parlor room of the Jays' large house in Washington Square and talked over the events of the day. When Uncle Arthur came in, he joined them for dinner and listened in an absentminded way to their discussions. Lydia felt very comfortable with her genial uncle and he was glad for her company. By that time, Henry was off at Harvard and Emily had already made a suitable marriage and was living with her husband, a lawyer named Timothy Davidson, on East Eighty-fifth Street.

From the beginning, Lydia's father had been horrified by Katherine's suggestion.

"You must be mad, Katherine, if you think I'm going to let you continue to drag her down there to that hellhole. What you do is your own business, but I cannot allow you to keep this up with my daughter."

Katherine called his bluff. "Very well, then, Charles, go back to doing things your way. But remember, she hasn't been confined to her bed once since she started working with me. Dr. Stevenson thinks it's the best thing for her."

He knew she was right, but he couldn't bear to watch it, so in the spring of 1905, he took an extended trip to Europe. It gave Lydia the excuse to move permanently down to Washington Square. It also meant that her father wasn't there to witness her first relapse. Katherine and Arthur took her back to the sanitarium in the middle of a warm night in June.

"The fire occurred three years ago this month," Katherine told Dr. Stevenson. "Her nightmares started again last week. She seemed to be better during the day when she was distracted, but I notice she hasn't been eating well and she's doing that old business with her hands."

"Tell me, has she had any contact with her Uncle James?"

Katherine frowned. "No. As far as I know, James is still living in Paris. I expect my brother-in-law, Charles, has been to see him and he might have written to Lydia about it, but that would be all. Why?"

"Just an idea," Dr. Stevenson said with a shrug. "Leave her with me. We'll start the same regime with her. I'm sure it won't take as long this time."

He was right. Lydia was back on her feet in a month, and after a week of rest in the country, she was ready to start work again.

"Wait until the fall," Katherine had cautioned. "Until the weather cools off."

"Please don't baby me," Lydia said steadily. "I'm ready now."

Katherine acquiesced. Dr. Baker, who had been briefed by Katherine, greeted Lydia matter-of-factly, as if she had never left at all. That August she and Aunt Katherine worked steadily through one of the worst dysentery epidemics in the city. Their moment of triumph came when Dr. Baker informed them that five hundred fewer babies died in their district than in any other.

Dr. Stevenson's sanitarium was closed in July of 1906, just two months after Lydia had finished the journals and carried them with her back to the second-floor bedroom on Washington Square. His final cure worked for almost two years . . . until the day Dr. Baker led them to an address on Norfolk Street.

From the very beginning, the street seemed oddly familiar to Lydia.

"I feel as if we've been here before," she told Katherine as they followed Dr. Baker into the first building.

"We might have been," Katherine said. "I can't keep track anymore."

"The name is Arrezini," Dr. Baker said. "The baby is only three days old. You first, Lydia," she added, stepping aside.

The routine was a familiar one to the three of them now. With a handful of sweets and some quiet reassurance, Lydia managed to convince the thin dark-eyed girl to open the door.

The room was lit by one dingy oil lamp in the corner. The three children stood in a row shielding their mother. Between their legs, the women could see the back of a body lying curved around the baby, whose high-pitched screams were the only sound in the room. When Dr. Baker took a step forward, the children drew closer together, creating a small defiant wall of protection.

"The doctor won't hurt your mother," Lydia said softly. She reached into her pockets and pulled out another handful of suckers. At the sight of the candy, the children came forward tentatively. While Lydia sat on a burlap bag on the floor and talked to them, Dr. Baker and Aunt Katherine worked with the mother.

After a while the doctor called Lydia over. "She does not want to let me hold the baby, Lydia, and I have to examine him."

Lydia knelt down on the floor by the pile of old cloth that served as a mattress. "What is your name?" she asked gently in Italian. The woman rolled over at the sound of her own language.

"I speak English," she said. "It is Maria."

Neither of them spoke for a moment.

"You have been here before," the woman said, her pain forgotten. "You were a little girl then. A man brought you to see me."

Lydia sat back on her heels. "How do you remember me?"

Sister Maria smiled, proud of herself even in her position, curled on the dirty pallet around the baby, who had finally been quieted by her breast. "I never forget when I have read the cards. They were not good for you."

"What's all this, Lydia?" Aunt Katherine said.

Lydia had begun to tremble. "She speaks English. She will let you see the baby. I need some fresh air, Aunt Katherine. I'll wait downstairs."

She sat on the steps under the awning that still said "Sister Maria," although the letters had faded. Was that the same room she had sat in, the one draped in scarves and stinking of the small bitter cigar? Fire, the cards had said. Fire and death. Lydia twisted her hands together. Nellie still haunted her. Had she lured Uncle James away from Lydia's room that evening in June? Is that why Lydia had found them together, why the woman could look at her so calmly with Uncle James scrambling into his clothes in a corner of the room and the noise and heat of the fire just behind them.

"You're trembling, Lydia," Aunt Katherine said, lifting her to her feet. "I'm taking you home. Right now."

"I'm fine, I really am," Lydia said, but her voice shook.

The old nightmare came back that night and she woke screaming for the first time in years. Arthur Jay returned to the house the next evening with the news that Dr. Stevenson's sanitarium had been closed.

"Is there no forwarding address?" Katherine asked.

"Nothing. He's disappeared without a trace."

"We've got to do something for her before Charles gets wind of this. He'll blame the whole thing on her work again."

"Send her to the country," Arthur said. "To the Morrises. Isabelle will be marvelous with her."

Katherine kissed her husband unexpectedly on his cheek. "Sometimes, darling, you are positively brilliant."

Isabelle and Taylor Morris lived in a big yellow house on the main street of the small town of Farmington, Connecticut. They welcomed Lydia but left her alone, and she spent long hours sitting with a sketch pad in a chair in the garden.

At the age of thirty-two, Isabelle Morris had come down with rheumatoid arthritis and she now spent her days in a wheelchair, her swollen legs hidden under a blanket. She was the most cheerful person Lydia had ever met and they became fast friends in a matter of days.

"I remember your mother. We grew up in New York together and I used to visit her up at Faraway, that big house on the Hudson River. What a place. Your grandfather was a sweet man but no match for Mrs. Livingston. She could stop him with just a look. It was always the most delicious fun. She made us put on plays and musicales and everybody had violent arguments on the most obscure topics, so you came down to breakfast ever so carefully because you never knew who was still talking to whom. Did you know your grandmother?"

"Yes," Lydia said. "I spent every summer there when I was a child, but by then she was confined to a wheelchair because of her weak heart and she couldn't hear at all. She died two years ago."

"Yes, Katherine wrote me about it. Your mother was a lovely creature to look at. Katherine and I used to be terribly jealous of her. I think it's what made the two of us such good friends from the beginning."

"What do you think she would have thought of her

162

daughter?" Lydia asked with a wry smile. "My hair has started to go gray and I'm only twenty-two."

"I suppose people have suggested you tint it."

"Only my cousin Emily. But she and I have never seen eye to eye."

"Well, to be honest with you, I like it. It makes you look like a woman to be reckoned with."

"Do you mean that?" Lydia asked shyly.

"I expect we're going to be good friends, Lydia," Isabelle said. "And if we are, you'll discover that I always mean what I say."

The party was for Lydia's benefit, although she never knew it.

"Introduce her to some eligible older man, dear Isabelle," Katherine had written in her introductory letter. "Although I would not like her to know it and I would never breathe a word of it to her father, I am concerned for Lydia's future. She is twenty-two years old and has buried herself in our work together. I think quite frankly it has been the best possible thing for her, but I don't want to see her ending up like my beloved Dr. Baker, who has never married and whose whole energy is directed toward saving the children of strangers.

"The whole business of the fire and her illness has made her wise beyond her years. (Her hair has even begun to go gray, although I've pretended not to notice.) She is contemptuous of the men she's met in New York and I must say I don't blame her. They are looking for wives who are content to stay at home and arrange flowers, and God knows, there are enough of them to go around . . . silly girls with no brains and even less conviction. Lydia has both and isn't afraid to show them."

"I've got just the man for her," Isabelle said to her husband when she'd finished reading the letter out loud.

"George Webster," Taylor said.

"Well, isn't he perfect? Ever since Miss Bunting died, he's holed himself up on that farm like a hermit in a cave. It's not natural. He must be over thirty."

"So what's wrong with that?" Taylor teased. "I was way past thirty when I married you."

She turned the wheelchair back to her desk so she could write a reply to Katherine.

At dinner, Lydia was seated next to George Webster, who was introduced as a neighbor of the Morrises.

"You live next door?" she asked.

"About twenty miles that way," he said with a nod to the right. "I've got a farm in Northington."

"Where I come from, one's neighbor lives on the other side of the wall," she said.

"New York City?"

She nodded.

"I couldn't stand that," he said. "I lived in a city for a while. New Haven."

"What were you doing?"

"I went to Yale. I wanted to be a journalist."

"But I thought you owned a farm."

"I do now," he said.

"Tell me about it," she said.

"Not much to talk about. We started with a herd of twenty Ayrshires. Now up to seventy. I started growing shade tobacco last year."

"What's that?"

"Cigar-wrapping tobacco. It's grown under nets."

He grinned at her as if to say "Now what?" and she smiled back. Now it's your turn to ask me a question, she thought, but he said nothing. So she let him be.

When she asked him later what he remembered about their first meeting, he said, "The silences."

"What do you mean?"

"You didn't natter on the way other women often do. You didn't seem to think that people have to talk all the time."

She remembered his black hair, the flashing blue eyes in a face already weather-beaten by the sun this early in the summer, and the faint smell of manure. "It must have been on my shoes," he said with a laugh. "Halfway over, I realized I had forgotten to change them after milking."

"Miss Bunting would not have approved," she teased, because by then she had already heard quite a bit about his mother's cousin, the one who got him started in farming.

"I doubt she would have accepted the dinner invitation in the first place," he said coolly. "Especially during calving season."

At the age of twenty, George Webster had been summoned home from college to his father's bedside. Frank Webster was dying of pneumonia. When George arrived, his father sent everybody else out of the room and signaled for his son to pull a chair close to the bed. Once the boy was settled, the father took one of his hands and held it for a long time in silence. George was startled at first by the heat radiating from the old man's skin. They had not held hands since he was a child crossing High Street together, on the mornings when his father would walk him to the one-room schoolhouse that was connected with the university. For ten years, Frank Webster served as chairman of the History Department at the university and in due time he was rewarded for his loyalty by being appointed president, a post for which he was entirely unsuited and from which he was, mercifully, retired early. Since then he had devoted himself to a book on the Congress of Vienna, a lengthy treatise that was still unfinished. It occurred to George as he sat looking into his father's weary face that it would never be finished. George broke the silence at last, unnerved by the buzzing of a fly dying in the corner, by the heat, oppressive for a late September day, by the sweat of death in the hand he held.

"You wanted to speak to me, Father?"

The head turned back so that their eyes could meet but once again, the silence was unbroken through four endless gasping breaths.

"George, you must come home and take care of them. There will be nobody else."

"Yes, Father." George did not argue with his father about his dying. It seemed undignified and childish.

"There will be no money."

"What do you mean, Father?"

"I have made some very unwise investments"—another pause while the lungs searched for air—"in the West. The money is all gone. Your mother does not know. I don't want her to know until afterward. I could not bear the reproach.''

George took his hand away, the only gesture he allowed himself at that moment. He sat back in the chair and looked across his father's body at the opposite wall of the room. Here, he thought, lies my father, who was a failure at everything he tried. Incapable of running a university, incapable of finishing the book he started or making a sound investment with his money. And at the last, he was incapable of facing his wife with the news of his final failure. "God help me not to be this kind of man," he prayed.

George did as his father asked. He did not tell his mother until after the funeral that they had no money with which to care for her and the children. Emma Russell Webster had deferred to her husband on all the proper occasions, but she had been strong enough for both of them. She took George's news without flinching.

"We shall have to find some, then," she replied with a smile.

"Aren't you surprised, Mother?" George asked, which was the closest he ever came with her to a condemnation of his father.

"Your father always had the best intentions, but he trusted other people too much with his affairs." They left it at that.

She was the first to suggest that they sell the house to pay off the debts, a proposal that George and his older sister, Minerva, had already decided they could not make.

"Nonsense," Emma had said to her children's protests. "My family is made up of the people around me, not the house we live in." So they sold it, auctioned much of the better furniture, and moved into a smaller house that the university let to them for a nominal yearly rent. Minerva went to work at the university library, secretly delighted that her father's death and the family's reduced circumstances allowed her to escape the boredom of home. Emma Webster insisted that George finish Yale with money that she borrowed from her own mother's cousin, an eccentric spinster named Martha Bunting. Emma could not have chosen a better benefactor. Miss Bunting forgave the debt when George graduated from college on the condition that he go to agricultural school for one year.

"I have always wanted a farm," Miss Bunting announced to everybody's amazement, "and I have decided that George will run it for me."

George suggested he might serve Miss Bunting better if she wished to own a newspaper. She glared at him with an expression that he would come to know well, a mixture of haughty indignation and barely suppressed laughter.

So they went into partnership, the seventy-six-year-old lady and the recent college graduate. The day he finished agricultural school, the two of them set off in her buggy looking for land. She had very definite ideas about the kind of place she wanted, and it seemed to George that they would spend the rest of her life at least looking for it. They covered most of the eastern part of the state in one summer, answering advertisements in the local newspaper and in a small magazine called *The Rural Farmer*, and it was on those long drives that he heard her ideas and began to understand what an obsession farming had always been for her.

"We must never be scared to experiment, George. I have ordered most of the recent bulletins from the Department of Agriculture in Washington. Every month they are coming up with new ideas about fertilizer, irrigation, sanitary conditions for a dairy farm. I want us both to read up on these things regularly."

It also became clear to George during those rides that she truly intended them to be partners. He would share in the ownership and she would share in the work.

"But you can't mean you intend to milk the cows and plow the fields with me?" George asked, incredulous.

"That is precisely what I mean," she said. "I have wanted to work a farm all my life and you are giving me the chance to do it. I don't ever want to hear you talk about any work being too hard for me, George Webster, because if I do, I'll buy you out and throw you right off the place."

They found the farm in the township of Northington on a rainy day the first week of October.

"Fifty acres of land with house and outbuildings," the advertisement had read, but the owner said it was closer to eighty. "That land over near the river's never been properly surveyed," he added, working his cigarette from one side of his mouth to the other with his lips.

The house itself had been let go, a white clapboard farmhouse too long without a woman in it.

"Why are you selling it?" Miss Bunting asked. In her enthusiastic inspection of the barn, her hair had begun to float out of its twist in a wispy cloud.

"Too lonely here without Mildred. She died three years ago. Diphtheria. Going to live with my sister over in Simsbury." The man's lips, which had barely moved during this speech, went back to work on the cigarette.

They returned three more times to "walk the fences" before they decided to take the place. The farmer, who seemed to have lost the energy either to sell the farm or to farm it, stayed in the kitchen whenever they came. He nodded silently as they passed by, discussing plans for the orchard or a renovation of the barn. The farm was unique, as Miss Bunting pointed out, because of the variety of land contained in its borders. There were plowed fields, a dairy barn, an orchard, considerable acreage turned to pasture as well as frontage on the Farmington River. The freight and passenger trains from New Haven to Hartford stopped in the small town of Northington twice a day.

So, in the end, they took it. Miss Bunting, displaying a shrewdness in money matters which surprised George, offered a sum considerably lower than the asking price, and after the weakest kind of protest, the man accepted it. He moved out within the week.

"I have no respect for a broken kind of man like that," Miss Bunting said as they stood on the front porch and watched his wagon drive away. In the back, the rocking chair swayed with each step of the horse.

"Who knows? I may leave like that," George said. The dead look in that man's eyes told him far more about the trials of farming than any book about irrigation problems or the destructive effects of hailstorms.

"Not I," Miss Bunting said, turning into the house and leaving him alone on the porch, feeling like a fool.

They moved in the following spring—Miss Bunting into the main bedroom on the second floor, which looked south toward the river, George into a small room at the opposite end of the house. The dour German cook named Vin took the bedroom off the kitchen, a place which must once have been used for storing the harnesses, as it had an odd smell of leather that never did respond to any of Vin's efforts to remove it.

That spring, they bought a herd of twenty Ayrshires and planted two fields in corn and one in alfalfa. By September, five of the cows had died of Bang's disease, contracted from a herd in a neighboring pasture, and the corn was wiped out by a freak hailstorm in late August.

Arthur Rutwell, their closest neighbor to the west, came over to survey the damage. "It could have been worse," he muttered. "Two years ago we had a tornado."

"Thanks for your encouragement, Mr. Rutwell," Miss Bunting remarked wryly.

George glanced at her with a smile. Because it was easier, she now wore her hair in two long silver braids that hung down almost to her waist. The first day she had arrived at the barn looking that way, George had had a hard time concealing his surprise.

"Go ahead and stare," she snapped. "This is what an old lady's hair looks like."

"It's just that I didn't know there was so much of it tucked up on top," he replied, for once unflustered, perhaps because, for once, she was.

She borrowed a pair of his overalls, and on the days visitors weren't expected, she wore them going about her chores, much to Vin's disapproval. George grew quite used to seeing her like that, and it was only on the odd day when someone dropped by without warning that he saw her through their eyes. Arthur Rutwell had done a certain amount of staring when he first arrived, but Miss Bunting endured it without a word. She had never minded being different.

That winter, one of the worst old Fred Howard, the station agent, could remember, the temperature dropped to 17 below and Miss Bunting suggested bringing the cows in the house to keep them from freezing to death.

"I'm more worried about you than I am about those blasted cows," George said. She had grown thinner in the last year, and the summer sun had left lines in her face because she refused to be bothered with a hat. The bones in her arms stood out so thin and brittle he wondered why they didn't crack like tree branches in an ice storm when she brushed against something.

They planted five fields the second year and replaced the dead cows. Four calves were born that spring, and George learned firsthand how to turn a calf that had gotten stuck in the birth canal the wrong way. They laid in the piping for a primitive irrigation system, so when the long dry spell settled in the middle of July, they were able to keep the three corn fields wet enough to pull them through.

"We're on our way, George," Martha cried that September when the two of them had been accepted into the local Grange to the strains of "Dear Old Farm" and the first payment had come in for the corn. "And what's more," she said, "I've got you hooked."

"What do you mean?" he asked, glancing up from his magazine.

"Remember last winter you were still reading *Vanity Fair* whenever you had a free moment? Well, look at you now," she cried.

He hurled the copy of *New England Farmer* at her and she ducked, laughing. That night, as he had so many others, he went up to bed wishing that she were fifty years younger.

In the early spring, the time a farm takes all the hours of the day and then some, they discussed the day's work over breakfast as usual. Angelo, the dairyman, hired last fall in the first flush of profits, was coping with the cows, which left George free to plow the four corn fields.

"What's your plan today?" he asked Martha one day late in March.

"The garden. I have staked out the potato patch. I plan to turn that over today and put in the peas. We should have enough food to keep us going most of the winter." She glanced across the table at him. "Why the frown?"

"I noticed those stakes yesterday when I came up from the orchard. It looks to me as if you plan to double the size of the garden in one day."

"Potatoes need room," she replied, and stood up to

keep him from saying more. They turned out to be her last words to him, and the garden was where George found her when he went down to see why she had not come up for lunch. She was lying where she had fallen, on her side in the half-dug potato patch, one braid flung irreverently across her mouth. He picked her up and carried her, still breathing, across the lawn, past Vin, silenced for once, up to her bedroom. Hour after hour, he sat there, even after the doctor had warned him that she would not wake up again, waiting for her to sit up and tell him how in hell he was supposed to go on without her.

His mother and sister came up to be with him, but George was alone with her the evening she died. Her dying was quiet, a small gasp of something that sounded like surprise and then silence. He put his head down on her chest against the stiff white muslin of her nightgown, against the thin bones, and cried. Minerva found him there and took him away.

"I never told her but I loved her," George whispered to his sister. "As a woman."

"I know," Minerva said, and her acceptance of what had seemed to him an unacceptable secret comforted him and allowed him to sleep.

She had left him everything in her will as well as instructions in a separate letter that she wished to be buried in the orchard. "I shall not haunt the place, dear George, not even if you sell it, unless I feel you giving up on yourself and creeping away from life like that broken spirit who sold us the farm. Thank you for letting me have my dream, letting me plow myself right into the earth."

When he read the letter, he did not cry again. He put it with an old photograph of her in a top drawer where, years later, Lydia would find it. And he went on without her.

"Did Grandfather sweep you off your feet?" Molly asked.

"I doubt your history teacher is interested in those kinds of details," her grandmother replied.

"Social history," Molly said. "Courting practices in the olden days."

171

"Oh, hush, you nasty girl. No, he didn't. Your grandfather was a very good-looking man but standoffish in the beginning. But then so was I, so we suited one another, I suppose. He once told me he liked me because I didn't babble away like other women."

"And why did you like him?"

"He smelled of manure."

Molly giggled. "Is that all?"

"No, but it was very important. I never have been able to stand perfumed men. He was older, he had fabulous blue eyes, and there was a sureness about him. Now that's enough. I don't want to talk about it anymore."

Throughout that year, they met a number of times at the Morrises'. He came down to New York for a visit, and she sat through an uncomfortable dinner while he described the farm to her father.

"Shade tobacco sounds like a very risky business, Mr. Webster. You say the crop has been destroyed once by a flood?"

"It wiped us out in one day. But that was just a freak thing, Mr. Franklin. On a good year, it can be very profitable. And of course, I have the dairy business to back me up. I have a good herd of Ayrshires."

As Lydia listened, they circled each other like animals staking out territory.

"You sounded defensive with Father that first time," Lydia said to him much later.

"I was. I knew already that I wanted to marry you and I knew he knew it too."

"Somebody might have told me," she said with mock indignation.

He had shown her around the farm before he asked her. "Mud season is the worst of all," he said, driving her back to Farmington. "Nothing moves and the loneliness can be terrible. And of course, the farm takes all my time and then some. It will not be an easy life after New York."

"Are you asking me to marry you, George?" Lydia said, jostling along next to him in the open carriage.

"Yes."

There. She had made him come out and say it. Now

172

what did she think? Did she want to leave her work in New York, her dear Aunt Katherine, comfortable Uncle Arthur. Certainly, they would never put her out, but she didn't want to be the maiden niece with the graying hair ensconced forever on the second floor.

She liked this man. She liked the way he looked, his laconic voice, the earthiness of him. He seemed sure of himself, easy with animals, with farm machinery, with natural disturbances. She felt safe with him. The old nightmares would not trouble her here, she was sure of that.

It would be lonely. He had already warned her about that. And she would miss her work, although lately even that had made her restless. She knew she didn't want to become a nurse, but she was tiring of her role as interpreter and entertainer of children. But what work could she possibly do here on a farm? Even though she loved the thought of him hitching himself fearlessly up next to a cow's rump, she didn't see herself there. What if he expected her to be another Miss Bunting?

"Should I take your silence as a refusal?" he asked.

"I thought you liked women who didn't natter on," she said quietly, still buying time.

He pulled the horses to a stop in the middle of the road. "Don't tease at a time like this."

"I think I'm scared of cows, George."

"I didn't ask you to come work on the farm, Lydia. I asked you to be my wife."

"And that's not the same thing?"

"Not in my mind."

"All right, then," she said after a deep breath. "I will marry you."

"Good. That's settled," he said. Later, when Lydia got to know him better, she would hear him make the same pronouncement when he shook hands on the purchase of a good milker.

He twitched the reins again and then reached over and kissed her right there in the middle of the road, with the horse still moving forward on its own.

173

12

"Tell me about the first time you came to the farm," Molly said.

Lydia laughed. "Is the tape on?" she asked.

"Yes."

"Good. It's a funny story. Tony Delbianco picked us up in your grandfather's little red Fiat at the train station in New Haven."

"Rudy's grandfather?"

"That's right. Funny short man with bright black eyes. He gave me a wide smile and sort of bowed when he saw me. I spoke to him in Italian and his smile got about four or five miles wider. *'Signora, parla Italiano—bene, bene,'* he announced, and chuckled to himself all the way home."

"Did Grandfather speak Italian?"

"No. I think your grandfather disapproved of my speaking to the workers in their own language. Maybe he thought it started us off on the wrong footing. He had a way of cocking his head to the side when he didn't like something I did. He handed me into the back seat of the Fiat, and I had to stare at that cocked head all the way home to Northington, which in those days was a very long ride, I might tell you."

"He made you sit in the back? That wasn't very gallant."

"As it turned out, it was easier because the car broke down every two miles. We had three flats on the way home as well as problems with the carburetor or some such thing. Every once in a while, the engine would just sputter to a stop and the two of them would clamber out, groaning, lift up the hood and study the situation, scratching their heads all the while. It was really a very funny sight. The first couple of times, I crawled out too, just to show my interest. Remember, I was the young bride,

174

eager to share in every experience. But after the third
time, it got a little ridiculous, so I sat in the back, stared
at the scenery, and wrapped one leg around the other. I
desperately needed to go to the bathroom, but I felt it
would hardly be appropriate for the new Mrs. Webster to
go squat behind a tree." At that point, Lydia burst out
laughing, which set Molly off, and the tape had to be
turned off until they recovered themselves.

When Lydia first arrived that night in 1909 after the
interminable ride in the car, she saw nothing of the house
and she brushed past George, who looked as if he might
try to pick her up and carry her over the threshold. She
had no time for that.

"Good evening," she said to the maid, who had opened
the door as soon as she saw the lights of the car sweep
across the driveway. "Can you show me directly to the
bathroom, please?"

The trouble with Vin the cook started the very first
morning. When the new Mrs. Webster sent down word
that she would always take her breakfast tray in her
bedroom, the woman stomped around the kitchen, slamming silverware about and muttering that "Miss Bunting
would be horrified by such a thing." Eve, the kitchen
maid, had only been hired two days before and Vin
terrified her. At last, when she took the tray up, she
knew there would be trouble. The egg had been hard-
boiled, the toast was black and the coffee cold. Lydia was
sitting in bed, fuming.

"Whatever took so long, Eve? I'm ravenous."

"I'm so sorry, ma'am. Vin seemed awfully put out
about something."

Lydia looked at the tray that the maid slid tentatively
across her knees. "This is unacceptable," she said.

"Yes, ma'am. I'll take it back."

"Never mind. I'll take it down myself. Might as well
beard the lion in her den."

George had warned her about Vin. "She's used to a
bachelor who's not very fussy about his food. And my
cousin, Miss Bunting, often ate in the kitchen with her

because she was in such a rush to get back out to the barn."

"I shall be very diplomatic, darling. I promise."

Vin did not turn around from her place at the sink even though Lydia knew she must have heard her coming. "Vin, I am Mrs. Webster," she started in as friendly a voice as she could muster. "I know you must have heard about the car trouble we had last night."

"I couldn't wait up any longer. I'm on my feet all day."

"Of course you are. I certainly didn't expect you to. The roast beef you left suited us fine. I always do like it on the cool side anyway." Strike one, Lydia thought to herself. The woman still had not turned around.

Lydia put the tray down on the large table in the middle of the room that served as cutting board and serving place. She walked over to the sink and plunged her hand right into the soapy water, searching for Vin's. Their hands met and came up, clasped together. "So nice to meet you at last," Lydia said, with her most radiant smile. "Now, about my breakfast. I like the eggs done for four minutes."

"They need five here," Vin said, wiping her hands on her apron. "They come from right down the road. Chickens laid them this morning."

"Five, then, is perfect. Ten is too much. And my toast should be done lightly and buttered. A little jam and salt and pepper on the tray would be awfully nice. And please send my coffee up in a thermos bottle so that it does not grow cold on the trip up the stairs."

Vin was cornered and she knew it. "Yes, ma'am," she said.

"As soon as I've finished breakfast," Lydia said, "I shall be down to discuss the menus with you. Mr. Webster has been very complimentary about your cooking and I am certainly looking forward to sampling it."

By the time she got back upstairs, Lydia would have been just as happy to eat in the dining room, but now that she had laid down the gauntlet, she knew she had to follow through.

Poor Eve's legs were very tired by the end of the

morning. Mrs. Webster sent the tray back twice more before she finally found everything to her satisfaction.

"I'm afraid that Vin will be a cross for me to bear, George," Lydia said tentatively. "She is determined not to like me."

"Give her some time. She just doesn't like change."

Lydia said nothing more. Very well. She would wage her own battles cheerfully and save all her real feelings about the sulky, unresponsive gnome in the kitchen for her weekly letter to Aunt Katherine.

"Please, Aunt Katherine," she wrote a month after her arrival in Northington, "could you make sure that the epitaph on my gravestone reads: SHE KEPT HER HUSBAND'S COOK, as I do not expect to get any credit in this life for the daily trials she subjects me to. I have taken to ordering my own meat when the butcher wagon comes, as she invariably picks the cheaper cut or conveniently forgets that I requested lamb for dinner. She looks on me as an extravagant New York girl who is sure to ruin her beloved Mr. Webster unless she takes it upon herself to thwart me at every turn. Eve, the waitress, left yesterday in tears. Of course she was driven to it by Vin's nasty criticism and I don't know how I'll find somebody else on such short notice. Mr. and Mrs. Morris will be coming for dinner Saturday night, and as this is my first official dinner party, I am very anxious that it do credit to George and myself. Vin will make every effort to sabotage me in some way, I am sure of it.

"How is your work going down on Carmine Street? I often think of you starting out in the morning just as I am settling down with Vin in the kitchen for our little morning talk. My times with you and Dr. Baker are what I miss most of all. I hope soon to find a place for me here, something beyond the concerns of the household to occupy my mind and my hands."

Lydia arrived at the farm in the middle of its busiest season and during the first three months of her marriage she saw very little of her husband. The first afternoon she decided to visit the barn at milking time without waiting for his invitation. George watched her picking her way down the wide aisle between the cows' swishing tails, her skirts lifted to the boot tops, with a bemused expression on his face.

"The lady of the manor, I presume," he said.

"I promise I won't be in the way," she said. "I wanted to see what you do all day." She didn't say: It's lonely in the house. I waited for two hours for you to come in at noon before Eve told me that your lunch is always sent out to the barn.

He sat her on a milking stool and taught her how to pull the teats down again and again with a steady rhythm until the milk squirted directly into the empty tin bucket. After some hesitation, she learned how to lean her forehead against the cow's furry side, to plant her feet firmly in the wet hay so that if the cow shifted weight suddenly, she was not knocked off balance.

"Not bad for your first time," he muttered, which she realized later was an enormous compliment from him.

"Miss Bunting did the milking with you," she said.

"Yes. But that was a long time ago. I told you before, I don't expect you to."

It felt like a rebuke. After a decent amount of time and some feigned interest about the best milkers, she fled to the house and soaked the smell of manure and wet hay and cow off her body in a long hot bath, so that when they sat together at dinner, he was the only one who smelled like the barn. She did not go down there again for a long time.

After that, she spent her days nesting, claiming the house as her own. She rearranged the furniture in the living room so that the piano she had brought with her fit next to the picture window. She hung new curtains in the bedrooms and rolled out the rugs her father had sent on from the Thirty-eighth Street house. As a wedding present, George had given her a pony named Max and she took him driving in the afternoons, exploring the roads around the farm, venturing a little farther out each day.

One day, when she saw Smack the gardener weeding the flower bed, she went out to talk to him. Startled by her sudden appearance, he stepped on a new peony bush in his rush to back out of the bed. Together, they inspected the damage. He snapped off the broken stems and patted the earth firmly down around the roots, talking to the plant in a soothing undertone the whole time.

At last, when he stood up, she said, "I didn't mean to startle you. I wanted to ask your advice about something."

"*Sí, signora?*"

"I want to plant a tree here next to the house. Something that will grow very tall. Something my grandchildren will play under."

He broke into a wide smile at the word "grandchildren." Most of his front teeth were missing and his face had a shiny scrubbed appearance that made it look as if the skin had been stretched too tightly over the bones.

"I want to plant it here, Smack," she said, selecting a spot just six feet from the dining-room wall.

"*Sí, signora.*"

"What kind of tree would be good?" she asked.

"Elm," he said. "Thick leaves. For the grandchildren."

"Perfect," she said, and they beamed at one another again.

When she showed George the place they had picked, he was not as enthusiastic. "It's awfully close to the house," he said. "I was thinking that if we ever had to expand, this would be a good place."

"But we can't build on here, George. It would block our view of the lawn and the orchard from the living room."

"Very well, but move it farther out from the side of the house. Roots can do a lot of damage to a foundation."

They planted it in the rain because Lydia could not bear to wait another day, and by that time, Smack had already fallen deeply in love with the *signora* and agreed to anything she said.

"Now I feel as if I've put down some roots," she said, tossing away two stones exposed by the newly turned earth.

Smack did not understand much of what she said, but he heard the determination in her voice and, underneath, the loneliness.

"A good tree," he said, and the tips of their fingers touched as they leaned their weight on the dirt.

"I have one good friend so far," Lydia wrote to Aunt Katherine. "His name is Smack, and no matter what I say, he agrees to it. He is teaching me about the garden, and although it is too late to plant anything this year, we have very ambitious plans for next."

A month after her arrival, George took her to her first Grange meeting. Driving over in the pony cart, he gave her a short lecture about the people she would meet.

"These are old-time Yankees, and until they get to know you, they can be as stony as the land they've had to farm. I've lived here for over ten years and they've just begun to accept me. Don't be too enthusiastic with them."

"You mean, don't go overboard the way I did at the church supper," she said. She had bought every antimacassar in sight, and despite the blank expressions, had stuck her hand cheerfully out and introduced herself to everyone. "Hello, I'm Lydia Webster. I'm so awfully glad to meet you. George has told me so much about you." Most of the time, she had received only a reluctant handshake and a silent nod in return.

She took her place on the women's side of the room and behaved herself very well until the end, when the whole group rose to sing the farewell song. A terrible fit of the giggles overcame her as they started the third chorus about the dear old farm, and even though she dug her fingernails into her palm to make herself stop, she knew that Mr. Rutwell across the way was watching her shaking shoulders with a stern expression of disapproval. Afterward, she stood demurely next to her husband, who was discussing a new bull he was thinking of buying from a breeder in Canton.

"Send him down on Wednesday. He ain't the kind that travels good," George said in a flat New England voice, and she looked up at him with amazement.

"You never talk that way to me," she teased him on the drive home. She had insisted on taking the reins because after this last month Max was used to her. With George, he positively poked along.

He shrugged. "I slip into it sometimes. Comes naturally to me now. It didn't in the beginning."

One August morning, they began the canning.

Dorothy, the young girl who had replaced Eve, was

sitting on a wooden stool in front of a pile of green beans. When she was done with that, she had to start on the cucumbers and the first tomatoes. She looked tired already.

"How are you doing, Dorothy?" Lydia called out from across the room where she was helping Vin maneuver the glass jars into the pot of boiling water with a pair of tongs.

"All right, I guess, ma'am."

"It's a pity we have to can on the hottest day of the year," Lydia said. It was only nine o'clock in the morning and already she was drenched in sweat even though she had picked out her coolest cotton dress.

"We do it when the vegetables are ready," Vin declared. "And they are ready now."

"Oh, I know that, Vin. I'm used to heat. New York's Carmine Street on an August afternoon would make this kitchen feel as cool as the bottom of a well."

"Maybe Mr. Smack planted too much," Dorothy said.

"We'll see if you say that next February," Vin spat. "Last year I used every last jar of tomatoes. Mr. Webster is partial to the way I do them."

"Yes, Vin," Lydia said sharply. She resisted the temptation to catch Dorothy's eye across the room. After her childhood when the servants were often her only companions, she felt easy with them, but even Aunt Katherine had cautioned her about becoming "too familiar." It was especially hard to change her ways up here in the country when George was gone all day and Isabelle Morris, her closest friend, was a good forty-minute pony ride away even in the summertime.

George dropped in at noon to see how the work was going. "You don't have to do it with her," he had told Lydia that morning.

"I'm not doing anything else today," she replied testily. "If Miss Bunting could do the canning, then so can I."

George had said nothing more, but now he frowned when he saw Lydia's pale face. "Why don't you sit down for a while?" he whispered when Vin was turned away at the sink. "You're not used to working in this heat."

Elizabeth Winthrop

"I just finished telling Vin how hot New York can get in the summer," she said loudly. "Aunt Katherine and I worked every single day, right through the month of August—" Suddenly she couldn't talk anymore and the lines of his face began to blur. "My God," she heard him say as her knees gave way.

She woke up and stared at the ceiling of her bedroom for a moment without moving. She remembered fainting and her first reaction was fury with herself. How could her body have given way like that? This had never happened to her before. And after all that ridiculous boasting about the heat of the city. "George," she called softly, and looked about the room. She was alone. He must have carried her upstairs and gone right back to the barn. What if she had never come to again? What if something were really seriously wrong with her? By the time he did finally return after milking, she had worked herself into a steely rage.

"How are you feeling?" he asked over dinner.

"Fine," she said.

"The cows seem awfully sluggish. Must be the heat."

"Must be," she said.

She was beginning to sound like a Yankee farmer herself, but what made her even angrier was that he didn't seem to notice. Dorothy cleared the table and he sat back to fool with his pipe. What an irritating human being, she thought as she swept past him into the living room and plunked herself down at the piano. The repetitive rhythms of Bach's Prelude in C calmed her and she stayed at the piano as long as she could stand it. When at last she turned around, he was sitting in his favorite corner chair reading *New England Farmer*.

"Do you ever think of anything else but the farm?"

"The farm?" he repeated without looking up. He wasn't listening.

"Yes, blast you, THE FARM." Her shriek finally forced him to lower the magazine. "I could have been very sick, you know. It was just lucky that it was a little fainting spell, because nobody paid any attention to me at all. You went right back to that beloved barn of yours. Why don't you start sleeping out there if you love it so much?"

She stormed out of the room, carrying with her the

memory of his surprised face. The first hour afterward her anger propelled her around the bedroom. In case anybody was sitting outside the door listening, she slammed the wardrobe door two or three times just for good measure. But after she had settled into bed to read, she began to calm down. She was being ridiculous. When he came in, she would apologize for her behavior.

She sat up most of the night waiting for him. Finally, as the birds began to chatter just before sunrise, she dressed and went looking for him. He was nowhere in the house. Outside, the rooster on the farm across the road had already begun to crow. It was the coolest hour of the day, and for a moment she forgot the sleepless night behind her. Standing on the edge of the orchard, she inhaled the scent of the wild rose bush that grew along the fence and the sweet grass which Smack had mown just the day before.

As she stood there, Aunt Katherine's words came back to her. "Your mother was really a child, Lydia. She never grew up." Well, she would face it in the empty sweetness of this morning. She had been acting like a child. George had never pretended that the farm would be any less important to him just because he had married her. Before she came along, it had been his whole life. So now she was here and she had to find a life in it.

As she stood there, the side door of the calf barn swung open and he stepped out. Of course, she remembered now. He had a bed up in the office for calving season. She had told him to go sleep in the barn and that's just what he had done. She smiled as she watched him stretch, hitch up his pants, shove his black hair back from his face using his two palms the way her father used his silver brushes.

She waited as he headed up through the orchard, loath to interrupt the peace of his morning. He did not see her until he had almost reached the fence she leaned against.

"Good morning, George," she said quietly, and he glanced up warily as if he might be able to read from her expression some sign of another explosion.

"It's over," she said. "The storm has passed. For now. Maybe for good."

"I hope not," he said, looking up at the sky. "The

183

farm needs rain every now and then." At first, she thought he had misunderstood, but when his face came back down to hers, she saw the wide teasing grin spread across it just before he kissed her.

She always wanted him to hold her more. But that's all she ever wanted. Just the holding. He was that much taller than she so that their bodies fit together well, her temple against his cheek, and sometimes if she stood on tiptoe, her chin hooked over the muscles of his shoulder the way an umbrella rests securely on a doorknob. "Tighter," she would whisper, knowing he was being careful because his arms were powerful but wanting to be crushed against the wall of him so tightly that nothing could ever slip between them. She felt safe and surrounded when he held her and she loved it most when he caught her on the way out to the barn and pulled her back into the dark hallway downstairs where Vin or Dorothy would not surprise them. Those times, they both were dressed, ready for the day, and even though she sometimes felt his body stirring to hers, his beloved cows were waiting, and she knew that the holding would have to do for the moment. Until that night.

Lydia never made a sound when George's hands slipped under her nightgown. She lay still, her eyes closed. She insisted on darkness, and while she was waiting for it to be over, she talked herself out of the panic that sometimes threatened to overwhelm her. George loved her. He was doing this because he loved her. She reminded herself of all the differences. The tips of his fingers were everyday work rough. His skin smelled of pipe tobacco and hay and leather and saddle soap. And his hands were different. He did not seem to know how to be gentle with her, and in an odd way, she was relieved by that. The hands that used to touch her were too slow, too languid, so that unless she held herself absolutely rigid, her body would betray her.

Once he was aroused, he entered her quickly. Her comfort came afterward, when they lay together, skin against skin, bone knocking bone, and she felt him relax into sleep against her shoulder.

*   *   *

Their first night together had been the worst. Charles Franklin had insisted on taking a suite for them at the Waldorf-Astoria, and they both felt foolish in the lavishly decorated rooms. George came to her directly from the bar, and when he tried to take off her nightgown, two buttons popped off in his clumsy hurried fingers.

But she didn't even mind that. It had been the smell of him that made her shrink from him in horror. George was not a drinking man.

"What have you been drinking?" she asked.

"Whiskey. Some gentlemen in the bar downstairs were toasting me."

She pulled the shoulder of her gown back up over her shoulder. "You don't normally drink, do you, George?"

"I didn't know it bothered you so much. I only had one."

"I hate the smell," she said with a sudden shiver.

"I'll go and rinse my mouth out again," he said.

When he came back, she had turned the gas way down and she was waiting, prepared to be very good. "I doubt you'll enjoy it," her Aunt Katherine had explained just two nights before. "But that doesn't matter. It's over with quickly enough. And they mean well."

And she was proud of the way she had behaved. In the darkness, she felt Nellie's understanding eyes resting on her the way they had that night of the fire. Only the smallest whimper escaped from her when he pushed himself higher up into her.

"I'm sorry, I didn't mean it to hurt," George whispered when it was over.

"Just please hold me now," she said quietly. "Tighter. Tighter." And he held her as tight as he dared until finally she stopped trembling and fell asleep.

In 1909, the town of Northington had a little railroad station, a stationmaster, and four trains going north and four going south every day. The freight cars brought grain and supplies to the farmers and to the fuse factory on the edge of town. Hartford was only nine miles away, but in order to get there, a person had to take the train fourteen miles south to the town of Plainville. There the passenger sat in the baggage room, talking in a companionable way to the cheerful baggagemaster while they both waited for the Dinky, a funny little two-car train which traveled east from Bristol toward Hartford. The entire trip took close to two hours each way.

The town itself consisted of a general store, the Congregational church, and various houses which belonged to the more prosperous members of the community, such as the minister, the manager of the fuse factory, and the owner of the store, a man named Jack Gardner who also served as postmaster from behind a small grilled window next to the candy counter. The teacher for the one-room school came from Southington, boarded in Northington during the week, and went home again on the weekends. In addition to its monthly meeting, the Grange held square dances twice a year. The only other regular evening entertainment were the church suppers sponsored by the Ladies' Aid Society. The Northington Strawberry Festival supper was famous in the county. People drove in from miles around, balancing home-baked pies on their laps, hitched their horses in the church shed, and joined their neighbors at long tables piled with quantities of potato salad, cold sliced ham, and rich strawberry shortcakes.

In 1909, there were three hundred people enrolled on the town's list of active voters. "Of course, that doesn't include the women," Lydia said with a honeyed smile, "because we're still classified with the criminals and the insane." George did not answer.

It also did not include the Italian immigrants or the Irish who had come in the late 1800s; only the New England Yankees, those independent, thrifty people who tipped their hats to nobody, who were not afraid of hard work, of living off the land, but who were terrified of showing any emotion, either pleasure or sorrow. They were rugged individuals whose only abiding fear was that if they should run out of money, they would be "sent away" to the Poor Farm, a tumbledown house just over the hill in Farmington. Their humor was dry and their laughter rare and they did not take to strangers.

"Winter has closed in here," Lydia wrote to Aunt Katherine early in December. "Am I just imagining that it has come so much earlier than it does in New York? The first snow two weeks ago was a lovely surprise, a white shroud over the lawns and fields that would not be trampled into gray mush the way it always is in the city. But we have had two more heavy storms since then. The high drifts next to the house and the heavy rubber boots I must pull on just to go out to the butcher wagon, make me feel trapped and lonelier than ever. How I long for someone to talk to during the day. When I finish this letter, I have decided to walk over to the general store (which also serves as the post office) to mail it. At least it means I will be able to exchange a few words with Mr. Gardner on the subject of the weather or the reasons that my order of muslin material hasn't arrived yet."

"What do you want to do that for?" Vin asked when Lydia walked through the kitchen in the heavy boots. "Smack will take your letter over in the afternoon as usual."

"I need the walk," Lydia said.

The store appeared to be empty, but Lydia could hear voices in the back. She rapped sharply on the wooden counter, and after some shuffling of feet and the scraping of a chair, Mr. Gardner appeared.

"Morning," he said with a noticeable lack of enthusiasm. "What can I do for you?"

"Good morning, Mr. Gardner," Lydia said. "I need to mail this letter. Could I buy some stamps, please? And I'll pick up our mail if it's ready."

"Hasn't been sorted yet," he muttered as he lifted the gateway to the post office section of the store.

"Well, I'll wait, then." As she moved to the right, she could see a group of men gathered around the stove in the back.

"Don't know when I'll get to the sorting," he added, taking the letter from her.

"Oh, I'm in no rush. In fact, the walk over has chilled me. If you don't mind, I'll just warm my feet by your stove for a while."

She ignored his look of alarm and swept past the counter into the back room, his inner sanctuary, which she was sure had never been invaded by a woman. The three

187

men sitting there in companionable silence as they waited for Gardner's return looked equally horrified at the sight of her. They took their sock-covered feet from the lip of the stove and made a few halfhearted attempts to rise, but she slipped quickly into the only available chair.

"Please pay me no mind," Lydia said. "I'm going to warm myself for a minute." She pulled off her boots and propped her own stockinged feet up where theirs had just been. Nobody moved or spoke as they cast glances of bewilderment and dismay at one another. An elephant might just as well have walked into their midst, as Lydia reported that night to George.

The silence continued, punctuated by the occasional shift of a heavy body in a chair or the clearing of a throat. She recognized them all. Besides Gardner, there was Nick Wilson, the blacksmith, Arthur Rutwell, the farmer whose land bordered the Websters', and Harold Butler, the Republican town chairman. It was rumored that Mr. Butler paid people two dollars apiece for their votes, controlled everything that happened in the town, and was nominated for any position he wished to hold by six of his henchmen.

Gardner did not come in to reclaim his seat, and Lydia knew that soon they would all get up and find some excuse to get back to work if she did not act quickly.

"How's your health, Mr. Butler?" she asked. "I hear your foot's been feeling poorly." Good Lord, I'm getting like George, she thought. I've never in my life used the word "poorly."

He did not answer at once, and Lydia could see that he was wrestling with the obvious betrayal that a reply would represent. In the end, the thought of a fresh audience for his medical complaints won out.

"Doctor's talking about an operation," he said, shifting his weight to the other hip and carefully sliding the foot forward.

"How terrible," Lydia said. "It's a bunion, isn't it?"

"Yup. Hurts fierce in the cold weather."

Gardner dragged in the postmaster's stool and settled himself on it. Lydia leaned forward. "May I take a look at your toe? I've done a little nursing."

Mr. Wilson groaned. Now they were all in for it. With

obvious delight, Butler pulled off the thick wool sock and lowered the foot into Lydia's cupped hands. With care, she touched the swollen lump on the side of the big toe.

"It does look bad," she said as he withdrew the offending foot and slid the sock back over it.

"You don't want to have no operations," Wilson said, irritated that Butler had managed to grab the spotlight. "My wife went to some butcher over in Hartford for a little bump on her shoulder. It didn't seem to me to be much of anything, but he convinced her she had to have an operation. That was three months ago and the pain's still so bad she can't lift that arm properly. I told her all along it was a bunch of nonsense. If I ever need help, I'll go to the vet. From what I've seen, he treats the horses better than them doctors treat people."

Lydia settled her backbone carefully against the struts of the upright chair, as Gardner continued the theme of the conversation with a story about his poor mother's last sickness. It looked as if the men had forgotten she was there. In time, they went on to other subjects. Bert Fish had been keeping company with Miss Carey Davis for four years now. Did anybody know when he would ask her the crucial question? The whole situation was beginning to look a little foolish. After all, Miss Carey must be close to forty years old, but of course Bert had promised his dying mother that he would take care of that crazy sister of his and Miss Carey refused to live in the same house with her.

"What else did they talk about?" George asked over dinner that night.

"The foolishness of planting shade tobacco," she replied. "I knew they had really forgotten me when they got started on you."

"Yes?"

"Well, they said that you were always reading pamphlets on this and that and trying all those newfangled methods when they knew well enough how to farm the land without those fancy folks from the Department of Agriculture telling them what to do. After all, they'd done fine up to now and their fathers before them."

George grunted. "Not Gardner's father. His farm went bust twenty years ago. And as for Harold Butler, he couldn't make a weed grow no matter how hard he tried."

"It was mostly Arthur Rutwell talking and everybody else agreeing."

"Doesn't surprise me. Arthur would love to see me fail. He has the most uncanny nose for disaster. He appeared out of nowhere the day Miss Bunting and I discovered the first case of Bang's disease and the broken fence down by the river."

"I expect Miss Bunting put him in his place."

George nodded without any further comment. He knew that Lydia was oddly jealous of the ghost of Martha Bunting. She had a right to be. In many ways, Lydia reminded him of his mother's cousin; her forthright manner, her courage, even the gray streaks in her hair.

"Will you plant the tobacco again this year?" Lydia asked.

"Yes, ma'am. Two fields more than last."

"But I thought you said you were disappointed with the yield."

"That turned out to be a miscalculation on my part. The tobacco settles during the sweating process more than I thought. That's why I'm planting more this year. Pass that on to your friends down at the store," he added with a grin.

But Lydia said very little during those sessions around the stove. As long as she didn't talk too much, the men seemed to accept her presence. She had found the perfect place to learn about the life of the town without asking the intrusive questions that would continue to set her apart as a foreigner. At night, George helped her sort out the subjects of the stoveside discussions, and little by little she began to form a picture of the town and its inhabitants.

By February, she was ready to take on the ladies.

"They'll be tougher than the men," George warned her.

"Oh, I know that," Lydia said gaily. "In a funny way, the men remind me of my father. Crusty exteriors but they're soft inside. I expect the women are crusty all the way through."

She took tea with Mrs. Ridley, the fanciest lady in

Northington, who hired weekly help and in the summer months sat on her front porch with her blond hair rolled into stiff curls. During their visit, Lydia had to vacate the only comfortable chair in the parlor to make room for Mrs. Ridley's dog, an ancient, drooling bull terrier named Chuffy. On another day, she left jars of Vin's strawberry jam for Miss Carey Davis, who, for some reason, was never available to see her. She sat and listened to Mrs. Beaman's endless description of the best method of making Bar-le-duc, which turned out to be currants cooked for three days in the sun. "And how is your daughter, Mrs. Beaman? Do you think she'll be having a child soon?"

"Not yet, Mrs. Webster. Olive doesn't know her husband well enough."

"Whatever did she mean by that?" Lydia asked Isabelle Morris. "The daughter's been married for two years."

Isabelle put back her head and laughed heartily. "Oh, Lydia, you are getting a big dose of New England in one year."

"No one laughs like you," Lydia said in despair. "There is no joy in these people. They perform a duty, but to have a zest for living, to feel a reckless passion about anything seems to be 'not nice.' They keep company for years in a gentle contented fashion with such an attitude of patience, such a sense of duty. No children will be born out of those marriages."

"I expect you're right, Lydia," Isabelle said with mock solemnity. "It's the passionate Mrs. Webster who shall be populating the town of Northington, I think."

Lydia stirred uncomfortably. She wondered if Isabelle guessed that the passion she showed about gardening and painting and people did not extend to the bedroom. "It's the Italians who will be having the babies," she said. "At least they know how to laugh. I think I'd rather be with them than those stony-faced Yankees with their monosyllabic replies." She stood up. "Well, now that I've exploded, I'd better get home to my farmer husband. He's off tomorrow for a three-day trip. You know he's decided to run for state senator next fall."

"I'm delighted to hear it," Isabelle said as she pushed the wheelchair through into the front hall. "Taylor and I have been after him for years to get involved politically. We need young people to replace those old fossils in Hartford.''

Lydia kissed the older woman on both cheeks. "Thank you, Isabelle," she said. "I don't know how I'd survive here without you. You're my Connecticut Aunt Katherine.''

"You'd better go along," Isabelle said with an embarrassed wave of her hand. "I don't want you driving that stubborn pony home in the dark. Everybody says you go too fast anyway.''

"In this frozen town, it's my only way of being reckless," Lydia called back from the bottom of the front steps.

Except for the other way, she thought on the long trip home. Except for looking into that black hole inside, the place that threatened to swallow her up if for one moment she stopped playing at farmer's wife. Sometimes, when it felt safe, when she was lying in bed next to George, who fell asleep so easily, she imagined herself walking around that pit, like a person exploring the edge of a lake. She peered into the blackness and saw her anxious face peering back and she had to close her eyes in order to break the endless ricochet of reflections that would get smaller and smaller until there was nothing left of her.

Once she had tried to tell George about the hole.

"I mean, am I just the things I do?" she asked, already regretting the conversation because he was looking so confounded by it. "If I weren't married to you and I weren't planting things in the garden and sketching and playing the piano, who would I be? Nothing. I'd disappear.''

"I don't know what you're talking about. You are Lydia Franklin Webster, my wife.''

"I know that," she said. She let the matter drop then. She had told George once about the fire but only briefly; and never about her illness or Uncle James. Only Dr. Stevenson knew what had gone on with Uncle James. Dr. Stevenson and the journals safely tucked away in the box under this bed.

But it isn't enough to be your wife, she told herself when he had turned over and gone to sleep. I've got to do more with my days. It will help keep me sane, help me guard against slipping toward the edge of the hole. That fierce craving for control reminded her of the old nightmares about the doors, but she lined her body up against George's and forced herself away from them, down into sleep.

13

By 1910, George Webster had already begun to make a name for himself as a farmer. With a herd of seventy breeding and milking Ayrshires as well as six fields planted out in cigar-wrapping tobacco, and a crew of twenty men, the farm had turned into a sizable operation. In the mornings after an early breakfast, he met with Nort Hart, his foreman, in the office over the calf barn. Nort was a long, spare man with a bony face and a thin twang. Born in Northington, he moved out West as a young man, where it was rumored that he had drunk away a fortune made from panning gold. When he reappeared in town one day, twenty years after he left, people cautioned George against hiring him.

"You can see the trouble in his eyes," Arthur Rutwell said. "He'll run off again one day. You never know. His father was a bad sort too."

But George trusted his own instincts better than Arthur's doomsday prophecies and he hired the laconic man. If Nort did any drinking he kept it to himself. He lived in a tumbledown shack on the other side of town out beyond the fuse factory, but despite the fact that he walked the six miles to the farm every morning, he was always waiting in the office when George arrived. He drove the crews hard, but the men trusted him and worked well for him, and although he rarely offered an opinion that differed with the boss's, George had learned to listen carefully when Nort spoke.

In the mornings over a thermos of coffee brought down from the big house, he and George laid out the work for the day. The Italians were divided into two crews, one for the dairy herd and the other for the tobacco.

The work on the tobacco started in April, when the first group of seeds were planted in starter trays in the two greenhouses. The seeding was repeated once a week for a month so that the tobacco would ripen in weekly waves across the summer. Once the seed broke ground, Smack walked through with a pair of tweezers and thinned the plants so that the healthier ones could find more root room. By the third week of May, when the plants had developed at least five leaves each, they were ready to be set out in the fields by hand. The tobacco acreage was divided into "bents," areas approximately thirty feet square. The day before the planting all the available men were sent out to the fields to raise the yards of cotton gauze up onto the poles which stood at the corner of each bent.

The planting crew was under Smack's direction, and in the beginning, the younger men complained.

"They know he doesn't have too much upstairs," Nort said, tapping his right temple with his long index finger. "They don't like working under him because he's so fussy with the plants."

"Damn them. What do they want? A college professor? I picked Smack because he's a genius with growing things. As long as I've got him starting the plants, I know I've got the best chance for a healthy crop. So tell them to do exactly what he says or they'll be out on their tails."

"Yes, sir," Nort said, a smile twitching the corners of his mouth.

By the end of June, the plant blossoms had to be topped so that the upper leaves could achieve a fuller growth. A week after that, the men were sent back into the fields to remove cutworms and to snap off the suckers, the tiny offshoots that appeared in the leaf joints. The tops and suckers, too gummy for commercial use, were left on the ground to rot.

"Can I come watch?" Lydia asked the morning of the first harvest.

"Certainly," George said. "But don't wear your fancy clothes. The dust gets kicked up by the constant movement of the wagons."

They started picking early in the morning to avoid the

worst heat, as the cotton tents increased the temperature by at least fifteen degrees. The leaves were carefully plucked from the stalks in bunches and laid in the canvas baskets that the pickers dragged along behind them. Besides the regular crew, Nort Hart hired all the boys in the neighborhood because they did not have to walk in a stooped position in order to reach the plants. They dragged the baskets to a waiting wagon, which drove its load along the edge of the field to the two sheds that had been built in the spring to cure the tobacco. There the women sat in the shade carefully sewing each separate leaf onto a string, which was then attached to a lath. When they were done, the laths were passed up to the men who slid them along the movable beams of the shed. The tobacco hung there curing for almost two months.

Lydia stood in the corner of one of the tents watching the pickers move slowly down the rows. When she slipped out for a breath of fresh air, Tony Delbianco called to her. He was driving one of the wagons. "I'll take you over to the barn, *signora,*" he said in Italian. "You can watch the women stringing the leaves."

"Thank you, Tony. Do the pickers stay under those nets all day?"

"*Il Gaioffa* gives us a break in the middle of the day. We go down to the river and swim then."

"*Il Gaioffa?*"

He grinned. "That's our name for the boss. Mr. Pockets." He stood up on the wagon seat, stuck his hands in his pockets, and shifted his weight onto one hip in a perfect imitation of George.

"Tony," Lydia said in mock indignation as she covered her smile with a dusty hand.

"You don't tell, *signora?*" he said as he settled back down on the seat and flicked the reins.

"No, I won't tell."

"Go see Louisa," he said when they reached the shed and the men began to unload the baskets. "She's the best stringer," he added with obvious pride.

Lydia knew which one Louisa was. She came to the big house on Thursdays to help with the laundry, but whenever Lydia tried to engage her in conversation, Vin intervened with some irrelevant question about the dinner menu. She seemed to agree with George that it was inappropriate for Mrs. Webster to become too friendly with the Italians, so after a few attempts, Lydia gave up. She knew it would only make Vin take out her fury on Louisa, who didn't deserve it.

She greeted the other women quietly as she made her way down the row to Louisa, who sat at one end of the long wooden bench, her dark head bent over the pile of tobacco leaves in her lap. Although the roof of the shed kept the women out of the direct sun, the dust from the constant wagon traffic hung thick in the air. Louisa had tied a kerchief around her mouth.

"Buon giorno," Lydia said quietly as she slipped into an empty place across from her.

Louisa pulled the smudged cloth down over her chin. *"Buon giorno, signora,"* she said, struggling to get to her feet.

"Don't get up," Lydia said. From where she sat, she could see Louisa's belly bulging out above the pile of dark leaves. "You are having a baby?" she asked.

"Yes," the other woman said, and she broke into a wide smile. "In October."

"Your first?"

"Yes." Louisa glanced over at the foreman and went back to her work.

"I don't want to disturb your work," Lydia said. "Tony tells me that you are the best stringer."

"Yes," Louisa said. "My fingers are very fast, but now it is hard because of the stickiness." The leaves when handled released a gummy substance that coated the skin and the needles. "You speak Italian very well, *signora.*"

"Thank you," Lydia said. She felt a sudden warmth for this woman who had welcomed her at the stringing table with more grace than Miss Ridley had shown in her fancy drawing room on Main Street. "I think maybe I will have a baby soon too."

"Truly?" Louisa said, her face up again.

"I haven't even told Mr. Webster yet, so please don't say anything. Not even to Tony. It's too early to be sure."

"That would be very good. A son in the big house."

"Can you show me how to do the stringing?" Lydia

asked. She regretted saying anything about the baby. It was like breaking a good-luck charm.

Louisa handed her a needle and a piece of thread. She showed Lydia how to pierce the leaf at the very top so it was not damaged, how to push the leaves carefully along the gummy thread with two fingers, how to tie the thread to the end of each lath. While they worked, they talked quietly. Louisa told her about marrying Tony, about her trip across the ocean in the old boat called the *Giuseppe Verdi.* "We were given a little sack with a spoon, a fork, a knife, and a tin dish. We stood in line to get our food. We slept in bunks in a room full of people. I was so sick on that boat. It never stayed still, always rolling back and forth. I won't ever go back to see my mother. I couldn't stand that ride on the boat."

"Maybe she will be able to join you here."

Louisa nodded, and although she kept her head down, Lydia could see the tears standing in her eyes.

"But I am better here. Tony is a good man. He works hard and he makes me laugh."

The bell rang for the lunch break. The other women put down their work and stood up to stretch. Louisa did not move, and Lydia sat working across from her until their laths were finished and the men had hoisted them up onto the beams above their heads. As soon as each beam was filled with laths, it was pushed along the rafters to make room for the next one.

"Do the beams ever fall?" Lydia asked Nort.

"Sometimes. But the boys are very careful."

Lydia walked back to the house along the dusty road, passing the crowds of pickers who were headed to the shed to pick up their lunch and then down to the river to wash the sticky tobacco juice off their skin. She held her own hands out from her dress as she walked and wondered where Louisa would go to wash.

"Nort tells me you helped with the stringing today," George said when he came in after dark.

"Yes. Louisa Delbianco showed me how. You know she's having a baby, George."

"Is she?"

"It's so hot in that shed with all the dust. I hope she'll be all right."

198

George didn't reply. She knew what he was thinking. Don't interfere. Louisa is my best stringer. She didn't say anything more.

Lydia's suspicions were confirmed by Dr. Ramsay when she went to see him the following week.

During the embarrassing examination, she had closed her eyes and pretended to disappear, her old childhood trick. At last, he pulled down her dress and turned away to wipe his hands. "The baby is due in February," he said. "Of course, these early months are the risky ones. Be sure to get a lot of rest and do not engage in any arduous work."

"I can still garden," she said.

"It wouldn't be advisable."

Nonsense, she said to herself on the way home. Look at Louisa working right through the hot picking months. She was not going to lie in her bed and wait for a baby to grow. She felt oddly resentful of this foreign person inside her. She and George were happy now, just the two of them. She didn't want another human being to come between them, but she knew that was an unwomanly thought, one she could not share with anyone. Maybe it's because my mother died so early, she thought. Maybe you have to know your own mother in order to want to be one.

The second picking went off so well that George decided he could be away for the third.

"A whole week," Lydia cried. "But that's longer than you've ever been gone."

"Gino Togni will be spending two weeks at the Springfield Fair with the cows and I want to be up there the first week to choose the milkers. Then I have to meet with some of the Republican people down in the southern part of the state. There's rumors that the nominating convention in September is going to turn into a real fight."

She was lying in bed watching him brush his hair, the two ivory-backed brushes moving in unison on either side of his head. The sun was just coming up and she knew he was impatient to be gone. After all, milking must be almost done by now, because an hour had passed since Gino and the other dairymen had brought the cows down from the fields where they spent the summer nights. She studied his reflection in the mirror, looking at the line of his firm chin, now so familiar. When he was gone she was always surprised to find that she could not put all the parts of him together in her mind. She remembered only details, the crinkles in the corner of his eyes when he smiled or his loose-limbed walk.

She had meant to tell him this morning about the baby, but when he leaned over to kiss her goodbye, she decided it was not the moment. She wanted him all to herself without even the word "baby" coming between them. She clung to him longer than usual until he gently undid her hands and pulled away. "You'll break my back," he said.

"When will you go?" she asked.

"Tomorrow. First thing."

The garden was her current obsession. All spring, she had hovered over the tiny perennial seedlings in the greenhouse, thinning them with great reluctance and only because Smack was firm with her about it.

"It makes the brothers and sisters much stronger," he said. "You have to throw some away so that the others will last. Like the elm tree. For the grandchildren," he had added with a grin, and then she had agreed.

The day George left they started the third tobacco picking, but Lydia stayed in the garden. She did not want Nort to think she was watching him, and besides, she had a queasy feeling in her stomach that she knew would grow worse with the heat and dust in the sheds.

The air was still. Lydia knelt on a cushion between the baby's breath and a stand of phlox, working in the dusting of lime that Smack said the soil needed. In the distance, she heard a voice calling. Too early for lunch, she thought, sitting back on her heels. Someone was calling her name. A child appeared around the corner of the house, running.

"Come, Signora," the boy said. "Hurry. An accident."

She struggled to her feet, cursing the skirts that had tangled themselves in the heel of her shoe.

"One of the beams in the barn fell," the boy cried, his eyes wide. "Mr. Hart says to hurry."

At the shed, the work had stopped. The crowd of women drew back when Lydia arrived.

Nort appeared at her side. "One of the beams fell and hit Louisa. She is unconscious. Tony has gone for the doctor."

"Bring me some water," Lydia said. Gently, she lifted Louisa's heavy dark head into her lap and bathed the dust away from her skin.

"Where was she hit?"

Nort knelt beside her. "I'm not sure. I was outside when it happened. The other women would know." He motioned for one of them to join them.

"Where?" Lydia asked Dora Togni in Italian.

"On her side. And here," Dora said, pointing to the side of Louisa's dark head. When Lydia touched the spot, the cloth came away smeared with blood. Dora began to cry.

"Nort, let's get her to the house. Bring one of the wagons right up into the shed. I want a board slipped under her body so that we can lift her without changing her position."

It seemed to take hours for the men to back the wagon into the entrance of the shed and to find a piece of wood that was wide and yet thin enough to slip under the unconscious woman's body. At last they started off with Lydia sitting in the back, Louisa's head still in her lap. The damp cloth that Lydia pressed to the head wound was now completely red.

"Be as careful as you can," Lydia cautioned Nort, who had taken the reins. "I'm worried about the baby."

Halfway home, Louisa came to with a groan.

"It's all right, Louisa," Lydia whispered in Italian. "We're taking you home. Tell me where it hurts."

Louisa's eyes grew wide with pain. "The baby," she cried.

"Never mind the bumps," Lydia said to Nort. "She's in labor. Just get us there as fast as you can."

The labor was long and painful. Lydia sat next to Vin's bed in the room near the kitchen, where they had put Louisa to avoid the trip upstairs. The hours went by.

Lydia bathed Louisa's wet forehead, held her hand, rode with her as she headed up into the next pain, through the deep breath, then the scream, the endless clawing scream that came at the crest of each wave as the birth muscles closed down to force the baby out. How could anybody bear this? she wondered. Even when Dr. Ramsay arrived, Lydia did not leave the room, and at the end, she put her head on the pillow next to Louisa's ear and whispered to her in Italian. "Push, Louisa. Let this baby go. You will have other babies."

When the baby girl finally came, Lydia wrapped her tiny dead body in a blanket.

"Let me see it," Louisa cried.

"That would not be wise, Mrs. Delbianco," Dr. Ramsay said in a stern voice. "You must rest now."

"Please," Louisa cried, her arms out. Ignoring the doctor's warnings, Lydia took the baby to her.

"Goodbye," Louisa said, reaching out to touch the small wrinkled forehead. "Give her to Tony."

Lydia nodded.

Tony was waiting on the back porch. He took the bundle from her without a word and walked away down the driveway.

Lydia sat down on the top step and cried for the first time in that endless hot day. Vin found her there, and more gently than usual, she led her upstairs to her bed.

"What time is it, Vin?"

"Five o'clock. The men are just coming in from the fields."

"Did the picking go well?"

"Yes. Mr. Hart stopped by a little while ago. He said the tobacco is all hung. Do you want Dorothy to bring you up some dinner?"

"No, Vin, not now. I'm not hungry. You must sleep upstairs in the end bedroom. Dr. Ramsay told me Louisa has two broken ribs, so she will be staying here until she can be moved."

When Vin had left, Lydia kicked off the sheets and slid her cotton nightgown up to her waist so that if the air stirred at all with the setting sun, it would blow across her hot skin.

*   *   *

Louisa stayed in the house for ten days. At first, she lay in the bed without moving or speaking. Lydia came and sat with her in the afternoons. She sketched the vase of garden flowers that she had placed on the dresser where Louisa could see them without turning her head. She did not push Louisa to talk. After what they had been through together, there seemed to be no reason to fill the air with chatter.

"The room smells of boots," Louisa said unexpectedly one afternoon.

"Stivali?" Lydia said. She could not remember what it meant.

Louisa pointed to Lydia's feet.

"Oh yes, boots," Lydia said in English. And then in Italian again, she explained why. "My husband says the old farmer used to keep his boots and the harnesses and saddles in here. No matter what she uses, Vin can't seem to get rid of the smell. I expect she's grown used to it."

"Boots," Louisa repeated the English word. Then she pointed to the vase. "Flowers?"

"Yes," Lydia said. "I brought them in from the garden."

"Tell me some more names," Louisa said.

"Of the flowers?"

"No. Of everything. In the room."

She looked around. "Bed. Chair. Table."

"Slower. I want to learn the names in English."

So Lydia pointed to each piece of furniture and repeated its name slowly in English until Louisa had memorized it. By the end of the afternoon, she knew twenty new words.

"We'll do more tomorrow," Lydia said, getting up.

"The women all want to learn English," Louisa said. "You will teach us?"

"I'm not a teacher," Lydia said.

"But you know how to speak Italian. And English. We could learn from you."

"When you are better, we'll talk about it," Lydia said. "You can ask the other women and see if they agree."

"So you will do it," Louisa said with a smile.

"If they want me."

"They will want you," Louisa replied. She shifted her weight too suddenly in the bed and winced with the pain.

"It still hurts," Lydia said.

"Only when I move." She touched her head. "And up here. When I think too much. About the baby."

"The doctor says you can have more, Louisa."

"Next time, I will not sit under the beams," Louisa said.

"Next time, the beams won't move. I plan to talk to Mr. Webster about it."

"Do not make him angry at me, *signora*. I want to string the tobacco again. We need the money."

"Of course he won't be angry. You are his best stringer."

George came back in the middle of the night. She woke from a light sleep to the sound of his footsteps in the hall and pulled the covers up over her. With the heat, she had taken to sleeping naked and she felt exposed and embarrassed that he would find her that way. They always made love in the darkness, under the blankets, sometimes even under her nightgown. She did not want to see the look on his face when her body aroused him.

"Lydia?"

She did not answer, preferring to take refuge in a feigned sleep.

He moved about the room carefully. She knew that he was laying his pants and jacket across the back of the chair, twisting the cuff links out of his shirt and dropping them into the china box on the top of the bureau, setting his shoes side by side at the end of the bed. George dressed well, the only farmer in New England who ordered his suits from a London tailor, the only man she knew who could look elegant when he stank of manure. He also took good care of his clothes. He teased her about the way she dropped things carelessly over chairs when she undressed.

"You may not always have a maid picking up behind you," he warned.

"When that happens, I'll do it myself. But not until then."

He slipped into bed and rolled over next to her. When his hand touched her bare back, she stirred.

"You were awake, you devil," he muttered as he pulled her close. "And naked as the day you were born."

"It was hot," she said. She was so glad he was home. If only he would just hold her. "I didn't know you were coming back tonight."

"Well, I shall have to surprise you more often," he said before he kissed her.

In the morning, he stayed in bed later than usual. "The hell with the cows. If the boys have been milking without me for ten days, they can milk without me for one more."

"I am honored," she teased. "Did the fair go well?"

"Very. We won three prizes and I bought four new cows and a bull."

"And the meeting with Roraback?"

"As well as could be expected. He's suspicious of me because I'm not one of his boys. J. Henry likes to hold the reins very tightly. I'll only get his support if he can't put in one of his henchmen to run against me. Now tell me the news of the farm."

She told him about Louisa. "Something has to be done about the beams, George. It's much too dangerous to slide them along the rafters that way. Couldn't they be fixed?"

"You can't hang as much tobacco that way," he said. "In the future, the girls should sit outside to do the stringing."

"But you know how dusty it is when the wagons come up from the fields."

She felt him stiffening. He could take suggestions from Nort Hart but not from his wife. "Louisa is still with us. I had the boys bring her into Vin's room because she went into labor in the back of the wagon and I didn't want her to bump all the way down the road to their house. Dr. Ramsay came yesterday. He says she should be able to move back home in the next couple of days."

"Good," he said, and she wondered whether it was praise for the way she had handled the crisis or relief that Louisa was moving.

"She lost that baby because of the beams, George," she said in as calm a voice as she could muster. "A baby is more important than the tobacco."

"I heard you, Lydia."

Dorothy knocked on the door. "I have your breakfast, Mrs. Webster."

George pulled the covers up to his neck.

"Set it down on the table in the sitting room, please, Dorothy," Lydia called. "I'll be out presently."

"I've got to get down to the barn. Half the morning is gone."

"There's one more piece of news, George," she said. "Since the subject has come up anyway. I'm going to have a baby."

She relished the look of amazement that came over his face.

"When?" he said.

"In February."

"How long have you known?" he asked.

"About a month."

"Why didn't you tell me?"

"I'm not sure how I feel about it," she admitted. "I have to get used to the idea."

"Yes," he said, getting out of bed. "I think I do too."

Honest George, she thought later, when she went out to the garden.

They started the English classes at the end of August after the last tobacco harvest. The other women came reluctantly at first.

"We must meet in my house," Louisa said to Lydia.

"But I have more room here."

"They don't want to come here."

Lydia was silent. "I understand. Very well. Wherever you say."

The Delbiancos lived with two other families in an old house that used to be a hotel on the corner of Route 44. The Tognis lived in the back, the Mahaffys upstairs, and Tony and Louisa in the front. They all shared the kitchen, and on the first morning, Lydia found three women and Louisa waiting for her around the rectangular table when she arrived.

The women jumped to their feet and Louisa introduced them.

"This is Dora Togni, Gino's wife. And Francina

Mangelli. Her husband works over in the factory. And Rosita Rutigliano. Her husband is one of the dairymen."

Lydia shook hands all around. "Good morning. How are you?"

They all sat down again except for Lydia, who stood at the head of the table. "I told Louisa that I've never taught anything before, so we'll all have to muddle through together. I think it would be best for me to speak English as much as possible, so I will only switch into Italian when you really don't understand. I suggest we meet twice a week for two hours in the morning. Will you be able to manage that?"

Rosita and Francina held a whispered consultation and then nodded their heads. "But I have to bring my babies after this," Rosita said. "My sister cannot look after them again."

"Certainly," Lydia said. "Why don't you bring your sister too?"

Rosita shrugged.

In the beginning, Lydia started with simple vocabulary as she had with Louisa. Table. Spoon. Floor. Window. Wood. Milk. After a while, she moved on to short conversational sentences. At first the women were embarrassed to try out the unfamiliar words in front of one another, but as the days went on, they grew more comfortable with their mistakes. Lydia had to be tough about sticking to English."

"No, Louisa, remember, I don't understand Italian. Say it in English."

"You wear a pretty dress today, *signora.*" Giggles all around.

"You are wearing a pretty dress. Why, thank you. I like yours too. Rosita, how is the baby?"

"He does well. No more—" She stopped, looked around, and made a vomiting noise. Everybody roared.

"I am glad he is over his illness," Lydia said with a smile.

Word of the English classes spread quickly, and some days there were as many as ten women crowded into the little kitchen. Because many of them could not read or write, their lessons were confined to conversation, which gave Lydia a clear picture of their lives. They talked about

207

nursing their babies, how much they missed Italy, their fear of the hospital, the snow that made them feel so trapped, Lydia's growing belly.

"The baby will be a boy," Rosita said one day in December. "I can always know."

"How?" Lydia asked in surprise without bothering to correct her grammar.

"It is a gift to me. From my grandmother."

Although Louisa was younger than many of the others, they seemed to look up to her. She organized them and bossed them around and told them how to stand up to their husbands and in February she took over the classes for Lydia.

"Louisa, don't be ridiculous. I can still come to class."

"No, now you must wait for the baby. The snow is thick."

"Deep," Lydia corrected with a smile.

"The baby will come anytime."

"I can't think of a better place to be than in that kitchen if the baby comes. You women know more about childbirth than Dr. Ramsay."

"You will stay home now," Louisa said, with such conviction that Lydia gave in.

When the labor pains started in the middle of a snowstorm, Lydia asked George to get Louisa.

"But what about the doctor?"

"Send for him too. But I want Louisa to be with me. She knows what it feels like."

"Push, *signora*. It is almost time now," Louisa whispered in her ear when Lydia felt that she could never push again, that the bottom half of her body would explode into a million pieces. And it was Louisa who cried, "A boy. Rosita always knows," when Dr. Ramsay held up the squirming red baby with the shock of black hair. And it was Louisa who wrapped him in the blanket and handed him to Lydia.

14

"You children came not as a gentle rain from heaven," Lydia told Charlotte years later. "But as a torrential flood. Oliver and George were less than two years apart and then you twenty-one months after Oliver. You and the war in practically the same breath."

"That was hardly our fault, Mother."

"I'm not complaining, dear, only explaining. Your father used to say the whole house stank of dirty diapers. Thank God for Margaret Cameron. I doubt I could have made it through those years without her."

"You? What about us?" Charlotte said.

"Was I that terrible?"

"You weren't there. If it wasn't a political rally for Father, it was the English classes or the Americanization Committee."

"But that didn't affect you, Charlotte. You were only two when I took on that committee."

"Then I must have been four with the suffragist cause and five when you started the Connecticut League of Republican Women and ten when you ran for the legislature."

"You've been reading the old scrapbooks. Revisionist history," Lydia scoffed.

"That's why I said thank God for Margaret. I still remember the day she left. I hated you with all the hatred a ten-year-old can muster when you fired her."

Lydia sat back. Why did these conversations with her daughter always turn poisonous? She remembered that day clearly too, Margaret standing at the door like a tree while Charlotte clung to her skirts. It had brought back horrible memories for her. She could still feel Uncle

Elizabeth Winthrop

James's arms slipping around her from behind and dragging her away from Nurse.

"You never gave Agnes a chance," Lydia said, lowering her voice. They were sitting in George's study in the new wing that ran along behind the kitchen. The one that had been built too close to the elm tree.

"You're right, I didn't," Charlotte said. "But how could I? It would have been a betrayal of my memories of Margaret. After all, she was my real mother."

Lydia interviewed Margaret Cameron in the sitting room outside her bedroom. The red-haired girl had come out from Hartford on the train and now she sat clutching her handbag on the edge of the couch, her feet planted side by side on the rose pattern in the rug. Her black hat had slipped to one side, but she did not seem to notice it. Despite her slightly disheveled appearance, there was a straightforward, almost dour look about her that made Lydia feel as if she were the one being interviewed.

"Miss Cameron, I shall be honest with you. You seem awfully young for this job. Have you had a great deal of experience with children?"

"Yes, ma'am. I am the oldest of four. My mother died of diphtheria just after the last baby, so I was the one who had to take care of the lot."

"That must have been very hard for you," Lydia said, but Margaret shrugged it off.

"You do what you have to, ma'am."

"Mrs. Fox at the agency says you have not been in this country for long."

"I arrived last summer. I have been staying with my cousins in Torrington, but they are not able to keep me, so I must give up the day work and take a job living in."

"The farm can be a lonely place."

"I come from Kirkcaldy in Scotland, ma'am. My father was a sheep farmer. I am used to the country."

"Yes, I expect you are," Lydia said. "Come in, Dorothy. Give the baby to Miss Cameron to hold, will you?"

"To be honest, I do not think she likes me very much," Lydia said to George later that day. "But she held little George in such a natural way. That's what decided me."

* * *

Margaret Cameron trusted nobody over the age of sixteen. Forced to grow up too early, she was happy only in the world of children, and for them, she was a fearless leader, a Robin Hood, a Pied Piper whose magic tunes only children could hear. She gathered the Webster children under her wings like a mother hen, and although she was always firm with them, their plans and dreams and secrets were treated with dignity and respect. The new wing was added to the house in 1922 in order to make room for Campbell, but in the preceding years, Margaret lived with the older three in a happy and huddled mass in the nursery. When little George decided at the age of six that he wanted to be a painter, the nursery was awash with murky paint water and countless of his dripping creations were hung on the walls. One summer, a corner of the nursery was given over to the potting of weeds because Oliver was playing gardener. When the children decided to put on a play, Margaret made the costumes out of whatever was at hand, including George's best shirts and, once, a satin slip of Lydia's which served very well as a ball gown for Charlotte, the majestic murdered queen. If a child came to her with a story in his head, Margaret wrote down every word just as he told it. If a child were sick, she read aloud by his bed all morning if it soothed him. In her thick Scottish burr, she taught them all her childhood songs, so that they went around singing about the "mun" and the "burrds" at the top of their lungs. When Aunt Minerva brought Georgie an antique magic lantern on his seventh birthday, Margaret cut paper to fit and asked the children to paint the pictures. After the children's supper, George and Lydia were invited to the nursery for a show and each child explained his creation with a solemn practiced delivery. "It is a pig caught in a fence," said four-year-old Charlotte in a loud clear voice. "This is his tail and this is his mother calling for help," she explained while the grownups stared in bewilderment at the mass of squiggles and lines projected on the wall.

"I want it to be a girl," Lydia said, eight months pregnant the third time around.

"You sound so fierce," George said. He was sitting up

in bed watching the nightly braiding ceremony. When she was done, the long thin ribbons of hair, their twists stippled with gray, hung down her back to the shoulder bones.

"I feel fierce about it," she said. "I've already been to see Rosita. She said another boy, but this time, I feel I'm going to trick her."

"The odds are in your favor. Nobody said you were meant to bear only sons like some Egyptian princess. Come to bed," he said. "I need the warm balloon of you next to me."

"Compliments have never been your strong point, Mr. Webster," she said as she pulled back the covers.

They had not made love for some weeks because of the pregnancy, and knowing that sex was not a possibility, Lydia felt playful and easy with him these days. But tonight she drew back when he nestled down next to her.

"You smell strange," she said. "What is it?"

"A secret."

She leaned over and sniffed him. "George, go on, off with you. Go wash."

"I will not. You have the most sensitive nose in the world."

"You smell like the sachet in my underwear drawer."

"It's the cologne Isabelle and Taylor gave me for Christmas. I thought you'd appreciate a change from the farm odors."

She shuddered. "It's awful. Please go and do something about it. In fact, go down to the barn and roll in the hay while you're at it. I never have been able to stand cologne on men."

He threw the covers off and stomped out of the room.

He smelled like Uncle James, she thought as she settled her ungainly body down on its side. Her uncle still haunted her even though he had died two years ago. December 1, 1912. He would have noted all the ones and twos in the date. An omen, he would have said.

Her father had written her about it when she was recovering from Oliver's birth.

"Poor James. They didn't find him for three days. Apparently he was living in the most grisly circumstances in some hotel on the Left Bank. I won't go into the details, but in any case, I thought you would want to know because you were always so close to him. Those years he lived with us were probably the best he ever had. If only I could have convinced him to stay on after the fire, but he was bound and determined to go. In some way, I think he held himself responsible for the maid's death, although everybody said he acted very honorably about her rescue."

"Is it bad news?" George had asked when she handed him the letter.

She had laughed, and the noise sounded shrill in the room. The baby woke and began to cry.

"No, it's good news actually. A relief. My father's younger brother died."

"Were you close to him?" George asked once he had read the letter.

"Everybody thought so."

She handed the baby to Margaret and turned over on her side without another word. George and Margaret exchanged a look that said "baby blues" and she tiptoed away with the baby, leaving Mr. Webster to comfort his wife.

Later that night when Lydia woke screaming, he came in to her from the dressing room, where he always slept when the babies were new.

"What is it, Lydia? What's wrong?"

"George, come here. I need you to hold me. As tight as you can."

He did as she asked that night and for months afterward. He moved back into their bed and sometimes he could feel the trembling start in her body before she even woke. He would take her in his arms and try to squeeze the fear out of her before it catapulted her up out of the nightmare into the scream.

"So Rosita was wrong," George whispered to her. The labor had been longer and more painful than the first two and she had fallen asleep without even looking at the baby.

Now Margaret brought in the squalling bundle and laid her in Lydia's arms. "I'll leave her with you for the moment," she said to Lydia. "The boys are wanting a story before bed."

"She's funny-looking," Lydia said to George. "Such a flat face. And no hair."

"They're always funny-looking in the beginning," George reminded her. "Oliver's head was as round as a melon."

"Now I've got her, I'm nervous. I don't know how to behave with a girl."

"The same as with the boys, I expect," George said. He slipped his hands under the baby and lifted her up next to his chest.

"I thought you didn't like to hold them when they're new," Lydia said.

"I've had enough practice by now," George said, and walked over to the window to look at his new daughter's face.

It's because she's a girl, Lydia thought. Fathers and daughters. Maybe this is the baby she should have been worried would come between them. Not the first one. Nonsense, she told herself. Judging from the last births, she would alternate between crying and laughing for the next weeks. She hated it when her moods were uncontrolled and spasmodic, when she felt as vulnerable as the newborn baby.

"I brought you the paper," George said. "Europe has gone to war. Wilson issued a Neutrality Proclamation yesterday. It's all in there."

Lydia weaned Charlotte much earlier than the other two, ignoring Margaret's obvious disapproval.

"They get sickly on cow's milk," she warned, looking grim.

"Don't tell Mr. Webster that, Margaret," she teased. "And don't frown at me that way. I've got my work to do. I can't always be rushing home in the middle of a class just because the milk has come down or the baby has switched schedules the night before."

"She's only six weeks old," Margaret said. "They all settle down sooner or later."

"Enough, Margaret. I've made up my mind. I want you to give her a bottle at the next feeding."

It wasn't the work. Although Lydia would never say it

out loud, it was the closeness. It was the girl's little mouth working at her nipple, the large contented eyes opening and closing in time with the sucking, that made Lydia strangely uneasy.

"You're too trusting, too available," Lydia whispered to her baby daughter, whose eyes widened at the intensity in her mother's voice. "No matter what else happens between us, Charlotte Webster, I will give you a tough shell, a way to protect yourself."

After a successful first term as state senator, George had run again in 1912, but this time on the Progressive ticket, out of loyalty to Roosevelt and his supporters in Connecticut. When they lost overwhelmingly, he declared he was through with politics.

Isabelle Morris tried to get Lydia to change his mind.

"There's a place for him in the Republican Party again. He could run for the legislature this time. I'm surprised at him. After all, he's just put his big toe in the water." She handed Lydia a cup of tea. "And all this nonsense about the farm taking so much of his time. Why, he's set things up so well, the place is practically running itself."

"I'd like to see him staying closer to home."

"What do you mean?"

"First selectman in Northington. Everybody in town is getting tired of Harold Butler's shenanigans as Republican town chairman. With George in as selectman, we might finally get somewhere with Roraback. But you're right about the farm. Nort Hart has turned into a first-class manager. We won ten ribbons at the Granby Fair last week." Lydia settled back into her chair. "Besides, George is getting restless. I can tell."

In the end, Lydia won out and Isabelle took the news of George's election with her usual good humor.

"All right, then, first selectman is a perfectly good jumping-off point for the legislature," she said to George. "I'll leave you alone for a year or two."

"It won't do any good, Isabelle. If you want a good candidate, you'll have to start working on my wife."

Isabelle threw back her head and laughed, a gesture that always reminded Lydia of her first visit to this house. "I've sunk pretty low in my time, George Webster, but I

215

will not dress up a woman in pants and march her before jeering crowds of men."

"Yes, I expect you'll have to give us the vote first," Lydia said.

"That won't happen for a long time," George said. "Old weak-kneed Wilson has his hands full trying to keep us out of this war."

"And for the moment I've got my hands full with this baby."

"I take complete credit for the recent dramatic increase in the Northington population," Isabelle said with a smile. "After all, I'm the one who seated you next to each other at dinner."

"Well, things are going to level off for a while," Lydia replied. "I have a feeling that Charlotte will be more trouble than ten boys."

For once, Isabelle allowed George to push her wheelchair over the doorsill in the living room. "Lydia, how can you say that? She's only a baby."

"Mother's instinct, perhaps. Who knows?"

As she went down the walk ahead of them, George and Isabelle's eyes met, hers with a question in them.

"Have the nightmares started again?" she asked in a quiet voice.

"No. She's had none since those months after Oliver's birth. I'm beginning to think it wasn't the new baby after all. It may have had something to do with the death of her uncle in Paris."

"That seems a little farfetched," Isabelle said.

"Come on, George," Lydia called. "We'll be late for dinner."

"Perhaps it is," he said as he leaned over to kiss Isabelle goodbye. "Best to Taylor."

At first, the farm was unaffected by the war overseas.

Margaret was the only one who waited tensely for news from home, as her younger brother Norman was fighting in France. In May of the following year, just after news came of the sinking of the *Lusitania*, the Webster boys took to the trenches. Margaret sat in a rocker on the lawn next to baby Charlotte, who spent hours examining a blade of grass twisted through her chubby fingers, while Georgie led Oliver and Frank Delbianco and two of the Togni boys up "over the top" onto the unsuspecting and ill-organized German regiment.

"We trounced them, Margaret," George would call out, waving his stick gun at her, and she would smile and wave back, with her thoughts on Norman, the wiry, sickly boy she had left in Scotland five years ago. He was only nineteen. Three of his letters had gotten through to her, and she carried them everywhere in the pocket of her dress like a talisman, believing in a childish, superstitious way that every time her fingers touched the same sheets of paper that his had touched all those weeks before, she was wrapping an invisible shield of protection around him. She read the letters only when they first arrived. They were too depressing to look at again, too far removed from the jewel-green lawn, the toy trenches of Connecticut.

Everybody on the farm knew what she was going through, and when Smack went for the mail in the afternoons, he always stopped by especially to tell her there was nothing for her that day. When the news she had been dreading finally did arrive one hot day in August of 1916, it came from Scotland by way of her father, who could not read or write. He had dictated the horrible words to the local minister, who added this message at the bottom:

"With the loss of his only son, your father is a broken man, Miss Margaret. We here have gathered around him and will do all we can to soothe his pain but I know he would dearly love to see your own sweet face before him."

When Lydia came in from a meeting late that afternoon, she found the children gathered in solemn silence around the kitchen table under Vin's care.

"It's bad news," George called out to his mother before Vin could stop him. Lydia's eyes met Vin's over the children's heads.

"Margaret's had a letter. From home. She's in her room. I've been up there twice but she won't let me in." She shrugged. "I suppose I don't blame her."

Vin's mother came from Berlin, and although Vin had never even been to Germany and did not speak the

217

language, she had characteristically taken a rabid pro-German stance as soon as the war broke out. She and Margaret had maintained a cordial, distant relationship before, but they had been unable to keep the war out of the kitchen. They had kept track of troop movements on a map of Europe taped to the back of the closet door in the hall until Georgie told his mother. Lydia put a stop to it.

When there was no answer to her gentle tapping, Lydia pushed the door open. Margaret lay on the bed, face down, arms and legs spread, and for a moment, Lydia was reminded of nuns dedicating their life to Christ, spread-eagled on the stone floor before the altar.

Lydia sat on the thin strip of mattress between Margaret's hip and the edge of the bed. She reached out to touch the other woman and then decided against it.

"I'm so sorry, Margaret," she whispered.

There was no sound from the bed, no muffled sobbing, no reply at all.

"May I see the letter?"

Margaret turned her face toward the wall. "It's on the bureau."

How curiously formal, Lydia thought when she read Mr. Cameron's words. "Word has been received that Norman, my beloved son and your only brother, died during the fighting at the Somme on the 2nd of July of this year. His captain wrote to me that he was brave and courageous under fire and that he was admired and respected by his fellow soldiers."

News did not travel fast during wartime. The boy had been dead over a month. All summer they had been reading about this grisly advance of the British Expeditionary Force under General Sir Douglas Haig. Margaret's brother must have died in the first wave of soldiers "over the top." He probably had no time to be brave, only to lift his head, scramble up the muddy slant, and be shot.

"He missed his birthday," Margaret said, her voice thoughtful.

"Would you like to go home?" Lydia asked, her mind already running through the possibilities. With her father's help, she could probably get Margaret on a steamer in the next week or so. It was no longer dangerous. Since May, the German U-boats had ceased their attacks on ships crossing the Atlantic.

"No," Margaret said. "I want to be left alone until tomorrow. Then I shall be working as usual."

"Would you like to go to your cousins at Torrington for a few days?" Lydia asked.

"No," and for the first time, Lydia heard the tears in Margaret's voice, so close to the top. She dropped her hand onto one stiff shoulder now jutting up from the bed like a piece of driftwood and rested it there for a while before she went down to talk to the boys about their trench warfare games.

Margaret did just as she said she would. The next morning she got up, dressed in her uniform, and went in to pick up Charlotte, who had been calling to her in an insistent voice for ten minutes. Charlotte was learning to talk much later than the boys, and when her first word came out "Marmar," both Lydia and Margaret claimed it as their name in different parts of the house, Margaret to herself, Lydia to George. "She's finally learned to say my name," Lydia told her husband. "Of course, her voice has that same strange Scottish burr to it that the boys learned from Margaret."

The confusion was only cleared up days later when, in front of Lydia, Charlotte screamed the word and held out her arms for Margaret.

This morning when Margaret opened the nursery-room door, she saw the same sight that greeted her every day: the droopy nightgown, the arms dangling over the edge of the crib, the bare feet poking through the bars, and that flat face filled with a look of such determined joy.

"Marmar," shrieked Charlotte triumphantly.

"Charchar," teased Margaret back, but even the small child heard her voice break and she put out her arms for the nurse. After a night of pressing the flat feather pillow against her stomach, where the pain seemed to locate itself, the girl's bony body felt so alive, so sympathetic that Margaret held her much longer than usual and much tighter until Charlotte squirmed to be let down.

"There's an end to it," Margaret lectured herself as

she was changing the child into her day dress. "I shall not mourn any longer. I shall put it behind me."

She lifted the child and carried her down the hall, the small pudgy bottom resting in its customary place on her hipbone, the two legs wrapped securely around her waist like a life preserver. In the days and months ahead, whenever she heard Norman's voice in her head or the last long scream that must have floated out of his mouth when he was hit, she reached down for Charlotte and planted the girl on her hip this way. To keep her from going under.

Marcus Holcomb's reelection as Republican governor of Connecticut in the fall of 1916 on a campaign of preparedness was a symbol of the growing belligerency of the state. By the time President Wilson sent his war message to Congress the next April, Connecticut was ready and waiting. Later that month, Holcomb appointed an eleven-man State Council of Defense to coordinate all war programs in Connecticut. To her amazement, Lydia was asked to join as coordinator of the Americanization Committee, an organization to transform aliens into patriotic citizens through education.

"Now I realize it smacked of terrible prejudice," Lydia explained into Molly's microphone. "During the First World War, patriotism was the name for all sorts of abuses against the immigrants. But I was the first woman appointed to the State Council and I was delighted to get the job."

"Why you, Grandmother?"

"It turned out I had Harold Butler to thank. Because he was Republican town chairman, he knew of my work with the Italian women and so he put me up for the Americanization Committee. Little did Governor Holcomb or even Roraback know that it would open the door for me to make further trouble for them later. In the legislature. But I'm getting ahead of myself."

"What about Grandfather? What was he doing about the war?"

"To his great disappointment, he was not allowed to enlist. He was too old and a farmer and a family man, all of which were strikes against him. But as first selectman of the town of Northington, he was responsible for the organization of the war effort in the town. He got all the Italians to join the Home Guard and he appointed Louisa Delbianco as head of the Red Cross in the town. Under her masterful direction, we' all knitted socks and sweaters and collected countless peach pits."

"Peach pits?"

"Yes, they were used to make the filters for the gas masks. It took something like seven pounds of pits to make one gas mask and we needed a million. After the war, I couldn't look a peach in the eye again for years. You know, by the time we finally got into the war, we were so ready for it that we did anything to prove ourselves. People gave up wheat and meat and using cars on Sunday. And the women went to work in the factories and on the farms. That was the best thing for the suffragist movement, actually. Once we had done the men's work, we didn't want to give up the power that came with it."

Lydia drove her small Model T Ford into her office in Hartford every day. She often did not get home until after the children had been put to bed.

"I feel badly about the children," Lydia said to George. "I see so little of them."

"That's their war sacrifice, then," George remarked. "Besides, Margaret is doing fine with them."

"I don't think I'm a natural mother," Lydia said.

"No, you're not," George said. His hasty concurrence irritated and goaded her.

"Today I am going to take you boys on a nature walk," Lydia announced the next Saturday morning when she came to the nursery.

"But I'm painting today," George cried.

"Never mind," Lydia said firmly. "You can paint again tomorrow."

"Why doesn't the baby have to come?" Oliver said.

"She's too small," Lydia explained.

Margaret said nothing.

They walked through the woods, Lydia in front with a bird book in hand, the two boys trailing grumpily along behind.

"There's a bird," Oliver called out, always the one who tried the hardest to please his mother.

"It's just a robin," George said. "We see them every day."

"Never mind," Lydia said patiently. "Now, where did you see it, Oliver?"

By that time, the robin had disappeared and they pushed on while Lydia pointed out the different kinds of ferns and the bird nests high in the branches.

"It would be much better if we lived near the jungle or the desert," George said disconsolately. His favorite book of the moment was *African Game Trails,* which Margaret sat and read aloud to him for hours. "Then we might see a nilghai or a gazelle instead of a stupid old chipmunk."

"You boys are terribly spoiled," Lydia said, hating the lecturing tone of her own voice. "Think of the poor children who live in the city and never get to see anything but pigeons and the occasional rat."

"I wouldn't mind a rat at all," said George.

"George, that's enough."

By the time they returned after a hot two hours in the woods, Lydia was relieved to hand them back to Margaret, who plunked them right into the bath and washed them down with yellow soap, her cure for poison ivy.

"She's washing away something else too," Lydia said out loud over dessert. "My influence on them."

George looked up, startled. "I've never heard you say anything as ridiculous as that. What's wrong?"

"I don't know. I think I'm jealous. Maybe I should give up my work and stay home with them."

"That's the second most ridiculous thing I've heard you say."

They left it at that.

15

The tobacco harvest that year was the best ever. "Seems obscene somehow with our boys dying in the trenches," George said to Nort Hart.

"They've got to smoke something, Boss," Nort replied with that deep private chuckle of his.

Louisa came back from her work in town to do the stringing. "I've never missed a day yet," she told Nort proudly. "Not since the beams were fixed in place."

"That was all your doing, Louisa."

"Mine and Mrs. Webster's," she reminded him, proud to have their names linked together over anything.

Her friendship with the Signora was as sacred to Louisa as her marriage to Tony and her three children. Because of their work together, almost all of the Italian women in Northington now spoke fluent English and most of them could read and write. The day Louisa went to Hartford to be sworn in as an American citizen, Lydia drove her over the mountain in the Model T. On the way over they sang a silly song about going round the mountain and riding six white horses that Lydia assured her was "very American." When Frank, their second child, was born in 1913, Lydia offered her the small white cottage at the end of the lane across from the calf barn. Louisa was delighted. A house of her own at last, after six years of sharing a kitchen with two other women. It was too good to be true.

And now she had taken the job as head of the Red Cross in Northington even though her third child, Sol, was only a little over a year old. "It's a great honor, Louisa," Tony told her. He still spoke Italian at home and insisted that their children do the same. *"Il Gaioffa* skipped over all the dried-up Yankee ladies to pick you. You have to say yes."

She had never considered doing anything else once Rosita had agreed to watch the children.

Some days after their work was done, Lydia walked down the lane to visit with Louisa. The children trailed along behind her, looking for companionship with the Delbiancos, whom they hadn't seen since rest time. On the warm days, the two women sat out on the little green hillock of a lawn in front of the cottage and drank dark sweet coffee while the children chased each other around the house.

"I'd rather sit here than anywhere," Lydia said one afternoon in the early fall.

Louisa's eyes filled with sudden irrational tears. She kept silent.

From where they sat, they could hear the evening train coming.

"The train," the children shouted, and ran down the lane to hang over the fence and watch its passing along the opposite bank of the river. This one didn't stop in Northington but barreled right through on its way to Hartford. The distant muttering grew and grew until, with an explosion of silver, it became a line of deafening noise stretching the whole width of the horizon across the river. Clinging to the wooden fence, the children waved and the whistle blew. Then gradually the noisy slash rolled up on itself as the last car passed and then nothing but the lingering echo of the tracks rattling and the wind starting up in the trees.

"Takes my breath away every time," Lydia said, stirring in her metal chair.

"More coffee?" Louisa asked.

"Yes, please. I can get it." In her own house, Lydia would not have moved but would have rung for Dorothy.

"No, Clara will," Louisa said. The dark-eyed girl, just turned five, took the cup from Lydia and bore it into the kitchen.

"Are you sure you don't want some cake? I made it last night."

"No, thank you, Louisa. You must be proud of Clara."

224

"She's a big help. She dresses the baby for me in the mornings."

Up at the big house, the screen door slammed. Margaret came down the porch steps with Charlotte in her arms.

"Margaret carries Charlotte too much. I've told her time and time again that the child will never learn to walk if she doesn't give her some practice," Lydia muttered, aware of the note of irritation that had crept into her own voice.

As if she had heard Mrs. Webster, Margaret slid the girl off her hip, set her down, and slowed her pace to match the three-year-old legs. They paused while Charlotte squatted to examine something in the road. From where she sat, Lydia felt the impatience rising in her throat. She would not have been able to wait for the baby, would have wanted her to march along.

"She's a stubborn one," Lydia said.

"You too," Louisa said with a smile. "It's good for a woman to be stubborn."

Clara came back with the cup of coffee.

"Grazie," Lydia said. *"E molto buono."*

"You make me learn English and you speak Italian to my children," Louisa said. "It makes no sense."

"I didn't make you learn English. You insisted I teach you."

They laughed, but Lydia was still aware of her daughter getting closer. Toddle, waddle, squat, hands up to show Margaret something, Margaret staring with great concentration, the red head close to the little one, dignifying her discovery with the time expended inspecting it.

When they reached the edge of the small lawn, Louisa slid down the slope and picked up Charlotte. Unlike Lydia, who lost the weight between babies very easily, Louisa had widened, and when she sat down, her lap was large and soft. She took each of Charlotte's small hands in her own and clapped them together, singing a song in soft Italian.

"We were having a walk after her dinner," Margaret explained. "The boys should come in soon for their bath."

"Yes," Lydia said. "They've been waving at the train. I suppose it's getting late." But she didn't move, so

Elizabeth Winthrop

Margaret went down to call in the children and herd the
Webster boys back up toward the big house. In the field
behind the calf barn, the cows butted heads in a bored,
lethargic way, pushing one another aside to get to a
better patch of grass.

"Do it again," Charlotte said when Louisa's song was
finished.

"No more, darling," Lydia said, putting her cup down
in the grass and getting up at last. "We've got to go back
up to the house."

"Can't you leave her with me?" Louisa asked. "The
children and I will bring her back in a little while."

"Another time. I want her to walk up with me. I
haven't seen her all day."

"You come see me soon again, Charlotina," Louisa
said, kissing Charlotte on her forehead and setting her
down next to her mother.

With the little fingers inside her firm hand, Lydia forced
herself to walk slowly, to adjust as Margaret had to the
irregular pace. "Look, Charlotte, the leaves are turning.
Fall is coming." But Charlotte liked to look down. The
leaves high in the trees were too far away for her small
eyes to focus on. With a sudden jerk, she squatted in the
dust and drew a line with her forefinger. Lydia waited.

"Bug," said Charlotte, chasing it with her dirty finger.

"Yes," said Lydia. She saw George walking across the
field from the big barn and waved. "Come on, darling,
Papa's coming home."

But the beetle was more fascinating, more immediate
than the distant figure of her father. She caught it square
in the middle of its black back with the tip of her finger
and pushed down. Crippled, the beetle dragged itself out
from under the pink skin while the child watched.

"Charlotte, come along. Right now." Lydia leaned
over, took the child's hand in her own again, and started
off.

But Charlotte would not straighten her legs and Lydia
was stopped by the dead weight of the child hanging from
her arm.

"No, I want to see the bug," she cried.

"Charlotte."

226

With a sudden about-face, Charlotte put out her arms. "Carry me," she demanded.

"No. You're three years old. You can walk. Come on, we'll skip up the lane," Lydia urged.

"Carry me," she cried again, her small sandaled feet dancing impatiently in the dust.

Behind them, Lydia could hear Margaret and the boys marching along to some Scottish ballad. She felt exposed and humiliated by her daughter's defiance, and without any warning, she lifted the child by her two hands and set her back down in front of her.

"One, two, buckle my shoe, three, four, open the door." The child was not distracted for long by the familiar words because the tone was harsh, impatient. She played for a few steps and then let her knees buckle again.

The three Scottish marchers passed them on the right.

"Come on, Charlotte, we're having a parade," Oliver called. "Come join the parade."

The idea caught the little girl's imagination and she twisted out of her mother's hands and ran to catch Oliver's. At the head of the line, Margaret did not break step or turn around but marched them straight up onto the porch and into the house while Lydia watched, with a mixture of fury and relief.

That winter Vin suddenly went crazy. In the beginning, they called it absentmindedness when she left the food out of the icebox overnight or burned the roast so badly that even the barn dogs wouldn't eat it.

"She must be close to sixty-five," George said when Lydia complained about it. "We've got to be a little understanding."

"I don't mind so much about the cooking. But now it's the war," Lydia said. "She's adopted the Germans. Nort found her in the post office yesterday ranting and raving at Mrs. Ridley. With all the hysteria about patriotism in the air, I'm surprised she wasn't arrested on the spot. Besides, it couldn't be more awful for Margaret, who has managed up until now to ignore her. You've got to speak to her, George. She won't listen to me."

That evening after dinner, he went to see her in the

kitchen. They talked about Miss Bunting, about the old days, and gradually he brought the conversation around to her health.

"Are you feeling well, Vin?"

"No complaints. Some been saying I'm poorly?"

"No. But Mr. Hart told me you had quite a conversation with Mrs. Ridley down at the post office. You know I don't tell anybody what to think," he said gently. "But you're living in America and this country's got its back up. If you choose to support the Germans during this war, I'm asking you to do it quietly."

She had a wild look in her eye when she turned around from the stove. "It's a free country, ain't it?"

"It's supposed to be. But right now, 'free' is a relative word. This craziness they're calling patriotism will pass soon enough. But for the moment, you'd do best to lay low. Besides, you're getting my back up," he said, trying to tease her.

"Very well, then, I'll leave tomorrow, Mr. Webster. I get the drift of your message."

It took him a good hour to convince her that he did not mean she should leave, and by the time he joined Lydia upstairs, he was exhausted and baffled. The next day, when Dr. Ramsay came by to see her at George's request, Vin locked herself in her room.

"I know what it is," Margaret told Lydia. "An aunt of mine went off like this. The brain just gives out in a funny way. I don't know the right name for it, but the person thinks everybody's against them. At the end, my aunt locked herself in her house and wouldn't let anybody in. My father had to break through one of the windows. They took her away to a home down in Edinburgh."

"The problem of Vin has finally been solved," Lydia wrote to Aunt Katherine in March 1918. "Dr. Ramsay found a couple up in Winsted who have agreed to take her in for what seems to me quite a princely sum, but we were desperate. George and I drove her up there yesterday, telling her that it was just for a short time, that she needed a rest. Who knows whether she will get better?

"In the end, she was totally unable to get the meals on

the table. She would lock herself in her room in order to write long notes to herself. She was suffering under some strange delusion that we were all French spies. If it hadn't been so disruptive to the whole household, I might have been able to laugh at the situation. Perhaps I will when I look back on it. Poor George is beside himself. She has been so fiercely loyal to him up to now. Just two years ago, when we had that awful hailstorm in June and it looked as if the whole tobacco crop had been destroyed in one hour, she brought him her savings book, plunked it down on his desk, and told him it was all his.

"But we found we could not keep her anymore. The children were terribly frightened of her, as her behavior has grown increasingly erratic. Last week, I came in to find her threatening them all with a wooden spoon dripping with hot melted chocolate.

"The oddest thing was that in the end she seemed to have decided that I was her only friend, the only person loyal to the German cause, the one who could be trusted. She no longer spoke to George at all but told me long crazy stories about troop movements and casualty figures. After all my years of complaining about her with such venom, I feel very sorry for her. Yesterday, when we left her in Winsted, I put my arms around her and gave her a hug. She submitted to it in stony silence, but when I looked at her face afterward, she was crying for the first time ever.

"George says that she has no family that he knows of, so I expect we shall be responsible for her, for better or worse. The whole situation seems so ironic. Perhaps it was her bitter hatred of people that turned her mind in the end. Who knows?"

Vin's mental condition never improved, although her body continued as strong as ever. Three years later, when she attacked the woman in Winsted with a knife, the couple refused to keep her anymore and Lydia went up and drove her down to a home in Hartford. She lasted there for eleven years, and although George's visits tapered off quickly, Lydia went to see Vin every month. She brought her flowers or a box of hard candy and told her the news of the children while Vin sat sullenly in her chair, her gray hair spread out in wild disarray about her face.

"Couldn't you comb her hair?" Lydia complained to the nurse. "I think she'd feel better about herself if she looked more presentable."

"Not me, miss. I don't go near her. Sometimes she throws things. Last week, she bit the night nurse."

"You've done your duty, Lydia," George said when she reported back to him. "Why do you keep going? She left us eight years ago now. And when she was here, you two were continually at war. It's as if you're doing penance for something else."

He was probably right. Penance for Nurse and Nellie. Even for Margaret. "I think she recognizes me. I can't stand to think of her all alone in there day after day with no change in the routine, nothing to look forward to."

When the nurse found her dead in her bed in the middle of a cold February night in 1932, she called Lydia, the only person listed on Vin's records. George and Lydia brought her back to Northington and buried her in the little cemetery behind the Congregational church. As far as anyone knew, she had never set foot in a church, but they didn't know where else to put her.

When peace was finally declared on the eleventh hour of the eleventh day of the eleventh month, Lydia quit the Americanization Committee. Harold Butler tried to get her to stay.

"The work is not done yet," he said grumpily when he found her cleaning out her office. "With those damn Bolsheviks digging in in Russia, we've got to be even more careful over here. Root out all them foreigners."

"Harold, that's not the kind of work I wanted to do and you know it. The country's getting crazy about this business of the Reds. Soon they'll be seeing one behind every tree. Besides, I've got more important work to do."

"And what would that be, Mrs. Webster?"

"The women. At last, we are going to force you men to give us the vote. And I want to be sure the women are ready when that day comes."

"Hah," he said and spat a stream of tobacco juice out

of the side of his mouth into the brass spittoon which had been left behind by the previous occupant of the office. Lydia patted his shoulder with as patronizing and concerned an expression as she could muster and carried another pile of papers out to her car. When she got back, he had left.

"I'm taking a whole month off," Lydia announced to George. "In January, I shall go to work full-time for the Suffrage Association. But for the moment, I want to be with you and the children. And I want to plan our Christmas party. We shall have everybody here. My father and John and the Morrises and Aunt Katherine and your sister, Minerva."

"Oh dear," George said. "You mean the family is your project for the next month. I hope we survive."

"George, darling, don't be so cynical," she said, and they didn't pursue the subject. It was a touchy one for both of them. George had often said that the household seemed to run more smoothly when Lydia could direct all her energies on the outside world.

"Whenever Mother meddled at home, it was as if we became her cause for that week or that month," Charlotte told Molly years later. "She waded in and attacked the problem of our inadequate vocabulary or our laziness about the vegetable garden with the same kind of administrative furor that worked so well in the legislature or the Suffrage Association. She just never realized that families can't be organized the way committees are. And you know your grandmother. She's never done anything halfway."

"That's what I like about her," Molly said.

"I suppose it's an admirable trait when viewed from a distance," Charlotte replied coldly.

"I want the children to put on a play at the Christmas party," Lydia told Margaret early in December. "We shall all work on it together."

"Yes, ma'am," Margaret said.

"Do you think you'll be able to muster a little more enthusiasm than that in the days ahead?" Lydia asked.

"Pardon me, ma'am?"

231

"Oh, nothing, Margaret, I was only teasing you," Lydia said. She knew Margaret shared George's dread of her forays into nursery life. I could get to feeling quite sorry for myself, she thought, watching Margaret's expressionless face. But I shall choose not to.

The next morning, Lydia called a meeting in the nursery and the children gathered around her in an excited circle. "A play?" said Georgie. "I want to be the pirate."

"Then I get to be the king," Oliver shouted.

Lydia smiled. "There won't be any pirates or kings. This is going to be a play about votes. For women. I figured it out last night. Georgie, you shall be a soldier returning from the war. And Oliver, you shall be President Wilson."

"Father says he's stupid," Oliver said. "I don't want to be a stupid person."

"And, Charlotte, you shall be a suffragist, carrying a banner in front of the White House. But you'll have to take your thumb out of your mouth by then," Lydia teased.

From her perch on Margaret's lap, four-year-old Charlotte surveyed her mother with a placid expression on her face. She said nothing.

They practiced every afternoon at teatime. Georgie, who was almost nine and who had shot through the first three grades at the little one-room schoolhouse in record time, was able to memorize his lines, but Lydia finally gave up and allowed Oliver to read his. With a little encouragement from Margaret, Charlotte finally got into the swing of things and paraded up and down in front of the President, waving her banner and shrieking "Votes for Women." Even Margaret summoned up some enthusiasm when Lydia gave her the run of the upstairs closets and the attic for costume material.

"She ought to be dressed totally in white with a yellow banner across her front. You can use those old curtains from the nursery. They were yellow, weren't they?"

"It's tough for one little four-year-old to represent all womanhood," Margaret remarked to Dorothy in the kitchen. Dorothy agreed, but she was too preoccupied with the problems of learning how to cook a turkey. When Vin left, she had taken over the cooking because

Lydia could not find anybody else with the women all at work in the factories, but she was ill suited for it.

"I can't make everything come out at the same time," she wailed. Then Lydia would sit down with her again and write lists, which was the only way she could think of handling the problem, since she had less idea than Dorothy of how to cook anything.

"This has all the makings of a disaster," George said in a sepulchral voice one evening. That afternoon he had passed through the kitchen in the middle of another session with Dorothy. "We could postpone the whole thing until next year."

"If you say that one more time, I shall murder you," Lydia said, and he took cover behind his newspaper.

After a while, he peeked out. She was knitting, but he could see the smile twitching at the corners of her mouth. "Still mad?" he asked.

"No. But I wish you'd be a little more encouraging, darling. I feel like a conductor trying to manage a very raggle-taggle orchestra."

"Yes, dear," he said, momentarily distracted by an article on the front page.

"Charlotte has turned into a ferocious little suffragist. I can't wait to see the expressions on the ladies' faces when they see her. That will be my Christmas present to myself."

But he wasn't listening. "This influenza business has gotten quite serious," he said. "It says here that it's spread to forty-six states."

"I know. The Togni twins both had it, but they've recovered. From what Gino told me, it comes out of nowhere. Already it's killed more people than the war." She spread the wool out along the needles and admired her work. "Thank God nobody else on the farm has gotten it. The worst outbreaks have been in the city, so we may be spared."

"I hope so."

233

16

The guests began to arrive two days before Christmas. Katherine and Arthur Jay stayed over in Farmington with Isabelle and Taylor Morris. Minerva moved into the room Dorothy had vacated to go into Vin's. The bed in George's dressing room was made up for Lydia's father, who declared himself very satisfied with it. Charles Franklin, now sixty-four, had grown quite portly and complained of gout in his knees, but to Lydia's amazement, he was very tolerant of the children and in fact encouraged them to swarm all over him, looking for the money he had hidden in funny places in his suit. At the last minute, John wired that he couldn't come.

"I expect it has to do with that nurse he's been seeing ever since he got back. A nice enough girl. Family's from Long Island." Lydia's father took the telegram from her, snapped it out, and read it through his bifocals.

"I'm so disappointed, Father," Lydia said when she took back the paper and threw the crumpled ball of it onto the fire. "In a way, he was the whole point of the party. The triumphant return of the soldier."

"You have such a dramatic streak in you, Lydia. It reminds me of your Uncle James."

She was silent. He had been dead for over six years, but just the sound of his name still sent a shudder through her.

"Uncle James was a very special person for you, wasn't he, Lydia?"

"Why do you say that, Father?"

"I expect I wasn't much good as a father. I know he tried to take my place."

"No, you weren't very good. But I survived. That's all there is to be said about it," she added. "Come in,

234

Minerva," she called to the figure passing in the hall. "Father and I were just having tea."

Christmas morning was suitably chaotic, and for once, Lydia allowed herself to get caught up in the merry confusion of it all without insisting that each child watch the other "open." With shrieks of joy, the boys tore into the wrapping paper, while the grownups watched from above with remembering smiles on their faces. Charlotte sat on her father's lap with her thumb in her mouth, pulling at the ribbon trailers with her one free hand. Margaret had stopped Lydia in the upstairs hallway before breakfast.

"Charlotte's looking peaked. She didn't want to get up this morning."

"I'm sure she's all right, Margaret. It's probably a result of the confusion. So many new faces for her to see."

Margaret shrugged. "I think it's more than that," she said, but went away to dress the child in her red velvet pinafore. Lydia took the boys aside and made them practice their lines one more time. "Now, remember," she warned. "Not a word to anyone about the play. It's our secret."

"Yes, Mother. Can we just look under the tree to see what's there?"

"You know the rules, Oliver. No peeking until after breakfast."

And breakfast had seemed interminable to the children, with their father deciding at the last minute to have just one more cup of coffee if only to torment them. Finally, in the Webster tradition, the whole household lined up at the parlor door, youngest first. With the guests and Margaret and Dorothy, the line snaked down the narrow hallway until Grandpa Charles, the oldest, ended up back in the dining room. Unlike her brothers, Charlotte had no memory of previous Christmases, of the glittering treasures that lay on the other side of the door, so that Oliver had to talk her through the ritual of turning the brass knob. She showed no interest at all but stood looking at her shoes.

"Can't I open it for her?" Oliver cried in exasperation at his mother.

"No, Oliver," Lydia said patiently from her place in the line. "She must do it herself."

"Come on, Charlotte, open the door," Oliver said.

At that point, as the tension rose in the dark front hallway, Margaret stepped forward and whispered something to Oliver, who in turn whispered to his sister. She took her thumb out of her mouth and stared up at him.

"You promise?" she said.

Oliver turned back to Margaret with a question on his face. She nodded.

"I promise. Just open the door."

And finally she did.

"Good God, Margaret, you're a miracle worker. Whatever did you say?" George asked as the grownups filed into the room.

"I told Oliver that there was a doll waiting under the tree for her."

"Did we give her a doll?" George asked, knowing his wife's oddly irrational prejudice against them.

"I did," Margaret said simply before she turned her attention back to the children.

And this was the box that Charlotte was now undoing on her father's lap.

"What do you think it is?" he whispered in her ear.

She shook her head and finally pulled the thumb out with a bubbly pop so that she could set about unwrapping in earnest. From across the room, Margaret watched while pretending to help George with his train set.

Charlotte reached deep into the box and lifted out the doll, a soft blue-eyed baby with straight brown hair just like Charlotte's. Ever since Margaret had seen the pattern in the Sears catalogue last fall, she had been working on this project in secret. The doll was dressed in a red Christmas pinafore that matched Charlotte's own and underneath the tissue-paper bed lay four more outfits modeled after Charlotte's.

The little girl cradled the doll's head next to her ear, slid the thumb back into its cozy place, and leaned against her father's warm chest with a happy sigh. Across the

236

room, Margaret allowed herself a small satisfied smile and turned back to Georgie's track-switching problems.

When all the unwrapping was finished and the grown-ups had exchanged socks and pipe tobacco and shaving soap with suitable expressions of interest, Margaret began to gather up the children and their toys. They would eat their lunch in the kitchen and come back into the parlor after the grownups were finished with their own lunch around the table. To Lydia's relief, the smell of roasting turkey already filled the house.

George stopped Margaret on her way out. "Charlotte seems so listless. Do you think she's getting sick?"

Lydia overheard the question. "George, she's just overexcited. Margaret and I have already talked about it. She's going to have a little rest and she'll be fine in the afternoon." Margaret went out without saying anything.

Louisa traditionally served her Christmas meal in the evening, so she had offered to come up to the big house and help Dorothy serve. Lydia found her basting the turkey.

"Merry Christmas," Lydia said, resting her hand for a moment on her friend's thick shoulder.

"And to you, Signora," Louisa said, baster still in hand.

Despite all they had gone through together, Louisa still called her, "Signora."

"Does it look all right?"

"Oh yes. Dorothy's done an excellent job. Very moist." She straightened up. "Something's wrong with Tony," she said, a slight frown starting on her forehead. "Says he feels all weak. I don't think he should drive down to Farmington to pick up the rest of your family."

"Never mind. I'll tell Mr. Webster he'll have to go. Do you think you should call the doctor for Tony?" Lydia asked.

Despite her worry, Louisa allowed herself a small smile. "The doctor? In Tony Delbianco's house? Are you crazy, Signora?" For all Louisa's adjustments to their new country, Tony held firmly to many of the old beliefs, particularly the one about the uselessness of doctors and hospitals. "He was up most of the night, helping Gino with that sick cow. Maybe he's just tired."

237

"We could probably manage without you, Louisa, if you wanted to stay with him," Lydia said, against her better judgment. She did not see how Dorothy could possibly cook and serve the meal. And she had wanted the party to be so elegant, such a triumphant return to normal life after the grim meals of wartime.

"Nonsense. What would I do but fuss over him and he can't stand that. Clara will come up if he needs me. Now, show me which serving dishes you're going to use for the vegetables."

It seemed to Lydia that George went off to Farmington with great relief while she and Minerva set the table for lunch and her father settled himself by the fire. She envied him his solitary trip in the cold air. The house seemed hot and crowded to her and she still had the lunch to face. But after that came the play, her little surprise. If only the children didn't let her down. It would be a perfect ending to the day.

Around the table, the talk was all politics.

"So, Lydia," Aunt Katherine said. "What's your plan now that the war's over?"

"To work with the Connecticut Woman Suffrage Association. I've been a member for years, but I've never worked actively with them. The time has come."

"They may not have you," Isabelle said. "From what I understand, Kate Ludwell has instituted a loyalty regime. If you didn't work for the war effort through their channels, you're considered suspect. Many of the more disgruntled women went over to the National Women's Party last year so that they could concentrate on the federal amendment."

"Trust Isabelle to know the ins and outs of everything," George said with a chuckle.

"Who? Me?" Isabelle hammed. "The arthritic old lady shut up in her house all day?" The table roared with laughter.

"Well, I shall present my services and see what happens," Lydia said. "Now that the federal amendment has passed the House and the war is over, the pressure will be on the Senate. And then back to the states for ratification."

"You'll have your work cut out for you," Taylor Morris said grimly. "When the suffragists allied themselves with the munitions workers over in Bridgeport, they lost a lot of friends in the Republican Party. You're going to be walking a very skinny tightrope, trying to stay loyal to your party and your sex at the same time."

"A lot of fossils in the Republican Party, Taylor," George said from his end of the table. "I've come up against a number of them in my time."

"They may be fossils," Taylor said. "But they're the ones in power right now."

Behind her, Lydia heard the children trooping down the stairs. She rang the bell for Louisa to clear and stood up.

"The children and I have a little surprise for everybody. Let's adjourn to the parlor room."

As directed, Margaret had hung a homemade curtain across the back half of the parlor so that Lydia, stationed on the piano, would be hidden behind it. The boys and Margaret were waiting for her.

"Where's Charlotte?" Lydia demanded.

"I shall have to take her place," Margaret said in a voice that sounded as if it expected an argument. "I've left her sleeping. She's got a fever."

Margaret as her suffragist, Lydia thought. How ridiculous. She hesitated for a brief moment. A tiny voice inside argued with her to give in to this, but she swept it aside. Margaret always coddled the child. This was just another example of it.

"I'll get her. Georgie, you go out and tell the audience that there will be a slight delay."

"What's a delay?"

"For God's sake," Lydia said. "Don't discuss everything with me. Just say it."

Her cheeks were flushed pink, but children always woke up sweaty, looking as if they'd run a race. Lydia talked to her in an encouraging voice while she pulled the white costume over her head and adjusted the yellow silk banner with short impatient jerks. Charlotte did not want to stand up or walk, so Lydia carried her downstairs wrapped in a blanket and around the outside of the

239

house so that the audience wouldn't see her before her triumphant appearance on the stage.

In the beginning, things went fine. Clutching his papers, wrinkled from so many practice sessions, Oliver stood on a wooden box and delivered his presidential speech. Meanwhile Georgie marched back and forth in front of the White House fence, which consisted of two fire screens wired together. The audience whispered encouragement and clapped for the boys. Then Lydia switched into a marching song and Margaret opened the curtain for Charlotte, who was supposed to stride across the stage screaming "Votes for Women" and shaking her fist at the President.

Blinking, she stood just in front of Margaret, her poster leaning on her shoulder, staring out at the people. She didn't think she could walk, because her legs felt like pudding. If only her head would stop that banging for a minute. Her father waved at her from the opposite side of the room and put out his hand. Was that where she was supposed to go? She couldn't remember. She had to try very hard to remember, because Mother would be awfully angry if she didn't do it right. The music stopped and started again and she knew that meant she was supposed to go somewhere. She would go to Father, then. She started out, but with no warning her knees gave way and she sank suddenly to the floor just beneath the President. Everybody stared. I've done it all wrong, she thought, before she stopped thinking.

Behind the curtain, Lydia didn't know what had happened until Margaret stepped forward and picked up the limp body. "Votes for Women," Margaret said with an embarrassed smile. "This little suffragist isn't feeling well, so I think we'll put her right back in bed. Good day, Lieutenant Webster. Good day, President Wilson." And with that, she swept off the stage to the audience's enthusiastic applause mingled with murmured concern about the little girl.

George got up from his armchair and pulled the curtain before everyone else caught sight of Lydia, who had put her head right down on the piano keys.

*   *   *

As it turned out, they both had it. The little girl shivering in the upstairs room in the big house and great strong Tony Delbianco calling out for his mother on the worst days of the fever.

"It seems to run its course in a week," Dr. Ramsay told Lydia when he came the next morning. "Whichever way it goes."

"What can we do for her?"

"When she shivers, wrap her in blankets, and when she sweats, bathe her with cold compresses. I'm sorry. I honestly don't know what else to tell you. She'll probably get delirious when the fever goes up too far." He shook his head wearily. "I've never seen anything like this disease. In Hartford Hospital, they've got people lying on mattresses in the hallways. But there's no reason to take her in. They can't do any more for her there than you can right here."

"Would you mind going down to Tony Delbianco, Doctor?"

"Mr. Webster just asked me the same thing. I understand he's not too partial to doctors. Well, none of those Italians are. I'll check back with you tomorrow."

He saw that she had already returned to her chair by the bed. She must have been there all night. Her eyes had a dazed, sleepless look.

"Your wife needs her sleep too," he told George Webster downstairs. "The weaker she gets, the more susceptible she is to the thing."

"I'll see to it," George said without much conviction. He knew that Lydia had worked out the terms of her own penance and there was very little he could do to convince her that the debt was paid, or much less that no debt was owed. From the beginning, her feelings about Charlotte had been so intense and yet so incomprehensible to him that George had learned to leave her alone to work them out for herself.

Margaret also had the sense to stay away, busying herself with the boys in the children's dining room. They drew pictures for their little sister and sent them upstairs on a message track constructed out of two pulleys and a long piece of string attached to the banister rail of the back stairs. When the message reached the top, a small brass bell would ring, and if Lydia were free, she would come and pick up the pictures or the notes that read: "Dear Baby Charlotte, Get better soon and I'll show you the book about the aardvark. Love, Georgie," or "Dear Mother, Dorothy wants to know what you would like for lunch. Please write back soon. Love, Oliver." Much as Margaret wanted to sit next to the child's bed and bathe her forehead, she knew that Lydia belonged there, so she accepted the second-best position, which meant keeping the boys occupied and away from the dangers of the sickroom.

The nursery became Lydia's world. She grew to hate the yellow flowered design of the wallpaper, the brown stain on the ceiling where some mysterious mold had come through the wall during the previous rainy spring, the wearying tick of the cuckoo clock. Mercifully, the cuckoo itself had given way years ago to Georgie in one of his "fix it" moods. This week following Christmas, the world seemed to be encased in ice because of an unusual early thaw and the icicles outside the eastern-facing window dripped all morning and refroze in the afternoon.

In the bed, the little girl slept most of the time, which in itself terrified Lydia. How could a body as strong and willful as this one give way so completely to sleep and survive? When the fever was at its highest, she tossed and moaned, tugging at the linen pillowcase, and sometimes, to Lydia's amazement, while still asleep, Charlotte rolled up one corner and sucked on it. During the illness, she never put her thumb in her mouth.

"Don't you want the thumb, darling?" Lydia asked once when her daughter seemed awake and alert. "It might make you feel better."

"I don't like the taste," Charlotte whispered, her eyes widening at her mother's suggestion.

She never sucked it again.

When the fever began to drop, the girl's body shook so hard that Lydia tried holding parts of it: the bony knees, the shoulders, sometimes even the mouth, where the tiny teeth clicked together so continually that she thought the top ones would wear away the bottoms. Finally, she gathered the whole body into her arms and pressed it against her own, but Charlotte cried out that her skin

242

hurt and Lydia laid her gently back on the bed, certain that she had held her too hard.

She longed to hold her more, to make up for the times when she had been in too much of a hurry, when the child had asked her to look at something but she had been on her way out the door. She knew that all mothers standing watch over a sickbed must feel this way, that guilt flowed through the umbilical cord as freely as blood. She also knew that she would do it again, that if she went downstairs now and Georgie called for her to admire his painting, she might feel that stab of irritation at having to stop, but she was too tired, living too far out on the edge in this winter sickroom, to be forgiving to herself.

One night when she had cracked the window open to freshen the air and had fallen into a restless sleep on the couch, a cry woke her. She was standing by Charlotte's head before she was fully awake and was surprised to find the little girl sleeping comfortably. Her forehead was cooler than it had been in the afternoon. The cry came again, a horrible keening wail from out in the darkness. And she knew instantly what it was.

She woke Margaret, who rose fully dressed, and directed her to sit by Charlotte. "I'm going down to the Delbiancos'," she said. "Something's happened."

Tony had died with a groan in the middle of a fitful sleep. By the time Lydia got there, slipping and sliding her way down the icy lane, Louisa was uncontrollable. The children stood weeping in the corners of the room, while she threw herself on his dead body and screamed his name.

Lydia caught her by the shoulders and dragged her back away from the bed. With a strength she did not know she had, she turned the other, larger woman into her arms and crushed the rhythmic wailing into silence when their bodies met, breast to breast, rib to rib.

George came soon after and settled the children back into their beds while Lydia poured hot coffee down Louisa.

"He was such a strong man," Louisa said, the last unshed tears waiting at the corners of her eyes to tip down her cheeks. "How could this take him?"

Lydia didn't speak. She knew they were both thinking of the tiny bony body in the nursery room up the lane.

"How is the baby?"

Lydia would not lie. "I think her fever broke this evening. She is resting more comfortably."

"Thank the Lord," Louisa cried, but the cry was mixed with renewed anger at her own loss, and Lydia understood. Why should her child be spared when a grown man, a father of three, Louisa's beloved Tony with the sparkling mischievous eyes, be taken?

"He was the first Italian I met when I came here," Lydia said to George much later that night when they lay in each other's arms for the first time in days. Margaret had promised to stay by Charlotte for the rest of the night and Lydia had given in because, at last, the girl's breathing seemed to have cleared. "I still remember the two of you fussing and cursing over the Fiat's engine on that endless trip from the New Haven station. Oh, my God, I shall miss him."

George didn't answer. At first, she thought he had fallen asleep. And then dimly, in her exhausted state, she began to comprehend that he was crying, holding the sobs so deep in his chest that the muscles in his arms were trembling with the effort of it. She pressed his dark head against her breasts and rocked him like a baby, as much in love with him at that moment as she would ever be.

The next morning, Lydia slept. George had left instructions that nobody was to wake her, and the household whispered and tiptoed its way through the morning. The boys were bundled up and sent out by Margaret to take Frank and Clara Delbianco sliding on the big hill behind the barn. Dorothy went down and brought Sol up to play at her feet on the kitchen floor until Rosita came and took him away with her. The news of Tony's death had spread quickly through the Italian community, and all day long, the people came to pay their respects to Louisa, some on foot, some in buggies. That afternoon, when Lydia finally woke, clawing her way up through thick dreams to the strange sight of the sun flooding the western side of her bedroom, the first sound she heard was the squeak of wheels on the road below. Dressed only in her wrinkled nightgown, she stood by the window, her forehead pressed against the cold glass, and watched the hearse go out the driveway. How many times had Tony taken that corner himself, always a little too fast for George's liking, his hands easy on the reins and, in the last year, on the wheel of the new farm truck?

"Oh, Louisa," she whispered.

Her next thought was for Charlotte. She dressed quickly and hurried down the long upstairs hallway to the nursery. The door was closed, but she could hear voices singing. She turned the knob carefully.

With her back to the door, Margaret sat in the same ladder-back rocking chair where Lydia had spent the last week. Charlotte sat in her lap and the doll was perched on Charlotte's knee. They were singing the child's favorite song about a white horse on its way to Edinburgh. They didn't notice Lydia until she came around into their sight.

"She's better, then?" Lydia asked.

"Yes, ma'am," Margaret said, breaking off in the middle of a line. For once, she allowed her emotions to show. Her voice was excited, almost jubilant. "Feel her forehead. It's cool."

Lydia knelt beside Charlotte, who gazed down at her with a solemn expression. "How are you, darling?"

"Fine, Mother. And so is Marmar."

"Margaret hasn't been sick, thank God."

"No, Marmar," Charlotte repeated. She picked up the doll and made her floppy cloth legs dance a little dance on Margaret's uniformed knee, which jutted up between her own small legs.

Of course. Lydia had forgotten the doll's name. "That's right. Marmar has been keeping you company. So have I." She wanted to put out her arms but was too scared that the child would cling to Margaret, would refuse to come to her, so instead, in an oddly penitent gesture, she leaned over and kissed both of her knees. "I'll come back and eat supper with you, darling."

Margaret picked up the tune just where they had been interrupted and began to rock in rhythm to it. Lydia left the room without looking back.

17

In June 1919, nearly eighteen months after the House vote, the United States Senate finally approved the Nineteenth Amendment awarding the vote to women. At that point, the emphasis in suffrage organizations throughout the country switched to state ratification. Every committed suffragist wanted her state to be one of the thirty-six to ratify.

Connecticut was no different. All through that summer and fall, suffrage leaders put pressure on Governor Holcomb to call a special session of the state legislature to ratify the Nineteenth Amendment. In their zeal, the women solicited the support of a wide range of individuals and organizations. They allied themselves with labor groups and other left-wing associations and took the risk of angering the narrow-minded Yankee Republicans in order to win ratification before the elections in November 1920. Lydia was in the thick of it, and just as Taylor Morris had predicted, by the end of the fight she found her loyalties were deeply divided. But in January 1919, she presented herself humbly at the Hartford offices of the Connecticut Woman Suffrage Association, ready to accept whatever job they gave her, no matter how menial. She took Louisa with her.

"Well, Mrs. Webster, we finally meet," said Kate Ludwell, thrusting out her large hand, blackened with typewriter ink. She was the president of the organization, which was housed in four small rooms on the second floor of an old office building on Asylum Street. "Appropriate name," Miss Ludwell liked to point out to her visitors, "since women are classified with the insane when it comes to voting."

An imposing woman of forty with closely cropped black

hair, Ludwell had a long history of involvement in the suffrage movement. She was a founder of the Cosmopolitan Club in New York, a trustee of the Connecticut College for Women, and one of the organizers of the Old Lyme Equal Franchise League. When she moved to Hartford in 1917, she took over as president of the state Suffrage Association when its former leaders defected to the National Women's Party and the fight for the federal amendment. Now the fight was coming back to the states and Miss Ludwell was ready.

After they had been invited to perch on the front of two broken-down armchairs that were already piled high with papers, Lydia explained why they were there.

"I understand the CWSA's position on loyalty. Although I've always been a paying member, I have not worked through the organization, for my own reasons. I'm ready to do that now."

Kate Ludwell looked at her visitors with an amused expression on her face. The women were coming in in droves now that the war was over. And Lydia Webster was a welcome addition to the ranks. After all, she had been one of the few women to serve on the State Council of Defense during the war. She was known around the state and she had a unique connection to the large group of immigrant women, who, once properly educated and awarded citizenship, could swell their ranks considerably.

"All past sins are forgiven," Miss Ludwell said with a smile. "You are very welcome and so is Mrs. Delbianco. As you know, we have a fight on our hands. It cannot be too long before the Senate passes the amendment. We spent all last year working hard to get the votes in a legislature sympathetic to our cause and for the most part we succeeded. But Governor Holcomb is a rabid anti-suffragist and the legislature can do no good if he will not call them into session. Our plan now is to mount an enormous speaking campaign throughout the state in anticipation of his foot dragging. You'll both have to do a considerable amount of traveling. Is that possible?"

"Of course," Lydia said, putting her hand on Louisa's to still her objections. "You may not realize that Mrs. Delbianco was in charge of the Red Cross effort in the town of Northington during the war. She has considerable administrative abilities as well as connections to many Italian organizations throughout the state. And of course, because she speaks both languages fluently, she will be invaluable to us."

"I have no doubt of it," Miss Ludwell said with a smile. "Mrs. Webster, as I recall, you are a registered Republican."

"Yes."

"Well, just so we all are clear about where we stand, I am a Democrat who probably leans toward socialism. I was the one who pushed through that support of the Bridgeport munitions workers' strike last summer. I know that move was not a popular one with Republican women throughout the state."

"It was a question of judgment, Miss Ludwell," Lydia said evenly. "Alienating Mr. Roraback and the Republican machine may not be in our best interests."

"The vote is the goal," replied the other woman. "I don't care how we get it. I suspect your loyalties are more divided."

"Perhaps," Lydia said, rising to her feet. "But for the moment, I see no reason why we can't join forces."

"I agree. Now come. I'll introduce you to the rest of our group."

On the way home in the car that afternoon, Louisa exploded.

"You are crazy, Mrs. Lydia Webster, if you think I am going to stand up and make speeches in front of a lot of other people. I just learned English a couple of years ago—"

"Six," said Lydia firmly. She had been expecting this. Louisa had been too quiet all day.

"Well, I don't care if it's six or ten, I refuse to do it."

"Let's give it a chance, Louisa. As I understand it, we always go out in pairs because someone needs to hand out pamphlets and collect contributions while the other speaks. I'll do the speaking in the beginning." She smiled at her companion. "It sounds like quite a bit of fun."

"You'll do the speaking in the beginning, the middle, and the end. I should be staying home with my children."

"Doing what? Laundry? Embroidery work?"

"Am I going to be paid to do this?" Louisa flashed back.

"Yes. I'm not sure what our salaries will be yet." Lydia didn't say anything more. She knew that the suffrage organization had very little money and she had to show them that Louisa was invaluable in order to get her on the payroll. If it didn't work, she intended to pay her out of her own pocket if Kate Ludwell would agree to let the money pass in and out of the CWSA checking account.

After a few forays into the pro-suffragist, upper-middle-class neighborhoods of West Hartford, they were dispatched to the small mill town of Winsted, where many immigrants had gone to work in a shoe factory.

"Your contact is Helen Bennett," Kate explained. "She has been trying to drum up interest among the women in the factories, but she's having a hard time because she comes from a totally different background and they are suspicious of her."

"They're Italian?" Lydia asked with a gleam in her eye.

"Most of them, from what I gather. Some Poles also."

"Put that grin away, Mrs. Webster," Louisa said on the way up Route 8. "I'm not doing anything but handing out pamphlets."

"Of course," Lydia said.

She backed the car up to the factory gates and they draped it with the traditional white, green, and purple banner. "What do these colors mean?" Louisa had asked Kate when she first saw them. "White for purity, green for courage, and purple for justice," was the answer. "I wish it were all green," Louisa had said.

When the closing bell rang, the doors at opposite ends of the factory opened to disgorge the workers, women on the left, men on the right. The two groups mingled in the middle of the yard and filed out past Lydia, who stood in the back of the car, bullhorn in hand, and spoke to them about the cause. Louisa circulated through the crowd, handing out pamphlets and translating the headlines into Italian. Despite the cold and the growing darkness, a small group gathered by the car. "Go back to the kitchen," a man called in Italian.

Bristling, Lydia turned and answered in Italian. "I've been there too long," and at that, Louisa caught her eye and laughed.

"What will the vote do for us?" a woman asked.

Lydia tried to explain, but as she began to stumble over the vocabulary for social legislation, the questioner turned away. Even Louisa could see their long trip was going to be wasted. The workers were cold and hungry. With another jeer, the men led their wives toward the darkening street.

"Give it to me," Louisa said, snatching the bullhorn. "You pass out the pamphlets." After years of calling her children in from across the lawn, Louisa knew how to project her voice. "Such a frightened bunch of women," she thundered in Italian. The crowd hesitated.

"You do the same work as the men. You don't want the same rights they have?"

Some of the workers turned back from the street to listen.

"Tell them your story," Lydia whispered.

Louisa talked about Italy, about her trip on the *Giuseppe Verdi,* her work on the farm. By the time she was done, the women were cheering, drowning out the taunts of the few men who had stayed. When Louisa finally sat down in the seat to catch her breath, the crowd gathered around her, chattering in Italian.

On the way home much later that night, Louisa slid down and rested her head against the back of the leather seat. Tony would have been so proud of her. He would have caught her eye from his place in the crowd and raised his fist the way he did when the dairymen beat the fuse factory boys in their annual baseball game. She began to cry silently. The tears tickled their way down her cheeks, but she did not lift her hands to wipe them away.

"Well, Mrs. Delbianco, next year we'll run you for President," Lydia said in the darkness. "But right now, you'd better get out that map. I think we're lost."

*   *   *

Two weeks later, after Louisa spoke to two more crowds in Bridgeport, Lydia went to see Kate Ludwell about her.

"I understand she's quite effective," Kate said.

"She's remarkable. Besides, she is our only link to the working classes and the immigrants. Face it, Kate, the women in the suffrage movement are mostly educated upper-middle-class people like you and me."

"I agree. What do you want me to do?"

Lydia told her about Tony's death and Louisa's financial situation. "She is living in a cottage on our land, and of course George and I are willing to help her out financially, but she's too proud to take charity. I told her you'd be paying us a salary."

Kate put back her head and laughed. "A salary? I can barely afford the rent for this space."

"But I know you pay the secretaries. They're important to the cause too, but someone like Louisa could really make the difference. She gets all the milk she needs from the farm and wood in the winter. She doesn't need much."

"All right, I'll figure out something."

The next week Louisa went home with her first regular paycheck.

"Don't look so smug, Mrs. Webster," George teased her that night. "You were lucky things worked out exactly the way you wanted them this time."

"Lucky?" she cried in mock outrage. "What would you say if I called your tobacco harvest lucky? You'd stick my head on a pole out in the field for the crew to laugh and jeer at. I knew all along the stuff Louisa is made of. It was just a matter of getting the right people to recognize it at the right time."

"You're beginning to sound more and more like a politician," said George.

"Perhaps," Lydia said. "Tell me, how is Margaret doing?"

"Don't tell her I said so, but I think she loves it. She's in her element with six children to manage. I came in the other day to find them all on a cleanup brigade. First they reported to the munitions officer, where they were awarded with a dust mop or a broom or some such

251

instrument of battle, and then they were assigned a corner of the nursery to attack."

Before Lydia even approached Louisa about working in the suffrage organization, she had asked Margaret whether she would take on the Delbianco children in addition to the Websters. Their discussion took place in the basement, where Margaret was putting the children's laundry through the ringer.

"Of course, we will raise your salary."

"I don't care about the money," Margaret said with her usual dour expression.

"And Nancy can help you," Lydia said. Nancy was the new chambermaid who had been hired right after the disastrous Christmas party. With the men coming back from overseas, women were out of work again.

"I don't need any help. But the same rules apply to all of them," Margaret said.

"Of course."

"Frank will be the problem," Margaret predicted.

"I expect so. Louisa says he misses his father terribly," Lydia said.

"That's no excuse for bad behavior," Margaret declared, and turned back to the washtubs. She picked up one of Georgie's shirts and fed it neck first into the slot between the rollers. As usual, Lydia felt dismissed, and as she climbed back up the rough wooden stairs, she realized that Margaret was probably delighted.

After the Senate passage, Kate Ludwell sent the two women out on the road almost every day. In the summer and fall of that year, the suffragists were looking for signatures on a petition pushing Holcomb to call the legislature into special session. By the following spring, Lydia had founded the League of Republican Women and was putting her energies into the education of new voters.

"I don't care whether Connecticut is one of the thirty-six states," she told Kate Ludwell in April. "We know the amendment is going to be ratified sooner or later, probably before the election in November. We've got to develop a strong voting bloc within our parties. The women have to be organized if we're going to be dealing with the Rorabacks and the Holcombs."

Kate tipped back in her chair. "There's a growing feeling among the suffragists that because of Holcomb's refusal to call the special session, we should put all our energies into opposing Republican candidates throughout the state until the amendment has been ratified. If we vote to go ahead with that plan, will you join us?"

Lydia had heard the talk. The gap between her loyalties had finally widened too much. She was like a woman in a river with her feet planted on two logs that were drifting slowly apart. She knew she had to choose one or the other or she would end up in the water.

"Kate, it's political suicide. This state is still controlled by the Republican Party and I don't see any sign of that changing. We've got to work within the party if we're ever going to get any power. Getting the vote shouldn't be the end of our road, just the beginning. If the CWSA votes to go ahead with that, I'll have to resign."

"What about Louisa?"

"I don't know," Lydia said.

On June 3, the Connecticut Woman Suffrage Association declared that they would oppose the Republican Party in the coming campaign. Lydia resigned. Louisa stayed with them.

"It's absolutely crazy," Lydia stormed to George that night. "The thirty-sixth state will ratify and then what will the organization do? Dust the office, sweep the floors, and go back to darning socks at home. Some people cannot see beyond the end of their noses."

"It's Louisa that's really making you mad, isn't it?"

Lydia didn't answer but went on brushing her hair with short angry jabs.

"You'd better prepare yourself, Lydia. She might even register Democrat when the time comes."

"She's her own person," Lydia said. "I've always known that." But the words had to be spat out one by one, like teeth that had been knocked loose in a fight.

Those were the years that Charlotte started to run with the boys. Georgie and Clara Delbianco always held themselves apart from the younger children. They were the only ones who went to school then and they walked down the road together, swinging their books over their shoulders, aware of the three pairs of jealous eyes that watched them from the front gate. Sol was still too young to know about school. He was content to squat down and inspect Margaret's shoes while the rest of them watched.

That left Charlotte with Frank and Oliver for the rest of the day. She was the youngest of the three but soon established herself in a leadership position. It all started with Helen Ratty.

"I am the queen of a secret kingdom," Charlotte announced one day.

"Yes?" Margaret said, putting down her sewing and looking up expectantly.

"The kingdom is up the mountain beside the brook. I am queen and Helen Ratty is my assistant. She calls me all the time on an invisible telephone and we decide what to do."

"I don't believe you," said Frank.

"You don't have to," said Charlotte, who was already used to Frank.

"Can we go visit the kingdom?" Margaret asked.

"Yes," Charlotte said. "Helen Ratty says we can come tomorrow for a picnic. Even if we don't see her, she will be watching us."

"Can I come, Charlotte?" Oliver asked. "Please."

She stared at him for a very long time as if trying to decide.

"Yes. Helen Ratty wants to take a look at you. She may have a job for you to do."

Oliver smiled. "Really? How does she know about me?"

"I told her."

"It sounds stupid," Frank said again. He was shooting marbles in one corner of the nursery. They were Oliver's marbles, but Frank played with them most of the time. "I'm glad I don't have to go."

Margaret looked at him. "We're all going, Frank," she said firmly. When she turned back to her sewing, he made a face at her. Oliver closed his eyes. He hated it when Frank defied Margaret. It scared him.

"Making faces at me will do no good," Margaret said, without looking up. "If it's a full moon, your mouth just might get stuck that way."

The next day, the five of them trooped up the mountain path. Frank dawdled along behind, snapping twigs off and tickling Sol with them on the backs of his chubby knees until Margaret made him the leader. Charlotte and Oliver fell into step behind him, marching to his barked orders. They all loved to play soldier.

It was the first warm spring day and the trees were fuzzy with the promise of new leaves. While Margaret and the boys ate their sandwiches on the blanket, Charlotte went behind a rock to consult with Helen Ratty.

"She wants you to come and stand right here, Oliver," Charlotte said. "You mustn't try to look for her or she'll be scared off. It's very important that nobody ever see her face."

While Frank snickered, Oliver did as he was told.

"All right, turn around," Charlotte commanded from her position by the rock. He showed Helen Ratty his back.

"Good. That's enough."

"What did she say about me?" Oliver asked when Charlotte came down from the rock.

"She thinks you might do. She will call tonight."

"And what about Frank?" Margaret asked. She and Charlotte looked at one another for a moment without speaking.

"She didn't see me," Frank said from his corner of the blanket.

"She watched you leading us up the hill," Charlotte said. "She'll call about you too."

For once, Frank did not scoff. That evening, they sat around the nursery waiting.

"I hope she calls soon," Oliver said. "We'll have to go to bed in a minute. And the others will have to go home."

"They're spending the night here," Margaret said. "Mrs. Delbianco and your mother are speaking at a rally down in the southern part of the state. They can't get home until tomorrow."

Helen Ratty took her time. She called after the lights were put out. The ring of the invisible telephone sounded suspiciously like the little china bell from the dining room sideboard, but Oliver didn't notice. Charlotte carried on the conversation from her bed in a conspiratorial whisper.

"What did she say?" Oliver hissed from across the room.

"I'll tell you tomorrow," Charlotte said. "Very important news."

"Aw, come on," Oliver pleaded. "Tell me before Frank." The Delbiancos had been put to bed in the big guest room at the other end of the house.

"Quiet," Georgie said. "Margaret will be in here in a minute."

"Tomorrow," said Charlotte.

The next day, after the older ones had been waved off to school, Charlotte called a council of war.

"Helen Ratty says there is to be an enormous fight between the German dogs and cats that live on the top of the mountain. She says whoever wins will be part of my kingdom and we want the dogs to win. Oliver, you have been made spy for our side. Every day, she will call in your orders."

Oliver beamed. He had been chosen.

With an uncanny sense of timing, Charlotte said nothing about Frank. She watched him squirm, not wanting to ask and yet dying to know. Had Helen Ratty said anything about him?

"First we must draw a map of the battle area. Get some paper and pencils."

Oliver jumped up. Frank couldn't bear it any longer. He wanted to be part of this. It sounded like fun.

"Did Helen Ratty talk about me?"

Charlotte glanced up from her desk. With feigned surprise, she clapped her hand to her forehead. "Of course she did. How could I forget? You are to command the troops along the left flank. Oliver will be your front man."

In the days that followed, Helen Ratty called every afternoon just after rest time. Nobody was allowed to watch when Charlotte spoke to her. Frank and Oliver waited breathlessly for the latest news, and the little girl used her communications with Helen Ratty to torment the two of them.

"Helen Ratty does not answer," she would say. "She must be out," or "Helen Ratty says there has been a council of war but I must not tell anybody about it yet. It's a secret."

"We're good at keeping secrets," Oliver groaned. "We're on her side."

"The bad spies have been getting across the lines," Charlotte reported. "Everyone is under suspicion."

Despite her horror at the children's knowledge of war and its jargon, Margaret watched these games with a secret pleasure.

"Helen Ratty's got them wrapped around her finger," Margaret confided to Mr. Webster when he stopped in for his evening visit to the nursery. "Such a clever little fox, Charlotte is. If she had been the one giving the orders, they would never have paid the slightest attention to her. As it is, they are turning cartwheels for Helen Ratty, the tyrant of Northington Mountain. Even Frank."

George smiled in return. "How is Frank doing otherwise?"

Margaret shrugged. "It's toughest on him. Sol was too young to really know his father and Clara seems content to read and play dolls and tag around after Georgie. But it seems as though Frank's always got his fists up."

"I know. I'm going to do some work with him when he gets older. Take Tony's place a little if I can."

"That would be good for him," Margaret said. "He's going to need a man's hand on his shoulder."

Summertime was the best time on the farm for the children. After the dark, cold cooped-up days, Margaret let them run free as long as they reported in and got their chores done. The chores consisted of picking the vegetables, helping with the tobacco harvest, and when they got old enough, milking one cow each every afternoon. When Charlotte turned seven, she went with her father to the barn for the ceremonial selection of her cow.

"I want a nice one," she said, skipping along beside him. Although he never appeared to be in a hurry, his long legs covered a lot of ground in a short time.

"A nice one? Well, I'm not sure about that. I only buy mean cows. Nice ones don't give as much milk."

"You're teasing, Father," she said, slipping her hand into his. She liked to run her fingers along the edges of his calluses. The skin there had toughened so much that he couldn't feel her tickling him.

He pushed open the giant sliding door just far enough for the two of them to slip through the crack into the dim rustling cave of the barn. She had always loved it here. The cows seemed friendly when they turned their brown eyes toward her, their bells clanking against the stanchions, their tails swishing at the flies that settled, buzzed away, and settled again. She pattered along behind her father, who stopped every now and then to speak to one of the men or to inspect a hoof, a distended udder. The barn was his kingdom and he swung easily down the hay-strewn aisles of it. The men knew when he came in even if he hadn't spoken. They dragged their milking stools in a little closer, pulled down a little harder. And the cows knew when he was there. Charlotte was sure of it.

He led her down to the very end. "Now, Charlotte," he said. "One of these five can be yours. They're all good milkers, so we'll expect a lot from you. Now that we've won the contract for Hartford Hospital, we've got to keep up our quota."

To her delight, he spoke to her the same way he did to anybody else. She had no idea what he meant half the time, but she could pick up the thrust of the message from his voice, the serious frown on his forehead. She went down the row, rubbing the stiff hair just above each cow's dusty black nostrils. She took the time to look each one in the eye, then inspected them from the rear.

"This one," she said at last, pointing to a slightly smaller cow with a brown friendly face.

"Brandy," he said without bothering to glance at the ear tag. He knew them all by heart. "A good choice. All right, then, no time like the present. Pick out your stool and your pail."

She took to milking easily. She liked the rhythmic movements of it, the satisfying drumming noise that the stream of white liquid made when it hit the bottom of the tin pail, the cow's rough-haired belly pressed against the top of her head.

"Let her know who's boss," her father said, giving Brandy a sharp slap on her right haunch when she began to move too close to Charlotte.

"So you've got your cow, Charlotte." They both looked up to see Lydia standing in the aisle watching them.

"Yes, Mother. Father says I'm good at this."

"I'm sure you're better than I was. Do you remember my one trip to the barn, George?"

"Sure do. You were fine too, but as I recall, you didn't have the stomach for it." Charlotte felt their eyes meet above her head and knew they were smiling. Grownups always had these secret ways of talking to each other. Sometimes they spoke French or used fancy words. And if nothing else worked, they sent the children from the room.

She poured her milk into the tank, cleaned out the pail and hung it on its proper hook.

"Goodbye, Brandy, see you tomorrow," she said with a last rub between the ears.

The three of them walked home together. Charlotte took her father's hand and then, more tentatively, her mother's. Above her head, they were talking about Lydia's work. Charlotte didn't understand the words and didn't much care. She was imagining herself to be a hammock strung between the two trees of them. She wished the walk down the barn lane and up the driveway could last forever.

"So many of the women have done just as I expected," Lydia was saying. "Gone home to their men and their kitchens. I can't seem to convince them that now we've got the vote, we've got to damn well do something with it. And the only action in this state happens in the Republican Party."

"Watch your language, Mother," George said, glancing down at the bobbing head between them.

She stuck her tongue out at him and went right on. "The women like Kate Ludwell have veered very sharply to the left. They're pushing for the right to—" She stopped herself and mouthed the words "birth control information" over her daughter's head. Down below, Charlotte grinned at the brief gap in the sentence. Her mother must be saying something secret again. Lydia went on. "I agree with them, but you cannot possibly organize a movement around an issue like that."

"My God, Lydia, you ran thirty-four women for the

legislature last year when you'd only had the vote for four months. What do you expect?"

"And how many of them won?" she said sternly.

"Four, as I recall," he said.

"Precisely. And three of the four were Republicans. I rest my case." She leaned down to Charlotte. "This is a Republican state, my dear, and I'm glad it is. So when are these foolish women going to come down off their socialist soapboxes and work within the party?"

"Tomorrow, Mother," Charlotte replied firmly, because the question seemed to demand an answer.

"There's my girl," she said, squeezing her hand. "No time like the present."

"It may not stay Republican," George said as they went into the kitchen.

"Well, I want a crack at it before things switch around. I'm thinking of running for the legislature."

In the silence that followed that declaration, the two trees dropped Charlotte's hammock strings and became parents again. She caught the look of surprise on Margaret's face across the room and stole away to the safety of her lap.

"Let's go in the other room," George said quietly. "I expect that rascal Isabelle Morris has put some more crazy ideas in your head."

"What's the legis . . . whatever Mother said?" Charlotte asked.

"Part of the state government. People elect other people to go there and decide things for them," Margaret explained. "Hop off my lap. You've gotten too heavy for me."

"What will happen if Mother does what she said? Will she get very tired from the running?"

Dorothy burst into laughter. "She sure will, honey, but not for the reasons you're thinking of. In my opinion, a woman should stay where she belongs. Right here in the kitchen."

Margaret took Charlotte's hand and led her into the little dining room out of earshot. "Now, to answer your very sensible question, when a person runs for government, they don't actually run along the road. It means they go around the countryside making speeches and trying to convince people to vote for them."

"But Mother's already been doing that."

"Yes," Margaret said. "But that was to get women the right to vote. This would be to make the people vote for her."

"I don't want her to do it," Charlotte decided. "I think she'll get grumpy if she does that."

Margaret smiled. "Knowing her, she'll get grumpy if she doesn't. I've never known a woman to—"

"To what?" Charlotte prodded.

"To have so much energy," Margaret finished and stood up. "Time to set the table. Call the boys."

Charlotte did as she was told, but she knew Margaret meant to say something else. Charlotte was already very good at figuring out what people meant just by listening to the tone in their voices or watching the way their foreheads crinkled up when they said something. Like an insect, she had emotional antennae and feelers that helped her pick up the invisible messages, the ones that told her which way to act so people would approve of her.

18

When Lydia got pregnant in the spring of 1922, she did not take it as a sign from God the way Dorothy the cook thought she should but as a betrayal of all her dreams. The day that Dr. Ramsay confirmed her suspicions, the whole household tiptoed around trying to shut out the pounding of her angry voice from the upstairs wing. Nobody met Mr. Webster's eye when he stormed down the front stairs and went out to the barn. The children played very quietly in the little dining room downstairs until Georgie and Frank got into a wrestling match over a card game and Margaret marched them all outside for a walk in the rain.

From her bedroom window, Lydia watched them troop down the barn lane like so many puddle ducks. Now there would be another straggling along behind. She slammed her fist against the window frame. Damn her body. Damn George Webster and his wanting her so much. She was to have started her campaign for the legislature in two months. It would be hard enough for the voters in this district to swallow the idea of a woman representing them. But a pregnant woman? Impossible.

In the beginning, the children had helped keep her away from that hole inside. Months went by when she forgot about it. After all, she was not only a wife but a mother. Mothers don't dissolve, disappear overnight. They endure because they have to. Somebody needs them. But once the babies became toddlers and talkers and even readers and their problems could not be solved with a breast or a gentle rhythmic push of the cradle, they seemed to require too much of her, more than she could give, and she felt slammed against the wall of herself by them.

To her horror, the small daily accidents of her children sent her into a rage that grew from a feeling of helplessness. "Don't be so clumsy," she would snap at Oliver, who was always bumping into things, and the pain of the bruised knee or the skinned palm would be increased because of that note of irritation that she could not seem to keep out of her voice. Sometimes she hid out of sight when she heard a cry, knowing that Margaret would take the time to inspect the wound, rock the shaking shoulders, that Margaret could endure the wailing voice next to her ear until it cried itself out in its own time. And she stood behind the doorway or to the side of the upstairs window, allowing the soothing voice to ease the child's pain and her own confused fear at the same time.

So it was the work that had restored her, lifted her out of this bedlam of emotions. Now that was being taken away. She was slipping backwards again, losing control, hanging on by her fingernails.

Down below, Louisa's black Ford turned into the driveway and drove slowly down toward the cottage. At last. Somebody to talk to.

Louisa had registered Republican when the women got the vote, a move which surprised Lydia.

"I expected you to follow Kate's lead and go with the Democrats," Lydia had said.

"I wanted to vote for Mr. Webster for selectman," Louisa told her. "Besides, I've been listening to you. The power in this state is in the Republican Party."

Once the vote fight was won, Louisa got the job as secretary to the Connecticut League of Women Voters, the organization formed to educate women about their new enfranchisement. She worked three days a week.

She had already settled herself down at the kitchen table in the cottage with a glass of milk when Lydia knocked at the door. She waved Lydia in.

"Milk, Signora?" she offered. "Or coffee."

"Neither one," Lydia said as she slipped into the other seat. "Am I disturbing you?"

"No. I'm making gnocchi for dinner but I'm not ready to start. Where are the children?"

"Margaret's taken them all out for a walk in the rain.

If they get pneumonia, it's my fault. I've been in the most terrible rage and everybody in the house is running for cover."

"What's wrong?" Louisa asked. The skin rolled away from under her black eyes in thick folds. Since Tony had died, she had gained weight.

"I'm going to have another baby."

Louisa's smile of delight was instinctive, the natural expected response, and yet it hurt Lydia. Not even her good friend understood her sense of powerlessness, of a thing done to her. The loss of control over her own body brought back the bad memories.

"It means, of course, that I'll have to give up the idea of the legislature," she said wearily.

"Just for now," Louisa said, reaching across the table to pat her hand. "The legislature won't go out of business in the next year. So you'll run for it later."

"George says the same thing. I don't want to wait, Louisa." Her voice changed pitch. "Dammit," she said, crying. "I don't want to cry about it either. I don't want another baby. What's wrong with me?"

Louisa did not move from her seat. She continued to stroke Lydia's hand but she did not speak, and through her tears, Lydia grew aware of the pop of the wet wood in the stove, the drumming of the rain on the roof, the distant cries of the children coming back from their walk.

"You think I'm crazy, don't you?" Lydia said as she pulled a handkerchief out of her pocket and blew her nose.

"I think that God is stupid sometimes."

"Louisa!" Lydia knew how important the other woman's religion was to her.

"God forgives me. I talk to him every day. He knows what I mean."

"Well, what do you mean?"

"He gives you what I want and he gives me what you want. I have the job, no possibility of more children. You get the children, no possibility of the job. For now."

"The 'for now' applies to you too. There are other men in the world. You might remarry."

Louisa glanced around the room. "You know, I sit here at night after the children go to sleep. Sometimes I think I hear Tony calling to me from the calf barn. He used to do that when he was helping Gino during calving season. He would call my name and I could hear him from the bedroom. This voice floating across the road to me. I still hear the voice," she said, her eyes shining.

The kitchen door banged open and Clara led her two brothers into the room. "We made mud pies," Sol shouted as he threw his dripping body against his mother. She picked him up, muddy hands and all, and set him on her lap.

Over his head, she met Lydia's eyes and shrugged. The kitchen felt close and crowded suddenly. Lydia slipped out the door and trudged back up the driveway with no thought for the puddles.

This pregnancy turned out to be much worse than the other three. In the mornings, Lydia could not lift her head from the pillow without first stuffing down the three dry soda crackers she kept on the bedside table. They tasted like sawdust in her morning mouth, but they seemed to settle the rolling sensation in her stomach. To stand for any length of time made her feel faint, so she either walked or sat. In the afternoons, she lay on her bed listening to the muffled noises from the other end of the hallway. She was unable to sleep, but dragging her body about the house seemed just as impossible. At first her brain kept going, making lists in her head, going over the letters she had to write, the people she should get in touch with, but eventually even her mind seemed to thicken, as heavy and lethargic as her body, and she dozed in and out of slow waking dreams in which she was always running but never fast enough.

George began to plan an addition to the house to make room for the new baby.

"It's just your way of apologizing," Lydia said one night when she found him sketching elevations at his desk.

"What for?" he asked.

"This baby."

"Don't talk nonsense," he muttered, and bent back over his pictures. He was flipping the whole house around, so that the old nursery would become their bedroom suite while the children would move into the new wing above the living room.

"You'd better not damage my elm tree," she warned as she peered over his shoulder.

"I'll do my best, but I recall telling you not to plant it so close to the house."

In the twelve years since she and Smack had first put it in, the elm tree had shot up and filled out enough so that when she stretched out under it to read, only her ankles and feet stuck outside the circle of its shade.

"Soon it will be big enough for a picnic with the children," Smack had said to her just last week. "All the children," he added with that crooked, toothless grin. News about any kind of babies travels fast on a farm, Lydia thought.

Smack had aged a good deal in the years since she had known him. Because of the arthritis in his hips, he had developed a rolling bowlegged walk that made him look more like a sailor than a gardener. He and Signora Leedia, as he called her, still shared a love of growing things and in the spring she spent hours with him in the greenhouse.

"Smack and I feel strongly about that tree," she said to George. "It's the very first thing we planted together."

She had meant to tease him, but there was no softness in her voice. He threw down his pencil. "Lydia, I'm tired of this game. Don't talk to me at all if you can't be pleasant. I know you're disappointed about the timing of this baby but stop blaming it all on me. Haven't you ever been told to make the best of a bad situation? You're acting like a spoiled child and I've never known you to do that before." When he stood up, the ramrod snap of his long legs knocked over the desk chair. He strode away without righting it.

She picked the chair up, set it in place, and adjusted the papers on his desk. Then she walked quietly up the stairs and closed herself in her room for the rest of the night. He slept in the calf barn.

"It might as well be New Year's," she wrote to Aunt Katherine the next day. "Because last night I had a sharp talk with the bad side of myself and I made new firm resolutions. George has told me that I am acting spoiled and he is right, much as it galls me to admit it. There are so many women in the world who want to be in my position. I must put my selfishness aside and be grateful for my loving husband, my healthy children, and the new baby on the way. If it means that for the time being I am not allowed to want anything for myself, then so be it. I shall be the best, most self-sacrificing mother there ever was."

"Oh dear," Katherine said when she read the letter out loud to her husband. "Lydia never does things in moderation, does she?"

Georgie and Oliver now traveled to school every morning in the delivery wagon that took the milk in to Hartford Hospital. Charlotte wanted to go too.

"You can't," Georgie said. "It's a school for boys only."

"It's too bad for you," Oliver said without much genuine remorse in his voice. "The ride in is so much fun. We get to sit up next to Smack and we all sing Italian songs and we bounce along."

"Except when Gino comes along too. Then there's no room for Oliver and he has to sit on the step on the side."

"Next time, it's your turn to sit out there," Oliver snapped at his older brother. "Especially if it's raining."

"I'm the oldest, so I don't have to sit out there ever," Georgie taunted, and they were off, chasing each other around the kitchen until Dorothy banged her wooden spoon on the table to make them stop.

Now Charlotte walked down the lane with Frank and Clara and Sol to the one-room schoolhouse, but no jealous eyes watched them from the gate. When she turned around to look, there was only Margaret left behind to wave and blow kisses.

This year, Charlotte liked school. Miss Templeton, the teacher, seemed to be very young, but she was firm.

On the first day, Charlotte had cringed when she heard Frank passing a ball under the desk to one of the Togni boys. The first day was always the most important. If the teacher didn't take care of the problems then, the rest of the year was a waste. Miss Templeton glanced up at the scuffling sounds and put up her hand for silence. Gradually the other children stopped their recitations and the noises in the room faded away until all that was left was Frank's giggling and the scraping of his feet. At last, he noticed that he was the only one moving.

"Bring me the ball, Frank," Miss Templeton said. She had pinned a name tag to everybody when they first came in, which was one good way of keeping control. Usually, it took two weeks for the teacher to sort them all out.

"What ball?"

Charlotte covered her ears. This was the bad time, usually. Frank would get her involved in an argument while Nick Togni hid the ball and then the boys would have won when she couldn't find it. Charlotte looked at Miss Templeton. Her lips weren't moving. She wasn't saying anything. Everybody waited. And waited. It looked as if they might sit like that until lunchtime. Finally, Nick couldn't bear the silence anymore. He stood up and threw her the ball. Miss Templeton caught it quite deftly.

"Next time, you may bring it up, Nick. Now, Frank, come up here. I want you to hold the ball while one of the younger children spells the word on his chalkboard."

The children giggled at the sight of big gangly Frank, the bully, holding the ball out in his hands while his little brother, Sol, solemnly scratched out the letters beside him. Frank was supposed to be in fourth grade, but he had not been moved up because he still couldn't read very well.

That was only the beginning of the battles between the teacher and Frank and Nick, but as the year went on, Charlotte began to relax, because most of the time, Miss Templeton won.

She didn't run the schoolroom as strictly as the teacher before her, who had drawn chalk lines on the floor to separate the different grades and who made the fourth be absolutely silent while the third read aloud. Miss Templeton seemed content with the buzz of different children's voices, and in each grade she appointed one leader who was responsible for listening to the others and making corrections in their work. In January, Charlotte was chosen as leader of the third.

"No, thank you, Miss Templeton," Charlotte said in a firm voice.

"It's an honor to be chosen as leader, Charlotte. Your reading has improved so much since the beginning of the year and you are the first to memorize the multiplication tables."

"Yes, but I don't want to be leader."

"Can you tell me why not?"

"It's a secret," Charlotte said in a low voice. Everybody seemed to be listening.

"Can you whisper it to me?"

"It's because of Frank. He's older than me. He won't listen to me," she mouthed into the pretty curled ear of Miss Templeton. She felt the lady's gentle hand come down on her shoulder like a bird landing on a branch.

"I'll take care of Frank," Miss Templeton whispered back.

The next day, she announced that Frank was going to be leader of the whole school. At the beginning of each day, he carried the flag around the room while the other children marched along behind him and sang a song called "Blessed Country, Land We Love." He was also given the job of raising and lowering the outdoor flag, and he took it upon himself to make a little ceremony out of it by saluting Miss Templeton when he came back inside. Like a general acknowledging a trusted subordinate, she saluted back and indicated his seat with a slight bow.

It was a stroke of genius on Miss Templeton's part. Frank still loved to play soldier better than anything, so he stamped his feet and marched and saluted with such vigor that by the time he came to the learning part of school, he had worked off most of his extra energy. If he didn't exactly apply himself to the numbers and letters, at least he sat still. For the most part, he left Charlotte alone.

One morning in March, Lydia met the children at the gate.

"I'm coming to school with all of you today," she said gaily. Clara reached up and slipped her hand into one of Lydia's.

"Why?" Charlotte asked, suspiciously.

"To see what kind of an education you're getting," she said.

Usually, they dawdled up the road, stopping to poke sticks in the muddy ruts or to wait for Sol, the one with the shortest legs. But Lydia took Sol's hand in her other one, and this morning they marched sharply along while she chatted with Clara. Charlotte walked behind, watching the rhythmic sway of her mother's hips. Margaret said there was going to be another baby in the house. Maybe it was already there, hidden under her skirts, Charlotte thought.

Miss Templeton met them at the door.

"I'm delighted to have you, Mrs. Webster," she said pleasantly. "Line up for the marching please, children."

Charlotte could not concentrate on anything all morning. Her mother chose a seat in the corner quite far away from her group, but Charlotte felt the eyes resting on her the whole time and she kept making mistakes during the spelling bee. Silly mistakes that made that little frown of dismay wrinkle Miss Templeton's forehead. Lydia left abruptly in the middle of the day when Charlotte was busy correcting the younger children's addition problems, and she wondered whether the silent departure meant her mother was satisfied or angry. For once, she couldn't tell.

The verdict didn't come for a week, and when she thought about it later, Charlotte remembered the feeling that discussions about her were being held in the grownup rooms.

"Darling, I'm going to teach you at home from now on," Lydia told her Sunday night.

"Why?" Charlotte asked in her abrupt voice.

"I think Miss Templeton is doing the best job possible considering the numbers of children, but you are not learning enough there."

"But I like Miss Templeton. I like my school," Charlotte said.

"There is talk of two ladies starting a good private school for girls in Hartford, but until that becomes a reality, I think I can really do a better job for you than Miss Templeton. It will be fun, darling. We'll get so much more done here, just the two of us, than in that chaotic classroom. And you won't have to correct other children's work."

Charlotte nodded because she knew that was what she was supposed to do. She didn't say that she liked the correcting part, that it made her feel as grownup as the teacher. In a small gesture of defiance, she took her hands away from her mother's grasp and stepped back.

"We'll have our meetings down here in the parlor, where we won't be disturbed by all the comings and goings. I've already ordered some books from New York, and I've given your father a list of supplies that he can buy in Hartford when he goes in tomorrow on business."

The next morning, Charlotte did not stand with Margaret to wave goodbye to the daily parade that was now composed entirely of Delbiancos. She watched from the kitchen window while she blew hot fog circles on the cold windowpane and rubbed them away. It seemed that she was always being left behind.

Georgie and Oliver were driving to school with their father today. They got to ride with him up front in the Packard and help him dig it out when it got stuck in the mud, which always happened this time of year. And here she was singled out from everybody else. The girl who went to school in the parlor. With her mother as teacher. It wasn't fair.

She wandered upstairs. It felt funny to be in the house during the day without the other children. Nancy was standing on a chair dusting the upper moldings in the hallway, and Charlotte lounged against the wall, watching her rock about on the rickety chair, her uniformed arm stretched so high that it threw her continually off balance.

"What are you doing?" Margaret said, coming up behind her. Charlotte never knew whether it was her shoes or the way she walked, but Margaret made no sound when she moved.

"Waiting for school to start," Charlotte muttered.

"Well, your mother's tray just went up, so you can come help me clean out the nursery."

"Is the nursery dirty?" Charlotte asked, grateful for any job as long as it would help pass the time.

271

"No, but the construction of the house will start soon, so your mother wants us to clear out anything that's unnecessary. We're going to be moved up to the other end. At least, the baby and I will. You'll have a bedroom that looks over the garden. Next to the elm tree."

"That will be nice," Charlotte said dreamily. She didn't like to think about the new baby getting to sleep in Margaret's room. "Maybe I'll be able to crawl right out my window onto one of its branches."

"I expect you will," said Margaret. "Put out your arms. I'll make a pile of the clothes you don't need anymore."

"Why can't I go to school with Frank and Clara anymore?"

"Your mother thinks she can do a better job with you at home," Margaret said. Her voice was even, although Charlotte could not see her face.

"Do you think so?"

"Pile these things in the trunk over there. Put them in carefully, please."

Charlotte did as she was told, but she was still waiting for an answer. "I think the school is perfectly good," Margaret said at last, "but your mother needs something to do."

"That's what I think."

At the same moment, they heard her sharp footsteps moving down the hallway. Rap, tap, rap. Charlotte's mother walked with short, businesslike steps. She never wandered. She always had places to go, things to accomplish.

"Go along with a smile," Margaret said softly. "It might be fun."

She didn't sound very convincing.

At first, it was fun. Her mother had a way of telling stories about history that helped Charlotte with the dates and names. For English, Charlotte copied sentences out of a storybook and diagrammed them, circling verbs and putting squares around the nouns. It seemed an odd game, very different from the spelling bees and the reading aloud Miss Templeton used, but Charlotte was good at it. She liked knowing that every word in the sentence

272

had a place on the funny trees her mother made her draw. In later years, this talent would serve her well.

"You see, this is the trunk of the sentence," Lydia would explain, making a line under the noun and verb, "and the modifiers are the branches. We used to do this for Mr. Gridley when I was your age." Lydia had actually forgotten that Charlotte was still only seven, wouldn't be eight until August. She was teaching her a year above herself, but the child was managing to keep up.

Charlotte tried to imagine her mother as a little girl. "Was Mr. Gridley a nice teacher?" she asked.

"I don't honestly remember him, darling. All I remember was the awful pinafore I had to wear. Since my mother was dead and my nurse didn't know any better, I went off to school every day in a pinafore while the other girls were always dressed in these elegant dresses with little bows and tucks. I hated it."

Charlotte never thought at all about what she wore. As long as she could pick up her skirts and run as fast as the boys, she was happy enough. Imagine caring so much about clothes.

She liked arithmetic, and on the first day, she proudly recited her multiplication tables all the way through the twelves. "I'm the only one who can do that in my grade," Charlotte said proudly, but her mother didn't seem to care.

"Very good," she said in a distracted voice. "Then I won't have to go over numbers with you. I never did like them myself."

The trouble began with penmanship. Lydia sat and watched while Charlotte laboriously copied over a paragraph from the newspaper. Miss Templeton had worked hard with her over the handwriting, but she couldn't seem to control the pencil. Sometimes the loops just flew away from her.

"You curl your arm so far around the top of the paper because you use the wrong hand," Lydia explained. "The position is most unnatural. How silly of me never to notice that before. We shall have to retrain you. Try copying over the same paragraph with your right hand."

"It feels funny," Charlotte said tentatively as she slid the pencil up and down between her fingers. Every letter took a very long time to form, and when she was finally done with the first sentence, it looked as if a five-year-old had written it. They both studied it in silence.

"I like my left hand better," Charlotte said as she switched back.

"Which hand do you use to hold a spoon?" Lydia asked.

"This one," Charlotte said, raising her right.

"And to throw something?"

Charlotte thought for a moment, pretended to pick up a ball. "Same one."

"You see, that's it," her mother said. Charlotte felt like a small scientific discovery. "Your right hand is so much stronger that in time it will control the pen better. You need to strengthen the muscles a bit. Switch the pencil back and try the next sentence."

For Charlotte, penmanship became the black hole in the middle of school, the time that divided the dreading part of the day from the relieved part. Her mother did not act angry or irritated when the letters did not improve, the muscles did not strengthen quickly, the hand jerked its way up along the paper and back down again like a small tired climber against the face of the mountain. But she did not give up either.

"I hate my right hand," Charlotte said to her father on their way back from the barn.

He picked it up and inspected it. "Looks fine to me."

"The muscles aren't strong enough for writing."

"That's what your mother says?"

"Yes," Charlotte said hopefully. Maybe he would try to convince her mother that hands were made equal, that left-handed writers did not have to be switched around in the middle of their lives.

"Well, your mother must know. She's the teacher," he said, and she gave up the hope. He was not going to come to her rescue.

George had decided not to meddle in this latest project of Lydia's. He knew she was trying hard to forget her disappointment about the legislature, and when he thought about her from a distance, he was touched by her childlike determination to be good. But ever since that night when he spoke to her so sharply, they had been nothing but excessively polite to one another. After dinner when he brought up an article in the newspaper or a problem with the town budget, she put down her knitting and looked at him with an expression of exaggerated attention on her face.

"Stop looking at me that way," he muttered one night.

"What way, darling?" she asked.

"That way. As if you're listening very patiently to a stubborn child," he said, folding the newspaper with as much noise as possible.

"You're imagining things, George. I was only trying to concentrate."

Very well, he thought. Two can play this game as well as one. He began to attend the evening meetings of the Northington Finance Board when he had never seen the need to go before. He sat out in the calf barn talking cows with Gino. In May, he went on a long fishing trip in Vermont with Taylor Morris. If Lydia were hurt, she said nothing to him about it. When her belly began to swell, he moved into the narrow bed in the dressing room on the pretense that she would be more comfortable if he left. She agreed without an argument.

Now that Charlotte was the only child at home for most of the day, the hours dragged by. She worked with her mother at the back desk in the parlor from nine until twelve, when Margaret came to get her for lunch. The parlor room was dark and silent, and in those agonizing minutes that went by while she toiled over the letters, she grew aware of each infinitesimal sound beyond the wall of her mother's even, attentive breathing: the bump of a cabinet door in the kitchen, the scratching of a mouse in the wall, the spine-tingling scrape of Smack's rake against the bricks on the terrace outside. Scrape, lift, reach, scrape, she recited in her head, trying to adjust her litany to his timing.

"Now dot's," her mother would say, and she would slip the pencil from her stiff hand and fan the fingers out to release the knots before she bent her head back down over the paper. When the clock bell rang, she counted the quarter hours, sometimes even the seconds if the ticking were loud enough, while her fingers turned the

Elizabeth Winthrop

corners of the letters. Margaret came to get her at twelve, always right on time. They ate lunch together in the children's dining room, and then Charlotte drifted noise-lessly about the house, waiting for the others to get home while her mother napped.

At the end of June, she was released with the boys. "You've done very well, darling," her mother said on their last morning together. "I know it's been hard for you, but we have had our fun too, haven't we?"

"Yes, Mother." But her voice was dull.

"You see, it's awfully important for a girl to be strong in life. You probably won't understand what I mean for a long time, but one day you'll remember and be grateful. I want you never to be afraid of anything the way I was as a child. If you are afraid and you show it, people can take terrible advantage of you."

Charlotte lifted her head. It didn't seem possible that Mother could ever have been afraid. "What were you scared of?" she asked.

Lydia settled back into the chair. "Of the dark. And other things. People, sometimes. I had a very lonely childhood. My brother, John, was quite a bit older and we never got along very well. You're lucky to have Georgie and Oliver. And the new baby next fall."

"It doesn't feel lucky sometimes," Charlotte said.

Lydia laughed. "No, I expect it doesn't. But I want to finish what I was saying. So any little weakness such as this business about your hands, we must catch early and take care of. I once knew a woman who had a deformed hand. It was a terrible thing for her. Of course, yours is not half as bad. And I'm so proud of your pluckiness about it. You haven't complained once."

"Will we have school in the parlor again?" Charlotte asked, crossing her fingers behind her back.

"I'm not sure, darling. It will all depend."

Darling. There was something about the way she leaned on the *r* in that word that made it reverberate and jangle in Charlotte's ear. She wished her mother would say her name instead of that word.

She had been trained to wait to be dismissed. Mother had turned toward the desk, but she didn't seem to be writing anything. Her shoulders were shaking, and Charlotte reached out to touch one as an act of exploration rather than compassion.

When the bone of her finger touched the bone of her mother's shoulder, Lydia stiffened, straightened her back. "That's all, Charlotte," she said sternly, her voice constrained and muffled. "Go along to Margaret now."

She *was* crying. Charlotte could tell because she had often held back her own tears when Georgie or Frank teased her. Why was Mother crying when she talked about being strong? I did something wrong again, Charlotte thought. She's crying about my weak hand, the one that touched her shoulder. She hid the offensive thing in the pocket of her dress and backed out of the room, waiting to see what else might happen. But her mother must have sensed that she was still not alone, because she did not show her face or let her back relax into a curve.

"Go away, Charlotte," she said, the voice as rigid, as packed with emotion as her ramrod back. But Charlotte did not move fast enough.

"GO!" she screamed, and her face when it finally turned was like the exaggerated mask of a scary circus clown, the mouth open, the eyes sliced into slits.

Charlotte fled.

19

The next week construction began.

"Thank the Lord it's happening in the summertime so you children can be out from under," Margaret said at supper. "Don't mash your beets, Oliver. It will not make them taste any better."

"I know, but it makes them go down easier," Oliver said defiantly.

"Oliver."

He put a chunk of beet in his mouth and moved it back and forth without chewing to see if it might miraculously dissolve.

"I'm going to help the men," Georgie announced. He was eleven this summer. He still held himself apart from the others. When the vegetable-picking season began, he was planning to pay Frank to do his share.

"Did Father say you could?" Oliver said, the beet forced down at last. His throat felt sore from the lump of it.

"I didn't ask Father," Georgie said.

Charlotte watched them argue without really listening. She was planning to spend most of her summer in the barn. Her father had given her two cows to milk because she was so good at it. She was going to stay out of the house, away from the dark parlor and the tapping of her mother's feet and the growing feeling that no matter how hard she tried, she would never be able to please her. She turned the fork in her right hand into a pencil and wrote her name on the tablecloth. Her hand still felt clumsy and stiff. And weak. She held it up and looked at it. It didn't look any stronger, but then you can't see the muscles underneath the skin.

"Stop playing, Charlotte, and eat up. If everybody

278

finishes soon, we can walk down to the swimming hole and back before bed," Margaret said. "But if we all dawdle and dandle over this pork roast, we'll have to march right upstairs."

"Do my hands look different?" Charlotte asked, holding them both up.

"They look dirty," Georgie declared.

"They do not," said Oliver. "That's ink."

"Does this one look deformed?" she asked as she waved the left one at them.

"Stop fussing about your hands," Margaret said, her eyes narrowing. "I've never heard such nonsense."

The swimming hole was really just part of the river. In the late afternoons, the farmhands swam down there to wash off the tobacco juice and the cow dust, but during the day the children claimed it. If it were a hot summer, the river dried to a measly trickle by August and they had to be content with wading. But now, at the end of June, the water was deep enough so that whoever dared could climb up the rickety ladder nailed to the poplar tree, grab the thick rope, and swing out over the hole until the right moment came to let go.

Now they stood in a row on the bank and looked down into the glistening black water. "Are you going to try it this year?" Georgie asked Oliver. Oliver was scared of heights.

"I guess so," he said, but he didn't sound very convincing.

"I'm going to use the rope," Charlotte said, and then instantly wished that she could suck the words back into her mouth. She hadn't meant to say anything out loud. It was supposed to be a promise to herself. After all, a girl with a weak hand would never dare trust her weight to the rope. She would prove to Mother that she really was strong. The boys stared at her.

"You're too little," Georgie said in that grownup voice that she despised. "I didn't do it until I was eight and a half and you don't turn eight until August. And Oliver is ten and he hasn't even done it yet."

"I don't have to wait for Oliver," Charlotte said. Her father had taught her to swim in the cow pond up in the pasture last year, but only babies kept on swimming there. She had joined the boys down at the swimming hole as soon as she could dog-paddle across the little pond. For her, swimming was easy.

"Charlotte says she's going to jump off the rope at the swimming hole," Oliver said breathlessly to his mother when she came in to kiss them good night.

"Really? Good for her."

She doesn't think I'll do it, Charlotte thought. But I'll show her.

Oliver the blabbermouth told Frank the next day, which meant he started to torment her about it. He was still mad that she didn't have to go to school with them anymore.

"She's never going to do it," Frank said in the middle of July when all she had done was go up the ladder and stare down into the brown water until everybody began to clamor for their turn and she had to jump or get out of the way. "Gino says if we don't get rain soon, that hole won't be bigger than a puddle. It'll be too late."

The week after that, he had the farmhands betting on her until Louisa got wind of it and made him stop.

It wasn't the height of it that scared her so much. It was knowing when to let go. Because of Frank's constant jeering, Georgie swung over to her side. His father had told him to stay out of the carpenters' way, so Georgie decided his summer project would be teaching Charlotte the jump. "It's just timing," he said. "Watch. You grab the rope, push off, swing out and then back a little before you drop." The echo of the last word followed him down until it was swallowed by his splash. And if you hang on too long, you miss, Charlotte thought as they all waited for that magic moment when he resurfaced.

"I wish I'd never said anything about the rope," Charlotte confided to Margaret.

"You don't have to do it," Margaret said. "Nobody really cares. They'll forget in a few days."

Mother won't, Charlotte thought to herself. She wants me to be strong.

Some days, when she wasn't too tired, their mother went down to the swimming hole with them to get away from the sawdust and the incessant hammering. The baby was sticking out pretty far in front. Her mother didn't walk normally anymore, Charlotte noticed from behind. She waddled.

"Maybe Charlotte will do it today," Oliver said one afternoon. "Now that you're here to watch."

"Do what, darling?"

"Jump from the rope, Mother," Oliver said. "Don't you remember?"

"Oh yes. Well, she's awfully young to try that."

She forgot all about it, Charlotte thought, her fury rising. "I'm not too young," she announced in a loud voice.

Her mother turned around and put out her other hand in a conciliatory way, but Charlotte scuffed along in the dust without taking it.

"So you'll do it today?" Oliver asked.

"Be quiet, Oliver. I'll do it when I do it."

With everybody waiting down on the bank, she took her daily trip to the top of the ladder. Georgie was coaching from below.

"Here now, I'll swing the rope to you. Don't lean out too far to get it. Wait. I'll do it again."

Her arm clung to the top rung, and on the second swing the rope came right for her. She reached out and stopped it before it hit her in the face. Down below, Frank was lying on his back in the grass.

"She'll never do it," he jeered, his arms folded under his head. Her mother looked up, her two hands lifted to shade her eyes from the sun.

A breeze stirred the leaves around Charlotte's head, and down below she could see ripples on the surface of the water. She shivered. The thick rope felt scratchy in her palm. How could she possibly let go and give it all her weight? What if the muscles in her bad hand weren't strong enough yet?

"Don't look down," Georgie called.

This was the time. She knew she had to do it this once or she would never crawl up this ladder again all summer. She would never come down to the swimming hole.

Her mother was not looking anymore. She was fiddling with something in the grass. She was tired of waiting.

"Mother, watch," Charlotte screamed just before she pushed off, her fingers wrapped around the fat rope but sliding a little, just a little, as she plummeted down the arc, up again toward the trees on the other side of the river, then backwards.

"Let go now!" Georgie ordered, and out of fear she obeyed. Before she hit the water, she saw that they were all sitting bolt upright, staring at her. With her arms straight up, she shot down into the murky green like a stone hurled off the edge of a bridge until, to her surprise, her feet touched the slimy leaves at the bottom and she was able to push herself back up toward the light.

"She did it," Oliver was yelling as she surfaced.

Her mother watched her with an odd smile as she scrambled up the muddy bank. "Were you awfully scared, darling?"

"No, Mother," Charlotte lied. She wrapped herself in her towel.

"Isn't she brave?" Oliver asked proudly.

"Very brave," their mother said. "But the bravest thing of all is to do something that you're very scared to do."

"What did she mean by that?" Charlotte asked Margaret that night when she came to tuck her in.

"I expect she was just talking to herself," Margaret said. She was not. She was talking to me, Charlotte decided. It wasn't good enough. The jump wasn't good enough for her. She went to sleep with the pillow bunched up like a hot-water bottle against the sick, sad feeling in her stomach.

One night, Lydia dreamt that she was growing a stone inside of her. When she beat on her belly in her nightmare, she bruised her knuckles against the hard wall of it. She woke, gasping, and reached for George. But he wasn't there beside her. He didn't sleep with her anymore. With the construction disrupting everything, he had moved down to the office in the calf barn for the summer.

It was an excuse, of course, the way the pregnancy had been. They could have both moved down to the calf barn or over to the Morrises'. But they barely spoke to one another, and the stone inside her was a growing hardness against him. He had abandoned her, let go of her hands, and she was sliding away from him toward the lip of the black hole inside.

"It's the renovation of the house," Isabelle Morris said when Lydia went round for tea and consolation. "I can't understand why George insisted on doing it at this moment with you in this condition. Surely, one little baby could have been squashed in somewhere. Taylor slept in a closet until he was four, or so his mother has led me to believe."

Lydia smiled at the picture and then, without any warning, she started to cry. "I'm sorry," she said. "I don't know what's wrong with me. I must be tired."

Action was Isabelle's solution to everything. By that night, she had moved Lydia into her old room on the second floor, the one she stayed in when she and George were courting. "Complete bed rest is what you need. George may come and visit and the children occasionally, but I shall be your guard dog and growl at anybody else. From what I understand there is nothing a mother needs more than a mother at a time like this. So I've appointed myself. Even though I don't know a thing about it." She showed Lydia the bell rope and left her to rest.

Isabelle kept her promise and drove everybody away. All through the month of August, hotter than usual, and into September, Lydia let herself drift. The baby grew and twisted inside her, butting its head up against her ribs and then turning somersaults and using its feet. She thought of the baby as an it and herself as a boat bearing the cargo, the stone, slowly, inexorably toward the shore.

When George came, he sat on the far chair like any other visitor, twisting his Panama hat round and round in his hands while he told her about the progress on the house or the daily small calamities on the farm. She listened politely, the way she would pay attention to a companion at dinner, and when he asked her for a decision on anything, she told him to make it.

"We must decide what's to be done about Charlotte's schooling," he said one afternoon. She had closed her eyes against the distance in his face, the courteous attitude of his straight back. "The two ladies in West Hartford have sent me notice that their school will open in

September. I think we should enroll her. She could go in on the milk wagon with the boys."

"Yes," Lydia said, the air of the word escaping like a whistle through her lips.

"Yes, what?"

"Yes, send her to school in West Hartford. Yes, George; no, George; anything you say, George."

He stood up and she opened her eyes again. They stared at one another, and for a moment, she thought he might do something violent, molest her with his mouth or slap her across the face, she didn't know which.

"When will you move back?" he asked.

"When the house is ready, I suppose. And how about you? When will you move back?"

"Whenever you do."

"I don't mean your body, George. God knows, I have no use for that right now." So cruel, I didn't mean to be so cruel. I take it back, George. But she didn't. She went on. "When is your heart moving back in with me?"

He jammed his hat on his head and walked out without answering her.

In the afternoons, she sat in the garden and watched the trees give up their leaves. She was sketching again, an occupation she had put aside when she went to work, and she found pleasure in it. She told George that she wanted to use the porch off their bedroom for painting. "Little Georgie and I shall work there. I think he's quite talented, don't you?"

"I suppose so," he said warily. "I haven't paid much attention. Charlotte's now milking two cows."

"The family dairymaid," she scoffed. "Charlotte's got to learn other skills as well." The angry words dropped out of her mouth like small pellets, babies to the great stone.

"The children miss you, Lydia."

And she felt that old knife slipping into her ribs, that old twist of helplessness. Isabelle had taken her in, allowed her to enjoy some respite from it.

"Thank God for Margaret," was all she said.

"They want to come see you," he said. He had mentioned this before.

"No," she cried, suddenly wild. "No. Not yet. I couldn't bear it. I need this peace."

He went away again, shaking his head.

"There's something very wrong with me," Lydia said to Isabelle one morning in the garden. "Louisa rejoices in her children, gathers them to her like a mother hen and doesn't care whether they're bleeding or muddy or their hands are sticky. I seem to have no patience at all for mine. I don't miss them, Isabelle. I don't want to see them."

"That's why you've got Margaret," Isabelle said in a matter-of-fact voice.

"I know. And I resent her for being able to do what I am incapable of doing. After all, Margaret lost her mother when she was just a child too. If I use my motherless childhood as an excuse, how is it possible that she's so good at taking care of my children?"

"Because they're not hers," Isabelle said, swinging her wheelchair around to move her face out of the sun. "Lydia, this brooding is doing you no good. God gives us all talents in different directions. You wouldn't berate yourself like this if you found you were unable to drive a motorcar or paint a picture or speak in public."

"But women are supposed to be mothers."

"I'm not." They looked at one another. "The reasons here are not physical, Lydia," Isabelle said quietly, "although I am content to let everybody believe it. I could have borne a child if I had wanted to. Remember, I am confined to this wheelchair because of arthritis. I am not in any way paralyzed."

"How did you—" Lydia stopped. The question was too intimate.

"Taylor and I came to an understanding long ago," she said. "And I think our marriage has survived because of it. Whom he sees and what he does when he is not with me is of no interest to me." She turned the chair again, and Lydia knew it was her way of ending this particular conversation.

"Mother is never ever coming back," Oliver announced mournfully. They were all in the vegetable garden, picking the squash. It was a boring, dusty job, and even

Georgie had to do it because Frank said he didn't care about the money anymore. There was nothing to spend it on anyway.

"Don't be ridiculous, Oliver," Georgie said. "She's gone away for a rest."

"It's very hard work making a baby," Charlotte said. "We're too noisy for her."

"I wish my mother would have a baby," Clara said in her soft voice. Charlotte made a face at her behind her back. Clara was a Goody Two-shoes. Her dress wasn't even dusty, whereas Charlotte looked as if she'd been making mud pies all afternoon.

"Your mother can't have a baby," Georgie scoffed.

"She can too," Frank said defensively. "Anytime she wants to." He was throwing the squash at the basket from the end of his row, and half the time he was missing. Dorothy was going to be furious.

"She needs a husband to make it with," Charlotte said firmly. Oliver had just explained all those things to her last week.

Frank stood up and marched threateningly down the row toward her. "She does not. My mother can do anything she wants," he yelled.

"Uh-oh," breathed Oliver.

"Forget it, Frank," Georgie said wearily. They were all sick of his moods.

"Anything, you hear me," he screamed in Charlotte's ear.

"Not this," said Charlotte very quietly, still hunting in the squash vines. The next thing she knew she was sitting on the ground on her bottom.

"Watch it, Frank," Oliver shouted.

"Come on, sissy, what're you going to do about it?" Frank yelled.

Without any warning, Charlotte grabbed him around the knees, and with a sudden shift of her weight, she was able to knock him off balance. He landed in the middle of two rows of corn. Then without waiting around to see what he'd say next, she took off in the direction of the barn. She had always been a good runner, and the first time she looked back, he was still struggling to his feet, pulling uselessly at the stalks of corn for support. The second time he was headed her way and closing fast.

Around the corner of the barn, down the long side past the tiny windows crusted with hay and dirt and right past her father, who was walking in the opposite direction. She wasn't going to take her troubles to him. In their world, that was against the rules. But he reached out with a long tan arm and stopped her dead.

"Tollgate," he teased. "Pay the toll."

"Let me go, Father," she gasped.

"Pay the toll."

"What is it?"

"Information," he said. "What are you running from?"

"Frank," she said, and twisted away, but he caught her again, this time by the collar.

"Never run from trouble," he said. "Turn around and face it."

"He's bigger than me."

"So? Goliath was bigger than David."

Frank came around the corner of the barn, but at the sight of Mr. Webster, his sprint slowed to a fast walk.

"I understand that you two have some business to conduct," her father said.

"She knocked me over," Frank shouted.

"You did it first."

Her father stepped back and shrugged. "It's your fight to settle," he said. "Don't look at me."

"You mean it's all right with you if I beat her up?" Frank asked, astounded.

"Charlotte's old enough to fight her own fights."

It was too late to start running again, but she could dodge. She was good at that too. Frank was big but slow. When he lunged at her the first time, she squatted down and he threw himself right over her. His booted foot caught her in the chin and she felt the blow travel up through her jawbone. When he threw himself back on top of her, she kicked and squirmed away before he could pin her down. She had no time to look directly at her father, but out of the corner of her eye she could see that his position hadn't changed. He really wasn't going to stop this.

The fight seemed to last forever. Georgie and Oliver arrived breathless and joined their father. Over and over in the rutted side lane, he jumped and she twisted away. They both knew the rules. Whoever could pin the other down for a count of ten won. At last, he managed to get to eight, counting fast, before she lifted her head and sunk her teeth into his dusty wrist.

"Not fair," he cried, rolling away. He sat up and rubbed at the wound.

"Anything's fair," she spat, on her feet again, swaying back and forth in a crouch.

"Oh, go away," he said. "You're just a stupid girl who fights dirty."

"Are you giving up, Frank?" Oliver cried.

"You're next, sissy," Frank muttered, but they all knew it was a false threat. He struggled to his feet and walked away without another word. When he was safely out of sight, Charlotte sank to the ground with a grateful sigh.

"All right, boys, go on back to work," her father said, and they obeyed. She liked to think that they were glancing over their shoulders at her with a new look of respect.

"Ready for a swim?" her father asked, lifting her under the arms like a rag doll until she found her feet and felt steady on them.

"The swimming hole's dried up," she said. She was grateful for his arm around her shoulders. Her muscles were already beginning to ache.

"We'll go up to the pasture. To the cow pond. Afterward, we'll help the boys drive the cows down for milking."

"All right," she said. "I'll go change."

"Nonsense. You can swim in your clothes. It'll wash you and them at the same time. That should please Margaret."

She giggled at the thought.

They didn't say a word to each other all the way up through the pasture. He slowed his walk to match hers, and when she looked behind, she could see the tall grass that had been flattened by their passing already rising slowly back up to its natural position.

"What was the fight about?" he asked once they had swum the width of the pond.

For a moment, she couldn't remember. "Babies. I said his mother couldn't have one because she doesn't have a husband. I was right, wasn't I?"

He grinned, a private joke. "Yes, you were right. But remember, Frank has lost his father and he feels it keenly enough. He doesn't need reminders."

Sitting on the bank, she squeezed the water out of her skirts, twisting one section and then another.

"You fought well."

She didn't answer but filed the compliment away to be brought out later and savored.

In the distance, they heard the shouts of the men coming up into the pasture. "Time to go. Those cows are ready for milking."

She took his hand on the way down, something she hadn't done in a long time. "When is Mother coming home?" she asked.

He let his breath out evenly in a long vibrating whistle. "I'm not sure, Charlotte. Soon. When the house is done. The noise and dust bothers her."

"Oliver says she's never coming home."

"That's nonsense." But he said it so quickly that she heard the worry in his voice.

"She went away because of me," she said in a small voice. "I make her very angry sometimes."

"So do I," he said, looking straight ahead. "But we can't help who we are, can we? None of us."

It was a peculiar answer, not the one she had expected at all. She decided that she had stumbled over a grownup truth, an important treasure. When she got home, she wrote her father's words down on a piece of paper and stared at them. After a few days, their significance faded away and she realized he had said that just to keep her quiet. Of course, people could help who they were. They had to fix the wrong things, make them better, change themselves when someone else wanted them to.

The baby was born in the middle of a warm October night across the town line in Farmington. Taylor went for George himself, but by the time the two men returned it was all over.

"It's a boy," Isabelle whispered. "Don't wake Lydia.

It went quickly, but the pains were very bad. Thank God the midwife lives close by. Dr. Ramsay still hasn't turned up." She wrapped the blanket more tightly about the child and handed him inexpertly up to George. "Here you go," she said. "I don't feel exactly comfortable with this. She said to tell you she wants his name to be Campbell. It was the closest thing to Isabelle she could come up with."

They smiled at one another over the sleeping baby.

Lydia came home two weeks later and moved into the sumptuous new bedroom at the opposite end of the second floor from the nursery. Under Margaret's direction, the children had all written her welcome letters.

"Dear Mother," read Georgie's, "I hope you like your lukshureows new budwar. Oliver says funny things in his sleep. I hope Baby Campbell doesn't talk in his sleep or you will have to stay up all night like me and you will be very tired."

"Dear Mother," Oliver wrote, "Whatever Georgie says isn't true. I wish I had a room to myself like Charlotte's. I'm glad you're home. I got everything right on my arithmetic test yesterday."

Charlotte didn't want to write a letter.

"All right," Margaret said, knowing why. "Draw a picture, then."

"I'll draw one for the baby," Charlotte said, which is what she did. If Lydia noticed that there was no letter from her daughter, she never mentioned it.

20

Charlotte wanted to hold the baby all the time, but she was sure there was something wrong with the feeling. After all, she had put her doll away last year, stuffed her in the very bottom of the trunk that smelled of mothballs. But this was a real baby that drooled and hiccuped and clung to her hair or her nose with an indiscriminate sweaty grasp. This was a baby with blanket lint caught in the damp folds of his fingers.

Margaret let her help whenever she wanted.

"It's good practice for you," she said.

But when her mother came into the room and found them, Charlotte felt uneasy, as if she had been caught doing something wrong, something dirty. Her mother seemed to like the baby. She hung over Campbell's changing table and talked baby talk to him while Margaret stood aside and waited.

"Did Mother talk that way to me when I was a baby?" Charlotte asked.

"Yes," Margaret said, giving her a steady look. "Mothers always do that with their babies."

"When do they stop doing it?"

"When the babies don't need it anymore."

"How do they know that the babies don't need it anymore?" Charlotte asked.

"Because the babies get up and walk around and talk and read and ride bicycles," Margaret said in her teasing voice, and Charlotte went away to think.

The nursery was Charlotte's favorite place, her haven from school. Miss Norton and Miss Wentwood turned out to be very dry, humorless teachers.

"Cross your fingers that you don't get Norton," Ellen,

291

her new friend, whispered to her. "She's the absolute worst."

Charlotte did as she was told and she got Norton.

"Stand up straight, Miss Webster, or your shoulders will become permanently curled. Breathe in, breathe out, breathe in, breathe out." Elocution was very important to Miss Norton. Correct pronunciation. "The lifting of the diaphragm," she would say in a high voice that had peculiar lifts of its own. She did not hesitate to punish children who didn't try hard enough. Charlotte turned herself inside out for Miss Norton, but she could never please. In March, after nine agonizing months of Miss Norton, she began to stutter.

"I don't know where it comes from," she confided to Margaret one night, close to tears. "I open my mouth and the word just hangs there on the edge. I can't spit it out, so I just keep saying it over and over."

"This is ridiculous," Margaret said, in a real fury this time.

"Please, please don't do anything. Don't tell Mother. I'll get better. Do you promise, Margaret? If you tell Mother, it will just get worse."

Margaret promised. "I won't do anything for now," she said.

Charlotte stopped talking in front of people. She smiled and nodded and shook hands firmly as she had been taught.

"Such a sweet, shy child" was the verdict of Mrs. Ridley, who came one afternoon for tea.

"I've never thought of my daughter as sweet or shy," Lydia reported to George that night. "I don't like it. Makes her sound mousy."

"Our," said George.

"Our what?"

"Our daughter," he said. They exchanged a look. "I don't think she's very happy in the school," he went on. "Those two women look like carved pumpkins that have been left out on the porch for too long. Their faces have caved in." He pulled in his lips and made an appropriate imitation. She smiled an appropriate smile.

After the birth of Campbell and her return to the expanded house, the two of them had worked their way back toward each other like people lost in a snowstorm, hands in front, calling out, listening for echoes before trying another direction. They talked easily of politics as they always had but tested the waters of other subjects hesitantly. Charlotte had barely come up at all, which was a relief to George. Lydia's spotlight had swung in another direction for a while, back onto herself and Republican state politics. Although she had not yet announced it publicly, she was intending to run for the legislature in a year.

"It's certainly much better than the local school," Lydia said now. "Charlotte's bright and she deserves schooling that's just as good as the boys'. Unfortunately, I don't have the time anymore to tutor her myself. It's all I can do to keep up the painting classes with Georgie on Monday afternoons."

"Why don't you teach painting to all the children?" George asked.

"Because Georgie is very talented. He's the one who can most benefit from it."

George had seen to it that Lydia got her painting porch. It opened up off their bedroom and faced south over the orchard and the calf barn, toward the town of Northington. In the winter she could see the spire of the Congregational church and the Farmington hills in the distance through the bare black branches of the elm tree. "It should be northern light, of course," she said to Georgie, "but we shall have to muddle through with what we've got."

The other children pretended to pity Georgie when their mother came to pick him up for the "painting class."

"Poor Georgie," they said when they heard her feet tapping along the upstairs hallway. The children always gathered in the nursery after school to do their homework while Campbell hitched himself around the floor under their feet and Margaret supervised.

Charlotte was secretly envious of Georgie, although she was careful not to show it. One of the unspoken rules of the house was that you couldn't say how you really felt about anything, particularly if it upset Mother. If you wanted to paint and Mother didn't want you to, it was best to pretend you didn't care one little bit about painting.

But Charlotte did love to paint and she longed to show Mother how good she was in order to make up for the uneven handwriting, which now Miss Norton found unreadable. Sometimes, secretly, she went back to using her left hand, but it had stiffened up too, so that neither one seemed to work smoothly for her when she had to form letters. But painting was different. The large white expanse of paper and the liquid flow of the paint released all the tightness in her hands. Margaret hung the pictures on the nursery walls, but her mother never commented on them. When it came to painting, she concentrated on Georgie. After all, he was the most talented.

"What does talented mean?" Charlotte asked Margaret.

"That you're good at something," said Margaret.

What am I good at? Charlotte thought, but she didn't say it out loud. In the old days Margaret might have guessed at the unspoken question and answered it, but now with the baby always on her hip or in her lap, she was more distracted. She didn't have as much time to figure out Charlotte's thoughts. Charlotte missed their times alone together, but then she loved baby Campbell. How could she want him to go away and love him at the same time? It was very confusing.

Charlotte managed to keep the stuttering a secret from her mother for almost a month.

Lydia's fledgling organization, the Connecticut League of Republican Women, had languished in her absence, and now she turned the full force of her energy on reviving it with an eye toward the next state election. J. Henry Roraback was still in complete control of the Republican Party in the state, and the last thing he wanted was an organized group of females who were not under his thumb. In May, Lydia traveled from one Northington house to the next, begging the women to register and vote in the caucus which Roraback had called to elect the new Republican town chairman. Harold Butler was Roraback's candidate. Lydia supported a young fellow named Nathan Green. To everybody's surprise, the women turned out in large numbers to elect Green as Republican town chairman and Lydia as vice-chairman.

After the caucus, an impromptu party was held at the Websters' and the children were brought downstairs to say hello.

"I don't want to go," Oliver said grumpily. "I hate getting all dressed up."

"Mother is practically the president," Georgie announced.

"Not quite," said Margaret as she bent over the white satin bow on Charlotte's dress. "But well on her way to it."

"I'm scared of all those people," Charlotte whispered, but not loud enough for anybody to hear.

The front parlor room was filled with strangers who all seemed to be shouting at one another. Their mother stood in the corner by the piano. She was surrounded by a group of enthusiastic supporters. Charlotte tried to catch her father's eye, but he had bent his head close to a gray-haired man who was lecturing him about something. Georgie led the way through the tightly packed bodies with Margaret and Campbell bringing up the rear. Oliver hung on to Charlotte's sash and would not let go no matter how hard she tried to shake him off. The news of their arrival preceded them.

"Children," Lydia said in an approving voice. "Here you are." She reached out her arms and Margaret passed Campbell over their heads. "Now I want you all to meet Mr. Green, our new Republican town chairman. This is Georgie and Oliver and my daughter, Charlotte."

Dutifully, they put up their hands, and the tall man shook his way down the row. When he got to Charlotte, he squatted down in front of her so their eyes were at the same level.

"Now, little girl," he boomed. His hot breath tickled her nose. "What do you think of your mother's success?"

The crowd about them quieted as they waited for her answer. She smiled and nodded without saying anything.

"Come on now, Miss Charlotte, you must have some word to give us. Whenever anybody asks your mother a question, she certainly has a lot to say." Everybody laughed, and Charlotte was sure they would go back to their talking. But the noise subsided, and she realized they were all looking at her again. What did they want her to do? She didn't even understand the tall man's question. Margaret's hand came down to rest on her shoulder, and she leaned back against it.

"Darling, Mr. Green asked you a question," her mother said.

"I-I-I—" She closed her mouth firmly again. It was the "I" that always repeated itself like that, bounced up and down over and over again in her mouth like one of Georgie's balls against the wall of the house.

Lydia handed Campbell back to Margaret and knelt down in front of Charlotte. Some of the people had begun to whisper to one another. Charlotte shivered.

"Take your time, darling. What did you want to say?"

But Charlotte would not try again. She knew from Miss Norton's elocution classes that each time she attacked the word, the bouncing in her mouth only got worse. She pulled backwards, and before anybody could reach out a hand and catch her, she snaked her way along the tunnels between the people, jostling a silk dress here, a suited elbow there.

Margaret found her an hour later hiding in the branches of the elm tree. She settled herself on the windowsill and looked through the yellow green leaves down to the terrace below.

"It's nice up here. A good hiding place."

With the bones of her back pressed against the bumpy bark, Charlotte pulled her knees further into her chest. "My secret place," she said.

"Your mother wants to see you before you go to bed," Margaret said.

"Do I-I-I have to go?"

The question was silly, and Margaret didn't bother to answer it. Down below, some guests were saying good-bye. They shook hands with George, kissed Lydia on both cheeks with that smooth practiced dipping of heads that reminded Charlotte of a rooster strutting around the chicken yard.

"She's going to be angry at me," Charlotte said.

"Not angry," Margaret said. "Concerned."

"She wants to fix things about me. Like my hand."

"You're not a bloody machine," Margaret muttered with such ferocity that Charlotte looked up in surprise. "I'll have a talk with her first."

"No, please don't. Don't make her angry," Charlotte cried.

"Who's that?" called Lydia's voice from below. Charlotte shrank even farther back, praying to disappear.

"It's me, Mrs. Webster," Margaret said. "I'm just helping Charlotte get ready for bed."

"All right. Send her down to my room when you're done, please."

She insisted on going alone, dressed in her cotton nightgown and her favorite slippers, an old red pair of Oliver's. Margaret stood in the doorway and watched the small brave figure turn and wave at the corner the way she used to do when she walked to school with the Delbiancos.

"I'll wait here," Margaret called, and Charlotte nodded to say she had heard.

She came back just twenty minutes later, just as bravely, her bony shoulders pulled back so far that even Miss Norton would have approved.

"We're going to meet every day," she said, trying to sound cheery. "It's called stuttering. Mother says it's very easy to correct. Just like-like-like"—she stopped, took a deep breath—"my hand. Every day in the porch. Right-right-right after Georgie's painting class."

Margaret nodded without touching her, knowing how fragile the child's nonchalant façade, how close to crying she must be. She tucked her into bed and left her staring up at the ceiling.

Charlotte hadn't told Margaret everything her mother had said. "One day, you might grow up to be like me, darling. You might have to travel around the country making speeches," she had said. "I couldn't make speeches if I spoke that way, could I?" "No, Mother," Charlotte had said, but inside a little voice of defiance cried: I don't ever want to be like you. And the inside "I" did not bounce around, repeating itself. It came out just fine.

At the other end of the hall, George was watching Lydia undress.

"Such a strange thing to have her suddenly start this," Lydia said as she rubbed cream into the dry spots at the corner of her eyes. She had never been vain, but she was more aware of her looks than ever before. The gray hair pleased her now because she thought it made her look experienced.

"I noticed the stuttering a while ago," George said. He was sitting up in the bed with his bare arms crossed behind his head. In the warm months, he went to sleep dressed only in his boxer shorts. "Margaret says she's scared of Miss Norton."

"I'm sure we can correct it perfectly easily. I've made some time for her after the painting class."

That will be a disaster, George thought, but he said nothing. The caress of her hand across her own face was beginning to arouse him, and he was reluctant to argue with her about Charlotte now. Lydia was full of energy and confidence after the excitement of the caucus, and he had learned over the years that her body yielded most to his when she was in this mood.

Later, when he had given her a last kiss and rolled away into sleep, she lay awake, celebrating her victories. She was really on her way now, back in control of her life after the queasy, unsure months of her pregnancy when all she could do was lie on her bed and think. She could organize the women, get the votes out, make love with George with grace if not real pleasure, and still give her children the attention they needed. So many different Lydias to call on, so many walls of defense erected against the old black pit inside.

During the forty minutes that Lydia spent with Charlotte every afternoon, the whole house seemed to freeze and listen. In the nursery, Margaret was distracted, her ear cocked to the open doorway, her hands soothing Campbell with uncharacteristically hurried gestures. The older boys learned to whisper over their homework during that time or else they would catch it from Margaret. Nancy, the maid, was the only one who had any excuse to go near there. She brought Mrs. Webster the tea tray in the painting porch. There was always a glass of milk and a plate of cookies for Charlotte, but Dorothy noticed they usually came back untouched.

"Poor little chicken, she's trying so hard to say the words the right way, it's no wonder she doesn't eat anything," Nancy reported to the group assembled in the kitchen.

"Does Mrs. Webster get angry?" Dorothy asked. She loved details.

"No, not exactly. Just very firm. 'Try it again, Charlotte. Use the muscles in your mouth to control the words. I want to go to the island.' And then the little girl starts in again." Nancy shrugged. "It doesn't seem to me to be getting any better."

"It's not," said Margaret in an icy voice.

She had been to speak to Mr. Webster about it more than once, because she had promised Charlotte she wouldn't say anything to her mother. The most recent conversation had occurred just a week before.

"She doesn't sleep well at night, sir," Margaret said. "I hear her repeating things to herself when I go by the room. Won't the stuttering just disappear on its own if we don't pay any attention to it? I have a feeling it's getting worse."

George did not look directly at her, because he agreed with her and he was sure she would see it in his eyes. Lydia was fanatic on the subject of Charlotte's "little problem." And her patience with the child was unbelievable. She never lost her temper, never got discouraged, always found the time for their session together no matter how full her day had become.

"Mrs. Webster knows what's best," he said, and Margaret stood up without another word and walked away.

As for Charlotte, she watched the seasons change in the paintings on the porch. On winter days, Smack came up and lit the little wood stove in the corner of the room around noon, so that it was toasty warm once the painting class began, and when Charlotte arrived at four-thirty, the smell of linseed oil and turpentine had mingled with cedar smoke. Georgie's latest painting would be resting on his easel next to his mother's. They painted their way through the year: the stark white horizon pierced by the church spire in the winter, a vase of flowers from the perennial garden in the summer, falling leaves in the autumn. Sometimes, her mother would still be standing to the side studying a painting with tilted head when Charlotte came noiselessly into the room and found her seat.

"Now, here's a good judge," her mother would say to Georgie. "Tell us what you think of the angle Georgie's picked, Charlotte. I think he's looking at the scene from too far above the ground."

Charlotte would think and think, trying to create some perfect sentence about the painting, and then she would work it out of her mouth through the grate of her clenched jaw. They listened respectfully and then continued their discussion without asking her opinion again.

She grew to hate the smell of the paint. Margaret unknowingly gave her a very special set of oils for Christmas, thirty-six smooth little tubes in a wooden box with a separate palette that lifted out. Underneath the palette in a scooped-out tray that was just the right size, she found two boar's-hair brushes, a palette knife, and a miniature bottle of linseed oil. The year before it would have been her absolutely favorite present.

"Thank you so much," Charlotte had said from her place by the tree. "It's beautiful."

They both knew without saying anything that it was all wrong.

"What a lovely thing for you to do, Margaret," Lydia said. She was sitting in her customary corner of the sofa, waiting for everybody else to finish. She always saved her presents until the end.

Charlotte pushed the paint box away and reached out for Campbell, who was trying to grab an ornament from the lowest branch of the tree.

In the summer of 1924, Lydia started her campaign for the legislature. As she told George, not a single human being in the Northington district wanted her to run.

"Not even the women?" he asked.

"No. They could stomach the idea of a woman as vice-chairman but a legislator? Never." She grinned. "I like a good fight. I shall simply badger them to death."

And she did. She sat in their kitchens while they made

bread, she pulled their children onto her lap and let them play with the change in her pocketbook, she followed their men into the barn and sat on the milking stool talking while they worked.

"I think I'm getting somewhere," she reported in July. "Even Jack Gardner has said he'd rather vote for me than a Democrat. And thanks to Louisa, every eligible woman in the district is registered to vote."

As her days began to fill up, she gave up teas with Isabelle, sometimes even the painting class, but never the sessions with Charlotte.

George tried once more. "Give her the summer off, Lydia. She needs to have some fun too."

"She has fun all day long, George. I'm surprised at you. And I think we're really getting somewhere."

"You are too fanatical about it," George warned her, but he didn't say any more because he had his own problems to worry about. For the second year in a row, a late June hailstorm had wiped out the tobacco crop. "In one day," he said to Nort. "All that goddamned money down the drain."

"It's a pity, boss."

"You have a remarkable capacity for understatement, Nort," George said in a rare moment of sarcasm. "Well, we're done with the goddamned thing. Finished. We're going to let those fields go back to pasture next year. If I'm lucky, I'll get some money back from the sale of the laths and the tents. Put that into cows."

"What about the men? We'll have to let some of them go," Nort said.

George nodded. "I'll go over and talk to Pete Winston in the fuse factory. He'll take them on there. Jesus, Nort, don't look at me like that. I can't keep throwing money down the drain for nothing. This is supposed to be a business."

Nort shrugged. "Them Italians don't like to work inside. They're farmers, not factory workers."

On Charlotte's tenth birthday, Margaret took the children to the tower field for a picnic. The tower stood at the very top of Northington Mountain. You could see it from the center of town, from the calf barn, from the river, from Route 10 as the road wound out of the valley. A wealthy German baron had ordered it built at the beginning of the century as the first wing of his country house. Once the tower was finished, he brought his wife to see it. This was going to be her escape from the noise and dirt of the city, her little piece of the country. But she hated it, so the baron abandoned the whole idea and sold the tower to the town of Northington for a dollar.

Northington was proud of its tower. It put the little town on the map. A picnic up in the field and a climb to the top, where you could look down over the whole valley, was a child's idea of a perfect Sunday outing.

"Can we climb it today?" Oliver asked on their way up the path.

"Ask Charlotte," Margaret said. "It's her birthday."

"Can we, Charlotte?"

"No," said Charlotte. "We won't have time." Not if we have to get back for my class with Mother.

The day was blue and brisk, one of those days that come in August to remind you that fall and school and dry leaves are just around the corner. But the sun was hot and the children played a game of tag in the newly mown field. Even Georgie forgot his important thirteen-year-old self and chased after the others, shrieking when they pulled his shirt and rolling down the hill with the rest of them. At the bottom, they lay on their backs and waited for the sky above to stop twirling. As the day wore on, Carlotte pulled out of the games.

"We'd better go back," she said to Margaret. "Mother will be waiting."

"We're not going back today," Margaret said firmly. "It's your birthday. No class on your birthday."

"Did you ask Mother?"

"No. It's my decision. Time for cake, everybody," she called to the others, and they came running to flop themselves down on the blanket. "Think of your wish now, Charlotte," Margaret said. "You and the wind will be blowing out the candles together."

"What is it?" Oliver asked. He had grown close to his sister in the last year. They shared secrets and defended one another against the loftiness of Georgie, the intrusions of Campbell. They were lumped together in the

302

middle of the family, and although their fights were fought with great ferocity, their truces were just as meaningful.

"You aren't supposed to tell your wishes," Georgie said.

They all looked at Charlotte and waited. "I-I-I—" She stopped.

"Ready to blow?" Margaret asked gently.

"I"—she took a deep breath—"wish that I"—this one with iron jaw—"stop stuttering soon."

"Everybody make a wall around the cake to block the wind," Margaret said. They pulled together in a tight circle, heads together, and in the silence that followed, Margaret lit the candles as fast as possible.

"Blow quickly, Charlotte," Oliver cried, and she did, but the wind must have gotten to some of them first, because her wish didn't come true.

Lydia had been waiting for an hour on the back porch. By the time she finally saw them straggling down the pasture path, she had worked herself into a rage, and the sight of Margaret, stepping calmly along in front, singing one of her marching songs, fueled the fire. The woman knew damn well what time it was.

The tension had grown between them lately. Lydia knew Margaret did not approve of the afternoon sessions, although she had never spoken to Mrs. Webster directly about them. In fact, she had grown almost insolent in the last months. She received her instructions in silence and spoke to Lydia only when it was absolutely necessary. Lydia had let the situation slide along, but it was time to put a stop to it.

"Where have you been?"

Margaret walked silently up to the top step. Lydia had to retreat in order to make room for her on the porch. "We've been on Charlotte's birthday picnic," she said.

Scattered down the steps behind her, the children peeked around at their mother. She was aware of their eyes, the flush of sun on their cheeks, the frowns just appearing as they heard the exchange.

"I came home early for my class with Charlotte," Lydia said. Every word had a distinct ending to it. The two women were standing very close together.

"All of you go upstairs," Margaret said, patting each one on the head as they passed. "Charlotte, please change Campbell's diaper. I will be up in a minute."

Charlotte hung back when she reached the back steps.

"Come on," Oliver whispered fiercely.

"Take Campbell," she said, and handed him over.

"Charlotte is not going to have any more classes," Margaret said as they walked into the empty kitchen. "Not as long as I am still working here."

"Margaret, I don't think I understand you."

"I will not see that child tormented any longer. I have spoken to Mr. Webster three or four times about it and the only reason I have not come to you before is because your daughter begged me not to."

"I *know* you are not telling me how to bring up my children," Lydia said, and from her hiding place, Charlotte cringed at the patronizing tone in her voice. Didn't her mother hear how she sounded to other people?

"That's exactly what I am telling you," Margaret said.

"Will you come through to the living room so that we can sit down and talk this over, please?"

"No," Margaret said. "I feel more comfortable in the kitchen."

At that point, Oliver came down the dark stairs and dragged Charlotte back up with him. They both knew if she fought him or cried out, the women in the kitchen would hear.

"Why did you do that?" Charlotte asked, feeling angry and relieved at the same time. Margaret's cold, sure voice had scared her even more than her mother's anger.

"So you wouldn't get caught," Oliver said. "Now, come change Campbell. I don't know how to do it and he smells awful."

"Something terrible is going to happen," Charlotte whispered, listening to her own words with horror.

She unpinned the baby's diaper, dropped it in the bucket, and replaced it with two new ones. Campbell lay on his back on the changing table with his feet hanging off the edge.

"Shouldn't he start going to the bathroom like the rest of us?" Oliver asked. Campbell was trying to poke his older brother in the eye.

"Soon," Charlotte said, keeping her answers short. It seemed to her that the voices in the kitchen had moved closer to the back steps. "There," she said as she lifted the baby down with a swift movement. "You take care of him. And don't try to stop me, Oliver. I-I-I've made up my mind about something."

They were still in the kitchen when she tumbled down the back steps. "I'm ready for my class, Mother."

"We'll skip it today, Charlotte. Please leave me alone with Margaret."

"No." Too small a voice, Charlotte thought. "No," she said in too loud a voice, and the two women stared at her.

"Go along, Charlotte," Margaret said. "Do as your mother says."

She shook her head, terrified to try another "I." The first one had been so successful.

Nobody said anything for a minute. At least I've stopped whatever was started, Charlotte thought. Through the open kitchen windows, they heard a tractor making its slow, noisy way up from the calf barn. Somebody shouted. In the distance, the train whistle blew.

Lydia rested her hands on her daughter's shoulders, and Charlotte was surprised by the lightness of their touch. "Look at me," she commanded, but her voice was soft. Charlotte obeyed, fixing her eyes on the determined point of her mother's chin.

"Margaret says that she will not stay if I keep up the classes with you. She says that I have been cruel to you."

Oh, Margaret, Charlotte thought, how could you? How could you have told our secret?

"You know, Charlotte, why I'm doing this. We've talked about it, haven't we? You know how busy I am these days. But no matter what, I come home every day to be with you. And we are making progress. The stuttering is getting better. If Margaret chooses to leave, we will all be very sad, won't we? But we will cope. Because I am your mother, darling, and I must make the choices for you, even if they are difficult ones."

With her head still tilted up, Charlotte froze. The muscles in her neck were as stiff and unresponsive as her fingers curled over the handwriting, her jaw locked over the words. From behind, Margaret's arms slipped around her waist and pulled her back away from her mother into a swift, fierce hug. "This is exactly what I mean, Lydia Webster," Margaret spat in a voice that nobody had ever heard from her before. "I will be leaving tomorrow morning, as soon as I can pack. If I possibly could, I would take this child with me. I cannot bear to stay here and watch you torment her with your insane ideas about perfection. She is not a machine, something that constantly needs fixing."

"I-I-I-I—" The bouncing words came out of Charlotte's mouth in a long wailing scream. She could not stop them, she could not take a breath, she could not lock the gates of her mouth over them. Before her, she saw her mother's face curl and crumple in shock before her head was pressed so firmly against the familiar uniformed wall of Margaret's body that the ricocheting of her mouth was finally stilled.

That night before she put Campbell to bed, Margaret gathered the four children in the nursery. By then, they all knew what was happening, that she really meant to leave.

"Hold hands in a circle. Sitting down," she explained. "Yes, Georgie, even you. I want us all to be touching one another."

"Are we going to pray?" Oliver asked.

She smiled at him. "Not exactly. I'm going to show you a trick my mother taught me just before she died. Now, close your eyes, hold on tight, and think about each person in the circle. Good, Campbell, close your eyes and think about me. Remember my red hair and my blue eyes and the little blue bump on my lip."

On the other side of Margaret, Charlotte held on very tight and concentrated. She had always wondered what Margaret thought of her little blue bump. She had never mentioned it before. I have to think of all the questions that I want to ask tonight. Before she goes away.

"What is it going to do?" Georgie asked.

"When we're not together anymore, it means we'll be able to remember exactly how the other person looks. Oliver, think first about Charlotte. Her straight brown hair and her eyes and the flatness of her face and the way her eyebrows go up in the middle when she's surprised and her long, strong arms hanging on to the rope when she's swinging out over the swimming hole." The voice went on, and Charlotte listened very hard to the description of herself, fitting each piece together as if she were assembling a jigsaw puzzle. By the time Margaret moved on to Oliver, she felt complete.

"Does it work for you?" Oliver asked weeks later after Margaret had left. "Can you still see her?"

"Yes," Charlotte said. "All the different parts. But it's hard to make them fit back together in my head."

When Margaret made her rounds that night, she saved Charlotte for last.

"You don't understand, do you?" Margaret asked when she lowered herself onto the bed. The window was open, but the air was hot, breathless. In the morning, there would be fog in the fields.

"No," Charlotte said. "Why did you say anything? It doesn't matter about the classes. They're not that bad."

"I was hoping that your mother would change her mind when she saw how strongly I felt about them. I took a chance and I lost."

Charlotte rolled her eyes. "Mother never changes her mind about anything. You should know that by now."

In the half-light from the hallway, Margaret sat looking out the window. A little wisp of an idea was forming itself in her brain, and she said it out loud before she could stop herself.

"I couldn't take it anymore," she said softly, more to herself than the girl on the bed. "Watching what she was doing to you. But you're stronger than I am, I think."

Charlotte's eyes were wide with surprise. So maybe Mother's doing the right thing, she thought. I must be stronger than I feel.

"Where will you go?"

"To my cousins in Torrington for a little while. And then home. I've saved enough money for the passage."

"Will you ever come back for a visit?"

"Oh yes," Margaret said, knowing it was the first lie she had ever told to Charlotte. "I must see how you're all

307

getting along. I'll just surprise you one day when you're least expecting it."

Charlotte threw herself against Margaret and gave her a brief, fierce hug. "Good night," she said, turning away toward the window. She liked to fall asleep watching the elm tree. Margaret slipped away without another word.

Later on, still awake, Charlotte realized she hadn't asked any of the questions. Was Margaret born with the little blue bump? How old was she when her mother died? Who would take care of Campbell now? And the last one. The most important one. How could Margaret go away and leave Charlotte behind?

21

Mrs. G. Webster's advertisement in the employment section of *New York Lady*, a weekly magazine, read: "August 12, 1924. Responsible woman needed immediately to care for four children on isolated farm in central Connecticut. Must have experience and be willing to work hard. Photograph and references required."

Not many people in Seneca Falls, New York, read the *Lady*, but then Agnes Becker had always been different, according to her twin sister, Edith. And restless.

Agnes took two days to write her reply. Before she mailed it, she had a photograph of herself taken in one of her mother's battered hats so that she would look older than she was, because, among other things, she had lied about her age in the letter.

Seneca Falls, New York
August 22, 1924

Dear Mrs. Webster,

    I expect you will be surprised to be receiving a letter from upstate but I read the advertisements in the *Lady* with great care and I found yours most interesting. I grew up on a farm just west of this small town. I am thirty years old and a widow. My husband was recently killed in an accident and I find myself alone and without resources.

    Although there are many possibilities for employment here, I am interested in moving to a new part of the country in order to leave some sad memories behind and to try to start my life over again.

Elizabeth Winthrop

* * *

"You mustn't sound too mopey," her sister Edith said when she read the letter. "Who wants a weeping widow coming to take care of small children?"

"I'm going to leave that part," said Agnes. "It makes me sound determined and energetic in the face of troubles."

> I am the oldest of three children [the letter went on] and have had much experience caring for young ones. Hard work does not scare me nor does the isolation of a farm. I am used to both. I am enclosing my address and a letter of recommendation from a Mrs. Gilbert, whose children I have cared for for many years.
>
> Sincerely yours,
>
> Agnes Becker

"The Lord will strike you down, Agnes, for all these lies," Edith said. "I can't understand why you want this job to begin with. You could be perfectly happy here working in the pump factory, going to the church supper dances with me and Joe on Saturday nights."

"You don't know what would make me happy," Agnes replied. "Even though we're twins, it does not mean that our thoughts and wishes are the same."

"You're running away from this town because Harry ran away from you."

Agnes wanted to smack that self-satisfied look right off her sister's face, but she shoved one hand inside the other and held on. "Perhaps you're right," she said, her voice a controlled, acquiescent singsong. "And I'm also running away from a small gravestone in the corner of the Lutheran churchyard. But whatever my reasons, I know you'll want to help me, because you want me to be happy. I'll write the Mrs. Gilbert letter. All you have to do is sign it. That shouldn't be hard, after all, because it is your name." Agnes could be cutting too.

* * *

310

"She no more looks thirty than the man in the moon," Lydia said, handing the photo across to George. "She's put on that ridiculous hat to make her look matronly."

He thrust the small sepia picture up close to his desk lamp and studied it. The face looked directly out at the camera, which was probably held by a Mr. W. T. Marion, judging by the imprinted golden signature in the corner. Her eyes were wide with an expression that fell halfway between surprise and defiance. The hair poked out in loose curls from under the preposterous hat and the lower lip curled down, not in a pout, but just because there was too much of it.

"She's not pretty, but she looks pleasant enough, I suppose," George said, handing it back. "Although how you can tell anything from a picture, I don't know. Why are you interested in her instead of the others?"

"She sounds like she's got pluck. And she says she grew up on a farm. The other letters are all too smooth and practiced. They sound as if some agency woman has dictated them. I want someone young and energetic, not a snooty lady with high-blown Washington Square references."

We had someone young and energetic, George thought, but he didn't say it. The night Margaret was fired, he had tried to persuade Lydia to change her mind, but she was unmovable. Just hours after Margaret left he went up to the Springfield Fair with Gino for the first time in years, and when he returned, he moved back into his dressing room. Lydia was just as glad, as she told Isabelle Morris. What with the campaign and the ordinary demands of the household, she had her hands full without the demands a petulant husband could make. She didn't admit to Isabelle or even to herself that she couldn't stand the accusation in George's eyes.

"I expect we'll have to pay her way down for an interview," George said now as he turned back to his desk. "Doesn't sound as if she's got much money."

"Did you see where she lives?" Lydia asked.

"I didn't notice the name of the town."

"Seneca Falls. The place where the first Women's Rights Convention was held."

"So that's why you're interested in her," George said,

311

his back still turned. "It's not the glowing recommendation and the homely face."

"Don't be silly," Lydia said. "Anyway, I suspect she wrote the recommendation herself."

After the interview, Lydia suggested that Agnes might want to have the rest of her things sent down from home.

"You mean you're hiring me?" Agnes asked, incredulous. The size of the house and the fancy lilt in Mrs. Webster's voice had daunted her. This was not exactly the kind of farm she had imagined.

"Yes. As I mentioned in my letter, I am in the midst of a campaign for the legislature, so I need help right away. Since the last nurse left so abruptly, things have been in a bit of a muddle. I would appreciate it if you could start immediately. Unless, of course, you've decided the position is not right for you."

"Can you give me some time to think about it?"

"Absolutely. Sit right here. I'll be in the next room when you've made up your mind."

The children seemed perfectly well behaved. Georgie, the oldest one, would be going off to boarding school next fall, according to Mrs. Webster, so she would not have much to do with him anyway. Oliver she knew she could win over. She had seen the books about fishing in his room when she had her tour of the house. Agnes was an accomplished fisherman. Campbell looked sweet and shy with his neat bowl of brown hair and his coy smile. Thank God he was a boy, Agnes thought, when she saw him. No connections.

The girl would be the problem. From what Agnes could gather, the previous nurse had left under difficult circumstances. What did that mean? Had she been caught stealing? Or sipping sherry? In any case, the children, particularly Charlotte, were very attached to this Margaret and "the adjustment period may be difficult," as Mrs. Webster put it.

She allowed herself to sink back into the deep cushions of the sofa. "You won't be sitting here ever again if you take this job," she told herself, "so you might as well enjoy it now." The room smelled of furniture wax and the rotting threads of antique rugs, of charred wood left over from last night's fire, and a wisp of Mrs. Webster's perfume. The walls were cluttered with oil portraits of ancestors and dark engravings that hung askew. Her prospective employer was clearly not particular about the cleaning. From where she sat, Agnes could see a cobweb spun in the legs of a chair across the room, and when she touched her fingertip to the surface of the end table, she lifted away a circle of fine dust. The furniture was "good." Real antiques. Not the kind of thing that Edith picked up at the odd barn sale and called antique. She liked the rich feel of the place. She would be busy, of course, with the four children, but these days that's what she needed more than anything. To keep herself busy with new people and new places so that she could drive Harry Becker and the little one straight out of her mind.

She knocked on the study door and told Mrs. Webster that she would take the job.

Agnes settled in easily enough, adjusting her rhythms to those of the household. Dorothy, who was growing stout from too many dippings of the spoon into the gravy pot, was delighted to have someone new to gossip with. Nancy had proven to be a poor companion, as she was always sure that someone was listening just around the corner. Margaret had held herself apart from the kitchen discussions, although once in a while she would add an acerbic comment that showed she had missed nothing. Agnes proved to be a sympathetic listener, mainly because it helped her to understand the undercurrents of the household. Dorothy was the one who told her why Margaret had left.

"Why did she interfere?" Agnes asked. "If Mrs. Webster chooses to hang a child by his toes, it seems to me that's her right. After all, she's the mother."

"Margaret was crazy about Charlotte from the beginning. That little girl could do nothing wrong, and according to Nancy the sessions up there are pretty tough on her. They still go on."

"Every afternoon at four-thirty, I understand," Agnes said. She had already witnessed the stony look on the little girl's face when she came back to the nursery from the painting porch.

313

"You all right, Char?" Oliver had asked.

"Yes, I-I-I'm all right. Just don't talk to me."

"You have to remember that Mrs. Webster is off most of the day with this campaigning business," Dorothy said as she pulled herself to her feet. Something was burning. "And before that it was the English classes for the Italians and the votes for women and I don't know what all. It's no surprise that Margaret became so attached to the children. She was their mother, in a manner of speaking." She settled back on the stool. "You have any children?"

The question was so sudden and unexpected that Agnes heard herself telling the truth without thinking first.

"I had a little girl," she said quietly. "She died two years ago. Scarlet fever."

"Oh, dearie, I'm so sorry," the other woman said, but Agnes pulled her hand out from under the sympathizing one.

"Please let's don't mention it again," she said, her voice hard.

"Yes, I can understand your wanting to put something like that behind you."

You don't understand anything, Agnes thought, but she changed the subject quickly. "What's Mr. Webster like?"

"A real gentleman," Dorothy said. "Not your normal farmer. He dresses very fine and has good, old-fashioned manners, don't you know? The men like him, although some of the Italians have gone to work in the fuse factory since he gave up on the tobacco operation."

"He grew tobacco?"

"Cigar wrappers. Right up until this summer. We used to have the biggest parties when they brought in the first harvest. The Italian women sat in the barn stringing up the leaves so they could dry. But two years in a row we had these sudden hailstorms late in June and the crop was wiped out in a day. All that money down the drain. So next year he's going to give the field back to the cows. Some of the Italians are real mad about it, but he's done what he can for them. Found them some work on the farms on the other side of the valley. He made sure the rest were hired by the fuse factory, but they hate that

314

kind of work." Dorothy shrugged. "They should be happy. Five years ago the factory was refusing to hire any foreigners at all. You know, during all that Bolshevik business."

Agnes nodded, but she didn't really know. Five years ago, she was nineteen years old and crazy in love with Harry Becker. All she cared about was meeting him on Saturday afternoons in the back of his cousin's barn, where he blew in her ear and made all sorts of wild promises that he never intended to keep.

She stood up. "Time to get the little boy up from his nap," she said. "The others will be home from school soon."

"I'm so glad you're here," Dorothy said effusively, patting Agnes's hand with a rapid clapping sound. "This place won't seem half so lonely."

Agnes did not reply. Why had she taken on this whole family with all its complications? she wondered as she climbed the back stairs. Well, she knew she wasn't going to make the same mistake as that Margaret. Mrs. Webster was the children's mother and she was welcome to the job. Agnes never wanted that to happen to her again. A child just tangles herself right up with you so you don't know where her pain ends and yours begins. After all, this was a job just like any other. She could leave whenever she wanted to, whenever the atmosphere got too close.

In the summertime, when the family traveled down to New York to see Mrs. Webster's aunt and uncle, Agnes took the train home to Seneca Falls. Edith and Joe always fussed about how glad they were to see her, and the first summer she wondered whether she should move back, but as each year passed, the old landmarks of her childhood in the town seemed dustier and more remote and the small back bedroom in Northington seemed more like home.

"Agnes seems to have settled in well," Lydia said to George a week after she arrived.

"I suppose so."

"She took Oliver down to the river to fish yesterday."

George didn't answer.

"George?"

He put down the newspaper and stared at her. "What do you want me to say, Lydia?"

She shrugged. "That I made the right decision."

"About Agnes, yes. About Margaret, no." He snapped the paper and raised it again.

"Do you think Margaret will ever come back to see us?" Charlotte had asked him the day before.

"Scotland's a long way away," he said.

"I don't like Agnes," Charlotte said.

"You don't have to," he said. They didn't speak about it again.

As a surprise, George rented a radio on election day so that they could listen to the results. In the afternoon while Lydia was down at her makeshift campaign headquarters, which consisted of one dingy room above the pharmacy, a man brought it out from Hartford and set it up in the living room. The two of them sat up most of the night, passing the one set of earphones back and forth and keeping track of the numbers on a pad of paper.

"We look like an old couple playing some newfangled parlor game," George said, and Lydia laughed. It was the first time they had shared a joke in months.

Coolidge won, and Lydia Webster, the female Republican candidate in the Northington district, rode in on his coattails. "Twenty-nine votes," she remarked to George when the numbers came in. "Hardly a landslide."

Election night, George came back to her bed, although he was now equipped with shields. No more babies, Lydia said, and she meant it.

When George gave up growing the tobacco, he knew exactly what he wanted to do next but he kept it to himself for a while.

Lydia was deep in the work of her first term in the legislature. Roraback had used his considerable influence to keep her off the important committees such as Finance or Appropriations. She was assigned to the Committee for Humane Institutions, but the day the legislature convened, a resolution was passed which prohibited the consideration of any bills by that committee.

"It was ingenious," she reported to Isabelle. "He put

all three women on Humane Institutions and then made sure we had no work at all to do."

"Satan shall find mischief for idle hands," Isabelle said with a smile. "Go to all the committee meetings. Make trouble in each and every one."

George agreed. "The one where all the work gets done is the Committee on Cities and Boroughs. Political appointments. Dirty linen. And nobody ever bothers to read the bills, because Roraback tells them how to vote. Why don't you make it your job to inform the other members about exactly what's in those bills."

She teamed up with Marjorie Shelden, the representative from Manchester, and the two of them pored over the bills, dissecting them. She was much too busy to pay much attention to George. The day that he found what he was looking for, she gave her first major speech on the floor of the legislature.

"Everyone was in an uproar," she reported, her eyes shining.

"What in God's name did you say?"

"I merely ran through the highlights of the Derby bill for them. Roraback had four of his political henchmen slated in there for very expensive and unnecessary jobs. Marjorie was the one who actually figured it all out. I'm just better on my feet than she is. It must come from my practice as a suffragist speaker."

"What happened?"

"The bill was tabled," she reported with glee. "If I hadn't spoken, it would have been passed, pro forma. Now what's your news? You look like the cat that swallowed the canary."

"I didn't think you'd noticed. I've found something I want to buy."

"What is it? Another bull. A new tractor? You can have anything, darling. I'm feeling magnanimous today. Besides, my little bit of money from Father should be coming through soon."

Charles Franklin had died of heart failure the summer before at the age of seventy. "Very properly done," John told Lydia when he telephoned her. "He was so terrified of becoming senile. The cook reported that he went early to bed complaining of indigestion, and when she went up to check on him, he was dead.''

"I want to buy a newspaper," George said, savoring the look of astonishment on her face. "The Plainfield *Herald* is up for sale. It's a small Republican daily, circulation of ten thousand. I think I could make something of it."

"Are you mad, George?"

"If you remember, I always wanted to become a journalist. It was Miss Bunting who deflected me to farming. Thanks to my father's mismanagement of his affairs, I had no choice back then. Now I do."

"What about the farm?"

"Nort runs it very well. I don't have enough to do, Lydia. With Gino overseeing the cows and the tobacco all gone, the farm can't exactly run itself but close enough. I'll spend part of the morning here and the rest over in Plainfield."

"Do we have the money?"

"We will if I get what I want for the Sinclair bull. He's turned into a very good investment. That plus the money from the tobacco supplies and perhaps a little help from your side. The *Herald* is cheap right now, from what my cronies tell me. Old man Sandler has gotten bored with the business and he's willing to unload it quickly."

She raised her hands in a gesture of despair mixed with amusement. "Life with you has never been dull, George. I married a farmer and now it looks as if I'm going to end up with a newspaperman."

This kind of banter between them was rare, and tonight she stayed longer than usual at the dinner table. In too many of their conversations the subjects they avoided rested between them like boulders in the road. Every married couple must feel this way after fifteen years, but on a night like this when his blue eyes rested approvingly on her, she opened up and flirted with him like a young girl.

In April 1925, George bought the Plainfield *Herald*, and for a year the family barely saw him at all.

"Why don't you sleep at the paper?" Lydia said groggily when he crawled into bed at two in the morning for the third night in a row.

"Hush," he said. "Go back to sleep. I'm just getting the hang of the thing. It won't always be this way."

But he was obsessed, like a child with a new toy. He loved the clatter of the machines, the smell of the printer's ink, the ebullient call of the newsboys on the corners. Sometimes he even followed them surreptitiously to see how well *his* paper was selling.

In the beginning, he announced to the staff that he would leave the editorial affairs to them. He was the publisher, the businessman, the fellow in the upstairs office who worried about advertising revenues and the circulation roller coaster. But at six in the evening, when the reporters began to file their stories and the city editor paced the length of the open room and screamed expletives at them from his desk, George would drift quietly into the room and watch the proceedings from a corner. At this hour, the newsroom resembled the central waiting room of a large city train station. The people were on the move and they all looked angry and urgent as they ripped the copy paper from their typewriters and slammed it down on someone else's desk. The phones rang continually, the chair legs scraped back on the worn wooden floor, pencils were dropped and sworn at. When the boys ran in from the Linotype room waving the first mock-ups, everybody gathered around to check their article, the placement of their byline, the look of the thing. Even though he owned the newspaper, George stayed in his corner and watched from a distance. This was their moment of glory. He wasn't a part of this and yet he longed to be.

On Saturdays he brought Charlotte into the office with him, and she roamed through the building, making sure to stay out of the way. Her favorite place was the Linotype room, where the three operators sat at their machines, setting the copy that the boys brought down from the newsroom. She stood against the wall of the concrete-floored room watching the metal slugs drop down into the catch tray. Every so often when one of the men made a mistake, he would stand up, pull out the incorrect slug, and toss it to her. The best ones she would save for her collection at home. The others she slipped back into the melting lead pot so she could watch the thick silver liquid swallow them up again.

In another room down the hall, the printing press sat poised over a hole like an enormous metal toad.

"What's the hole for?" she asked her father.

"If the press breaks down, the men need to get down under it in order to fix it."

The pit fascinated and terrified her at the same time. Sometimes she was tempted to make her way down the short flight of steps to see what the underside of the press looked like, but she never dared go for fear the huge machine would shift for some inexplicable reason and crush her.

On Saturdays the paper was put to bed by one in the afternoon. Once the newsroom had cleared out, she borrowed a corner desk and practiced her typing on one of the reporter's black Underwoods.

"I wish I had a typewriter," she told her father. "Then Miss Norton wouldn't be able to say another word about my stupid handwriting."

"I'm going to give her one of the old ones for Christmas," George told Lydia.

"Don't be silly, George. Miss Norton can't be expected to accept typewritten work from Charlotte. Every student is supposed to develop good handwriting. She can't make exceptions."

"Oh, pooh to Miss Norton. I'll give it to her anyway. She can play with it at home."

Charlotte loved the typewriter, and in no time at all, she taught herself to type with her eyes closed. She wrote letters to George at school (he rarely bothered to answer) and to her Aunt Minerva in Middletown (she always wrote back), and the summer she turned twelve, she published a newspaper called the *Webster Weekly*.

"Who's going to read it?" Oliver asked.

"The household," Charlotte said, undaunted by his gloom. "It shall contain news of interest to all."

The headlines on the first issue read: "Stray Dog Hit by Car on Route 10," "New Calf Born to Webster Herd," and "Agnes Becker to Travel to Hartford on Her Day Off."

"That's hardly news," Agnes said. "I go there almost every week as long as Smack will give me a ride in."

"Well, I was desperate to fill out the page," Charlotte admitted with a grin.

"Very accurate reporting," Agnes said when she had finished the paragraph. A grin from Charlotte was a rare thing and she wanted to show she had been grateful for it.

"Maybe someday you'll come in here and work alongside of me," her father told her one day when they were leaving the office. "I want to keep this paper in the family."

She slipped her hand into his. Their times in the barn had been replaced by Saturdays at the paper. He still treated her as an equal, although now, instead of milk quotas, he discussed with her the problems of selling advertising to small businesses or the new advances in Linotype machines. These afternoons together made up for an entire week of Miss Norton.

Once her mother had been elected to the legislature, she declared that Charlotte was cured of stuttering and they could give up the classes. Although Charlotte was relieved to be done with that painful daily ritual, she resented her mother even more. Margaret had been gone for only three months, and in one day her whole reason for leaving had been erased.

Charlotte's speech had improved. She had learned to take a deep breath and set her jaw before she started speaking. Sometimes, she got through two days without the "I's" bouncing out of her mouth, and when they did come, she pushed through to the end of the sentence anyway while everybody looked down at their laps and waited until she was done.

22

The summer that Charlotte turned fourteen, her father decided to teach them all how to shoot.

"Everybody over the age of ten," George announced at the dinner table to his older three children. Six-year-old Campbell was the only one who still ate in the little dining room. "The Delbianco children too if Louisa will let me. Children growing up on a farm need to learn how to use guns properly."

"I learned skeet shooting with Johnny Bradley," Georgie said. He was in his third year of boarding school, and Johnny Bradley, his new friend from outside of Boston, seemed to start every one of Georgie's sentences. *Johnny Bradley is taking me to his parents' place in Georgia. Johnny Bradley is taking me sailing in Maine. Johnny Bradley's father is a good friend of Charles Lindbergh's.*

"If he says that name one more time, I'm going to throw up," Charlotte told Oliver.

"I think he made him up. If Johnny Bradley is Georgie's best friend, why doesn't he ever come here to visit?" Oliver asked.

"Because we live on a farm, silly. We're not as rich and superior as Johnny Bradley. We embarrass Georgie."

"Good," George said to his oldest son across the dessert plates. "Then you'll already know some of what I intend to teach you. But we'll be starting with a rifle. A .22."

Clara Delbianco did not want to learn how to shoot. "The noise scares her," Louisa said by way of explanation. "Besides, she'll be working over at the hotel this summer."

"Still a sissy," Charlotte said.

"Never mind," said Oliver. "It'll be more rounds for

us." The noise scared him too, but he would never admit it. He was trying to sound tougher than he felt to ally himself with Charlotte.

In the last four years, Charlotte had grown five inches. "On the outside too," Lydia said as she wrote her daughter's name and date beside the pencil line on George's closet door. The height measurement was an annual event, held the first of every year.

"What do you mean by that?" George asked.

"She's thick-skinned like an elephant."

"I don't think so," he said. Their eyes met in the mirror, and Lydia was the first to look away.

She had made some mistakes. She could admit that now. Didn't every mother try too hard to smooth the way for their children? Perhaps she had been too insistent about the stuttering. But after all, Charlotte had gotten better. And that was all behind them now. No use bothering with regrets.

The first shooting lesson was held behind the barn. Lydia came down to watch, George taught them how to hold the rifle, how to load it, how to press the butt firmly into their shoulders so that their aim held steady. They lined up in a row, starting with Georgie and going down by age. Oliver, Frank, Charlotte, Sol.

"This is like Christmas morning," Oliver said. "Why do we always have to do everything by age?"

"Because it's easier," his father said with exaggerated patience. "Georgie, shoot once, reload, and hand the gun on." The target was a round paper circle attached to the barn wall.

By the end of the morning, they could all see that Charlotte was the best at it. Perhaps those years of retraining her fingers had paid off, because her hand was steadier, she knew how to sight down the barrel without wavering, she squeezed the trigger instead of popping it. Georgie was more interested in the picture he presented than in firing well. Oliver cringed and blinked just before he fired. Sol's arms weren't quite strong enough. Frank's shots went wild and he was too loose with the rifle.

"Frank, when you are not using the rifle, rest it in your

right hand with the butt tucked under your upper arm," George reminded him for the third time.

"But it's not loaded," Frank said.

"It's a good habit to get into. Guns are a serious business. We're not playing with toys here." George's voice was sterner than he meant it to be, but he was disappointed in Frank. In the nine years since Tony's death, George had worked very hard with the boy. He had taught him how to run the tractor, how to swim, how to ride a bicycle, all the things he did with his own sons. But Frank was arrogant, impatient. He assumed he could learn faster than the others. He wanted to own the equipment before he had perfected the skill and yet he was easily bored. The bicycle they had given him for Christmas last year had been left to rust in the rain. Louisa was apologetic and defiant about her son at the same time. Frank was one subject Lydia avoided when she walked down the road to visit with her friend.

Before the lesson was over, Agnes brought Campbell down so that he could watch from a safe distance.

"I want to see Charlotte do it," Campbell called from his perch on the lowest branch of a tree. In the weeks between Margaret's departure and Agnes's arrival, Charlotte had taken care of Campbell with only a little help from Nancy, the chambermaid, who admitted to being "nervous" with babies. Ever since then, Charlotte was firmly established in Campbell's mind as his hero.

"Quiet, Campbell, you mustn't interrupt," Lydia said.

"Anyway, it's not her turn, it's mine," Frank said.

"Frank, dammit, stop waving that gun around," George shouted. The boy turned and his eyes locked with George's. After a long silent look, he put down the .22 and stepped out of the line.

"I know how to shoot without you telling me," he shouted. "You can just stop bossing me around from now on. You're not my father, you know."

George said nothing more. They all watched, their eyes drilling into Frank's back as he stomped away from them down the barn road and around the corner. The line shifted nervously and waited.

"Pick up the rifle, Charlotte, and take your shot," George said in a voice barely above a whisper.

She hit the edge of the paper circle, two rings away from her previous shot. Sol said he didn't want to do it anymore, although no one knew whether it was from fear, exhaustion, or loyalty to Frank.

"We'll meet here again tomorrow at the same time," George said, and they dispersed.

Campbell ran to Charlotte and she put out her hand for him.

"You were the best, weren't you?" he asked.

"She was," Oliver said glumly.

"You always think I'm the best," Charlotte said to the little boy. Agnes came up beside them, but she did not reach out for Campbell's other hand. She still gave Charlotte all the room she wanted.

On the nights when the Websters went out to dinner and the older children joined Campbell and Agnes for supper, Charlotte rarely entered the conversation. She listened to Oliver's enthusiastic rendering of the day, she set Campbell's knife and fork straight on his plate, sometimes she even smiled at one of Agnes's jokes, but in the last year she had begun to hold herself farther apart from the rest of them. Agnes remembered her own need for privacy when she was that age. She had shared a tiny bedroom with Edith, who always poked through her drawers and stared at Agnes when she changed into her nightgown. Charlotte's body was developing. Everybody in the house could see that.

"That girl is growing up," Dorothy had remarked to Agnes just the day before. "And she's not even fourteen yet."

"Nothing she can do about it," Agnes had replied. "The body picks its own time.

"I used to shoot rabbits with my father," Agnes said now.

"Did you kill any?" Campbell asked, his eyes wide.

"Now and then. But they're pretty fast when they want to be."

"Why did you shoot rabbits?" Charlotte asked, looking straight ahead.

"Because they got in the garden and ate the vegetables. So we ate them. Rabbit stew."

"Ugh," said Oliver.

"They didn't taste bad. Like a tough, rangy old chicken," Agnes said, winking at him. Oliver liked her despite himself, despite his loyalty to his sister. After all, Agnes knew how to fish better than anybody except his father and she had taught him how to tie his own flies.

"Poor rabbits. Too bad you couldn't have just built a fence," Charlotte muttered as she leaned down for Campbell. He liked piggyback rides. They galloped away with him cracking an imaginary whip above her head.

Behind, Lydia and George followed the troops across the lawn.

"Frank worries me," Gerge said. "He feels to me like a bomb about to explode."

"It's his age, George," Lydia said. "Boys are supposed to rebel and he doesn't have anybody but you to rebel against."

"Gino told me he caught him making fires out behind the calf barn one day. That's the kind of rebellion I don't want to hear about."

But Lydia was thinking of something else. "Campbell was right. Charlotte is the best, isn't she?"

He nodded. "She's got a steady hand. It doesn't surprise me."

"Why?"

"She'd do anything well if it would satisfy her mother," he said with a glance in his wife's direction.

"You're wrong, George. She doesn't care what I think anymore. There's a devilish, mean edge to her that I certainly never encouraged. You ought to hear the way she talks to Agnes sometimes. She's figured out how not to be actually rude, so I can't reprimand her, but she fires off these quick biting comments." Lydia shrugged. "If I were Agnes, I probably would have quit a long time ago."

"Agnes is too smart," George said. "She knows if she shows that it hurts, Charlotte will just go on doing it."

Charlotte knew that Frank was watching the shooting lessons from behind the barn. Once, when she whirled around to follow the arc of the clay pigeon in the sky, she caught sight of his dark hair, the glint of sweat on his naked shoulder, and she missed the black disk completely. After that, without seeming to ever notice, she kept an eye out for him. He was there spying on them, almost every day. She wondered if her father knew. If he did, he said nothing about it.

That summer she spent a long time studying herself in the mirror. The shape of her body was something that nobody, not even her mother, could control, and although during the day she hid it under layers of clothing, she liked to stand naked and look at herself when she was alone. In the last year, her breasts had developed quickly into firm handfuls and her nipples stood up and puckered when she let her hand slide across them. Her legs were long and thin, tapering down from the curve of a buttock that never used to curve. She remembered her father giving her a playful spank on that flat childish bottom. Now he was careful not to touch her.

She had grown her hair down to the shoulders, and when she was playacting in front of the mirror, she let it fall across half of her face and tickle her skin. Was she pretty? she wondered. No. But the way her eyes slanted up at the corners was interesting. And her thin lips opened up and glistened when she smiled.

Later, she would sit up in the crook of the elm tree and stare moodily down to the orchard. Sometimes, Frank would come out of the front door of the cottage. That summer, he never wore a shirt. He was helping with the haying in the upper pasture, and he seemed to like to show off his sweaty chest as if it were a mark of his manhood. They avoided each other and yet they were watching each other too, like animals stalking enemies or mates. On the days when she did not see him, she felt oddly disappointed, out of sorts, as if the sight of him confirmed in her some sense of who she was, of how they were different and yet the same.

Lydia was watching Charlotte too that summer.

"She stretches like a cat," she remarked to George one afternoon when she looked down on her daughter from the painting porch. "It's those movies she goes to on Saturday mornings."

Just the year before, Harold Butler had built a movie theater in the center of town next to the post office. Now that Hollywood was making talking pictures, it looked as if the cinema would make Harold a much richer man than politics ever had.

George joined her at the window. "Your little girl is growing up," he said. "Nothing either of us can do about it."

She didn't move or answer and eventually he went away. She was remembering the day Nellie forced her to give up the chemise for a corset with shoulder braces. She was only thirteen then. And Charlotte would turn fourteen in August.

"Charlotte, you're getting too old to kiss your father," Lydia said the next morning after George had left the breakfast table.

The girl looked up. "Yes, Mother," she said, but she did not drop her eyes. She was sitting up very straight this morning in her chair, and Lydia could not help but notice the swell of her new breasts under the cotton shirt.

"As a girl grows older, she must be more aware of herself. Take care with her appearance."

Charlotte noted her mother's discomfort and savored it. Her own questions and answers were not so childishly abrupt anymore. In the years since Margaret had left, she had learned even more about the twists and turns of conversations, the different tones of voice a person could use. "I know, Mother. That's why I've decided to work very hard on my posture. It's my new resolution. Miss Norton agrees with me."

Lydia stirred her coffee so vigorously that a small brown wave slopped over into her saucer. She did not bother to mop it up. "That's admirable, darling. But at the same time, you must realize that members of the opposite sex will look at you differently. It's up to you to set the standard. Your body is not something to be flaunted. It is merely the physical housing for your soul and your intellect."

Charlotte dropped her head and allowed herself a small smile. Mother was getting awfully tangled up with her words. She sounded as if she were giving a speech to her fellow legislators.

"And women who do use their bodies as enticements are terribly weak and foolish creatures. They are to be pitied and, of course, they don't command a man's respect."

That word again, Charlotte thought. Weak.

Lydia pushed her chair back from the table. "I'm glad we were able to have this little talk, Charlotte. It's the kind of thing I missed when I was your age because I didn't have a mother. Nobody to protect me."

Charlotte puzzled over that last remark for a long time. Protect her from what? she wondered.

When she knew that Frank was out of the house, Charlotte liked to go down and sit with Louisa in her kitchen.

Now in her mid-forties, Louisa had given up her work with the Connecticut League of Women Voters and taken a cooking job at the local private boys' school which had been opened just two years before by an eccentric spinster named Myra Waldrop.

"But a cook, Louisa," Lydia said. "Your talents will be wasted back in a kitchen."

"That is exactly where my talents lie," Louisa said. "I really wasn't cut out for the political life, much as I've enjoyed it. Your only problem, my dear friend, is trying to make everybody like what you like. You love being a politician. I love being a cook. And it also means that I will have the summers off to be with my children."

Charlotte loved the Delbianco kitchen. It was cluttered and messy and she was allowed to stir things and lick bowls and crack eggs.

Louisa was happy to sit and talk to Charlotte while the last traces of batter hardened in the unwashed mixing bowl and the room filled slowly with the sweet smell of rising cake. For her, cooking was a process, not a product, and although the cake might overflow onto the tin shelf or stick to the edge of the inadequately greased pan, it always tasted good.

The little house had a living room, but Louisa only sat there when friends joined her on Thursday evenings for a game of mahjongg, the latest rage. "Funny game for Italians to play," Agnes had said. "Italians," Louisa replied with feigned indignation. "We're all Americans now." Most of the time, visitors sat in the kitchen around the

Elizabeth Winthrop

wooden table Tony had built himself when they first
moved to this house. The room was close and cluttered.
A visitor on one side of the table had to jump up and
stand aside whenever Louisa needed to open the oven
door. A painted porcelain relief of the Virgin Mary hung
over the sink next to a drawing of Tony that Lydia had
done the year before he died.

"Mother told me that I was sick with the same influenza as your husband," Charlotte said one afternoon.
Tony seemed too intimate a name to use for him. After
all, her only memory of Louisa's husband was his thick
fingers tweaking her nose when they encountered one
another on the farm.

"Yes. She was up in the old nursery room watching
over you and I was down here. Seems like just yesterday
and ten years have passed. Clara's already working. And
Frank's grown into a young man." She shook all over
suddenly, like a dog after a bath. "Now you've gotten me
thinking sad thoughts."

"And I'm a young woman," Charlotte said, more to
herself.

Louisa looked over. Her eyes traveled down the length
of Charlotte's body, and Charlotte squirmed. "Getting
there," she said at last.

"Mother says it changes everything."

Louisa hoisted herself to her feet. She punched her
hand deep into the bowl of rising bread dough and the air
escaped with a barely audible sigh. "Changes some things."

A silence that was not uncomfortable hung between
them. Each one was waiting for the other to say the next
thing. Charlotte thought about Frank. He slept in this
house, just on the other side of the thin wall behind the
icebox. She wondered what it was like here in the evenings with Louisa and her two sons. Did they play checkers? Did Frank prowl the small rooms or go out into the
night? She knew he was hanging out with the older boys.
Nick Togni still. The Rutigliano boys, who worked in the
fuse factory. Oliver liked to tag along too even though
Frank barely tolerated him anymore. Suddenly this room
seemed close, suffocating, and she scrambled to her feet.

"Frank was brought up like a brother to you and the
others," Louisa said, still working over the bread. "It

330

wasn't right. I'm not blaming anybody but myself. But he's got to go his own way now. Can't always be following other people's orders."

Had Louisa read her mind? "Nobody ever said he should," Charlotte muttered, feeling defensive, although she wasn't sure why. "I'd better go," she said abruptly, and let herself back out into the hot sunny afternoon.

23

The elm tree worked well as an escape hatch. One breathless night, Charlotte left pillows plumped in the shape of her body, wound her way down to the lowest branch, and dropped off noiselessly. Through the picture window, she could see the silhouettes of her parents in their usual evening positions on the sofa. She ducked down and scuttled along until well past.

The night was humming with cricket noise. In the summer, the herd was left out all night in the pasture, and down along the orchard fence, she heard the huff and blow of a cow, the crush of the dry grass as a hoof was lifted and lowered again.

She was dressed in her usual summer costume, an old pair of Oliver's pants and a shirt. She trotted along the fence and then turned down the road toward the river. Of course. She would go for a swim. The thrill of it made her shiver. She was breaking so many rules. To swim alone was strictly forbidden. But last year, in the dry season, her father had ordered the hole dredged, so that now they could swim right through August. The moon was out. It was almost as light as daytime. There would be no real danger. Just the thrill of breaking rules, of being outside under the late-summer moon, her body moving easily the way it always did in boy's clothes.

The night did not scare her. She had grown up on the farm, and the turn of a stone in the road, the tree shadows, the call of the whippoorwill from the edge of the river were all familiar to her. Once on the forest path, the moonlight was blocked here and there by the high, heavy-leafed branches and she hopped playfully from black patch to light as if crossing a river on a road of rocks. Then, to her surprise and sudden fear, she heard an unfamiliar noise. A voice, somewhere up front. She froze in a dark part of the path. Another voice, a high falling cry, and then a splash. Somebody was down at the swimming hole. More than one person.

She hesitated on the path, ready to turn back, and one voice sang out louder than the rest. "Geronimo," it cried as it fell away to the water. Frank. Of course. His favorite war cry from the days of their Indian games. Well, she could be a good Indian too, she thought with a grin, as she made her way silently down the path toward the water.

The river was slow and easy in the moonlight. She stole up toward the voices and dropped to her hands and knees long before they could hear her. Flattened like a snake with her belly to the ground, she inched forward.

She counted five of them. Three around the edge in the shadows, Frank just scrambling up the side of the bank, and Nick Togni on the platform above. The moonlight glistened off Nick's wet back, and as he grabbed the rope and swung out over the black water, his naked white buttocks winked at her before his body slapped the surface and slipped under.

She closed her eyes, frightened for the first time that night. They would all be naked. If they caught her now, they would kill her. She should slide backwards right then and tiptoe away before anybody knew. But she didn't want to. It was too much fun, having this secret look at them. The thrill of it sent a shiver through her body even though she had already seen more than most girls her age.

After all, she used to take baths with her brothers when they were little. And sometimes, on Agnes's day off, she still bathed Campbell and watched him soap himself down there, rolling his little marbles around between his fingers and giggling. And worse than that, she had come upon the barn dogs rolling in the dust, that raw pink thing hanging down between their back legs even after they were done.

Frank headed up the ladder. On the platform, he stood poised for a long time in the moonlight, shouting taunts at his friends down below, and she stared hungrily, shocked at herself and yet eager not to miss anything. His whole body shone, the water from his last jump still gathered in wet patches in his hair, on his shoulders and arms. His torso was divided, the upper half dark from his shirtless summer, the lower half almost babyish-looking, sheathed in its shiny white skin. Between his legs, she could see nothing but a shape and dark hair behind. When he raised his arms to catch the rope, she saw the shadow of more hair in the exposed armpits. "My Frank's a grown man," Louisa had said. This is what she meant, then.

"Oh, go on and jump, Frank," someone yelled from the side, and she recognized Oliver's voice. So he was sneaking out at night too. There were three orange spots in the bushes where the others sat. Somebody coughed. They were smoking. Oliver was smoking. In the midst of her shock, she smiled. He was probably the one who had coughed. Frank's body hit the water, but she did not inch forward from her hiding place to see him surface.

She stayed for as long as she dared and she could not take her eyes off Frank. He was the ringleader. He took a cigarette from Nick and drew the smoke deep into his chest. With a towel draped around his waist, he stood on the edge of the bank and posed, one knee bent, a hip jutting out, his movements loose and confident. His voice seemed deeper than she remembered it. When was the last time he had said anything to her? Maybe this is what she had been hoping to see all those afternoons when she huddled in the elm tree and stared at his house. Him up close.

Before the moon went down, she got away safely and scrambled back up the tree to the open window. For a long time, she sat on the windowsill until she heard voices down by the Delbiancos' and then Oliver making his way up the back stairs.

By the side of her bed, she posed as Frank had, her hip slipped to one side. There was a sense of power in his swagger, in the way he let his cigarette dangle from his lip. She wanted to be a part of his world, but not as an admirer like Oliver. As an equal.

He quit school that fall. Just walked out of class one October day and never came back. George went down to talk to Louisa about it, but he got nowhere.

"My Frank's the man in this family now," she said mildly. "He's got himself a good job working down in Bronson's Garage."

"He'll get a lot further with an education, Louisa. You know that as well as I do. The boy's only fifteen."

She shrugged. "Nick dropped out two years ago. Frank was the oldest one still there. He felt stupid with all those little kids reciting their alphabet. Sol will stay, though. He's my book learner. Frank needs to get out and work. It will drain away some of that extra energy of his."

"I give up," George said to Lydia. "I've got enough children of my own to worry about."

Charlotte spent the fall following Frank. She got to know his hours. Sometimes she made up excuses to stop at the drugstore next door to Bronson's Garage on the way home from school. They talked about the engine he was working on or he showed her some new part he had learned how to install. She could tell he knew what he was talking about. His black eyes stared at her insolently and she looked right back without flinching.

After dinner, he and Oliver went down to the empty stalls in the back of the calf barn to smoke. One night, she followed them.

"Did you bring the cigs?" Frank asked in a low voice.

"Sure, I did. But I can't keep on buying them, Frank. Sooner or later, Mr. Gardner is going to remember that my father doesn't smoke. Besides that, I'm running out of money."

On the other side of the door, Charlotte smiled to herself. That's why Frank tolerated Oliver these days. He kept him supplied. She heard the scratch of the match on the stone floor and then the silence while they puffed. A cough. She slid the rolling door back a crack and slipped through. When he saw her, Oliver dropped the cigarette and jumped up, brushing ashes off his front. Frank didn't move but stared at her coolly as if he had been expecting her.

"You've been spying on us," Oliver said angrily.

"Want a smoke?" Frank asked with a grin. She nodded, not trusting herself to speak.

"She doesn't know how to," Oliver said.

Elizabeth Winthrop

"Neither do you," Frank said without even looking at him. "I bet your sister's a fast learner. I've been watching her. Come sit here," he said, patting the hay bale next to him. "I'll light it up for you."

The smoke made her feel light-headed, but she held it down the way she had seen him do, letting it drift in wisps out her nose.

"A tough lady," he said admiringly, and she trembled with the praise, the look he gave her, the thickness of his arm next to hers.

"It burns a little," she admitted, and he shrugged. "You'll get used to it," he said.

It didn't take her long. They met down in the barn on and off all fall.

"How's rifle practice?" he asked one night.

"All right. My father took me out quail shooting. I got one."

"You look pretty good at it," he said, blowing the smoke toward the rafters in a single concentrated stream.

"She's the best," Oliver said, and Charlotte was embarrassed by the childish sound of his voice.

"Cut it out, Oliver," she said, lighting one cigarette with the next.

"No, he's right," Frank said. "You looked like the best to me."

"You were watching us," Charlotte said. "I saw you hiding behind the barn."

He didn't answer.

"I could teach you," she said but immediately wished the words back into her mouth. She would have to sneak the gun out of her father's study.

"That's right," he said with a smile. "After all, I taught you how to smoke."

"Next spring maybe," she said. "It's too cold now."

"All right. I won't forget."

"You're crazy," Oliver told her on the way back up to the house. "You know Father has forbidden us to touch the gun closet. How are you going to teach him?"

"I'll think of something," she said. "With the newspaper, Father's hardly ever home anyway. Or maybe Frank'll forget."

"Frank never forgets anything," Oliver said gloomily.

She glanced over at her brother. He was Frank's slave. Do this, Frank said, and Oliver jumped.

"You shouldn't hang around with Frank so much," she said suddenly.

They were standing on the back porch under the light. Oliver's pale brown eyes stared out at her. They looked to her like the eyes of a small wild animal, frightened, alert. "Why?" he snapped. "You want him all to yourself?"

She shook off a shiver that did not come from the cold. "Don't be stupid," she said. I don't like the way Frank treats you, she wanted to say. When you're with him, you seem weak and pitiful. I don't want to be responsible for you.

She sniffed the sleeve of her sweater. "We both smell of smoke. Better get upstairs before Mother finds us here."

"Miss Norton reports that Charlotte is not doing well in school this year," Lydia told George after dinner one night. She was sitting at the piano, playing scales, and the repetition of the notes irritated George. He didn't answer.

She lifted her hands from the keyboard and swiveled around. "It's Frank Delbianco, George. She's spending too much time with him."

"What about Oliver? He tags along behind Frank like an eager puppy. Maybe we should have sent him off to Groton with Georgie. In any case, I think Bronson's Garage is the best thing for Frank. It seems to have straightened him out. As Louisa reminded me, he never did very well at school."

Lydia walked over to the sofa and curled into the corner of it. She felt very tired these days. Her term in the legislature was just winding up and she had decided not to run again. The endless skirmishing with Roraback had lost its appeal for her. "I'm sure I'll go back in at some point," she told Isabelle. "But I want to stay home for a while. Get to know Campbell. Keep an eye on my daughter."

My daughter. These days she could not look at Charlotte without wanting to fix something about her. Her posture, which seemed exaggerated, almost wanton. The brown lank hair which was forever slipping out of its pins and falling into her eyes. That strange sly smile which came over her face slowly as if the girl were remembering some nasty barnyard joke. She knew she treated Charlotte differently than the boys, spoke to her in a tight voice which masked her own mysterious rage. Her chin would shake and the tears would sit at the corner of her eyes while she lectured her daughter about something. It was almost as if she were two people at the same time, the mother berating and the child being scolded. Meanwhile, Charlotte would smile her secret tight smile and eventually, with dreadfully slow, floating movements that seemed to Lydia to be even more disrespectful than refusing to obey, she would pin back her hair or tuck in her blouse or rewrite the thank-you letter.

In some incomprehensible way, Charlotte had gotten the better of her in this contest between mother and child. And yet when she was alone, Lydia daydreamed about changing everything. She had imagined that it would be just the opposite, that Charlotte would be her closest companion, the one dearest to her heart just as she would have been for her own mother if Elizabeth had lived. She remembered the sleepless nights when the little girl sweated and shook her way through the influenza and Lydia could touch and hold her with nobody knowing, not even Charlotte herself. Then she would resolve that their next meeting would be different. They would have a cozy chat over a cup of tea and discuss Charlotte's homework assignment. Or they would go for a walk down to the river and collect leaves and make rubbings of them the way Margaret used to do. Or they would paint together. Charlotte used to love to paint. But now she said she hated the smell of the oils. "We'll use watercolors," Lydia would say in the bright sweet voice of her daydreams. But Charlotte would still refuse.

"I think we mishandled the whole business of the Delbianco children," Lydia said to the ceiling. She knew by the rustle of papers behind her that George had not left the room. "It was my fault. I was so eager to take care of Louisa after Tony died that I forced this household to absorb them. It was not fair to any of the children, theirs or ours. It muddied the waters."

IN MY MOTHER'S HOUSE

"I agree," George said in a small still voice. He knew what an enormous admission this was on Lydia's part. "But there's nothing to be done about it now."

"I am just going to forbid Charlotte to see that boy. And Oliver too."

George pushed his chair back. "I think that's foolish. If you tell the children that they can't see Frank, it will turn him into some kind of hero for them. Ignore this. It will go away."

"You and I have never agreed about Charlotte," she said, opening the old sore. "She's still your shadow, your perfect little girl. You can't see what she's turning into."

"And what's that?" he asked.

"A little—" But she couldn't say that word.

"A little bitch?" he asked. "Whore? Slut?"

She put her hands up to her ears. "Stop it, George," she spat. "I never said that."

"Well, that's what you're thinking, isn't it?" he said in a cold voice. "I'm just naming your thoughts. You are the one who's thinking them."

Lydia said nothing, pretending to herself that she was not dignifying his accusation with an answer.

"You are talking about a bright, accomplished, not very pretty child," he said. His voice sounded patient as if he were embarking on a long explanation of a mathematics problem. "She is fourteen. She can shoot a gun better than any boy of that age or older. She can milk cows, write on a typewriter, add up sums, swim like a fish." Although still controlled, his voice began to escalate. "She has developed breasts as girls are wont to do. For all I know, the hair is growing under her arms and she bleeds every month." And louder still. "There is nothing that you or she or I can do about that. So what in God's name do you want of her?"

The conversation between Lydia and Charlotte on the subject of Frank Delbianco took place on the painting porch on an icy January day. Lydia had gone back to painting now that she had more time at home, and on days like this the heat from the stove and the steamy human breath fogged up the windows until ice crystals formed delicate patterns on the inside of the glass panes.

Charlotte stood at the door waiting for her mother to finish a stroke and turn around.

"Come in, darling, and shut the door behind you," Lydia said at last, sitting back and cocking her head at the canvas on the easel, a portrait of Campbell.

Whatever you're going to say, Charlotte thought, don't ask me what I think of the picture. She lowered herself onto the wooden chair in the corner. Without even turning around, she knew just where it would be from that year and a half of stuttering classes. Back then she used to tuck her feet around its legs and now she was surprised to find her own legs were too long.

"What do you think of my attempt at portraiture?" her mother asked.

"It's fine," Charlotte said abruptly. She wasn't going to play that old game of trying to think of the perfect painterly comment. "It looks like Campbell."

"Well, that's good," her mother said with a quick smile that faded just as quickly. She dropped her brush into the jar of turpentine, slipped off the smock, and swiveled around on her stool. Charlotte put on her tentative smile, the mask she used during these little talks with her mother to cover up her fears. What was it this time? What had she done wrong now? With the ice-covered windows and the closed door, Charlotte felt completely shut away from the rest of the world, as if she and her mother were two people trapped in a glass bubble.

"Darling, you know me, I like to get right to the point. Your father and I—" She hesitated. "No," she corrected. "That's not being honest. *I* have decided that the less you see of Frank Delbianco, the better for both of you."

When Charlotte did not reply, her mother rushed on. "You know, when I got Louisa to work with me that year, I thought that moving her children up here with all of you was the best solution for everybody. It's so much easier to see things in hindsight. The Websters and the Delbiancos are different. We come from different backgrounds, we have different values, different educations. Now that all of you children have gotten older, you must separate and go your own ways. Do you understand?"

"Father doesn't agree with you," Charlotte said, poking at the weak place in the armor.

"Well, of course, he's concerned about Frank too. And we both think that this job of his was actually a good move, although we hate to see someone give up on his education. What I'm trying to say is that Frank and you come from different walks of life. And the world being what it is, you should each keep to your own side of the fence."

Charlotte looked down at her feet, crossed at the ankles. Louisa had said pretty much the same thing to her. Different. Her mother must have used that word five times in the last five minutes. Different because Frank is a boy and I am a girl, she thought. That's what's different.

"What about Oliver?" she asked.

"In the fall he will be going off to Groton."

"Just for one year?" Charlotte said, distracted by this new development.

"No. Actually, he will be repeating fifth form. To give him a little extra time before college." Lydia crossed the room to hang her smock on its hook. "But I'll be speaking to him separately about all that. Do you understand what I'm saying to you about Frank?"

"I suppose so," Charlotte said. She took a deep breath and tightened her jaw to guard against the stuttering. Lying always seemed to bring it on. "I hardly ever see him anyway."

"Why, that's strange. I understand from Smack that you often ask to be dropped off at the corner on the way home from school." The words dripped like honey. "And didn't I see you talking to Frank at the garage one day last week I went into town to run some errands?"

Charlotte nodded. "I-I-I—" She clenched her hands into two balls. "I was just talking to him. You mean I'm not supposed to even talk to him? If he says, 'Hello, Charlotte, how's school?' I-I-I should just walk past with my nose in the air?"

"Don't be dramatic, darling," her mother soothed. " 'Fine, thank you,' you can call back and keep on walking. Don't seek him out. That's all I'm saying. Spend more time with your school friends. I'll be home much more now. You and I can find things to do together."

"Yes, Mother," Charlotte said. The room felt close, the smell of turpentine suffocating. "Is that all?"

Elizabeth Winthrop

"Yes. Would you like to stay up here and have a cup of tea with me?"

"No, thank you," Charlotte said evenly. "I've got some arithmetic to finish."

That was better, Lydia told herself as she stared at the empty chair. I didn't scream at her. And she dropped that awful smile.

Her mother's rule about Frank wasn't hard to follow. In the winter, people on the farm rarely saw each other anyway because it was usually too cold to linger outside. After school, Charlotte went right up to her room. Her father had given her his old desk, which she set up in the corner by the window. She had always been a neat person. She liked pictures that hung straight, pens that lined up right next to the ink bottle, a blotter with no spots. That winter, she spent hours in her room, rearranging the furniture, practicing her typing, lining up the discarded metal slugs from the Linotype machine across the top of the desk. The backwards letters made her eyes cross if she looked at them for too long.

"What are you doing in there?" Oliver would call through the door. "Nothing," she would call back. "Just tidying up. Leave me alone."

She was like an animal, hibernating. Waiting for the spring.

It came very early that year, which meant the mud season lasted longer than usual. "Next time I go back into the legislature I'm going to request the Committee on Roads and Bridges," Lydia announced to the family at dinner. "And I've already figured out my campaign slogan. 'It's time to get the farmers out of the mud.'"

"That's very good," George said. "I'll make sure the paper puts in a good word for you."

"That's not fair, Father" Oliver said solemnly. "You're married to Mother. That's hedonism."

George put back his head and roared with laughter while they all watched. Their mother was the only other one who understood the joke and she didn't seem to think it was that funny. "Nepotism," he corrected, still sputtering. "And it's not really that either, because she doesn't work for the paper. But never mind. I was only teasing your mother, Oliver."

Charlotte said nothing. She had seen Frank on the road that afternoon and he had given her the old sign. Two fingers up and waving. Around an imaginary cigarette. That meant they were supposed to meet down at the barn after dinner.

"Are you going?" Oliver asked when they ran into each other in the upstairs hallway before dinner.

She shrugged. "I-I-I don't know. I haven't decided yet."

"Remember Mother's rule," Oliver teased. "Well, I'm going. I haven't seen Frank all winter."

In the end, she went too, but she shook her head when he offered her a cigarette.

"Gone sissy on me?" he asked. His face looked pale against the black hair. She liked him better with a tan.

"I've given it up," she said with a smirk.

"But you're keeping your promise, right?"

"What promise?" She was hoping she could barter with him. No cigarettes, no shooting lessons.

"Rifle practice. In fact, I've got a better idea. I think we should go hunting squirrels up in the woods. Take the trail up to the old tower. Some Saturday."

Oliver and Charlotte were both quiet. Oliver was scared, but Charlotte was enticed by the idea. An outdoor adventure after the months of being cooped up inside. Her father usually went down to Plainfield on Saturdays. It would be easy to take one of the .22s. She would have to be strict with Frank about it, how he held the gun and all.

"I'd be in charge, Frank," she said. "I'd be the one carrying the gun and loading it. That's the only way you'll get me to show you."

He raised both hands as if someone were pointing a toy gun at him right then. "You're the boss, Miss Webster," he said. "Always been that way, always will be." They stared at each other for a long time. He was the first to break the spell with a poke in her ribs. "You don't laugh at my jokes anymore," he grumbled. Then she grinned too and shivered at the same time, because it was the first time he had touched her since last fall.

* * *

They picked a day in April. It hadn't rained in at least a week, and the dirt road had finally solidified from rutted quagmires to a solid-packed clay, damp on the surface but holding underneath. On their way up the pasture road, Oliver squatted down to write his initials in a flat moist place.

"Come on," said Charlotte irritably. "We don't have all day." She was nervous. The rifle was balanced comfortably under her crooked arm, barrel down, but she didn't like the silhouette they presented in the open field. She wanted to get under the cover of the woods as soon as possible.

Her father had left for Plainfield later than usual. He had been up most of the night before helping Gino. It was calving season, and much as the paper had become his preoccupation, watching a cow give birth took precedence over everything else. "You coming in with me today?" he asked Charlotte over his late breakfast. Her mother had already left for a political luncheon in Hartford. "I'll let you type up my editorial for Monday's paper. Now that I've finally put my toe in the water, Dick Holden says he'll let me do one editorial a week."

"Well, you should, Father. After all, you own the place. He's just the managing editor."

"But he knows a lot more about his job than I do about writing. Never mind. The question at hand is: Are you coming?"

She shook her head. "I can't. I promised Oliver I'd go up to the tower with him."

"I don't blame you," he said. "It's much too beautiful a day to sit inside. Go on, then. Have a good time."

She hated lying to her father. He knew her face better than anyone else, and during the last weeks when they were planning this little excursion, she had not been able to look directly at him. But he hadn't appeared to notice anything odd about her this morning. Perhaps he was too tired from his night in the barn.

Waiting for him to leave reminded her of Christmas morning, when he always took that last cup of coffee to torment the children.

"Still here?" he asked as he headed out the side door.

"Oliver's doing something."

"See you later, then. Maybe we'll shoot skeet in the lower field when I get back."

Her heart filled her throat and she couldn't speak.

The guns were kept in a small study directly under her bedroom in the new wing of the house. It was called Father's hunting room. Audubon prints of birds hung in rows over the small fireplace, and his favorite fly rods were displayed over the sofa. The locked glass gun case took up one whole wall of the room. The place where the key was hidden was supposed to be a secret, but many times she had watched him lift it off the hook behind the first picture. He trusted her.

She had the .22 halfway off its rack when she heard footsteps approaching from the kitchen. There was no time to put it back and try to hide.

"Oh, Charlotte, I thought you were upstairs," Agnes said. "What are you doing?"

"Father asked me to clean his Winchester for him. We're going shooting this afternoon." Her voice was steady, almost authoritative. But she couldn't meet Agnes's eye and pretended to be studying the trigger mechanism.

"Fearful-looking thing," Agnes said thoughtfully. "All right, then. I guess I don't need to tell you to be careful. I'm taking Campbell into town to the post office."

"See you later," Charlotte said.

The sky was not blue but pearlized and iridescent like the inside of a seashell. Charlotte was glad she had brought a sweater. A day like this in the spring could turn suddenly cold.

Frank was leading the way up the path, establishing himself in some position of power since he could not carry the rifle. He still has to be the general, Charlotte thought. Oliver dawdled along behind.

"Remember our picnics up in the field with Margaret?" Charlotte asked.

"Yup. She was a tough old bird. Never let us get away with anything."

"Never let you," Charlotte said. "You were the troublemaker."

Frank turned around. "Me?" he roared with mock indignation. "You and that stupid old Helen Ratty."

Charlotte grinned. "That didn't make trouble. It kept us all very busy."

"How much longer to the tower?" Oliver asked, coming up behind them.

"We'll get there when we get there," Charlotte said evenly.

"Easy for you to say. You're just carrying the rifle. I've got the lunch."

Oliver's complaints brought them back to the purpose of the trip and they trudged on.

"What are we going to do with this squirrel when we shoot him?" Oliver asked farther on.

"Squirrel stew," Frank called from the front. "I'm sure Mama knows how to make it."

Charlotte was always amused to hear big strong Frank call his mother by that baby-sounding name. "And what are you going to say when she asks about the squirrel?"

"I'll say I found it," Frank said.

"With a twenty-two shell in it," Oliver muttered. "That sure is lucky."

They ate lunch in the clear space at the foot of the tower. Nobody talked about climbing it today. They didn't want to take the time. Frank was eager to get his hands on the gun, and Charlotte was already nervous about when her father would be getting home.

Back on the woods path, she handed the rifle to Frank unloaded and showed him how to clear the bolt, how to load, how to press the weapon into his shoulder.

"Yeah, I remember all this now," he said. "Let's load it." She took it from him, broke open the barrel, and slipped the shell into place. She handed it back to him with the safety on.

He stalked ahead like a hunter, the .22 balanced loosely in his right hand. "There's one," he whispered as he brought the rifle up to his shoulder and squeezed the trigger. Nothing happened.

"What's wrong?" he barked.

"The safety's on. I-I-I forgot," she lied. "Be careful when you swing the rifle around, Frank."

"You sound just like your father," he said.

They walked on in silence for a long time. She knew Frank was eager to take a shot. They were getting too close to the farm again. Somebody might hear.

The woods seemed oddly quiet, as if the animals were watching their progress. Oliver moved up beside Charlotte. Frank was still in the lead. He stopped suddenly, dropped to his knees, and shot up into the branches. The crack of the bullet rang out in the stillness.

"I didn't see anything," Charlotte said.

"Practice," Frank said as he got up again. "I hit that branch. Just where I wanted it to go. Give me another bullet."

She handed it over reluctantly. "Only one more," she said. "We're getting close to home."

He snapped the barrel back together and swung around. "Let's go back into the woods, then." The rifle was pointing directly at them. Charlotte moved up next to him and put her hand on the barrel. "I'll take it back now, Frank."

"No," he shouted. "I've got one more shot."

She knew she shouldn't try to wrestle the gun out of his hands. It went against everything her father had taught her, but his grip seemed loose and relaxed. I just wanted to slip it away from him for a while, she told herself later. I didn't know he would hang on. I didn't know his finger was still on the trigger.

The second shot rang out. With her ears still vibrating from the noise, she felt him let go of the rifle. Good, she was holding it now. But why was Oliver all curled over himself on the ground. Had he fallen?

"Char," Oliver screamed. "You shot me."

She dropped the rifle on the ground and ran to him. Later, she would always remember that expression of pain and confusion when she lifted his head and pulled it close, that growing dark stain behind his hands, which were pressed, one on top of the other, against his belly.

"You stay with him. I'll go get somebody," Frank said, and he was off, his big legs pumping and scrambling down the path ahead of her.

Oliver did not move again. He's not dead, she whispered to herself over and over again. He's gone to sleep so the pain won't hurt so much.

How long did she sit there, she wondered later, the .22 in the path ahead of them, its empty barrel still pointed ironically in their direction? What did she say over and over again to herself? It's not my fault, I didn't do it, oh God, please be okay, Oliver, I'm sorry, I'm sorry, I'm sorry.

Once they lifted Oliver off her body and Gino and her father carried him down on a stretched-out coat, her mother took her hand in one of her own and the rifle in the other and led her down the path like a baby. Or a criminal.

"Are you all right, darling?"

Charlotte nodded.

"You weren't hurt?" Another nod. When would she start screaming at her about stealing the rifle?

But nobody had anything to say about the incident. Not that first afternoon when her parents had gone with Oliver into the hospital and Agnes put her to bed. And not in the days and months that followed when Oliver went back and forth to the hospital for this operation to fix his bladder and that one for his kidneys. Everything inside of Oliver had been rearranged by that .22 long rifle, the shell she had selected at the last minute because it was a little more powerful, more accurate, had a longer range.

But no grownup ever spoke to her about what happened that afternoon. It was too big, too enormous for a scolding or a spanking or any childish punishment. There were simply no words that could possibly hold the hugeness of what she had done.

PART III

1971–
MOLLY

24

In the Webster family, the women's lives were threaded in and out of that white farmhouse in Northington like the piece of string a bird weaves into its nest.

The house had never been considered distinguished. From the front gate, it always looked as if it were leaning toward you, as if the top floor measured slightly wider than the main floor.

"It looms at you," Lydia said to George a few months after Campbell's birth. They were standing together on the small steep hill across the road staring at the proportions of the new addition. She had to hang on to his arm for support, as her feet, ankle deep in dead wet leaves, kept sliding gently out from under her.

"Looms?" George said. He had developed an irritating habit of repeating what she said in order to give him a little extra time to form an answer.

"Looms," he said again.

"Yes, looms," she snapped back. "Leans, looms, lurches."

"Never mind," said George. "It looms friendly."

For the first time in months, they shared a smile.

For Lydia the house had always loomed friendly, and when she stepped into the narrow dark hallway after a trying meeting or a long drive, it used to remind her of the cool silence of a church on a surprise weekday visit. She came home from Hartford grateful for its peace and safety.

Charlotte returned for different reasons. Even when she had married Jack Taylor and moved six miles away, she often dropped by on her way home from work. She would pull her car into the driveway and sit looking at the house, unmoving, the way a cat watches a bird. In the early days of her marriage, she stopped there in order to put off listening to the children's suppertime fights or seeing the glaze over her husband's eyes like the thin ice over a black pool. In the last years, since the children had moved away, she turned in to stave off for a while the dark silences of her own empty rooms.

For Charlotte, the house of her childhood did not "loom friendly," and she rarely went in but sat watching Agnes, who was exposed in the bright light of the kitchen as she moved unhurriedly from the stove to the tin-topped table, preparing Lydia's supper tray.

Molly came back too.

"Why?" Charlotte asked her daughter once. "Why do you keep going back there?"

"Because it feels like home," Molly replied.

These days Charlotte stopped by to check on Agnes. Lydia had been dead just over a year now and the family was concerned about Agnes living there alone. She had turned seventy last January, and they all assumed she would go over to New Jersey to join her sister soon after Mrs. Webster died, but she asked to stay on.

Charlotte pulled the car into the driveway, slid down in the seat to rest her aching head against the hot leather, and lit a cigarette. She was up to a pack a day and the dentist had chided her about it during her appointment that morning.

"You're fifty-seven years old," he had said, scanning her charts.

"As of yesterday," Charlotte said.

"Have you tried to stop smoking?" he asked.

"Countless times," she said. "It works for a few weeks and then I slip back to it."

"Give it another go," he said.

She nodded and leaned over to pick up her purse.

"Just a moment, Mrs. Taylor. I have a few more questions. You did mention to the nurse that you have headaches. How often?"

"Every day," she said with a shrug.

"Do you take something?"

"Aspirin."

"How many aspirin do you take in a day?" he asked.

"You're making me nervous, Dr. Peters. Can someone get hooked on aspirin?"

He smiled. "Well, actually, you can. But my concern is the number and severity of your headaches. You mentioned a clicking sensation and pain in your jaw. The wear pattern on your teeth indicates you have a condition called TMJ. It comes from grinding your teeth at night and grinding usually comes from tension. In order to give you some relief, we'll need to fit you for a night guard."

Sitting in the car now, Charlotte smiled to herself. She had enough tension for twenty sets of teeth. She and Oliver were in the middle of final negotiations with Sol Delbianco for the sale of the farm. The compositors had just called a strike against the paper. And on top of all that, Molly was coming back to the farm to live with Agnes.

Charlotte opened the car door and ground the butt of the cigarette into the macadam driveway. The light had just snapped on in the kitchen, which meant that Agnes was starting her dinner. Better get on with it.

Agnes followed the same patterns that she had lived by for the last forty-seven years in this house. The laundry on Monday, the kitchen floor and downstairs on Wednesday, white bedroom curtains washed in the fall, dark curtains sent to the cleaner in the spring. She ate at six-fifteen, just as she always had. It gave her just enough time to eat before she had to get dinner on the table in the dining room or, as she had done in the last years, on the tray and upstairs to the boudoir couch.

Mrs. Webster had wound down slowly in the months before her death. She had become obsessed with the bathroom and would sit on the toilet for hours waiting to "do her business."

"Are you finished in there?" Agnes would call, not quite daring to open the door and invade her privacy.

"It won't come out," the other woman would cry.

"With the amount you eat, there isn't anything to come."

In the end, she died of a stroke. Woke up one day with

just half her body working and died the next. The way to go, Agnes thought now.

From the upstairs hallway, she saw Charlotte's car pull into the driveway, but she didn't hurry downstairs. Charlotte always sat and stared at the house for a while, as if she had to steel herself to come in and check on the old lady. There, she was lighting up a cigarette. That meant she'd stay out there until it was finished. Everybody in the family knew how Agnes hated the smell of smoke in her clean house.

Besides, Agnes already knew what Charlotte had come to tell her. Molly had called with the news last night.

"Hello, Agnes," Charlotte said, putting her hand out behind to stave off the slam of the screen door. It never came. "I see Frank still hasn't fixed this spring."

"That's right. Frank is a busy man, as he's always quick to tell me. I can't quite see what he does all day, but then I'm not his boss." She turned from the sink and glanced quickly at Charlotte. "Just about ready to have my dinner."

"Go ahead and start. I would have come sooner, but there were problems at the office."

"Nothing but soup," Agnes said, stirring at the stove. "You want a bowl?"

Charlotte hesitated. It would be nice to hitch the white stepladder back up to the old tin-topped table. "Stop slurping," Margaret used to say all those years ago. "No, I'm sure there's something waiting for me at home," she lied. The cleaning lady left dinner only two nights a week, and if Charlotte remembered correctly, this was not one of them. "You go ahead."

She leaned her elbows on the pockmarked tin surface and watched Agnes's precise movements that came from years of working in this particular kitchen with these particular tools. She had turned out to be a much better cook than poor old Dorothy, who mercifully gave up the job just before the war.

"How are things going?" Charlotte asked.

"Fine," Agnes said quickly. "Man came to clean the furnace. He was here all day banging around in the cellar. He says the old thing isn't going to last much longer."

"It won't have to," Charlotte said, deciding this was just as good a time as any. Agnes went on ladling soup into a crockery bowl. "We've got a buyer for the place, Agnes. There are still details to go over, but Oliver and I thought it was time you knew."

She rested the ladle against the side of the large black pot and settled herself at the other end of the table from Charlotte.

"I figured it was coming," was all she said as she dipped her head for the first spoonful of soup. "Who's the buyer?"

"Sol Delbianco and two others. He wants to turn it into a golf club. I think they'll restore the calf barn because it makes a picturesque backdrop for the ninth hole, but they'll take down the big barn. With that and the front pastureland that we've been renting to the nursery, they'll have all the land between the road and the river."

Molly had not known who the buyer was. Agnes grinned. "That Sol has always been a shrewd one," she said. "Much smarter than his older brother."

"Remember, Frank quit school in the tenth grade," Charlotte said. "And even then he was a year or two behind."

"Well, I'm not just talking about school," Agnes said. "When do I have to be out?" she asked with her customary abrupt swerve of subject.

"Not till next June. About ten months. We told Sol we wanted to give you as much time as possible and he understood. Besides, as I said, we're still doing some haggling over the price. Oliver thinks its worth more than Sol's last offer."

Even though her head was still bowed to the soup, Agnes could see Charlotte's hands opening and shutting. Arthritis had swollen the joints in her hands and wrists and she did this to unlock them. In the last few months, it seemed to have become a nervous habit.

"Mother is the one behind it, of course," Molly had told Agnes on the phone the day before. "Remember, she was talking about selling the place the day after

Grandmother's funeral. And Uncle George supports her decision. He says it's ridiculous to keep the farm going just for old times' sake. The Websters can no longer afford this kind of luxury," she had intoned in a perfect imitation of George's lawyerly voice. "Uncle Oliver and Uncle Campbell are dead set against it, but it seems they've been overruled as romantic sentimentalists."

"You know we really can't afford it anymore, Agnes," Charlotte said. "The upkeep on the house plus paying Frank and Angelina—"

"And me."

Charlotte hesitated. "It doesn't make sense anymore."

"Charlotte, you don't have to justify yourself to me. Remember, I'm just the help."

"I hate it when you talk that way," Charlotte said, straightening up. "There's one more piece of news," she said. "I spoke to Molly yesterday."

"Yes, I know," Agnes said. "She called me."

"How long will she be staying?" Charlotte asked, adjusting the shoulder strap of her purse.

"From what you tell me, no more than ten months. But I didn't ask and she didn't say," Agnes said as she pushed herself away from the table. "She knows she's always welcome here."

"We all know that," Charlotte said. "Which is why she always comes running back."

"She's only been here once since your mother's funeral," Agnes said.

"Well, I'm sorry it didn't work out with Eliot," Charlotte said. "He seemed awfully nice. Certainly a lot better than Chris. What a spineless man he was."

"She told me she's bored stiff with Eliot," Agnes said. "Apparently, he wants her to marry him."

"A perfectly nice man proposes to Molly and she bolts. That sounds typical." It was time to stop this conversation. She and Agnes always faced off over Molly, and tonight Charlotte didn't have the energy to get into it. She longed for a cigarette and a hot bath. "When is she getting here?"

"Day after tomorrow," Agnes said. "Sometime in the afternoon. She's bringing all the painting business. She says she has a lot of work to do."

"Tell her to call me when she gets in," Charlotte said. "Good night."

Agnes picked the checkered dishrag out of the soapy sink water, squeezed it, and mopped the tabletop with wide slow sweeps of her hand while the headlights of Charlotte's car journeyed across the pale yellow walls of the kitchen. When Agnes looked up from her work, the two red brake lights blinked at her from the end of the driveway before they disappeared.

She finished up in the kitchen, turned off the lights, and made her way slowly up the back stairs. Normally she settled herself in the faded chintz chair in the corner of the children's dining room to watch a television show across the top of the scarred wooden table. After all these years, the chair cushion was molded to the particular dips and lumps of her body, and in the evening after her work was done, she sank gratefully into it. But tonight she felt restless and she traveled up into the dark recesses of the house where she could hear the echoes of Mrs. W.'s voice and the sharp tapping of her heels on the bare floors.

"So, Molly's coming back again," she said as she plumped up the fat cushions on Lydia's bed.

"Take care of her, Agnes," she heard Lydia say.

"Don't I always? Haven't I given that child more love and attention than anybody else in this family? And she's the only one who repays me. At least, she tells me the truth about things. A golf club," she snapped. "In a year or two, some perfect stranger will be lying in some ugly modern bed right here in this room. Probably his hair grease will wipe right off on the pillowcase and nobody will care." She shuddered.

"Perhaps it would be better if they knocked it down," said Lydia's voice in her head.

"And where am I supposed to go?" Agnes demanded, swerving again. "Parceled off to live with Edith in that cluttered apartment in Fort Lee, New Jersey, with those terrible photographs of her grandchildren and all her fake antiques. How will I ever be able to stand it after this place?" she asked, her voice winding down to a small bewildered whisper.

For a moment, she stood there in the silence, the

357

house creaking and stretching around her. The night was warm and cricket-filled, and through the open windows she could hear the distant hum of the cars on Route 44 as they made their way over the mountain. Ever since the people who worked in Hartford had discovered this quaint rural town just on the other side of the mountain, the buzzing background noise of the traffic had grown a little louder each year. One by one the farmers had given in to the development fever, and the pastureland slowly filled up with rows of identical houses surrounded by packaged trees and swing sets and turquoise-blue pools that sat up above the ground looking like wading pools for giants.

"Oh, get on with it," she whispered to herself. "No use moping around over things. Charlotte's made up her mind and nothing is going to change it."

At that remark, she half expected a sharp reply from Mrs. W., but nothing came. She followed the twists of the hallway back to her own bedroom and undressed for bed. Propped up against the pillows, she read her meditation for the day in the *Daily Word* and then slid down between the cool sheets to wait for sleep.

"Charlotte worries me," she said out loud. "There's a crazy kind of look in her eye."

"You're imagining things."

"Easy for you to say," Agnes said. "She's not your problem anymore, is she?"

In 1943, George Webster suffered a heart attack while driving home from Plainfield. The police telephoned the farm from the hospital, but nobody answered. The year before, Lydia had been hired by Governor Baldwin to run the Women's Land Army, and she was still in her office in the State Armory. Agnes was down in the vegetable garden.

"I'll call the *Herald*," Sergeant Gardner told his partner. "The daughter works over there now and all the boys are overseas. Well, all but Oliver, of course." Nat Gardner was the son of old Jack Gardner, who had run the general store in town for a good thirty years. He and George Webster had been long-standing rivals for years, the congenial kind that small-town living breeds.

The switchboard operator at the newspaper put the call

right through to the news desk, where Charlotte was filling in for the managing editor, who had reported in sick.

"It was a miracle the car didn't hit someone, Miss Webster," Nat said. In the confusion, he had forgotten her married name. "He went off the road at that sharp curve on Route 10 and fetched up against Rutwell's fence."

"Is Dr. Ramsay there?" Charlotte asked.

"Yes. But some young guy's in charge. I wrote down what he said. Want me to read it to you?"

"Yes, please."

"Massive damage to one of the main arteries. The patient is conscious, but the heartbeat is still irregular. I guess you'd better come right in."

When Charlotte thought back to those six days between the first heart attack and the second, fatal one, it seemed to her that all they talked about was the paper. And Oliver.

"I want you to take over as publisher, Charlotte," her father said. "No matter what happens, the doctor says I'm not up to the work anymore. I knew this was coming. Remember the chest pains I told you about last month, Lydia?"

She nodded and patted his hand in an effort to calm him. Charlotte looked away. Seeing her mother sitting by this sickbed reminded her of Oliver's long convalescence.

"I've trained you to do it, Charlotte. You know the business now."

"Let me take over the editorial side when Rex Linscutt is done, Father. We'll bring somebody else in as publisher. I want to keep on writing. That's what I'm really good at."

Her father struggled to find a more comfortable position in the bed. Lydia shot her a dark look that meant: Don't argue with him, not now of all times.

"Charlotte, I don't want this paper to go out of the family. We've held on to it through the worst times. Remember the Depression and all the people I had to put out of work then? When Oliver comes back from Washington, he's going to need a job. We all know he's got to work for someone who understands his physical problems. You've always been much better at the business end of the thing. Keep him on the editorial staff. You'll be able to write the occasional editorial the way I always have.''

But she wanted more than the occasional editorial. When she had started working for the *Herald* the first time, the year after her graduation from Smith College, she had been a conscientious but tentative reporter. Rex, the managing editor, had burst out laughing one afternoon when he found her outlining her article first on a yellow pad. ''Throw the paper in the typewriter and start writing,'' he roared. ''We're on deadline here. No time for this schoolgirl stuff.'' Although the other reporters pretended not to hear, she felt the room quiet around her. With red cheeks, she picked up a piece of typing paper and rolled it into the Underwood. Her father had said she would have to prove herself. This was the first test.

Slowly, she had become a reporter. Even though it embarrassed her to ask the obvious questions, she persevered, often to discover that those questions produced exactly the answers she was looking for, the answers everybody thought they already knew. Her recent series on the road-building scandals in Danbury had gotten a lot of attention.

But it wasn't just the reporting. She loved the buzz of the newsroom, the sense of camaraderie that didn't seem to exist in the upstairs offices, where the floors were carpeted and the problems related to numbers not people. She loved the way Charlie Pursino, the police reporter, took to shouting at her across the newsroom. ''Hey, Lottie baby, you got that burglary story?'' She loved the slam of the file drawers, the constant ringing of the black phones, the smell of typewriter ink, the genial, chaotic coziness of the newsroom. For the first time, she felt as if she belonged somewhere. And now her father wanted to send her upstairs. All along, even though he had insisted on training her in the vagaries of advertising and circulation and how to read the budget sheets, she never thought he meant her to take over.

''I'm too young to take it over now, Father,'' she said.

"You and Rex can work together to begin with," he replied. "And don't worry, I'm not gone yet. I'll be hanging on here a little while longer. I hope that God will give me enough time to put the finishing touches on you."

But God had other ideas. Her father died less than a week later. The second attack came when he stood up to take his first walk down the hospital corridor.

Eighteen months later, when Oliver came back from his desk job in Washington, Charlotte was firmly ensconced in the second-floor office, the youngest newspaper publisher in the state of Connecticut. And the only woman.

Charlie Pursino was sent upstairs to interview her for the *Herald*'s feature page.

"So, Lottie baby," he muttered. "Give me the scoop. You like it up here in these posh offices?" He took a quick swivel in his chair, and when his face reappeared, he wore the expression of a surprised child. "Now, this is living," he crowed, and went around again.

"I'd rather be back downstairs with you, Charlie," she said. "It's a little lonely up here. But we'd better get on with the interview. I've got a budget meeting at three."

He asked the obvious questions, and she talked about the direction the newspaper would be taking now that the war was finally over and the boys were coming home. When Charlie asked about her father, she launched into a long speech. Her vehemence surprised him. "He wanted this paper to tell the truth above all. He wanted it to serve the people as a pipeline. Leave the big national stories to the big newspapers, he used to say. This paper's got its own special readership with their own special needs and interests. We are here to serve the farmers and the housewives and the factory workers of this valley. I intend to carry on in the same way."

"Now for the human-interest side," he said. "You're the only woman publisher in the state, after all. Better tell the fans how old those kids are and how you're managing to juggle motherhood and management. Like the sound of that?" he added with his old twinkle.

She glanced at her watch and stood up to search for some papers on her desk. "Well, of course the children are very young. David is just seven and Molly is five. But we have a wonderful woman taking care of them, and my

361

Elizabeth Winthrop

husband, Jack, is very understanding. Sometimes I think he's better than I am with the children," she added with a short laugh. "Certainly more patient."

"He used to work at the *Herald,* didn't he?" Charlie asked.

"Yes," she said. "I met him when I first came here." She did not say what his job had been, and even Charlie knew enough not to put in the article that the boss's daughter had married a typo, one of the men from the composing room. It killed him. The readers would love an angle like that. But she wouldn't. And now she was the boss.

The interview was still in the files somewhere. Marge, the archivist at the *Herald,* was fierce about the morgue, and even Charlotte had to admit that, from time to time, some of the old articles had proven useful, although lately the idea of all those stories, all those words resting on top of one another in yellowing manila folders, had begun to oppress her.

"When Marge retires in January, I'm going to have the files cleaned out," Charlotte told Oliver the morning after her visit with Agnes. "Now that we're going to be clearing out the farm, we might as well do it all at once. Sit down," she said, nodding at the chair. "We've got a lot to cover today."

Oliver lowered himself ever so slowly into the armchair, using his arms for support. She ducked her head down and pretended to search for the pencil she had dropped on purpose because she hated watching the way he moved his body around. It was as if everything below his waist had to be shifted about like fragile furniture. Some days were better than others, but she knew from Susan, his wife, that he had been having trouble with his bladder again. She never asked Oliver directly about his physical problems. She wished she didn't have to hear about them at all, but Susan made a point of letting her know every detail. Charlotte had often wondered whether her sister-in-law was totally insensitive or whether she had been sucked into the unacknowledged family conspiracy to help Charlotte pay her penance.

Oliver had married Susan Collins in 1946. She was a

local girl. Her mother had been an acquaintance of Lydia's, and if she were a little bland, her voice a little whiny, well, what did it really matter? They should all be grateful that Oliver had found someone to take care of him. Lydia had welcomed her into the family with such enthusiasm that Charlotte grew to dread even more the obligatory family dinners and holiday gatherings.

George told Charlotte she was just jealous because their mother paid so much attention to dull, dutiful Susan, and Charlotte had decided not to dignify his pronouncement with an argument. He was married and living in New York. Georgie the painter had turned out to be a corporate lawyer with an apartment on Park Avenue and a weekend house on Long Island. And he was very prone to pronouncements.

"So, Char, what's on your mind? I've got a desk piled high downstairs," Oliver said as he ran his hands nervously through his thinning hair. Sometimes when he got caught in the rain, the strands lay in dark separate lines on the top of his head.

"The compositors' strike. From what we hear, they're definitely going out tomorrow. We've got some people lined up to replace them for a while, but it's going to be chaotic. For the duration, I want to bring out just one edition a day. Skip the Newington–West Hartford one."

"Fine by me. It makes my life easier," he said. "We'll put a note on today's editorial page about it. By the way, I've had to push your editorial about the regional high school plan off till next week. We just don't have room for it."

She shrugged by way of reply. He played this game with her all the time. Write an editorial, Charlotte. Sorry, it's too long, Charlotte. Can't fit it in today, Charlotte. Sometimes she fought his decisions, but on days like this, she swallowed her fury and gave in. After all, as he liked to remind her under the guise of teasing, he was the managing editor. He never knew that Charlotte had practically bribed Rex Linscutt to stay on way past his retirement age in order to put off Oliver's promotion to the job. "He's really not ready for it," she used to tell her husband. "He's too inexperienced. And his writing is so bombastic and opinionated." And I want it to be me, not him, she sometimes still admitted to herself.

"About the house," she said. "Sol Delbianco called me this morning with his final offer."

"What is it?"

"Six hundred and seventy for the whole shooting match. Pending the results of the zoning board, of course. That shouldn't be any problem since Nick Togni heads up the board and is a silent partner in this venture." She threw her pencil down on the blotter and leaned back in her chair. "The irony of this whole business never fails to amuse me. The sons of the Italian tobacco workers are buying out the children of the man who brought their fathers here. Life does come full circle, doesn't it?"

"Well, Char, you're the one who started all this. I still don't understand your desperate rush to sell the place. And now you're talking about clearing out files. God knows what's next," he grumbled. "I'll probably see an ad for your own house in the *Courant*."

"It ran yesterday," Charlotte said. "I've decided to move to the Cape." At his look of horror, she added, "I'm only teasing, Oliver. You've lost your sense of humor."

"What did you tell Sol?"

She steeled herself. "I accepted his offer."

"Just like that? Without consulting the rest of us? I do think you've gone mad."

"Perhaps. But I didn't see any reason to keep on fiddling around. The land and buildings together are appraised at six-ninety. Twenty thousand dollars divided four ways isn't worth hassling over, for God's sake."

When he tried to shift in his seat, his jacketed elbow slipped off the wooden armrest and he winced with a sudden pain.

"Are you all right?" Charlotte asked.

"Yes, dammit. I'm so sick of women hovering over me. Susan is driving me mad these days, so don't you start."

Charlotte said nothing.

"Campbell is going to be furious that you've gone ahead without consulting the rest of us. Georgie won't give a damn, of course. He's like you. All you two care about is getting the money."

Underneath the desk, she fanned her hands and curled them closed again until the sharp points of her nails left small dark dents in her palm. Oliver's voice was droning on and she could see his mouth moving but she did not hear the words. Lately, she had found a new way to shut out the world when it got to be too much for her. She turned on a song in her head. It was as easy as flicking the volume dial on a radio. The one that kept repeating itself these days was the hymn they had sung at her mother's funeral. "The strife is o'er, the battle done, the victory of life is won. The song of triumph has begun. Alleluia." The more Oliver gestured and rumbled at her from his side of the room, the louder the song grew until she began to sway ever so slightly in her seat.

"Char!" Now Oliver was really shouting. "What the devil is the matter with you? You haven't heard a word I've said."

"No. I haven't. I guess we'd both better get back to work. Why don't you call Campbell and moan with him about your incorrigible sister. It might make you feel better."

Oliver struggled to his feet. "I hate it when you get sarcastic," he said. "This was a family decision and the whole family should have made it. It's not the money, it's the principle of the thing."

"Then call Sol up and tell him you're having me committed and the offer doesn't hold because I was temporarily insane." She couldn't stop herself. Teasing Oliver had always been fun even when they were little. Had he seemed so whiny to her then? She couldn't remember. He looked as if he were going to ignore the last comment and stomp out of the room. "There was one more thing on the agenda," she said, raising her voice slightly. "Molly wants to come back and live with Agnes for a while."

He turned around in the doorway. "Why?"

"I know she sublet her apartment in the city when she moved out to Danbury with Eliot. Now she's leaving him, she probably needs a place to stay in the interim."

"I thought they might get married. He seemed nice

enough. Wasn't he the one she brought to Mother's funeral?"

"Yes. I get all my news about my daughter from Agnes, who reports that Molly's bored with him."

"Oh well, children aren't our strong point, are they?" Oliver said. "Richard called last night asking for money again. You'd think at the age of twenty-four, the boy could start supporting himself."

Oliver and Susan had adopted children soon after they were married. The boy had struggled all the way through school, and Sally, the younger one, had moved back home after graduating from college. She was supposedly looking for a job, but for the time being she was working part-time at her mother's antique business, which they ran out of the barn in the back of the house. Oliver blamed the girl's problems on Susan, who coddled her. In her worst moments, Charlotte blamed herself because, of course, if it weren't for her, Oliver could have had his own children.

"At least Molly's made quite a name for herself in the art world," Oliver said. "Two shows in a well-known gallery in New York. Not bad for a thirty-one-year-old woman."

"Yes," Charlotte said, her voice softening. "Although the reviews in June were hard for her to take after the wild success of the first show."

"Life has its ups and downs," he said. "The sooner she learns that, the better."

25

Molly Taylor sat in the hall chair, staring at one of her old paintings. When she first moved in with Eliot, he had insisted on hanging this self-portrait by the staircase, as if by giving her art some prominent space in his house, he was also making room for her. She had appreciated his gesture at the time, but the painting had begun to grate on her. It was the first in a series done in oil, and now she could see that the colors looked too scrubbed in, the lines tentative and muddy. By contrast, her thick red hair attracted too much attention in the painting. Even her pose seemed forced as she faced the viewer, elbows resting on knees, chin jutting out as if she were saying, "So what do you want?"

"You're letting those reviews get to you," Andrea Fenton had said to her on the phone that morning. Andrea owned the gallery which showed Molly's work. The two women had become good friends. "Nothing's making you happy these days."

"Because the reviews were right. Miss Taylor's work seems to have lost its energy in the last year—"

"For God's sake, don't start quoting them to me again. I've never known an artist who memorized her bad reviews instead of the good ones."

"It's all your fault," Molly said with feigned petulance. "Introducing me to Eliot Duncan. Getting me stuck out here in the country with this damn lake staring at me all day like a one-eyed monster."

"When I introduced you to the man, I never expected you to bury yourself with him in the country."

"Well, I've decided to dig myself out again."

"You're coming back to the city. Thank God. It's all

367

that beautiful nature that's sucking the energy out of your work."

"No, actually, I'm headed deeper into the hinterland. To my grandmother's house in Connecticut. My mother's put the place up for sale."

Andrea was full of questions, but Molly had squirmed out of the conversation quickly because she wasn't sure of the answers herself yet.

Now she lifted the self-portrait off its hook and turned its hostile face to the wall. "Now you've been a bad girl," she said out loud. "You must stay there until suppertime. Or breakfast. Or the middle of next winter. Because the farm will be sold. And there's nothing you can do about it."

In the last ten years, just knowing that the house and her grandmother and Agnes were all still there had made her feel less crazy on the bad days, more jubilant and celebratory on the good ones. The farm was her amulet against the evil spirits. How many times had she run back there to sit with Grandmother over the tea tray in the sun porch or huddle with Agnes around the wooden table in the dining room? Too many, her mother would say.

She picked up the phone again. Agnes answered after six rings.

"It's me," Molly said. "It's Tuesday, which means you were cleaning the upstairs bedrooms. Did I make you walk all the way down the back hallway?"

"Yes. There's something wrong with the telephone in your grandmother's room. Wait. Let me catch my breath."

"Take your time."

And Agnes, being Agnes, did.

"All right, now I've collected myself."

"Thank heavens," Molly said with a grin. "I thought you'd died. Spending twenty cents a minute to listen to someone expire is not my idea of a good time."

Agnes didn't reply, but Molly knew she was smiling. They had the same sense of humor.

And of course, Agnes wanted her to come. She sounded as if she'd been waiting for just this phone call, as if she knew before Molly even did that she would be coming back. They went on talking until Molly saw Eliot's car turning into the driveway. He hated her to be on the phone when he walked in from work, and she was determined to make their last few days as peaceful as possible.

"Agnes, I'll be there day after tomorrow. Sometime in the afternoon. Eliot's coming in now, so I've got to go."

"I'll be here. Got nowhere else to go," Agnes said, and as Molly put the phone quietly down, she heard Agnes's goodbye drifting back up to her from the receiver.

That night over dinner Molly told Eliot she was leaving.

She packed all the next day, sorting through the piles of sketchbooks she had accumulated in the last two years. The pages seemed choked with pictures of leaves and sunsets and the lake.

She left early the next morning. Once the car was packed, she pointed its nose down the steep driveway and took off with a start, the tires spitting gravel like loose teeth. Eliot would rake it again this evening when he got home.

"Goodbye, Eliot. The careless gravel sprayer has just gone out of your life." And to her surprise, she drove the next five miles through a mist of steady tears.

"We ought to have windshield wipers for our eyes," Rudy Delbianco had said to her at her grandmother's funeral when he handed over his damp handkerchief. "It's not clean, but it's better than your sleeve."

The thought of Rudy cheered her a little. She kicked off her shoes and turned the radio way up. You're not supposed to cry when you're going home, she told herself. Only when you're leaving.

The drive to the farm took a little over two hours. She'd made the trip many times, and each familiar landmark eased the gnawing in her stomach. At the halfway mark, she stopped at her usual coffee shop and bought herself a doughnut and a pack of cigarettes, her first since the move to the country. Eliot hated the smell of smoke, so she had given it up to please him.

"Miss, you'll have to move. This is a no-smoking section."

"I'll put it out," she said. "Do you smoke?"

The waitress looked at her suspiciously. "My boyfriend does."

"Give him a present," Molly said, pushing the pack across the damp counter. "I've just given it up."

Agnes hated the smell of smoke too.

She saw the flash of Agnes's wave from the window above the kitchen sink as she turned into the driveway. With the car door open, she swung her bare feet out onto the macadam, which felt soft from the heat of the afternoon sun. The smell of the freshly mown lawn mingled with oil fumes. That odd mixture of farm odors was enough, every time, to send her back to the games under the copper beech tree when she was ten, back even further to the splashing in the plastic wading pool on the lawn while Agnes watched to be sure she and David didn't slip and drown in the six inches of water. Agnes was watching her now, although their eyes had not yet met.

Molly dropped her first load of canvases by the kitchen door. Agnes didn't turn around. She always made you cross the room to her. It was her way of saying: If I've stood at this sink and waited all this time for you to come, I can wait a little longer.

"Hello," Molly said, putting her cheek down on the curve of Agnes's uniformed back. Agnes seemed to be shrinking as she got older, and Molly noticed that the hump of bone between her shoulders had gotten bigger in the last year.

"Hello yourself," Agnes muttered, reaching around awkwardly to pat the top of Molly's head. Her hand dripped soapsuds and Molly felt their tiny poppings against the skin of her forehead. "Have you eaten anything?"

"Just a doughnut and some coffee. But I'm not really hungry now. I'll wait till dinner." She pulled the white wooden stepladder out from under the kitchen table and collapsed on it. "I'm tired."

"It's a long drive."

"It's been a long year." She spread her bare arms out against the tin tabletop that had been battered over the years by children's spoons and heavy platters and rolling pins. The pocked metal surface felt cool against her hot skin. Coming home reminded her that this would be the last time, and without any warning at all, she began to cry.

Agnes went about her business, dried her hands slowly

with the plaid dish towel, rinsed the sink one more time, adjusted the shade pull against the lowering sun. A green truck turned into the driveway.

"That's Frank come to pick up the garbage. Late as usual."

She reached into her pocket, and on her way past the table, she put three neatly folded tissues next to Molly's face. "I'll keep him outside," she said.

They ate dinner in the children's dining room sitting side by side at the round dark table.

"Here's the place where David worked his knife into the wood," Molly said, running her fingers back and forth across the deep scar which had blackened with time.

"He was awful mad at me," Agnes said. "All over a small pile of peas."

"It wasn't like David, was it? He was always the good boy." Molly smiled.

The green and white squares of linoleum ran from the kitchen right through the doorway into this room, where, for years, children had dropped knives and forks and spilled milk and thrown food at each other when the grownups weren't looking. The pictures had hung in the same place on the walls for so long that their frames had ground circles of dirt into the wallpaper. Molly knew them by heart. The Dutch country village scene painted on tin, the charcoal sketch of some distant uncle sprawled in a garden chair the year before the war, the six post-card scenes of Venice at the turn of the century. The glue had dried up behind the bottom right-hand card and it hung askew.

"I walked through this house in my mind all winter," Molly said.

"You could have come for a visit," Agnes said. She lined her fork and knife up side by side.

Agnes was not pretty. Probably when she was younger her face had been more tightly gathered together, but now the loose skin hung down from her neck and upper arms like tissue paper that had been scrunched up and smoothed out straight again. Her white hair was thinning, and one week after her regular Thursday visit to the House of Beauty, it stood up from her scalp in

separate clumps. Her thick glasses magnified the size of
her blue eyes, so that if she looked up at you suddenly,
straight on, they gave her the appearance of a slightly
surprised frog. She looked that way now.

"I should have. I missed you. But I had the feeling that
once I came back here I would never be able to bear that
suburban house by that dark lake. And I didn't know
then that I wanted to leave Eliot." Molly rested her chin
in her elbows. "Doesn't make much sense, does it?" she
asked. "But you know me and goodbyes. I'd rather just
skip right over that part."

"Hellos aren't exactly your strong point either," Agnes
said.

"Has Mother told you anything more about the house?"
Molly asked. "How much time do we have?"

"Till June if the deal goes through. And by the way,
the interested party is one Sol Delbianco."

"Rudy's uncle?"

"That's right. He owns the big motel on the corner
with two other partners. He wants to turn this place into
a golf club."

"That's awful," Molly said. "It would be better if they
knocked the whole thing down. I can't stand the idea of
fat men in spiked shoes marching in the door on Saturday
afternoons." She shuddered. "Don't you think that's
awful?"

"I suppose so." Agnes shrugged. "What's the difference, really? Once I go, I'm never coming back."

"Where will you go?"

"To Edith's in Fort Lee if she'll have me. I haven't
phoned her yet. Been putting it off."

Molly reached across the table and squeezed the other
woman's pale veined hand. She knew there was no love
lost between Agnes and her twin sister. "Why don't you
stay here in Northington? I'm sure that Mother and I can
get you one of those apartments right in town above the
stores so you can walk everywhere. And maybe Frank
could drive you into Hartford every week the way he
does now. Wouldn't that be better?"

"I don't know. I'll think about it." Agnes twisted her
hand out from under Molly's. "You know, you give your

whole life to a family and a place, but when the time comes, you're put out on the back stoop like the cat."

Before Molly could answer, Agnes stood up and stomped out of the room, her fat-heeled black shoes beating an angry path into the kitchen. She was right, after all, Molly thought. For all her own sentimental yearnings about the farm, she had that apartment in New York, she was young, she could make her way in the world. How old was Agnes now? At least seventy. After forty or more years of service in this huge old house, she was being pensioned off to live with her sister.

"We'll figure out something," Molly said later when they stood side by side, drying the dishes. "I'll talk to Mother."

"Nothing more to be said," Agnes whispered. "We both know they can't keep this place going just for an old housekeeper. I should have died when your grandmother did. It would have been more convenient for everybody. Including me."

"Agnes, I hate it when you talk that way."

"Why not? It's the truth."

Molly put her arm around the sloping shoulders and squeezed her once. She was right. Nothing more to be said.

Once the dishes were done and put away, they walked down the rutted farm road to the river. The jumping platform at the swimming hole had begun to sag at one end from years of use.

"Does anybody use it anymore?" Molly asked.

"I reckon the neighborhood kids come down here. And Rudy brings his three on the weekends. They always have dinner with Frank and Angelina Sunday nights."

"Boy, did I hate it up there," Molly said. "Everybody tormenting me to jump. Even Mother. Uncle Oliver used to tell me that Mother first jumped when she was eight years old. I didn't do it until I was fourteen and Rudy was the only one who saw. Remember that?"

Agnes smiled. "He came busting into the kitchen screaming at the top of his lungs, 'She did it, she did it!' I thought you'd flown to the moon and back, the way he was carrying on."

They turned away from the water and followed the

forest path. "Daddy never bugged me about things like that," Molly said quietly.

"No, he didn't," Agnes said.

Back at the porch, the screen door swung open on a sudden breeze.

"The spring's gone. Frank's been promising to fix it, but he forgets," Agnes said. She took the steps one leg at a time, leaning over the upper bent knee for support. Molly knew better than to offer any help.

Agnes went in the house and flicked on the porch light. "You coming in?"

"Not quite yet. It's a pretty night."

"Lock up when you do."

She sat at the top of the steps and watched the night fall. From inside, there came the flickering half-light of the television. Agnes was watching one of her shows. The phone rang. Molly tensed. It rang again. The third time, Agnes picked up. Molly tiptoed inside and stood at the doorway, listening.

"Yes, she's here. Just a minute."

"Eliot?" Molly mouthed.

Agnes nodded. Molly shook her head.

"She can't talk to you right now, Eliot. Maybe tomorrow. . . . Yes, I know. . . . Yes. I'll tell her."

She hung up and went back to looking at her show.

"What did he say?"

"Said to tell you he loves you."

"That's the trouble," Molly said as she went to lock up.

As usual, she chose to sleep in her mother's bedroom. The windows looked through the branches of the last surviving elm tree on the place. Beyond, the lawn flowed like water down around the vegetable garden and the old clay tennis court her grandparents had built in the late thirties. The green leaves of the elm seemed to grow right over the windowsill and into the room because the walls were covered with paper "designed by a maniac," as David used to say. Ivy tendrils curled in and out of the metal triangles of a chain fence from the baseboard right up to the ceiling. It had always made Molly feel like a baby bird, safe in its nest.

She lay in bed, listening to the familiar rustlings of the house that meant mice or dry wood or loose shutters.

She thought about Eliot. It was too early for him to be in bed. Usually, it took him hours to unwind from work. He would play the piano, fix a lamp, hang upside down like a bat from the bar he had installed above the bathroom door. When he finally came to bed, ready to cuddle and play, she would already be asleep. Her first sleep of the night was always very deep, and if he tickled or stroked her into consciousness, she would be enraged and push him away, trying to find her way back down by giving herself space alone in the bed. Lately, she had not slept well, but she had been pretending.

Lying on her side wth her knees bent and the pillow pressed the length of her stomach, she wanted to have Eliot there just to hold him for a moment without speaking. To comfort the part of him that felt like her.

At the other end of the house, Agnes lay awake in the darkness, thinking of Nort Hart. How long had it been since he had come visiting in her mind? "It must be Molly," she said out loud. "She's always on the lam, always running from something. Just like Nort."

They had kept company for close to ten years, right up to the beginning of the war. He used to stop by on Thursday nights in his old Ford pickup and drive her over to Simsbury to the movies and after that to the Blue Wagon, a dim bar on the edge of town. He was a hard drinker, and she often had to drive him home, even though she never did bother about getting a license.

In the beginning, Agnes had dreamed about marrying him and moving across town where he had some land. He would build her a little house. They might even have a child, a little one to erase the shadow of the girl she had buried back in Seneca Falls. But she was careful not to let on that she had any expectations. After Harry Becker, she had learned her lesson. Men got edgy when you tried to tie them down. So she pretended to be perfectly happy with their one or two nights a week. After all, he was a good-looking man, and even though he didn't talk much, he could say things to surprise you. He liked rocks, for example, and knew a lot about them.

"It comes from digging so many of them out of these fields," he told her with a chuckle.

The first time she had insisted on driving him home, he was furious.

"I've driven myself much farther than this on a couple of drinks," he stormed.

"You can drive yourself anywhere you want," Agnes told him. "But not me."

"And how will you get yourself home?" he asked.

"I'll fix you some coffee and sober you up. If that doesn't work, I'll take the truck back to the farm. And won't you look a little sheepish, coming over in the morning to fetch it?"

He didn't want her to come inside the house, but she pushed right past. The liquor seemed to loosen up everything about him, so that his voice grew as wobbly as his legs and he propped himself up by the front door and watched her take over.

The house, a shack really, was surprisingly neat. His rock collection was laid out on homemade shelves along one wall of the main room. There wasn't much else to look at in the way of furniture. An old bureau, an iron bed neatly made, some photographs which she pretended not to see. A man has a right to some privacy.

He drank the coffee obediently, but the whole time he watched her with shining eyes and she felt uneasy about being there with him and yet mischievous too. They sat next to each other on the narrow wooden bench in the kitchen, and she was aware of their bodies lined up close together while they sipped the black coffee.

She was turning to ask him for sugar when he took her into his arms. She should protest, she told herself. This was wrong, of course. And yet, hadn't she known this might happen when she drove him here? Wasn't this just exactly what she wanted after so many years? Her body stirred to his, and then suddenly, abruptly, he pulled away.

"You'd better go now, Miss Becker," he said. "I'm not in control of myself right now. You take the truck. I'll come for it in the morning."

"I'll finish my coffee first," she said, ducking her head. And then we'll see, she told herself.

It turned out that he still wasn't in control of himself after the coffee, but then neither was she, and what she loved most about that night and the ones that came after was the loose easy grin on his face when it hung over hers in the bed.

He made no promises, no proposals, and she asked for none, although she made very sure he took the necessary precautions. They fell into a pattern. She drove to his house from the Blue Wagon, and once the coffee and their roll in the hay, which is what he liked to call it, had sobered him up, he drove her home to the farm.

At first, Nort was amazed at his good fortune. A woman who made no demands on him, who took him for what he was with no complaints, whose body fit well with his on the narrow bed. But after a while, he began to berate himself. He should do right by her, of course. People in town were beginning to snicker about them. He knew they were the subject of idle gossip in the post office or on the barstools at the Blue Wagon, and Agnes was a good woman. She deserved better, and in his mournful moments, he tried to tell her that.

"I'll decide what I deserve," she told him.

Then one night when he had more drink in him than usual, he asked her to marry him.

She got out of the bed without saying a word and dressed herself.

"I want you to ask me again in the morning," she said. "When you're sober."

"You don't believe I'll go through with it," he said, itching for a fight, something to wipe out what he had said.

"Yes, I do. But I don't want to take advantage of you when you're under the influence."

"Now, there's a switch," he said with a harsh laugh. "Usually it's the man that takes the advantage."

That night she drove herself home alone. He never came to pick up the truck. He was gone in the morning.

"The shack is cleared out," Gino reported to Mr. Webster in the kitchen.

"Did he give you any hint that he was going?" Mr. Webster asked. "I can't understand his leaving after all these years."

Around the corner, Agnes stood in the pantry, mashing the same orange half over and over again until the thick skin of it finally broke against the ribbed glass of the juicer.

"Agnes was out with him last night," Gino said. He didn't know she was listening. Mr. Webster said something in a low voice, and they went out onto the porch.

Nobody ever heard from him again. There were rumors. Someone had seen a man just like Nort working in a logging camp up in Maine or somebody else's cousin was with him in Florida during the war, but Agnes paid no attention to the stories. She knew better than to waste her time waiting for him to come back. "When they go, they don't come back," she told Mrs. Webster one of those nights alone together when they met after dinner in neutral territory to keep each other company. "I know. I had one like that before. Left me when he heard I was pregnant."

"What happened to the baby?"

"It was a little girl. She died when she was two. Scarlet fever."

"So that's why you came to us," Lydia said. "Tell me. Did you write that letter of recommendation?"

Agnes grinned. "Yup. Mrs. Gilbert was my sister."

"I thought so."

All these years later, Agnes still wondered what Nort Hart would have done if she had accepted him that night.

"He would have bolted anyway," she said out loud. "Another Harry Becker all over again. And Molly's a bolter too. I seem to attract them. Bees to honey."

She knew what Mrs. Webster would have said. "It's because you let the men have their way with you, Agnes." Who knows? Maybe she should have kept her body from Nort in the vain hope that he would marry her to get what he wanted. The shack had been bulldozed years ago when they ran the new road through that way, but maybe Nort would have built her the little dream house and she'd be sitting there now in her own kitchen. Her own place that no Webster or Delbianco could take away from her. Maybe Nort would be there too. How old would he be now? Seventy-five or so. She giggled. He'd

378

probably take his teeth out at night and fart in their bed.

But knowing Nort, he would have dropped her or run off anyway and she would have been left with nothing but her pure body and the memories of all those wasted nights behind and a lifetime of them stretching before her. No, thanks, to that. She was glad for what she'd done.

26

In the morning, Molly went down to the vegetable garden to help Agnes pick the first tomatoes and the last beans. She took her sketchbook, and when the work was done, she asked Agnes to sit on an overturned bushel basket.

"Sit?" said Agnes. "Now that's an easy order for me to follow these days. Stand, trot, gallop. Those are all harder."

"You always talk when I sketch you," Molly said.

"It makes me nervous to have a body staring at me," she said. "Is this painting business going to go on the whole time? I'm not sure I can bear it. It's like having your grandmother back again."

The year she turned fourteen, Molly lived at the farm, and every afternoon when she got home from school, she and Grandmother painted together for an hour. One day it would be a still life, another day a portrait. Once they had descended on Agnes in the kitchen and made her sit on the white stepladder next to the window while they sketched her from different angles.

"The dinner's going to burn up, Mrs. W."

"We're just doing quick sketches, Agnes. Five minutes each. I've got the timer going."

The bell of the timer would ring and the two artists would flip over the pages of their sketchbooks and move their chairs to work from different angles.

"Try the next one in charcoal, Molly," Grandmother said. "Remember to make broad, bold strokes. Use the whole page."

"It's a good thing I had my hair done yesterday," Agnes grumbled. And later: "I can smell the roast. Don't blame me if the lamb is overdone at dinner. You're the one who likes it pink." And finally, she couldn't stand it anymore. She slid off the stool before the timer rang and marched back to the stove.

"Agnes," Lydia wailed. "I was just doing your mouth with that pouty expression."

"When I was hired for this job, nobody said anything aobut modeling for amateur artists."

"I loved the way you and Grandmother used to talk to each other," Molly said now, tilting her head one way to stare at her work and then the other.

"You look like your grandmother when you do that," Agnes said.

"Terrible," Molly said, and flipped the page. "I've been drawing trees for so long, I don't know how to do people anymore."

"Enough," said Agnes as she struggled to her feet. "I've got my morning's work cut out for me. I'm canning today."

"It's so hot, Agnes. You'll expire." Molly lifted her hair off her damp neck and twisted it up into a knot on top of her head. "I was thinking of having all this chopped off."

"I wouldn't do that. Summer will be gone and then you'll have a cold neck in the winter. The landlady here is very sparing with the heat. From the sounds of it, the furnace might not even make it through the winter."

"You take the beans and I'll bring up the tomatoes," Molly said. "Go on ahead of me."

Agnes took the smaller basket and walked slowly away, her body leaning toward the slight incline, the hem of the pale blue uniform lifting and falling a bit with each step. Beyond her, a black pickup truck turned into the driveway and parked down by the calf barn.

"I'll be up in a minute, Agnes," she called, setting the heavy basket down on the uneven ground. "I want to say hello to Rudy."

Agnes plowed on ahead without acknowledging that she had heard.

Molly trotted across the lawn, thin freckled legs churning under her, elbows pressed close to her sides. She didn't shout his name until she was sure he would hear, and when she did, he turned ever so slowly from the door, his head cocked as it always was toward his right shoulder, the grin spreading across his face as he recognized her.

Of course, he expected her to stop and shake hands, and if they had met somewhere else, in the kitchen under Agnes's watchful eye, for example, Molly would have done that. But out here with the heat and the exhilaration of her run and the excitement of seeing him, she threw her arms around him with such fervor that he was almost knocked off his feet.

"Molly Taylor," he said into her ear as he lifted her a few inches off the ground and then set her back down on her feet. "I heard you were coming back."

She stepped away, a little embarrassed. His face was square and open, as available as a road map or a hand at cards. The thick eyebrows, the sideburns, the hair curling up out of the neck of his T-shirt all made him look older than he was. "It's good to see you, Rudy."

"I guess so. How are you?"

"Breathing in and out," she said. "And you. How's Rosa? And the kids."

"Fine," he said, but his voice sounded odd. "Kids are growing up."

"I hear that's what they do," she replied with a smile. "You know about the farm, I guess."

"I've just come from a meeting with Uncle Sol. He's asked me to renovate the calf barn."

"Your beloved calf barn," she said, and he smiled.

"I've still got your picture of it. Remember when you gave it to me?"

"Of course I do. And I still have the cherry-wood palette you made me that year." She looked away. "So they've definitely closed the deal," she said, her voice low.

"Sounds that way." He put out a hand to her but withdrew it before he touched her. "It must be hard for you."

"I came back to say goodbye, I guess," she said.

"How's—" He paused, searching for the name.

"Eliot. Left behind. I'd better go. Agnes is determined to put up vegetables today and she's waiting for the tomatoes."

"Need a hand?" he asked.

"No, it's all right," she said. "Painters develop big muscles from hauling all those canvases around."

"Rosa and I will get you over for dinner soon," he said.

"I'd like to see the kids," she said, but they were both being polite. "See you." She turned and jogged away, aware that he was still standing by the truck watching her pumping legs and the thick knot of her hair as it came undone and spilled across her shoulders.

When they were growing up, she used to go down to the cottage for supper once a week. She sat next to him at the small kitchen table that had been covered with flowered Con-Tact paper, fringed at the edges. They ate spaghetti swimming in the sauce his mother made with hot sausages and red peppers, and after dinner Angelina would braid her hair while Rudy watched.

"Where did you get it?" Rudy asked her once while she sat in the straight-backed chair, swinging her legs back and forth.

"What?" Molly said, allowing her head to be tugged about by Angelina's hands.

"The red color."

She shrugged. "It came with me," she explained.

Angelina put back her head and roared with laughter. "You silly son of mine," she said. "Did you think it came out of a bottle like shoe polish?"

He had jumped up and run away to hide in the tree house.

"Come down, Rudy," Molly called from below on her way home. "I don't think it was a stupid question."

But he wouldn't, and that night she had to walk up the driveway by herself.

Agnes was standing at the stove over two enormous vats of boiling water. Her white hair was tied up in a ridiculous red bandanna.

"You look like the Wicked Witch of the West," Molly said as she lowered the tomato basket to the floor.

"Speaking of that, your mother just called."

"Agnes, I'm shocked. That's no way to talk about my dear darling mother."

"Sorry, I couldn't resist," Agnes said with a rare grin.

She dragged the stepladder out from under the table and lowered herself onto it. "She's coming by this afternoon. Where have you been with my tomatoes?"

"Talking to Rudy. Apparently the Delbiancos and the Websters have reached an agreement, because Sol has told Rudy to go ahead with a renovation of the calf barn."

Agnes looked up and neither of them spoke for a moment. "Done deal, then," she said, and went back to snapping the ends of the beans.

"Do you want some help here?"

"No. Go along with you," Agnes said. "I'm not too old to can a few tomatoes by myself."

"Is it all right with you if I use the painting porch?"

"Go right ahead. Nobody's looked in there since your grandmother died, so you might do a little cleaning out while you're at it."

Molly wandered slowly up the back hallway, checking the rooms to reassure herself that, for the moment, all was still the same. Here was the guest bedroom where she taught her brother, David, how to smoke, and of course Grandmother had caught them. "Darling, what did you expect me to think when I found the pile of butts in the empty fireplace?" Here was the upstairs wood chest where her father had once managed to hide during a terrifying game of Murder in the Dark. Here was the attic staircase, which still smelled of cedar and drying leather and Grandmother's potpourri. And here was the boudoir where Grandmother ate her breakfast on the chaise longue while Molly leaned against the rose chintz side of it and finished her last bit of homework before the school bus came.

At the one end of the large light room stood the cast-iron stove that Frank started up on winter mornings when he brought up her tray. The flowered couch under the windows was always called the judgment seat. Badly behaved grandchildren and sons in debt and maids who had been caught lifting the silver had all known their day of reckoning on that couch. Molly had sat there all too often, her feet planted firmly on the peach-colored rose in the hook rug, her back straight and unsupported, while Grandmother went over her report card, stopping every once in a while to glare over her bifocals at her granddaughter.

"I thought you liked history, darling. How could you possibly have gotten a C? A C is such a middling kind of grade. Get an A or a D, for God's sake. Don't be mediocre."

"Really, Grandmother?" Molly asked.

"If I thought that enthusiasm meant you'd try for the A, I'd say yes. But knowing you, you'll throw up your hands and sink down to the D. So no, I don't mean it, you rascal."

"It's so hard to concentrate in history. Miss Nutting has no imagination. She tells me I'm impertinent when I ask questions." Besides, I'd rather draw in the back of the textbook when she's not looking, Molly admitted to herself.

Her parents never paid much attention to her grades, but Grandmother insisted that they go over every report card very carefully. She never did it with David, but then David didn't need the extra attention. David was the hero in the family, the perfect boy.

The mirrors along one wall of the room hid a row of closets where in the evenings Agnes would burrow through a tightly stuffed rack of dresses, searching for the emerald-green velvet or the red chiffon. Grandmother never threw anything away and she had no idea about fashion. "It fit me then, it fits me now," she used to say as she sat at the dressing table, poking in the U-shaped hairpins with sharp jabs and talking to Molly all the while.

In those days, her grandmother's gray hair was pulled up in a flat bun anchored by the black hairpins that crept out and were pushed in all day long. Her skin hung loosely on the bones of her face, which gave the large smile and the head thrown back in laughter plenty of room. The ears and nose matched the grandeur of her gestures. They were all too big, out of proportion with the small shoulders, delicate hands, the thin waist. "A Gibson girl with the face of an elephant and the sweep of its trunk," she used to say about herself without bitterness. When she died, that quote made its way into her obituary in the Hartford *Courant,* with the comment that

385

such a description was appropriate for one of the leading Republican women in the state.

The door to the painting porch had swollen with the August humidity. Molly had to kick it hard in the lower right-hand corner three or four times before it finally gave way. The smell of oils and turpentine contained for so long in the closed space flooded over her like a perfume. She took a deep breath and walked to the center of the room.

Nothing had been moved. The easel was set up in the corner, the paint box opened on the tray beside it. On the palette, a brush lay stuck in a dried-up puddle of turquoise, one of her grandmother's favorite colors. Grandmother had always been very careful about her equipment and had instilled in Molly a love for the materials and for the rituals of cleaning up. She must have put the paintbrush down for some minor interruption like a phone call or a trip to the bathroom. She must have been planning to come back very soon and she never did and here was the evidence left for Molly to discover like some fossilized dinosaur print.

Molly lifted the brush as carefully as a dressing on a moist wound, but the thin black hairs, trapped for over a year in the frozen paint, tore away from their aluminum holder. "I'm sorry, Grandmother," Molly whispered. "I'll have to throw away the palette too. It's not worth saving."

In another corner of the porch, some stretched canvases were propped up against the closet door. Apple blossoms fuzzy and pink against the wall of the calf barn, the barn silos, a vase of flowers on the dining-room table, the sun porch in the spring with the freesia blooming in the corner pots, the boudoir with Frank standing awkwardly by the wood stove.

The closet was a jumble of stretchers, rolled-up canvases, sketch pads of various sizes, cans of turpentine, two watercolor sets. Molly was sitting on the floor going through the sketch pads when she heard her mother's voice calling to her from the hallway.

"I'm in here, Mother," Molly yelled back. "On the porch."

"My God, what a mess," Charlotte said as she rounded the last corner.

"Have you noticed that she always comes into a room talking?" David had asked Molly once. "It doesn't ever occur to her that something else might have been going on when she wasn't there, that she might be interrupting. She must think we stop breathing if she's not there to watch our chests go up and down."

"Hello, Mother," Molly said from the closet floor. She threw up her hands in a gesture of helplessness. "I'd get up, but I'm a little overwhelmed."

"I can see. What is all that stuff?"

"Grandmother's sketchbooks mostly. Look at this picture of Agnes," she said, holding out one of the larger books. "She caught the mouth perfectly. You know the way her lower lip hangs down."

Charlotte took the sketchbook and leafed through it quickly. "Not bad," she said without enthusiasm as she handed it back. "This place hasn't changed," she said as she walked the perimeters of the room, ran her finger along the windowsills. "It's hot as hell in here. I guess Frank didn't bother to put up the screens this summer."

"No reason to," Molly said. "But I'd like to move my stuff in and get to work soon. Is it all right if I ask Frank or Rudy to do it?"

Charlotte whirled around. "Rudy doesn't work for us, Molly. Only Frank."

"All right, then, Frank. No big deal." She piled the sketchbooks to one side and struggled to her feet.

"Have you seen Rudy?" her mother asked.

"Yes. He came by this morning to look at the calf barn."

"Sol is hiring him to do it over," Charlotte said.

"So I heard. I understand you've all agreed on a price. I didn't think it would happen so quickly."

Charlotte laughed, a sharp harsh sound that bounced off the glass walls. "Neither did your uncles. But it was ridiculous to drag the business out any longer." She took another turn around the room and settled at last on her mother's painting stool. "God, I haven't been in this porch in years."

"Grandmother and I used to paint here in the afternoons," Molly said.

"You weren't the first," Charlotte said. "The first was your Uncle George. Every afternoon at four o'clock until he went off to boarding school. 'Georgie has real talent,' Mother used to say. That word 'real' always made me cringe."

Molly watched her mother's hands fanning open and shut. "How's the paper?" she asked.

"Tough times. The compositors have called a strike against us. Automation is beginning to threaten their jobs. To be honest with you, Molly, I'm fed up with the whole damn thing."

"I know what you mean."

"Yes. You got fed up with Danbury, I understand."

"Not Danbury exactly. Suburbia, the lake. And Eliot. It wasn't for me." She lifted her hair off her neck. "It is hot."

"So it's over for good with Eliot?"

"I think so, Mother." With her arms still up in the air, she waited.

"Well, that's that, isn't it?" Charlotte said.

There, Molly thought. I got what I always get. Pleased to meet you, meeting's adjourned, sincerely yours, discussion closed . . . next?

"So what's next for you?"

"I'll stay here at the farm for a while. Help Agnes with the work. Get back to my painting. The last show was a disaster. Uncle George bought one of my landscapes, which was sweet of him, but Andrea says nothing much else is moving. Of course, August in the art world is dead, but I don't really think that's the problem. It's the work I did in Danbury that's really dead. So if I could stay here for a while and live off my sublet money, it will give me some breathing space. I want to get back to portraits. I might even paint you, Mother. Doesn't the paper want something for the boardroom? There's one of Grandfather, isn't there?"

"Darling, I don't mean to be cruel, but the kind of portraits you do wouldn't hang well in a boardroom, would they?"

Molly smiled. "I can always count on you for the truth, can't I, Mother?"

"Absolutely. Remember, I was a reporter first."

"I remember after Daddy left and David came to see me here on his first vacation from boarding school. I asked him, David, does the truth make you safe?" Molly cocked her head as if eyeing a painting. Her mother was looking in her purse for a cigarette. She always busied herself with something when Daddy was mentioned. "Do you want to know what David said?"

"What?"

"Safer. The truth makes you safer."

Charlotte lit up and dropped the dead match onto the palette. "Sounds right," she said, but she stared out the window down toward the calf barn.

"I've been painting garbage," Molly said. "So if I go back to my crazy people, with their wild eyes and their split-apart heads, then maybe I'll get closer to the truth again. It's like your reporting, I guess. We all have different ways of tracking down a story. And don't forget, Mother, you're really the one who got me started on painting."

"What do you mean?"

"Remember the paint box? The one you gave me for Christmas when I was eight."

Charlotte's look of bewilderment shifted slowly to recognition. "That's right. Margaret, my old nurse, gave it to me years ago. There was a brief and fleeting moment in my life when I wanted to be a painter." She stood up abruptly. "I've got a dentist appointment," she said. "Walk me downstairs."

"I'll have to defend you from Agnes if she finds you smoking in the house," Molly said.

They stood by the car for a moment while Charlotte ground her cigarette out with the toe of her shoe.

"Are Rudy and Rosa doing okay?" Molly asked. "He acted a little strange when I asked about her."

"Fine as far as I know," Charlotte said. "But I'd steer clear of the Delbiancos, Molly. With this house business, the whole situation is a little touchy."

Molly nodded, but she had no intention of steering clear, not this time.

Charlotte got into the car. "I'm off to have a nightguard made," she said cheerily. "It seems I've managed to throw my jaw out of whack because I grind my teeth at night. I expect I shall look like Frankenstein."

"Do you have to wear it all the time?"

"Only at night. Nobody to see me then." Their eyes met briefly and slid away. "Take care, darling. I'll be in touch."

27

Rudy was seven years old when the Delbiancos moved back to the cottage. Although his mother explained to him that he would be sleeping in his father's old room, he did not know that his father's memories of this little house at the bottom of the Websters' driveway were not happy ones.

Soon after the shooting accident, Louisa had packed up her children and her life and moved over to an apartment on the other side of town. The Websters saw very little of the Delbiancos in the years before the war, although town gossip kept them all up to date on each other. Sol graduated from school and went on to college at the University of Connecticut. Clara married a solid young man named Ricky Calabrese, and in no time at all, Louisa had three grandchildren. Louisa continued her cooking job at Miss Waldrop's school, going on half pay during the Depression when the enrollment fell off. As for Frank, he stayed on at Bronson's Garage, where Lydia and George exchanged pleasantries with him when the gas tank had to be filled or the automobiles serviced. Just before he was sent overseas during the war, Frank married a girl from Simsbury named Angelina Mazzarella. George and Lydia were invited to the wedding.

"What's she like?" Charlotte asked her mother. By that time, she was married herself with a one-year-old son.

"Seems perfectly nice. Louisa looked pleased." And that was all she would say. Charlotte had not dared ask for more.

Something happened to Frank in the war. He still loved to march and drill as much as he had as a child and the guys in his platoon used to kid him about it. But he

391

had gone crazy with a gun one morning and began shooting everything in sight. That was the rumor. All anybody knew was that he came home before the other boys with a mental discharge.

One day Angelina came to Mrs. Webster and asked if she and Frank could move into the cottage.

"Frank could work on the place again. He knows it very well, of course, and with Mr. Webster gone and the farm all closed up, you probably need a man around."

"Does Frank know about this, Angelina?" Lydia had asked.

She looked into her lap. "Not exactly. But he's having a hard time holding down a job. You know, something happened over there during the fighting. He won't talk about it, but he's jumpy all the time, yells at me and Rudy. He was fired last week from the school because he chased after one of the kids who made fun of him. Miss Waldrop only took him on there because of his mother. And Mr. Bronson won't take him back at the garage. He says Frank's too surly with the customers. We don't need much, Mrs. Webster, but I heard nobody's living in the cottage right now and Rudy could help too."

Lydia stood up. "Let me think about it, Angelina. I do need somebody to help out. I'll let you know."

"Why start it all over again, Mother?" Charlotte said. "We're finally untangled from each other."

"In a way we'll never be untangled, Charlotte. When Louisa got sick last year, she kept talking about her Frank. What was he going to do with his life? That last day, she kept squeezing my hand and whispering his name."

"Mother, don't tell me you're fulfilling some deathbed promise."

"Charlotte, you can sound so cruel sometimes," Lydia said quietly. "Louisa's been dead a year and I still think about her every single day. Frank's always going to be a problem. The least I can do is try to take care of him now that she's not here."

"You're meddling again, trying to fix things," Charlotte had said.

"Perhaps."

*   *   *

392

When Frank learned that his wife had been to see Mrs. Webster, he was enraged.

"What did you throw yourself at them for?" he roared. "If you think I'm going crawling back there to pick up their garbage and wash their cars, you're crazy, Angel. Never. Do you hear me? Never."

But Angelina knew they would go. What other choice did they have? She also knew that the more she argued with him, the worse he would get, so she said nothing although the muscles in her cheeks tightened and twitched as his voice grew louder. Their neighbors upstairs would hear. She hated people to know how crazy Frank could be.

Just like all the other times, he came around to her way of seeing things and took it for his own. She patted his arm and told him how smart he was and how lucky she was to have such a man. And Frank moved down to the cottage with a strange mixture of fury and relief, because he was going back to the place where it all started, where nobody had ever trusted him, which was good, because after what he had done that morning in France, he didn't trust himself anymore either.

When the Delbiancos returned to the farm, Rudy had the run of the place. The ghost farm, he called it, but he didn't care, because it was all his.

He moved into the room next to the kitchen that used to be his father's. It looked out across the small laundry yard through the strong fence of the bull pen to the fat white silos of the main barn. He had never minded being alone, and as the years went by and no little Delbianco babies came along to keep him company, he took more and more pleasure in his own company because he had no choice. After school, he roamed through the empty, hay-dusted stalls of the big barn beneath the agitated chatter of the swallows, who huddled together for warmth in the winter and pushed their babies off the rafters in the summertime.

Mrs. Webster had sold off the cows the year after her husband died. "You can keep the cows or the paper," her son George told her. "Not both." So she elected to sell the Ayrshires because despite all her years on the farm, she had never learned enough about running the place to make a go of it and they had never found a manager as good as Nort Hart. And she knew that would have been George's choice if he had ever had to make it.

The empty calf barn was Rudy's favorite place. He loved the lines of it, the old peg-and-dowel construction, the fanciful cupola at the top. It seemed kind of silly to him that someone had gone to all this trouble to put a roof over a lot of mother cows giving birth, but in the absence of calves, he turned it into his special hideout. He dusted off Mr. Webster's old desk in the office upstairs and put some of the treasures he had found around the farm in the drawers—rusted parts of old tractor engines and the blue tag from a cow's ear and three glass milk bottles with the head of an Ayrshire painted on the curved surface. The office was his secret place, and when his mother called him in for dinner, he slipped out the side door that faced the lower field and came around the long way so that she could not see where he had been.

He started at the Northington Elementary School in the second grade, and when the big school bus dropped him off at the end of the driveway, he took to stopping at the kitchen in the big house for a cookie and a glass of milk. In those days, his mother was working as a cleaning lady over at the motel and his father was usually out in the afternoons, running errands in the pale green pickup truck. Frank did the odd jobs around the place, and as the years went on, he needed less and less direction from Lydia, which was a relief to both of them. He put in the vegetable garden and mowed the upper fields and replaced the mortar in the brown stone wall that ran along in the front of the house. Wintertimes, he plowed the driveway out and did repairs on the big house. A gutter here, a leak there.

He was not as good a gardener as Smack, but then, he never had cared about plants the way Smack did. The flowers especially seemed like a foolish indulgence to him, although he had a grudging respect for Mrs. Webster's knowledge.

So Rudy had his turn perched on the white stepladder with a glass of milk and the pale brown cookies that Agnes pressed out onto the sheet in flower shapes. Those afternoons, the kitchen smelled of sugar and vanilla and drops of batter burned black on the hot walls of the oven. "It's good to see a child here again," Mrs. Webster said when she found him there on her way through from a meeting in Hartford or a bridge game over in Farmington.

But he wasn't the only child at the farm. Her grand-children came to visit all the time, and Charlotte's two, Molly and David, spent every Tuesday night in the big house.

"I don't like him hanging around up there," Frank told Angelina at night when they thought the boy had fallen asleep. "He'll get into some kind of trouble."

"Oh, don't always be finding trouble where there isn't any," Angelina said. "He's got no children to play with. What's the difference if he goes up there? Besides, he helps out the two old ladies."

And he did. Gradually, it began to develop that it was his job to keep the upstairs cupboard full of firewood during the winter. And once a month throughout the year, he sat down with Agnes and Angelina and helped them shine all the silver in the house. Mrs. Webster seemed to like having him around, because she was al-ways thinking of little jobs for him to do. "Rudy, would you help me move this box of books?" "Oh, Rudy, yesterday, one of the pictures fell down behind the pi-ano. Can you slip back there and get it? I can't reach it." She seemed to enjoy his company and he could under-stand why. On winter days, when the sun set early, the old house seemed larger and darker and more ghostly than usual. Agnes stayed in the kitchen, where the stove and the good smells made you feel warm, but Mrs. Web-ster didn't spend much time there. The kitchen was a place she always seemed to be passing through, a place where she talked to Agnes about food and where the heels of her shoes made brisk hammering noises on the linoleum floor.

She had company for dinner once or twice a week, and sometimes when Rudy snuck out after dark to make snowballs for the freezer or for a last ride on his bike up to the road and back, he would see the fancy ladies and gentlemen sitting around the dining room with the can-dles burning and his mother waiting on table.

Mrs. Webster liked to ask him about school. Did he

read well? Did he have neat handwriting? What was he studying in history? What was his favorite subject? "Shop," he told her once in fifth grade.

"Shop?" she asked. "What in heaven's name is that?"

"Carpentry. I'm making a box for my father for Christmas."

"Show it to me when it's done."

He brought it up before he wrapped it, and she turned it over and over again in her hands, admiring the way he had set in the two hinges, the neatly mitered corners, the rich color of the stain he had selected. The next month she gave him one corner of the cellar for his birthday.

"I can't remember whether it was Georgie or Campbell who took up carpentry," she said as she led him down the stone steps and around past the old washing machine with the hand wringer to a small wooden door. "Anyway, Mr. Webster set up a shop for him down here. Nobody's used it for years, so I thought I'd turn it over to you."

It was Rudy's dream come true. The tools had all been left hanging there on the dusty pegboard. It took him almost a month of afternoons to put things right with a broom and a pile of dustrags and a box of steel wool to clean the rust off the blades. His father took the saws and the plane to the hardware store in town for sharpening, and Mrs. Webster gave him enough nails and screws to make two dozen wooden boxes.

He started off with small projects. Weak chair backs where the glue had dried up over the years of sitting too close to the fireplace or wobbly night tables with legs split from dry heat and too many books piled on their surfaces. He became acquainted with the inner workings of furniture, with the intricacies of turnbuckle braces, of dowel construction, of mortise and tenon joints. On Saturdays, he hitched a ride with his father to the lumber mill and hung around, listening to the men talk wood. His favorite carpenter was a short fat man named Luigi Dalbon.

Luigi knew wood better than anybody else. "This Douglas fir, I always liked this wood. Better than pine even. Spits back the rain. Never seen any water damage with fir. Used to be, you could get lots of different woods at the yards," Luigi told him. "Woods you never hear about anymore because it don't pay the mills to cut them. The carpenters these days don't know anything about trees and they don't care. Just give me the wood and I'll slam the house together, they say." He turned his head aside and spat a yellow stream of tobacco juice mixed with contempt at the ground. It barely missed his own boot.

Rudy didn't do well in school. "How is it that he can read one of them furniture books all through the night and never bother with the English homework?" his mother complained to Mrs. Webster.

"Rudy has a gift, Angelina. Who needs novels and history if you can work the way he can with wood?" Lydia replied.

"I wonder if she would say the same about her own grandson," Frank remarked bitterly. "Carpentry is a good enough trade for the Delbiancos, but what if David Taylor decided to work with wood the rest of his life? I told you, Angel, it does Rudy no good to hang around up there. Don't you think I learned anything from growing up down at this end of the driveway?"

Although Rudy didn't understand why Mrs. Webster seemed to make his father angry, he knew enough to keep quiet about his activities up there, to talk about school or football at dinner, to keep the door to the workshop closed so Frank wouldn't see him when he came down the cellar steps to wash out the garbage cans. Rudy loved his father, but he also understood without being told that Frank had to be handled gently and patiently.

In any case, it was too late to change Rudy's ways now. He was addicted to the big house. He loved the rich feel of the materials, the grand sound the piano made when Lydia practiced in the late afternoons, even the musty smell of the dead flower leaves in the china bowls on the magazine table. Everything about the place reminded him of the past, of the days when houses and furniture were built with care and people appreciated trees. Growing up alone had made Rudy smart about adults too. He was given the run of the big house because he understood his place. If Mrs. Webster were having ladies in for tea, he stayed in the kitchen or down in his workshop in the cellar. If she were practicing the piano, he tiptoed quietly through the big room to carry out a chair that needed repairing. If she stopped to chat with him, then he stopped what he was doing. He took his cues about how to behave from her. And that included his attitudes about the Webster grandchildren.

In the beginning, he stayed away from the house when Molly and David Taylor came for their Tuesday-night visits with their grandmother. One evening, Mrs. Webster sent Agnes down to the cottage to find him.

"She wants Rudy to have dinner up at the big house tonight," Agnes said to Angelina.

"But the grandchildren are there," Angelina said.

Agnes shrugged as if to say: I've long ago given up trying to figure out people's reasons for doing things. "Can he come?"

Angelina hesitated. Frank would be angry. It was just the kind of Webster summons that enraged him. But he was over in Northington tonight at a meeting of the volunteer firemen. She nodded at Agnes. "He'll be along in a while."

"Now, don't go telling your father," Angelina said to Rudy as she brushed the black hairs off his gray sweater.

"Why do I have to get all dressed up?" Rudy asked. He was wearing last year's church pants, which pinched him at the waist.

"It's special. You're eating with her grandchildren."

It didn't seem so special to Rudy. They ate in the little dining room around the wooden table. No candles. None of that heavy silverware he helped to shine once a month.

"Did Mrs. Webster eat with you?" his mother asked him when she put him to bed later that night.

"No. She was going out for dinner. She came in all dressed up and sat with us while we ate dessert. That was good. Vanilla ice cream with hot-fudge sauce."

"And the children were nice to you?"

Rudy shrugged. "I guess so. The boy read a book the whole time. He's a year older than me."

"Yes. And what about Molly? Agnes tells me she's Mrs. Webster's favorite."

"She was fine." He didn't tell his mother that the girl with that amazing colored hair had spit peas at him when

Agnes wasn't looking. He didn't know what to do about it so he pretended not to see. The next time Agnes turned her back, the girl had stuck out her tongue at him.

After that, he ate dinner with them regularly. David paid him very little attention. He did homework or played backgammon with his grandmother, and so Rudy was thrown in with wild, red-haired Molly, who led him on safari expeditions through the cluttered attic or played Murder in the Dark with him in the upstairs bedrooms. Sometimes she came down and ate dinner at his house, and he noticed for the first time how sullen and angry his father seemed at the table or how stupid it was that his mother tacked up pictures from magazines on the kitchen walls. But Molly did not seem to care. "I like your house," she told him when he walked with her back up the driveway. "It smells friendly." What strange things she said.

Molly seemed to live with her grandmother most of the summer.

"It's because her mother works so hard at the newspaper," Angelina explained to Rudy. "It's lonely for the little girl, so she comes here."

They played together outside in the summertime. They swam in the river, and she watched him jump off the platform and swing out over the water on the thick rope, but she never wanted to try it herself and he didn't make her. They explored the empty barn stalls and played barefoot, uncoordinated sets of tennis when the grownups weren't using the court and endless games of pretend in the tree house his father had built for him in the oak tree in their backyard. Once when he was the husband coming home from work, she kissed him at the top of the ladder.

"What did you do that for?" he demanded.

"Because that's what the wife is supposed to do when the husband gets home from work."

"Well, if you do that again, I won't play," he said.

She talked about Daddy all the time. Daddy traveled a lot for his business, she told Rudy. Sometimes when Daddy was between one trip and another, he came over to the farm to see her, and Rudy knew that he should leave them alone together, so he sat in the tree house and watched her dancing along beside the tall dark-haired man who always walked with one ear cocked to her chatter. And when Daddy went away again, Rudy knew that she would be sad for a while and that anything he said would be the wrong thing. Her mother came too, but Molly didn't seem to care about her so much. She didn't even want to stop playing with Rudy to go in for tea.

"Your mother doesn't like me," Rudy told Molly one day.

"I know," she said, to his surprise. "But I don't care." And they dropped the subject.

She spent a lot of time painting with her grandmother. They set up their easels in the strangest places. Once in the middle of the driveway, so that Frank had to drive the pickup truck around the back way by the main barn in order to get to the cottage. "We were sketching the calf barn," Molly explained to Rudy later. "And Grandmother wanted that angle because of the afternoon light."

She showed him her pictures, and when he got brave enough, he showed her his workshop. "This is all yours?" she said as she walked around the cellar room touching each tool with a special reverent kind of gesture that pleased him.

"Yes. Your grandmother gave it to me. It used to belong to one of your uncles."

"What do you make down here?"

He unveiled his latest project, a simple wooden palette. "It's her Christmas present, so you can't tell. It's made out of cherry. My favorite wood. She thinks I'm crazy because I had to go out and measure her arm. A palette is a very special thing. It's got to fit just right."

"I know that," Molly said. "And I promise not to tell if you make me one too."

"All right," he said.

"Here's my arm. You can measure me right now."

"Hold it the way you do when you paint," he said, stretching out his measuring tape. "Away from your body."

She closed her eyes and let her arm drift to its normal painting position while he measured the distance from the crook of her elbow to her thumb, which would stick up through the palette to balance it.

"Done," he said.

That Christmas they exchanged presents late in the afternoon when he got home from his Uncle Sol's house. They met in his secret room on the second floor of the calf barn.

"Close your eyes," she said when she heard him coming up the stairs. "Have you got my present?"

"Yes."

"I've got something for you too, but I don't want you to see the shape." He heard the scrape of a desk drawer. "Come on in. I'm ready."

He had made her palette out of cherry too, although he had to work five extra hours on a Saturday job with Luigi to earn the money for the wood. "Mine will match Grandmother's," she said, delighted. She made him close his eyes again, and she put the flat package in his hands. He knew from the moment his fingers closed around the edges of the frame that it was one of her pictures, but he pretended to be mystified until the very end. It was the picture she had done of the calf barn from the middle of the driveway. She knew it was his favorite place.

"Thanks," he said.

"You don't like it?"

"I like it very much."

"I like it very much," she mimicked. "You sound like your best friend just died. How about a little enthusiasm, Rudy Delbianco?"

"Stop teasing me," he said, and led the way back down the stairs. Sometimes he couldn't figure her out at all. She could ruin a perfectly nice time with a comment like that.

He did not dare hang the picture on the wall of his room because he knew his father would say something mean about it, so he kept it hidden under his bed. One day, when he was at school, his mother had pulled it out with the dust mop and then pushed it back again. From then on, she was careful when she cleaned his room.

The year after that, when Molly turned fourteen and Rudy fifteen, she stayed at the farm all winter. He remembered the exact day she came because for the first time ever, Agnes asked him to use the outside steps to get down to his workshop.

"Molly's here," she said. "Mrs. Webster wants to be alone with her, and I know if she sees you . . ." Her voice drifted off, and Rudy backed out of the kitchen with his hands up as if to say: You don't need to explain.

Rudy worked very quietly that afternoon, listening for sounds from upstairs. Once he heard the sharp rapping of Mrs. Webster's heels on the kitchen floor above his head and then some muffled talking between the two old ladies, but nothing more. He went home early.

It was November when she came, and for the first week or so, Rudy didn't even see her. In the early mornings, he walked up to the end of the driveway to wait for the school bus, swinging his book bag nonchalantly, all the while checking the windows of the house to see if she were looking out. Blank glass and the shadow of curtains stared back at him.

His parents were careful to avoid the subject of Molly in front of him, but one night he heard her name from the kitchen and cracked his door to listen.

"It's all very strange, if you ask me," his mother was saying. "A girl should live with her mother. How long is she staying here?"

There was a silence, and although Rudy could not see him, he knew his father was throwing up his hands the way he always did when his wife brought up the Websters. "What does it matter, Angel?" he asked. "I keep trying to make you see that their affairs are none of our business. And I want the boy to stay away from her."

"It's something to do with the father, I know that. He was a bad one from the beginning, I can tell you that. Imagine Miss Charlotte picking someone like him out of all the rest."

"Yes," said Rudy's father. "Imagine." There was a quiet drift to his voice that Rudy did not remember hearing before. He took a chance and peeked out. Across the small hallway, he could see his father tilted back in one of the metal chairs. His thick arms were folded across his chest and he was gazing at a spot just above

402

the door with a quizzical look on his face as if he was trying to remember something.

"Agnes told me the girl will be staying for a while," his mother went on. "She's up in her room as if she's sick and the mother comes visiting every afternoon. And Agnes has got her thick lower lip all tucked up as if she disapproves of something. You know the way she can look."

"Yes, Angel, I do," his father said as he let the front legs of the chair bounce back down on to the linoleum. "And I'm sick of talking about the Websters."

The next morning, she was waiting at the end of the driveway. From a distance he could see her back. The long red braid and the one fallen knee sock and her shoulders, hunched against the early cold, all made him feel oddly protective toward her.

When she saw him, her return wave was tentative, and the closer he got, the more she seemed to close in on herself.

"Hello," he said, searching her face for some explanation.

"Hi, Rudy. Your bus stop here too?"

"Yes."

She leaned out and looked down the road. "Well, I hope the driver doesn't forget to come for me. It's freezing."

Then he didn't know what to say, so they both watched as he flicked a small stone back and forth from the toe of one shoe to the other.

"I'm going to be staying with Grandmother this winter," she said, and this time when their eyes met, hers were filled with tears. He froze at the sight of them.

"Is everything okay?" he asked, thinking: What a stupid question.

She hugged her loose books against her chest and said, "No. Everything is horrible, but I don't want to talk about it."

And then his bus came and his friends stared down at her curiously from their high seats.

"Hey, Delbianco, who's your new girlfriend?" they called out as he walked up the aisle to a seat by a rear window. She stared up at him, and at the last moment, as the driver searched for first gear, she stuck out her tongue. He grinned and managed a quick wave just before the bus pulled away.

But still she kept to the house. He took the outside entrance to the cellar without being asked. One afternoon, Agnes called down to him from the top of the kitchen steps.

"Yes?" he called back, holding himself very still, so that he could hear her.

"Can you come up, please? Mrs. Webster needs some help. She's in the painting porch off her bedroom," Agnes said as he ducked his head on his way past. "You can come in through the kitchen again if you want," she added.

"I just thought—"

"It's all right now. Things have settled down. Besides, I need somebody to empty out this cookie jar. Molly doesn't have much of an appetite these days."

"Okay. Thanks."

He had not been on the second floor of the house in a long time, not since his last game of hide-and-seek with Molly the summer before last. In Mrs. Webster's boudoir, where the clothes were draped untidily about on the chairs, he felt as if he were pawing through somebody's private business. Some article of underwear, her hairpins scattered on the glass surface of the dressing table, even a pile of unopened letters made him feel awkward and uncomfortable.

"We're out here, Rudy." Mrs. Webster's clear voice, so close by, startled him.

She was standing in the middle of the porch in a long painting smock that was dyed the same color as her hair. Molly was there too. At first, he didn't notice her, she was sitting so quietly in the corner on a high stool.

"We need to do some rearranging here," Mrs. Webster said to him. "Molly and I are going to set our easels side by side, so if we move that trunk up to the attic and that old chair down to the cellar, I think there will be enough room, don't you?"

"Yes," he said, deliberately leaving off the "ma'am." Suddenly, with Molly watching, he didn't want to look like a servant boy. For the next hour, while he moved furniture about at Mrs. Webster's bidding, he was conscious of Molly's eyes on him, although they didn't say one word to each other.

Gradually, as the days passed and the weather grew colder, they fell into their old ways with each other and Molly's face seemed a little more lively, a little more like her old self. Rudy learned the story of what had happened in bits and pieces from things that she and Agnes told him. Her beloved Daddy had gone away. Moved to California. Her parents were getting a divorce.

"But you'll see him again. He'll come back to visit," Rudy said. They were walking down to the river during the January thaw. She was wearing her grandmother's black boots, and the mud squished up over the edge with every step.

"No. I don't think so," she said, and her voice had a note of bewilderment in it as if she didn't even quite believe her own words. "I don't think he's coming back."

"Why?" Rudy asked indignantly. "That's ridiculous."

"Because Mother hates him. She says he won't be allowed to ever see me again."

Then her face darkened, and he said nothing for fear another question would make her close up again.

"I hate Mother," she spat, and without knowing he was going to do it, he took her bare hand and squeezed it tight inside his glove. "I'm glad Grandmother brought me here to live with her and Agnes. I wish I could stay here forever."

She left her hand in his, and later that night, when he was lying in bed and thinking about their conversation, he promised himself that part of her wanting to stay at the farm meant wanting to be with him.

"Our Molly is two people these days," Agnes confided to him one afternoon when Molly wasn't there. He was on his second piece of chocolate cake, and Agnes was leaning against the sink watching him eat it, but she had a faraway look in her eye.

"What do you mean?" He was pleased with the "our." It must include him. The two old ladies and him, they all had an equal stake in keeping her happy.

"Well, with us, she's a little like a wounded bird. Somebody to keep an eye out for. At school and with her mother and even with David, she's a tough little so-and-so. Don't bother me, I'm trouble."

He knew what Agnes meant. He had seen the look of determination that came across her face when her school bus pulled up to the gates before his. She reminded him of the lady saint he had studied about in Christian doctrine classes on Saturday mornings. Joan of Arc flipping down her metal helmet before she went into battle.

"Is it true her father isn't coming back?" Rudy asked.

Agnes folded her arms across her chest. "It seems that way."

"Molly misses him an awful lot."

"I know and I don't understand it, considering—" She stopped herself when she heard Mrs. Webster's footsteps in the dining room. "Here comes another kind of trouble," Agnes said, but she was smiling. Rudy slipped off the stepladder. He was washing his plate at the sink when Mrs. Webster burst into the room, stepping briskly along as usual. She seemed younger than she was because she walked so fast.

"Hello, Rudy," she said.

"Hello."

"You're still tilting your head over that way. I think there's something wrong with your eyes. Did your mother take you to the eye doctor?"

"Yes," he said, taking the dish towel from Agnes and pushing it around the damp plate. "The doctor says I'm twenty-twenty."

"Oh, don't be so nosy, Mrs. W. The boy likes to wear his hair long, and he's got to tilt his head over that way so the hair stays out of his eyes."

Rudy smiled to himself as he put the plate in the cupboard. Agnes was absolutely right, but he didn't think anybody had noticed. He liked to hear them arguing over him. It made him feel as if he belonged.

"Are we having green beans with the roast, Agnes?"

"You already asked me that this morning."

"I did? Well, what was the answer?"

"Yes, we are."

"Good. I'll be back by six-thirty, then. I'll pick Molly up from school on my way home."

Rudy took a job that summer helping Luigi do the cabinetry work on a house over in Simsbury. Luigi said the man building it was a millionaire.

"It sure is big enough," Rudy told Molly. "There must be ten bedrooms in that house. Sort of a waste."

"I wish you didn't have to work," Molly said for the tenth time.

"The Delbiancos live at the bottom of the driveway," he said. He hadn't meant it to sound bitter, but it did.

"And my grandfather brought your grandfather over from Italy in 1907 to work in the shade-tobacco fields. One-way passage, all the milk and wood they needed for a year. I learned that from my interviews with Grandmother this winter."

He looked at her. "And what's it supposed to mean?"

She shrugged. "That you and I are a perfect example of the melting-pot theory. That's what I wrote in my history report," she said, and walked away. For once, he was seeing her tough side, the one she usually saved for the others.

When he got home from work, they swam down at the river.

"Soon, I'm going to get the nerve to jump," she told him one day in August when he had thrown himself off the platform for the third time in a row. He stood on the bank drying himself off with a towel.

"It doesn't matter to me whether you do it or not."

"Oh yeah? Well, it's beginning to matter to me. I don't want to be a sissy anymore."

When her hair was wet, it turned a dark brownish red that made her pale face glow in ghostly contrast. "You look like the saints in my doctrine book," he teased. "So pale."

"Saints don't have freckles." She pointed to her legs. "Look at this. I even have them on my knees."

Next to her, he felt suddenly thick and awkward, aware of the dark hair which had begun to sprout on his chest and on his face. She reminded him of a delicate piece of wood, one of the thin curved spindles from an antique chair that could so easily break in his clumsy fingers. She was staring up at him with a funny look on her face.

"I'm going to do it now," she announced, throwing down her towel.

"Don't, Molly. You might hurt yourself."

"See, even you think I'm a weakling." She scrambled up the ladder like a squirrel straddling the bark of a tree, and before he could stop her, she was standing on the edge of the platform with the thick rope in her hand.

"Goodbye, sweet prince," she cried, and jumped. He watched her waft out over the trees and back toward the hole of brown water with his hands pressed illogically over his ears. "Rudy," she screamed, and hit the water like a bullet. When she didn't come up, he began to shout her name over and over again.

"I fooled you," she called from the side. He had forgotten how good she was at holding her breath.

"Were you worried?" she gasped.

"You did it," he cried. "You were great."

She scrambled up the bank, and he threw his arms around her wet body and picked her up and twirled her about with an exuberant war cry. Still in his grasp, her body slid down against his until her feet found the ground again and she grew still and so did he. She rested her wet hair against his cheek and he began to tremble.

"Rudy?" she whispered.

"Mmm."

"Nothing. Just don't move."

"I'm not."

When he kissed her, he saw that her eyes were closed and that her long eyelashes were still wet and clung to one another. He let his hands slide down her damp arms and then took a step backward. By the time she opened her eyes again, he was gathering the towels, afraid of what he would see in her face, afraid that the kiss had meant more to him than it ever would to her.

He started off at a swift trot for the house.

"Where are you going?" she called.

"To tell Agnes that you jumped."

"Wait. I want to tell her."

"Better hurry, then, because I'm going to beat you."

The race lasted all the way up to the house and she almost caught him at the last minute, but he took the porch steps two at a time.

"Wait," she cried, but he thought it was just another ploy to win, so he burst through the back door without stopping.

"Molly did it," he cried to a startled Agnes.

"Did what?"

"She jumped from the platform."

"Oh, God," said a voice from the corner. "Is she all right?" He swung around to see Mrs. Taylor sitting in the ladder-back chair by the window.

"Yes, Mother," Molly said as she let the screen door bang behind her. "I'm fine."

In the awkward pause that followed, he realized that he was dripping river water on Agnes's clean floor and that Mrs. Taylor was staring at him with a look of apprehension, the way you eye a wet dog about to shake. In his cutoff shorts, he felt large and naked and clumsy in front of these silent women. "I'd better go."

Nobody said anything to stop him.

She moved back home the next week, and he barely saw her before she left.

One afternoon, he found her down by the vegetable garden, sketching.

"Did I do something wrong?" he asked.

"No." But she wouldn't look at him.

"Then what's going on? Why don't I see you anymore?"

"I'm moving back home," she said in a small voice. "And in two weeks I'm going away to boarding school."

"Where?" he asked.

"Some backwater town in Maryland," she said, and at last she looked up. The skin around her eyes was red as if she had been rubbing it. "Mother really wants to get rid of me."

"It's because of me," he said. "I told you she doesn't like me."

"It's not just you. She's been planning this for a while. Even Grandmother can't get her to change her mind. I just found out they've been fighting about me for the last two months." Molly closed up the sketchbook and stretched. "If you don't like your daughter, then send her away. After all, it worked with Daddy. Then why not me?"

He could think of nothing to say.

"She says that my friendship with you is inappropriate. I heard them arguing about it last night after dinner. My mother said, 'After all that's happened with the Delbiancos, Mother, I cannot believe you have allowed this business to go on.' Apparently, you and I are a business."

"What does she mean, all that's happened with the Delbiancos?" Rudy asked.

Molly shrugged. "You tell me. I don't know."

After she left, he asked Agnes what that meant, but he couldn't get anything out of her. It was his mother who told him in the end.

"But who fired the gun?" Rudy asked when he had heard the whole story.

"Nobody knows. Apparently your father and Miss Charlotte were fighting over it when it went off. Now don't say a word to your father. He doesn't like anybody talking about it. Your Uncle Sol is the one who told me."

Rudy never mentioned the story to his father, but this new knowledge made him feel even more solicitous and protective toward him.

Molly wrote him from boarding school, but he never answered. Even though she was scornful about the silly traditions and uniforms, there was something about her round girlish handwriting and the pale blue stationery that made him feel uneasy and awkward the way he had that day in the kitchen. Once he sat down and wrote her the whole story of the shooting accident, but he tore it up without sending it.

When Molly came to visit her grandmother during the holidays, they greeted each other stiffly. The wall between them was fragile, Rudy was sure of it. It would just take a poke in the ribs, a tease about her freckles to set her off, to bring back the old Molly, but the moment never seemed to be quite right and so he let it go each time, waiting for their next encounter.

Many years later, at her grandmother's funeral, he had found her all alone in one corner of the living room and had given her his handkerchief with some silly comment about windshield wipers. She had smiled up at him in the old way, helmet off, but just then he had felt Rosa at his elbow. His wife always stuck close by him in the Webster house.

"You know my wife, Rosa?" he asked, still looking at Molly. "This is Molly Taylor."

They shook hands and Rosa murmured appropriate condolences while he looked past their bobbing heads to the crowd of people gathered at the other end of the room.

"Rudy?" Rosa was saying. "Miss Taylor asked you a question."

"How's business?" Molly asked for the second time.

"Good," he said, his eyes drifting back to her, to the hair which she still wore in a long braid down her back. "We'd better get home, Rosa. I promised Lina we wouldn't be too long."

"Lina's our smallest. Rudy is much too soft with her," Rosa said. She must be awfully nervous today, he thought. Rosa had never been one to talk about her husband in that patronizing way other wives used.

He and Molly had shaken hands and parted, and she rejoined a tall man he had seen her standing with in the church. "Eliot Duncan," Agnes explained to him a few days later with a roll of her large eyes. "The latest flame."

And that was the last time Rudy had seen her. Until their meeting the other day by the calf barn when she had thrown her arms around him. Having her back reminded him of the old days.

"Molly Taylor's come to live at the farm for a while," he told Rosa one afternoon when he came in from work. He was washing his hands at the sink. "I thought we might invite her for dinner sometime."

Rosa looked over the heads of the children at him, her flat dark eyes wide with surprise.

"Why?"

He shrugged. "It must be lonely for her in that big house with just Agnes for company."

It had been a stupid idea of his. The only people they ever had for dinner were family. Otherwise, they met their friends at Al's Pizza House on the other side of town. The children all came too and chased each other around the table, pizza slices clutched in their hands, the tomato sauce oozing up through the small, tight fingers.

His two sons' discussion over a water gun suddenly exploded into an argument.

"Ma, Louis hit me."

"I did not."

"Liar."

He pulled them apart with his wet hands, eager for the distraction of their argument. "Cut it out, you two. Come over here and wash your hands for dinner." Rosa was still watching him. When she turned away at last to set the plates down on the oilcloth, he shut the water off.

"Leave it on, Pa. I want to wash the dishes," Tony said.

"Not now. It's time to eat," Rosa said from across the room. She never raised her voice. Its stillness cut through the noise of the children and silenced them more quickly than his yelling.

Later that night, when they were lying in bed, the light of the television reflected on the ceiling above them, she said, "When do you want her to come?"

"Never mind," he said. "It doesn't matter."

"I don't mind, Rudy. We can have her."

"You know, she's different from the other Websters."

"What do I care about that?" Rosa said. She flicked off the TV with the remote-control box and turned toward him. Her dark head fit comfortably into the hollow next to his shoulder bone. He made love to her slowly and carefully the way he had in those months right after the babies were born, but her body under his was still and thoughtful.

She would remember now. She would have Molly for dinner as if it were a homework assignment she had been told to finish. She would do it the way she had done so many other things in the last months just to make him happy. And the more she watched him with her dark eyes and adjusted herself to his latest mood, the more he longed to run. And the more he hated himself for it.

28

Molly had gone to Bard College over everybody's objections.

"What in God's name are you going to learn there?" Charlotte had said.

"How to take care of myself," she had replied without a moment's hesitation.

"But, darling, I wish you'd pick something a little more conventional," Grandmother said after reading through the catalogue. "It says here that you don't even have exams. How can there be a college without exams?"

"Grandmother, my term paper in art can be a painting. I've never done well in exams anyway. I've found the absolutely perfect place for me."

And then of course, having fought so hard to get there, she never could admit how lonely the place made her feel. She came home on vacations dressed in black with wild scarves tied about her head and silver earrings so long and heavy that if she tilted her head the slightest bit to the side, they rested against her shoulder. She had taken up yoga and Buddhism and spent hours in the lotus position on Grandmother's living-room floor.

"Darling, as always, I'm interested in everything you have to say, but I will not allow you to burn that ghastly-smelling stuff in the house."

"But, Grandmother, the incense is better than Mother's cigarettes and you let her smoke in the house."

"Yes, well, that's different."

In her junior year, Molly enrolled in Allen Reckler's painting class. The rumors about him were the usual. He was tougher than the other teachers and all he wanted to do was to get the "lady painters" into bed with him. She didn't mind the toughness, she told herself. She was ready for it.

Elizabeth Winthrop

In those days, she was confident, almost arrogant about her work. She had done well in her classes. Those afternoons with Grandmother seemed to have paid off. The first two years, the work had all come from assignments. The teacher would hand her two sticks and a ball and say, "Make a picture out of this." Or the class would draw a model. Over and over again. In charcoal, in pencil, in pastels. Five-minute sketches, half-hour drawings. She was told what to do, she turned her assignments in on time, and she was good at it. But when Mr. Reckler looked through her sketchbooks, he didn't seem as impressed as she wanted him to be.

"Of course, these are technically good. You can draw," he said.

"You make that sound like an insult," she said, taking back the portfolio.

"It is. As long as you continue to render effectively onto the paper what you see, you are just that. An illustrator. A renderer. I want more from my students than that. I want to see you taking some risks."

"Are you saying there's no room left in the world for realism?" Molly asked, full of her own brashness. She had always gotten away with talking to teachers like this.

"Of course not. But there has to be a metaphor behind the realism. The trouble with realism is that it screams a narrative."

She pushed doggedly ahead, trying to prove him wrong. If she just took enough courses, if she learned to work in wood and papier-mâché, if she sharpened her eye, she was sure she would get his approval. Her last year, she was admitted into the senior seminar where the teachers worked side by side with the students, struggling with the same problems of form and space. They all critiqued each other's work, and with Molly, they were merciless, hammering away at her to make some leap. She felt tormented by them and began to cut the class. In February, Allen told her there was a chance she might fail the course.

"I don't give a damn," she screamed, aware that her voice was carrying through the closed door to the students waiting outside. "You've all ganged up on me just because you want me to create the same meaningless

414

ugly messes on my canvases that you do on yours. You're the one who said that there are as many ways to paint as there are painters."

To her fury, he was smiling at her. "Do you realize that you've never raised your voice at me before? Now go back to the studio and scream onto the canvas."

She slammed out of the room and stayed away from class for a week. She felt betrayed, as if the three and a half years of work had been wasted. But deep down, she had an uneasy feeling. One weekend night when the campus was deserted, she went down to the studio. The janitor found her there in the morning.

"You been here all night, miss?"

"I guess so," she said, looking up with a start. "What time is it?"

"Seven o'clock. You waited too long to do your homework, huh?" He was looking at the canvas, which was a jumble of color. She stood behind him and looked at it with his eyes.

"What's it called?" he asked, hitching up his green pants.

"The scream."

"That's what it looks like."

When Allen saw it, he said nothing for what seemed like hours. "Is it finished?" he asked.

"You're the teacher," Molly said. "Is it?"

"You're the painter," he replied. "Anyway, it's a good start. I think you've begun to understand what I've been telling you for the last two years. But it's still too intellectual."

One painting seemed to give birth to the next. She turned the shapes inside out so they mirrored one another, mixed colors that jarred and fought like prisoners shaking on their bars. Allen watched and commented, and in the end, he passed her in the course.

"For true, gutsy effort," he said in their last conference together. By that time, they had taken to going down to Pete's Bar in the middle of Tivoli, and they drank one beer after another and wrangled back and forth across the small table until the bartender threw them out. On their way up the hill to the campus, he put his arm around her shoulders and sang a dirty English soldier's song at the top of his lungs. "Uncle George and Auntie Mabel did it on the breakfast table."

She went home with him to his one-bedroom bachelor's apartment and they did it on his wide unmade bed.

"Now I've learned that both the rumors about you were true," she said the next morning.

"And what are those, my red-haired lady?"

"You are the toughest teacher on campus and all you want to do is get your students into bed."

"Who got whom?" he asked. "But yes, I am the toughest teacher on campus. Which is what I need to be or else you women will settle for marrying a famous artist and spending the rest of your lives grinding his paints."

"You're still drunk," she said.

"No. I have a headache from that fifth beer, but I am making perfect sense. Name me one woman painter who has had a solo show in a major New York museum in the last five years."

She couldn't, of course. It was an old theme of his, the futility of a woman's future as a painter. But she didn't want to sit in his drab kitchen and listen to his depressing lectures as if the night before had had no effect on either of them.

She stood up. "I'm off. I've still got packing to do."

"I'm driving you away," he said. "You want me to talk about what last night means to *us*." His expression was sarcastic. It reminded her of the cruel side to this man, the bitter teacher she had seen humiliating the more vulnerable students.

"Allen, don't be ridiculous. I'm a big girl," she said, but she almost choked on the words. He was only the second man she'd slept with, and the first had been a drunken experiment, a college girl's version of the trip to the whorehouse. Gentled by the drink perhaps, Allen had nestled with her in the bed, and his slow teasing had done so much more for her than the hurried fumblings of her blind date two years before. Although she would never admit it to him now, she had fantasized in his bed this morning that it would happen again.

"I have a present for you," he said.

He disappeared into the back room and returned with something wrapped clumsily in newspaper. She could tell from the shape that it was one of his linoleum blocks. "Don't open it until you get back to your room," he warned, and kissed her gently at the door. "I *will* miss you, Molly."

As usual, she walked away without saying goodbye.

"I think that's hideous," Eliot had said years later when she hung it up on the wall of the room he designated as her studio.

"Allen was never a great artist," she said, gazing at the rough lines of the boat he had carved. "But he pushed me further along than I would have ever gone by myself. So I carry this with me everywhere. It's my good-luck charm."

On the back of the block, Allen had scrawled the word "painting" and then crossed out the last four letters.

Now she hammered a tack into the siding of her grandmother's porch and hung the block with the words facing out.

As always when she was beginning to work again, she laid claim to the place. She sorted through her grandmother's paintings, kept the best ones for herself, and with her mother's permission, sent the rest to her Uncle George in New York, who was the only member of the family who had any interest in them. Once she had thrown away the ruined palette and the old matted brushes, she laid out her own tools: the thick pane of glass she used as a palette, the brush washer, the old paint box her mother had given her, which now served as a suitcase for her favorite oils. Next to Allen's woodblock she hung the palette Rudy had made for her years ago. She only used it when she was painting outdoors these days, but she often set it out in her studio because she loved the sensuous shape of it. Around the light switch, she pasted some of her favorite postcards—Mary Cassatt's portrait of her mother reading *Le Figaro,* a Modigliani nude, Picasso's "Woman Ironing," a Degas. One morning, she rushed off to the art-supply store and returned loaded down with supplies.

Agnes stopped by the porch later in the morning. "I'm going into Hartford with Frank," she said. "Do you need anything?"

"No, thanks. By the time you get back, I'll have at least ten canvases stretched."

At first, her fingers felt awkward. She'd forgotten the basic rules—to start the stapling in the middle of the long side, to pull the canvas tight enough for a clean edge but not too tight or the stretchers would warp. In the middle of the second canvas, she checked her grandmother's manual for the right proportions of gesso and water.

By the third canvas, she found the missing rhythm. Stretch with the canvas pliers, staple, turn the hospital corners, staple again. Just to have the paintbrush in her hand again made her giggle, and she spread the star of gesso on the center of each canvas with great care. The hours melted away. She sanded the dried gesso with a tunafish sandwich in one hand.

When Agnes came back that evening, Molly was still up on the porch waiting to sand the last canvas.

"A full day's work," Molly said, indicating with a broad sweep of her hand the eight finished canvases propped up on the windowsills behind her.

"Seems to me the work has just begun," Agnes said. "What are you going to put on them?"

"It just came to me. I'm going to paint the house. Make a record of it."

"I thought you were going back to doing people. Portraits."

"This will be a portrait of the house," Molly said.

Lectures on perspective in art school had always bored Molly, and now she struggled over the angle of each line as it moved from the sketch pad back toward her eye. She drove into Hartford and took books on architectural drawing out of the university art library. She dug out her grandmother's old camera and spent two whole days photographing the house inside and out.

"Now what?" Agnes snapped when Molly appeared in the kitchen one afternoon with the camera.

"Go right on working," Molly said. "It's not you I want. It's the kitchen."

"Thanks a lot."

"All right, then, say cheese."

Agnes looked up from the pie she was baking. "Whiskey. That's what we were always taught to say."

When the roll of film came back, Molly tacked the snapshot of Agnes up on the wall next to her postcards. She hoped Agnes wouldn't notice it there, because Molly knew she would rip it up if given the chance. Her lower lip hung down and the wrinkles showed on her hands, her upper arms, even her earlobes. But Molly loved the picture—the solid, no-nonsense stance, the easy way Agnes slid the checkered dishrag along the knife blade without bothering to look down, the pile of apples accumulating in the pie tin. The images honored Agnes's life in a way that appealed to Molly not only because of the symbols in the picture but because of the problems they presented to her as a painter. Still, she put it aside. First the house, she told herself.

One afternoon in late October, she was sitting on the fence sketching the calf barn when Rudy's truck pulled up. She waved but went on working. Two doors slammed, and when she next looked up, Rudy was striding toward her with another, shorter man behind.

"How are you?" Rudy asked with a smile.

"Fine," she said.

"You remember Luigi Dalbon? This is Molly Taylor, Luigi. Mrs. Webster's granddaughter."

She slid off the fence and put out her hand. "Of course. Rudy used to say you were the man who taught him everything he knew."

Luigi grinned with pleasure. "I remember your grandmother," he said. "A good lady."

"Yes, she was." A tiny nostalgic pause hung between them. "You're starting work on the barn, then."

Rudy nodded. "We brought the first load of lumber, but with this warm weather, I've got my hands full on two other sites. Trying to get them framed in before the cold weather comes. I see you're working too," he said, nodding at the sketchbook. "Can I look?"

She handed it over. "I'm doing a record of the house," she said. He tilted the book for Luigi to see, and with

419

heads close together, they studied her sketch of the calf barn.

"Look at the cupola," Rudy said. "I've never seen one like that with the gingerbread details going along the eaves too."

Luigi turned and spat. Molly was amazed at the amount of liquid that came out of his mouth.

"I don't like the sag," he said with a frown. "If we don't do this right, Rudy, the whole damn building could fall over on us."

"We'll do it right," Rudy said.

With a shrug, Luigi turned away and hitched off to the back of the truck.

"Can I look at the others?" Rudy asked.

She nodded. He flipped the pictures over, moving from front to back.

"What do you think?" she asked when he was done.

"I think you do best when you pick up a detail."

"What do you mean?"

"I like the one of Agnes's hands and the apples piled in the baking tin. And that old kitchen faucet."

She turned the pages back to an elevation of the western side of the house. "What about something like this?"

He looked at it again without answering. Luigi passed behind him, bowed under the weight of his first load of lumber.

Molly couldn't stand his silence any longer. "I know something's wrong, but I can't figure out what. I guess I got caught up in the technique. It's an old problem of mine," she said wearily.

"I'd better help the old man," Rudy said. "Before I forget, Rosa and I—" He hesitated. "Well, we were wondering if you could come for dinner sometime this week."

"Really? I'd like that."

"How about Friday?"

She nodded, and he went off to help Luigi.

Agnes was sitting on the kitchen porch in her red metal rocking chair when Molly stomped up the steps.

"Damn that Rudy Delbianco."

"What's he done?"

420

"Made me see something I should have figured out myself." Molly found the sketch of the apples and the one of the house. "Now you tell me. Which of these do you like better?"

"That's my apple pie."

"Right."

Agnes pushed up her glasses and squinted at both pictures. "I like the apple pie better. Even though my skin looks awful wrinkled."

"Exactly. I love the apples because they remind me of you and I remember good apple pies over the years and I love the way you handle the knife. So I put all those feelings in this picture. But I don't give a damn about this side of the house and it shows." She sat down with a bump in the other metal chair.

Agnes rocked. Her chair creaked. Someone in the woods started up a chain saw and the distant roar ballooned and then quieted as the metal teeth bit into the wood.

"Well, don't you have an opinion on all this?"

"Of course I do," Agnes said. "When I stop having opinions, I'll keel over and die."

"What is it?"

"That Rome wasn't built in a day, as your grandmother used to say."

"I know," Molly said. "I just wish I could get into gear."

They sat in silence as the light slipped away, leaving the land in shadows. The birds began to settle for the night, hunkered up next to one another in the top branches of the copper beech tree. Rudy's truck passed with a flick of the headlights and they waved back.

"Have you called your sister?" Molly asked.

"Not yet."

"Why don't we go look at those apartments in town tomorrow."

"I've got to clean the upstairs tomorrow."

"Well, we'll both clean the upstairs and then I'll drive you into town."

"We'll see. It's too cold to sit out here anymore," Agnes said. "Help me up. My bones have all stiffened in this chair."

That night after dinner, Molly pulled a floor lamp out onto the porch and painted Agnes's hand hovering above the apple slices.

"It's a start," she said at the end of two hours, and went to bed.

Agnes hated the apartment.

"You didn't even give it a chance," Molly said on the way home. "The bathroom was nice. I turned on all the faucets and the water pressure was great."

"How could I stand living over Manson's Drugstore? What a way to end your life, lying in bed listening to old men asking for hemorrhoid prescriptions."

Molly giggled. "You are impossible, Agnes Becker. No wonder you and Grandmother got along so well."

Later on, after a frustrating hour in front of the canvas, Molly came back downstairs looking for company. It took her a long time to find Agnes, who was sitting out on the sun porch in Mrs. Webster's favorite chair.

"I've never seen you sitting out here before."

"I've never sat here before," Agnes said, pulling her dark blue sweater across her sunken chest. "I wanted to see what it felt like."

"Are you cold?" Molly asked.

When Agnes didn't answer, Molly took Lydia's old lap rug and tucked it around the older woman's steely corseted bottom. Then she lowered herself into another chair.

The sun porch, which gave out onto a side lawn, was a larger version of the painting porch upstairs. Every spring, Frank replaced the glass with screens and covered the tile floor with disintegrating sisal rugs that someone had brought home from Africa too many years ago. Lydia had managed to keep her sweet olive plants blooming throughout the year, so that even now, in October, the air was still filled with the fragrant scent.

Agnes began to speak as if telling a story to an audience, her eyes fixed on the doorway to the living room. "You know, there was a time when your grandmother was invited to go on a boat ride out in the harbor in New Haven. It was that Mrs. Morris who invited her, the fancy lady with the big house in Farmington. You know the one I mean. She had arthuritis and was always in a wheelchair."

Arthuritis, Agnes always said, as if it were a disease contracted from living with a man named Arthur.

"I remember Grandmother mentioning a Mrs. Morris when I taped her talking about the old days."

"It was one of those big yachts," Agnes went on, "and I've never in my life been on any kind of a boat, and so I asked your grandmother if I could go too. Do you know what she said?"

Molly shook her head, thinking: And I don't want to know either.

"She said, 'But, Agnes, where in heaven's name would you sit?' " Agnes paused and drew breath, still looking straight ahead. "Where would I sit? It's the kind of thing you might say to a dog, don't you know?" Her eyes swung right, and Molly could see the glitter of tears in them. "So, Mrs. W., I definitely do need a place to sit right now," Agnes declared to the empty room, her voice rising, "and where do you think that should be?"

"She was wrong about a lot of things," Molly said in a quiet voice. "It was the way she was brought up."

"Don't you go making excuses for her. She doesn't need anybody to do that."

"Yes, ma'am," Molly said.

"And don't be impertinent either," Agnes growled, swatting at her wet cheeks with both hands at once.

"Do you want some tea? I'll bring the tray out here to you."

Agnes hesitated, obviously tempted for a moment by the idea. "No," she said, folding the lap rug. "I get mopey like this when I sit still. Besides, the kitchen is warmer."

29

Rudy stopped by on Friday afternoon after unloading another pile of lumber down at the calf barn. He knocked on the frame of the screen door and walked in when nobody responded.

"Agnes," he called. His voice sounded intrusive in the still, female house.

"I'm back here," she yelled back. "Ironing."

He wandered through the children's dining room and down the back hall, following the smell of the hot iron against cloth.

"Hello, stranger," she said without looking up.

"Hello, Agnes," he said. She seemed to have shrunk a little even in the few weeks since they had chatted in the vegetable garden. "Still ironing the tablecloths?"

"Yes, sir," she said, glancing up at him and then back down to the board. She wielded the heavy iron with confidence, poking its metal snout into the intricate lace borders, leaving behind a wrinkle and then sweeping back over the white damask to smooth it out again. As a boy, he had always loved to watch her ironing. The clean scorched smell, the hiss of steam, the thump of the iron on the board as she readjusted the material used to soothe him. Even then, he realized, he must have appreciated a piece of machinery in good hands. "What are you staring at?" she teased. "If you hang around too long, I'll make you shine the silver trays."

"Give that job to Molly," he said. "She was always trying to take it away from me, especially when it looked as if I was having some fun. Where is she? I came by to see if she wanted a ride."

"Upstairs on the painting porch, I expect."

"You know, I never thought—" He paused, but she

didn't look up. "I mean, if you'd like to join us, I know Rosa would be very happy."

"Oh, go along, Rudy," she said. "I can't digest those Italian sauces. You know that."

"Do you think she was hurt?" Rudy asked Molly later as she scrambled into the front seat of the truck.

"Whether she was or wasn't, it's too late now," she said. "Wild horses wouldn't make her admit it."

They slammed their doors at almost the same moment, and Rudy was aware of the dirty rags on the floor, the tool tray under her feet.

"Sorry the truck's such a mess," he said.

"Trucks are supposed to be messy," she said with a wide sudden smile. She bounced once on the seat. "I like sitting up high like this."

He shoved the black ball of the gear shift into first, aware of his arm near hers, knowing that under the layers of sweater and shirt, his skin was as dark with tan and its coating of black hair as hers was pale and freckled and fine. He started the engine and guided the truck out onto the road. On the way to the house, they talked about his children.

"Tony's the oldest. Named after my grandfather. He's nine, very smart, does well in school. He's sharp like my Uncle Sol, but fresh."

"My type," Molly said.

"Then there's Louis. He's seven. He's skinny, but he's strong. You should see him run. His heels come up and touch his bottom every step. Lina's the baby."

"Named after your mother," she said. She had pulled her knees up to her chin, and he drove carefully, fearful that she might bump herself against the dashboard if he braked suddenly.

"Yes. She's five."

"I bet you're a good father, Rudy," she said.

"Rosa says I'm too easy on them. I don't take them for granted, I suppose. They seem to feel like some sort of miracle to me."

When they pulled into the driveway, the children burst out of the kitchen door, screaming "Daddy." "Hold on to your hat," he said to Molly as the small bodies threw themselves at the car.

When he dropped off the high seat, they clustered around, ignoring his shouts for order, and with a last helpless glance at Molly, he held out his arms for them. With Molly trailing along behind, he waded into the kitchen, the little girl in his arms and each of the boys riding a leg.

Rosa stood with her back to the chaos, washing her hands at the sink. Suddenly, in the middle of this foolish parade, Rudy saw the way the pleats of her skirt splayed out across her bottom, and he was, in one instant, embarrassed for her and enraged at himself for thinking it. It was a mistake to bring Molly here, he thought as he busied himself with the children, all the while watching as the two women greeted each other. Rosa was shy, almost aloof, and Molly excessively polite.

Rudy had wanted them to eat later after the kids were in bed. "She doesn't have kids of her own," he had said to Rosa that morning. "She's not used to them."

"It won't bother her," Rosa said flatly. We won't change our ways for this woman is what she had meant.

They ate veal stew with tomatoes and polenta cakes that Rosa's mother made every week. They put their paper napkins in their laps and drank milk and made stiff conversation that was fragmented by the children's interruptions.

"Tony hit me with his elbow," Louis said, eyes bright.

"Cut it out, Tony. Behave yourself," Rudy said.

"Where do you live?" Tony asked.

"I'm staying at the farm with Agnes," Molly said. She pronounced each word carefully, the way adults do when they're uncomfortable with children.

"Where do you live when you go home?"

"New York City. Have you ever been there?"

"Have I, Ma?" the boy asked.

"Yes, Tony. But you were too little to know. Your father and I took you on a vacation there."

"You've been to New York?" Molly asked Rudy.

He shrugged. "Years ago."

"You should have called me. I would have shown you the town."

"When are you going home?" Tony said. He didn't want the attention shifted away from him again.

426

Nobody said anything for a moment. "When I decide I'm good and ready," Molly said with a grin. Tony smiled back. They were two of a kind, Rudy thought as he watched them.

"Bring the plates, children," Rosa said, sliding out of her seat. Molly had been eager to help before dinner, but now she sat without moving and let Louis take her plate and glass.

"It was very good, thank you," Molly said for the third time. She had not said Rosa's name once. But Rosa hadn't said hers either.

"What's for dessert, Ma?" Lewis asked.

"Apple pie. Agnes gave me the recipe," she said over the children's head to Molly.

Rudy helped clear and put the pie in front of Molly so that she could divide it up. He felt responsible for the awkward silence and kept running through possible subjects of conversation in his mind, but nothing seemed right. Her painting? That would make Rosa feel uncomfortable. His work? What was there to say about that? We framed out the back of the Hatcher house today. The new kitchen cabinets for the Lawrence job are going to be held up at the factory. That was the kind of thing he and Rosa talked about over the heads of the children, but it seemed mundane, ridiculous in front of Molly.

Rudy gulped his pie while the two women clucked over the problem of Agnes, where would she go, how could she move after all these years. He got up suddenly and went out the back door. Lina padded silently after him, and the screen caught her full in the face. She fell onto her bottom with a wail, but he picked her up and swung her outside with him before anybody else could move.

She quieted down, comforted by the rhythm of his step, the lifting and falling of the hip she rode on. He let her slide down the side of his leg and they walked up the road, hand in hand. Little Lina had her mother's stillness and she was comfortable with her father, content to trot along beside him without talking. They often went out on a walk like this after supper, just the two of them.

Before he and Rosa were married, they used to go out and walk along the back roads, next to the tobacco nets. In those days, there were still three farms that grew shade tobacco in the Northington Valley and in the evenings, just before sunset, the gauzy white nets made the fields mysterious, more like oceans than land. Sometimes he and Rosa stood under the white cotton and stared at the rows of tobacco plants stretching away from them, interrupted only by the poles that held up the cloth.

"It's a crazy way to grow something," she had said once in that soft voice of hers. He was so much taller that he often had to tilt his head in the old way to hear her. She spoke so rarely that he began to feel every pronouncement of hers was somehow prophetic.

He and Rosa had known each other their whole lives, in the way that children do when their parents are friends, when they end up in the same church, the same Christian doctrine classes. Rosa was the oldest of three girls, and to everybody's surprise, she went away to secretarial school in Boston after high school.

"It was my father's idea," she told Rudy much later. "I would be the boy for him. He let my other sisters be girls. But I had to get a skill."

She was miserably unhappy there. When Rudy saw her at the firemen's picnic the summer after she graduated, she was so skinny that he barely recognized her. He started in with her as if she were a homework assignment. He knew Rosa pleased his father. By falling in love with her, Rudy had finally acknowledged the gulf between the big house and the cottage at the end of the driveway.

Around that time, with Mrs. Webster's permission, he moved the workshop from the cellar room into the old office in the calf barn.

"We'll miss the sound of a man in the house," Mrs. Webster had said. He saw that she was flirting with him and it made him angry. Had he just been a houseboy for them all those years? Maybe his father was right. Maybe Mrs. Webster had no respect for the Delbiancos.

"It will be easier for me to work out of there," he explained.

"You're doing well, then," she said, still cheerful despite his sullen face.

"Yes." The work was trickling in. He had started as a carpenter after the two years of trade school. The jobs were small to begin with, so he lived at home and put his money in the bank. A bookshelf system for one family, then a kitchen renovation which led to a two-room addition to a house. He had gone back to school at night and learned plumbing, wiring, structures. He had even taken a drafting course so that if his clients did not want to bother with an architect, he could draw them a reasonable picture of what they were getting. He began to bid on larger projects, and the business grew by word of mouth.

In those years, he saw very little of Mrs. Webster and Agnes. One day, he took Rosa over to meet them. They greeted her warmly enough, but he saw that they kept to the kitchen.

"It looks like a very fancy house," Rosa said as they walked back down the driveway. He didn't answer.

Molly came for occasional weekends. If their paths crossed at all, they were stiff and awkward with one another. One November afternoon, he was helping his father take down a split limb of the copper beech tree when Molly's car sped into the driveway. Even now, he could remember the car. It was bright red, a small foreign model. The front right bumper was crumpled and beginning to rust. She jumped out, a bright scarf tied around her neck, her hair piled on her head. He remembered thinking that she would catch cold in that thin sweater and the skinny short skirt. She looked like some exotic bird that had just landed on the branch of their lives, and he stared at her without calling out while she trotted across the driveway and up the porch steps with a backpack over her shoulder.

"Agnes, where are you?" she called, and then the door slammed behind her.

"Foolish girl," his father said under his breath before turning back to his work.

That night, lying in his narrow bed in the cottage, Rudy thought of her again, of how separate their worlds were, of how easily she moved from the farm to New York City to college and even to Europe, where she'd gone on a trip with Mrs. Webster the summer before. A restlessness boiled up in him, and when he had tossed back and forth for an hour, he got up and let himself quietly out the front door. The big dark house drew him, and he went and stood next to the elm tree, underneath her bedroom window. Her light was still on, and he could hear the faint murmur of a radio. He prowled along the edge of the house, like a dog sniffing its territory. After all, this was his bigger world, this house. This was his New York City and Europe and college all rolled into one, the only piece of it he would ever touch, and he was filled with a sudden despair about the life that was laid out ahead of him. Rosa and the Northington Volunteer Fire Department and maybe a trip to northern Italy when they had retired, to see the town his grandparents came from. He wanted Molly's freedom, her easy flight over the surface of the world, her spontaneous landings in places where the furniture was beautifully made and the air smelled of fresh flowers and perfume. And he hated himself for wanting it because it meant that his father was right. He was still addicted to the Websters, still the poor little boy from down the road with his nose pressed against the window of their dinner party.

The next night when he drove Rosa down the river road after the movies, he asked her to marry him with an intensity that made her hesitate.

"Let's do it soon," he said.

"What's the big rush?" she asked, laying her hand over his because he seemed to be shaking.

"Because I can't stand it another minute," he said, pulling her body close to his. She had smiled to herself, and for the first time, she let him slip his hand under her shirt, despite Father Dionne's warnings about chastity, because it couldn't still be a mortal sin if the boy had just asked you to marry him.

So when Rosa told him two months later that she was pregnant, Rudy had to crawl back up to the big house and ask Mrs. Webster for a loan. The bank wouldn't give him one just because he *thought* he was going to win the contract for the new development over in Plainfield, and he couldn't afford to put down the money for the construction trailer he would need as well as the small house they had picked out on Barnett Road.

"We'll live with my parents, then," Rosa had said. "I don't mind. My sisters will help with the baby."

But Rudy was stubborn about it. He would rather borrow money from the Websters than start out his married life with the Valentis, who already looked down their noses at Frank Delbianco, the caretaker. Besides, he had no intention of telling Mrs. Webster about the baby. It would be strictly a talk about his business.

Mrs. Webster was recovering from a broken hip.

"It's her first day downstairs," Agnes explained. "She's waiting for you in the living room."

She sat in her usual corner of the couch.

"Hello, Rudy. Have a seat. I would struggle to my feet to greet you, but it would take much too long."

"How are you?" he asked.

"Well enough for a clumsy old lady. But I feel as if my bones have suddenly turned to plastic."

He pulled a desk chair from its position against the wall rather than sink intimately down into the soft cushions at the other end of the couch. That place was reserved for her lady friends who came out from Hartford for tea.

The three-tiered maple tea caddy stood in its customary position to the right of her knee. He knew about the tea parties from the preparations he used to watch in the kitchen. Molly and David always complained when the bell rang for them to join her because they would have preferred to stay with him, dipping the sugar cookies into their mugs on the tin-topped table, dribbling a little so Agnes's sponge could shoot out and wipe up the drops.

"How much money do you need?" she asked, continuing the conversation he started and had hoped to finish on the telephone.

"Ten thousand."

"Rosa is a very nice girl, Rudy, but I can't quite understand your rush to get married. She's only about nineteen, isn't she?"

He looked down at his hands. A bank would not have asked him this kind of question. "This is the turning point in the business," he said. "It really looks as if I'm going to get the contract for the new development on Route 16 over in Plainfield. I'll need to hire more people and buy a construction trailer for the site. And at the

same time, Rosa and I want to have our own house. I've
saved every bit of money I've made since I started, but
with everything happening at once, I'm going to need
some extra capital." He pulled a folded sheet out of his
back pocket and laid it on the sofa next to her. "I've
figured it all out here. I'll be paying you back at the same
interest rate the bank would charge me."

She had stopped listening somewhere in the middle of
his speech. "Have you noticed the elm tree outside Mr.
Webster's study door?"

"Yes," he said.

"I planted that with Smack the first year I moved here.
In 1909. Fifty-three years ago. I remember I asked him if
my grandchildren would see it, and he promised me that
they would. You're too young to remember Smack, I
suppose."

He shook his head. Her mind must be going.

"Smack was right. The tree has lasted as long as he
said it would. But we planted it too close to the house.
Of course, he couldn't know that we would build the new
wing out in that direction in the twenties. In any case, the
roots are pushing their way into the foundation. Last
year, your father took me down to the cellar and showed
me the cracks in that wall."

Still he said nothing. Was she asking him to do another
job for her? Move this chair for me, Rudy. Move this
tree for me.

"You won't be building houses like this one, Rudy.
Your houses will be small and efficient. They won't have
enough room to hold the past." She sank even farther
back into the corner of the couch. The room had grown
dim. "In this generation when everyone is so restless, the
roots cannot grow that deep. I sit in this living room
every afternoon with a cloud of witnesses. We share the
secrets of half a century."

"Do you want me to cut down the tree?" he asked at
last.

"Not while I'm alive," she said as she painfully shifted
her body into a more comfortable position. "This house
will go on this way as long as I'm here. After that, who
knows? You still tilt your head to the side. I told your
mother to have your eyes checked years ago."

"About the loan, Mrs. Webster?"

"I'll give you the money, but I want it to be a partnership, Rudy. I don't make loans, I make business deals. I think you're a sound investment. I will take ten percent of the profits. When I die, you can pay the principal back to my heirs in monthly installments at the going interest rate. Fair enough?"

He was shaken by her suggestion and said nothing for a minute.

"Are you trying to figure out how long I'll last?" she asked with a smile.

"No. I just need to think about this. It's not the kind of arrangement I had expected."

"In the beginning, you'll have the use of the money interest-free," she said. "If you do as well as I think you will, I stand to make a little money on the deal. After all, the valley is filling up with houses. All those people who work in Hartford want to get away from the city. They'll be coming over here eventually. Think it over. If you decide to go ahead, you can call Mrs. Taylor over at the newspaper. She'll have a document drawn up that we can both sign."

"But what if I don't show a profit right away?"

"No business does. I'm willing to take a gamble."

He stood up and took her outstretched hand. Her skin felt like soft paper wrapped too loosely around the dull bumps of her bones.

She lived for nine more years, long enough to dedicate the town library that he had built. They drove her to the ceremony in a horse and buggy and she insisted on taking his arm to walk up the flagstone path. She clung tightly to him, and he bent his knees a little to adjust his height to hers.

"I hope you did a good job on this one, Rudy. Since it's named after me, I want it to last a while." By then, she was eighty-four years old, but she still had a mischievous twinkle in her gray eyes.

"Best job I've ever done."

"Did we make any money on it?" Before he could answer, she stopped right there in the middle of the path while the townspeople lining the path continued to clap respectfully. "This could be considered a conflict of interest, couldn't it? Does the town planning board know about our partnership?"

"I don't think so."

"Well, in any case, I certainly did not use my influence to get you the job." She slipped her thin arm out from his to greet the first selectman, who was waiting for her on the top step, and Rudy stepped away to take his place in the crowd beside Rosa.

That was the last time they ever spoke together. She wrote him a note when she received the last check for her share of the profits.

"I'm impressed," was all it said in black loopy letters. He put it in the file marked "LW."

If she ever bothered to count the months between his wedding day and Tony's birth, she didn't mention it to him.

"Papa, pick me up, my legs are tired," Lina cried.

He scooped her up and turned back toward the house.

When he set Lina down on the doorsill, he could see that Rosa was sitting stiffly at the kitchen table with her back toward him.

"She's drawing a picture of Mama," Tony sang out from his place at Molly's elbow.

"You were gone so long," Rosa said, forgetting her pose and turning to glance at him.

"Sorry." He walked around behind Molly to look down at the sketch. She was using one of the children's black crayons and a piece of his business stationery.

"She's a terrific person to do," Molly said half to herself. "The line of the jaw is so strong and the space here is good too," she said, laying a finger between the picture's two eyebrows.

"I don't think it looks like Rosa," he said abruptly, and moved away. He didn't like the proprietary way that Molly was talking about Rosa, but most of all he didn't like what he saw in the picture—the wide full face, the thickness of his wife's bones under Molly's thin skillful fingers.

"I do," Tony said. Now that he was Molly's friend, he had attached himself to her with all the fervor of a crusader. She could do no wrong in the boy's eyes.

"What do you think is wrong with it, Rudy?" Molly asked, still tilting her head back and forth while she held the piece of paper at a new angle to catch the light.

Rosa stood up suddenly. "Children, it's way past your bedtime," she said.

"I'm sorry. I totally forgot the time," Molly said. She put the sketch down on the kitchen table. "There's my house present," she said. "Thank you for having me."

Rosa said goodbye. She took Lina by the hand and called out for Louis, who was hiding in the front room. Rudy noticed that his wife avoided looking at her likeness, which stared up at them from the table.

Molly was very quiet on the drive home. When he pulled the truck up beside the porch steps, she asked him if he wanted to come in.

"No, thanks," he said. "I should get back to help Rosa put the children to bed."

"Did I do something wrong, Rudy?"

"What are you talking about?"

"You seemed very angry tonight."

"It has nothing to do with you, Molly."

He watched as she walked around the front, half expecting her to stick out her tongue at him in the brief glory of the headlights. But she kept her head down all the way up the porch steps.

When he got home, Rosa's picture had been removed from the kitchen table, and he assumed she had destroyed it until a few days later when he found it taped up on Tony's bedroom wall.

Now that Rudy was working on the calf barn, he stopped by to see his mother more often. She seemed to be getting thinner and complained constantly of a stomachache. The television was always on, but she didn't pay much attention to it. "It's just for company," she told him. Her favorite occupation was still the newspaper. She had given up tacking pictures on the kitchen walls, but she still took the Hartford *Courant* as well as the Plainfield *Herald* and pored over them every day, cutting out recipes that she rarely used and Ann Landers columns and marriage announcements and news of the Websters to paste in her scrapbook. The articles had yellowed with age, but they loyally traced the achievements of the big house.

Lydia Webster Reelected for Third Time as Republican Town Chairman. Model Barn on Webster Farm Opened to Public for Weekend. Webster Boys Fighting in Europe. Charlotte Webster Married to Jack Taylor of Simsbury. George Webster, First Selectman of Northington for Thirty Years, Succumbs to Heart Attack. Webster Ayrshire Herd Sold Off. Lydia Webster Appointed to Board of Directors, Hartford College for Women.

And so on. The Websters shared space on each page with the Mazzarellas and the Antonuccis and even occasionally the brief obligatory announcements about the Delbiancos. Baby Son Born to Delbiancos. Delbianco-Valenti Wedding Planned. "Mr. and Mrs. Frank Delbianco of Brook Road, Northington, have announced the engagement of their son, Rudy, to Rosa Valenti, the daughter of Mr. and Mrs. Antonio Valenti of Southington."

"You'd think I'd done nothing at all between getting born and getting married," Rudy said to his mother.

"Don't be ridiculous," she said, but Rudy suspected she wasn't even listening.

On Sundays, they always went over to his parents' for dinner. It was one of those rituals that had begun to grate on Rudy. Although his mother professed to love her grandchildren, they made her uneasy. "It comes from having just one of my own," she explained to Rosa. "And Rudy was so quiet, you know. Not like your boys."

So Rosa had taken to feeding the children ahead of time and sending them outside to play.

The Sunday after Molly had been to the house, the four adults sat out on the lawn in front of the cottage, wrapped in sweaters. The weather was turning. This weekend the clocks went back.

"I don't know what that girl does up at the house all day," Angelina said to Rosa.

"She's painting, I guess," Rosa said, catching Rudy's eye. He looked away.

"Remember when she used to come down and have dinner with you, Rudy?" his mother asked. "I loved to braid that child's hair. It was so thick. I don't know where that red came from. Certainly not the mother. Or the father either. Rudy once asked her if it came out of bottle."

"Hush, Angel," said Rudy's father from his metal chair under the oak tree. His voice sounded weary.

They sat in a row, staring out at the dim forms of the children playing tag on the lawn across the driveway, and after a while, Angelina started again.

"That father was a bad one from the beginning. I remember thinking that when I served at their wedding reception. He was such a nervous type, with his eyes shifting around and the drink always in his hand. Imagine Charlotte picking him, of all people."

"Whatever happened to him?" Rosa asked.

"He was killed in a car accident about six years ago, wasn't it, Frank?" Angelina said. "Out in California. Charlotte should have married again. Makes a woman hard to live alone like that."

"She was hard to begin with," Frank said from beneath the tree. In the deepening twilight, he was nothing but a silhouette and a voice. Rosa glanced over at him with a question on her face, but she didn't ask it.

A door slammed up at the big house, and they all looked to the left. Molly was standing at the edge of the kitchen porch, watching the children. Tony saw her and bounded up the steps to greet her. They talked, and then Molly looked down the driveway toward the cottage. She waved, and Angel waved back. After another word with Tony, Molly went inside.

"Louis learned to ride his bike this week," Rosa said. "He did it all by himself on the driveway."

"Imagine that," Angelina said.

Rudy pushed himself out of his chair and went to gather in the children.

30

After eight weeks, the compositors' union had gone back to work with a new contract.

"We should celebrate," Oliver said when he dropped by Charlotte's office on his way out. "How about dinner?"

"No, thanks, Oliver. I've got a lot to finish up here."

"You don't look well, Char. Susan was saying the same thing just the other day. Why don't you take some time off?"

She glanced up at her brother. "Where would I go?" she asked.

"She looked just like a lost child when she said that," Oliver told his wife over dinner that night.

"Imagine her living alone in that house all these years. I remember that sweet man from Farmington was interested in her, but she wouldn't have anything to do with him," Susan said. "He was a teacher in the high school, wasn't he?"

"Well, as they say, once burned, twice shy," Oliver said. "I expect if you've made a mistake as catastrophic as Jack Taylor, you'd never really trust yourself to choose right the second time around."

In the last year, Charlotte had taken up swimming to try to ease the pain of the arthritis, which had spread to her shoulders and her hip joints. The pool at the Y stayed open until ten o'clock most nights, which meant she had a place to hide out on the evenings when she couldn't face the empty house. Like an aging frog, she did the breaststroke up and down the fifty-meter lane as younger women churned past her, their arms rising and falling in the rhythms of their crawlstrokes. In the beginning, she had been embarrassed by her body, by the way the skin hung so loose on her legs, by her clumsy, slow progress, but in the last few months, like so much else, even that feeling had fallen away from her. It was part of not caring about anything anymore.

Her visits to the steam room gave her the most pleasure.

There the women lay naked on the moist white tiles, exhaling evenly, brushing the hot drops of water off their skin with casual movements, easy with their exposed bodies in the anonymous fog. Usually nobody spoke and the sound of the regular breathing was drowned only by the occasional rumbling of the steam machine as it released another hot cloud into the close atmosphere. Sometimes in her dreamy dozing, Charlotte fantasized that this room, the whole building in fact, had been set down on top of an underground hot spring, a continually bubbling eruption whose original source was actually the core of the earth.

Tonight, Charlotte secured her favorite spot, an upper shelf space in the corner, and lay there with her legs fully extended. The door opened and closed as newcomers changed places with the women who were finding their way out. Charlotte allowed herself more time than usual. She had been through a hell of a day. There was nothing to go home to but a cold bed, her night guard, and the pile of photographs she'd decided to weed through.

It was rare that anybody disturbed the peaceful, almost spiritual silence, but tonight, without any warning, a voice from the opposite corner said, "We must look like bodies in a morgue," and Charlotte began to laugh.

It started out as just a giggle, but the giggles led to short barks and then higher shrieks that seemed to last forever. Charlotte listened to the wild, hysterical sounds as if they did not belong to her, as if they were issuing from someone else's mouth or from the dark tunnel that led down through the floor to the mysterious source of steam. This noise could not possibly be coming from me, she thought. But why do my sides ache so? She rolled over and held her belly. Nobody moved or spoke as the raucous, obtrusive noise began, at last, to subside, to wear itself out. The laughing had disturbed the peace of the room and made people uneasy. One woman got up and left and then another. They're getting away from me,

Charlotte thought, the same way people move down from
the crazy lady who mutters to herself in the back of the
bus.

"Are you all right?" asked the same disembodied voice
from the other corner.

"Yes," Charlotte whispered as she pushed herself up
to a sitting position. Like a penitent, she made her way
out of the cloudy room, away from the silent women,
who would probably start whispering about her the moment the heavy glass door settled safely back into its
frame.

She followed her usual path into the dark house.
In the mornings when she left for work, she flicked
on the porch light. From that pool of safety, she
moved to the switch over the kitchen counter and
from there to the hall chandelier. The dark upstairs still
waited for her, of course, but she would put that off.

She made herself a bowl of tomato soup, crumbled
some crackers onto the thick surface, and carried it into
the study, where this morning she had left the bottom
drawer of the desk hanging open. Molly had called last
week asking for photographs, and Charlotte had promised to weed through them.

"What do you need them for?" Charlotte asked.

She was glad Molly had asked for the pictures because
she was suddenly eager to clear things out. She had been
too much of a pack rat all her life. After Jack left, it had
taken her three years to send his old suits to the Salva-
tion Army.

"What in heaven's name are you waiting for?" her
mother had asked.

"Maybe David could use them," she murmured.

"For God's sake, Charlotte, don't be morbid."

She knelt by the open drawer and plunged her hand
into the layers of loose photographs. Up came a fistful of
the formal Christmas photographs, one of those Webster
traditions that Charlotte had insisted on perpetuating,
although now, sitting on the floor and looking at the stiff
sad faces on the sofa, she could not imagine why. Pale,
solemn David stared obediently out at the camera, his
thin shoulders pulled back in an imitation of the little-

man stance that he thought pleased his father. Molly was about eight and, as usual, slightly out of focus, because she never could bear to sit still. She was leaning against her father, one elbow planted on his upper thigh. And Jack was drunk. Charlotte recognized the look as if she had seen it yesterday—the thin, arrogant grin; the arm draped loosely around Molly's shoulders in that proprietary attitude he always assumed with his daughter. This one's mine, it seemed to say. You can have the boy.

And Charlotte herself. Her own face peered out at her from more than twenty years ago. How determined it looked. How convinced that if you just lifted your chin, smiled for the camera, and looked straight ahead, then everything would turn out for the best. By the time this picture was taken, things had been going from bad to worse for a long time. Jack had lost two or three jobs, and every night when Charlotte got home from the office, Jessie, the housekeeper, met her at the kitchen door with rolling eyeballs.

Suddenly, she pulled the whole drawer out and tipped it upside down. She was struck by the incongruity of the cascade as single faces slid across group pictures, formal shots across candids, barns and tennis games and Christmas trees tumbled out together. With hurried nervous fingers she fitted the drawer back into its slot and then spread the pictures out across the rug the way David used to sort through his baseball-card collection, looking for one specific face. It took her ten minutes to find it. A picture of Jack taken the day she'd met him at the annual *Herald* picnic, which was always held in the field below the calf barn. She was just three days out of Smith College and one day away from her first job as junior reporter on the news staff.

"There," she said to herself. "You weren't crazy. He *was* the best-looking man you'd ever seen."

The smooth young skin, the jaunty dark mustache that he shaved off an hour before they were married without warning, the black black hair, thick and wavy, the way his blue eyes fixed on you and stayed without embarrassment for as long as they needed to take you in.

"Who is that?" she had asked her father when she noticed Jack watching her.

441

Her father looked up from his place behind the sandwich tray. "Which one?"

"The one who's staring at me right now," she said under her breath.

"That's Jack Taylor. He's a typo in the composing room. His father's Sam Taylor, my arch rival in Plainfield because he's as confirmed a Democrat as I'm a Republican. He owns the elastic webbing factory, one of the biggest industries in town. Jack coming to work for us was a real slap in his old man's face."

"What's he like?" Charlotte asked.

Her father shrugged. "Quiet. Seems to have some kind of chip on his shoulder. A lot of tough talk and bravado, but it doesn't amount to much. He's a good enough worker when he pays attention."

From the beginning, Charlotte loved the arrogance and the swagger, the flag tattooed on his upper right arm, the thick shoulders, the cocky way he walked through the newsroom to say something to her. The composing room was in the basement, so normally the reporters never saw the typos. Charlotte remembered her Saturday-afternoon visits to that dark room when she was a child. Now she went down there after work to meet Jack.

He was so different from the boys she had met at Smith, tall blond boys who smoked pipes self-consciously and made plans to go to the North Shore for the weekend. She knew Jack felt uncomfortable in her parents' house and that all his drinking and bluffing was just his way of covering that up. From the beginning, her mother made it clear to Charlotte that Jack Taylor was a perfectly nice fellow, but, of course, she wasn't serious about him.

"I'm dead serious," Charlotte said. "He's the only man I've ever met with any strength."

"You're confusing brawn with strength," Lydia said. "And eventually you will miss the brains, darling. The animal attraction can't last forever. Besides, that tattoo on his arm is perfectly revolting."

"I have enough brains for both of us, Mother. And they don't seem to make me any happier."

* * *

Over everybody's objections, they were married one year after they met in the Congregational church in Northington, and two weeks later Jack quit his job at the *Herald*. It was the second of the many surprises she grew used to over the years. The first had been the mustache.

"Did my father ask you to quit?"

"No," he said. "It has nothing to do with your father. It has to do with my pride. The *Herald* isn't the only paper in the world. I'll find another job where I won't just be the guy who's married to the boss's daughter."

It turned out to be a very foolish mistake. In 1936, the country was still trying to get back on its feet, and although prices and production were up, there were still eight million unemployed. Jack didn't find another job for six months.

"I'm sure you could go back to the *Herald*," she suggested tentatively when he came back discouraged at the end of another day.

"That is the last goddamned place I'll go," he muttered, and slammed out of the house again.

In January, he found a job working for the Southington *Press*, a small daily in the area. David was born a year later and Molly in 1940. The little girl with her tufts of red hair seemed to take his breath away, and many nights, when Charlotte came padding down the hall to check on her, she found him sitting in the baby's room with a beer in his hand. He looked like a night watchman.

"Is she all right?" Charlotte asked the first time. "Why is the light on?"

"I didn't want her to be scared if she woke up," he said. "She makes such strange noises when she sleeps."

"Babies do," Charlotte said with a smile. The mechanics of baby care did not frighten her at all after her time taking care of Campbell. Jack lifted his head for another swig of the beer and she left the room.

When the call went out for men to register in October 1941, Jack was the first in line. But even the Army didn't want him. They turned him away because of his asthma, so he went up to Canada, where it was rumored they were signing on rejected Americans for the British Army.

"They took almost everybody," he told Charlotte the night he got back. "I told them I hadn't had an asthma

443

attack in two years, but they gave me some breathing test and told me to go home."

"I'm glad," she said, touching his hand. He jerked it away as if he had been bitten.

"I'm going to be the only goddamned man under the age of sixty in this town in a few months. Then you won't be so glad."

She stole upstairs without another word. He never came to bed at all that night. Soon after that, Charlotte dropped by her father's office.

"Got any work for me?" she asked.

"You've got two babies at home," he said.

"I'll find someone to take care of the children," she said. "I need a job."

"What is it, Char?" he asked. "What's really wrong?"

"Nothing, Father. Except that we could use the money. And I miss the work. You always said you wanted me to learn the ropes around here. Well, I've come back to finish what I started."

"She's like me, George," Lydia said. "Being at home with two small babies will drive her mad. Besides, you need people now that the younger reporters have been drafted."

"I'm sure you're right. But there's another reason too," George said. "She's living with a man who's lost his self-respect. She's got to get out of the house so she can think about something else."

So he took her back, and three years later he died, leaving her to run the *Herald*.

Those early years of serving as publisher, she came home most nights long after the children were in bed. Her dinner was often stuck to the plate because Jessie had left it in a warm oven so many hours before. Jack would be sprawled in his chair in the study with the Plainfield *Herald* draped over his front like a flag over a casket.

To her surprise, Jack did not complain about his involvement with the children. The other men she knew would have refused, would have insisted that the picture they present as a couple be what was considered "normal." His sense of pride seemed to have nothing to do with what other people thought of him but with what he thought of himself. He obviously enjoyed the children. And they adored him.

Charlotte was the one who worried that it was unnatural. Children are supposed to go to their mothers with their arithmetic papers and their scraped knees and the rip in their Halloween costumes. But Jack was the one who told Jessie she could go on home. He was the one who started the baths and read the bedtime stories and went back upstairs for the absolutely last good-night kiss.

When he got fed up, he asked Jessie to stay late and went over to Plainfield to make the rounds of the bars. How could she possibly complain when he fell into bed at three in the morning, smelling of bourbon and muttering excuses? It was his way of letting off steam and, after all, it didn't hurt anybody. They didn't have much of a social life anyway, except for the obligatory evenings with his parents and the painful dinners with her mother when Jack was the only man around the table who was not dressed in a dinner jacket.

"I refuse to get suited up like a monkey just to please your mother," he said.

"I never said you had to."

Charlotte sat rigidly through those meals trying to concentrate on her dinner partner's conversation but all the while keeping her eye on Jack, who was usually seated next to his mother-in-law. "How's your work going, Jack?" Lydia would ask with what the family called her party face.

"What the hell does that mean anyway?" he asked his wife on the way home. "How is my work going? It goes the same every day."

When he barked questions at her like that, all Charlotte wanted to do was press her hands over her ears and run back to the office, where the answers seemed so much simpler. Sometimes she admitted to herself that she used the job as a shield against all sorts of unpleasant things.

"What a pretty picture, Molly. What is it?"

"It's a dragon, Mother," Jack said, turning it upside down and then sideways. "Can't you see the flame shooting out the front?"

"Daddy," Molly said with a giggle. "Stop being silly. I already told you it was a flower."

"It's a flower dragon, then," he said, and she climbed up into his lap and whispered to him. Charlotte felt left out of the fun when she sat across the room from the pair of them. She longed to hold out her arms for Molly, but she was too scared the child would curl closer into her father's chest. She was such a skinny bony thing and now, because it was summertime, the freckles on her face and arms ran into one another. They made an odd pair, the one so dark and thick and the other pale and thin. Jack was a physical man. It seemed to come naturally to him to touch his daughter, to run his black-haired hand up and down her arms, to pull her thick hair up and blow on her neck, which made Molly giggle and snuggle closer. They played a tickling game together. Molly would sit in his lap while he counted to three. If she didn't get away before he stopped counting, he would tickle her all over until she shrieked for it to stop.

But Charlotte flinched when he touched her.

"For God's sake, sometimes I feel as if I'm making love to a washboard," he said one night. "Loosen up."

"I'm trying," she whispered as if it were a problem she could solve if she just applied herself harder.

Most nights, she let herself very quietly into the bed, hoping he wouldn't wake.

When did the drinking get out of hand? She couldn't pinpoint the exact time now, as she sat on the floor surrounded by the photographs. She remembered the Christmas day on the way home from the farm when she made him stop the car and wash his face in the snow.

"Why does Daddy have to do that?" nine-year-old Molly had asked. "Is he sick? Is he going to throw up?"

Molly was always asking questions like that. She could never just sit still the way David did, looking straight ahead, pretending that there was nothing strange about your father stumbling around in the snowbank on the side of the road.

"Daddy's feeling a little dizzy, that's all. I'm going to drive."

"Why is he dizzy?"

"No more questions, Molly," Charlotte said in a voice that held warnings David heard and Molly never did.

"Shut up, Molly," David hissed from his corner of the back seat.

"Oh, shut up yourself."

Jack began to lose jobs, one after another. It turned out that he had been reporting in late for work, sometimes not at all, and once the men started coming home from the war, employers found they could use more reliable people. He went on scouting trips to look for new opportunities, "business trips" as he told the children. Charlotte asked Jessie to live in with them.

"But when will you be back, Daddy?" Molly wailed. "Where are you going?"

"I've got some new work down in Pennsylvania, sugar. Big new deal. I'll bring you a present when I get back."

Charlotte wasn't sure where he went or what he was doing there and she knew enough not to ask, because those days he was like a powder keg. For a while, he talked about some kind of import business, then he decided to go back to trade school at night and learn carpentry. As a gesture of support, Charlotte gave him a table saw for Christmas and he set up a shop in the basement, but after a few faltering months he gave it up. Finally, he took a job in his father's factory. That's when the drinking began in earnest. The family all knew that Sam Taylor took his son back more out of pity and the need to teach him a lesson than anything else. Demand for elastic webbing had dropped once the war ended, and the plant had laid off close to a hundred workers in the last few years.

Charlotte began to dread what she would find when she came home at night. He was still loving and attentive to Molly, but she and David seemed to be the targets of his irrational anger. Sometimes when she went into David's room to say good night, the boy was lying rigidly in the bed, staring blankly at the ceiling.

"What's wrong, David?"

"Nothing."

She ruffled his straight brown hair. How much easier it was for her to touch this child than the other. "Come on, you can tell me."

"Daddy is mean."

"What did he do?"

"He yells at me about everything. He never yells at Molly. David, pick up your shoes. David, stand up straight. David, use your arm when you throw the baseball. Watch Molly do it. Blah, blah, blah."

"Daddy's very tired, sweetheart. He works hard."

He flopped over on his side away from her. "I wish you were here when we got home from school."

"I'll get home earlier, David. I promise."

So she did. But even that seemed to make Jack angry.

"What are you doing?" he roared. "Spying on me?"

"Of course not. I was able to get away earlier today. I thought I'd do something special with the children."

"They've both got homework to do. You probably forgot about that."

He was right. She didn't know how to fit herself into the pattern of a child's afternoon. Did they want to take a walk with her? Could she take them into town for ice cream? She was like the special uncle who flew in occasionally, gave them a kiss and a surprise package, and flew away again. So she went back to work and told herself that things would sort themselves out.

And sometimes they did get better. Jack was mopey and often remorseful, and he kept promising Charlotte that he would stop, he would "make it up" to her. And he was so sweet with Molly. In the sixth grade, she was the center fielder for the softball team. She and her father spent hours in the backyard practicing.

"Throw the ball again, baby," he said. "Let your arm unfold. Use your wrist. I don't want you throwing like the sissy girls."

He made sure he got to every one of her games.

"For God's sake, Charlotte, get rid of him," Oliver said whenever she complained about one of Jack's binges. "He was the wrong man for you from the start. How much of this are you going to put up with?"

"I'll handle it myself," she would reply coldly, and turn back to discussions of the budget or staff problems. The whole family agreed with Oliver. Jack Taylor was a disgrace.

"But he's a very good father," Charlotte said to Lydia. Actually mother, she admitted only to herself, I'm the father in this family, the breadwinner with the briefcase who gets home just in time to kiss the children good night. If she divorced Jack, who would go to the softball games? Who would hold that girl the way her father did?

"There are other men in this world, Charlotte."

"Don't you worry about the stigma of a divorce?" Charlotte asked.

"Not in your case," Lydia said, lifting her chin. "You married a sloppy drunk with a lousy employment history. You have a right, in fact a duty, to throw him out of the house."

But still she held on. Jessie quit, saying she wanted to move back down South with her brother. Charlotte wondered whether it had something to do with Jack's drinking, but she didn't ask any questions. She hired a cleaning lady who left casseroles for the week in the freezer.

When David turned fourteen, she sent him off to boarding school in Massachusetts.

"Why?" Jack said. "So he can turn into another snob like those friends of your brothers?"

No, she thought, so he can have some relief from your criticism. But she said nothing, because talking with Jack when he was drinking got her nowhere.

"Well, you're not shipping our daughter off like some package. She's staying right here."

"I have no intention of sending Molly to boarding school," she said.

Of course later, when she found out the real truth about him, she understood so much more. "But how could I know then?" she asked the circle of photographs. "Was there some change in Molly's face that I missed, some clue that would have given it all away?"

The ashtray was already overflowing, but she lit another cigarette without bothering to empty it. She had no idea what time it was. These days, she rarely went to bed before midnight because that left her too many hours to count off before she could get up again.

She would look for the clues now, she thought, getting up on her knees. It took her almost an hour to weed out all the pictures of Molly, and once she had arranged them chronologically on the rug in front of her, she was amazed to see how many there were. Molly's seventh-grade class picture. Molly and Jessie carving the Halloween pumpkin. Molly with her father after the final softball game of the season the spring before he left for good.

Charlotte studied that one for a long time. The girl leaned into the crook of her father's arm with an easy languor. He was wearing her cap and had turned it around so the brim hung out over his left ear. The silly grin on his face could just as easily have been pleasure over his daughter's fielding prowess rather than a glass of bourbon in some bar before the game. If something had been wrong between them all those years ago, wouldn't Charlotte see it now? Wouldn't the girl have been stiff, her expression a frightened one? Wouldn't Molly have told her mother something?

"How could she tell you, Charlotte?" Lydia had said. "You were never home."

How could your own daughter tell you the kinds of things her father did with her all those afternoons you left them alone together, when she had never told you anything before, when you had never been there for her to tell?

That November afternoon. She had been interrupted in the middle of a meeting in New York. Come directly to the farm, Lydia had dictated to the secretary and had then taken the phone off the hook, so Charlotte had no choice.

By the time she arrived, Molly had already been moved into her grandmother's house, the neglected child taken away from the unfit parents. It was Tuesday. When the school bus did not drop Molly at the farm for her usual night at her grandmother's, Lydia had driven over to find her. At first she thought there was nobody home, but the living room was a mess.

"Bourbon has such an ugly smell," she said to Charlotte, wrinkling her nose. "The whole house looked as if a hurricane had blown through there. Papers everywhere. The pillows on the floor. Your husband"—the words held such disdain—"was gone by the time I got there."

"What about Molly?"

"I found her upstairs in her closet. She was singing a little song to herself. Her blouse was ripped at the shoulder, and there are some bruises on her neck." Lydia's hands were twisting round and round in her lap. "The poor child," she whispered. "This has obviously been going on for years."

"What did she say happened?" Charlotte pressed.

"That she and her father had a fight," she said. "Of course, she couldn't tell me what had really happened. I mean, there's no way to put something like that into words."

"Oh, my God, Mother, what are you saying to me?" Charlotte cried. "Are you saying that Jack—" She couldn't finish the thought out loud.

Lydia came and sat next to her daughter on the stiff sofa. "You mustn't blame yourself, darling," she said, putting her arms around Charlotte. "You've done the best you could all along. Now we have to pick up the pieces and go ahead. Molly will stay here with me where she can feel safe until her father is dealt with."

When Charlotte went upstairs later to talk to Molly, the girl was turned toward the window, staring out through the bare branches of the elm tree.

"Hello, Molly."

"Hello, Mother." She didn't turn around or reach out her arms the way Charlotte wanted her to. To sit on the bed she would have had to push her daughter's thin body aside, so she dragged the desk chair over.

"Daddy didn't do anything wrong," Molly said quickly. "I don't know why Grandmother's acting so funny about it. He just scared me a little, that's all."

"I know that, darling. But I think Daddy will be going away for a little while."

Molly turned over then. Her face looked pale, almost ghostly with its circle of dark hair. In the wintertime, out of the sun, her hair always darkened. "Is he mad at me?" she whispered, and Charlotte thought her heart would break.

"Darling, of course not. Nobody's mad at you. We just want to be sure you're all right."

"Call me Molly. I don't like that word 'darling.' "

"Of course," Charlotte had said, ready to agree to anything. "Agnes and your grandmother want you to stay here with them. Do you want to?"

"Yes," she said, and turned to the window again.

Charlotte followed her gaze. "That elm tree used to be my secret hideout."

Molly didn't answer. Charlotte leaned over and kissed her cheek tenderly. "I'll come back and see you tomorrow."

Propelled by his mother's commands, Oliver was the one who dealt with Jack. He found him late that night in a bar in Plainfield. Apparently, it didn't take very much to convince him to leave quietly. "He was terribly remorseful, as usual," Oliver told his sister when she could bear to listen to the story. "He doesn't really have a drinking problem, he'd just let things get out of hand, all the usual excuses that you must have heard a hundred times. When I brought up the business about Molly, he looked horrified. 'I couldn't have done that, Oliver. I couldn't have, you're making it up.' But he did admit to occasional blackouts. You know, in the end, I think he was relieved that we were stepping in and dealing with him. As if he couldn't do it himself."

Like a package, Jack was put on a plane to California, where he said he was going to get a whole new start in life.

When he telephoned Charlotte from the airport, he sounded sober. "You're sending me away just like David," he told her. "But I'll show you. I'm going to turn things around now. Your family has always thought of me as nothing. I'm going to prove them different. When I come back, I'm going to see my children. You can't take them away from me just like that. For God's sake, Charlotte"—and his voice broke—"I'm their father."

"Please just go away, Jack," she whispered into the receiver before she set it gently back down. The next day, she called the phone company and requested an unlisted number.

Sitting on the floor now, Charlotte thought about the grown Molly safely ensconced once again at her grandmother's house. Whenever she was around, Charlotte was forced to remember that the child had even tried to warn her. At least once.

She was just home from work, flipping through the mail on the front-hall table as usual. It was part of her arrival ritual.

IN MY MOTHER'S HOUSE

Molly had materialized out of nowhere. She must have been eleven then, maybe just twelve. "Something's wrong with Daddy," she had announced in that dramatic way of hers.

"What do you mean, darling?" she asked without looking up from the pile of envelopes.

"Sometimes, he gets so mad at me. And he wanders around the house at night. I hear him breathing."

"Don't be silly, darling," Charlotte said, still distracted. "You're imagining things." She ripped open the letter from the electric company. They'd been arguing over this bill for three months now, dammit.

"I don't imagine things," the child said in a hard, clear voice. "Unless I want to."

When Charlotte looked up again, Molly was gone.

"Stop it, Charlotte. Stop tormenting yourself," she said to the empty room. She gathered the pictures together, lifted them up like a messy pile of fall leaves and headed for the garbage bag in the kitchen. Along the way, one slipped out and then another, so that by the time she reached the kitchen she had left behind clues of her progress like Hansel and Gretel with their bread crumbs. And here comes the hungry bird, she thought, as she retraced her steps to the study, dipping and snatching at the loose pictures until they were all gathered back together. They were Molly's now. She could have them all. Let her sift through these remnants of their history together as a family and use them however she would. She tied up the ends of the garbage bag and dragged it like a dead body out to the car. Tomorrow she would leave it at the farm on her way to work.

That night, she dreamt her usual dream. Somebody was crying to her for help, it was one of the children, she was sure of that, but her legs weighed too much, something was dragging her back and she would never reach them in time. She woke up two or three times during the hours and tried to talk herself out of the dream, force her thoughts in some other direction, but when she fell back into the sleep, the nightmare would pick up again, just where it had left off.

31

Molly was the only one that fall who noticed the colors of the leaves. Everybody else, even Agnes, began to wonder if the snow would ever come. Usually she hated the winter, because she said it made her bones stiffen up. But this endless muggy weather was worse. It hung over them like a bad omen.

The flowers in the garden had been blackened to rotting green stalks by an early frost.

"Aren't you going to put the garden to bed?" Molly asked Frank one day. "Grandmother always used to cut down the perennials and spread branches over the roots."

"No point," he mumbled as he moved the cold pipe from one corner of his mouth to the other. "Sol is talking about building an addition out this way. The whole place will be a mess by next summer."

"Oh no, Frank," she cried. "Not right on top of Grandmother's garden. She kept this going ever since she first moved here. More than sixty years."

"Not just the garden. First thing Sol's got to do is take down that elm tree."

"Why the elm?" Molly asked.

"I told your grandmother a long time ago that the roots are growing right through the foundations of the house. Took her down to the cellar and showed them to her."

"What did she say?"

"This old house has got to last my lifetime, she said. I can't help what happens to it after that."

"That's the truth," Agnes said when Molly stomped in the kitchen and reported the conversation to her. "I remember her saying it."

"Well, she must be turning over in her grave right now," Molly said as she headed back upstairs.

One day in late October when it felt as if the weather were finally going to change for good, Frank had replaced the painting-porch screens with the glass panes. When he first arrived with a bump of the ladder and a fistful of tools, he and Molly had greeted one other pleasantly, but they each returned with relief to their work. They didn't normally spend so much time in such close proximity.

Frank was irritated by the whole procedure. He had just put up the damn screens at the end of August, when she first arrived, and now he had to take them down again. Why the hell couldn't she paint in some other room where the windows opened normally.

"I hope this cold weather holds," she called out as he hammered in the last nail, and he nodded.

But it didn't. The next day when the temperature climbed back up to sixty-five, Molly felt as if she were going to pass out either from the heat or from the smell of turpentine.

"I hope that fire extinguisher still works," Molly said when Agnes dropped by in the afternoon. "This whole place may explode with me in it."

"Your grandmother had it checked every six months. Frank replaced it last June." She fanned her face with a piece of newspaper. "You'd better stop for the day. These fumes are dangerous."

"And when the cold weather comes, I'll be freezing to death. What a crazy way to live," Molly said.

"Move inside, then. Lord knows, we've got enough rooms."

"No. I feel Grandmother with me when I'm up here."

I feel her with me everywhere, Agnes thought, but she didn't say it out loud. It sounded ridiculous.

Every day that passed, Molly felt herself slipping backwards, away from the free risky shapes and colors that people had admired in her earlier work. When her mother delivered the green garbage bag of photographs, she had dropped it in a corner of the porch, where it still sat unopened.

"What a peculiar thing to bring them in," she said when her mother pushed it out the car window toward her.

"If you hadn't asked for them, I might have put them in the garbage," Charlotte said.

"Everything all right, Mother?" Molly asked, trying to keep her voice light. The dark circles under her mother's eyes scared her. She looked a little crazy.

"I'm not sleeping well these days," Charlotte said. Their eyes met. "Lots to think about." She pulled back into the car, reminding Molly of a turtle retreating. "Talk to you soon," she said, shoving the gear shift into reverse. Molly hoisted the garbage bag over her shoulder and waddled across the driveway, pantomiming an old hobo with his sack on his back. Maybe it would make her mother smile, Molly thought as she turned to wave. But there was no answering wave, only the screech of the car's tires as they took the corner from a dead stop.

So the garbage bag sat in the corner while Molly tried to find her subject. When she did the landscapes in Danbury, she had become fascinated by patterns, but now they felt cold and intellectual to her. In her loneliest moments, she followed Agnes around, alternating pushing the vacuum cleaner with sketching her. She had begun to move the sketch of Agnes and the apple pie onto the canvas, but the work wasn't going well.

"I had so many ideas about the painting when I started," Molly complained to Andrea on the phone. "I wanted to honor the symbols of Agnes's life. I loved the curve of the apples, the problem of showing their different shapes when they actually have very little color. Agnes's lower lip hangs down when she's listening to you and the inner skin always glistens a little. And her hands are so full of texture. Skin like tissue paper, the veins like mole's tunnels. But it's not turning out right. My lines have lost all their confidence, their sharp edges. I'm so scared that I scrub everything in."

"Nonsense," Andrea said. "You always talk like that. Just keep at it, Molly. Do you want me to come up and cheer you on?"

"No, thanks. You'll be too much of a distraction. I

already have this terrible feeling that the days are rushing by."

On Thanksgiving Day, Charlotte joined Molly and Agnes in the children's dining room for the ceremonial turkey, but there was a mournful, uncomfortable feeling around the table. It reminded Molly of the time she found Agnes doggedly watching television in this room during the reception after Grandmother's funeral. Behind her clear-rimmed glasses, her eyes had reflected the blank light of the screen. She was in a rage.

"I never thought I'd live to see the day when a bunch of strangers were invited to barge around in my kitchen as if they owned the place," Agnes barked at Molly in the middle of a commercial.

"Mother thought that having the meal catered would make it easier for you," Molly explained. "It's been a rough week with so many people here."

"She didn't think that I could even cook a last meal for—" Her voice broke and she sat working the muscles of her face in a hopeless attempt to hold back the tears. Molly went over and squeezed herself into the same chair, just the way she used to do when she was a child. She put her arm around Agnes's shoulders and left it there through most of *The Edge of Night*. When the rest of the family finally came looking for them, they were giggling helplessly over a rerun of *My Three Sons*.

"What did David say when you asked him up?" Molly asked.

"Too much work," Charlotte replied.

"So what else is new?" said Agnes.

After he graduated from law school, David had gone to work in Washington. He was now the legislative aide to Perkins, one of the more liberal senators on the Hill.

"I can't seem to walk through this house without wondering how we're going to get rid of all this furniture," Charlotte said over her slice of pumpkin pie.

"Mother, for God's sake, Agnes and I are still living here. You sound as if you might shove us out with the upstairs clock or roll us up in one of the rugs."

"Not a bad way to go," Agnes said with one of her rare smiles.

"Have you called your sister, Agnes?" Charlotte asked.

"Yes. She's happy to take me if I want to go."

"Well, there's still time to decide," Molly said.

"Yes," Charlotte said quickly. "Of course there is. By the way, I thought I would invite everybody to come back here in December. Perhaps at Christmas, if that's the most convenient time. I've figured out quite a good system for dividing everything up if my brothers will agree to it. We'll have an appraiser come in to split things into four equal lots and then pick straws. People can always trade back and forth if they want."

"Sounds fine," Agnes said as she got up to clear the table. "If you four have to haggle over every single item, you'll still be arguing by the time Sol Delbianco drives his bulldozer across the lawn. Good Lord, remember the fights you used to have over the marble collection? This one stole such and such a marble. I've never heard such nonsense."

"Did they fight all the time when they were little?" Molly asked as the three of them trailed out to the kitchen with the dirty plates.

"Not all the time. George was practically off at boarding school by the time I arrived, but the middle two were always scrapping. Weren't you, Charlotte?"

"Were we?" Charlotte asked. "I remember Oliver and myself as quite good friends in those days."

"You and Oliver and Frank," Agnes said clearly over the sound of the running water.

"Frank Delbianco?" Molly asked, and the question dropped into the small pool of silence in the kitchen.

Agnes turned from the sink and took the last plate from Charlotte. "You did go down and sneak cigarettes with him in the barn. Oliver too."

"You knew that?" Charlotte asked.

"Of course I did. It was my job to know things."

"But why didn't you ever tell on us?"

Agnes shrugged. "There didn't seem to be any harm in it."

"You know, Frank was nothing to me," Charlotte said, the indignant fourteen-year-old girl again.

Molly lowered herself ever so quietly into the chair in the corner, hoping they would forget she was there.

"Well, if he was nothing to you, why did you agree to steal the gun? He must have put you up to it. It wasn't the kind of thing you'd ever do on your own."

"It was a deal we made that fall," Charlotte said quietly. "He taught me how to smoke so I would teach him how to shoot. Oliver and I kept hoping he would forget about it. But he didn't. Frank never forgot the things he wanted to do. Just the chores or his bicycle rusting in the rain." Her eyes were fixed on a spot above the window. When Agnes turned the water back on, it seemed to break some sort of spell.

"How did we ever get into that conversation?" Charlotte said. "I haven't thought about all that in years."

With the warm weather still holding, Rudy was working his crew overtime to frame in as many houses as they could. It was often late in the day before he and Luigi got down to the calf barn.

"There are two ways we can do this job," he had said to his Uncle Sol when he was first hired. "The right way and the cheap, half-assed way."

"How about something in between?" Sol asked with a grin. "We both know the half-assed way won't last, and with you, the right way will cost too much and take too long."

They had settled on the in-between price, but Rudy was doing it the right way, which meant jacking the barn up one section at a time, removing the rotting beams and replacing them. Luigi was the only carpenter Rudy knew who would agree to his methods.

Even though Rudy spent most of his time managing other people now, he had never lost his pleasure at working with wood. He loved the sweet smell of sawdust when he made the first cut, the clean connection when one perfectly measured length of lumber kissed another, the proportions of a building that had been well constructed. He built a tree house for his children with as much care as a new home for a client. Luigi had taught him that each step had to be done well or the next would not make up for the sloppiness of the last, so he sanded as carefully as he measured, he drove each nail in straight, he sharpened his chisels, searched for the angle, and attacked the wood cleanly. The only complaint that people made about his work was that he took longer than anyone else to finish.

"What's the difference between a carpenter and a cabinetmaker?" Molly asked him one day. She had taken to stopping in on them on her way back from the river.

"Easy," he said. "One does finer work than the other. More detailed. I dabble in everything. Furniture making, cabinetry, rough carpentry. Luigi's a real cabinetmaker."

The other man, bent over his work on the floor of the barn, snorted with disdain.

"Come on, Luigi, let's take her over and show her your boxes," Rudy said.

"What boxes?" Molly asked.

"You'll see. Let's go, old man. The light's fading anyway."

They drove to Luigi's house in Rudy's truck, Molly squashed between the two men in their overalls, which smelled of sweat and sawdust. Before they all climbed in the truck, the men had taken off their leather tool belts and dropped them in the back. Otherwise there would have been no room for her between them.

"Tell her about the boat, Luigi," Rudy said. He wanted Molly to like Luigi. He was showing him off as proudly as he had his children.

"What boat?"

"The one you built with your grandfather."

"We made a boat together when I was ten years old. Long time ago now," he said with a wink. "How old are you?"

"Thirty-one," she answered. "And a half."

"Well, I'm close to eighty. Bet you don't believe that."

"I don't."

"Stop flirting," Rudy said. "Get to the boat." With Molly's body pressed along his side, he felt giddy and reckless. He liked listening to the two of them teasing one another, to Luigi listing off all the different kinds of wood in that ten-foot rowboat.

"Nowadays, you can't get woods like that from the mills," Rudy told her. "It doesn't pay the guys to cut them. It's a real pity."

"I guess it would be the same thing if they stopped making my favorite oil colors," Molly said.

"Yup," Luigi said, bracing himself against the dashboard with a thick gnarled hand as Rudy took the last corner. "Pull in next to the back door," he said to Rudy.

Rudy let them slide out first while he pretended to be putting the keys under the front seat. Rosa would be wondering where he was, but, as usual, she would say nothing when he came in late, just set his dinner down on the table and take the other chair. Wait for him to tell her the one thing he didn't dare say but that she had already guessed.

The basement room was lined with shelves, and the shelves were crammed with boxes of every size and description.

"I started making them for my kids when they were little, but they didn't care. They banged the things up and threw them around, so I wouldn't give them to the kids no more. Made them for myself."

He stood, shifting with embarrassment from one foot to the other, while Rudy took Molly around the room. Each of the boxes had its own special place on the shelf, and Rudy took down his favorites and showed them to her.

"This one is the absolute best," he said. "Open it up. See the burly maple inlay. The dividers are made out of rosewood."

"How long does something like this take you?" Molly asked.

The old man shrugged. "Depends. A week of nights. Sometimes a month. You ask the people in town. Ask Rudy's father. They think I'm crazy. Some people get mushy about animals. I'm crazy about trees. The birds sit in the branches and the leaves come out on them every spring. When you cut down a living thing that's as beautiful as a tree, you'd better make something beautiful out of it."

"What a wonderful speech that was," Molly said on their way back to the farm.

"Luigi is unique in a town like this," Rudy said, pleased with her reaction. "Everybody wants aluminum siding and plastic furniture and things done yesterday and who

461

cares if it falls apart tomorrow. Luigi is a true craftsman. Those boxes belong in a museum."

"You're lucky to have him," Molly said quietly.

"He's like a father to me."

"That's what I meant."

Finally, in the beginning of December, the weather changed. An inch of snow fell and was melted by a day of freezing rain.

"Now we're in for it," Agnes said that night over dinner. She looked tired, and when she started to get up to clear the plates, Molly put a hand on her arm. "It's my night, remember? Stay there and read the paper."

Molly stood at the sink, her hands warming in the soapy water. Somebody turned in the driveway, and in the brief illumination of headlights, she could see that the tree branches were encased in ice.

"Who was that?" Agnes called.

"I think it was Rudy's truck," Molly shouted back. "Maybe he dropped by to see his parents."

"Odd time," said Agnes as Molly wandered into the dining room with a dish towel and pot in hand.

"It must be treacherous driving out there," Molly said. "Everything's covered in ice."

Once the dishes were done, Molly settled across the table from Agnes and sketched her working the crossword puzzle.

"I had a scary dream last night," Molly said.

"What's a seven-letter animal beginning with *a*?"

"Try aardvark."

"That's eight letters."

"Don't you want to hear my dream?"

"Yes," Agnes said, but her voice was still distracted. "Tell me your dream."

"I was painting—"

"Naturally."

"Don't interrupt, Agnes, it's rude. I was painting the ocean. Not the top like a landscape but underneath. It was like a great underwater carpet of light and motion. Up above me, I could see the shadow of a boat. You know how in dreams you can see things from the top and bottom at the same time?"

Agnes nodded.

"Well, the boat was empty and the oars were cocked. I kept wondering whether I was supposed to be in the boat. But the worst thing was that somebody was watching me the whole time. Whenever I turned around to see who it was, he was gone. So I would hurry to finish the painting, but the canvas was enormous and my arm didn't seem to be long enough." She shuddered. "It was horrible."

"Sounds it," Agnes said. She pushed the newspaper away and took off her glasses to rub her eyes. "Who do you think was watching you?"

"I keep thinking it was Daddy," Molly said. "I don't know why. I just had a feeling about the person the way you do when somebody's watching and not saying anything."

"Sounds like your father. He used to sneak up on me in the kitchen. Gave me the heebie-jeebies."

"What would he do?" Molly asked.

"He would come in the back door when I wasn't looking," Agnes said, "and then hide in the pantry. When I went in there to get something, he'd poke his nose out from behind the door and yell boo or something. Made my heart jump out of my skin."

"Daddy loved games. Remember Murder in the Dark in the attic? And Sardines. Mother never liked to play."

"I don't think I'd want to play a game either after a full day's work."

"Daddy worked too."

"Not as hard as your mother did," Agnes said sharply. "And not as steadily."

Molly rested her head against the wooden back of the chair. Nobody ever understood her father the way she did. She knew he drank too much. He was probably even an alcoholic, but there were worse things in life. Daddy never hurt anybody but himself with his drinking. He was drunk when his car went off the edge of that road in California six years ago. Right down a cliff the way you see in the television movies. She still remembered exactly what she was doing when David called to tell her. Making popcorn for her current lover, a weak puppy dog of a boy named Chris, and a friend of his. Chris spent that night holding her and whispering to her that it was all right to cry when she didn't feel like crying. The next day, he moved his things in when she was too stunned to stop him. It took her a year to get him out again.

"Why do you think Mother married him?" Molly asked.

"He was good-looking," Agnes said. "And different from the other boys."

"Do you think she ever loved him?"

"She married him, didn't she?" Agnes said. "But you should be asking your mother these questions."

Agnes got slowly to her feet and made her way to her usual chair in the corner.

"I'm going to mke myself some tea," Molly said. "You want some?"

Agnes shook her head without speaking. When Molly came back into the room, she had dozed off. Molly sat at the table, keeping her company until the clock in the back struck ten. Then she nudged the older woman awake.

"What is it?"

"I think we ought to go up to bed. You're going to get stiff sleeping in that chair."

"Have you locked up?"

"Yes, and I've done the lights in the other part of the house. I'll turn these out once you've started up the stairs."

"Help me up," she said, putting out her arms. Molly tucked her hands under the bumps of Agnes's elbow bones and hoisted her gently to her feet.

"Stiff," Agnes muttered.

"I shouldn't have left you sleeping so long. I'll follow you up."

"You may have to push from behind," Agnes said.

In unison, they took one steep step at a time, Molly's face close to Agnes's thin rustling bottom.

"The winter's come. I can smell it," Agnes said at the top.

"I don't smell anything different," Molly said.

"You have the eyes and I have the nose," Agnes said.

"You okay?"

"Of course I am. Go along. Good night."

Impulsively, Molly touched Agnes's hair. "Time for the House of Beauty."

"That's right. Tomorrow if the roads are clear of ice. No sense breaking our necks over a head of gray hair."

"Good night, Agnes."

"Night."

Agnes undressed slowly. She was thinking about Molly's questions tonight and those journals of Mrs. Webster's she had tucked away in her closet last year. She pulled the box out and looked at the top. MOLLY WEBSTER TAYLOR it read in her own block printing.

"I guess I ought to give these miserable books to Molly right now," she said out loud. "Or throw them away."

She thought she could hear the familiar rapping of feet in the back hallway, the echo of her name. "Agnes, where in heaven's name are you hiding? I've got to dress for dinner and I have no idea where my black velvet skirt has gotten to. Did you put it up in the attic?"

"I'm in the closet with these awful books of yours, Mrs. W. What am I supposed to do with them?"

"Just leave them there for now."

That is what she would say, of course. Just like the elm tree. Leave it there. Let somebody else take care of it later.

"I still remember the day you brought Molly home to us to stay," Agnes said quietly. "When I saw you leading her out of the car, I knew that something had gone wrong. She looked like a frightened little bird."

"How could you ever forget something like that?" said the voice. "To think she'd been in that house alone with him all those years."

"Well, then, why didn't you give her these books?" Agnes said. "After all, you both went through the same awful business. You with that Uncle James. Oh, hush. I don't want to hear any of your foolish excuses. This family keeps too many secrets."

Before she climbed into bed, Agnes sat down at the narrow desk in the corner and wrote Molly a note that she taped to the top of the box.

32

Molly had gone back to the painting porch. She started off in bed, but lying there, she thought about the angle of light glancing off Agnes's glasses while she dozed and she crept down the back hall to the canvas to see if she could use that.

Now that the cold weather had really settled in, she had hooked up an electric heater to back up the Franklin stove. Last week, in the shopping center, she had found a pair of bright orange fingerless gloves. "They're perfect, because they'll keep my hands warm but leave my fingers free to work the brushes," she told Agnes in great excitement. When she worked after dark, the black panes of glass reflected her image, and tonight she reminded herself of a goofy scarecrow with Day-Glo hands.

For the first time in months, she lost herself in the work, and when at last she shoved the brushes back into the jar of turpentine, it was past midnight. The painting was taking shape, she told herself when she turned around one last time at the door to look at it. She had worked out the problems of the light on the contours of Agnes's face and had become absorbed for what seemed like hours in the folds of the checkered dishrag.

She walked down the hall pleased with herself, ready for bed. At the door to her bedroom, she noticed the glow of a light up the back stairs. The same light she had turned out when they came up a few hours before.

"Agnes," she called. There was no answer, but some other noise floated up to her. A clunk. Somebody moving in the house. Agnes often went to the bathroom in the middle of the night, but this came from the first floor.

The old house made lots of noise, and she woke often to listen to it the way a mother checks her newborn baby.

She would lie tensed in the darkness until she could identify each twitch of the beams, each shrug of wind. "That's the loose shutter on the dining-room window," she would tell herself. Or "Calm down, it's the screen door on the back porch again."

But this noise came from a person.

"Agnes," she called again. The door to her bedroom was ajar, and the bed was empty. Molly slipped down the stairs. In the kitchen, the glare of the fluorescent light blinded her for a minute, and when the room came into focus, the first thing she saw was Agnes's bare feet under the table. She was sitting upright against the stove, her hair wet, her small veined hands twisted into the flowered nightgown.

Molly knelt beside her and looked into the blue eyes she had been painting just minutes before. They were wide open and staring.

"Agnes, what is it? What's wrong?"

The head moved almost imperceptibly back and forth. A drop of water made its slow way across the wrinkles in her forehead. Molly stopped it very carefully with her finger. "The pain," Agnes groaned. The lips barely moved, but the words came twisting out of some deep hole of fear inside her. "In my head."

"I'll be right back," Molly whispered, and ran for the blanket which always lay folded on the armchair in the little dining room. She covered up the stiff flowered body, tucking the wool, which seemed suddenly too rough, around under her back. There was a sour smell in the air which Molly recognized as vomit. Agnes began to tremble. Molly longed to pick her up and carry her to the couch, but she was terrified that whatever was happening inside the shrunken body would burst or break and overwhelm her. "I'm going to call the doctor," she said, hating to leave her there on the cold linoleum floor. "I'll be right back. I don't want to move you."

In the pantry next to the wall telephone, she found the list of emergency numbers scrawled in Grandmother's handwriting on a yellowed, curling index card. A stubby pencil swung from a string nearby.

"Dr. Barlow's line. Can I help you?"

Molly explained the situation.

"Well, I will try to reach him, but I suggest you call the ambulance service as well." The calm nasal voice read her the number, which Molly repeated twice because the pencil hadn't been sharpened in years.

The ambulance operator took down the information.

"You've got to hurry. I think she's having a heart attack or a stroke. Something very serious," Molly said, trying to keep the hysteria out of her voice.

"Have you covered her up?"

"Yes, but she's sitting on the kitchen floor. Would it be safe to move her?"

"No, don't do that," the voice said. "We'll be there as fast as we can, but the roads are very icy. There's been a big accident out on Route 44."

"Agnes, I'm right here," Molly said in a loud voice. "I'm just calling Mother."

No answer there. No answer at the Delbiancos' down the road, even though Molly let it ring for what seemed like hours. They must turn the phone off at night. Rudy. He was close by.

Rosa answered the phone on the third ring. Her voice sounded thick as if she'd been crying. Or sleeping.

"Rosa, it's Molly Taylor. Something terrible has happened to Agnes." She kept her voice low so Agnes would not hear. "She's on the kitchen floor. I've called the ambulance and the doctor, but apparently the roads are very slippery. Could Rudy come down here and help me? Frank and Angelina aren't answering their phone and I don't want to leave her to go get them." She took a deep breath. "I think it's very bad. I'm scared."

"Rudy's not here," Rosa said, her voice clearer now. "What's wrong with her?"

"I'm not sure. She's complaining about a terrible pain in her head. I found her on the kitchen floor. The ambulance operator told me I shouldn't move her."

"I can't leave the children alone," Rosa said.

"Where's Rudy gone?" For God's sake, it's the middle of the night. Where is he?

The silence at the other end of the phone seemed to last forever. "Never mind," Molly said. They had both begun to talk at once. "I'll wait for the ambulance."

"Try Rudy's parents again. Or why don't you walk down there?"

"I can't leave Agnes alone for that long," Molly said, her words tumbling out in her frustration. "I must go to her now. Goodbye."

Agnes's feet were peeking out the end of the blanket, the toes curled. Molly took an old wool coat off the hook by the back door and tucked it around them. She could not imagine that the pain had centered itself only in Agnes's head, and so each time she touched her body, she was scared of sending a shock wave of more pain traveling along the road of her bones.

Agnes's eyes stared back at Molly with an expression of alarm and fear. Her lower lip was caught between her teeth.

Molly settled down on the floor as close as she dared, thinking that her warmth might leap the inch between them and enter the stiff, trembling form. She reached under the blanket and took Agnes's hand without moving her arm away from her body.

"I've called Dr. Barlow. He's on his way and so is the ambulance. I was just up in the painting porch and it felt warmer tonight," she lied. "The roads will be clear." Please God, let somebody come. I can't sit here talking about the weather forever. Please let her be all right.

Molly talked on, her voice even and soft in Agnes's ear. She talked about the picture on her easel.

"I think I finished it tonight. You're going to like it, Agnes, I know you are." The sound of her steady voice reeled out like a rope ahead of them, leading them through each minute of their vigil. Agnes groaned sometimes, a very low noise that seemed to push itself past her clenched lips, past what must have been her desperate need to hold on to her dignity.

When the knock at the back door came at last, Molly didn't know whether they had been sitting there for an hour or five minutes. "Someone's here," she said. She laid Agnes's hand gently down on her thigh and went to unlock the door. It was Dr. Barlow, dressed in an overcoat and pajamas. In the distance, she heard the sound of sirens coming closer.

"Thank God you're here," Molly whispered as she led him back toward the trembling body on the kitchen floor.

When she went back to the door to let in the medics, she was surprised to see Rudy standing with them.

"She's in there," Molly said, pointing out the way to the medics. "I called Rosa, but she said you weren't there," she said to Rudy.

"I heard the siren," he said. "I was down at the calf barn. What's wrong with Agnes?"

Molly leaned back against the yellow kitchen wall, her arms folded across her chest. I will not cry, a voice said in her head.

"Are you all right?" he asked, resting his hand on her shoulder, cupping the palm around the curve of her bone.

She studied his face for a moment, wondering who he was, why he was there. Her mind had catapulted forward to a time beyond the hospital when she would bring Agnes home and take care of her. Give her back some of the years of trays and cooking and doing for other people.

"Molly?"

"Yes, I'm all right. I don't know what it is, but she's in terrible pain and there was nothing I could do but talk to her."

"I'll go with her to the hospital," he said.

"No, I want to do that," Molly said.

"All right, then, I'll follow you in my car. It might be a long wait. You'll need her social security numbers, Medicaid, things like that. Where would that information be?"

"Up in her room, I guess. In her tan purse on the bureau or hanging on the back of the closet door. Will you get it? I don't want to leave her for too long."

The doctor joined them. "I'm pretty sure it's an aneurysm," he said in a low voice. "You were right not to move her. If it ruptures, we're in trouble. Do you know why her hair is wet?"

Molly shook her head. "I think she threw up. Maybe she was trying to wash the smell out."

"Where's the phone? I want to call the hospital."

Molly led him into the pantry and went back to sit with Agnes. She could hear Rudy pounding down the back stairs.

"The ambulance is here," she said. "I'll go to the hospital with you."

"It hurts so much," Agnes whispered, every word separate and defined.

"I wish I could take it away," Molly said, and her voice broke for the first time that night.

When the medics returned, they motioned Molly aside and opened their bags, exchanging instructions and information in quiet voices. The equipment looked ominous. Bottles and needles and tubes.

"They're starting an IV in case she goes into a coma on the ride in," Dr. Barlow explained.

"Why can't they do something about the pain?" Rudy asked. He handed Molly the tan purse.

"We can't do anything until we're sure of the situation. If it is an aneurysm, the blood is seeping out of the vessel and there's no place in the head for it to go. It's the pressure that's giving her the pain. With the roads in this condition they've got chains on their tires. The ride in is going to be very hard for her."

Ever so gently, the men lifted Agnes's body to slip the stretcher under her and she screamed for the first time that night.

"Oh, God, do something for her," Molly cried.

Rudy took her hand, and they followed the stretcher so that Agnes could see them from her propped-up position. She cried out again as they lifted her and slid her between the open doors of the ambulance like one of her cookie tins going into the oven.

"Hop in front, miss," the medic said. "The doctor and I will be riding in the back with her."

"Tell her where I am, please. I promised her I would stay with her."

She died that night on the operating table. Molly heard those words over and over in her head in the hours leading up to the funeral. *Yesterday she was here and she squeezed orange juice and complained about the paint stains on my jeans, and today she is gone. Today and tomorrow and forever after.*

When her mother arrived in the waiting room later that night, it was already over. She took Molly's hand

and led her to the car, with Rudy behind, carrying Agnes's purse. They talked across the top of her head in whispers.

She took the white pill her mother gave her and slept for the rest of the night and into the morning, the kind of sleep that shuts out all thoughts. When she woke to the gray sheet of a cloudy noon sky, her jaw ached as if she had clenched her teeth together to keep the demon nightmares from walking in and out through her mouth.

Her mother had been to the farm already. She had packed Molly a suitcase, which included a dark wool skirt for the funeral, and enough clothes to last her a week. She'd even remembered her sketchbook. When Molly walked downstairs, Charlotte was on the telephone.

"No, I don't need to come and pick it out. We want something very simple." Pause. "Fine. And listen, Mr. Ordway, the coffin will be carried out of the church by my brothers and the Delbiancos. No wheels, do you understand?" Molly went into the kitchen and poured herself some coffee.

She had just settled herself down at the table and taken her first searing sip (now her tongue would be tender for days) when her mother bustled in.

"Everybody will be arriving today. I've asked Frank to meet your Uncle George's train from New York. Alice can't come with him because she is down in Florida staying with her mother and it would be ridiculous for her to fly all the way back up just for this. Campbell will be driving down from Williams, of course."

"Mother, you sound as if you're arranging a dinner party," Molly said. "This is Agnes's funeral."

Her mother's face flinched as if she'd been slapped. "I know that," she said, lowering her voice. "I've just had so much to do that I—" She stopped.

"I'm sorry," Molly said. "I shouldn't have said that. You're always efficient at times like these. I know somebody has to do it."

"David's coming tomorrow from Washington. It's the soonest he could get away. The funeral has been held until twelve o'clock so that he can make it. I thought you might meet him and drive him directly to the church."

Molly nodded. "What about Agnes's family?"

Charlotte lowered herself into a chair and propped her head in her hands. It felt good to be sitting like this alone with her daughter. Maybe now they could be friends, now that all the people who came between them were gone. "I've talked to Agnes's sister. For some reason, her name has flown right out of my mind."

"Edith," Molly said.

"That's it, of course. Edith. She will be arriving this afternoon. She says she's the only one left except for her two children, who won't be able to come."

"That's good," Molly said. "Agnes couldn't stand them. She said Edith spoiled them terribly."

"Well, Agnes was a hard one to please. It was one of her charms." They were both silent for a moment.

"I still can't believe it," Molly said in a small stunned voice.

Her hand lay on the table between them. It was only a matter of inches between that hand and her own, but Charlotte couldn't bring herself to reach for it. How terrifying it was to touch someone else, even at a time like this. "It must have been frightening to sit with her for that hour," Charlotte said in a gentle voice. "Was there any sign of it coming? Did she complain of pain earlier in the day?"

In her mind, Molly traveled slowly back through her last hours with Agnes. "Nothing, except that she seemed tired. She dozed off in her chair last night. But she used to do that quite often."

"Darling, I know it's hard for you to believe this right now, but it's really a blessing. We both know how much she hated the thought of moving."

Molly didn't trust herself to speak for a moment. For some irrational reason, she still hated it when her mother called her darling. It always sounded like a reproof. "I suppose you'll be deciding about the furniture this weekend since everybody's gathering here."

"It does make sense," Charlotte said as she stood up.

"So like Agnes to die at a convenient time," Molly whispered. She began to cry but went right on talking through the obstruction that seemed to have lodged itself in her throat. "Allows us to kill two birds with one stone,

Elizabeth Winthrop

so to speak. Or bury them. Sorry. I've begun to muddle up my metaphors, haven't I?"

"Molly, stop, please. You can be so cruel."

"I can," Molly said. "It must run in the family. Right through the women."

Charlotte began to sponge off the counters in a methodical way.

"People are always being taken away from me," Molly whispered.

"It happens to everybody, Molly. You were taken away from me, weren't you?"

"What do you mean, Mother?"

"This is the first time you've spent a night in this house in years. This was your home, you know." She was shrieking and she didn't mean to be. Sing to yourself, Charlotte. Turn away from that look on Molly's face and sing yourself a song. The strife is o'er, the battle done . . . I shall ask to have that sung at Agnes's service, she thought. But it's a Lutheran church. Perhaps they don't know that hymn.

"Mother?"

"What?"

"Thanks for bringing over my things."

"You're welcome. I like that painting you've done of Agnes. It's softer than the other ones."

"I finished it last night. Maybe that's why Agnes died. Like voodoo. Maybe I'm responsible."

"Darling, do stop saying things like that. You make things worse for yourself when you do."

"Let's make a deal, Mother. I'll try to say all the right things if you stop calling me darling. For some reason, I cannot stand it."

Charlotte lit a cigarette. "All right, it's a deal. Now that I remember, I couldn't stand it when my mother called me darling either. There was something terribly patronizing about it." They rested for a moment at this truce. Charlotte was the first to stir. "I'm afraid I've got to go into the office for a couple of hours. Will you be all right here by yourself?"

Molly stood up and stretched. "Yes, I'll be fine."

"Now that the other house is empty, you're welcome

474

to stay as long as you want," Charlotte said. She was pawing through her purse looking for the car keys.

"Thanks. I'll think about it."

"I'll pick Edith up at the bus on my way home."

As soon as her mother's car pulled out of the driveway, Molly felt trapped. The farm was her safe house, the place where she had dreamed about her father and had drawn pictures for him, and like the pioneer's wife waiting for word, she had made elaborate, secret plans to follow him West. The word never came, but over there, in rooms her father rarely visited, Agnes and Rudy had allowed her to hang on to her dreams of Daddy. Even Grandmother had kept silent when she talked about how much fun her father was, how one day he would be coming back to get her. But in this house where she saw him everywhere—lying on the sofa in the living room, throwing a softball at her in the backyard, rocking in the wicker chair on the porch—her carefully knitted dreams were always threatening to unravel.

She stood on the kitchen threshold, watching her mother's car disappear around the corner, and felt like the eleven-year-old who stood in the exact same spot every afternoon and listened to the heartbeat of the house.

"Daddy's mean," David used to say.

"He is not."

They never went on with the argument. It was better not to talk about it, for fear that one would prove right and the other wrong. But they became silent partners.

When David got home first, he waited for her in the kitchen.

"It's all right, Daddy's not home yet," he would say, or "He's out in the backyard," or "Steer clear, he's in a bad mood today."

But then David went away to boarding school and she had to do the listening all by herself.

When had she stopped running in the back door and calling out his name? "Daddy, I'm home. Daddy, where are you?"

"In the basement, Button," his voice would call back to her through the floorboards. "Come on down."

She was eight the year he set up the workshop. She loved to do her addition problems on the big wooden worktable down there, doodling with her fingers in the piles of sawdust. He sang while he worked. She brought down her cookies and milk, and he always had a glass of something that he sipped from. She felt closed in and safe with him in the cozy dark room. When David came in from baseball practice, they heard his footsteps in the room above them, but he never came down, which was all right with Molly because no matter what David did it seemed to make Daddy mad. Besides, it meant that Molly could have her father all to herself for a little while longer. In those days, he was more fun than anyone else.

When he was gone on one of his business trips, there was only Jessie to bug them about washing their hands before dinner, and sometimes Mother, who started in with them about their day at school. "And then what happened in history class, Molly? What are you studying this week?" Daddy never asked questions like that. "What did snooty old Valerie do today?" he would ask. He remembered the important things, that Valerie was the one who threw up in the middle of the spelling bee and Alice Morgan was the first in the class to get braces and that Molly won the most original prize in the art contest in fifth grade. He couldn't have cared less about history.

But things began to change. Once, after a long trip, Molly came home to find David waiting for her at the top of the stairs.

"Did Daddy get home?" she cried.

He put his finger to his lips. "He's locked himself in the bedroom," David whispered. "Leave him alone."

"Where's Jessie?"

"Down in the kitchen on the phone."

"Daddy," Molly called through the keyhole. "Are you okay? It's me. Molly."

She heard his footsteps moving heavily across the floor toward her. David ran and hid around the corner.

The door opened, and there was his face looking down at her with a funny crooked smile on it. Something was wrong. He was crying. Her big strong Daddy crying the way she did when David made fun of her on the school bus. That scared her more than anything else that had

476

come before. More than the shouting she heard through the walls at night, more than the time he stopped the car and rubbed the snow on his face, more than the tired, distracted look on her mother's face.

"Oh, Daddy," she whispered, "what's wrong? Please don't be sad."

He knelt down and gathered her into his arms. "You're not mad at me, are you, Button? You love your daddy no matter what, don't you?"

"Of course I do," she whispered into the familiar smell of his shirt. She wished he wouldn't hold her so tightly against him, but she did not move a muscle because she had to show him that, whatever he did, it was all right with her.

"Then I'm fine, Button." He held her away so that he could wipe the tears from his cheeks. "See now. It's all over. My Molly did the trick."

And from then on, she knew it was her job to make Daddy happy. Mother stayed at work and David ran away. But Molly could do the trick.

One time when she brought home Ellen Watkins, who was her absolutely best friend at the end of fifth grade, Daddy was lying on the sofa in the living room with the newspaper over his face.

"What's wrong with your father?" Ellen asked. "Is he sick?"

Molly backed out of the room, with Ellen still trying to see over her shoulder. "Nothing's wrong with him," Molly said.

"Well, why's he lying on the couch? Why isn't he at work?"

"He's got such an important job that he can come home whenever he wants," Molly announced.

"I don't believe you," Ellen said. "I think there's something wrong with him."

"There's nothing wrong with my father," Molly screamed back, and she kicked her best friend so hard in the shin that Ellen started to cry and Jessie had to call her mother to come pick her up.

The next day Ellen started whispering with Valerie behind Molly's back. Molly pretended not to see, but after that she didn't bring friends home from school anymore. That way she could keep her daddy all to herself. She didn't have to see in other people's eyes what they thought of the way he dressed or talked or the way he cheered so loudly at her softball games.

In sixth grade, when she was center fielder, he wanted to come to all her games. After all, he was the one who had taught her to throw like a boy, using the wrist so that her arm snaked away from the shoulder as if it had ten joints instead of three. And he loved to watch her doing it.

"It's all right, Daddy," she told him at dinner one night. "You don't have to come tomorrow."

"Are you kidding? I wouldn't miss it for anything."

"How does your father feel about you skipping out of work so much?" her mother said.

"Hasn't said a damn thing to me about it," her father said. "Besides, nothing's more important than Molly's career as an outfielder," he added, raising his glass in Molly's direction. "Except for her career as an artist. Did you know, Mrs. Taylor, that we have a very talented child sitting here with us?"

"Stop it, Daddy," she murmured. When they were alone, she was glad that he was proud of her, but it always made her squirm when he talked this way in front of other people, particularly her mother. Now that David had left for boarding school, it was just the three of them gathered around the dinner table in the evenings, and Molly usually flipped through several subjects of conversation in her mind before she settled on the safest ones. But the big game was coming up tomorrow. She couldn't put this off any longer.

"Daddy, none of the other fathers come," she said quietly.

"Well, they should," he roared. "What kind of lousy, no-good parents are they anyway?"

Molly felt her mother watching her from across the table. When her father got up to pour himself another drink at the sideboard, she allowed her eyes to travel slowly upward to meet her mother's. They gazed at one another for a long moment without expression. Her father's hand landed heavily on her shoulder, and she flinched as if caught in an act of treachery.

"I'm sorry, Daddy," she said quickly. "I didn't mean it. Of course you can come."

"You bet I'll be there, Button."

But he was late. She stood in the field scanning the line of parked cars for the blue station wagon. In the middle of the fourth inning, she heard his car before she saw it, a screech of tires that made everybody on the field turn and stare at the idiot who had taken the corner much too fast. The car stopped with a jolt that lifted the driver up and dropped him back down onto the seat. Molly turned back to the game and stared fixedly at the batter, willing her father not to move or speak or shout her name. She never looked his way again, not when he cheered her on from his hunched position on the hood of the car, not when she speared the line drive that ended the game, not even when she was bundled triumphantly off the field and into another car.

When she got home much later after the celebration party, he was sitting in the wicker rocking chair on the porch. She came up from behind, careful in her approach.

"We won, Daddy."

"I saw." His voice slowed her even more. The dark brown liquid in the glass between his legs swayed sloppily from one rim to the other with each tip of the chair. "You couldn't even come over and say hello to your old father, who killed himself to get to that game."

"Where were you?" she asked. "I was looking for you."

"You fucking well were not."

"Daddy!"

His face changed with hers, and she saw mirrored there a moment of sadness, of wishing he could suck the word back into his mouth.

"Come here," he said quietly.

No, Daddy, I don't want to. Please let me go upstairs.

"Come here, Button," his voice even softer.

He reached out his hand for hers, and she gave it to him because after all, he mustn't see that he was making her sad. Wasn't it her job to keep him happy?

"Don't ever lie to me again, Molly," he whispered. "I can't stand people to lie to me."

She nodded numbly while he pulled her polo shirt down over her shorts to straighten it out. The stretched material exposed the barest beginnings of her breasts, the soft bumps that she covered with her folded arms whenever she remembered them. She felt naked standing there in front of him. At last, he let her go and sat back again.

"So tell me about the beginning of the game," he said, picking up the glass with one hand and brushing the puddle of liquid off the rush seat with the other. She wanted to run upstairs, but even that seemed to amount to another betrayal, so she dredged up details of home runs and double plays to entertain him, to make him think she was giving him her full attention, until at last he seemed satisfied. The she walked quickly and quietly upstairs and shut herself in her room.

That bedroom. Molly wandered upstairs and pushed open the door. It never changed, but then the whole house had a vaguely neglected air about it. Venetian blinds sagged and slowly leaking pipes turned the wallpaper brown and there were always holes in the caned chairs in the dining room. For Charlotte, a house was merely a roof over her head, a place to rest between the end of one day at the office and the beginning of the next.

"I can't be bothered with it," Charlotte said defensively. "I just don't look too closely."

The schoolteacher's desk that her Taylor grandmother gave her for her twelfth birthday was still covered with the green spotted blotter, the books on the shelves were left over from seventh- and eighth-grade English classes; *The Mill on the Floss, The Poetry of Elizabeth Barrett Browning, Ethan Frome, The Odyssey.* On the bottom shelf, a pile of her earliest sketchbooks leaned against a wooden box filled with her old china horse collection. The curtains were the same, the dressing-table skirt was still untacked in two places, so that it hung down unevenly from its frame and gathered dust balls in its folds.

"I don't want to sleep in my room anymore," Molly had told her mother that August in 1955. She had moved back from the farm just two weeks before she left for boarding school. "I'll use it as a study."

"You know you're safe here now, darling," her mother

said in a small voice. "Nothing is going to happen to you again."

"I'm not scared, Mother," Molly said firmly. "Of anything."

But she was. She was scared of the closet. She asked her mother to move all her clothes into the guest room and then never went near the door again. The fear was an irrational, childish one. It reminded her of David, who used to jump into his bed from two feet away so the monster hiding underneath wouldn't be able to grab his foot.

She walked over to the closet now and yanked the door open. There it was. Just a dark empty space with the hangers dangling from the pole and the dusty shelves for shoes. Nobody pounding on the bedroom door. No teenage girl curled against the back wall singing to herself while she waited for someone to discover her hiding place.

Grandmother had been the one who found her all those years ago, Grandmother who had wandered through the house yelling her name. Molly had not bothered to answer because she knew Grandmother was thorough, she would find her in the end. And she did.

"Molly, what is wrong?"

"Nothing. I'm just hiding. This is my secret place. Is Daddy here?"

"No, he's gone out, Molly." She knelt down then and touched Molly's shoulder. "Did Daddy hurt you?"

"He wanted to play with me, but I didn't want to play anymore." Where were the tears coming from? She didn't mean to cry. After all, there was nothing to cry about. "I'm too old for that, Grandmother."

"Of course you are, Molly. Come with me. I'm going to take you home to the farm. Agnes made brownies this afternoon."

"Will Daddy be angry?"

"Don't you worry about your father anymore," her grandmother had said as she led her out of the room. "I used to push the bureau in front of my door," she whispered. Suddenly, she took Molly into her arms and hugged her. Grandmother's never held me like this before, Molly thought to herself as she leaned against her bony chest. She feels so fierce.

"Let's go quickly," Molly whispered. "Before Daddy comes back. He doesn't like to stay here alone when Mother's away. He likes me to stay with him. But it's my night at the farm. It's Tuesday night, isn't it, Grandmother?"

"Molly, please come down," her mother called. "Edith's here."

"Yes," Molly whispered. She closed the closet door and leaned her weight against it. "I'm coming."

33

Molly had met Edith once or twice before when her husband, Joe, drove her by the farm to see Agnes. She was a smaller, more bewildered version of her twin sister.

"Why do things like this keep happening to me?" Edith asked when Molly settled her on the sofa in the living room. "We buy the apartment and then Joe dies. Now Agnes." She shook her head and her curls jiggled. "I was making room for her. We were going to be back together after all these years."

"I'm so sorry, Edith," was all Molly could bring herself to say. I'm glad you didn't know how much Agnes was dreading it.

It was remarkable that the small daily habits of sisters who saw each other so rarely could still develop in the same direction as they grew older. They wore the same clear-rimmed eyeglasses, and it looked as if their hairdressers used the same-size rollers to turn up their silvery gray hair every week. Anybody who didn't know Agnes as well as Molly did would marvel at the sisters' likenesses, at the blue eyes and the dangling lower lip, the long, wrinkled earlobes. But Molly could see that Edith was a pale version of her beloved Agnes, who was so much stronger, so much less frightened. Edith had leaned on her husband all her life and had been getting ready to lean on Agnes. And Agnes had known it.

Molly stayed close to her during the evening while the rest of the family drifted in. Uncle Campbell drove down from Williamstown, Massachusetts, where he was chairman of the English Department at the college. A thin, blond man with a slightly ridiculous mustache, he was Molly's favorite uncle. There was something carefree and childlike about him that brought out her playful side.

Always the extravagantly emotional one in the family, he lifted her right off the couch and kissed her on both cheeks.

"I'm glad to see you, Mo," he said. "And you must be Agnes's sister. I am so terribly sorry," he whispered as he leaned over her. "You know, Agnes took care of me right from the beginning. I hadn't seen enough of her in the last years, but I have a picture of her on my bureau. I look at her face every morning and I can hear her telling me to stand up straight and comb my hair. We all loved her very much, didn't we, Mo?"

Edith seemed overwhelmed as much by his old-fashioned dignified manners as by his message.

"Mother's making tea in the kitchen, Uncle Campbell," Molly said.

"What about George and Oliver?"

"They'll all be here in time for dinner," she said.

They made awkward, halting conversation around the table. The subject of the sale of the farmhouse came up and was quickly dropped as if Edith would be offended by it.

"Thank you for sending along those paintings of Mother's," Uncle George said to Molly. "They're really very sweet, aren't they? Alice and I have decided to give one to each of the children and put the rest in the house on Long Island."

"She was quite a prolific painter," Molly said. "I was surprised at how many things were tucked away in that little porch."

"And how is your work going?" Uncle Oliver asked. "I never know whether that's a fair question to ask. It's like asking a novelist what their book's about or a sculptor if they've started chipping away yet."

"Oliver, don't ask somebody a question and then go right on talking," Campbell said.

There was an uneasy pause around the table.

"It's going very slowly," Molly said.

"Do you have a show coming up?" George asked.

"Andrea is hoping to schedule something next June if I get enough work together. But the last show was such a flop that we're both feeling a little shaky about another."

"If you'll excuse me," Edith said in her birdlike voice. "I think I'll just go on up to bed. The bus trip tired me out."

"Of course," Charlotte said, getting up so quickly that she knocked the knife off her plate.

"I'll take Edith upstairs, Mother," Molly said. "She'll be in my old room, right?"

"That's right."

"I hope I'm not putting you out," Edith said at the top of the steps.

"Oh no," Molly said. "I'll be right across the hall if you need anything. Sleep well."

David Taylor's plane landed twenty minutes early. He settled himself on a bench by the taxi stand, grateful for the extra time to collect his thoughts. He hadn't seen his sister for over a year, and he always looked forward to their meetings with a mixture of excitement and anxiety. They were very different people really, and yet, their odd childhood had made them comrades-in-arms, particularly in the last years he lived at home. They had worked out secret signals to warn each other of their father's movements about the house. Thumbs up if he were gone, down if he were home and on the first floor.

But no matter how badly their father behaved, Molly would not tolerate one word of criticism against him. Her beloved daddy.

A horn blared twice and he recognized his mother's car. Molly was waving impatiently at him through the windshield.

"Hello, Mo," he said. He was the only one besides Campbell who used her old nickname. They kissed briefly and awkwardly across the top of his duffel bag.

"Hello. We're going right to the church. I hope Mother warned you."

"Yes." He put his head back against the leather seat as she maneuvered the car into the stream of traffic. "I can't quite believe that Agnes is dead. In my mind, she's forever standing at the kitchen window waiting for me to drive in with another crowd of unruly friends from college."

Molly said nothing. He glanced over at her. "Mother

told me you'd come back to the farm to do some painting. How's it going?"

"Slowly. How's your work?"

"Same as ever. Enough for six legislative aides instead of me and one assistant. How's Eliot?"

"I talked to him a while ago. But it's basically over between us."

"You too?" David asked. "Jean moved into her own apartment two months ago. Back to bachelorhood."

"I'm sorry to hear that, David. We don't seem to be very good at making things stick."

"No, we don't. But we didn't have a very good model to follow, did we? Is Mother all right? She sounded even more compulsive than usual on the phone. She was talking so fast I had a hard time understanding her."

Molly didn't answer for a minute. She seemed to be concentrating on making the left-hand turn into the church parking lot. "We're early," she said, turning the engine off. "Might as well wait in the car. Now, what did you ask me?"

"Mother."

"A little strung out, I think. You know, she's the one who's really pushed through the sale of the house. George agrees with her, but Uncle Oliver and Campbell are furious."

"She told me on the phone that she wants to divide up all the furniture this weekend," David said.

"That's right. It makes sense, I suppose, since everybody's here, but she seems to be in a terrible rush about everything."

"Oh, Christ," David said in a weary voice. "I'm not sure I can deal with all this."

"Want me to drive you back to the airport?" Molly asked. "You always were good at running away."

"You're one to talk," David muttered. "You lived half your life at the farm. Look at you. You're still there."

"Oh, shut up," Molly said without much conviction.

The hearse pulled up to the back of the church, and the driver, wearing dark glasses, went inside to confer with the minister.

"Poor Agnes," David whispered.

Molly rested her hand on top of his.

"The last funeral I went to was Daddy's."

"Don't remind me," she said, taking her hand back.

She had refused to go, so David had flown out to California with his grandfather, who ordered one drink after another from the pale, nervous stewardess. "That damn son of mine never amounted to anything," Sam Taylor had said suddenly just before they landed in Los Angeles. David turned away and stared at the exit sign until the red letters blurred together.

They buried him out there in a small cemetery on a hill. A simple stone marker was ordered.

"We'd better go in," Molly said now. "I see Mother and the uncles."

David sat up. "I just thought of something, Molly. Nobody ever checked to see if Daddy's marker was delivered. I mean, we ordered it when we were out there, but nobody went back to see the grave. You remember Grandfather died the year after that and—"

"Please shut up, David. This whole day is gruesome enough without bringing up things like that. He's dead, isn't he? What else matters?"

She got out of the car and slammed the door with a kick of her foot.

Molly stood next to Edith in the front pew. The old woman clung to her arm when Rudy and Frank Delbianco and the four Webster men carried the coffin back down the aisle to the entrance of the church, where the hearse waited, its doors propped open like the minister's hands at the last blessing. She was buried in the little cemetery outside the church in a short graveside ceremony. Molly stayed behind as everyone wandered back to their cars, talking quietly to one another. She stared down into the freshly dug hole at the shiny rectangle resting in the dark earth, her arms clenched over the ache in her stomach. Her mind kept walking back through the kitchen door of the house, past Frank's front room where the shoes used to be polished, past the coat hooks, to the point where the wall turned a corner, and Agnes's familiar figure would not be standing by the tin-topped table.

"Agnes, what will I do now? Where will I go?" she whispered.

She felt somebody's arm around her and knew without looking up that it was Uncle Campbell. He tried to lead her back to the car, but she shrugged out of his embrace.

"Tell Mother I'll drive myself home in a little while."

"Are you sure?"

She nodded.

Car doors slammed, loud erratic pops in the cold afternoon. With an irreverent roar, the engines started up and moved away. The undertaker's assistant rolled up the plastic-grass cloth, folded the metal chairs and packed them away with the flowers into his truck. When he left, one of the gravediggers approached her, his hat in his hand.

"Are you ready, miss?"

She looked into his face. He had a job to do.

"Yes."

"Are you sure you want to watch?"

"Yes, I promised I would stay with her."

He shrugged and nodded at another man, who stepped forward. Together they attacked the mound of fresh dirt with their shovels, their bodies swaying in an easy regular rhythm. After a while, they forgot she was still standing there and began to talk.

"We were lucky with the warmer weather last night," the first one said. "Softened the ground."

The other man grunted. "Another one to fill in over there."

The last corner of coffin disappeared under its load of earth. Would the box crack and give way under the weight of the dirt before the moisture and worms softened the walls? Underneath it all lay Agnes's face, her tissue-paper skin, her thin aching bones, her feet uncurled now that the pain was over, her large surprised eyes, closed at last.

Molly was doing penance now, making up for the other time when she had been too chicken to go all the way out to California and stand over her father's coffin. All that weekend she had visualized David and her grandfather flying back across the country with a flag-draped casket like the men she saw on the evening news who went out to Vietnam to bring home their dead soldier. And then

David called to tell her it was done and their father had been buried in California.

For some reason, that had freaked her out more than any other part of his death. She had been consoling herself with the thought of visiting his grave, as if that would make up for the eleven years of not knowing where he was or what he looked like anymore.

"David," she had cried into the telephone, "all the Websters are buried in the Congregational churchyard in Northington. Why couldn't you bring him back?"

"Molly, Daddy was not a Webster," David had replied in a cold, weary voice just before he hung up.

She meant what she said earlier in the car. If Daddy couldn't be here near her, what did it matter if his California grave was unmarked? She didn't plan to go looking for it.

When the last spadeful of dirt was tamped down and the two men had moved on to their next job, she walked slowly back to the parking lot. Rudy was standing beside her car, waiting for her. He put out his arms and wrapped them so tightly around her that his body absorbed her trembling and their bones reverberated together. The loosened knot of his tie pressed against her right temple and he rested his chin on her head. She felt like a package, tied and taped. I can stay here all afternoon if I want, she thought.

A car turned into the parking lot. She stirred and he loosened his arms.

"Thanks, Rudy," she said. "I think you squeezed all the tears out of me."

When she looked up into his face, she saw that his eyes were red from crying too.

"It was too sudden," he said. "I didn't have time to say goodbye to her. I never thought when we went into the hospital that we wouldn't be bringing her home."

"I know," she said. "I keep thinking about walking in the back door of the farm."

"I've got to get back to work," he said.

"I've got to face the family. They're all staying for the weekend." Neither one of them moved. "Rudy, why weren't you home when I called that night?"

He shoved his hands deep in his pockets and jingled

some loose coins. "I've moved out for a while. I'm staying in the office down in the calf barn. There's an old mattress in there and I've rigged up a heater."

"Oh, Rudy, I'm so sorry."

He shrugged. "Something that's been brewing for a while. It's not Rosa's fault. It's mine. My father says she's too good for me."

"What about the children?" she asked, and his eyes filled suddenly with tears again.

"Rudy," she said, but he waved her away and jogged off to his truck.

He needed that hug as much as I did, she thought as she drove back to her mother's house.

Charlotte's headache grew steadily worse all weekend.

"So much for your night guard, Dr. Peters," she fumed as she set the thing into place over her teeth. "I look like Godzilla, I feel like a twelve-year-old in braces, and I still have the headaches."

"It doesn't look so bad, Mother," David said when he ran into her in the hallway the first night. They were sharing a bathroom. Edith had gone home on the afternoon bus, which meant David had moved into Molly's old room. "It just looks as if you don't have any lines between your teeth. As if they're made of plastic or something."

"Go to bed and stop trying to make me feel better," she said with a smile. "Tomorrow promises to be a long and grisly day."

They started off in two cars right after breakfast.

"A funeral procession of Websters," Campbell said from his place in the front seat next to Charlotte. She was driving. "Come to divide the spoils. I imagine the Delbiancos are gathered at the end of the driveway, peering up at us from the windows of the cottage."

"The fall of the house of Webster," David intoned from the back seat. "When is Uncle Oliver coming? Is that his car?"

"No, that's Molly's."

"I saw her packing her case this morning, Mother. I think she's moving back over here."

"Not surprising," Charlotte said in a voice that ended that line of conversation.

Molly was driving her Uncle George.

"Your mother seems awfully tired, Molly. It's too bad this business with the house has to fall squarely on her shoulders."

"I know. I'll help with the cleaning out, of course. But when it comes to the financial end of things, she always ends up doing it. Uncle Oliver just seems to hand things over to her."

"She's too efficient for her own good," he said. He leaned down to look through the front windshield at the farm as Molly swung the car into the driveway. "The old place needs a paint job, doesn't it?"

"Yes. I guess the Delbiancos will have to worry about that now," she said quietly. "Let's go in the side door. I can't face the kitchen without Agnes quite yet."

When everybody had gathered, they started upstairs in Lydia's bedroom.

"What's the system, Char?" Campbell asked. "I assume you've figured this all out."

"I had figured it all out, but I didn't have enough time to put my plan into effect. I wanted the whole business appraised and divided into three equal lots. Then you boys could just pick straws for a lot and trade back and forth if you didn't get something you wanted."

"Three, Char? Who's missing?"

"Me," she said. "I only want a very few things. The furniture from Margaret's old bedroom and Father's desk. The rest is yours."

Everybody began to talk at once. Molly and David stood off to the side. They felt uncomfortable as the only representatives of their generation.

"I feel like the dogs at a banquet table waiting for scraps," David said under his breath to his sister.

"I think Mother just gave away the banquet," Molly said. "Do you want anything?"

"Yes, come with me. I'll show you what it is."

He took her into their grandmother's bathroom. In the corner stood an old-fashioned contraption with a motor and a belt which Grandmother must have used long ago to shake the weight off her waist. David hooked himself up and turned it on. "Remember when we used to do this as children?" he called over the noise of the motor. "I figure this would make a great conversation piece in my apartment."

"Let me try it."

The motion soothed and tickled at the same time, and Molly leaned back into the leather belt, feeling the muscles in her lower back relax against its vibrations. "This is fabulous," she called. "Mother needs this more than you."

"Needs what?" Charlotte asked from the door.

"This," Molly said, flicking the switch. "It's very relaxing."

"Can you two come back and pay attention, please."

"Why, Mother?" David asked. "We don't have rights to anything."

Molly felt an irrational rush of nostalgia for him, for their old sibling partnership. "Yes, Mother," she said. "It sounds as if you've just given everything away."

"Well, my brothers are suggesting that you two might have a say in it. They're picking certain things for their own children."

"Why don't you want anything?" David asked. "There are some nice pieces of furniture in the house. Good rugs. The grandfather clock."

"I feel about this house the way Molly must feel about mine. It's full of ghosts that I have no wish to drag along with me." She lifted her chin and stared at the two of them with a cold smile. "I understand you're moving back here, Molly."

"Yes."

"It makes sense, I suppose. All your supplies are over here. Your paints, your brushes, even your good memories." She took a step backward, feeling with her shoe for the doorsill. "Can we go back now? It seems a little ridiculous to be holding discussions in your grandmother's bathroom."

Once their mother had turned around, David rolled his eyes at his sister. With a mother like this, Molly thought, you never stop being a child.

*   *   *

The division took all day. Whenever somebody showed the slightest interest in a piece of furniture, the others wanted it too, for no reason at all except perhaps to settle old debts, to keep the scores even. Charlotte stayed out of it, trailing along behind like a weary governess while her brothers haggled. When the final decisions were reached, she put colored stickers on the pieces of furniture and entered the correct names on her legal pad. She forced herself to print the names. Over the years, her handwriting had not improved.

At lunchtime, Molly and David made tuna sandwiches at the tin-topped table, and without any warning, Molly began to cry.

"Whatever you do, don't weep into the mayonnaise," he teased, rubbing her between the shoulders. "Are you sure you want to stay over here all alone? I think you're nuts. Too many ghosts."

"Got to face them square on," she said.

"Mother sure is strung out," David said. "Why does she do that business with her hands all the time?"

"Her joints are swelling with the arthritis, but I think it's become kind of a nervous habit."

"For God's sake, Oliver, you've never given a damn about Father's study before. Can't you let me have the hunting prints without another wrangle," George said as he led the others through the dining room.

"If you get the prints, then I want the guns," Oliver said, his voice ballooning suddenly against the bare walls of the kitchen.

"The guns?" Charlotte echoed in the stunned silence. Her heart began to pound in her ears, and she wondered if the rest of them could hear it. "Why do you want the guns?"

Oliver ran his hands nervously through his thin hair as the group's eyes turned on him. He leaned over and picked up a sandwich.

"I thought I might start collecting them," he said with a sharp laugh. "Seems appropriate, doesn't it? Unless that's the one thing in the house that you've decided to keep, Charlotte," he said.

David's hand closed slowly over Molly's wrist. Everybody else seemed frozen in place like children in a game of statues.

"What are you saying, Oliver?"

He shrugged. "Father always said you were the best shot in the family. So I thought you might like to take up the sport again."

It was a test, Charlotte thought. Like the impossible tasks given to heroes in fairy tales. If she took the guns, if she dared to live under the same roof with them, then it was clear once and for all that she wasn't guilty, that she had not been the one to pull that trigger. "Yes," she said with a steady voice. "You're right, Oliver. I think I will take the guns. If that's all right with the rest of you."

George and Campbell nodded in unison, obviously eager for this to be done with.

"Mother—"

"Hush, Molly. This doesn't involve you," Charlotte said, still staring at Oliver.

He shifted uneasily under her gaze. "Then you and I *will* have to wrangle over the prints, as you put it, George," Oliver said.

"You can have them," George said mechanically. "Anything to be done with this business."

"These sandwiches look good, kids," Campbell said as he reached across the table and picked up two halves. "For some reason, family discussions always make me hungry."

With that, the bubble of tension popped and people began to find chairs and worry about eating. David released Molly's wrist and went to see if there were sodas in the pantry.

The afternoon progressed more quietly.

"They've lost the fighting spirit," David said when they were driving back to their mother's house for dinner. He had been given the vibrating machine from Grandmother's bathroom and the bureau and bed from Uncle Campbell's room. Molly asked for the furniture in her bedroom.

"At the end, I think they just wanted to get it over with in one day," Molly said.

"Will you go back to the farm tonight?"

"Might as well. I never have slept well in Mother's house."

Charlotte couldn't wait for them all to leave. Lydia used to love the rituals of one meal after another, and over holiday weekends, when everybody gathered at the farm, it seemed that they moved from lunch to dinner with only time for a nap or a short walk in between. "Let's just skip dinner," Charlotte used to say. "Nobody has room for it anyway." But her mother wouldn't hear of such a thing, and even when Charlotte begged off because the children were too small to be kept up late, Lydia had treated her absence from the table as a betrayal. She liked the circle of family faces around her to be complete, like the covered wagons around the campfire.

Oliver went home, pleading exhaustion, and Charlotte sensed a slight unuttered sigh of relief from her other brothers when he left. David came in the kitchen to help her with dinner.

"I had no idea you knew how to cook," she said to him when he offered to make the vegetables.

"No other way to keep my strength up on my pittance of a salary," he said.

"It's hard having all these people in the house," she said. "I'm so used to being alone. One English muffin, one dirty plate and a glass. It takes me a week to fill up the dishwasher. We've already run it twice since yesterday."

"You sound tired, Mother," David said.

"I am. To be honest with you, I wish I could go somewhere, pull the covers over my head, and sleep for a week. But I can't, so there's no use talking about it."

"Why can't you?"

"The paper's in a turmoil right now. My general manager just left, so I'm trying to put the new budget together myself. And the strike settlement is going to mean higher advertising rates.

"What about Uncle Oliver?"

"Oliver's no good at all with the figures. He never has been."

"Is there any bourbon, Mother?" Molly asked from the door. "Uncle George is asking for it."

Elizabeth Winthrop

"No," Charlotte said. "I never keep it in the house. I hate the stuff."

There was a pause, and under the harsh fluorescent lights, they all looked at each other and then away again. It feels as if a ghost just passed through the room, Charlotte thought.

"Can you toss the salad, Molly? I'll go light the candles."

On her way into the dining room, Charlotte saw the house from above like a child who flips up the roof of her dollhouse and looks down on the family of dolls, each one frozen in action, plastic limbs bent into appropriate attitudes. Uncles at the hearth smoking pipes, their heads tilted toward one another, brother and sister in the kitchen preparing dinner, mother bent over candlesticks in the dining room.

"Poof," Charlotte said, blowing out the match. "Gone. No more family. No more houses to close up and people to bring together around a table and traditions to maintain and fronts to preserve."

"What is it, Mother?" Molly asked. "Do you need another match?"

"No. It's all done. Dinner, gentlemen," she called through the door to her brothers.

Molly got it over with quickly. In the back door, past Frank's shoe-polishing room and the coat hooks, past the little dining room to the light switch, which she flicked on, and there she was standing in the sudden harsh brightness of the kitchen. The first thing she saw was the one purple blossom on the African violet that Agnes had been nurturing for years in the north window. Her eyes roamed across the porcelain sink, the high, shiny faucet, the salt and pepper shaker on top of the stove, Agnes's apron dangling from a cupboard door.

"Agnes," she shouted. "I'm home."

She pulled out the white stool and put her head down on the tin surface of the table. It felt cool against her forehead, reminding her of that afternoon in August when Agnes had put the Kleenex down next to her and gone to divert Frank. The house waited for her. Clocks ticked away in empty rooms (Agnes always did the winding on Sunday afternoon), food aged slowly in the refrigerator, the roots of the elm tree moved imperceptibly into the foundations, one destructive millimeter after another. In the years since Grandmother had died, Agnes had gone on cleaning and cooking and caring for this empty temple because it was what she had been hired to do and it was all she knew to do. The size and history of the house pressed down on Molly as she sat in its center, and she was reminded of the weight of the earth on top of Agnes's coffin.

Once her small suitcase was unpacked, Molly walked through the house, locking the doors. She had gone through this ritual every night with Agnes, so it was familiar to her, but tonight she counted them as she went: the sun porch, the side door off the small front hall that her mother always used, the two glass doors in the dining room, the one that led to the garden from Grandfather's study, the door to the cellar, the kitchen door. Seven in all. Would she ever get used to living alone in this great sieve of a house where a thin bolt was no real protection against an intruder?

In the kitchen, she poured herself a tall glass of water from the jar in the refrigerator. She narrowed the path of light as she went, so that it ran from the kitchen, through the little dining room, up the back stairs, past the phone in the hall to her bed. The door to her room had loosened in its hinges. She had to lift and push it firmly against the jamb so that the latch clicked and held.

All her life Molly had used sleep the way her father used his bottle. She was addicted to it. If she just slept well, she knew she could face anything the next day. Sometimes at night her father would wander around the house. She woke with the sense of a person moving along the dark hallways or the distant rise and fall of raised voices. When the arguments grew so loud that the hard-edged words seeped in under her doorway, she would tiptoe down the hall and slip into the extra bed in David's room. The first time her father discovered she was not in her bed, he woke the whole family with his shouting.

"Molly's gone. She's run away. She's been stolen."

"I'm right here, Daddy. I'm in David's room."

Her mother turned on the hall light, and they stood there in a sad circle, blinking at one another.

"Why are you sleeping in there?" her father asked.

"I was scared, Daddy."

"It's all right, Button. You come wake me up when you're scared."

Her mother and David had turned away from the two of them huddled together in the sudden light and gone back to bed.

After that, she lay awake and tried to talk herself out of her night fears. She didn't want to go into the dark bedroom where her parents lay so close together in the double bed even when they barely spoke to one another at the dinner table.

Now she heard the wind rising and the scratch of the elm branches on the pane. Winter would seal her into the house like a body into a tomb. If the work went well, she would survive it. But she couldn't work without sleep. She took one of the white pills her mother had given her and lay stiffly in the bed talking herself out of things.

34

The next morning, Molly was sitting over her breakfast at the kitchen table when Frank came in as usual to take the trash out.

"You'll be staying here all alone," he said.

"I'm going to try it.

"You know about the bell by Agnes's bed?"

She shook her head.

"There's a bell we rigged up there when your grandmother got old. It's a black button right above her pillow. It's very loud. Sometimes Angelina and I don't hear the phone."

"I know. I called you the night Agnes got sick, but there was no answer."

She pulled the trash can out from under the table for him.

"So you going to be cleaning this place?" he asked.

"I guess so," she said.

"It's a big place. My sister Clara used to come up and help Agnes off and on. You want me to see if she can come again?"

Molly grinned. "You don't think I know how to clean, Frank?"

"Big place," he said again.

"I guess it's up to my mother. I'll ask her."

He tipped the can over and emptied it into the green plastic garbage bag.

"I was sorry to hear about Rudy and Rosa," Molly said tentatively.

"What about them?" Frank asked with a blank stare.

"Well, I thought—"

"Rudy's just living down there till the weather turns," he said. "Wants to get that barn finished. I don't know why he's fussing over it so. He's always been like that. Has to do things right."

She didn't say anything. In Frank's mind, she had no right to comment on his son.

"I'll get the rest of the garbage now. You still want the wood upstairs for that stove on the porch?"

"Yes, please. But the woodbox is full, I think. Besides, it's Sunday. You should be relaxing today."

"All right, then. I'll do it tomorrow."

In the refrigerator, Molly found the leftovers from their last dinner together, the Tupperware containers labeled in Agnes's spidery handwriting. Agnes recycled everything, so that the carrots from one dinner were used the next night in beef stew. She rotated the soup cans and the noodles and the packages of walnuts on the pantry shelves and cooked with whatever was in the front row, so nothing went out of date or grew stale. Molly felt inadequate in the face of Agnes's organizational methods. She threw the leftovers away and made a list.

She went down the aisle in the grocery store slowly, pushing the cart that seemed grotesquely large for one person, distracted by the patterns on the cookie packages, the fat content on the yogurt containers.

"You on a diet?" the checkout lady asked as she rang up Molly's items and moved them along the conveyor belt to the packer.

"Not really. I just hate to cook."

"Me too." They smiled at each other, and Molly thought: Savor this conversation. It may be the last one you have today.

Back at home, with the food put away, she went upstairs through the hallways to the painting porch with Agnes's old radio under her arm. The outlet was too far away and it took her twenty minutes to fine an extension cord. The door to the painting porch stuck as usual. She fell into its cold turpentine-scented air as the swollen corner gave way suddenly with the pressure of her body. With the chatter of music and advertisements behind her, she crawled up on the stool and stared at her portrait of Agnes.

"I miss you," she whispered. "What do I paint now? What do I have to say?"

Every finished painting feels like the last one you'll ever do, she once told Andrea. You have an idea, and what you make is never as good as the idea, but you see that it's the closest you'll get. So you're doomed to put that painting away and start again. But before the next painting comes to you, you wait. "And the waiting is the loneliest part," she said now, out loud, to the ghosts in the room.

She propped Agnes up on the chair rail of the porch next to an empty canvas and replaced her with the largest sketch pad she could find. Charcoal frees you, Grandmother used to say. Make broad bold strokes. Molly searched through the clutter on her table for the box of charcoal. The thick stick felt smooth in her cold fingers. She broke the white space of the newsprint page with the long curved line that runs from under a woman's arm to her ankle. The width of her body was defined by another line. The arms and elbows, the crotch.

She flipped to a new sheet and began to fill it in from one corner with the charcoal lying on its side against the minuscule bumps of the page. Back and forth, no white spaces left, like a mop swinging in a wide arc across the kitchen floor. When the first page was done, she did another from the opposite corner, stopping every now and then to blow off the black dust. On the third page, she pressed her blackened hand against the white and outlined it with a stick of charcoal. She turned over her other palm and ran the longest, fattest piece against it, filling in her hand the same way she had filled in the page. She used to hate the mess of charcoal. Today, she was taking a bath in it. She pressed both palms against the white page and smeared them back and forth, taking joy in the dusty trails they left behind, dark at first and then lightening out. Finished, she stood up and stared. "Now, that is art," she said out loud, her voice breaking.

She washed her hands and made lunch even though she wasn't really hungry. Everything she did seemed to take a very long time and yet the hands on the clock barely moved. Would it always be this bad? She had never realized before how much she had relied on Agnes's constant presence in the house and in the months before on Eliot's arrival. Dependable, punctual Eliot, whom she used to tease so cruelly. And before that, when she lived in the city, she was teaching and the phone rang and the man in the apartment below her composed his electronic music until she got so fed up with the noise that she jumped up and down on her living-room floor in her high-heeled boots. Maybe she was crazy to stay here in this ghostly old house.

In the middle of the afternoon, the phone rang and she ran for it, terrified that the person would hang up before she got there.

"How are you doing?" her mother said.

"I'm all right. I keep the radio on all the time."

"I used to do that. I left it on all day so the house wouldn't be so quiet when I got home from work."

How many years had her mother been coming home to an empty house? Ever since Molly moved over to the farm for that winter. Sixteen, seventeen years. Why hadn't she ever sold the house? Or married again?

"Well, they've all left. They said to say goodbye to you."

"You sound relieved," Molly said.

"Yes, I guess I am." There was a pause, the click of her lighter and the first deep pull on the cigarette. "Did you sleep well last night?"

"Yes. It was all right, thanks to your pill."

"Do you want some more?"

"No, thanks, Mother. I don't want to get hooked on them. Frank came by this morning. He said his sister Clara might be able to help me clean the house. Is that all right with you?"

"Certainly. I'll call her about it."

"Thanks." The conversation was winding down, which meant Molly would be left alone again.

"All right, then. Call me if you need anything."

"I will," Molly said, and put the receiver down in its cradle.

Late in the afternoon, she pulled on her grandmother's mud boots and walked down to the calf barn. The air was cold and dank. Four-thirty in early December felt like nine o'clock on a summer evening. The shortest days of the year had closed down around them like a cloak.

Rudy's truck was parked around behind the barn. She hesitated at the foot of the office steps. Up above, the light shone out from under his closed door.

"Rudy," she called once and then again a little louder.

He opened the door and looked down. "Hello," he said with a smile. "Tony's here. Come on up."

"Hi," Tony said, shoving his head through the space between his father's rib and his arm. His grin matched Rudy's. "Come see Daddy's room."

The office looked the same as it had all those years ago when she and Rudy had exchanged Christmas presents up here. The old rolltop desk where the farm manager had kept the accounts had been pushed to the opposite wall to make room for a chair and a lamp. A thin mattress was laid out on the floor in the other corner under the window.

"Isn't it neat?" Tony asked eagerly.

"Very neat," she said, catching Rudy's eye.

"Tony thinks it's almost as good as camping out in his tree house," Rudy explained.

"It's better. I don't have any light in the tree house. Except my flashlight."

"Well, this arrangement can't last forever. At some point we're going to have to jack up this end of the barn."

"You'll move back by then anyway, Daddy."

It wasn't a question, so Rudy didn't answer it. He looked at Molly instead.

"How are you doing?" he asked. They were standing just a foot apart, and she knew if Tony had not been there, she would have walked back into the comforting circle of his father's arms. She wanted to have as much right to be there as the boy did and grew jealous now as he leaned up against Rudy like a puppy staking out the boundaries of his territory. Tony had liked her in the beginning but now he saw her as a threat.

"Molly, are you all right?"

"Yes. Just tired. The house feels strange without Agnes. I came running back to be with her, and now that she's gone, I'm wondering why I'm here."

"Do you have somewhere else to go?"

"Yes. I have friends in New York I could land on. And if I gave him a month's notice, I could always kick the sublet tenant out of my apartment if I wanted to be nasty. But I'm going to hang in here a while longer. Everything's set up in the painting porch. I'm ready to go if I could just figure out what the hell I wanted to paint. If you'll excuse my language," she said to Tony.

"That's all right. My father's crew says bad words all the time."

Molly met Rudy's eyes over the boy's head. His look said: I can't help it, I love him, and she smiled back, touched by the easy affection he had for his son.

"I finished a painting of Agnes last week," she went on. "The night she died, in fact. You should come up sometime and take a look at it, Rudy."

"I'd like that. Can I give you a ride up the driveway?" he asked. "I promised to get Tony home before dinner."

"No, thanks," she said. "I'm going to walk down to the river and back."

"Be careful," he said. "It's pretty dark down there."

She had forgotten to leave the porch light on and found her way back up the driveway by the light of a half-moon. The house waited for her like a great animal hunkered down in the road, and she climbed the back steps wearily. Only one day had passed. It felt like a year. Halfway through dinner, she remembered it was clock-winding day.

"The hell with it," she said to herself. "I'll get up when I wake and eat when I'm hungry. And if I'm tired in the middle of the day, I'll sleep. As long as I have to sit here and wait, I'll do it on my own time." Before she went around the house checking the doors, she unplugged the wall clock in the kitchen.

That night she tucked her hands under her arms and rolled from side to side as if to rock herself to sleep. It was an old trick of hers from childhood and sometime in the night it worked.

The weeks that followed Agnes's death passed in a timeless haze. Molly got up when the light woke her.

Frank lit the stove upstairs for her every morning, and after a big breakfast she forced herself to crawl up to the painting porch and sit on the stool. The first snowfall came as a relief, and affirmation that the days would pass and after winter came spring. But on the porch, the reflection of the sunlight off the white landscape blinded her like the unexpected pop of a flashbulb. That day, she went back to bed and slept until dinnertime.

Clara came in on Thursdays and did the downstairs. Molly cleaned the second floor in a haphazard way, rushing about with the dust mop when she couldn't bear the row of empty canvases lined up accusingly on the chair rail.

"For God's sake, Molly, come back to New York," Andrea said. "Just for a visit. I'll take you out for a big lunch and we'll go to some galleries. There's a wonderful show of skulls up at the Graham. That should fit your mood perfectly."

Molly was tempted but only for a moment. "I can't, Andrea. I'm so scared if I leave here I'll miss something."

"Sounds as if you're sitting in an empty theater waiting for a movie to start."

"It feels that way. There's something about the house and Agnes and Grandmother that I want to put down. I'm just not sure what it is yet."

"All right, I'll leave you be. The old gang misses you. By the way, I saw Eliot last week."

"How was he?" Molly asked.

"The same. Eliot doesn't pack too many surprises. He does have a new lady in his life."

She took a breath. "Who's that?"

"Marilyn something. Seems very nice but a little dull. She works in his office. I guess he's sworn off the unreliable artist type."

Molly said goodbye and hung up. She felt odd, as if the air had suddenly been sucked out of her stomach. Andrea had acted so casual about it, assuming, of course, that Molly didn't care anymore. And Molly was surprised at herself.

"Did you think he would hang around in Danbury waiting for you to come back?" she demanded of herself.

"No, of course not," she answered. "It just hurts to know there's someone else in his bed. I don't deserve to feel sad or bruised or replaced, but I do. So I'll just feel it. Funny how I was the one who left but now I'm the one who feels left behind."

She walked down to the calf barn, but Rudy's truck wasn't there. "Just as well," she told herself later. "God knows what nonsense you would have started."

Her mother called every day, and Molly found herself looking forward to the interruption. They talked about the newspaper or moving details.

"I've told the church they can come in April and take away everything that isn't marked," Charlotte reported one day in the middle of December. "They'll put on a big sale on the lawn. It'll give us a tax deduction, and it means we don't have to go through the junk in the attic or your grandmother's clothes or the pots and pans. All that clutter."

"Sounds good," Molly said. She was rolling a tassel on her grandmother's counterpane back and forth in her fingers.

"Oh, by the way, the lawyer opened Agnes's will yesterday. She wrote an addendum in August 1970 that leaves you a cardboard box in her closet. She doesn't say what's inside. Do you have any idea what that could be?"

"No," Molly said.

"Well, whatever it is, it's all yours. Also, somebody has got to sort through Agnes's belongings. I frankly don't think I can face it. Shall I ask Clara and Angelina if they'll come up?"

"No, Mother. I'll do it. I think that's what she'd want."

"Yes, I suppose you're right." In the brief silence that followed, Molly could hear the clatter of typewriters and phones ringing in the background. Her mother was calling from the newsroom, where she went at one o'clock to proof the front page of the paper.

"Molly, are you all right?" her mother asked. It sounded as if she were trying to muffle her voice with her hand.

"Mother, why do you keep asking me that? I'm a big girl now."

"I just think it would be awfully lonely rattling around in that big house all by yourself."

"It is lonely. But I'm beginning to feel that's good for me. Sort of like a dose of castor oil."

The door to Agnes's room was closed. Molly stood in front of it for a while, hand on the knob, forehead pressed into the raised center section of the wooden panel.

This moment of preparation reminded her of the other time she stood outside a door and steeled herself for the unpleasant job ahead. Freshman year in college she had been assigned a red-haired roommate from Texas, a bouncy overweight girl who bumped into furniture, cluttered the room with curlers and makeup and worn issues of *Glamour* magazine, and stayed on the phone for hours at a time with various boyfriends back home. Molly took responsibility for her, perhaps because Lynne's chaos was so threatening to her own carefully constructed world. She cleaned up after her, posted a schedule of her classes, reminded her about overdue assignments. But Lynne was like a whirling dervish, turning faster and ever more frantically on herself.

The night of the annual spring mixer on campus, Molly came back to the dorm early, tired of making conversation with strangers over the drummer's pounding. Somebody was crying in a booth in the communal bathroom.

"Hello," Molly called out, her voice echoing against the cold white tiles. "Who is it?"

The crying stopped instantly, like a gum bubble sucked back inside a child's mouth. Molly leaned over to look under the booth and saw Lynne's bare feet. She recognized them because of the ten splotches of bright pink polish which Lynne had labored over on her bed earlier in the day, her knee crooked up next to her chin, the little brush shaking in her hand. In the middle of one of her smooth-skinned feet, there was a dark flat spot that looked like blood.

"Lynne. It's Molly. What's wrong?"

"Go away."

"Tell me what's wrong."

"Don't go into the room," Lynne cried out. "Promise me you won't go in the room."

507

"If you don't come out of there, I'll crawl under."

With a snap of the bolt, the white partition swung open. Lynne was sitting on the toilet, both wrists slashed, the gray slimy insides that must have been muscle and tendons bulging out through the unnatural openings. Molly stopped the scream, the contorted expression of disgust before it reached her face.

"Do you think you can stand up?" she asked.

Lynne shook her head.

Molly wrapped two towels as tightly around the wounds as she dared. Then she led Lynne down the hall to an empty room and made her lie down on the bed while she called the infirmary.

"Promise me you won't go into our room. I'll come back later and clean it up."

"I promise," she said, stroking the other girl's forehead.

Once Lynne was safely in the ambulance, the doctor took Molly aside.

"Do you know her well?"

"She's my roommate, but I've only known her about four months. Is she going to be all right?"

"Yes. You did just fine. She was serious, though. Most people cut this way," he said, laying the side of his hand across his wrist. "The only way to really do it is her way." He turned his hand so that it lined up along the track of his vein.

When the ambulance left, Molly climbed to the top floor of the dorm and zigzagged back down, collecting all the rolls of paper towel from all the bathrooms. She stood outside the door of her room for what seemed like hours, holding the soft tubes, a bucket of water at her feet, reminding herself that it would only be blood.

It was everywhere. On the walls, the windows, the bedspreads, the mirrors, Lynne's shoes. After an hour of mopping, with the soggy brown paper towels piling up next to her bucket, Molly began to think of it as fingerpaint. For months afterward, she found dark dried patches of it in unexpected places.

Molly swung this door open, wondering what traces Agnes had left behind for her to uncover and mop up. The shadow of the older woman hung in the room. She was the last person to smooth this bedspread, adjust that picture, prop the *Daily Word* open on the bedside table.

In the far corner of the closet, beyond the four pairs of shoes, she found the box. An envelope with her name scrawled on it was attached to the top. She tried to strip off the strapping tape to take a quick peek inside, but Agnes had done her usual efficient job of sealing the package. Molly decided to save it for later.

It didn't take her long to dismantle the room and divide Agnes's life into neat piles. Edith would get the good clothes and shoes, the silver bureau set, the antique clock, two brownish-gray photos of their parents. The neon-colored stickers winked at her from the surfaces of the furniture. Uncle Campbell would be getting the bed and dresser and Uncle George the night table, the rug, and the chairs. Like the rest of the house, the contents of this room would be spread about the east coast all the way from Massachusetts to New York City. It seemed to Molly a violation that Agnes's careful, neat life inside these walls could be scattered about like dry leaves in a sudden wind.

She dragged three large cardboard cartons up from the basement, filled them with the various piles, and marked them: one for Edith and on the other two she wrote "church sale" in large black block letters. She was done, and when she looked about the stripped room, she saw an absence of possessions: the lines left in the dust by the picture frames she had removed from the bureau, the empty hangers clustered together at one end of the dress pole, the exposed mattress, yellowed with age. Agnes had lived here for over forty years, and in the space of an afternoon, the room had been emptied and packed away in the cardboard cartons. Molly picked up the box marked with her own name and found her way down the hall to the porch.

December 3, 1971

Dear Molly,

I discovered these journals under your grandmother's bed after she died. Maybe I should have thrown them away when I found them, but I like to think she kept them under that bed all those years for a reason. And I've decided you're the reason. I can't stand to watch you reading them. That's why I've left them to you in my will. When I move myself down to Edith's cluttered little apartment, I expect I'll take them along with me and shove them in the back of my closet there.

You'll have to make up your mind what's to be done with them next. Whatever you do, don't let your mother see them. I don't think your grandmother would like that.

Love,
Agnes

Pasted inside the front cover of the first volume, Molly found an old photograph of her grandmother. She was leaning against an ornate column and a rose dangled dramatically from her clasped fingers. Half of her long dark hair was pulled up into a large satin bow that seemed to perch on her head like a pale bird. The rich velvet dress opened in a V from the waist to the shoulders to reveal a high-necked frilly underblouse. Her smile was unsure, tentative, almost fearful, as if she were worried that it might displease the photographer. Underneath was scrawled a note in Lydia's loopy, girlish handwriting. "A picture Uncle James had taken of me on my thirteenth birthday."

The journals opened with this paragraph: "Dr. Stevenson and I have concluded that my assignment during this visit (which we both hope will be my last) is to write down in these books everything that happened between me and Uncle James. It shall be an attempt to exorcise whatever devils still haunt me from those years and will, he hopes, cure me completely of my nightmares and the continuing bouts of nausea. He does not intend to read what I write, which will allow me to put down absolutely everything without any fear. He says that is the point of this exercise. Nobody shall judge me except myself. When I am done, Dr. Stevenson hopes I will not need to look at these words or ever think of them again. Lydia Franklin, May 6, 1906."

Before she read any further, Molly called her mother at the office.

"When was Grandmother born?" she blurted out as soon as Charlotte came on the phone.

"Eighteen eighty-six. In April."

"And when did she and Grandfather get married?" Molly asked. She was scribbling the dates on a pad by the phone.

"In 1909, I think it was. Why all the questions?"

"I'm doing some research," Molly said. It wasn't far from the truth.

"What did Agnes leave you?"

"Nothing very exciting. Some old books of Grandmother's. Thanks, Mother. Oh, by the way, I've cleaned out Agnes's room and put it all into boxes. I'll take Edith's to the post office in the next few days."

"I didn't mean you had to do it right away."

"I wanted to get it over with. See you."

She did some quick figuring on the pad. Grandmother was twelve years old in 1898, twenty in 1906, twenty-three when she got married.

It took Molly most of that night and half the next day to read through all four books. Unlike Agnes, she read night and day. She took them downstairs and read them in the kitchen while her bread was toasting. She took them into her bed and fell asleep with the black book sliding off the edge of her chest and woke suddenly two hours later, feeling for it. There were times when she wanted to stop, when the thought of the little girl trying to twist away from her uncle made Molly feel like vomiting. But she forced herself to keep going. If her grandmother had found the strength to write these things down, then Molly would make herself keep reading them.

When she was done, she put the journals back into the box and carried it into the porch.

She pulled on her coat and boots and walked out to her car. "Where are you going?" she asked herself. "Anywhere but that house," she answered.

She drove through town and out into the country, taking whatever turn appealed to her, choosing her route by the name of the town or the curve of a stream. She stopped to fill the car with gas and, at dusk, to eat in a roadside diner, one of the old ones with shiny metal sides. After a dinner of scrambled eggs and a cup of coffee, she found her way home again along roads dusted with a light dry snow.

"You see, you big old monster of a house, I can leave you. Anytime I want."

She didn't even bother to try to sleep that night but sat up watching an old Western movie on television and then the Johnny Carson show. Anything not to think about those journals, about the little girl who couldn't get away.

Sometime in the night, Molly wandered up to the painting porch and drew the boat from her old nightmare. The empty boat. Was it waiting to go somewhere? Was it waiting for someone to climb in? Had someone just fallen out? She didn't know. She yanked a canvas off the chair rail and threw it on the easel and painted the boat again, this time larger and more menacing. The lines were dark and thick and she did not pick up the rag to scrub them in. She went to bed when the sun rose.

She woke up late in the afternoon and made sluggish plans to go out, do her errands. The market, the post office with the box for Edith. But she couldn't make herself do it. Her coat was on, her bag swung from her left hand, she had found the car keys, but she didn't want to go out of the house. She forced herself to unlock the kitchen door and open it. The air was heavy, the skies overcast. It smelled like snow. She would do the errands tomorrow. They could wait. She would eat sliced bananas on oatmeal tonight. Agnes used to make that for her when she was sick.

When Frank came in the next morning, she was watching television.

"You've got the door locked," he said.

"Yes." She didn't look up.

"You feeling all right?" he asked. "You look kind of pale."

"Just a cold," she said. "Are you going into town today, Frank? Would you mind doing some errands for me?"

"Won't be till the afternoon."

"That's fine."

He stomped off through the house. By the time she heard his footsteps coming back, she had written out her list and left it with some money and Edith's package on the kitchen table.

For the next few days, she slept in snatches, sometimes at night, sometimes in the middle of the afternoon. When Clara came by on Thursday, she stayed in her room, feigning sickness. One day she made a list of her fears in big black charcoal letters on the sketch pad. I am afraid of: the dark, crying, sickness, water, swimming, empty canvases, unlocked doors, clowns, throwing up, drunkenness, roller coasters, being left behind, losing myself. On the right side of the page, she made another column, which said: I am not afraid of: blood, insects, money (not having enough), the cold, the heat, thunderstorms. She taped the sheet of paper up on one white paneled wall and crawled back down the hall to her bed.

Over and over again, she dreamt she was sitting in a bar or a restaurant or at a county fair, some noisy public place. She was with her father and she was a little girl again. She clung to his arm and called his name. Sometimes he would look her way and smile, but his attention was continually diverted by the woman on his other arm. He bent his head close to that other woman and whispered secrets in her ear and laughed at her jokes. "Isn't this great?" he would call to Molly over the noise of the band. "Isn't she terrific?" "No," Molly would scream back at him, but the baffled expression on his face showed he hadn't understood her. She woke each time, exhausted with her efforts and shivering and sad.

Once in a while, she would rush down the hall like a patient about to vomit and smear something on the page of a sketchbook. The pictures themselves were abstract, the colors dark and sick, and the curves and forms insinuated themselves onto the page as if the voices in her mind were squeezing the paint right out of the ends of her fingers. She had relinquished all control over the process.

She saw Rudy's truck parked down by the barn in the late afternoons. Sometimes he stopped and looked up toward the house, his head tilted, shielding his eyes against the snow glare. She would duck out of sight then and watch him scanning the horizon of the house for a glimpse of her. He had promised to come look at her painting of Agnes. Why didn't he come? she wondered. Maybe his father has told him how strange I am these days, Molly thought. Maybe it's a blessing that he stays away.

35

One day, her mother dropped by without any warning. Molly was curled up in a nest of blankets on her bed, and she held herself motionless as the footsteps approached. She had a wild, irrational urge to hide in the closet, but she knew how ridiculous that would be. After all, her car was parked in the driveway. Her mother would search and search until she found her.

"Molly." The call was singsong. On her mother's tongue, the syllables in her name seesawed back and forth in the hallway. "MO-LLY."

"I'm in here, Mother. In the bedroom," Molly said in a quiet clear voice that stopped Charlotte before she went too far. Molly did not want her to go onto the porch. She might pick up one of Lydia's journals and start to read it or flip through Molly's sketch pad. Molly knew it was her responsibility to keep all those ugly things hidden away from her mother. Hadn't Agnes said as much in her letter?

"Are you all right?" her mother asked, tiptoeing suddenly as if into a hospital room. "Why have you got the curtains closed in the middle of the day?" She started across the room to open them.

"Leave them, please," Molly whispered. "The light reflects off the snow. It's too bright."

Charlotte hesitated midway and sank down on the edge of her daughter's bed.

"What is it, darling? What's wrong?"

"Mother, please don't use that word. Darling," she mimicked in an exaggerated voice. "Don't you hear how it sounds?"

Charlotte folded her hands in her lap. "Talking to you

is a little like walking through a minefield," she said. "I never know where to put my foot down."

"Eliot used to say the same thing."

"Are you sick?"

"No. I think I've just pulled the covers over my head for a while. I'm waiting. Sometimes, there seems to be no other way."

Charlotte smiled tentatively. "Sounds quite soothing to me. I wish I could join you."

Molly grinned back. "Pick a bed. That's one thing we've got plenty of in this house."

"I probably wouldn't last long. Not doing anything scares me too much. In any case, Oliver would find me sooner or later."

"I've let all the clocks wind down. What time is it?" Molly asked. "For that matter, what day is it?"

"About four o'clock. December twenty-first. I came by to see what we should do about Christmas."

"Couldn't we skip it this year? I'm not in a very festive mood."

"Oliver's invited us both over to his house for lunch. Your cousins will be there. How long has it been since you've seen them?"

"Ages. But I really couldn't stand it, Mother."

"No, you don't look as if you could," Charlotte said quietly. She fanned her hands out. "Let me take you home and put you to bed, Molly. I'll make you a tray. We can watch some idiotic television show or play dominoes or you can just sleep if you want to."

Molly pulled her knees up against her chest. "Mother, I know it sounds crazy. But I have to stay here and wait this thing out."

"Will you call me if you change your mind?"

"Yes. But I meant it about the beds," Molly reminded her. "You could always come join me here."

Charlotte trembled. "I can't, Molly. I can't be in this house."

"I know," Molly said. "You're too scared to stay and I'm too scared to leave."

It was a bad night. She pulled on wool socks and a heavy sweater over her nightgown, but she could not stop the shaking. When she cried, the sobs were raw, cutting as they came up, sounds that, once released, hung in the room above her bed. At the end of it, in the stillness, her body felt limp and thin, but still she couldn't sleep.

Sometime in the night, she got up and crept down the hall to her grandmother's room, feeling her way with her right hand, palm flat against the rough surface of the plaster walls. She pushed each black button as she went, leaving a trail of light behind her. On her grandmother's bed, the three pillows sat up one behind the other, the white counterpane smoothed and still. The December wind pressed against the house. The panes of glass seemed to move back and forth in their wood frames as the air outside alternately pushed and sucked on them. She slid into the bed and tucked the extra two pillows against her belly, trying to press down the fine stomach hairs that stood up in the electrified emptiness under her nightgown. It was no warmer here. The air moaned as it eked its way through some crack under the porch door, but for the moment, she felt cradled, held in and comforted by the history of this bed.

Rudy was keeping himself very busy. He was working Luigi too hard, he knew it.

"I'm going to get some of the other men in to finish up the interior work on the barn," he told him the week before Christmas. "You need a rest."

"You don't mean other men," Luigi growled. "You mean younger men."

Rudy shrugged. It was the truth, of course. "The joists are heavy, Luigi. You shouldn't be moving heavy lumber like that at your age."

"No better way to go, I figure. After all, my wife had her heart attack over the kitchen stove. Just where she wanted to be."

In the beginning, the little room in the calf barn had seemed cozy and warm and welcoming to him. Just like the tree house for Tony. When he dragged himself up the rough wooden stairs, he barely had enough energy to turn on the heater and drop into bed. He took showers at the cottage, and his mother had begun to stir herself around the kitchen now that he was in and out all the time. But he would have to find an apartment soon. This was no way to live.

The children came over some nights for dinner with their father and their grandparents. Without Rosa, he hovered over them, aware of his mother's jumpy heart, reprimanding the children for their sloppy table manners before she could say anything and hating himself later when they looked confused or hurt by the sharp tone in his voice. After dinner, they all pulled on their boots and went for a walk on the snow-covered lawn before he took them home again.

"Is that lady still here?" Tony asked one evening. "The lady from New York."

"Molly? Yes, she's still here. She's living up at the big house."

"I don't like her anymore," Tony announced, and Rudy glanced over the heads of the other two children at his oldest son's profile.

"Why not?" he asked.

Tony shrugged. "Just don't." He was setting up his boundary lines, Rudy thought. Sorting things out for himself. Liking Molly must amount, in Tony's mind, to some sort of disloyalty to his own mother.

Rosa was usually standing at the kitchen window when he brought the kids home. He could see her body silhouetted against the bright yellow walls that they had painted together the first weekend that they moved in. He wondered how long she stood there waiting. She did not come out to greet him, and he sent the children alone down the short path from the headlights of his truck to the back door.

When they did talk on the phone about plans for the children, he heard in her voice the same quiet sadness that he recognized from the months before he left. If only she would get angry or scream at him, it would make the whole thing easier. But of course she knew that. Rosa had always known before he did what he was thinking. She never tried to push him in one direction or another. Being with someone who knows so much makes the walls close in on a person. It was as if everything about him, about his future, was already decided and he was powerless to change any of it.

Rosa must know, then, that he thought about Molly all the time. Keeping himself away from her was a way to take back the power, to show himself that what Rosa thought he would do did not necessarily lock him into that course of action like a missile into its trajectory.

Sometimes, after dinner, his father would walk with him around the barn and he always brought up "that girl."

"She's acting sickly," Frank said just the other night. "I guess she keeps to her bedroom most of the time. The house is filthy. Your Aunt Clara spent two extra hours there last Thursday cleaning the upstairs."

From his distance, Rudy watched for signs of her. Sometimes he saw her shadow ducking across the glass wall of the painting porch. At night he could follow her progress through the house by the lights that went on and off. But the car hadn't been moved in days. He stopped to brush the snow off it one morning on his way out of the driveway.

At night, in the brief moments before sleep, he thought of her in that large dark house just yards away across the lawn buried in snow. He thought about her red hair fanned out across the white pillow, her pale skin with the fading winter freckles, her long fingers dappled with paint. Sometimes in the screen of his mind, he saw his own hands reaching for her, his own fingers twisting open the buttons of her blouse and slipping into the dark hidden warmth beyond, and he would roll over onto his stomach with a groan.

On Christmas Day, after a big lunch with Uncle Sol's family and a short visit with the kids, he pulled the truck up alongside the house and knocked on the back door. He had a present for her, one of Luigi's boxes. He had even found some wrapping paper in the back of his mother's closet, and when Angelina asked him who that present was for, he had mumbled a lie. "Little Lina," he had said. "She needs a place to keep her crayons."

Nobody came downstairs to let him in, but the door was unlocked. He hadn't been in the house since Agnes had died, and now he tiptoed along the pale wall of the kitchen like a burglar. Outside, the light was fading and dust motes danced in the last rays of the sun slanting across the shelf of African violets. Although the counters and the tabletop were clean, the room had an unused look and the dead smell of a kitchen where nobody cooked anymore.

"Molly," he called tentatively as he passed through the pantry and the dining room, as dim and peaceful as a chapel. He didn't want her to be scared, but he didn't want to be sent away either.

"Molly," he said again from the top of the stairs.

"Rudy," she called back. Her voice was small but clear, and he twisted his way along the hall toward it with the box hidden behind him.

"I'm in Grandmother's bedroom," she said. "Don't come in, please."

He hesitated halfway across the boudoir. "I've got a present for you. I came to see the painting of Agnes."

She didn't answer for a long time. "What day is it?"

"Christmas, Molly. It's Christmas Day." He tiptoed closer and peeked. She was lying down in the bed, her back toward the door. Her arm lay along the line of her hip bone.

"Molly," he said. "What's wrong?"

She didn't turn over. "I told you not to come in, Rudy," she said, but her voice sounded weary and defeated. "I didn't want you to see me like this. Every day, I kept thinking I'd get better but—" The sentence drifted off into silence.

He sat down gingerly on the flat space between the lump of her foot under the covers and the edge of the bed. Her hair across the pillow looked matted and dull. The air in the rom smelled stale, used up. It reminded him of a hospital. Why didn't she turn over? He began to imagine that her face was covered in scars or open sores and he didn't think he wanted to see them.

"I'll leave the present here, then," he said quietly. "At the end of the bed."

She lifted her face from the pillow and gazed down the length of her body to him. "You were sweet to bring me something, Rudy," she said. "Don't you want to stay to watch me open it?"

He brought the present around to her. Her skin was unscarred, but he was struck by the glassy look in her eyes as she dragged herself up to a sitting position. With sluggish gestures, she ripped into the present, scrunching the paper into a wadded ball inch by inch with her fingers. He was careful when he opened presents. He sliced the Scotch tape with a fingertip and folded the paper into neat squares before he allowed himself the pleasure of the present itself. His kids liked to tease him about it. "Papa, hurry up," they would cry in exasperation. They tore the paper apart with fevered glee, not like Molly, who looked now as if she were bent on the slow destruction of something. The sight of the box brought a smile to her face.

"It's my favorite one," she whispered.

"I could tell," he said. "Luigi's too. He didn't want to give it up until I told him it was for you."

She lay back on the pillow again and stared at him with shining eyes. "Thank you, Rudy," she said, and she was still looking at him when the shine in her eyes tipped over into tears. She didn't seem to have the energy to wipe them away, so he blotted them with the corner of the linen sheet.

"What's wrong, Molly? Are you sick?"

"I must be," she said. "I'm so tired. I don't sleep anymore. I haven't taken a bath in days. I don't have the energy to do anything. I'm scared I'll never get up again."

He stared at her for a long moment without speaking and then stood up abruptly.

"Are you going?" she asked.

"I'll just be a minute," he said.

When he got back to the room, she was still sitting in the same position with the box cradled in her arms. He carried in the towel, the basin of warm soapy water, the hairbrush he had found on her dresser, and the clean nightgown from her drawer.

Her eyes followed him around the room while he hung his jacket over a chair and rolled up his sleeves.

"Once, Lina was sick with a high fever," he said. "We had to get her up and bathe her every two hours. I'm very good at sponge baths."

During the whole procedure, she lay on the bed without saying a word. Every so often, the soundless tears would start again and he would stop whatever he was doing to wipe her face, down the curve of her cheeks until the one moist track met the other at her small, determined chin. He lifted the thick hair, wiped her neck, and then blew the fine damp hairs dry. He pulled the covers away, sponged down her legs, and ran the cloth in between each toe. Slowly, without any warning, she worked her nightgown up over her bottom and then pulled it all the way off.

Her breasts were small, the nipples puckered and dark, and she shuddered as he worked his way down from her neck to sponge each of them with the warm cloth. Her hip bones jutted up above the flat stomach. A line of pale red hair disappeared into her scant cotton underpants, which were decorated with girlish flowers. Her body was all he had dreamed of those nights in the barn, but he treated it now with great tenderness. To touch her in any other way would violate the traditions of this ceremony, this silent ritual that echoed centuries of one human being ministering to another. He was a nurse, a spiritual healer, a loving parent easing fever, a grieving spouse anointing a body for the last time.

She rolled over so that he could do her back and then lifted her arms obediently while he worked the clean nightgown down over her body. He straightened the sheets and tucked them back in around her.

"Will you let me brush your hair?" he asked.

She nodded and pulled herself away from the pillow again so that he could work out the matted knots that had formed against her scalp. When the brush moved through the hair easily without snagging, he turned the thick hank into a single braid.

"Where did you learn how to do that?" she asked.

"From watching my mother," he said in a thick voice. "Don't you remember?"

"Yes, now I do."

He made her a bowl of chicken alphabet soup and brought it upstairs on a tray with some stale crackers he had found in the back of one cabinet.

"I don't think I can eat it," she said.

"Try it. Go through the alphabet one letter at a time. That's what I used to do."

He moved about the room cleaning up so she wouldn't

feel self-conscious. He had never liked people to watch him eat. Perhaps it came from years of his mother hovering over her only child at meals. When he had washed out the bowl in Mrs. Webster's bathroom and hung the towel and washcloth up to dry, he pulled a chair up and sat next to her.

"It tastes good," she said. "Want some?"

"Yes. If you've got a *c*."

"A *c*?" she asked, dribbling the soup off the spoon. "Why *c*?"

"For Christmas," he said.

"I hate holidays," she muttered.

"I don't. I'm very childish about them. But today was a tough one."

"How are the kids?"

"Confused. I wish Rosa would get angry at me. But she doesn't. She gives me a look that says: I understand, I know what you're thinking. It infuriates and humiliates me at the same time."

"Why did you leave her, Rudy?" she asked, her voice gentle.

"The walls were closing in on me. My whole life seemed set on one course. Northington, marriage, fatherhood, a trip to Italy in my old age." He shrugged. "I couldn't stand it anymore."

"It sounds kind of cozy and comfortable to me," she said. "Although these days, my judgment is not very dependable."

"My turn," he said. "What's happened to you? Is it Agnes's death?"

"That's part of it of course. But there's something else. Agnes left me a box of journals in her will. She found them under Grandmother's bed after she died. They gave me nightmares." She paused.

"Why?"

"Grandmother was molested by her uncle for years. She never told anybody and nobody ever suspected. It went on until she was about sixteen years old." Molly pushed the tray down across her legs to the flat space at the end of the bed. "I've eaten as much as I can," she whispered. "Thanks."

Rudy was slumped against the back of the chair. "God

in heaven," he said once and then again. "She wrote all this down?"

Molly nodded. "Every word of it. Apparently, she was in some sort of sanitarium and the doctor who was treating her told her to put her experiences into a journal."

Rudy was thinking of Lina, of some man's hands on her, under her dress. He shuddered. What would that do to a child? Molly was talking again.

"I don't understand why Agnes gave them to me," Molly said. "I wish to God she'd just thrown them away."

Rudy stared at Molly for a long time. Pictures dropped into his mind like slides into a carousel. Molly sitting next to her grandmother in the middle of the driveway in front of their easels, Molly's frown when her mother's car pulled up to the back door, Molly dancing along beside her father. That father. Could he have done something to her? Was that why Agnes passed on those books? But that was ridiculous. Molly was so fierce about him, so loyal.

"What are you thinking about, Rudy?" she asked.

"You," he said. "The old days."

She looked at him with a crooked smile. "They were fun, weren't they?"

"Yes, they were," he said, and her smile drove whatever connection he was starting to make right out of his head.

"Remember when I did that oral history of Grandmother the winter I lived here?"

He nodded.

"I know I asked her about her childhood, but she never mentioned an Uncle James. I guess I can understand why."

"Where are the tapes now?"

She shrugged. "Somewhere in my mother's house, I guess. Unless she's thrown them away. I wouldn't put it past her these days. Anyway, that's what's been happening to me. I feel as if I've been inside Grandmother's body ever since I read those books. I have these horrible dreams, Rudy."

"Have you painted anything?"

She nodded. "If you can call it that. More like vomiting on the page."

"Can I look?"

"Why not?" she said with a grin. "You've seen everything else."

He turned on the porch light.

"That's the picture of Agnes I wanted you to see," she called from the bed.

"I like it. You've caught that look of hers. You know, that 'this is who I am, want to fight about it?' look." He cocked his head. "The apples are good too."

"Do you really think so? I spent hours on them. I had to keep resisting the temptation to overwork them. I think I stopped at the right moment." She got out of bed and padded up next to him. "Brr," she said, "it's freezing in here."

He picked up the sketch pad and leafed through. The pages rattled as they settled slowly down on the back side of the pad.

"Grisly, aren't they?" she said.

"Yes. Like nightmares."

She took the sketch pad from him. "Now I look at them all in a row, I can see myself working something out here. I keep seeing faces in the background. Somebody watching from the back of the room. See here? And here again?"

He nodded. Beneath the pad, he could see one of her small bare feet curled over the other. "Come on," he said, taking her by the elbow. "Back in bed. Doctor's orders."

She let him lead her back into the room, but he could tell she was still lost in the sketch pad. She kept flipping back and forth between the pictures, and while he shoved the swollen porch door back into its frame, she began to rip out the ones she wanted.

"I'd better go," he said. "Back to work tomorrow."

She glanced up with a frown. "Do you have to go so soon?"

"Yes." He was ready to get out of the house now. Beyond this small circle of light, the ghost-filled rooms stretched away from them. And here sat Molly in the middle, wrapped up in her flannel nightgown and her nightmares. There was something about her sudden feverish involvement with the pictures that made him uneasy. She must have sensed it, because she put the pad away and stood up again.

"Goodbye, Rudy," she whispered as she gave him a quick hug. Before he could move his arms from where they were pinned under hers, she had pulled away. "My father was the last person who took such good care of me. I think you remind me of him."

He didn't know what to say to that. Molly's adoration of her father unnerved him. He wanted to say: The man went off and left you. He never wrote you. He never telephoned, he never came back to get you. Why do you keep him in such a holy place in your heart? But he didn't say any of it. "I'll leave this in the kitchen on my way through," he said as he slid the tray out from under her sketch pad. "I'll check in on you in the next couple of days."

The last glimpse he had of her, she had spread the pictures around her in a circle on the bed. He had the feeling she had already forgotten him.

36

January had always been Charlotte's worst month. When the ice and snow closed in around her, she tensed her body more tightly than ever to keep out the cold. At night, when she lay in bed and stretched her hands and heels down to release the pain in her joints, everything clicked and cracked. She woke up in the mornings sore from the hours of being curled into a rigid fetal position.

At the end of the month, she went for a checkup.

"How are you feeling?" the doctor asked when she sat down in his office after the examination.

"Exhausted," she admitted. "And terribly cold all the time."

"Are you sleeping well?"

"No," she said. "I have the sleeping pills, but they don't seem to help that much. I was wondering, is there anything you can prescribe for the daytime, Doctor? Something that will give me more energy?"

He didn't look up from his pad. "You know I don't believe in a lot of drugs, Mrs. Taylor. How about exercise? That might help you sleep better."

"I'm swimming twice a week already. That's all I have time for."

"You are under a lot of stress?" he asked, glancing up quickly.

She nodded eagerly. Maybe he had changed his mind. If she could just have something to get her through the days. "My mother's house is being sold, and of course, my job is always stressful."

He signed off on the papers and put them aside. "Well, there's nothing that I can see, Mrs. Taylor. I recommend you take some time off, ease up on the work a bit. Why don't you plan a vacation for yourself? Change your routine in some way. We all go through these rough times now and then, particularly this time of year." He got to his feet, which was his way of ending the conversation. She gathered up her gloves, which had fallen on the floor, and left the office without shaking his outstretched hand.

Goddamned doctor, she muttered under her breath as she waited for the cigarette lighter in the car to heat up. At least he hadn't started in with her about the smoking.

She knew it was more than the time of year. Even the work, which used to distract her from the loneliness at home, had become unbearable, and she dragged herself into the office every morning. The staff was watching her and whispering, but she kept the door closed and pretended not to notice. She didn't blame them for wondering. Some days, she sat through the morning editorial meetings, slumped in her chair with her eyes half closed, while Oliver droned on about the problems with the redistricting story, but more often than not, when she didn't think she could bear his whiny voice for another minute, she would insert herself into the deliberations over some insignificant decision that she normally left up to him. While the others shifted nervously in their chairs or tapped their pencils on the table, she and Oliver would wrangle back and forth until one or the other of them slammed out of the meeting in a rage.

"I've come to the end of my rope with Oliver," Charlotte told George on the phone one afternoon. "I can't stand it anymore."

"What are you going to do, Charlotte?"

"Here he comes now. I'll call you later."

Oliver knocked on the glass door and came in when she hung up the phone.

"Just the person I was looking for," she said. "Have a seat."

"No, thanks. We're on press. I brought up page one for you to look over."

She took it from him and spread it out on her desk.

"Cute picture," she said. "Dan's working out well as photographer, don't you think?"

Oliver shrugged. "He's all right. He goofs off too much as far as I'm concerned."

They couldn't agree on anything, Charlotte thought. She had hired Charlie Pursino's son over Oliver's objections two years ago. The boy was cocky. He came and went when he wanted. But he took good photographs.

"It looks all right to me," Charlotte said. She was lying. She didn't think the zoning board story was worth a two-inch headline. Oliver laid out the paper every day as if a new President had just been elected, but she knew better than to bring up that old argument.

"I'll take it downstairs."

"One minute, Oliver." At the door, he turned to look at her with a quizzical expression on his face. The age spots had begun to show on his shiny forehead. This brother of hers was a grown man. Why in God's name couldn't she treat him like one? Why did she always see instead the face of her responsibility, the sixteen-year-old boy who turned to look at her after the gun went off?

How could she possibly tell that boy the truth? We're through, Oliver. We can't go on like this, trying to march along in step with one another when we are shackled together by this newspaper, by our father's dream, by some freak accident that happened forty years ago.

"What is it?" he asked impatiently.

"Nothing," she said. "We can talk about it later."

Once he had gone out, she folded her hands on her desk and rested her head on the pillow of them. It's not telling the truth that's making you crazy, she whispered to herself. But where do I find the courage to do it? This time reminded her of those days with Jack when she knew she couldn't bear the sight of him one more day and yet the thought of throwing him out made her feel so desolate. And look what happened to Molly because you didn't have the courage to make that decision, said her mother's voice.

"Shut up," she screamed, so loudly that her secretary poked her head in the door.

"Did you want something, Mrs. Taylor?"

"No. I'm going out for the rest of the afternoon."

Molly had spent the month making collages, cutting up the photographs she found in the green garbage bag. She sat on the floor of her grandmother's boudoir day after day, surrounded by glue and paper and scissors and the twisted wreckage of the faces she had cut apart. She used an eye here, a chin there, constantly shifting and turning the face pieces until the shapes satisfied her. Collage had always served as a searching method for her, a way of taking notes, seeing the picture before she moved to the canvas. Sometimes she connected the scraps of paper with a drawing or a quick sketch in pastel. When she was finished with them, she taped the collages up around the walls of the painting porch. She had already done twenty or thirty, but she still was not ready to move onto the canvas. The fragmented faces stared down at her whenever she walked in to hang up another one, but they didn't seem unfriendly. They seemed to be waiting.

"I can't stop," she told Rudy on one of his visits. "It's another way of figuring out what I'm trying to say. I'm getting closer."

"I believe you," he said. "But my mother would die if she saw you doing this. You know how she treasures those photo albums of hers."

"I remember. But I already checked with my mother. She never wants to see any of these pictures again."

"I hope she doesn't regret it someday," Rudy said. He couldn't imagine anyone wanting to throw away the whole record of their lives.

Molly pointed to a pile of scrapbooks in the corner. "I found those in my grandfather's desk downstairs. I'm not going to cut them up, but there are some wonderful early pictures of my grandmother that I want to use."

Rudy leafed through them while she went back to her work on the floor of the adjoining room. The stiff faces stared out at him from their posed arrangements. He didn't recognize anyone except the occasional picture of Mrs. Webster as a child.

"Is the uncle here?" he called out to Molly.

"Yes," she said, coming back to join him. "I'll show you." She flipped backwards through the stiff cardboard. "Here. James Franklin. Paris, 1884. That was taken before he came to live with them."

A well-dressed thin man with a mustache struck a pose for the studio photographer.

"He looks harmless enough, doesn't he?" Molly whispered.

Rudy was aware of her breath in his ear and he didn't answer. He wanted them to stay frozen like this, hunched together over the album, lined up side by side for a minute. But she had regained her old energy and never stayed in one place for very long. "Back to work," she said, slipping away from him again.

"Me too." He patted her on the head as he went out of the room. She looked up and smiled.

"I love it when you come, Rudy," she called after him. "You're the only person I see for days on end."

"See you tomorrow," he called back, but he kept on moving away from her down the hall. She was happy to see him. He knew that. But he also knew that the pictures would keep her company when he didn't.

Molly didn't move. She was playing on the floor, and the best art she ever made came out of times like these. She had painted the landscapes to death. This time, she clung to the playfulness, hoping to dance it right onto the canvas.

Charlotte came straight to the farm from the office. She had stayed away from Molly all month and she didn't want to see her today. She had come to pick up her guns.

The day was clear and crisp and the plows had already cleared away the six inches of snow that had fallen the day before. Molly's car looked as if it hadn't been moved in days. Charlotte drove down and parked out of sight on the other side of the barn. She could see Frank's truck, but he didn't seem to be anywhere around.

The door to her father's study was locked, and in frustration, Charlotte kicked the corner with her foot. Nobody ever bothered to lock that door. She crept back around to the kitchen and let herself in. Gliding through the empty rooms like a spirit, she stopped every now and then to listen for noises. The distant hum of a radio drifted down to her from upstairs. Molly was hard at work.

After the accident, her father had put the gun right back in the same glass case where they had always been kept and hung the key behind the first picture. Charlotte had expected him to lock them up in the basement or even sell them. How could they all go on living in the same house with the gun that had shot Oliver? Or with the person who had stolen the gun in the first place?

But that was what she remembered most clearly about the weeks and months that followed the accident. Without speaking about it, they had all picked up and gone on the way pioneers in a snowy canyon pass start walking once their horse has dropped in its shafts. You just keep going. What else is there to do?

The only one who talked about the shooting was Oliver. Those days, he babbled incessantly about the day and the way the gun looked when it swung around toward him and the squirrel. "We never really thought we'd get a squirrel, did we, Char? That was Frank's idea, wasn't it? I bet his mother didn't know how to make squirrel stew. I wouldn't have eaten it anyway."

"Hush, Oliver," she would say. "Let me keep going with the book." She spent an hour every afternoon reading to him or playing checkers in his room.

"They all know it was Frank who pulled the trigger. I've told everyone. Even Louisa must know. That's why she moved away so fast."

"Oliver, please don't talk about it anymore," Charlotte would whisper, close to tears. "Please let me keep reading."

Maybe that's what made poor Oliver so bitter in the end, Charlotte thought now, as she unlocked the gun case. Nobody would talk to him about the shooting. There he was going on and on about it like a maniac and everybody was rearranging his pillows and staring at the ceiling and changing the subject. To be ignored like that could certainly make a person turn in on themselves.

She lifted the twenty-two out of its bracket, closed the case and locked it up again. Footsteps. Charlotte froze. Molly was walking through the dining room, humming a song to herself. She passed the door to the hallway and went on into the kitchen.

Charlotte slipped a box of shells into the pocket of her coat and let herself out the side door. She crossed the road at the far end of the fence and headed up the path toward the tower.

*   *   *

Sometime in the fifties, the water company had bought the tower and the land around it from the town of Northington. Charlotte wondered if people still came up here in the summer to spread their picnic blankets in the clear space at its foot. Once they were done with lunch, did they trudge dutifully up the curving stone staircase to the top to admire the view? Were the children still lifted up to the edge of the wall so that they could see the spire of the Congregational church and the red roof of the corner drugstore and the Ford dealership across the street?

"And that's the Webster farm," the people used to say. "First place around here to grow shade tobacco. In the old days, George Webster had the best herd of Ayrshires in the whole state. Imagine that. Mixing up cows and cigars."

Charlotte could hear them now as she leaned against the wall, her coat collar turned up against the wind. What would they be saying next year when they looked down on this view? "That's the golf course. Used to be the Webster place. George Webster was first selectman of this town for more than thirty years. You never heard of him? Well, times have changed."

That's where they had all rolled down the hill at her birthday picnic, she thought as she stared down at the snow-covered field. Margaret's last day.

From here the house looked like a plaything, a wooden toy that you could just pick up and move away. Out of sight. She loaded the gun, lined the peak of the roof up in her sights, and pressed the trigger with that same steady squeeze her father had admired all those years ago. "Watch Charlotte, boys. She doesn't jerk the trigger. She squeezes it." There was a high whine in the air as the bullet sped away from the barrel of the gun. The house was much too far away, of course. The bullet would lodge itself harmlessly in the upper branches of some pine tree. Or in the heart of an unsuspecting squirrel, the great-grandson of the one they had come up into the woods to shoot all those years ago. She shot again, loaded, shot twice more. The small gold shell cases dropped with a tinkle to the stone floor around her feet.

The motions came back to her surprisingly easily after

all these years. She loved the warm wood of the butt against her cold cheek, the faint smell of oil, the sure line of the track between the two barrels. Now there was something you could trust. If you put that little sighting mark directly between the two barrels and lined it up on your target, the bullet was sure to find its way. Suddenly Frank's truck came into her sight and she pulled the gun away from her cheek. He paused at the entrance to the driveway while a car went past and then steered the truck onto the farm road. He wouldn't get very far, she thought. Nobody bothered to plow out that road anymore. The truck disappeared under the trees and she heard, through the silent woods, the faint spinning of his wheels. There. He was already stuck, the fool.

She gathered up the spent cases and slipped them into her pocket. The light was failing already. Never mind. She had had her fun.

Frank heard the shots down at the calf barn.

"What the hell is that?" he shouted at Angelina, who had come to the back door.

"Some crazy hunter in the woods," she said with a shrug.

"Not hunting season," he muttered. "I think I'll go look."

He saw Charlotte before she knew he was there, and the sight of her swinging down the snowy path with the gun cocked open in her right hand stopped him in his tracks. People in town were talking about her, saying she'd gone around the bend with the sale of the house. Even Sol had mentioned something about it. He stood in the middle of the path without speaking until she lifted her eyes from the snow and saw him waiting there.

"Hello, Frank."

"I heard shooting. From up on the tower." His eyes rested on the gun.

"So you came up to arrest me?" she asked. Her coat hung open, the cloth hem wet with crystallized snow.

"Just came to check. Are you all right?"

"Me? I'm fine. I always did know how to handle a gun, Frank. Remember?" She took two steps closer. "This is *the* gun. Do you remember it?"

He turned away abruptly and started down the path ahead of her.

"Frank. Stop." His steps slowed. After all, she was carrying the gun, and for all he knew, she still had some ammunition with her. "We never talked about what happened that day."

"It's a long time ago," he said without turning around.

"You pulled the trigger, Frank. You remember that?"

"What difference does it make now?" he asked, still facing down the hill.

"It makes a difference to me. I just want to get it straight between us. I stole the gun, but you pulled the trigger."

"I don't remember."

She came up close beside him now and rested her hand ever so lightly on his shoulder. "I'm not going to say anything to anybody else about it," she whispered in his ear. He could smell her perfume. The woman was crazy.

"Yes," he admitted at last. "I pulled the goddamned trigger. It wouldn't have happened if you hadn't tried to snatch the gun away from me."

"Maybe," she said. "And maybe not."

She stepped away, and at last, he looked her full in the face. "What are you going to do with that gun now?" he asked.

She looked down in a daze. "Put it back, I guess." She shoved it toward him. "Will you do it for me? The key's behind the first picture over the sofa. The one of the pink bird."

He took the gun from her and slid it under his arm. They went down the hill single file, the only sound between them the swish of the snow past their boots.

He opened the door of his truck for her, and she struggled up to the high seat.

"I heard the wheels spinning," she said when he swung himself in.

"That was back a little ways," he said. Carefully, he steered the gun in over his knees and between them to the space behind the seat. "It's not stuck now."

Once the truck had been turned around and was headed down the hill, he spoke again. "Angelina and I want to go to Italy on a trip. We were planning to go in the summer, but my cousin's pretty sick, so we're moving it up. How about the middle of February?"

Charlotte glanced over at him. "That's fine with me if you can get somebody to cover around the place."

"I already talked to Rudy about it. He'll keep an eye on things. There's not much to do this time of year anyway."

Molly was standing on the back porch in her coat and boots when they drove up.

"She's been for her walk," Frank said. "She goes down to the river most afternoons."

Molly waved and started down the driveway toward them. "Do you think she's okay, Frank?" Charlotte asked. "You see her more than I do."

Frank shrugged. If you want my opinion, you're all crazy, he thought. "She was kind of sick-acting back before Christmas. But she's okay now. Doesn't eat much."

"How do you know?"

"No garbage," he said with a chuckle as he got out of the truck.

"I saw your car, Mother. What were you doing here?"

"I took a walk up to the tower," Charlotte said. "How are you?"

"Fine. Great, in fact. I hit the canvas today for the first time in weeks."

"Congratulations. You look very healthy. Pink cheeks and all."

"I went for my walk. Hey, Frank, what's the gun for? I thought I heard shooting up in the woods."

Halfway to the back door, he froze, the rifle still dangling from his hand.

"We were hunting squirrels," Charlotte said.

"Hunting squirrels? What did Mother mean by that?" Molly asked Frank when he came back out of the house.

"Guess it was a joke," he muttered.

"She looked strange to me," Molly said. "Her hair was standing up all over her head and her coat was undone."

"I found her up in the woods. She'd got one of your grandfather's rifles and was shooting at things from the tower."

"What do you think I should do about her?" Molly asked David that night on the phone.

"Get her in to a doctor."

"She just went for a checkup last week, she told me."

"Where's the rifle now?"

"Back in the case. Frank gave me the key. He said he didn't think she wanted to use it again."

"He's probably right. But you'd better keep an eye on her."

In January and February, Molly hit the good days. One afternoon she stretched twelve new canvases and painted them various pale colors to establish their grounds. From time to time, she was overcome with a need for order, and after vacuuming the second floor, she would clean up the porch, shifting canvases, soaking brushes, scraping and washing the three palettes thoroughly. By the end of the day, she settled back into the colorful, cluttered order like a hen on her nest. She loved the disarray of this room, the tools and smells of her profession, the lively row of pastels in their box, the white tubes of oil paint that were squeezed in the middle like little old men bending over a stomachache. The rest of the house, with its order and history and, on Clara's cleaning day, a smell of disinfectant, confined her gestures.

When Frank left, she started carrying her own wood upstairs for the porch stove. Rudy never knew that was part of his father's job, so she didn't mention it to him. She found the sight of his face in the house stirred her up and distracted her these days. This often happened to her when the paintings began to grow and take their own shape on the canvas. The innocent passing of cloth against her skin, the lift of an eyebrow, or a sudden burst of laughter could roil her up. "I am not to be trusted," she said to herself one morning as she watched Rudy walking along the hedge to his truck.

Once his parents left on their trip to Italy, Rudy moved into the cottage. Now when the children came down on Sunday to visit him, he made their spaghetti dinner in his mother's battered old pot. Everybody helped, even Lina, who liked to crumble up the hamburger meat and drop it bit by bit into the hot oil while her father stirred. Sometimes Rudy asked Luigi to join them, and the old man sat at the kitchen table chuckling to himself over the chaos.

"For a man who's so persnickety about his tools, you sure are relaxed about the mess in here."

Rudy grinned over the heads of the children. "I can afford to be. It's not my workroom. Boys, you dropped half the green pepper on the floor. Pick it up."

"Tony won't let me cut and it's my turn," Louis said.

"Here's another knife," Rudy said. "You can both chop at the same time. Just keep your fingers out of the way. I never did like fried fingernails in my spaghetti sauce."

"Daddy, don't be yucky," Lina announced in her solemn, matter-of-fact voice, the one that always made him put down what he was doing so that he could lift her up and squeeze her.

One night when he took the three of them home, Rosa was not waiting in the kitchen as usual, and he trailed into the house behind the children, who were calling her name. He admitted to himself that he had counted on seeing that silhouette at the window.

"I'm in here," she called from the living room.

The children stopped at the door. Rudy hung back. From across the room, there came the sound of a record playing.

"Mama's dancing," Tony said in a small, breathless voice.

When he peeked in over their heads, he could see her twirling in the other corner of the dim room. She was concentrating on the beat of the song and did not stop until it was finished. "And two and three and four," she counted out as she turned the final step.

When she looked up, flushed and out of breath, their eyes met. "Rudy, I didn't know you were here," she said.

"We didn't see you in the kitchen."

"I've been practicing my steps."

"What steps?" he asked.

"Folk dancing. I go on Tuesday nights to the high school."

He didn't know what to say. In his mind, she was

539

planted in this house as solidly as a tree. He couldn't adjust easily to the thought of her dancing under the bright lights in their old school auditorium.

"Go on up and get ready for bed, children," she said, and they filed out obediently. "Do you want some coffee?" With her back turned, she was putting the record away in its dust cover.

"Yes, thanks. We had spaghetti for dinner. The children helped cook."

He led the way into the kitchen. He always used to make the coffee in the mornings, but now he settled himself at the table, unsure of his rights. She put the kettle on.

"Your parents got off, then?"

"Yes. I drove them to the airport. Mother was very nervous and Pop didn't say anything at all. They shouldn't have waited this long to travel."

"The teacher wants us to come talk to her about Louis. He's not doing very well at school. She says he's distracted." Their eyes met. "You should take him off by himself one day, Rudy. He misses you terribly and he thinks you pay too much attention to Tony."

He felt that twist in his gut, the old knife of fear that used to turn and cut a little when one of the children woke crying in the night with a fever or a nightmare.

"Yes, I guess I should. I don't have much time," he said quietly.

"Have you finished with the barn?"

"Almost. It'll take a couple more weeks. We found four more rotten floor joists that have to be replaced. Uncle Sol is complaining about the time and the money he's having to put in on it. He's had surveyors crawling all over that land by the river. I guess they're laying out the holes for the golf course."

She put out his old mug and poured him a cup of coffee. Her movements were sure, familiar, and he felt a terrible longing to be with her again, but he didn't dare speak about it. She sat down on the other side of the table and looked at him.

"Molly Taylor is still in the big house?"

He nodded and looked down into the black circle of

his coffee. "I don't see much of her," he said, hating the way his voice sounded. Unsure, guilty.

"How long is she staying?"

"Until the spring, I guess. She's working on her painting. For the last month, she's been sitting on the floor of that big room on the second floor, cutting up photographs. I told her my mother wouldn't approve."

Rosa surveyed him silently.

"I think she's a little crazy," he said. "They all are. The mother too. Pop told me he found her up on the tower shooting one of her father's guns."

The children were calling. "I'll go up to them," Rosa said, and slipped quickly out of her seat.

He didn't mean to talk like that, to betray Molly to Rosa. He still thought about Molly, more than ever now that he had moved into the cottage. He had to admit it was her face that hovered over his in the darkness, but when he tried to push beyond that moment, the picture of them together dissolved. Once she left the farm, went back to her world in New York, he would be nothing to her. Even now he knew her photographs kept her better company than he could. "You have to do all the working out on your own," she told him once. "It's very lonely sometimes. But it's the only way I can be. I can't not paint." And she didn't look lonely anymore. She looked absorbed, even radiant, when she came out of the house for her daily walk to the river. "I'm pregnant with pictures," she cried to him just the other day. "They're pushing their way out of me. I've never felt this way before."

Rosa came back. "The children want you to kiss them good night," she said from the doorway.

He stood up. She didn't move, and he wondered how he would get past her without touching her.

"You look tired," she said.

"I miss you," he said.

She nodded as if she knew already and stepped aside, so that when he went by, the only thing that touched was their hands, which met, squeezed, and let go all in a matter of seconds.

*   *   *

Elizabeth Winthrop

When Molly first moved onto the canvas, she started with a portrait of her grandmother based on the photograph that was pasted into the front of her journals.

"In the beginning," Lydia had written in the journals, "Uncle James was the sun in the middle of my dark, somber, motherless world."

In Lydia's thirteen-year-old face, Molly saw such a look of hesitancy, of fear, of wanting desperately to please whoever was watching her, that she put the other characters in the painting. The photographer, a Mr. A. L. Bradley, with his body half hidden under the black drape of the stand-up camera, and over to the side, lounging against the wall, with an encouraging smile on his face, Molly painted in Uncle James.

Then Molly filled a sketchbook with the Uncle Jameses she had met in the journals. Uncle James coming home with flowers, Uncle James and Lydia lunching at the Claremont, Uncle James and Lydia at the fortune-teller's, Uncle James holding the white rabbit, Uncle James and Lydia taking a ride on the carousel. In that sketch, he was standing next to the girl's horse with his arm draped loosely around her waist.

She stared at that picture for a long time and then scrabbled through the garbage bag, looking for a certain photograph, one of the few she hadn't used in a collage. She was standing with her father after the final softball game of the season. Her cap sat cockeyed on his head and his arm was tucked easily around her waist. She was looking up and laughing at him while she leaned her whole weight against his.

He had made it to that game on time. She couldn't remember whether their team won or lost, but that was a day in the middle of all those other, uncertain days that they were happy together in the old way. His breath didn't smell of bourbon, and in the mirror of his eyes she could see herself growing and she could see that he was proud of her.

"Grandmother, a daddy like this one lets you love yourself better," she said to the other picture. "Maybe in the beginning, that's what Uncle James did for you."

Later, when she thought back on those weeks, Molly would remember the feeling of urgency, of some force

542

larger than herself pushing her toward something she didn't want to see, much less paint. Two sides of herself were at war. She could not take the time to eat or sleep, she could not be away from the work for too long for fear she would lose her way, and yet, each time the way was made clear she turned aside from it. It wasn't until months later, when the paintings at last hung side by side on the gallery walls, that she could see how tough and stubborn she had proved to be, how long she had held out against the truth.

So first she turned back to her grandmother and coaxed her slowly out of her shell. Lydia's eyes became less wistful, more direct, more suspicious. "You don't have to watch out for him all the time," Molly said. "The power is moving into your hands, Grandmother. Yours and mine. Next week, we'll let you get angry. And you can stay that way for as long as you want."

That was the week when the brush found a life of its own. Molly painted all over the canvas at once, and the strokes became freer, farther and farther away from the tight, balanced look of the earlier portraits. That last painting took days to finish, and she worked with a sandwich in one hand, stopping only for sleep, which she took in snatches when her legs gave way. She kept only one appointment. Every afternoon at four, she called her mother.

"What's on the easel, today?" her mother would ask.

"Same thing. Grandmother."

"Can I come see?"

"No," Molly cried, panicky. "Not yet. How are you?"

"The same as ever. You don't have to keep calling, Molly. I'm really all right."

"I believe you," Molly said, but she didn't. Her mother's voice had a dull, dazed tone to it. She wondered if Charlotte was taking drugs.

From this distance, propped up on the edge of the bed, she could see a way of fixing the light in the right-hand corner of the picture. "I'll talk to you again tomorrow," she said, and put the phone down, distracted again.

She finished the painting late one night and went to sleep for almost twelve hours. When she woke at two in the afternoon, she sat up in bed and called Andrea.

"I thought you'd died and gone to heaven," Andrea said. "What's up?"

"I'm getting somewhere. I finished a painting last night that you'll be happy with. At least I am."

"So, tell me about it."

"Well, I'm looking at it right now. I've moved into my grandmother's bedroom next door to the painting porch. The painting itself shows Grandmother standing in front of an easel on that porch. You're looking over her right shoulder at the canvas. She's working on a portrait of her uncle. You see the side of her face and the brushes gathered in one hand. But the uncle's the part I'm happiest with. At first glance, he seems to be just a handsome man. Blond hair, a dark mustache. But if you look closer, you'll see how she really feels about him. This is not a man to be trusted, says the painter. She might as well have stamped 'Danger, Keep Away' all over his face."

"Do I dare ask the history behind this painting?" Andrea said.

"I'll tell you sometime. When I get back to New York. Right now I'm going to take myself out for lunch and a movie before I start in again. I don't have much time left here. The ladies from the church are going through the rest of the furniture in early April. Then they put it all out on the lawn and have a big sale."

"How grisly," Andrea said.

"I agree. But I'm not thinking about that now. I've already got an idea for my next painting."

"What's that?"

"You know I don't work that way, Andrea," Molly said. "If I told you all about it, then I wouldn't have to bother painting it."

"All right. I miss you."

"I miss you and New York and galleries and garbage in the streets. Everything's too clean around here. I bet the snow is piled up on the curbs in great gray hillocks."

"That's right."

"Remember that line, as pure as the driven snow? You look out the window at Grandmother's lawn and that's what you think of."

*   *   *

In early March, the world began to show signs of spring. The fuzziness of new baby leaves covered the trees down by the river. One day the thermometer hit forty-five, and by three in the afternoon the snow was draining down the driveway in tiny streams that meandered back and forth, dragging the sand with them.

"Spring," Rudy said when he saw her standing at the edge of the lawn, sniffing the air.

"I know," she said. "I'm not ready for it."

"Why?"

"It means the end of things here. And my work isn't done. As long as the cold freezes me into the house, I'm like a bear hibernating in a cave. Nowhere to go, so the outside world doesn't distract me too much. Spring is distracting."

He smiled at her. "You sound like a grumpy old bear. What happened to all those paintings pushing their way out?"

She turned her head away. "Don't tease me, Rudy. Not today."

"All right," he said. "I'll get the garbage instead." He stomped up the porch steps and went into the kitchen. By the time she got inside, he had disappeared down into the cellar.

All the energy of the previous weeks seemed to have slipped away, and she could not figure out what had gone wrong. She had begun to work on the canvas with the images in the collages, and she had let herself go with the fragmentation of them, the shifting shapes of her family's features. When the first paintings were done, she was pleased with the abstract patterns she had made, but she also saw a cold, distant quality in them that upset her. They were too intellectual. They reminded her of the Danbury landscapes. After all this time, all this waiting, all this work, why was she losing her way again? What did she have to show for the seven months? Two good paintings and a lot of jumbled images.

One evening, she stormed her way down to the river in her grandmother's mud boots, swearing all the while at the melting snow. Rudy stopped her on the way back up. "How about dinner?" he said. "I make a mean omelette."

She hesitated. "I'm not very good company these days."

"Never mind," he said, taking her by the hand. "You can sit at Mother's kitchen table and kick your feet against the legs of the chair and nobody will braid your hair unless you want it."

She let him lead her inside and set her like a rag doll in the chair. He put a chunk of cheese and the grater in front of her. "You can help. That way everything will come out at the right time. And you don't have to talk unless you want to."

She jimmied off the boots and wiggled her sock-covered toes. Grating the cheese absorbed her. It reminded her of the palette preparation and the canvas stretching, all those mechanical jobs connected with painting that she loved. She felt the knots in her back begin to loosen, and she hunched over her work, pleased with the smells in the close, warm room, the companionable silence between them.

Rudy seemed to know his way around a kitchen. He chopped and stirred and slammed pots around with abandon. When he saw she really did not mean to talk, he turned on the radio and hummed along to a country and western tune.

"I hate that kind of music," Molly said matter-of-factly.

"So did I at first. But listen to the words," Rudy said. "Very basic emotions all laid out in simple words."

"She took the gold mine and gave me the shaft?" Molly repeated incredulously.

"You're actually smiling, Miss Taylor. I thought that was against the law," he said as he took the plate of cheese from her. "Good God, this is enough cheese for six omelettes."

She shrugged. "I get involved in my work."

"So I've noticed."

They ate slowly. Molly savored every bite. "This is good, Rudy. Particularly since I've been surviving on tunafish and yogurt and cereal. I eat out almost every night in New York. That's one thing I'm looking forward to."

"That sounds grim," Rudy said.

"Grim?" Molly asked. "It's fabulous. I can eat in a Chinese restaurant on one corner of my block and French on the other corner. And about three delicatessens in between. It takes so damn much time to buy food, put it away, take it out again, unwrap it, chop it up, and cook it. I'd rather go to a good movie. Or paint. Or go dancing."

He looked at her with amusement. "I hate eating in restaurants. I get homesick the moment I walk in."

"I used to like to cook. Daddy and I made dinner together at night. He was a terrible cook, but we had fun. Like now." She reached across the table and he closed his hand around hers.

"Molly, don't you ever get angry at him?"

"Why?"

"Because he never called and he never wrote and he never came back for you."

She tried to pull her hand away, but he held on tight. "Don't run away," he said. "Answer me."

"Why is everybody else so determined to ruin Daddy for me? My mother, my brother, my grandmother, even Agnes. And now you." She looked at him with a flash of intense hatred. "Let me go," she shouted. "The man is dead. Can't you all just let him be?"

"No," Rudy said, blocking her bolt for the door. "You've got to face up to him. You won't be able to stay in one place or love anybody until you do that. You won't be able to do anything, Molly."

"And what do you know about that?" she spat. "Clean up your own backyard, Mr. Delbianco, before you start in with the neighbors."

They stood inches away from each other. When she moved to the right, he moved to the left to cover her break.

"That was cruel," he said thoughtfully.

"I meant it to be," she replied. "Now, let me go, please."

He stood aside. She gathered up her jacket and hat from the back of the chair.

"I used to love the fact that you could always run away," he said quietly.

She struggled into her jacket without looking at him. "But you obviously don't anymore," she said.

"No. I don't."

She managed to walk out of the house without slapping

him or even slamming the door behind her. It took every
bit of control she could muster.

In the middle of the night, she gave up all pretense of
sleeping and lit the stove in the painting porch. She
gathered up the collages that had been positioned on the
chair rail and leaned their chopped-up faces against the
wall.

"I'll show Rudy Delbianco," she muttered as she adjusted the large sketch pad on the easel. With a thick
piece of charcoal, she began to draw her father from
memory.

He was smiling. He was reaching for her. His delight at
the sight of her was frozen on his face. It never changed.
That was the father she started with, the one she drew
and redrew for days, racing against time, against the
spring weather, against the closing of the house.

The sketches had no life, but she would not let herself
throw them away. She tacked them haphazardly on the
wall, so that now his blank eyes were the ones that stared
down at her. One day she started at the other end of the
picture and drew herself, the little girl racing for his
outstretched arms. Then slowly she let herself change
from one sketch to the next. The little girl's face grew
sullen, angry, and then turned away completely. What
would the daddy do now? How could he keep his arms
up like that when nobody was racing to jump into them?

"This daddy would bolt," Molly whispered to herself.
And she drew him turning to run, a look of alarm and
fear on his face.

She worked late into the night, painting by the garish,
flat light of two standing lamps. For once, she didn't care
about the source of light either in the paintings or in the
porch. She was rushing to stake her claim on the material
first, to nail it down before it blew away from her again.

She would paint it, she would see it, she would feel the
sadness of what she saw and then she would grieve. Or
maybe they would be all mixed up together.

Down on the tin-topped kitchen table, she stretched an
enormous horizontal canvas. Rudy found her there when
he came in early one morning to get the garbage.

"Hello," he said. His voice was wary. "You're up early."

"Or up late," she said. "I don't think I've been to bed."

He dragged the garbage can out from under the table and lifted the plastic liner. "Are you eating anything at all?" he asked as he held the bag up for her to see. "You're going to put me out of a job if you keep on this way."

She grinned. "I went out to a diner last night and ate two great big greasy rare hamburgers and a mountain of french fries. I'm ashamed of myself."

"And well you should be. Back in business, I see." He nodded at the canvas balanced precariously on the table. "This one looks big enough to decorate the side of a building."

"It will be more of a mural than a painting."

"How will you ever get it back to New York?" he asked.

"Take the stretchers off and roll it up."

"Doesn't the paint crack?"

"Not if you treat it properly. It's just like your business, Rudy. You've got to use the right tools in the right way. Could you hang on to that corner for me?" He held it while she tucked the canvas over on the opposite side and stapled it. "Thanks. I just have to do the straight sides now."

"How will you get this monster back upstairs?"

"Surprisingly enough, I thought of that," she said. "The only tight spot is the top of the front stairs, but I measured. It should just make it around that corner."

"Call me if you need any help. I'll be downstairs for about half an hour."

"Thanks, I will."

She hadn't apologized for the things she'd said before, but then neither had he.

She finished it in the middle of the night. She lifted the brush from the canvas for the last time and turned her back on the painting. With her right hand still full of brushes, she went to wash up in the sink in her grandmother's bathroom. This ceremony always pleased her.

She smeared a large blob of hand cleaner into her left hand and set about cleaning her skin and the brushes at the same time. The white goop was soothing, and she took delight in the slow, sensual spread of the cool cream across her palms, the way it slipped in under her fingernails.

She would not look at the painting again tonight. It would wait there for her fresh eye in the morning. But once the brushes had been lined up on the edge of the sink and her hands dried, she knew she couldn't sleep. She was filled with a sudden rush of energy and excitement, a need to share the triumph of the moment. If she had finished this painting in her New York apartment, she would have called up a friend and gone dancing.

Well, she had a friend here too. She would go pound on Rudy's door, wake him up, make him dance with her right in the middle of the driveway by the light of the new April moon.

Down at the cottage, the kitchen door was locked or else she would have slipped right in and pounced on him. Through the little panes of glass in the top of the door, she saw his long hair standing on end, the look of alarm that crossed his face when he saw her. Of course. He thought something was wrong.

"What is it, Molly?" he said as soon as he had wrestled the door open. "Are you all right?"

"Nothing's wrong. I finished a painting and I think it's good and I want you to celebrate with me."

He was dressed in a pair of work pants, which he must have pulled on hurriedly when he heard the knocking. He rubbed both hands through his hair and then across his bare chest in an effort to wake up.

"A celebration. Absolutely. How do we start?" And she was touched by his groggy enthusiasm.

"Turn on the radio. Our favorite country and western station. I feel like dancing."

He looked around the kitchen. "Not much room in here."

She turned him about and pushed him toward the bedroom. His skin felt warm and smooth, and she let go of him reluctantly. "Get a shirt on, Rudy. We're going to dance in the middle of the driveway. By the light of the moon."

He obeyed and returned wiping his face with a towel. "I always have a hard time waking up," he said sheepishly.

"Is this the right station?" she asked, cocking her thumb toward the radio.

"It sounds right," he said. "But I've never tried to find it at two in the morning before. I don't even know if they're broadcasting now."

She put her finger up to her lips so they could listen. "That's it. One of their favorite songs."

"I like the beat. I don't think I'll listen to the words." She turned the volume up so high that he clasped his hands to his ears, mouthing complaints at her.

"What did you say?" she shouted.

"What about the neighbors?" he shouted back.

"We don't have any. Come on." She took his hand, and side by side they squeezed through the narrow front door and tumbled down the small soggy lawn to the driveway.

He was a good dancer, although in honor of the occasion, he hammed things up, slapping his knee and bowing from the waist. She caught the drift and promenaded with her partner until they were both gasping and doubled over with laughter. The next song was slow, and he pulled her into his arms without hesitating. "Willie Nelson," he whispered in her ear, and as they swayed back and forth to the easy rhythm, he sang the song to her in his low baritone voice. "Maybe I didn't hold you all those lonely, lonely times. I guess I never told you I'm so happy that you're mine." At that, he put her away from him. "But you're not mine, are you, Molly Taylor? Never was and never will be."

"Nobody belongs to anybody else, Rudy," she said. "But let's pretend I am. Just for tonight."

She walked back into his arms, and he picked her up and twirled her in a long, slow circle.

Inside, he danced her past the radio, turned it off, and took her to his parents' room. "You smell of turpentine," he whispered as his mouth came down to hers and his hands began to make their slow, gentle way across her body. He undressed her carefully, the way he had before, but this time she felt his wanting her and she rose up from the pillow and pulled his body tight against hers.

He tickled and teased her with his fingers and his tongue, everything slow and drawn out the way she loved it. When they came the first time, she didn't know where she ended and Rudy began and she didn't care.

They made love all night, their bodies rolling over and over in a bed that seemed to have no edges.

He woke up first and lay stiffly, watching her sleep. Waking up next to a new lover in bed seemed to him more intimate than the sex itself. Besides Rosa, she was the only woman he had slept with, and he had been stunned and a little appalled by her energy, the noise and engagement of her passion. Even in sleep, her pose was full and extravagant, her arms spread wide, her legs tangled around his, half her hair across her face, the other half fanned across the pillow. She was still his for now, for this moment. Once she woke and they spoke, he knew she would begin her retreat, her dash up the driveway, back to the safety of the old house, of her crazy paintings. He looked at her face again. She was watching him.

"What are you thinking?" she asked, her voice hoarse.

He blushed. "I was wondering how long you would stay."

"All day if you want," she said, stretching luxuriously.

"I doubt you'd last," he said.

"Well, at least until lunch," she said, and pulled him back down against her.

He brought her coffee and toast at noon. She was sitting up in the bed, winding her hair up into a knot.

"I love it when you do that," he said as he slid the tray onto the bed and got back in beside her. "I keep watching to see whether it will come undone."

"It usually does when it's clean.

"What a strange place to be, here in Frank and Angelina's bed," she said. "Do you remember kissing me down by the swimming hole?"

"Yes."

"Look how many years it took us to finish what we started," she said with a smile.

He didn't respond.

"What's wrong, Rudy?"

"I'm going back to Rosa," he said. "I told her two days ago."

"When?"

"When my parents get home."

"So you're feeling guilty? About us?"

"Not exactly guilty. I feel as if I've fulfilled another of Rosa's silent prophecies. You're only mine here on the farm, Molly. We both know that. I can already feel you slipping away from me."

She pulled his head down against her shoulder and he rested there.

Later, when she went back up the driveway to the big house, she thought about what he had said. Maybe people like her, children of alcoholics, of fathers who were there one day and gone the next, were doomed to a lifetime on the road, slipping out of situations under cover of night before they could get too connected, too happy. She believed now that happiness was even more terrifying for her than loneliness because the happiness would end one day and she would have to face the edge of the black pit, the moment of jumping, knowing that, once again, there would be nobody to catch her. At least when you were lonely, the jumping part was all over.

He came up that evening to look at the painting. She stood in the corner, trying not to watch his face but peeking all the while.

The canvas was filled with figures running. Each one was pursued by a long trail of repeating mirror images of himself and each image varied slightly from the one before.

"You mean all four of them to be trailed by their own history, don't you? Bits and pieces of their past."

"That's right. I'm glad you see it."

"I like the way you've done it," he said. "Not just the people but the pattern of their running. It's as if you've actually painted echos."

"Can you tell how I feel about them, Rudy?"

"Terribly sad," he said quietly. He glanced at her. "Did I pass the test?"

"No, I did," she said, slipping her arms around his

waist and burying her head in his back. "Want to name it?" she asked.

" 'On the Lam,' " he said.

"Done."

"That's an odd name," Andrea said months later when they were going over the price list for Molly's show.

"A friend chose it for me."

"Want to tell me more?" Andrea asked.

"No," Molly said and changed the subject.

38

Late in April, the women from the church moved into the house, swarming over it like ants, calling to one another as they maneuvered the furniture and boxes of books and contents of trunks down the narrow attic steps and out onto the screen porch. They poked about the rooms pretending to be working, but Molly knew they were just snooping while they had the chance. She could hear their conversations as they made their way down the hall toward her.

"I thought it would be much fancier, don't you know? The beds are so simple, and you can get those white curtains mail order from Sears. My sister has them in her little girl's room."

"No telling how people are going to live," said another voice. The speaker sounded disappointed, as if the Websters had somehow let her down with their white iron beds and their simple curtains.

Molly turned up her radio to warn them away. She didn't mind them in the house, but she couldn't bear strangers looking at her paintings right now. They were too new and her feelings about them too raw. She was working on smaller variations of the big mural, playing with the colors and the shadows.

After their night together, she and Rudy gave each other room. "Are we avoiding each other?" she asked him one afternoon when his truck turned in the driveway.

"I think we're getting ready to say goodbye," he said, leaning his head out the window. She laced the fingers of her right hand back and forth through his and squeezed tight.

"I wish we could stay like this," she said, lifting their braided hands.

"It would never work, Molly. But we could prick fingers and mix blood," he whispered. Their heads were so close together that the breath from his voice blew across her eyes. Behind them, another car turned in the driveway and they pulled apart. "Your mother," Rudy said, glancing in his rearview mirror. He shoved the gear shift into first. "Come see me later. We've finished the barn. It's my turn to show you something."

"They're doing a good job?" Charlotte said as Molly walked her through the first floor.

"I suppose so. I haven't been keeping too close an eye on them. But the attic is almost totally cleared out. They've piled everything on the sun porch. The auction takes place next weekend, doesn't it?"

"Yes," Charlotte said. They stood in the middle of the living room. "The furniture trucks will be coming the second week of May, one for Campbell's in Williamstown and the other will go to New York to George's. If there's anything you want to send in that truck, just mark it."

"The bedroom furniture, I suppose," Molly said. "And some of my paintings if I could get them crated in time. I'd rather not take some of the big ones off the stretchers."

"How has your work been going?" Charlotte asked wearily. She propped herself up on the arm of the sofa.

"Very well. I'm almost ready to show it to you, Mother. This weekend when you come over for the sale, I'll set everything up for you to see."

"I'd like that," Charlotte said. "I promise not to say a word. As I recall, you hate any criticism when the paintings are new."

"Uncle Oliver called me this morning," Molly said. "He says you've begun to talk about selling the paper. Is it true?"

"Not exactly. I asked him to let me take over the editorial end of things. I'm sick to death of the publisher's job. I only took it all those years ago because of a promise I made to my father on his deathbed. Oliver turns sixty this year. I suggested he retire and help Susan out with her antique business. Let me have a crack at editorial for the next six or seven years, which is about all the energy I've got left in me."

"Could he take over as publisher?"

"No. He's never shown any interest in the business end of things. In any case, he's very angry with me right now. If we can't settle this thing amicably between us, I'm going to put the paper up for sale and walk away from it. I doubt poor Oliver would last a year with another publisher. His little sister has been a pretty lenient boss."

"Still wrangling," Molly said quietly.

"That's right," her mother said, standing up and stretching. "Like two children over blocks. My life has been one long atonement for one thing or another. At the age of fifty-seven, I've finally decided to give up the sackcloth and ashes."

"Tough decisions, Mother."

Charlotte gazed at her. "Do you think so? I feel as if I've stepped out into the clear air for the first time in my life."

"She looks different," Molly said to Rudy later on.

"How?"

"Peaceful. And far away. I felt as if she were speaking to me from a great distance and that she didn't really hear what I had to say. It was eerie."

He took her hand. "Get your mind off your mother and onto my barn for the moment. This is the crowning achievement of my career." At the sight of her solemn expression, he put a gentle elbow in her ribs. "I'm kidding. But Luigi and I are proud of it."

She watched his face as he talked about the joists they'd been forced to replace, the two-by-sixes they'd put in running in this direction, the new beam under the old office.

"It looks as if it will last another hundred years," she said.

"It better. After all this work. Luigi said he's really through now. I've gone and worn him out."

"Do you believe him?" she asked.

"No. I put in a bid for a big new house on the other side of the mountain. If I win it, I'll bring Luigi right back out of retirement. This man has enough money to do everything right. He wants handmade cabinets, solid-oak doors. It's a carpenter's dream. I just need to give Luigi a little sniff at the plans and he'll come running."

"I have a job for you, Rudy. I need crates made for my bigger paintings. There's room in the truck that takes my Uncle George's share of the furniture back to New York. I'll roll up the smaller ones, but I'd rather ship the big mural and some of the portraits as they are. Do you think you have the time?"

"When is the truck coming?"

"Second week of May."

"I'll manage it."

They walked down to the river, swinging hands.

"Next year at this time, the fields will be all green. Little flags, fat men in golf carts," she said. "I don't ever want to see it like that."

"I don't blame you. The kids and I will have to sneak around the long way to the swimming hole."

The sun had just set when they came back up the rutted farm road and the land looked even, dusky in the afterlight. "If I painted this, nobody would believe it," she said to him.

"You have to let some things just be," he said. "You can't hang on to them with a canvas or a camera. You just carry them inside of you."

They made love again that night. His hands on her were tender and ministering, and when they came at last, when their bodies caught the same rhythm and rolled down that long easy hill together, she began to cry without making a sound. Afterward, she curled against his warm taut back.

Two days later, when Frank and Angelina came home, he moved back in with Rosa.

Hours before the time set for the auction, cars began to file into the driveway. The policeman stationed at the kitchen door asked to use the phone. Molly could hear his insistent voice over the noise of the water running into the sink.

"I don't care about that, Steve. We need some people here to show them where to park the cars. There's only two of us and this young lady here, and the driveway's already filled."

"I'll go do it," Molly said to him as he came out of the

pantry, looking exasperated. "They'll have to go into the back field, won't they?"

"That's right. And when that fills up, send them across the street up into the old pasture."

"They could get stuck," Molly said. "That road hasn't been used since my grandfather's cows grazed up there."

The policeman shrugged. "That's their problem. Nobody told me the whole county was going to turn out for this thing. Anyway, thanks for your help. I appreciate it."

Directing traffic had always been one of Molly's secret fantasies. She stood out in the middle of Route 10, delighted with the power that a simple gesture of her hand seemed to wield. Into the parking lot she waved at her mother, the checkout lady from the grocery store, the librarian, and countless others who seemed to recognize her. They drew to a stop, listened to her directions, smiled their thanks, and turned their attention back to their driving. Often she heard the remarks they made about her as the car crept away. "That must be Mrs. Webster's granddaughter," they said to each other. "Charlotte's girl. Where'd that red hair come from?"

As she watched the cars pouring in, Molly realized that this amounted to a celebration, the last big party at the Webster house. It followed in the tradition of the picnic after the first tobacco harvest, the public inspection of the barn, her grandfather's wake, the reception after her grandmother's funeral. The town of Northington had a claim on the Websters, and the citizens were coming over to say goodbye. The ladies from the church set up lunch on long wooden tables under the copper beech tree. Two dollars admission bought you some good homemade food and a chance to pay your respects.

She didn't realize that she had been waiting for Rudy all morning until she saw his black truck top the small rise and coast down toward her. Could he tell it was her? she wondered as he drew closer. There were two dark spots behind the windshield. Rosa was with him. Of course.

He rolled the window down slowly. "Good morning," he said. "Looks like the whole town has turned out. Except the police force."

Elizabeth Winthrop

"I'm filling in," she said. Every word they spoke to each other seemed too intimate, and she forced herself to look beyond him to his wife. "Good morning, Rosa," she said.

"Hello," said the soft voice, over the head of the little girl who sat between them.

"I've got the boys in the back," Rudy said, as if she had asked for them. "Where should I park?"

"There should be some more places in the far corner. It's filling up fast."

"Let's go, Daddy," said the little girl.

"Your Uncle Sol came in a while ago," Molly said. "I think he's headed down to look at the barn."

He gave her a long thoughtful look and pulled the wheel over to make the turn.

Suddenly, she was tired of standing there, and without any warning, she walked off the job and wandered down to the lawn to buy herself some lunch.

The bidding started promptly at noon, and by four, everything was gone. Molly stayed as long as she could stand it, but when the costumes began to come out of the attic trunk, she fled upstairs to the painting porch. The people had grown more raucous, and all around she could hear them wondering out loud about her grandmother, her family, her history. It was like watching crows pick over a squashed animal in the road.

Toward the end of the afternoon, when the crowds had thinned, she looked out to see Rudy walking down to the barn with his uncle, a short, roundish man with a bald head. She watched as the two men came out the far side of the barn, and Rudy led his uncle into the field to look at the angle of the roof. Rudy pointed and talked and tilted his head, and the shorter man nodded and looked and listened. Then they walked back across to look at it from another angle, a turn in the road that hid them from her sight.

Down below, the women were folding the tables and gathering up the garbage in green plastic bags. Her mother came out to help. Across the hedge in the field, the cars were pulling out slowly, many with pieces of former Webster furniture tied to their roofs.

560

"Not with a bang but a whimper," she muttered, and went back to work. She had spent the day sorting through things, choosing the paintings she wanted Rudy to build crates for and taking some of the smaller pictures off their stretchers.

A little later, she heard her mother's voice calling to her from downstairs.

"Come on up," Molly shouted. She had promised to show her the paintings, and this would be as good a time as any. The tall canvas of her grandmother painting was set up on the main easel, and the long mural, which ran the entire length of the porch, was propped up against the wall under the molding. "Wait," she cried as her mother's footsteps came closer. "Don't come in yet." On the left-hand wall, she set up all the pictures she had done of Lydia, starting with the first one at the photographer's. "All right," she called. "Now."

If Charlotte had known that so many faces would be waiting for her in this room, she might never have come at all. The day had been filled with faces from the past, people from the town of Northington come to pay their respects, and in the last years of living alone, she had grown used to empty rooms, to silences, to the sound of that same old hymn playing over and over in her head.

She walked around the room twice very slowly. When she got to the mural, she hunkered down with her bottom close to her shoes and followed the characters across the canvas. She didn't notice the painting on the easel until her second turn around the porch. Then she backed off from it, pulled a chair from the next room, and sat just inside the door.

"This is where I sat while she painted," she murmured. " 'I-I-I want to go to the i-i-island. What do you think, Charlotte? Have I got the perspective right? Oh, well, never mind, darling, Georgie will tell me.' " She glanced over in the corner. "Why so many of your grandmother, Molly? You seem obsessed with her."

"They grew from that first picture," Molly explained. "The one of her at the photographer's studio."

"Who's that slimy character in the corner?"

"Her father's younger brother. Uncle James. Did she ever mention him to you?"

"Perhaps." Charlotte pulled a cigarette out of her pocket and lit it. "I remember her father, of course. He used to come up from New York for Christmas. He died when I was about seven. But I don't think she ever mentioned an Uncle James."

"That's him again," Molly said, pointing to the canvas on the easel. Charlotte got out of her chair and stepped closer to inspect. "Handsome," she said. "But untrustworthy."

"Good," Molly crowed with a clap of her hands. "That's what I wanted you to see."

Her mother picked up one of the sketch pads and began to leaf through it.

"That's filled with Daddy, Mother."

"I see," she said. Neither woman said anything for a moment as Charlotte kept going. "The same thing over and over again."

"They get looser," Molly said defensively. "I was trying to knock him off the pedestal. It's hard to draw a statue from memory. Those led eventually to the big mural."

Her mother got to the end of the sketch pad at last and put it down. "Handsome," she said slowly, "but untrustworthy."

Their eyes met. "Why did you send him away, Mother? Was it the drinking?"

"That and all the rest."

The room had darkened as the sun set. Molly reached over and flipped on the standing lamp. Charlotte dropped her cigarette on the floor and crushed it with her shoe.

"Better be sure it's out with all the turpentine in here," Molly warned.

Charlotte leaned over, picked up the butt, and dropped it in the pocket of her sweater.

"I didn't mean you had to do that, Mother."

"I guess I'll be on my way. It's been a long day."

"What did you mean by 'all the rest'?" Molly asked. "What else did Daddy do that was so bad?"

"You tell me, Molly."

"I don't know what you're talking about."

"You do remember the time your grandmother called

me home from a business trip. The time she moved you in here."

"Yes." Molly looked down at her hands. "Daddy was really drunk that afternoon. He thought I was seven years old again. I didn't want to crawl in his lap and play the old tickling game. I was fourteen, Mother."

"But what about all the other times?"

"What other times?" Molly asked, her heart beating.

"The other times he touched you, played with you," Charlotte said.

"Mother, are you crazy? Are you trying to say that Daddy molested me? He never touched me like that. Never."

"But you told your grandmother—"

"I told her what I just told you now. He wanted to play with me. Remember that game where I sat on his lap and he counted to three—"

"I remember," Charlotte cried, putting her hands up. "That was all? What about the other times you were alone in the house together? All those afternoons."

Molly lowered herself onto the stool. "He could be scary," she admitted in a low voice. "When he was drunk. And nobody ever talked about his drinking. Why didn't you tell me and David about it? Why didn't you make Daddy stop?"

Charlotte didn't answer. She was staring out the window.

"Sometimes, when I came home, he was crying. Once I brought home a friend and he was passed out on the sofa. Another time, he said 'fucking' to me. I'd only heard that word from a friend of David's who was trying to be cool. Daddy felt terrible about it afterward. He wasn't mean to me when he drank too much. He was sweet and kind of pathetic. But he never ever did what you're talking about. He never touched me that way."

Charlotte took another turn around the room without saying anything.

"Why did you ever think that about him?"

"It was your grandmother, Molly. That's what she told me."

"Mother—"

"No, don't say anything more. Go on with your painting. I've got to go home. I've got to get away from this house."

Molly sat on the porch for a long time after she heard her mother's car take the turn out of the driveway with a squeal. She's driving too fast, she thought, but there's nothing I can do about it.

The whole thing made perfect sense now. That's why Agnes had passed the journals on to her. That's why her grandmother had hugged her so fiercely that afternoon. She thought they were both victims, sisters of a sort. Because Lydia was powerless to banish her Uncle James, she had banished Jack Taylor instead. "So you were the one, Grandmother," Molly said in astonishment. "You were the one who sent Daddy away."

And that's why, all these years, Mother had kept her distance. Better to stay away than make another mistake.

Those three women who watched Molly grow up must have been wondering all the time where she had hidden the unspeakable memories of her father's hands. She wrapped her arms around herself and rocked back and forth in the chair. Nobody to run to tonight. Rudy would be sitting at the head of the family table with Rosa's dark eyes on him.

"Oh, Daddy," she whispered to the black panes of glass. "Why didn't you ever come back for me?" She walked over to the mural and squatted down in front of it the way her mother had done just hours before. "Everybody running away from each other, our pasts spinning out behind us like ribbons in the wind," she said as she passed her hands over the bumps of paint. "Just as I painted it."

Much later, she woke out of a doze in her grandmother's bed and sat up. "In the beginning, I was glad you went away, Daddy. Sometimes you scared me so much." The truth said, she fell asleep again.

39

Charlotte drove all night. One half of her brain was occupied with the mechanics of operating the car, which left the other half free to float. There was so much history that needed revising, so many expressions and gestures that she had misread. She cried easily, the tears making their way down her cheeks and then drying to a salty film when she did not bother to wipe them away. She was crying for all the might-have-beens. Would she and Jack ever have been able to make it if she had agreed to move away from Northington, away from her mother, from her crippled brother? He had asked her that one time after the war. Florida, he said. A newspaper had offered him a job. He had written them in secret because he knew how angry she would be. It was out of the question. By then she was publisher of the paper and her father was dead and she was not brave enough to commit herself to a life with Jack so far away. She was never really married to Jack and he knew it. She had tried to live with one foot in each world, never daring to choose until the choice was rammed down her throat.

"The poor child. This has obviously been going on for years," her mother had said with such conviction. "Foolish of you not to see it, Charlotte. I don't want you to see Frank anymore, Charlotte. A little weakness like this is so easily fixed. Try it again, Charlotte. Form the letters again with your right hand. More slowly. I-I-I-I hate you, Mother."

The phone woke Molly.

"Your mother didn't come in to work this morning." It was Uncle Oliver. "Molly."

565

She cleared her throat before she spoke. "What time is it?"

"Sorry to wake you, but it's nine-thirty." She could hear the disapproval in his voice. It *is* nine-thirty. "She never comes in this late without calling," he added. "There's no answer at the house."

"What do you want me to do?" Molly struggled to a sitting position and pushed her hair off her face.

"I'm awfully worried about her. She's been acting so peculiarly in the last months. The house and now this business about the paper."

"I'll drive over there, Uncle Oliver. She was very tired after the auction yesterday. Maybe she's just pulled the covers over her head for the day."

The car was gone and the house was unlocked. "She's not here," Molly said when she called him back. "The bed's made up. It looks as if she didn't sleep in it last night."

"I'm calling the police," Oliver said.

"I think it's too soon to do something like that," Molly said patiently. "She's a big girl, Uncle Oliver."

"Don't be fresh, Molly."

Molly held the phone away from her ear and took a deep breath. She was beginning to understand the kind of pressure her mother had been under all these years. "I'm not trying to be fresh. I'm just saying that Mother is perfectly capable of taking care of herself. I'll leave her a note and go back to the farm. She may turn up there."

Rudy came by that afternoon with the lumber for the crates. Together, he and Molly carried the largest paintings downstairs to the side porch.

"What about that one of your grandmother painting? It's still up on the easel."

"Leave it for now. There's one more thing I want to do to it. If we don't get around to crating it today, I'll do it myself later. The truck doesn't come till Monday."

"I brought you a hammer," he said, handing it over. "Might as well get some work out of you."

"I do better at cheese grating," she said quietly. They looked at each other. "I miss you."

"Leave it alone, Molly. Please."

"How is it being back?"

"We are terribly careful with each other," he said. "Like people who have been bruised."

She listened to his directions and bent over the hammering, glad to have work to concentrate on right now so she wouldn't get lost in watching him. The phone rang once and she twisted through the back hallway to get it before the person hung up.

"Your mother just called," Uncle Oliver said. "She's fine. Just took the day off."

"How did she sound?"

"Very calm. She'll be in tomorrow."

"Were you worried about her?" Rudy asked when she told him who it was.

"Yes. We had a strange conversation last night, and Mother left here very upset. Apparently Grandmother convinced her that Daddy had molested me. That's why they sent him away."

Rudy put his hammer down. "Molested you? When?"

"Lots of times, I guess. Because of that last afternoon when Grandmother found me in the closet."

"What did happen that day, Molly?"

She sat cross-legged on the porch floor, close to the crate she was working on. "It must have been a Tuesday, because I was supposed to spend the night here as usual. I remember I was going to be in a play the next day and I had forgotten some part of my costume at home. So I took the bus home and I figured I would call Grandmother and ask her to pick me up later. I didn't expect Daddy to be there. He had been away on one of his business trips for three days."

Those days with no David home to warn her, she had to get her own signals from the house. Noises or smells or just the eerie sense that someone was there. But that particular afternoon, she was in a hurry. She didn't bother to listen for long. The silence seemed complete. Just an empty house.

She dropped her books on the kitchen table and headed for the back stairs.

She felt him before she actually saw him and hesitated with her foot on the bottom step. He was standing in the door of the living room. Leaning against the frame. Waiting.

"Hello, Button," he said in that low voice. The glass, already drained at least once, hung down from his limp arm.

"You're back, Daddy," she said brightly, knowing the cheeriness sounded false. "I just came to get my apron for the play tomorrow."

"That's right. It's Tuesday. Molly's night out." He backed into the living room. "Come in and talk to me a minute, Button."

"I'm already late, Daddy. Grandmother will be wondering why I didn't take the bus there."

"Not even a little minute for your daddy?" he asked, and she gave up and followed him into the dark living room. The sofa looked as if he'd been sleeping on it. Newspapers were spread around on the floor. The bottle of bourbon stood on the table. He picked it up and poured the last inch into his glass. When he threw the empty bottle away, the wastepaper basket rocked back and forth. She caught it with her hand so it wouldn't tip over.

"So how was school?"

"Fine." Make him happy, but get this over with. She hated the sloppy look of the room, the smell, the shine in his eyes. Was he going to cry again? Those times were the worst of all.

"I've been thinking about the old days, Button. Remember when we used to draw all the time at the kitchen table?"

"Yes."

"And the tickling game. You loved the tickling game."
I didn't, Daddy. I just wanted you to be happy.

"Come sit on my knee. Let's play it now. Remember, I counted to five. Or was it three?"

"Daddy, I have to go now. Please."

"Oh, come on," he said angrily. "Your grandmother can wait five more minutes."

"Daddy, I don't want to play," she said. "I'm too old for that game."

But he had put down the glass and lumbered to his feet. His hand reached out and found her shoulder, and when she backed suddenly away, his fingers pressed down against her bone, and then, as he felt her slipping from him, he snatched at the blouse. It ripped.

"Daddy, stop," she screamed. "Leave me alone."

"I'm sorry, Button," he cried. "I didn't mean—" She turned then and ran away from him, up the stairs, into her room, into the dark safety of the closet.

"Did he follow you?" Rudy asked.

"Yes. I suppose he could have pushed through all the furniture if he had wanted to. He was a strong man. But Daddy would never have done that. He just sat outside the door for a while and called to me. I could hear him crying— What's wrong?"

Rudy shrugged. "Nothing. I thought I heard a car come in the driveway."

"Are you worried about being here? With me, I mean," she said.

"No," he said. She knew he was lying. Rosa would wonder. "Go on," he urged.

She aimed the hammer at the next nail. "That was it. I stayed in the closet until Grandmother found me."

"It makes sense, doesn't it?" he said thoughtfully. "She would put two and two together because of what she had been through. Because of her uncle."

"Yes. The only trouble was she came up with five. And nobody ever talked directly about it. Are you all right, Molly? Daddy's going away for a while, Molly. Did he do anything to you, Molly?" She stared out across the lawn. "It felt safe here," she said. "He did scare me, Rudy. I felt so responsible for making him happy."

Rudy stood up and started toward her.

"Don't," she warned. "Don't touch me. I have to get used to feeling it alone. We've both made our choices."

Much later, when she went over the whole scene in her mind, she realized that she thought Rudy bolted for the door because of what she'd said. But it wasn't. It was because, when he stood up, he could see everything.

"Rudy," she cried, "where are you going? What is it?"

"The painting porch," his voice came echoing back to her from the dining room. "It's on fire."

If he hadn't been in the house, they might have lost the whole shooting match. And her mother too.

"At first, I didn't see her," Rudy said when it was all over. "All I could think about was your paintings. But she was sitting there in a chair watching it burn. Without moving."

"Was it a cigarette?" Molly asked. "She was so careless with them."

"The turpentine went right around the easel in a clear circle. She must have poured it and then thrown the match. I don't think she had any idea how fast it would catch."

"Of course," Molly said. "The picture of Grandmother."

The ambulance driver tapped her on the arm. "Miss, the doctor wants to know if you'll be coming in with us."

"Yes, I will." She turned back to Rudy. "Tell the police that it was my fault," she whispered to him as her mother's stretcher was being lifted into the ambulance. "I was up there. The turpentine can was open. I should have told her not to smoke."

He frowned at her.

"Rudy," she whispered. "Please."

He shrugged.

Molly went with her mother in the ambulance. After a preliminary examination, the doctor told her that the burns on Mrs. Taylor's left arm were minor. "She's in shock, of course. I've given her a sedative. She's a very lucky lady," the doctor said, and Molly nodded, the tears of relief streaming down her face. As soon as Rudy got to her, he had wrapped her in the blanket that was always kept folded at the foot of Lydia's bed.

The family began to gather at the hospital. Oliver was first.

"I was worried about her, Molly. I told you something was very wrong."

"Uncle Oliver, it was my fault," Molly said, her chin high. "I should never have let her smoke on the porch. Not with the turpentine can open like that."

"No," he said, watching her. "We should have been paying more attention all the way around."

"That's right. But the doctor says the burns are minor. She'll be fine in a couple of weeks," Molly said.

Rudy came next. He greeted Oliver and then asked to speak to Molly alone.

"Are you all right?"

"Yes." But this time, she let him take her in his arms and hold her. "Thank you," she whispered into his ear. "Now let me go before Uncle Oliver comes back." He squeezed once more and then lowered her into the nearest chair.

"We were lucky. Thank God your grandmother kept that fire extinguisher on the porch."

"She was always terrified of fire." Of course, Molly realized now, remembering the last story in the journals. The fire. The maid's death.

"I told the inspector your version. I said you had just left the room for a moment or else he would have wondered why you weren't burned too. He wants to speak to you directly about it, but I doubt there'll be any trouble. Since I'm a member of the volunteer fire department, I think he's willing to let it go without any further investigation."

She nodded. "What's left up there?"

"You lost the painting on the easel," he said gently. "And a couple of sketchbooks. Except for some smoke damage, the rest of the things survived. The fire sergeant wanted to hose the whole place down just to be sure, but I wouldn't let him do it until your things had been moved."

"Thanks," she whispered. She had been imagining the worst. All the work of the last months destroyed in an afternoon.

"Here comes your aunt." From where he stood above her, he could see down the hospital corridor. "I'm going now. You know where I am if you want me."

"Yes, I do," she whispered as he loped off down the hall.

By the time her mother was ready to come home from the hospital, Molly had already moved over to her house.

"A person has to go to extraordinary lengths to get her daughter to come for a visit," Charlotte said.

"Now, Mother, don't start. Anyway, there isn't even a bed to sleep on at the farm." She didn't mention the smell of smoke. She didn't mention the fire at all. Her mother could bring that up if and when she wanted to.

Molly had taken over the dismantling of the house. On the day the movers came, she and Clara and Frank had stationed themselves in different rooms to be sure that the right furniture got into the right trucks. It took two days to sort everything out, and when it was all done, Molly took herself out for a big dinner. That night she packed the last things into the car, drove the five miles to her mother's house, and moved into her old bedroom.

"The place must look grim without the furniture," Charlotte said. "Mother was never good about keeping the place up. I imagine there's eighty years of grime on the walls."

"That's right," Molly said. "You can see exactly where the pictures hung, and there are stripes of black where the chairs have rubbed up against the wall. Sol is planning to repaint the whole place. Also some interior renovation, according to Rudy."

"I never thanked Rudy properly," Charlotte said. She was lying on the sofa in the living room staring up at the ceiling.

"I'm sure he knows how you feel," Molly said quietly.

"I'm sorry about your painting." She didn't look at Molly, and Molly was glad. How many days had she struggled over that one portrait of her grandmother, struggled to capture the expression of fear on her face? There was no way she could re-create it. That painting was gone forever.

"It felt like an exorcism," Charlotte said. "Once I had decided what I wanted to do, I felt so clear. So calm. It was your fault in a way, Molly. You painted her too well."

"What will you do about the paper?" Molly said, to change the subject.

"Oliver has agreed to my proposal. I'm buying out his interest and he's going to retire early. He drove a hard bargain, but I couldn't care less. He wants to put the money into Susan's antique business. They're going to open a store in the middle of town. Can't you see him fussing over eighteenth-century fire screens? It's perfect for him. But of course, now I'm scared I'll be a lousy

newspaper editor after all my years of fuming about
Oliver." She began to fan her hands open, one finger at a
time.

"Do you want your knitting?"

Charlotte nodded. She had quit smoking since her stay
in the hospital, and the doctor had suggested she take up
knitting to keep her hands busy. Molly handed her the
scarf.

"This looks like something a child put together," Charlotte said as she held up the narrow purple swatch that
ballooned in and out.

Molly smiled as her mother bent back over it. There
was something endearing about Charlotte's awkward stabs
with the needles. "Nobody said you had to be good at
it," Molly said.

Their ten days together passed slowly, peacefully.

"Are you going back to the farm?" Charlotte asked
when Molly began to pack her suitcase on the last day.

"I wasn't planning to." She glanced up at her mother.
"Why?"

"I thought you and I might drive by there once,"
Charlotte said. "For old times' sake."

"All right. If it's what you want."

They didn't go in but sat outside in the car and stared
at the blank windows, the peeling paint. "Sol will have to
do the outside too."

"Rudy finished his work on the calf barn. It's supposed
to be painted when the house is done. He did a great
job."

"Did Rudy go back to Rosa?" her mother asked, still
looking straight ahead.

"Yes."

"It's where he belongs, Molly."

Molly pushed away the surge of irritation. It wasn't
worth fighting about anyway. The cherry palette and
Luigi's box were tucked into a corner of the back seat.
That's all of Rudy she would take back to New York with
her.

"I used to come here on the way home from the
office," Charlotte said. "I'd sit here and smoke and watch

Agnes moving around in the kitchen. I was putting off facing your father."

Molly turned the key in the ignition. "It's getting late. I've got to get on the road."

The house rose up in her rearview mirror as she took the turn out of the driveway.

That night when Charlotte went upstairs, she found a cardboard box at the end of her bed. On the top was an envelope addressed to her in Molly's handwriting.

May 31, 1972

Dear Mother,

This is the box that Agnes left me in her will. It contains a set of journals that Grandmother wrote when she was twenty years old. Agnes told me that I shouldn't let you see them but I think she was wrong. I think more than anybody you deserve to know what's in them.

I love you,

Molly

ABOUT THE AUTHOR

A former journalist, ELIZABETH WINTHROP is the recipient of a prestigious PEN award for short fiction. The daughter of the late Stewart Alsop, she herself is a member of an old and prominent family, and she draws from many events and characters from her background for her novel. Ms. Winthrop lives in New York City.

⊘ SIGNET   (0451)

SENSATIONAL BESTSELLERS!

☐ **HER FATHER'S DAUGHTER by William J. Coughlin.** Victoria Van Horn. A
beautiful and daring woman in a sizzling novel of money and power.
What she wants most is to prove that she's as good as any man
in her father's company. When he dies, she gets her chance—only to
find herself involved in the high-risk world of a vast corporation where
power and corruption are locked in an unholy embrace. "Great
entertainment"—*Detroit Free Press*   (400372—$4.50)

☐ **THE TWELVE APOSTLES by William J. Coughlin.** A scorching novel about
the ravenous new breed of lawyers... big, juicy... This portrait of
modern life oozes with sex and scandal, glamour and greed... and all
the other things that go along with the world of money and power. A
Literary Guild Alternate Selection.   (136047—$3.95)

☐ **FAME AND FORTUNE by Kate Coscarelli.** Beautiful women... glittering
Beverly Hills... the boutiques... the bedrooms... the names you
drop and the ones you whisper... all in the irresistible novel that has
everyone reading... "From the opening, the reader is off and turning
the pages!"—*Los Angeles Times*   (160290—$4.95)

☐ **PERFECT ORDER by Kate Coscarelli.** Glamorous Manhattan forms the
backdrop for the sensational story of Cake, Vanessa, and Millie—three
beauties who move into high gear in the most super-rich, super-sexy,
super-powerful city in the world ... "Every woman over the age of
twenty ought to have three copies."—*Los Angeles Times*
                                                       (400038—$3.95)

☐ **LIVING COLOR by Kate Coscarelli.** From the highest reaches of posh
society to the lower depths of Hollywood and betrayal, this dazzling novel
traces the lives of twin sisters separated in infancy but drawn together
by an indestructible bond.   (400828—$4.50)

Prices slightly higher in Canada

Buy them at your local bookstore or use this convenient coupon for ordering.

NEW AMERICAN LIBRARY
P.O. Box 999, Bergenfield, New Jersey 07621

Please send me the books I have checked above. I am enclosing $_____
(please add $1.00 to this order to cover postage and handling). Send check
or money order—no cash or C.O.D.'s. Prices and numbers are subject to change
without notice.

Name_____

Address_____

City _____ State _____ Zip Code _____
Allow 4-6 weeks for delivery.
This offer is subject to withdrawal without notice.